Shlomo Kalo / THE CHOSEN

To the One whose name is Love

Joy and blessing to Rivka, my wife,
who did a sterling job in the work of copying
and her remarks - hit to the point

Shlomo Kalo

THE CHOSEN

Book I: **THE YOUTH**

Book II: **THE PROPHET**

Book III: **A MAN MUCH LOVED**

© All Rights Reserved
Y   D.A.T. PublicationsPOBox 27019,
Jaffa 61270, IsraelFax: +972-3-5070458
Email: dat@y-dat.co.il
www.y-dat.co.il

Original Hebrew title: *HaNivchar*
4th Hebrew edition, 2011
4th English POD edition, printed by Amazon, 2015

English translation by Philip Simpson
Cover design: Hagit Shani
Image: kwest/Shutterstock

ISBN: 978-965-7028-59-9

THE CHOSEN is available also in Hebrew and in Korean

PREFACE

This book, based on the Biblical story of Daniel, is not an academic treatise.

The protagonists of the narrative transcend their chronological context, and in them, in the air enveloping them, in their conduct and their speech, there is that which touches on the present and foretells the future.

The solid base, on which the plot is founded and where its developments unfold, is the Spirit. And it is a steadfast source of aesthetic satisfaction, engaged and profound.

Note:
The Scriptural extracts, quoted in italics, are not always complete and are in some instances supplemented, as required by the narrative.

Contents

THE YOUTH

BOOK I

THE ROAD TO ANATHOTH

He peered, unheeding, through the broad window – the sky high above and a cloud, only the one, as white as snow, drifting across the blue radiance like a thought imbued with a distinctive degree of composure and all of it with but one purpose: to convey pure tranquillity of consciousness, infinite, divine...

"Divine" – is it really so? Perhaps this thought is nothing other than a memory, drawing behind it another memory, and this one, another, and they skim one after the other over the broad surface of consciousness, without touching it, without staining it, without belonging to it and yet, as if acknowledging its sway.

He is sitting in his home in Jerusalem, facing the once opulent gate, so long neglected and not as it was in the past, before the Chaldeans came. Then the opulent gate had been thronged with men and beasts.

A mounted Chaldean patrol passes by in the straight, narrow street. Like most if not all of the Chaldeans, their faces are grim. They are stopping a Jew, grey-haired and with unkempt beard, leaning towards him and asking him something.

The Jew stares up at him, glassily, and their eyes meet. At once it is all clear to him: the Chaldeans are asking about him, looking for him, a Jewish youth who has barely come of age.

A week has passed since the rumour went about that the Chaldeans meant to gather him and his three companions, Hananiah, Mishael and Azariah, and other "children" in Chaldean parlance, scions of the royal family and sons of courtiers, "skilled in all wisdom and knowledge and understanding science, and fit to stand in the palace of the king." This was a persistent rumour, which did not fade with the passing of the days but grew ever stronger, constantly arising in the conversations of slaves and servitors, in the house and outside it.

And he and his companions are indeed the sons of courtiers, whose fathers used to serve the king as ministers and advisers. They had a teacher of the Torah in common too, who made every effort to explain to them the mysteries of the Scriptures and interpret them properly. He was a simple and humble man, and devout as well, but he lacked the inspiration to crack the shells of things and penetrate to their heart.

Under his tutelage they learned chapters of the Torah by heart, touched lightly on the books of the Prophets, but stopped short of studying the Writings. And they could expect nothing more than this. They were left as they were – thirsty for knowledge, a thirst that was not to be quenched, and used to oppress them, and after the lessons they used to meet together and go through the chapters they had learned and try to interpret in ways other than those of their teacher, or those of the priests engaged in divine service. And sometimes they succeeded and this brought relief to their minds and aroused that quiet pleasure which could be called the pleasure of understanding. At other times they failed in the attempt to interpret something, to break through the superficial, verbal cover of the holy verses, and the outcome then was dejection and disappointment, which accompanied them for days and sometimes even weeks.

Besides the teacher of Torah, he had another tutor, a man from the islands in the north who bore the strange name of "Theodoros", a man broad of face and broad of shoulder, fair-haired and fair-skinned, who at first did not understand even a syllable of the Holy Tongue. Theodoros came into their household by chance. One of those days, before the Chaldeans laid siege to the capital city, his father was riding through the bustling market when he saw three Jews manhandling a stranger and trying to overpower him, while he made every effort to free himself from their grasp. His father approached the assailants and asked them what sin the man had committed, and why were they so eager to detain him. They explained to him that the man had the audacity to enter the Sanctuary, thus defiling it since he was not one of the sons of Israel or of Judah, but an uncircumcised gentile, a pagan in every respect and deserving death by stoning. His father reminded them as if by the way, that there is no prohibition on a gentile visiting the Sanctuary, as it is said in the Torah that all nations shall worship the Lord, and the voice of anyone who prays to Him will be heard. The Jews were embarrassed, as their ignorance of the Scriptures was revealed for all to see. And then his father offered them three gold shekels, one for each of the assailants, in exchange for the man's release. They agreed, let the stranger go and held out shaking hands to accept the promised shekels, grabbed them while they were still in the air and made off in haste.

The stranger expressed his gratitude to his father who had saved him from his attackers with gestures of hands and body. His father tried speaking to him in Aramaic, Egyptian and Chaldee, but in vain – the man's language was not like any of these. His father took his leave of him and turned to go his way, but the stranger ran after him, clutching at the reins and pleading, with descriptive gestures of the hands and bodily gyrations, to be allowed to accompany his deliverer, if the latter had no objection. And so the fair-haired and fair-skinned one entered their household, first as a guest, then as a servant and finally as a tutor.

With surprising ease Theodoros became fluent in spoken Hebrew and Aramaic and even learned some Egyptian expressions which were common in the patois of the street. He came from a distant state, over the seas, called Athens, and the inhabitants of this Athens are devoted above all else to reason, trying to explain all phenomena by means of reason, and trusting in reason to an extraordinary degree, sometimes even more than they trust in their deity, or rather, deities – a whole pantheon of gods and goddesses, who invariably raised a tolerant smile to his lips, on hearing of their festivities and their rivalries, their liaisons and their escapades.

Theodoros taught him moderation, and clarity of tongue, and some physical exercises too, to strengthen the muscles and hone the body's systems, and a particular form of calculation, based on the dimensions of areas and shapes of all kinds, called "geometry" in the Greek language, and since there was nothing in these things to undermine his faith in God, they were gladly accepted and he showed himself an accomplished pupil. Finally, Theodoros converted, underwent circumcision and became "Doroz".

The Chaldean officer climbs the stairs, his footsteps echoing in the empty void of the tall, ornate house, the house of a minister of state and senior adviser to the king. A moment more and he will knock on the heavy door... and here comes the knocking, a sound speaking authority on one side, and striking terror on the other.

One of the slaves opens the door, and on hearing what the officer has to say, calls the young man's mother. After a short conversation, he is summoned to his own chamber, where the Chaldean is waiting for him. Sure enough, he is required to accompany him and go down with him to Babylon, where he is to be trained to serve the great king, Nebuchadnezzar.

One request he has, and one alone – that he be given time, half a day, to go to Anathoth, which is not far away. He is eager to obtain blessing for his journey from a man of Anathoth whom he has never met but of whom he has heard well, to prostrate himself before him on the ground and to see with his own eyes the prophet of God, the like of whom appears only once in a generation, or perhaps in many generations.

The officer can accompany him if he so desires, or send men to escort him.

The Chaldean warrior hears him out in silence, his head bowed. Then he raises his gloomy, indignant gaze and studies him from head to foot. There is bitterness in his eyes and it is clear that his posting to desolate Jerusalem is not to his taste.

Two of his soldiers will escort him, and he must return no later than midday, before the sun reaches its highest point in the sky. The three of them descend into the gloom of the cavernous, almost empty stable. The Chaldeans mount their small, pampered ponies, which are quartered here, while he takes the last horse left to the family after the persistent predations of the Chaldeans. A black mare which only a year ago used to delight all who saw her with her powerful frame, her proud and noble bearing. And now, for want of food, she is just a ghost, a pitiable skeleton.

The road to Anathoth. A steep ascent, which in the past the mare used to devour in one leap, with a whinny of delight, rejoicing in her strength, but now she needs twice and fourfold the time, as she pants heavily and drags herself along on tottering legs. He would not have ridden her at all had he not known that the exercise would be good for her, and his young body not too heavy a burden for her. The Chaldeans, accompanying him on their agile, piebald ponies, often have to pause and wait for him to catch up. They are tight-lipped and taciturn, displaying patience amounting to indifference – an attitude sometimes reminiscent of gravediggers.

The ride reaches its highest point, the ascent over, the tedious climb at an end. At their feet, somewhere, the low, white houses of Anathoth, huddled together like a flock of sheep, are turning gold in the rising sun. A fertile valley, with orchards and fields – but the crops have been harvested prematurely and now the ground is barren and black, a bare expanse in which the eye can find no point to focus on, but would grow weary in the attempt, skimming along the sharp line of the horizon, soaring aloft into the clear, and never-changing sky, as it always has been and ever shall be.

The mare has gained more confidence, treading slowly, cautiously, inspecting every stone that she encounters on her way. The path itself is a dust path, without any more ascents in the offing. It seems the mare has sufficient strength to cope with the descent.

This grove is well known to him and has been precious to him since the dawn of his childhood. There used to be rare birds here, and nightingales sang on fine summer evenings. But it was not the rare birds or the nightingales that drew him here, to this grove. He loved the fresh raspberries that grew there in abundance, the bushes giving of their bounty in the summer. He could fill a whole sack with them and amaze the other members of the household. The fragrant raspberry, young and sweet, its colour the colour of new Jerusalem wine. There were other varieties of woodland berries, and mushrooms in the autumn, and tall nut trees. They had just passed one of them, trunk standing erect and proud as a king. Indeed, its broad foliage was reminiscent of a crown.

This grove is implanted in his memory as a kind of ancient song about the girl, Nejeen, and about himself. Nejeen, daughter of Gamliel. Her father used to serve as an advisor to the king. A tall man, wrapped up in himself, of wise words which he was in no hurry to express, and only on rare occasions did a smile of astonishing brightness pass across his face, radiating over all those in his company a vibrant and delicious sense of fellowship, blended with respect and appreciation.

Often the two families, his and that of the king's advisor Gamliel, used to be the guests of one another. And he enjoyed listening to the words of his father the minister and of Gamliel, words of importance, each one pronounced precisely, and being surprised, a surprise which made his heart beat faster, by Gamliel's smile, which broadened his thin lips and lit up his eyes, whenever his youngest daughter Nejeen passed amid the assembled company for some reason or another. Thanks to her father, Nejeen was one of the very few of the daughters of Judah who could read and write, and she delved deep into the Scriptures, and long passages from the anthems of King David, gathered together in the Book of Psalms, she knew by heart. But much as she loved the psalms of David, she was entranced most of all by the Song of Songs of Solomon. Yes, she was truly excited when she quoted a verse or two from the Song of Songs, her rosy lips quivering, the pure gaze of her eyes revealing their depths, eyes a vivid shade of blue.

As if it was something obvious in itself the two of them used to meet here, in this grove, so grim today, perhaps – because of the presence of the Chaldeans, with their stern faces. And just a year ago it was so different – its air enchanted and all of it – like a legend of antiquity, tuneful, mysterious.

Sometimes they met with other members of the family in their home, the house of the minister Naimel. All of a sudden, his father and her father would decide to move from the parlour to one of the spacious rooms in the interior of the house, and it was a sign to all of them that their conversation was no longer public property, and the members of the two families used to disperse, his mother and her mother going to the kitchen, while he and Nejeen made their way down to the courtyard – an extensive courtyard with a fountain in the middle and rare flowers of luscious colours at its fringes.

In their conversation he would refer to the Book of Genesis, and the mysteries yet to be solved by those who take everything that is written at face value. She listened to him in silence, with close attention, her whole being in thrall. She quoted a verse from the Song of Songs which matched perfectly the words spoken by him and was as if summoned by itself. In the limpid air of a blue evening, the words sounded as if they stood in their own right, with images that lived and enchanted the imagination, and it seemed to him in these miraculous moments that he had found what he sought and did not know existed. And then he recited before her, in a voice that had not yet matured, the voice of a ten year child, the lines that came after and she looked up at him and poured into his eyes all the purity stored in the depths of hers, setting the heart a-quiver and infusing him with prodigious strength from an unknown source.

For a long moment they were both silent, a moment that grew longer still, and thousands of years perished in the blinking of an eye, and everything faded and disappeared, never to return.

Then his name was called. Once, twice. This was his tutor, reminding him that the time for study had arrived. Before parting from her he said:

"I'm very fond of the grove on the hill, on the way to Anathoth, there isn't a day that I don't visit it. Farewell!" And he ran as if he had sprouted wings to his good-natured tutor, who had been waiting for him a long time and hadn't dared disturb him.

Thereafter they used to meet in the grove on the hill, on the road leading down to Anathoth, a grove that seemed to them like a dense forest holding a secret, all of it sheer delight, enlivening the soul and cleansing it of all mundane dross.

And there were days of harvest too, and both the families had fields to the south of the wall, on the road to Jericho, and he and Nejeen were there with the reapers, listening to the sounds of their song soaring to the heavens, in harmony, making the hot air quiver, responding to their call and bringing them pitchers of water from the well by the wayside, whose waters are always cool, always refreshing, and earning hearty thanks and fulsome benedictions. And fine evenings, when the skies draw close to the earth in tenderness, as a lover is close to his beloved, and kiss her rosy fringes, they used to lie supine at the feet of the giant haystacks, staring up in silence at the plethora of great stars, sparkling above them and so close it seemed you could stretch out your hand, and a star would slide into your palm, living and lustrous, and bringing with it its other world, serene and pure.

The skies were like the song of angels, telling in measured rhymes, in a melody matching all the aspirations of the heart, legends of long ago.

And he asked her then if she knew the constellations of the sky, if she was aware of the conjunctions of stars that astrologers study and teach, as a means of foretelling the future of a person or of whole nations of the world. And she said she knew only a very little of all this but would be so glad to hear...

And she heard his voice, a voice clear and resonant, with pleasantly modulated words, telling legends of the heroes of old, who fought in the heavens and on the earth, and astrologers predicted their victory or their downfall by means of those gleaming stars. There they are – he pointed out the constellations one after another, and she following him with wide open eyes, her look expressing nothing other than submission to the infinite, and above all, something resembling admiration, frank and proud admiration, bringing a moist veil to her eyes. He absorbed all of this and recalled the verses of Solomon, son of David: *Turn away your eyes from me, for they overwhelm me.* He saw in his mind's eye the young Solomon and the young Shulamite, lying on their backs at the edge of a great hayrick, breathing the balmy air of the cropped field, looking up at the sea of stars gleaming above their heads, and Solomon, the future king, revealing to his beloved and cherished Shulamite the secrets of the firmament and she gazing at him with her deep, wide-open eyes, more beautiful than anything that bears the name of beauty, and at this very moment they are sparkling with a moisture that is nothing other than sublime, surpassing all else that is known as sublime.

Love is strong as death... if a man were to offer for love all his worldly wealth, it would be utterly scorned.

For some time thereafter they did not meet again. Indeed – their bodies did not meet, but beyond such limitations, he used to meet her and talk with her at all hours, by day and by night. She was in his heart, as a manifestation of what is "strong as death", clear, sharp and limpid and above all – uplifting the soul and laying bare the spirit, and opening the doors of the heart to that which never perishes.

There were moments when it seemed to him that meeting in the corporeal sense would spoil and impair those other encounters of theirs, continuing in constant succession, vibrant with the life of truth, in other words – life flowing without check.

And what a surprise it was to him, when after a whole month he went back to walking in the forest of Anathoth and met her near the rosy spring, so called on account of the pink marble rock from which it flowed, and the raspberry bush reflected in its clear waters.

This was the place where they met for the first time and where they had often met in the not so distant past. Her face was pale, but the moment she saw him it changed at once: a red flush spread across it, bespeaking tenderness and gratification, and she skipped gracefully towards him, and dipped the radiant purity of her eyes in his, which could not disguise his astonishment and were replete with overwhelming delight.

"How is this?" he asked awkwardly.

"Simple!" – she answered the question, and he accepted it, and she understood.

"Have you been here long?" – he almost stammered, disconcerted by the dark, bold blue of her eyes, enfolding him on all sides like a gleaming halo, like a mighty ocean bearing him on its pure waves towards a destination of its own choosing.

"And how did you know the time and the place?" – he went on to ask in his bemusement, without pausing for her reply, and beneath the many layers of his confusion seeing the truth and dreading it, unwilling to delve into its depths, fearing lest its joy upset his peace of mind forever.

But she left no room for doubt:

"I didn't know and I didn't guess," she replied.

"What then?" – his voice shook.

"I have been here," she answered him simply – "from daybreak till sunset."

"But Nejeen!" – he spoke her name and felt the tingling of his flesh and of hers with it.

"It's the truth," she guessed what his next question would be and answered it first.

"Every day?"

"Every day."

And then she held out her hand and he took it, a white, slender, firm hand. And all at once, as if a sign had been given and without a word spoken between them, they gambolled hand in hand down the slope that was all fields strewn with flowers of every hue and of strong and pungent scent, the scent of endless spring.

Here is the slope. They are approaching the first houses of Anathoth, low houses, huddled together like a flock of sheep, waiting for the storm to break or the wolf to pounce.

This is the kind of dejection which has descended upon so many members of his race, those accustomed to seeing themselves as the elect of God. The envoy of God came into the midst of this people, took his stand in its market-places and attended its gatherings, delivered his speeches in the bustling squares and in the hearing of the gentry, he even made his message known in the palace of the king. His words were clear and grave – and no one listened to them. Instead of this the nobles and the commoners, the ministers and the counsellors and the viziers, and the king himself and in person – they persecuted the envoy of God. Even men of the clergy joined in the chorus of abuse and rejection. The priests charged with the practice of divine service in the Sanctuary, their sons and their pupils, and the Levites, and the officially approved prophets, and the sages speaking out in support of the regime – all of them, as one man, persecuted the envoy of God, scorned him, and slapped his cheeks, and spat in his face.

This is the man he is going to see, the envoy of God who lives the life of a recluse in these dreadful times, in fear and in anguish, unable to leave his home.

His black mare has guided him directly to the house at the southernmost end of the silent, forbidding settlement, its inhabitants peering out through the cracks and crannies in shuttered windows, and half-opened doors, at this strange group, consisting of a Jewish youth and two Chaldean soldiers. They peer, and then slink back into their holes.

No living being has met them on their way, until it seems the settlement is neglected and abandoned, a habitation of ghosts. There is the southernmost house, standing a little apart from the others. Behind it – a broad meadow growing wild.

His heart is beating fast. Already he is prepared to climb down from his mount, to approach the house on foot, ascend the two flights of stone steps – untrimmed Jerusalem stone, coarse but lustrous – push open the light wicket, walk along the narrow path and knock on the massive, grim-looking gate, so heavy it seems no man alone could shift it on its hinges. But he is spared all this effort. Suddenly, without a sound, as if at the touch of a magic wand, the heavy gate swings open and in the dark void beyond stands a man of medium height, thin-fleshed, wearing a striped robe, like those worn by priests when not engaged in divine service. The man's hair, shoulder-length and longer, and his dangling, straggly beard are streaked with grey, his forehead high and beneath it, set deep in their blue-tinged sockets, those strange eyes are flashing brightly, eyes that are worlds in their own right, unexplored worlds, shafts of light that pierce the void of the universe – nothing can resist them, nothing stand against them, for their source is beyond the control of any mortal.

And the man was drawing closer, crossing the path and descending the two flights of the short stairway. And only then did the youth muster his courage and leap nimbly from the back of his black mare, quaking beneath him, and take two steps forward, to bend the knee and prostrate himself on the ground at the bare feet of the envoy of God, the vessel of the word of God.

The Chaldean soldiers also dismounted, and they too knelt and bowed, prompted by some sudden impulse, before this strange man, doing just as he was doing, the youth whom they were escorting, whether as a prisoner or as a future guest of their king.

"Rabbi, my master and my teacher!" cried the youth in a choking voice: "How many are my sins against him and against He who sent him! My sins, and the sins of my masters and my parents and my fellow-countrymen in all their teeming hordes!"

"You are not the sinner, Daniel sweet youth!" – the man interrupted him in his wondrously clear, courageous voice, with not a single note out of place: "You are blessed by the Almighty God whom I serve. It is He who has called me to come out and meet you, and told me your name, and commanded me to inform you that great mysteries will be revealed to you, and the most arcane of secrets you shall know, and His name you are to uphold in a distant land, and lords of the land and kings shall listen to the word of the Lord issuing from your lips, and great and mysterious things you shall accomplish for the sake of His glory and the holiness of His name, and many shall hate you and very few will understand you, and they are the ones who will be saved at the end of time.

"And now arise, young Daniel, and set out on the way that has been ordained for you!"

"Not until you have blessed me, father Jeremiah, prophet of God the most high!"

"May God be with you whatsoever you do and wheresoever you go!" – Jeremiah blessed the youth, and added with a faint smile: "Although that is not so much a benediction as a simple observation, for even before you were in the womb God was with you and to the end of your days on this earth He will not forsake you, for you are very dear to Him and are numbered among His children! He shall show the way that you must walk until you are gathered to Him, forever and ever, amen!" – and so saying the man leaned forward and lightly touched the head of the youth, then turned and with vigorous, measured tread, returned the way he had come.

When Daniel rose to his feet the void was empty again and the house silent and closed, as he had seen it just a short while before. The gate was locked, locked and bolted, heavy and forbidding.

He mounted his mare and realised he had done this with unwonted lightness, with agility, in high spirits even. The Chaldean soldiers followed his example and they too seemed more cheerful, as a sort of distant flush tinged the edges of their cheeks, areas untouched by their neatly trimmed beards. His brown eyes gleamed. He urged on his mare without giving a moment's thought to her debilitated condition but – and here was a positive miracle – she responded to his commands and settled into a steady gait, treading lightly as she climbed the incline of the road from Anathoth.

The words of the prophet reverberated in the turbulent soul of the young man. The lines of his face, delicately crafted yet bold, were enlivened by remarkable vigour, without revealing the merest hint of his innermost thoughts. Thus he had been taught by his tutors who constantly repeated to him one of the sayings of the wisest of men: *Better be slow to anger than be a mighty warrior, better control your temper than conquer a city.*

The young features were handsome, although expressing a composure at odds with his age. His hair was black, raven-black, silky-smooth and clean, combed back and falling to his shoulders, his forehead a startling white, high and smooth. The expression of his face spoke of absence of fear, as if cleansed of the last vestige of worldliness.

He called to mind once again the encounter that he had longed for so much, the words he had just heard, the words he had uttered. Everything so different from what he had envisaged, surprising and embarrassing, and continuing to perturb his spirit. Had the die really been cast, had he been assigned the far from easy task of preaching the word of God before the rulers of foreign lands? Would they believe him? He saw no purpose in attempting to answer his own questions, and they remained suspended in the void, a source of anxiety and stress – and of untempered delight.

He revealed to no one his wishes and his latent longings, and indeed there was no need for this, since He, his father in Heaven, his God, always listened to the meditations of his heart, and guided him on the way that led to Him.

He had heard tell of Jeremiah and knew he was the true emissary of the living God, and he took his side, sometimes in silence, sometimes with a sentence or two, inside his house and outside it. In time it became known to him that his father too was on the side of Jeremiah, but because of his exalted status and his respect for the king he could not express this publicly, only in the presence of the king and his inner circle of advisers. The king and his entourage, with the exception of his father and possibly his uncle too, his mother's brother, did not accept the yoke of the Chaldeans and refused to believe that they had brought it upon their own necks, with their departure from the Holy Torah and their rejection of God, speaking through His prophet and saying: *Not by might and not by power but through my spirit*, meaning – cleave to me, keep my commandments, and you have no one to fear and nothing to dread, for I am your defender, your redeemer and deliverer and no power on the earth, however great it may be, can do you harm.

They did not understand anything, or it would be more true to say – they refused to understand. Their pride was hurt, and instead of seeking out the source of their downfall in themselves, they accused God of abandoning them and forsaking them, and selling them to their enemies.

It was painful, looking into the faces of his father's friends, the ministers and advisers and leaders of armies, and seeing how their eyes flashed with resentment at the cruel fate allotted them. And when the Prophet appeared, the true emissary of the living God, and called on them to repent, and foretold the future, they vented their anger on him, blaming and abusing him, threatening him with torture, exile, imprisonment... and the man of God endured it all and was not deterred. Threats were of no avail, and yet those who threatened were unabashed and unrepentant.

That was when he began praying for the soul of his father, and the soul of the misguided king, and of the people, led astray through no malice of their own. And his prayers were heard and the way to salvation was revealed for all to see, but it was not as those destined for salvation had envisaged it; it seemed to them this was not the way of salvation but the way of suffering, of destruction and of ruin.

Before they knew it, they had reached the ravaged wall of the Holy City, the capital city of the people of God. This is the site of the Humble Gate, lowest of all the gates, with just enough space for a horse and rider to pass through it, and it used to be the pedlars' gate. Only a few years ago the place had been thronged with pedlars, hawking their various wares and blocking the path of anyone trying to pass by.

Today it is just an aperture with no breath of life about it. An aperture leading to a cemetery. Has the city of the faithful turned into a cemetery? Judging by the wraiths presiding over it, there is little to choose between city and cemetery. Graves – is that not what these houses are, houses where only the sounds of grief and bitter weeping interrupt their mournful stillness? Has this city breathed its last? Not yet. The Prophet Jeremiah predicted the renewal of its youth seventy years from now, when its inhabitants are cleansed of all their defilement and a new generation comes, the generation of great hope, and build upon its ruins, laying firm foundations of righteousness, truth and justice, and God dwells in it once again, as in the first days and as He promised to His people, the God who is love.

At home a surprise awaited him. His friends, Hananiah, Mishael and Azariah, were sitting in his room waiting for him patiently, their belongings packed at their feet, and faint smiles on their young faces, while beside them Ashpenaz, the chief eunuch and envoy of Nebuchadnezzar, who had come to collect "children" as he called them, children of outstanding talents, was incandescent with rage. He hurled all kinds of senseless accusations at his soldiers, denouncing them as wastrels and halfwits, deserving only the executioner's sword. And all this because they did not spur on their horses and arrive early. And there was no point in making excuses here, since Ashpenaz was clearly in no mood to listen to excuses. Especially as the officer who sent them had been transferred elsewhere and there was no one who would dare to remind the furious Ashpenaz that the riders were required to return not later than midday, and as it was not yet midday, they were in fact ahead of schedule.

When Ashpenaz the chief eunuch had expended his anger on his soldiers, he turned to them and commanded them to make haste to the square by the elegant gate, where the convoy about to leave for Babylon had been delayed by the irresponsible behaviour of two of his soldiers, who would yet pay the penalty, as would the officer who had authorised their absence.

The youth regretted the punishment that was in store for the Chaldean officer, but in his heart he rejoiced at the opportunity that he had been given, looking into the face of the true man of God, the dauntless prophet of his father in Heaven, hearing his blessing and parting from him in peace.

He bade hasty farewells to his mother and his two sisters and his brother in the cradle, his nurse and his grandmother and all the slaves and family retainers. His mother held back her tears, as did his nurse. His sisters were too young to realise what was happening, the slaves wept softly, as did the maidservants. He took his bundle and set out with vigorous tread for the main entrance of the house. An old slave trailed along behind him, and accompanied him as far as the outer door. From here he carried on with his three companions.

THE CONVOY

The commander of the convoy, a Chaldean officer, grim-faced like most of the all-conquering Chaldeans, put them, the four of them, on one of the wagons that were covered with canopies of cattle-hide for shade, and crammed with youths like themselves, the scions of noble families, summoned by the king of Babylon to serve in his palace.

The officer spurred his thoroughbred horse along the line of the convoy, composed of wagons, men and beasts, inspected whatever it was that required his inspection, retraced his steps and ordered his equerry to shoot off three burning arrows into the bright blue sky, the pre-arranged signal for the convoy leaders to move. And sure enough, as soon as the arrows had fallen to the ground and been extinguished in the whitish-grey dust of the roadside, a kind of stirring was sensed among men and beasts alike. Most of the people carried knapsacks on their hunched shoulders and walked, barefoot as a rule, close to the long wagons and leaning on them for support. The majority of the wagons were open to the blazing sun and carried all kinds of cargo and a few passengers. Besides the pairs of horses harnessed to the wagons, the pampered little ponies of the Chaldean cavalry, escorting the convoy of exiles, many of them artisans – were everywhere to be seen. About a dozen oxen, a source of fresh meat for the Chaldean army, and some half dozen milch-cows, for the provision of fresh milk, trailed along ponderously in the rear.

Their covered wagon occupied, so it seemed, prime position in the middle of the convoy, with six Chaldean horsemen, three on either side, escorting them. It soon became clear to them that this was the royal wagon, reserved for those destined to look upon the face of the great king, the conqueror of the world, Nebuchadnezzar the Chaldean, himself and in person.

Some residents of the city came out to accompany the convoy with their silent looks, while well-armed Chaldean troops kept them away from the travellers.

His eyes lingered on the faces of those looking on; sad, scared faces with bitter, veiled looks, the faces of his compatriots, the people of God who did not keep faith with Him, but strayed and led astray... and again his heart was filled with such a weight of grief that it almost stopped beating.

And then, somewhere, among the silent watchers, those remaining behind in the city that was doomed to destruction, he caught her eye. He knew it was her, and her gaze that was following him, the deep gaze of her eyes, blue tending towards violet, even before their eyes met.

Relief from an unknown source swelled his chest. His heart resumed its joyful beating, the vibrant joy that he knew so well.

Their glances locked together. This was a long moment which detached the two of them from their surroundings, erased all other faces and transported them to the limpid heights of another world, a world of their own, where no stranger could set foot.

His head was turned back, and his eyes still fixed on hers, eyes radiating comfort and confidence and peace. Could it be that the purity of the world, all that divine purity, bestowed upon man in abundance but rejected and trampled rudely underfoot, has found in these eyes its inexhaustible spring? – so he pondered, unable, and unwilling, to detach his gaze from hers.

The Chaldean horseman leaned across, trying, with a clumsy movement, to move him back into the interior of the wagon, while making every effort to avoid injuring the king's prisoner. His instructions were to show leniency and fairness towards the youths destined to look upon the face of King Nebuchadnezzar the conqueror of the world, and to serve him. And all the while the wheels of the wagon went on turning, moving slowly on the road with its coarse, unmatched paving stones.

Nejeen had to run behind the ranks of soldiers and a number of Jews standing at the roadside, and when she realised she could not catch up with him, she stopped and stood still and waved her hand to him, a familiar, white hand, that suddenly glowed in the stifling heat of the air like a source of tender light, a blast of invigorating chill.

He waved back to her energetically, then yielded to the pressure exerted on him by the Chaldean horseman and withdrew to the depths of the wagon, his eyes sparkling and his face burning. His companions stared at him, bemused.

The wagon was long, more so than any of the other wagons, and yet still the youths sitting in it were cramped together. There were eight of them, apparently all of an age. He sat between Mishael and Azariah. Hananiah tried to peer through the seam of the stitching at the rear of the canopy and observe, for perhaps the last time in his life, the ruined northern wall of the city, the wall which the Chaldeans had taken the trouble to reduce to its foundations, setting to work those inhabitants of the city who had not been slain nor exiled to Babylon, alongside such slaves as had survived.

Azariah asked him in a whisper:

"Nejeen?"

He confirmed this with a nod of the head, and spoke the name with a blend of reverence and exaltation of spirit:

"Nejeen."

And perhaps he will never see her again, never meet again. This thought seems to him strange and at odds with reality. He will meet her again. How and when – only God knows. Jerusalem the holy city, the land that he knows, his mother, his sisters and his baby brother – he may never see again. So his doleful heart tells him. But Nejeen... a current of warmth bearing with it a gentle beam of light, sweeps through his whole being and drives the dolour from his heart.

And what will become of Jerusalem? Will it be utterly destroyed, and never rebuilt? The Prophet of God decreed for it seventy years of desolation, after which it shall be built again. And great is the hope and bold is the dream, that the one that is to be built will never again be destroyed and it will be the city of God, the habitation of the faithful, inside and out. The city of God in which the people of God live and praise their Father who is in Heaven with psalm and anthem, with harp and viol, with cymbals, drum, lyre and pipe, extolling and glorifying Him all the days of their lives upon the earth, a people that will serve as a model to all races and principalities and nations and tongues, who will come from faraway to bow down to the one God and see His people with their own eyes, to learn from them and to be like them.

This people will beat its swords into ploughshares and its spears into pruning-hooks, and its best young men, God-fearers and God-lovers all, will no longer take up weapons, and among them there will be no commoners, no men of power and authority, no kings or nobles or dignitaries, no servants and no masters, no slaves and no free men, For all shall know me, from the least to the greatest, as God has declared through the lips of His prophet. And they will all be His children, in the words of King David: *I said, you are God, and all of you are children of the Most High*. There will be no more need of judges and constables and kings, and He will be their one and only unrivalled king.

The convoy was moving now at a faster pace. The big wheels of the wagon creaked beneath them, dust rose in spirals from the road, thick and cloying, hanging in clouds above their heads, in the void of the air, veiling the face of the bright sky. This dust made breathing heavy, seared the throat.

"What were you thinking about?" asked Mishael.

He glanced at him. His contemporary, swarthy of face and bright of eye, his hair black and curly, falling on both sides of his head and behind, *like a flock of goats coming down from Gilead* – the line from the Song of King Solomon flashes into his mind. The face of Azariah, on the other hand, was not at all swarthy, but very pale, a face not testifying to the best of health, eyes black, soft and deep-set, his hair almost smooth and tending towards ruddiness. It was said of him he was descended from King David. His family was one of the most distinguished in Jerusalem, but he for his part had little to say, being wrapped up in himself.

On his father's advice the former Theodoros, now known as Doroz, came to drill him with physical exercises.

Azariah detested such exercises, and was not outstanding in horsemanship either, but after their fathers had spoken together, Azariah's father approached his son and urged him to do these exercises. Azariah complied, thus upholding the commandment to honour father and mother, and listened to Doroz, who invested a great deal of effort in him and tried to persuade him to continue with these exercises, even when the trainer was not there. The results were visible – and for a few days a light reddish tinge spread over Azariah's cheeks, but only for a few days. Then the pallor returned and reclaimed its place.

Above all else, Azariah chose to sit in the Sanctuary, to spend as much time as he could under its high, domed roof, radiating the solemnity of holiness, his eyes staring in the shadowy void, and his lips murmuring the verses most dear to him: *Even though I walk in the valley of the shadow of death I shall fear no evil, for you are with me… I trust in the Lord, I shall not fear what mankind may do to me… From the straits I called upon the Lord, He answered me in the open spaces.*

Sometimes he joined Azariah in the Sanctuary, to sit beside him on one of the seats reserved for the royal household, and be as silent as he. Sometimes they sat like this, in silence, from daybreak to sunset.

The Shekhinah prevails between the high walls of the Sanctuary and they are both of them imbued with it, in their detachment from the outside, from what grieves them or gladdens them, in their loss of all awareness of time. In the end they rise from their seats and part in silent amity, each turning to go his own way.

It is not only within the Sanctuary that the Shekhinah prevails. It prevails outside it too, in the flickering expanse above the City of David and in its winding alleyways and in the hills and the fields surrounding it all around, in the dewy meadow of a spring morning, in the greening forests, in every single place where man serves his Father in Heaven with love and tells His praises.

"What were you thinking about?" – Mishael repeated his question, his voice distant.

"About all the sins that we have committed against our Father in Heaven. We dream of what could be good and beautiful, and we do what is wicked and ugly."

"But Daniel, we are not like that!" – Azariah turned to him, and his voice more quiet than usual, restrained to a degree, a restraint that was conscious and not natural.

In the tone of his voice there was pain and longing. Pain over what had happened in Jerusalem and what his eyes had witnessed, and this exile that had been forced on them, and the separation from parents, from brothers and sisters, and from uncles, from fields and vineyards, from enchanted mornings of spring and summer, autumn and winter... and longing to cling to God with all his might, with redoubled love, to trust in Him to the end and above all – to do His will without a moment's thought, and if it is possible, to sanctify His name, to sacrifice everything, to the end. Are this pain and this longing not the pain and the longing of all of them, of the four of them at least?

Hananiah returns from the crack through which he had been looking at the ruined buildings of his home town. The dust has already covered them, and there is no longer anything to look at. Hananiah tries to hide the tears welling in his reddened eyes.

"This dust!" he exclaims, when he realises that his three friends have discovered his weakness.

"It scalds the eyes" Hananiah insists, studying the faces of his three friends as if saying: "Try to believe me, make it easier for me! It's the truth that I'm telling – it scalds the eyes and damages them!"

"You have to beware of dust!" Mishael declares with dignity, and Azariah joins in, in the same tone of voice, as he explains:

"A few years ago Esther, our housemaid, was in floods of tears because she happened to be walking on a dusty road when a troop of the royal guard came riding along and kicked up clouds of dust. It took her a long time to recover. She needed cold compresses on her eyes for a whole month!"

"That's what dust can do, and there's no doubting it's as dangerous to the eyes as vinegar is to the teeth," he asserted solemnly – "and we'll have to be careful of it, especially seeing that we have a lengthy journey ahead of us, and it's not a matter of a day or two, or even a week or two. It's a long way, and it's all obstacles, dust and sand!"

"How long is it supposed to take?" asked Azariah eagerly, clearly intending to change the subject and give Hananiah the chance to attend to his tears. And Hananiah took his friend's hint, pulling out from under his sheepskin tunic a scrap of cloth and wiping his face and his nose with great deliberation. When he turned to face them again, his eyes were dry.

"About three weeks," he answered the one who had asked, and went on to explain: "So I have heard from those who have done the journey there and back – twenty-one days from here to there, from there to here, a little less."

"And perhaps they were horsemen in a hurry and not a caravan like this one of ours, which is mostly people on foot and a few wagons and horses, not to mention oxen and cattle trundling along at their own pace."

"A caravan just like this one," he insisted. "Since the Chaldeans came, several such have gone down to Babylon, and some of those escorting them have returned, and that journey was indeed a shorter one – no caravan, just horsemen."

"Chaldean horsemen?" asked Mishael.

"Correct," he answered him.

"Have you been fraternising with Chaldeans?" asked Hananiah, in a tone that suggested he had not the slightest interest in hearing an answer to his question.

"They were billeted on us," he replied – "in our house on the plain. They seemed to like the place, and we refused them nothing. Secretly, my mother was hoping the house would be spared, but in the end it was destroyed, like the houses of all those who opposed the Chaldeans and fought against them, and those who were close to the king."

"But the minister Naimel, your father, died in battle!" Hananiah pointed out.

"All the more reason," he replied with dignity.

"Our house is still standing," – one of the 'strangers' approached the group of four. "My father was killed fighting them too, but my mother convinced the Chaldeans that our house was not his but belonged to my grandfather, who had nothing at all to do with the king's ministers or advisers, but on the contrary – was among the supporters of Jeremiah."

"Did he really support Jeremiah?" he asked curiously.

The young man replied with a sly wink:

"My grandfather's eyes are failing and his ears stopped hearing anything a long time ago. To this very day, he doesn't even know that the Chaldeans are in Jerusalem."

"So your mother broke the commandment against giving false witness," Mishael commented.

"We had to choose between our home and this commandment.... and I don't know anyone who obeys it to the letter!"

The four of them looked down and were silent for a long moment.

"Don't pretend to be so righteous," another youth interjected from the depths of the wagon. "You people haven't been keeping this commandment either, you're just like the rest of us! No one is capable of keeping this commandment – and all the others!" he insisted.

"It's because of that kind of thinking that Jerusalem fell and the kingdom of David came to an end," Hananiah commented.

"Jerusalem will yet be rebuilt and there will be no end to the kingdom of David!" – he intervened hastily, before one of the others could reply to Hananiah. "You'll find it in the Scriptures, and it was Jeremiah's prophecy too," he concluded.

"What I mean to say," – added the youth who had spoken previously – "is that it's not in the nature of a man of flesh and blood to keep the commandments, and abiding by them is beyond his capabilities!"

"He who keeps these commandments – will be saved!" he insisted.

"Anyway, the whole world, with all its inhabitants and creatures, is surely doomed to destruction and will perish!" interposed a third youth, not one of his companions.

"The whole world will not be destroyed, nor will all creatures perish!" he answered him.

"Who are those who will be spared?" asked Hananiah curiously.

"Those who love the Lord," he said and added: "As it is written – *You shall love the Lord your God with all your heart and with all your might and with all your soul.* He who loves the Lord will be saved and the world will be saved for his sake."

One of the wheels of the wagon struck a hillock, and all eight youths were flung to one side. A cloud of hot, sticky dust drifted in, settling and drawing a chorus of hoarse coughing from the throats of the young men. The debate was suspended, as eyes were closed for a long moment.

Outside, someone could be heard cursing the wagon-driver in a coarse tone of voice. One of the Chaldean riders, evidently. Another Chaldean arrived and restrained him from laying a whip on the back of the hapless Jewish wagoner.

He peered through a chink in the canopy: a long straggling line of wagons, and beside them creatures who seemed to be from another world, walking blindly with heads bowed, a grey, winding column, slow-moving, ponderous and it seemed – without purpose. Dust is still spiralling upwards and the lines are blurred. The molten gold of the horizon is dulled, and the head of the column seems to blending into it and disappearing from view.

The wheels of the wagons creak, the horses whinny, the oxen behind utter their prolonged, guttural bellows, in which there is no defiance, only despair and a plea for mercy. The cows add their voices to the chorus, but their lowing is less discordant and less submissive. The hot, dust-laden air is impeding the progress of the convoy. The mounted Chaldeans shield their eyes, scanning the wide expanse. They can't tell anyone, not even themselves, where they are. Hands droop in resignation, and the caravan moves on. The Chaldeans try to calculate their position on the basis of the time that has elapsed: some four hours since they left Jerusalem, and the way still to be travelled seems longer than ever. Their reckoning is faulty. They wish one of the exiles would ask them how far they have travelled from Jerusalem and when they will arrive in Babylon, to which they will reply in true soldierly style, that this is no concern of his, and he should be so good as to continue to walk this narrow path and not impede the journey in any way, and mind his own business. Some day, and somehow, he will reach his destination, see the towering walls of the mighty metropolis of Babylon, draw near to them and enter by the tall gates. And there work awaits him, all kinds of tasks in the service of the great king, conqueror of the world, Nebuchadnezzar his name, and woe betide him if he is idle or fails to deliver or asks too many foolish questions! In the court of the king of Babylon such things are not tolerated. And he should take great care, and heed this friendly warning: for infringing these prohibitions there is only one penalty – the sharp sword of His Majesty's headsman.

But no one addresses a question to the soldiers of the king of Babylon, possibly because no one is in the mood for a lecture. They all know better than to ask unnecessary questions – questions with all too predictable answers. The swathed head of the Jewish exile, bowed against the hot wind, is laden with crude and corrosive particles of dust, and all his face, except a narrow slit for the eyes, is shielded with cloth against this treacherous dust, which settles everywhere and penetrates everything, only adding to the burden of gloom of the exiles.

NAIMEL

His father was of priestly lineage on his mother's side, and a man of Judah through his father. A family with roots stretching back to the son of Jesse on the one hand and the sons of Aaron on the other. His grandfather and his grandfather's father were counted among the senior advisers of the kings of Judah, as was his father too. A skilled archer was his father, and an accomplished swordsman, and a javelin thrown by his hand never missed its mark. Moreover he was a scholar and played on the lyre, and the anthems of King David were forever on his lips. No man dared compete with his father in horsemanship; while mounted on his horse he could shoot five arrows one after the other, and with each of them strike a target marked out for him on the trunk of a tree.

Before the coming of the Chaldeans, the king summoned his courtiers and urged them to compete among themselves in the arts of archery and horsemanship; shooting arrows and bringing down doves in flight, while riding a charger. The minister Naimel refused to take part in the contest, with the polite determination that was so typical of him. He saw no point in shooting arrows at blameless doves, he declared.

This was a reasonable argument to which the king had no answer, but there could be no doubt he was enraged by the refusal of his senior minister and adviser. Because he was not yet ready to dispense with his services, he allowed him to remain in his post. However, the king bore a grudge against him, and this grudge turned to open hatred when his father, the minister Naimel, supported Jeremiah, declaring him a true prophet through whom God was speaking, and saying it was a sacred duty to heed the voice of God and do His will, and not, Heaven forfend, be numbered among His enemies. Nevertheless, the minister Naimel allowed no one to speak ill of the king or revile him in his presence.

In a bitter moment during the siege, the king issued a stern edict according to which his senior minister and adviser Naimel was to be arrested, chained and imprisoned. And if the Chaldeans breached the wall – he was to be hanged on the nearest available tree. But all the ministers and advisers, and seasoned warriors, rose as one man in opposition to the king, even those who were the king's most avid supporters and the most implacable foes of Jeremiah the Prophet, spurning his prophecies out of hand. The edict was cancelled and never put into effect.

Thus, his father was reprieved, and not put in shackles, or thrown into a dungeon. And the king did not regret his clemency, for when the time came and the wall was breached, and the king fled for his life, Naimel stayed behind at his command in the abandoned palace, to defend its empty chambers and delay the Chaldeans for as long as possible in their pursuit of the fugitive king. Alongside the minister were a handful of the king's slaves and eunuchs, who had no training in warfare, and barely knew one end of a spear from the other. They quickly dispersed and left him to his fate, when the mighty Chaldean army smashed down the gates of the royal palace.

Melancholic memories come to mind: here is his father, teaching him to ride. In a few, short sentences, he explains what requires explanation, and demands, without a flicker of an eyebrow, that he perform for himself what has just been explained to him and demonstrated to him.

His father followed with an attentive eye every one of his movements, and every slightest twitch on the part of the horse, at that time a pampered mare, the best in their stable, and the most intelligent. His father had a thin and tranquil smile, a smile of composure blended with sincerity. His forehead was fair, gleaming, pure, testifying to wisdom and to a personality ignorant of the meaning of fear. The lines of his face symmetrical, carefully crafted, such as are found in those born to be kings, whose beauty bears the supreme stamp of the spiritual.

His father spoke little, and only of urgent matters. He met him but rarely, and every such meeting left a deep impression on his soul.

He loved his father, admired him painfully, revered him secretly, and did everything in his power to gain his approval and to be like him. And when he succeeded in this, as for instance in those riding lessons, and later when he was instructed in the arts of archery and of sword-play, and knew that his father was pleased with his progress, he was filled with elation such as he did not know existed.

His father never expressed his satisfaction or his dissatisfaction in words. Even the lines of his face showed no hint of what was happening inside him. But he knew for sure, without needing any hint, when his father was satisfied with him and when not. Instances of dissatisfaction he could hardly remember. And all this against the background of their rare meetings, in which they barely needed the spoken word in order to communicate with one another.

"Speech is superfluous," his father answered him once with that typical smile of his, redolent of charm and assurance together, and in spite of this, saying everything that needed saying.

"The more words are needed," his father explained, "the more foolish men are. The less they are needed – the wiser."

"And what about the Scriptures?" he asked.

"They are concise. Every word, every syllable, every letter, every dot – is in its place!"

His father never went out hunting, despite being a marksman. Nor did he eat meat, and in their family they never slaughtered a lamb or an ox or a goat. His father insisted on this, and so it was. And it aroused his curiosity to the point where, seizing one of those rare opportunities afforded by riding lessons, he asked what was the reason for this. In his typically succinct yet persuasive manner, which never failed to captivate and warm his heart, his father answered him:

"Read the Genesis Scroll, first chapter, verses twenty-nine and thirty."

As soon as the lesson was finished he ran home, found the Genesis Scroll and read: *And God said, Behold I have given you every herb bearing seed which is upon the face of all the earth and every tree in which is the fruit of a tree yielding seed and they shall be yours for food. And to every beast of the earth and to every fowl of the air and to everything that creeps upon the earth, in which is life, I give all herbs for food, and it was so.*

And the reading of this passage left him deeply confused. Did the Blessed and the Holy One really command man and beast to eat only vegetables and fruit? And yet, in the Scriptures there is also talk of sacrifices, and feasts, and the ritual of Passover... He had to muster all his patience and wait for the next riding lesson, which was, as it transpired, also the last, to put his questions to his father and mentor, making prodigious efforts not to reveal his inner turmoil.

And he obtained his answer:

"This is the law that is prior to sin. A true law. Man does not prey on beast, and beast does not prey on any living creature, and there is no sin."

"This could hardly be described as a law!" – he commented, tentatively.

"Without sin there is no need for law. The man who has not sinned is law personified."

"And at the end of days?" he asked.

"He will again be as he was before he sinned. Remember what the Prophet said: *The wolf and the lamb shall graze together, and the lion shall eat hay like the ox.*"

And then, and this is a moment he will never forget, his father turned to him and gave him a long look, different from any look he had experienced until that day and declared:

"*I do not delight in the blood of bullocks or of sheep*" – and these words too were unfamiliar to him, and in his efforts to grasp what it was that made this occasion special, something about his father's look and his voice, one word sprang into his mind and embedded itself there: warmth.

"And yet in spite of all this – there were feasts and sacrifices and the Passover ritual!" he exclaimed reluctantly, for he would have preferred not to have spoken at all, preserving at all costs the wonder of that moment. Nor was he expecting a response, but there was one.

"*Grace I desire rather than a feast, and knowledge of God rather than sacrifice*" – again his father quoted a verse from the Scriptures, this time from the Prophet Hosea.

"So what does it mean, when people still need meat?"

"It testifies to the sin that still prevails over them."

He remembered seeing his father one more time, the day before the wall was breached and the Chaldeans took Jerusalem.

At a late hour of the night his father came into his chamber, a little oil-lamp in his hand, and finding him awake, asked him if he understood that the soul is immortal, and death cannot come between those whose hearts are pure, who cleave to God and love Him with all their heart and might.

He nodded, assenting.

And without saying another word his father withdrew to the corridor and for some time he could make out the flashes of his lamp, until the light faded and was utterly absorbed by the darkness.

The following day the wall was breached, and the king commanded his father to stay in the palace, to repel the attacks of the Chaldeans and delay them for as long as was possible, to cover his own escape.

THREE BURNING ARROWS

The convoy climbed up to a broad plateau, the dusty road stretching across it straight as a ruler and with no obstacles to impede progress. Men and beasts quickened their pace and breathed more easily as less effort was required of them, and the jolting of the wagons subsided.

The young men were assailed by hunger.

He took from his knapsack a lump of sheep's cheese and a loaf of stale bread, cut off slices and distributed them to all the occupants of the wagon in equal shares. And they accepted their rations with gratitude and thanked him. Azariah passed around a small water-skin, Jerusalem water, which is not agreeable to the palate but refreshes like no other. And they pronounced the standard blessing over food. Most of them paid no attention to the words of blessing and thanksgiving addressed to their father in Heaven whereas a few, those accustomed to praying for a purpose, intoned the words one after the other, closely following their literal meaning.

"Is there is no meat?" asked one of the young men, not of their group.

"None," he answered him with a smile. Perhaps – the smile of his father, good-natured and yet at the same time warning against excessive closeness, and revealing a degree of firmness and resolution which never failed to elicit respectful acceptance.

Once he surprised his father when he was praying at home, found him kneeling, facing towards the Sanctuary, with hands joined. A most unusual posture indeed, the joining of the hands especially. He could not resist asking: "Why is this?" His father finished his prayer, rose from his strange kneeling position, a look in his eyes of distant serenity and without waiting for another question, he explained:

"This kneeling is the posture of an Egyptian slave who is devoted to his master with heart and soul, to the extent of utter self-abasement."

"And in this case," he construed – "it is our Father in Heaven who is our Lord." He intentionally used the plural forms, in the desire, repressed indeed but strong and emphatic, to be numbered, he too, among the beloved servants of God, and to abase himself before Him, like that Egyptian slave before his master.

In his accustomed way the minister Naimel confirmed his son's statement with a slight nod of the head which did nothing to conceal his satisfaction.

"And yet," the son saw fit to add – "this God to whom we cleave with heart and soul, will punish us for our sins against Him, however trivial they may be."

"This master," his father declared, his face turning suddenly grave – "will never punish, for the one and only name of this master is Love!"

Seeing his son's puzzled look, Naimel continued:

"God is love. Anger, offence, wrath and the like – have no place in God. Where these things are, God is not. Anyone who rejects God by behaving deceitfully, with hypocrisy and malice, brings upon himself a state of absence-of-God which some people have mistakenly defined as 'wrath of God'."

Here, in this jolting wagon, he would willingly have fallen to his knees and joined his hands in prayer to his Father in Heaven who is love, and thank Him for the joy that He has bestowed upon Him by the very knowledge of His existence, this knowledge being his inalienable property.

The jolting of the wagon went on. One of the youths, whose name was Adoniah, turned to him and asked:

"They say the minister Naimel abstained from eating meat... is that the truth, or merely a rumour?"

"It is the truth," he answered him calmly.

Adoniah asked another question, but he was no longer listening. Could this Adoniah ever comprehend the profundity of the truth, expose its hidden light and rejoice in it? Words are only dead weight. They are superfluous, and if silence is to no avail, then all the tongues of the world could not take its place and shed light on the tiniest particle of the divine, of the God whose name is Love.

The road was growing wider, and smoother, and the convoy proceeding at a satisfactory pace.

The sun inclined westward, and the far horizon, kissing the summits of a range of silent mountains, was ignited all at once into blazing fire, a sea of fire the colour of blood. The sight aroused the heart and left its impression upon those who witnessed it, but lasted only a few moments. The sea of fire began to pale, red-purple turning to orange, shading gently into yellow in the hallowed silence.

The commander of the convoy ordered his equerry to shoot three burning arrows into the clear skies of evening, the evening poised to descend on the world at any moment.

Slowly the convoy drew to a halt. Beasts, wagons and people stood silently, waiting. It emerged that the high plateau was crossed by a river, and the commander gave the order to water the animals and fill gourds with fresh water, take a hasty wash and eat some of the food that all were supposed to have brought with them.

The Chaldean soldiers clustered around their field-kitchen, heating up their rations on the brazier that they had brought along, on the spur of the moment.

The youths went down to the river, bathed in the refreshing water and disported themselves cheerfully, in the manner of the young. They dressed again, in clothing which, despite energetic brushing, were still ingrained with dust. In high spirits, they were about to sit down and resume their meal, when the order was given to harness and saddle the horses and start moving again. It seemed that the convoy commander was not satisfied with the distance travelled in the course of that sweltering day, and he meant to make up the deficit.

The cool, blue-tinged air of the evening was refreshing, and the commander's order aroused no resentment, overt or repressed. Oil lamps were prepared, fitted with brass shields, in case the journey continued into the night, and these were hung on the wagons and on the harness of the horses. Some of the walkers wore them suspended from their belts, while horsemen carried torches.

The youths raced one another back to their wagon, laughing and joking, and still laughing they climbed the high sides of the wagon and took their places inside.

Meanwhile the Chaldeans had brought back the draught-horses that had been watered and bathed in the river, and were harnessing them to their shafts with brisk and practised movement. The horses whinnied contentedly, thin vapour rising from their powerful bodies.

The convoy was about to move, when the deep silence of the evening was torn apart by a piercing cry. The young men froze in their seats. He was the first to recover his wits, and he jumped down from the wagon and ran towards the river, the source of the cry.

Between the river and the road, by which the convoy was to travel, he saw a man, a grown man, lying on the ground as a Chaldean soldier lashed him with his whip, lashed him repeatedly. Approaching the Chaldean, he cried in his language: "Stop!"

For a brief instant the latter froze where he stood. The voice was authoritative and untainted by fear or hesitation. The voice of a born leader and commander.

He seized the moment, hastened to the stricken man and bending over him, at once grasped the state of affairs: the man had fallen lame and could march no further. This, evidently, had aroused the wrath of the Chaldean.

The soldier recovered from his shock, and staring at the Jewish youth who had presumed to give him an order, he was incandescent with rage. He hissed a curse between pursed lips, raised his whip and was about to bring it down – this time on the back of the youth. At that moment, heard from above was the calm, deep-guttural voice of the convoy commander, also curious to discover the source of the commotion:

"Dismiss!"

The flustered soldier quickly disappeared in the blue-tinged shadows of the evening, dragging his long whip behind him.

The convoy commander, mounted on his piebald horse, turned to look at the young man, not saying a word.

"What is to be the fate of this man, who is unfit to travel further, who needs to rest for two days at least?" asked the youth, bent over the injured man.

"His head shall be struck off," declared the Chaldean.

"We shall care for him!" he cried with fervour, retaining such an air of firm resolution that the Chaldean officer could not but be impressed.

"That will not help!" he insisted.

"Let us try!" replied the youth.

The convoy commander pondered his decision. Clearly the youth was not to be easily swayed, and the orders given him had been most explicit: the "children" were to be delivered whole and healthy, unharmed, and in an equable state of mind, to the palace of the king. This being the case, petty disputes were to be avoided.

"Take him in your wagon!" he said, and rode back to the head of the column.

The other youths, who had followed and arrived on the scene after him, heard the conversation between him and the commander, and without a word said, approached the wounded and beaten exile, took him in their arms and quickly carried him to their wagon. They just had time to lay him down before the wagon lurched forward and was once more in motion, creaking stridently.

The name of the older man was Gershon. He was a calligrapher of scrolls by trade, whom the Chaldeans in their haste, as he explained it, had mistaken for a tanner, and therefore suitable for inclusion in the convoy of the exiles. The youths dressed his wounds and assured him that no harm would befall him, and he could travel all the way with them in the wagon, which while not an outstanding exemplar of comfort and luxury, would at least give some respite to his bare feet, which were not the feet of a peasant nor the calloused feet of a tanner.

Gershon did not know how to thank them. He blessed them, and blessed them again, with tears in his eyes, until the youths were so moved that they almost wept with him, while some of them had uneasy consciences, having not been as quick as Daniel to intervene in the episode.

Only a few moments had passed when at the command of the Chaldean officer their wagon was stopped. His stern face, framed by a wavy black beard, peered in through a gap in the canopy.

"You need to get rid of this man!" he declared, his voice deep and imperious. "The wagon can't carry all of you!"

"I don't mind lightening the load and walking alongside!" he retorted, in a calm but resolute tone of voice, no less authoritative than that of the Chaldean.

"I can't agree to that!" the Chaldean, adding by way of explanation: "It's my duty to deliver you, all of you, to Babylon, safe and sound and unharmed."

"Walking won't do me any harm," he insisted, and at this point Mishael and Azariah spoke up in his support, volunteering to ease the burden on the wagon themselves by walking alongside. And then Hananiah said:

"We can take turns walking, so no one will suffer any harm, no one will be over tired, and our esteemed commander can accomplish his mission and bring us to Babylon safe and sound – and refreshed as well since the atmosphere in the wagon is stifling and unhealthy, and it will do us all good to breathe a little fresh air outside it.

The senior officer had to admit that here too the Jewish youths had made a valid point. Whatever anger had arisen in his heart soon melted away and its place was taken by curiosity: How astute these young men are! – it was partly a question to himself, partly a statement. His lower lip twitched a little, in what was supposed to be a smile, faint and fleeting – yet expressing something that could be cautiously defined as sympathy.

"Who will be the first?" demanded the Chaldean in an even tone of voice. All four of the youths sitting in the forepart of the wagon sprang to their feet and made for the way out. Daniel stopped them.

"Please, good friends – let me the first to do this service!" – and without waiting for their response, he took advantage of the moment of indecision and jumped from the wagon. To the driver he shouted "Go!" – and began walking at a brisk pace.

The wide open space cleared, swallowing up, in a strange and inexplicable way, all the sounds emanating from the convoy; the creaking of wagons, the neighing of horses, the lowing of the livestock – oxen for slaughter and milch-cows, the orders given by Chaldean officers to their subordinates in peremptory tones, the gallop of horsemen patrolling the line of the convoy, the sighs and murmurs of those on foot.

The darkness thickened without impairing in any way the transparency of the air. The evening came down without a sound, stars glimmered. Suddenly, the sounds returned, to the relief of the ear. The transfer of watches between day and night was complete.

The convoy commander ordered the lighting of oil lamps and lanterns, and the torches carried by his horsemen. And the velveteen expanse was lit up by an infinite chain of points of glittering fire, responding to the greetings of the stars above, in their flickering radiance.

My Father in Heaven, my God, how can I be worthy of You, worthy of the abundance of Your grace that You have bestowed upon me? My Father in Heaven, my God, make me an instrument of humility in Your hand, for only in humility can I draw close to You, only out of humility can I serve You and do Your holy will!

He did not feel the ground under his feet, and it seemed to him at times he was hovering above it. The world melted around him and vanished, with all its shapes and marvels, as if it had never been, a world in which he had no interest. Within, the light broke through, shining on the surface of a sea of peace. He had no desire other than to live at all times and forever in this limpid light, to be, at all times and forever, a sea of peace.

When Abraham sensed that Isaac, his son, had captivated his heart, and his love for him was identical to his love for the source of all love, he decided at once to "sacrifice" Isaac – to put an end to this misunderstanding of love. For it was clear to him that any love not directed towards his Father in Heaven and his God, is a lie and a fraud, hypocrisy and pretence, which in the end will be shown to be the opposite of love. And when Abraham wields the "cleaver" of his love for his Creator, to put an end to the illusion of his love for his son, flesh of his flesh and blood of his blood and bone of his bone – then love personified, his Father in Heaven and his God – stays his hand, prevents the beloved one from putting an end to that which love personified has bestowed upon him – his son Isaac, who is flesh of his flesh and blood of his blood and bone of his bone. Falsehood will collapse on the spot, fall by its own agency, for this is its nature and its yardstick. Love will stand for ever, for this is its nature and its yardstick.

And once again the sign was given, and the convoy came to a halt, and the brief, vigorous, sometimes brusque orders were passed by liveried messengers, galloping on horseback on either side of the broad, dusty road. The air was cool but not too heavy to breathe, and as such was widely welcomed.

The column wheeled to form a circle – wagons in the middle, the exiles beside them and on the perimeter – the battle-hardened Chaldean cavalry.

The horses were tethered between the exiles and the low tents of the Chaldeans, and with them the milch-cows and the oxen destined for slaughter.

Camp-fires were quickly ablaze, and one of the oxen was butchered, its flesh roasted and distributed among the Chaldean soldiers. For a while there was heard the murmuring of people exchanging words about this or that, negotiating the loan of a bootlace or a kerchief. All were tired, including the livestock.

By order of the convoy commander, a large tent has been set up for the eight youths, who have brought their mats with them to be laid on the bare ground. Gershon has been left in the wagon, at his own earnest request, for fear of disruption and the chill of the night. The youths have left him a cloak and a goatskin rug, and he is more than satisfied with these, constantly thanking them and blessing them effusively for their generosity and nobility of spirit.

Inside the tent with its cattle-hide awning, the cold was not felt, and the air was gentle and pleasant. Hananiah lit one of the small lamps.

"Tomorrow we shall have more walking to do," commented Adoniah, hinting that the light was superfluous and they should take this opportunity to rest, thus rising in the morning alert and refreshed, ready to travel onward.

"Tomorrow it's my turn to march," Hananiah intoned in Daniel's ear, and put out the light. The white and radiant light of the stars was enough to distinguish between the shapes of the various figures.

"As you wish," the other replied.

They lay down on their mats and covered themselves with blankets of wool or goatskin. The four close friends bedded down in the innermost recesses of the tent, the others near the entrance. Hananiah lay beside Daniel, and at his feet Azariah stretched out. Mishael was curled up at Daniel's feet.

Hananiah was restless, and even the rigours and the upsets of the journey were not enough to bring sleep to his eyelids. He was pondering all kinds of strange and peculiar things, and in the process, stole a glance at his friend. Daniel lay supine, arms folded under his head, eyes open and staring into the dark void above him.

"Aren't you asleep?" Hananiah whispered

"No," the answer came.

"Have you noticed how closely we are being watched?"

"Yes."

"Why are we being summoned by King Nebuchadnezzar?"

"Ashpenaz the chief eunuch told us – we're to serve in his palace."

"Do you believe him?

"I do."

"I'm not inclined to believe him."

"Why is that?"

"You know – this is a pagan king, and I've heard about some weird practices."

"Such as?"

"Human sacrifices to Moloch, especially – boys!"

He grinned faintly, noting the emphatic supplement, so indicative of Hananiah's fears and misgivings.

"And I've heard rumours about women, especially – virgins!" he teased his friend.

Hananiah seemed offended. He was silent for a long moment and then whispered:

"The essential thing is to be prepared for this! I'm talking about sacrifice or anything of that kind."

"Meaning what?"

"Not bringing disgrace on the people of God, but sanctifying His name as is proper and fitting."

Slowly he turned his head towards his whispering friend. His face, sketched in the darkness with a few sharp lines, looked serious.

"There's no point discussing this," he remarked softly.

"Why is that?" Hananiah persisted.

"Because," – he turned and faced Hananiah again – "it's obvious."

Another prolonged silence. Hananiah replied with a sigh:

"It doesn't seem that obvious – to everyone, I mean," he corrected himself.

"If it isn't obvious to someone – explanations and sermons will do him no good."

"And what about someone to whom it is obvious?"

"He doesn't need them," he declared.

The muscles of Hananiah's body relaxed. He seemed relieved. He too lay on his back with arms under his head, but wasn't yet asleep.

A long moment passed and again Hananiah turned towards him and whispered:

"Asleep?"

"No."

"I looked at this Gershon and I felt a pang of compassion for him – over the beating he took and the deep wound in his leg and the whole thing – all the suffering that he's been through. I looked into his eyes, and saw nothing there but innocence. The innocence of a baby! Surely you can't say of such a man that he's a sinner or a criminal. He's one of our people. An artist. A calligrapher. And I suppose there must be many like him and yet – this dreadful scourge has fallen on him!"

"It wasn't the innocence reflected in the eyes of an artist like Gershon that dealt the people of God such a cruel blow."

"What then?"

"Lack of faith."

"Gershon was lacking in faith?"

"His teachers were."

"What have his teachers to do with it?

"He was swept along with them, believed in their teaching."

"What could he have done?"

"Turned to the source and asked Him."

"Turned to God and asked Him?"

He nodded in the darkness without turning to face his inquisitor.

"Perhaps his teachers didn't let him."

"No man can come between God and another man."

"He believed his teachers?"

"And didn't believe in God."

"They didn't teach him to turn to God."

"The thirsty man doesn't need to be taught to drink water."

"So why didn't he turn to God?"

"He wasn't thirsty for Him. It was convenient for him to listen to those who set themselves up as His envoys and His interpreters."

"Did they not set themselves up in obedience to the Torah?"

"The Torah which they neglected and perverted."

"A great blight on our people!"

"And the root of it – is pride."

"And yet – He chose us out of all the peoples!"

"It wasn't us that He chose, but a people that would follow Him and cleave to His truth. For as long as we followed Him and cleaved to His truth – we were His people, the people of God! When we stopped following Him and cleaving to His truth – we stopped being His people, stopped being the people of God."

"Scholars and teachers of the Torah don't share your interpretation!"

"That is why we have got to the state that we are in."

"What are we to do to set things right, as far as is possible?"

"Repent, cleave to Him, the Holy One, and live His truth!"

Hananiah pondered these words, pondered them at length and finally exclaimed:

"You are so right!" He felt his mind was now at ease, and deep, sweet slumber descended on him and closed his eyes.

The order to rise was given while it was still dark outside, and a few stars that had waxed and waned, and exchanged their brilliance for a dull red hue, were still suspended in the firmament. The moon had not yet withdrawn its lustre, and the chill was everywhere.

The exiles woke to the sound of the shouts of the soldiers, spurring their horses among the huddled forms on the bare ground.

A movement began towards the wagons and the livestock. Some had time to put on shawls and pray the dawn prayer, and some washed in the icy water, some paced vigorously back and forth, to shake the sleep from their limbs, while some lit small fires and tried to warm themselves with the meagre flames.

Meanwhile the draught-horses had been fetched and harnessed to the wagons, and the cattle were led to their position in the rear and hitched behind the open carts, and as the night retreated, and the distant pallor of morning rose to take its place, clouds of vapour rose from the mouths of the people and the bodies of the beasts.

And before sunrise, the convoy was marshalled into one long column, tensed for departure and ready to move on the giving of the order. The order was given, and three burning arrows pierced the silvery mists of the rising dawn.

The horses moved forward, people riding them, driving them or walking beside them. Somewhere, to the east, the point of a white-hot sword cleft the narrow line of the horizon above the heads of the silent mountains. The dark column of people, beasts and wagons shrank and dwindled to a mere shadow of itself. And in the wake of the gleaming sword there appeared a regal crown of gold on the head of the sun, and then the sun itself, and the people began the daily exchanges of opinions and speculations.

"Are those the heights of Gilead over there?"

"No. The heights of Gilead we've left far behind us!"

"On this side there's a fortress from the days of King Solomon, his august majesty!

"I can't see it!"

"Somewhere over there, at the foot of that hill, there's a peasant's cottage."

"You're right!" – another agreed, shielding his eyes to take a better view of the hill that they were approaching. "You're right!" he insisted and added: "Cottages... and all of them burnt out!"

"The handiwork of these friends of ours," – someone gestured with a raised shoulder towards the Chaldeans, and someone else nodded. A Chaldean officer yelled at a group of exiles who were milling around, making desperate efforts to work out where they were – and in the process lagging behind. At the sound of this cry the group of exiles dispersed and put on speed, catching up with the rest of the convoy and picking up the pace dictated by the Chaldeans, in their eyes – bitterness and repressed resentment. The convoy moved on in silence towards the distant, bright horizons.

Hananiah was walking beside the wagon, his hand on one of the struts to which the crude canopy was fastened – made of ox-hide that had not been adequately treated.

The youths crowded into the forward section of the wagon as it jolted along the way that had suddenly become rough, exposing sharp stones that had been hidden beneath the cover of grey dust.

He attended to Gershon's wound. The latter gave him a long, tormented and compassionate look.

"So, you are the son of the minister Naimel!" he said, dragging his body into a position intended to alleviate the pain caused to his injured leg by the jolting of the wagon. He helped him, putting a pair of cloaks under the leg for support, smearing the wound with oil and binding it in a clean cotton bandage.

"How did you know?" he asked, placing a folded kerchief under the knee.

"I asked," – Gershon sighed in pain or in sorrow, or both of them together – "and the lads told me, not all of them... there are some among them who are talkative, and some who are less talkative. The less talkative ones will do well in the court of the Chaldean king, Nebuchadnezzar. Those friends of yours, Hananiah the compassionate and Azariah the wise, and Mishael the humble. I know people and I take an interest in them. I used to have dealings with so many of them in my line of business, in the pursuit of my art. I even did a commission for the king, transcribing the sayings of the ancients on clean parchment. He wanted them read to him too, and he listened, heard and paid attention, but he did not uphold them. Even the word of the living God that the prophet from Anathoth preached before him – he would not accept!"

"And you?" he asked, helping him to sit in the corner of the wagon, close to him, and eyeing him calmly.

"I?.. Oh yes, I!" – he understood the question and replied: "To tell the truth, I myself did not heed or pay attention. A kind of thoughtlessness, an obtuseness of the heart that is beyond the strength of man to control."

"Such things are well within the strength of man to control," the young man declared calmly.

"Not always," the other replied. His denial was faint, hesitant. "How could it be believed that the people of God must bow down before these pagan Chaldeans?" And the older man went on to say: "I didn't believe it! I couldn't believe it"

"You didn't want to," the young man retorted without changing the tone of his voice.

The older man appraised him with a glazed look in his eyes:

"There were other prophets," he pointed out mildly – "and they prophesied otherwise."

"They prophesied what you wanted them to prophesy. If you had listened to the voice of your God, you would have recognised their deception."

"That voice didn't sound like the voice of my God!"

"Because you didn't believe it. You trusted in yourself – instead of trusting in Him."

"Perhaps," the older man sighed. "Everything is possible. Now, from a distance, things look different. I often examined my own mind, taking stock of myself, and some voice told me I was in error and my error was very grave – in that I refused to listen to the words of the man from Anathoth and to see in him the prophet of truth, but this voice faded and was quickly silenced. I stopped my ears from hearing. I was afraid of it. It was convenient for me to go with my friends and my relatives and – with the king! Are we not told, *the voice of the masses is the voice of Shaddai?*" He tried to grin, but the pain prevented this. He pursed his lips and ground his teeth. Drops of sweat sparkled on his narrow, wrinkled forehead. He wiped away the sweat with a kerchief.

"We have all sinned and done evil," Gershon went on to say after a short silence – "but we don't want to believe that we are no longer the people of God, that God is not with us, that He has abandoned us and turned His face away from us."

"God does not abandon anyone," the other declared and added – "but He doesn't force Himself on one who does not want Him."

"What does that mean, not wanting Him?" Gershon asked, fervently.

"Not keeping His commandments and making a mockery of His law."

"What you say is the truth!" Gershon responded after a pause for deliberation, looking up again at the void beneath the tattered canopy above him. "You are as wise a man as your father – and as brave!" He thought for a moment and then continued: "You need to know – I was told about your father's last moments. I heard it from an eye-witness. One of the king's slaves who was with the minister Naimel in the king's deserted palace, and fled for his life when the Chaldeans attacked them. The slave hid in a stone chest in the great hall that was used as a store for weapons, and he saw it all. And he couldn't help, or as I have no doubt you would say," – a bitter smile showed on the narrator's face – "he didn't want to help. The fact is, he was simply terrified... and when the Chaldeans had left the king's palace he slipped away and found refuge in my house. I have a large house, not far from the palace," the older man explained. If you want to know the whole story, I shall tell you," he offered, turning to look at him with his colourless eyes. The hair of Gershon's head was sparse as was his beard, and both were flecked with grey. His eyebrows thick, his expression sombre, and presumably this was how he had been even before he was injured. His body was lean, exceptionally lean, his cheekbones protuberant, and it seemed that the dark grey skin was their only protection.

He did not reply.

Gershon looked up again at the void above him and without waiting for a response from the youth, continued as if talking to himself:

"The slave, Manasseh by name, hid in that stone chest at the end of the great hall and against his will, truly against his will, he was a witness to all that happened.

"In the stone chest he was hiding in, there was a narrow slit at his eye-level, and through this he watched and saw it all, without intending to, as if he was compelled by some demon, commanding him: *Behold and see, and shame and torment of heart will be your lot, from now until the end of your days upon this earth.*

"The minister Naimel, mighty warrior that he was, fought ferociously against his assailants. At first there were six or seven of them, as the others were hunting for fugitives in the royal palace, in the parlours and the bed-chambers and the gardens. His back to the wall, the minister prevailed over his attackers and slew them. His trusty, battle-tested sword flashed back and forth, swift as lightning and just as deadly. Anyone who approached him was laid low by his sword, and when three knights attacked him all at once, in the twinkling of an eye not one of them was left alive. And it seemed that in just a moment the minister Naimel would carve himself a way through the hall and make his escape from the Chaldeans. And then two more of the Chaldean warriors rushed at him.

"'That long moment, that long fateful moment,' Manasseh the slave was crying to me, repeating it like a constant refrain – 'if I had burst out from the stone chest where I was hiding like a panic-stricken rabbit, if I had come out uttering a blood-curdling yell and taken my stand beside the minister Naimel! Just then, you see, there were only those two warriors to contend with, and I still had my sword at my hip and in a corner of the stone chest there was a spear that had been left behind. If I had come out of my hiding-place at that fateful moment, it's very likely the minister Naimel would still be with us, and I would have delivered my miserable soul from everlasting shame! How I wish I had been slain beside him! How I wish I had been slain!'

"And then the two of them uttered a cry fit to shake the foundations of the universe and it was answered by an echo, and at that moment Chaldeans seemed to pop up from every corner, in full armour and with drawn swords, and they streamed into the hall. And some of them had little bows, and were shooting arrows at the minister Naimel. The minister did not flinch or fail, but fought on, the sword flashing in his hand and sowing terror and death among the enemy, with three arrows in his body, two in the belly and one in the chest.

In the ranks of the Chaldeans there were two officers who stormed at him in a rage, refusing to believe that anyone with three arrows in his body would still have the strength to stand and resist his assailants..."

It was hot in the wagon, the air stagnant and heavy, and the jolting never ending. Some of the youths jumped out to join Hananiah, walking alongside.

"So they rushed upon him, those Chaldean officers," – Gershon continued his account, with no change in the tone of his voice – "and they were killed there and then. The head of one of them flew off and hit the wall, smearing his blood all over it, the other was run through the heart. For a moment – according to the eye-witness – the Chaldeans withdrew, stunned and confused at the spectacle unfolding before their eyes. In the opinion of the secret watcher, in this retreat of the Chaldeans there was an element of respect, besides the incomprehension and the fear. And then from behind them there appeared a veritable man-monster, a giant who would have dwarfed even Goliath the Philistine himself, and on his shoulder he was carrying a great stone ball, evidently a capital torn from a wrecked marble pillar. The giant hurled his ball at the minister Naimel, and the witness was sure that he must have been crushed beneath it. But he quickly realised that the man-monster had missed his mark, or the intrepid warrior had stepped aside just in time, and the stone failed to hit him. But then the monster charged at him, and the minister fought him ferociously, hacking at his legs with his sword until the giant fell face-forward to the floor, sprawling on him full-length and pinning him down with his body. At that moment hordes of Chaldeans joined the attack with wild cries and deafening yells, slaying both the man-monster and the saint of Israel trapped beneath him, the minister Naimel." With his narrow little hand Gershon wiped away two tears that had fallen from his colourless eyes, and he was silent.

Besides them, sitting at the front of the wagon were Azariah and Adoniah, out of earshot of the narrator – not that they seemed to be paying any attention.

"Something else I shall tell you," – Gershon suddenly resumed – "when that man, that slave Manasseh, told me what he told me, because he couldn't keep to himself what his eyes had seen, I felt a strong urge to strike him, if not with a sword, then with some implement or other, to stun him for a moment and see him sprawling helpless at my feet. And he, this unhappy slave, this Manasseh, sensed this – and how do you suppose he responded?" A note of curiosity crept into Gershon's agitated voice, and he turned to face the young man who was listening to his words, silent and unflinching.

"Don't you want to guess?" he exclaimed, knitting his brows in a supreme effort to control himself.

The narrator went back to staring into the void above him, the canopy of the wagon which never stopped flapping for a moment.

"I asked because I reckoned you would never guess, any more than me, any more than any rational and reasonable man. This Manasseh," – Gershon continued smoothly – "all of a sudden and without any warning – fell on his knees and barked at me like a dog: 'Do it, Gershon Ben-Caleb Ben-Judah, do it, I'm begging you!' And he wailed a piteous wail and broke into bitter weeping, the like of which I have never heard, nor ever hope to hear again. And he kissed the floor at my feet, and cried again: 'I wish I had died before I saw with my own eyes what I saw!' And he was wailing and sobbing at my feet, and yelling: 'Do this, Gershon Ben-Caleb Ben-Judah, do it if you're a man!' And I, you understand, couldn't do it, not that I didn't want to – I couldn't, I wasn't capable. And I don't regret this, I don't regret it in the slightest! I just feel sorry for that poor wretch. I have no doubt he was seeking his death and perhaps – since then he has found it. If it is so, let us pray to the Lord to have mercy on his soul and relieve him of that terrible burden.

"I shall join in that prayer of yours, and entreat my Father in Heaven and my God, not to abandon his unhappy soul but to grant him absolution."

The older man gave the youth a lingering, wondering look.

"I wish there were more in Israel like your father and yourself, men of compassionate and steadfast heart!" he said.

For a long moment silence reigned beneath the canopy of the wagon.

"And how has it come about," the youth asked, in a serene tone of voice – "that the Chaldeans have seized you and exiled you to Babylon as a tanner? Surely you are a calligrapher of scrolls, and the Chaldeans are not fools!"

"You are absolutely right," the older man replied and added: "They are not the world's brightest people, but they are not total idiots either."

"And yet?" the youth pressed him.

"As far as the Chaldeans are concerned," – the man turned to him with a smile, half cunning and half bashful sketched in his eyes, his bluish lips tensed – "Gershon Ben Caleb Ben Judah does not exist. They know of no such man! If you ask, they will tell you that my name is Jacob Ben Eliezer, the tanner."

"And there really is a tanner of that name?" he asked him, as if guessing what lay behind this statement.

"A tanner born and bred!" the other confirmed and went on to explain: "He is my brother-in-law, brother of my wife who passed away some ten years ago. The most wonderful among women was my wife – lovely as a gazelle, industrious as an ant, wise as a queen and yet, the Lord of all the worlds claimed her and took her from my embrace."

"That's no way for a man of faith to talk!" – he interrupted him gently

The one sprawled on his back once more turned to the youth with a look of wonder:

"You are right, of course!" he declared – "And I regret my over hasty tongue! This brother-in-law of mine is also a fugitive from the Chaldeans, and he came to seek refuge in my house. He has two sons, both of them adults, who fled from Jerusalem in time and found safety in Edom, with their great-uncle who was of Edomite origin but converted in the end and became one of the people of Israel. I am childless, and this brother-in-law of mine, Jacob Ben-Eliezer, besides his two grown-up sons has five more, three sons and two daughters, the oldest of them nine years old and the youngest of all – not yet turned two. Anyway, the man was on the run from the Chaldeans who were on his trail, intent on including him in the convoy of exiles due to leave Jerusalem a few days hence.

"Before dawn the man knocked on my door, and when I opened it for him, he pleaded with me in a tremulous voice:

" 'Please, my brother, my dear friend, may the Lord be your helper and make your ways straight, and preserve you from sickness and from foe, and prolong the days of your life in this world, so you shall know joy and peace and riches, and you shall be truly blessed!' All these salutations and we are still standing on the threshold, he trembling and I mystified, and then he suddenly bursts out with the cry: 'Save me dear brother from the Chaldeans, hide me in your house that the Lord gave you in His bounty! I have a wife and young children, and how can I abandon them and go into exile in Babylon, never to see them again, nor they to see me!' And his eyes filled with tears.

"I brought him into my house, locked the door behind him and pointed to the hiding-place, a dark alcove in the corner of the cellar that was used for storing winter firewood. As he was still on his way down the steps, and I closing the trapdoor behind him, there was a thunderous knocking at the main door, almost enough to uproot it from its hinges.

"I ran to the door, scared, a big oil-lamp in my hand, and asked who was there. The answer came in the Aramaic language: 'In the name of the King of Kings Nebuchadnezzar, conqueror of the universe, open at once if you value your life.' I valued my life.

"Seven men burst in, armed from head to foot, two of them wielding blazing torches.

"'Where is the tanner, Jacob Ben-Eliezer?'

"Thoughts were running riot in my feverish mind: if I say *He's not here!* – they'll turn the place upside down and find him, dragging me away to the scaffold, and him to Babylon. If I reveal his hiding-place to them, I'll have saved my skin but not his. He, my brother-in-law, is a man of substance and five children depend on him. Whereas I, by contrast – I'm childless and utterly useless.

"In those tense moments of fear and anxiety and indecision, I hear myself answering the soldiers: 'I am Jacob Ben-Eliezer the tanner!'

"A wild hoot of laughter broke out among the soldiers, a laugh of satisfaction and relief at a task successfully performed, or the finding of something that was supposed to be lost. In the gloom they couldn't see me properly or estimate my age, and even if they had seen me, they wouldn't have noticed the deception, as they didn't know what my brother-in-law looked like or how old he was.

'By command of the King of Kings, Nebuchadnezzar his name, pack your belongings at once and come with us. Fortune has smiled on you and you are to be numbered among the tanners of the glorious metropolis of Babylon, serving the greatest king in the universe!'

"Fortune has indeed smiled on me," the older man sighed. "Here I am, as you see, with you – Gershon Ben Caleb Ben Judah, calligrapher of scrolls, supposed to be serving the greatest of all kings in the universe, Nebuchadnezzar his name – as a tanner! It seems to me that if I make it to Babylon, and I'm not even sure of that, all I have to look forward to is a sentence of death!"

"Don't dwell on the dark side, my friend," the youth interposed: "After all, you saved a whole family from a cruel fate, and gave back to five children and a wife their father and husband and breadwinner!" They were both silent. Time passed.

One after another the youths climbed onto the wagon and took their places. The sun blazed down, the air was hot and sultry. Outside, Azariah was still walking.

One of the youths turned to him and asked something, but he wasn't listening and didn't respond. The vision of his father's death as described to him by Gershon was trapped in his mind, and he could not rid himself of it.

Yet again, perhaps for the tenth time, he saw everything that happened in the great hall of the palace, in all its most minute details, even those that were not mentioned in Gershon's account. Such as, for example, the pallor of his father's face, the pain reflected in his eyes, that he was so adept at suppressing, the pain of the arrows shot into him by the Chaldeans, arrows that could perhaps have been removed without causing further injury. It was all replayed in his mind's eye, vivid and alive, as if had not been a wretched slave who witnessed the episode but he himself, in person, crouching there in the chilly weapons store, watching all, seeing all.

He tried, and tried again, to detach himself from the series of images, to cleanse his mind of them, and could not do it. The bizarre spectacle repeated itself with searing clarity, with terrifying acuity.

If... if... if only – he was ashamed to finish the sentence with the words: I had been there – for this was a childish thought and not a mature one. "But *You* were there!" – he hastened to declare – "You, my holy Father in Heaven, my God, You whose name is love, You who are love, true love overseeing all, defending all, controlling all. And if You were there, and things transpired in the way they transpired, and ended as they ended, it means that everything happened in the proper and the foreseen manner, and what happened had to happen, and it was the good and the right outcome for your faithful servant, none other than my father in the flesh, the minister Naimel, the dauntless warrior. In my heart there is not a shred of doubt that my father in the flesh, Naimel, who cleaved to You with all his heart and all his might, at all times and always, and loved You with a love strong as death, as indeed do I, accepted what You decreed for him with gratitude, with joy and with love, and was aware of Your presence in those fateful moments, and came to You with joy and gladness, and sanctified Your name. And although he has left behind his broken body – He is in your presence and will be united with You forever, and be an inseparable part of Your living light!"

TAURUS MOUNTAINS

The road was straighter now, and the jolting less troublesome. Gershon dozed, while his fellow-travellers in the wagon whispered among themselves, trying not to wake him.

With an agile movement, gripping the side panel of the wagon for support, Daniel made his way to the aperture and jumped down into the dazzling light of a ferocious summer sun.

"Get into the wagon, Azariah, I want to stretch my legs!" – he smiled into his friend's gloomy face.

"It isn't time for the change-over yet, and you're not the one who's after me. It's Adoniah's turn next!"

"Go on Azariah, you need the rest!" – his voice was gentle and clear, but also firm and decisive, as irresistible as his genuine smile, the smile of one who has never known the meaning of deceit.

Azariah touched his shoulder, a friendly gesture, responded to his smile with a smile of his own, and climbed into the wagon.

The time was early afternoon, and the sun was beating down with undiminished vigour, but he was unaware of its scorching. His heart was filled with joy and his impulse was to break into song, a song of praise to the Creator of all, his all-seeing Father in Heaven, who spoke through the lips of his servant David, son of Jesse: *I said, you are God, and all of you sons of the Most High!*

The commander of the convoy approached him, mounted on his powerful steed. It was evident that the heat of the sun was not agreeing with him. He had removed some of his armour, the visor of his helmet was open, secured with a goatskin strap, and his face was roasting. Both horse and rider were sweating profusely.

"This isn't a fair sharing out of the walking duties!" he commented, adding: "I saw you yesterday, and I see you today. Where are your friends? What kind of friends are they?"

He looked up and answered him, his voice calm and even:

"It was my choice to walk!"

"Walking in the sun is not my idea of a pleasurable pastime," – the Chaldean spoke fluent Aramaic, seasoned with occasional words borrowed from the Holy Tongue.

"Pleasure is not dependent on the sun," he retorted in the same tone, turning away and looking straight ahead at the broad dusty road, the royal highway, built by the Egyptians and improved by the Chaldeans, nations locked in conflict for mastery of the world.

"What is it dependent on?" the Chaldean asked with some interest, clearly seeking some way of distracting his attention from the heat.

"The heart," he answered him.

"How is it dependent on the heart?" the Chaldean queried.

"If there is no joy in the heart – even in Paradise man will be miserable, and if the heart is singing joyful songs to its God – then Hell itself will be turned into Paradise!" he declared.

The convoy commander reined in his thoroughbred mount and paused to reflect on the young man's answer, turning it over in his mind. Then, with a light touch of his whip on the horse's handsome neck he moved on, keeping pace with the young man as he stepped out with vigorous tread.

On the eastern side of the road appeared another ruined Jewish village.

The convoy commander's horse was showing signs of distress, shying and bucking, rearing on his hind legs and whinnying repeatedly. It took considerable effort on the part of his rider, fine horseman that he was, to control and pacify him.

"Your horse is upset by what he sees!" the youth commented.

The Chaldean officer was more impressed than ever: "You understand horses too?"

"I do."

"It's as you say," the rider admitted, going on to explain: "This horse was present at the massacre that we carried out in the rebel villages!" There was a hard edge to his deep, guttural voice – a ploy to mask his unease. "They didn't heed the warnings, or listen to the voice of their God, speaking through their great prophet, Jeremiah!"

"The one who slaughtered these wretched peasants – was he listening to the voice of his God?" – asked the youth, fixing the Chaldean with a stern, reproachful look.

"King Nebuchadnezzar is our God, his voice we hear and his commands we obey!" the other snapped.

"Nebuchadnezzar is no deity but a man, flesh and blood, ruling by the grace of God. And if his actions are not acceptable to the One who bestows His grace upon him – he won't be a king for much longer!"

"The penalty for speaking out against our King and our God is death by hanging!" – the Chaldean threatened, but the menace in his voice was overridden by his amazement at the young man's reply. The more he spoke with him, the greater his wonderment grew.

"The man who kills for the sake of killing, is defying God!"

"How then are certain persons to prevail over others in battles and in warfare?" – the Chaldean shot at the young man, still walking alongside the wagon with confident mien.

"The one whose faith is true faith, and whose God is the living God, has no need to take human lives and burn down people's homes to prove himself the victor!"

"How can that be?" – the Chaldean's bemusement was sincere and he listened attentively to the words of the youth, leaning towards him in the effort to learn something of his wisdom.

Disregarding his question, the youth went on to say:

"Crowds will come flocking to such a man with joy and jubilation, and they will greet him with singing and dancing, and urge him to consent to being their leader, and they will make him their king, and he will be to them a governor and a mentor, ruling over them with justice, with truth and with love! His victory will be absolute and his praise – eternal praise!"

"You mean – a king who rules with the consent of his people, and not by virtue of royal and noble birth?" asked the Chaldean.

"I mean – a king who rules with the consent of the living God, who is love!"

"There are no such kings!" the rider declared, unconsciously tugging at the reins of his pampered horse, and the horse whinnied uneasily, rearing and stamping the hard ground with his hooves, before calming down again and submitting to the will of his master.

"There are no others!" the youth asserted, adding: "He who takes the lives of human beings and burns their dwellings to subject them to his rule – his faith is not true faith, and his God, not the living God!"

The Chaldean soldier was silent. He too was silent. What more was there to say? What he needed to say, he had said. The good seed was scattered. Whether it would flourish and prosper and grow tall, and ripen and bear fruit – this depended on the quality of the ground on which it fell.

They walked on, about the distance of half a parasang, in unbroken silence, side by side, the Chaldean horseman and the Jewish youth on foot.

The convoy commander took a long-necked jug from his saddle-bag, leaned towards the youth and said:

"Be my guest, take a drink of this pure water, fresh from the spring.

My equerry filled this jug a little while ago," and he handed it to the youth.

He took the jug, raised it in his right hand and drank from it in the ploughman's fashion – letting the water trickle from a height straight into the mouth, without the lips touching the jug. The water was cold, fresh and sweet to the taste, Galilean spring-water, renowned throughout the land of Judah.

"Thankyou!" – he returned the jug to its owner.

"And now I must make haste and see how matters are proceeding at the head of the column! It has been a pleasure talking to you," the Chaldean added, "and I am sure we shall meet again in the palace of King Nebuchadnezzar! My name" – he introduced himself – "is Or-Nego. May your God go with you!" And he spurred his horse and galloped away at the side of the long column and disappeared from view, kicking up behind him clouds of powdery, cloying dust, that hung suspended in the air.

Day followed day, according to well-established routine: setting out, on foot or on horseback, before the sunrise, a brief halt in the middle of the day, a snack at noon, overnight camp beside a lake or a river, washing of beasts and of people alike, evening meal around campfires, curling up and sleeping, reveille before the sun has risen and the last of the stars has faded, meticulous inspection of wagons, horses' hooves, cargo, weaponry, then the saddling and harnessing of horses, and the cycle of the day begins again.

They swallowed up the land, crossing over Judah and Galilee, climbed up to the heights of Ashur and left them far behind, proceeded slowly along the steep and narrow roadway to the forbidding Taurus mountains, and here one of the older horses perished, and one of the milch-cows fell into a deep crevice and was lost. From the Taurus mountains they saw the eternal snow on peaks far away to the west, and began the slow descent towards their destination, the kingdom of Babylon and the city of Babylon, the greatest city in the universe whose king, so it was said by all, had conquered all the nations of the world or cast his fear upon them, and there was no land and no people that did not pay him tribute in goods and in slaves.

The second week passed and then the group of young men realised that there had been no improvement in Gershon's condition; on the contrary – his health had deteriorated and he was a state far worse than that of before; his injured leg was swollen and he was plagued by fever, suffering hallucinations and muttering incoherently, sometimes turning to his God in prayer, sometimes staring blankly at the young men, eyes wide open but seeing nothing.

Adoniah suggested they appeal to the convoy commander, and ask him to send one of the surgeons in the service of the Chaldean army, to examine the invalid and pronounce whatever judgment he would pronounce. The suggestion was accepted.

Or-Nego heard him out in silence, and when he had finished, spurred his horse and rode away along the line of the column. Half an hour later, one of the Chaldean surgeons presented himself, asking to see the patient. Daniel pointed to the interior of the wagon. The surgeon went inside, leaned over Gershon, examined his wound, his leg that was swollen and turning blue, saw the seeping discharge, laid a hand on his sweating brow, withdrew in silence and climbed down from the wagon.

"There's no hope for him!" he told the young man. "Even if we amputate the leg, it would do him no good. The best treatment for him is a quick and merciful, painless death. His suffering will be over, and the progress of the convoy not impeded."

The surgeon reported to the convoy commander, and the latter came and asked the young man, solemnly, what he proposed to do with the casualty.

"We shall try to cure him!" was the brief reply.

"Do you have some treatment at your disposal that the surgeon does not?"

"We have."

"And that is?"

"Prayer."

The Chaldean gave him a quizzical look.

"He's holding up the convoy!" he declared.

"By God's grace he will be well enough to walk with the rest of them."

"And if not?"

"Then do with him as you see fit."

"Will three days be long enough to cure him?"

"Ample!" he replied.

The Chaldean turned his horse and sped back to the head of the column.

The surface of the road had changed and was rockier than before. Clouds of dust, rising in plumes in the wake of the charging horses and befouling the air, were a thing of the past.

When they halted for the night, he approached his companions, telling them of his conversation with Or-Nego and suggesting they pray together for the recovery of Gershon. They agreed, but with reservations. Adoniah reckoned there was no point bothering God in a hopeless case such as this, and his two friends, Matthew and Gabriel, supported him, albeit hesitantly. Uziel was silent, as if not caring either way. Azariah, Mishael and Hananiah supported Daniel enthusiastically.

"Let us pray!" – he said and knelt, putting his hands together and lifting them up towards the lofty, starry sky.

The youths stared at one another in amazement. His three friends, Azariah, Hananiah and Mishael, followed his example, kneeling, joining hands obediently and lifting them up to the sky and the great stars, twinkling with their enchanted light. Uziel also did likewise, kneeling and putting his palms together, but not raising them heavenwards. While Gabriel hesitated, Matthew and Adoniah sprang to their feet.

"This is nothing but idolatry!" cried Adoniah in a croaking voice, turning his back on the group. Matthew followed his lead and they both disappeared in the dark.

He did not respond to Adoniah's comment, did not even hear it. Nor did he pay any attention to the departure of Adoniah and Matthew, or to the way that Uziel was not raising his hands, while Gabriel was not putting his hands together but simply kneeling, as if unable to make up his mind.

"I pray, my Father in Heaven, in Your mercy and Your compassion and Your kindness and Your love – please heal your servant Gershon Ben Caleb Ben Judah, deliver his soul from torment, deliver him!" And this he repeated three times. He lowered his head and let his hands fall limply to his sides, then sank into a deep silence, that neither Heaven above nor the earth beneath could have broken.

Long moments passed. He rose finally, turned to his friends, standing there immobile, like shadows bereft of the life-force, and said to them:

"By the grace and the love of God, Gershon is cured!" And he turned, and walked to the camp.

They found themselves a place beside one of the campfires that had been well stoked, spread out their mats, curled up in their blankets, and fell asleep, shielded from the fierce chill of the night by the bright flames of the fire.

Not one of them dreamed, but all were aware of something limpid, intensely pleasurable, filling their entire being, and their lips eased into smiles and their faces lit up as they slept. And when the reveille was sounded and all were awakened, the youths emerged from beneath their blankets, washed hands and faces, covered the embers of the fire with dust, picked up their mats and climbed into the wagon, happy and invigorated – and saw no sign of Gershon.

"The man has disappeared!" cried Gabriel, who was the first into the wagon. And Uziel was quick to add:

"I expect he went out to relieve himself, and fell into one of the gullies and got himself stuck there, and even if some wild beast hasn't attacked him, you can be sure he's given up the ghost by now, returned his sinful soul to his Maker!"

"Or perhaps he went to the waterside to wash his hands and face, and give joyful thanks to his Creator, Hallelujah!" – an unexpected voice rang out behind them, responding to Uziel's words, a voice that made their hair stand on end.

"The invalid has risen from his sickbed, and lives by the grace and the compassion of God!" exclaimed Hananiah, pointing to Gershon who stood before them steadily on both his legs, a broad smile on his face and eyes sparkling with youthful light. The youths regained their composure and all of them, including Matthew and Adoniah who had popped up from somewhere, cried with one voice:

"Hallelujah! Praise be to the Lord Most High! Hallelujah!"

His eyes filled with tears, and he moved away from the group, found a secluded spot behind a bush and sat for a long while in silence, his whole being suffused with gratitude to the living God.

When he returned, he found the young men gathered around Gershon, intent on discovering, to the last detail, when and how the change had come about, when and how the debilitating fever had left him, and his rotting leg had healed and he had been utterly cured of all his ailments, his pains at an end, and his soul delivered.

And he was happy to oblige them, willingly answering all their questions, giving a full and detailed account of the miracle, how it had happened and when, and in what circumstances:

"I was in the grip of a fever, not knowing where I was, not knowing who I was, and great sinner that I am, I called upon the Holy One Blessed be He and begged Him to let me die, just so I should be spared further torment, the throbbing agony creeping up my leg, my head that was spinning like a wheel, my heart beating like a drum in my chest!

"I didn't expect, and it never occurred to me, there would be a change for the better, and I didn't imagine I had the right, or could find the courage – to appeal to the Lord my God to restore me to life!

"How I longed to stop being, to stop suffering, to die! And my pain grew worse, until all of a sudden, in a way I shall never be able to explain to myself, it stopped, all at once, as if it had been cut by a knife. It was over, finished, fading and disappearing as if it never had been.

"I was born again! At first I didn't believe it. I thought it was just a hallucination, a dream! I'm dreaming a dream that isn't real, I told myself, and I hope I'll never wake up! But what kind of dream is it – I asked myself – if I can feel my right hand holding my left, pinching my arm, and the pain, the exquisite pain! – spreading through all my limbs? So I'm awake! Awake and not suffering, not in torment! A miracle has been done here, a miracle!

"The Holy One Blessed be He – He has taken pity on me. Unbelievable! Well, I said to myself – let's have a look and see what's left of my rotting leg. And very carefully I unwrapped the cotton bandage, and already seeing in my mind's eye the vile discharge and bracing myself for the stench. And here is the leg! No discharge and no stench, no sign or trace of gangrene – all thanks and praise to the God Above! The limb is whole and healthy, as if it never was infected at all!

"So there it is my young brothers, my friends and my children! Praise and glory to God the most High, Hallelujah!" – and Gershon was leaping and cavorting, dancing before the group of young men, who were still staring in disbelief, and constantly touching his thigh and stroking his shin, as if refusing to believe the evidence of his senses.

And when Gershon and he came face to face, with no one else close by, Gershon said to him:

"I suppose this came about through the merit that I earned with that act of charity of mine, saving my brother-in-law from exile and coming in his place, and taking on myself his suffering and his anguish." If Gershon expected to hear approbation of this statement, he would be disappointed.

After a long moment Daniel looked up and gave Gershon a cool and incisive look, and answered him:

"That act of charity of yours, I've changed my mind about it. That wasn't an act inspired by faith."

"How is that?" – Gershon was bemused.

"If you had trusted in your God with flawless trust, you wouldn't have needed to deceive anyone. You would have turned to Him, your Father in Heaven and your God, and sought His mercy, and His grace and His love – and your brother-in-law would have been saved!"

"What was I supposed to tell the Chaldeans?" Gershon persisted.

"That you trusted in your God."

"And then?"

"They would have gone away without another word, leaving your house, and you could have stayed with your brother-in-law and not gone into exile, spared all your pain and suffering."

The older man gave him a silent, probing look and finally said:

"What must I do now?"

"Cleave always to your God, trust in Him and strengthen your faith!"

"How can I strengthen my faith?"

"By upholding His commandments and keeping your heart pure, avoiding all contamination by the world!"

Meanwhile the order had been given and the draught-horses were being harnessed to the wagons and the riding horses saddled, and the legs of the few remaining oxen and milch-cows unhobbled as they were led to their allotted place at the rear of the column, behind the ordnance wagons.

And between the beasts and the wagons thousands of people were milling about, voices rising in the chilly air of the early dawn – strident, grating-guttural, angry. And once again commanders were issuing orders in brusque, imperious tones to their subordinates, and the latter spurring on their horses and harassing the exiles, yelling repeatedly in their ears. And the rabble shuffled into a long and silent file, waiting tensely for the starting signal.

And the sign was given, and the convoy was in motion once more. This was the seventeenth day, and the sun had not yet risen but its blessed light, infusing energy and vigour, was already felt by those swarming bodies as they began the day's march, faces clearing and eyes turned eastward, in enchanted expectation of the rising dawn.

Before an hour had passed, somewhere the screen was lifted and the light spread swiftly along the line of the horizon, honing it and breathing life into it, bright light turning gold and turning pink and burning with purple fire, standing still like a royal guard poised to greet the king, and the king rises in all his majesty and splendour, lighting up the broad expanse of the land.

And so the day began, the seventeenth since their departure from Jerusalem, capital of the kings of Israel and Judah.

Or-Nego rode along the line of the convoy, his equerry riding beside him, and on reaching the wagon in which the youths were travelling, he approached Daniel and greeted him with a salute, then leaned towards him and inquired after the health of the invalid.

By way of answer, he turned and shouted to Gershon, walking on the other side of the wagon: "Gershon!"

The latter rounded the wagon and stood between it and the convoy commander.

For a moment the commander froze in his saddle, evidently dumbfounded. And when he had regained his senses, he leaned down again from his horse to take a closer look at the face of the older man. Without waiting for the order, the latter lifted his robe and revealed the perfectly healthy leg, which only yesterday had been oozing pus.

"Is this you?" the Chaldean exclaimed, making no attempt to conceal the astonishment which was untypical of him, and without waiting for Gershon's nod, ordered his equerry to fetch the surgeon.

The young men's wagon was moving on, and he and Gershon had to hurry to catch up with it. Or-Nego remained for some time behind them, sitting on his horse and wrapped up in his thoughts.

The equerry returned with the surgeon and reported to his commander, who ordered the surgeon to take a good look at Gershon; only yesterday this man had been an invalid with just hours to live, a suitable candidate for mercy-killing, in his own interests and the interests of the convoy.

The surgeon was flabbergasted. He spurred on his horse to catch up with the young men, then dismounted and walked beside Gershon, the reins in his hand and the animal trailing along behind. For a long time he was staring intently into the older man's face, studying his expression which showed nothing other than youthful alacrity.

The surgeon stopped Gershon, knelt down and exposed his leg, probed it and prodded it – a totally healthy leg. No one could have imagined that only yesterday it had been consumed by gangrene, a dead leg that even amputation could not have cured, since the infection was already spreading to other parts of the body.

The surgeon left the former invalid, rose from his kneeling posture and stared up at the clear sky, his eyes devoid of any expression. And suddenly he fell to his knees, at the feet of the astonished Gershon, in an attitude of extreme reverence, even prostrating himself on the ground, before rising and saying to Or-Nego, who had just caught up with them:

"This man is a saint, a veritable saint, and that is why he has been granted a complete cure by the grace of God! Either that, or the young man who prayed for him is no ordinary young man but the chosen envoy of God Almighty, and he is to be served, honoured and obeyed in everything he says and every commandment he gives, and he is not to be harmed in any way, since injury to the envoy of God is the same as the attempt to injure God Himself!"

"So what is all your learning worth, surgeon!" cried the convoy commander, showing clear signs of anger and disappointment.

"I am worth nothing, most esteemed commander, and my learning is as nothing!" – the surgeon answered him calmly – "In comparison with my creator and provider, the God who dwells in glory in the heights of Heaven, and in comparison with this youth, who is His chosen envoy."

"So there's no point in consulting you any more," Or-Nego commented, his annoyance dissipating and giving way to a mood of jocularity. "We shall have to turn to God, and no doubt He will save us!"

"Turning to God is best, but not everyone is fit to turn to Him and not everyone knows how to turn, and not everyone will have his prayers answered!"

"And can you not make yourself fit to turn to Him, so that you know the way to turn to Him?" the convoy commander went on to ask.

"It is not a skill that is taught in academies, Sir, and the knowledge of how to approach Him is not handed down from one man to another! These things God gives in His infinite grace, and He it is who decides who is fit for Him and who will know the ways that lead to Him. Anyway – no man of malice or avarice will be among His chosen ones!" the surgeon concluded.

The convoy commander looked at him keenly, as if this were a new man standing before him.

"You're to hold your tongue, and not tell anyone of the things you have witnessed!" Or-Nego declared, seeing fit to add: "Rumours like these are like fire, not easy to stop once it has taken hold!" and so saying he turned his horse and rode slowly towards the rear of the column.

Without another word, the surgeon mounted his horse and rode away in the opposite direction.

The rumour spread far and wide. And no one could have foreseen the events that would ensue, or have prevented them.

As evening fell a great crowd, exiles and Chaldeans alike, gathered around the young men's wagon, which was forced to slow down. All were clamouring to speak with the youth who had "cured by the grace of God" a man expected to die; according to some accounts, he had raised from the dead a man whose funeral had already taken place and who was about to be buried, restoring him to life. They were eager to feast their eyes on this miraculous youth, to touch his cloak, kiss his hand and ask him to perform a miracle for them too, not a spectacular or intimidating miracle, but a miracle nonetheless, since many of them were suffering from ailments and afflictions of various kinds.

Or-Nego reprimanded the surgeon, who claimed it was not his fault that the information had leaked; rumours such as these are passed in mysterious ways, not through any human agency, and are not to be prevented by any means whatsoever, and at the end of the day people are entitled to enjoy the grace of the God who brought them into this world for their benefit, and it is God Himself who is the source of rumours of this kind.

Not for the first time that day, Or-Nego stared at his surgeon with the bemusement of one who does not believe what his eyes are seeing and his ears hearing. And without responding directly to the surgeon's lengthy and somewhat impassioned address, he appointed him there and then to supervise those who sought an audience with the youth, to ask for a cure or hear his advice.

"Disperse the crowd!" he commanded – "And tell the people that when we camp for the night they can visit the young man, if he's prepared to receive them, that is!"

The young man, surrounded by a milling crowd, all of them jostling one another and competing to attract his attention, shooting questions at him in a veritable Babel of languages, with loud cries and wild gestures – took in the convoy commander's words, and raising his voice to make himself heard, he cried:

"I shall receive them with pleasure!"

The Chaldean officer and the surgeon exchanged a smile of satisfaction.

"There are sheets in the rear wagon," Or-Nego went on to tell his surgeon: "Put up a tent in an easily accessible place, for the young man's use, station a guard at the entrance to keep order, and admit people to the tent one at a time if they want to consult him. Fix a starting time and a finishing time and enforce them strictly!"

The crowd was dismissed and the convoy continued on its way.

When the signal was given for the overnight stop, and the convoy had halted, the surgeon chose a space resembling a large rectangle, and with the help of exiles and Chaldeans set up at one end of it a tent made of linen sheets and strips of leather, put a table and two chairs in it, one on either side, with two torches to light the interior of the tent. And then the surgeon presented himself to the young man and bowing low, asked him respectfully if he would be so kind as to take his place in the tent set aside for him.

The queue outside the tent was long and dense, a variegated throng of people of all ranks and social strata, speakers of weird and unfamiliar dialects, Chaldeans and Judeans and Edomites and Israelites, people from Tyre and Sidon, ages ranging from twelve years old to sixty.

There were those who waited their turn patiently, entering the tent in silence, sitting down facing the youth and fixing him with a staring look, and some burst into floods of choking tears and wailed incoherently. Some pointed to their distorted, painful limbs and appealed for relief, while others spoke of parents or grandparents left behind in the ruined city, sisters and mothers and wives bereft of support or livelihood, and they wanted to know how they were faring, and asked the young man to pray for them.

And there were those who put gold and silver coins on the table, with a sly smile, asking him to cast afflictions on their enemies, and some who sat in awe and reverence, staring at him with blurred eyesight, not uttering a word, eventually rising and leaving the tent just as they had entered it.

An awkward Chaldean soldier, who had taken off his armour and laid his weapons aside as a mark of his respect for the youth, limped into the tent, vehemently refused to sit in the chair offered him, knelt at his feet, and after a long silence, looked up and said:

"Have mercy on me, envoy of God the most High! In the battle for Ashkelon my thigh-bone was broken. It was set but it has healed in a crooked fashion, and since then it has caused me nothing but pain and anguish! I am in torment all day long, and at night it is no less severe. I cannot sleep by day or night and there is never a moment's respite, and I would rather die than live like this! Can you rescue me?" His tortured eyes were fixed intently on his face, the eyes of someone drowning in the sea, focused on a lifeboat far away, and gazing at it with the last remnants of hope.

"Do you believe wholeheartedly in the God who is love, and do you believe that through His grace and infinite mercy, I can heal you?"

"If that is the God you serve, then I believe in Him wholeheartedly, and I believe that through Him, you can deliver me from my torment!"

"It shall be as you believe!" the youth declared.

The Chaldean rose to his feet, and suddenly aware that he was no longer limping and his pain had been extinguished as if it never was, he fell to the bare ground again, kissed the young man's feet and left the tent on hands and knees, crawling backwards.

After the Chaldean, a Jewish exile came in, and set out before him at length and in a querulous voice all the blows he had suffered, and told of a large family, grandparents and father and mother, brothers and sisters, wife and sons and daughters, and he was the sole survivor, the carpenter from the street of the artisans in Jerusalem. And he was being exiled by the Chaldeans to a distant land, and even from his few remaining friends and neighbours he was being uprooted. What is to become of him? Can it be hoped that some time, in the next world, he will see again some of the faces he loves, his sons at least, his wife, daughters?

"Do you believe in God, who gives strength to the weary and vigour to the powerless."

"Is that the God who has inflicted all these disasters on me?" asked the man resentfully.

"It isn't God who does the inflicting, He is love. Mankind in his arrogance brings down upon himself all the disasters in the world."

"How can I believe in this God, when I'm in such despair and anguish?"

"By shunning pride, lies and guile, and the ways of avarice."

"And if I truly believe in this God whose name is love, and shun pride, lies and guile and avarice – will God show me the beloved faces of all those whom the Chaldeans have tortured and murdered and executed?"

"You will see them all, not here but in the hereafter!"

The Jew hesitated, looked down, turning something over in his mind, and without looking up, left the tent in silence.

And there was a Chaldean officer who fulminated against him, insisting there is only one God, Bel, who brought victory to the Chaldeans and defeat to the Jews, and the only envoy of Bel and his earthly regent is none other than King Nebuchadnezzar, conqueror and subjugator of the world, and he refuses, the Chaldean officer, to believe in any other God, least of all any God of the Jews! And in his rage and incandescent fury the officer raised his hand and brought his fist crashing down on the unplaned table, his dark eyes shooting fiery sparks of hatred at the young man. And when the Chaldean tried to get up from his seat and go, leaving the young man and his tent and his surgeon acolyte far behind, he realised that the hand which had struck the table was not obeying him, and his arm was hanging by his side, limp and useless, and any attempt to move it aroused only excruciating pain, searing the guts and the heart, inflaming the brain.

"What is this?" raged the Chaldean. He was approached by the surgeon, who touched the limp arm and gave his professional diagnosis:

"It's fractured all the way along the bone," he told the furious, suffering officer – "and perhaps after all you should appeal to the mercy of the young man's God whose name is love, because there's nothing I can do to help you."

"I'd rather die than plead for the favours of anyone, least of all the favours of some God called *love*, of all the weird names!" And he left the tent stooping, feeling his way and trying to protect his dangling arm from any further harm, and no one saw how his lips were contorted with pain as he slipped through the silent crowd waiting patiently before the tent, and disappeared into the darkness.

At around midnight, the surgeon came out to speak with those waiting outside the tent, and before ordering them to disperse, made a few reassuring remarks about the coming day, which would also bring blessing, aid and relief, even complete recovery, to those who needed it, just like today, and he reminded them that even this marvellous young man, envoy of the living God, needed bodily rest, and there was no doubt in his mind that all, Chaldeans and exiles alike, would in the end get into the tent and be received by the youth, and see his face, shining with a beauty that is not of this world, and lay before him all that pains their bodies and troubles their minds, and the youth will not deny them the mercy of God and His compassion, and he will cure them in the name of God, and will save them by virtue of His love and His might.

After the surgeon's impassioned speech, which was a little longwinded but accepted in good spirits, the crowds pressing around the entrance of the tent dispersed and turned away to rest in the places they had chosen for their night's sleep.

Meanwhile, the story of the Chaldean soldier who had been completely cured of his disability and relieved of his pain, emerging whole and healthy from the young man's tent, skipping and dancing and hymning the name of the living God and His mercy – spread quickly through the camp and there was no one who did not hear of it: starting with the breaking of the soldier's leg in the battle for Ashkelon and the way it was badly set, continuing with the conversation between him and the youth, and ending with the miracle done and the thigh-bone straightened and even stronger than before, and no more suffering, and the terrible pain which had kept the soldier awake for weeks and months, was as if it never was.

When he returned to his friends, who had spread his mat for him and put beside it his goatskin coat, he found them divided into camps. Adoniah and Matthew maintained vehemently that these acts of healing were nothing other than sorcery and idolatry, and the proof – a pagan like that Chaldean is granted full recovery, whereas a Jew, like that carpenter who lost all his dear ones and wants to know if he will ever see them again, is promised this on condition that he believes in some God called love, who demands of him all kinds of requirements that are contrary to commonsense and far from easy to comply with, such as eschewing guile, when it was by virtue of guile that the Children of Israel had the wisdom to ask the Egyptians for silver and gold vessels before their exodus to freedom, and not to return them or – demeaning yourself before the community and the people and all other peoples, the kind of humiliation that he calls "avoidance of arrogance".

He, the righteous Jew, circumcised in accordance with tradition and believing in the living God, was sent away disappointed, while the uncircumcised Chaldean, a pagan through and through whose law is not as our Holy Law, his ways not as our ways, his thoughts not as our thoughts – was sent away rewarded! We can have no confidence in this type of healing, supposedly performed through the grace of God, and our good friend Daniel needs to repent, immediately and wholeheartedly, give up his weird incantations, deny them, fast and be mortified, until the Lord grants him absolution and his apostasy is forgiven. And all the time that Adoniah was speaking, rebuking and denouncing, Matthew was nodding his head in agreement.

Against these two were ranged his three longstanding friends, Mishael, Azariah and Hananiah, and they utterly refuted the charges of Adoniah, declaring repeatedly that it was not in the power of sorcery or paganism or idolatry to perform the miracles that had been performed, since only God could do this, and Adoniah and Matthew should take care to avoid heresy and idolatry and profanation of the holy, and spurning the God who dwells in their hearts. If anyone needs to repent, it is they who should be working towards their salvation, bowing the knee and asking their Father in Heaven to forgive them for the slander they have spoken against His envoy, none other than Daniel Ben Naimel Ben

Judah, the purity of whose heart fills his face with precious light, and only one whose eyes are blinded by jealousy and whose heart is consumed by sanctimony, could utter such calumnies and condemn the innocent, and did not God command Moses: *And you shall love the Lord your God with all your heart and all your soul and all your might,* meaning that God is love and therefore only he who loves can draw near to Him and cleave to Him, and long for Him and believe absolutely and when the time comes – join with Him for ever and be Him for all eternity.

And Gershon sided with the threesome, quoting in their support a plethora of verses drawn from the anthems of King David which he, Gershon, the calligrapher of scrolls, knew by heart on account of his profession, having copied them innumerable times. As opposed to Gershon and his three friends, Uziel and Gabriel kept their own counsel and expressed no opinion either way.

When the speeches were done, all eyes were turned to him, including the eyes of Gabriel and Uziel.

"Sleep well!" he said with a bright smile, lay down on his bed, wrapped himself in his goatskin, closed his eyes and slept. And as he slept there was a smile on his face, a smile radiating soft and conciliatory light, and not one of the youths who saw him sleeping could help but feel the exaltation of spirit and exuberance of heart that his presence inspired.

The morning light broke and the convoy mounted the king's highway, descending slowly from the shoulders of the mountains towards their roots. All proceeded cautiously, man and beast alike, calculating each step as if groping in the darkness. Chasms yawned at their feet, sometimes to the right and sometimes to the left.

NAARAN

In the early hours of the afternoon the heat grew intense and the signal was given to bring the convoy to a halt. Orders were distributed and the people were instructed to take a short rest, resting the animals as well, and to eat a meal, and attend to their ablutions, sort out their clothing and clean their shoes, then return to their formations and continue the journey down the slope, which appeared to be a smooth and steady incline. But not everything proceeded as smoothly as had been expected. The convoy was delayed for a reason no one could have foreseen.

The young men had just finished their meal, washed down with cold mountain water, sweet to the taste, when a troop of Chaldean cavalry came speeding towards them, and without a word spoken, took up positions around the wagon beside which they were sitting. The soldiers were well drilled and equipped for combat, facing outwards with their backs towards the youths, bows in their left hands and arrows in their right, ready to unleash a rapid volley. The Chaldeans said nothing to the youths, who for better or worse were hemmed in from all sides, and gave no answers to the questions of Gershon and Hananiah and Adoniah, not revealing the reasons for this sudden deployment, or what peril they were poised to forestall.

Immediately following the encirclement of the wagon, there was uproar in the camp, as crowds of people, uttering high-pitched shrieks and yells, interspersed with sounds of weeping and lamentation, began moving towards the young men. They stood their ground, tense and anxious as they watched the impassioned hordes closing in on them from all sides with sticks and stones.

"Something unpleasant has happened in the camp," Gabriel muttered, with a sidelong glance at him.

"This is what comes of trying to give the grace of God to pagans and share it with heathens!" exclaimed Adoniah, his voice crackling between his teeth, and all of him hostility and hatred.

In the crowd there were exiles and Chaldeans alike, and they surrounded the wagon in a wide circle and did not dare come any closer, as the Chaldean soldiers had their bows at the ready and their commanding officer had announced, in a low but perfectly audible voice, in a manner leaving no room for misunderstanding, that anyone attempting to reach the wagon would be shot, and this by the explicit order of the convoy commander. There was nothing in the Chaldean officer's words to suggest anything other than absolute seriousness; he meant what he said and was prepared, if necessary, to put it into effect with speed and efficiency. And so the crowd stood still, encompassing the wagon which, it now emerged, had been isolated from the rest of the convoy.

But passions were unabated, and the yelling continued with redoubled intensity, echoing in the pure air. Amid all the clamour there was one cry that rang out with perfect clarity: "Death to the young sorcerer!" – and this was taken up and repeated in chorus, as the protesters shook fists and brandished clubs and even swords.

"Bring out the son of Satan and we'll deal with him, and there'll be an end to the evil in the camp!" was the cry of the exiles, who constituted the majority of the throng, and it was then that Or-Nego arrived on the scene in haste, at the head of two troops of cavalry, and set about dispersing the crowd without any further delay, threatening to charge directly at the dense ranks of the rioters.

Taken aback, the crowd began to withdraw, intimidated by the horses and recoiling from their persistent onslaught. Within a short space of time order was restored and the way ahead was clear, but still angry voices were piercing the air, and although distant and indistinct, the menace in them was still real and tangible.

Accompanying the convoy commander was the surgeon, and he paused to speak to the passengers in the covered wagon, explaining to Gershon and the boys that Naaran, the officer who had abused Daniel and his God, and in his fury, struck with his fist on the table with such force that the bone in his arm was split, and despite his excruciating pain refused to accept help – this officer, the surgeon told them, had hanged himself on one of the old oak trees at the side of the road.

Naaran's dreadful end aroused the soldiers of his platoon to action, and in their fury they resolved to avenge him, with the death of the lout who had impugned the honour of their officer, the valiant Naaran. But their intention became known to Or-Nego, who had his informers in all the units escorting the convoy under his command, and he lost no time in disbanding Naaran's platoon and sending troops that he could trust to stand guard over the young men, before it was too late. Among the exiles too there were many who resented the youth, including some who were dissatisfied with the treatment they had received from him and who denounced him as a braggart and a fraud, a liar with saintly pretensions. Chaldeans and exiles alike, all were agreed that he could be nothing other than a disciple of the devil, and as for the miracles that he had performed – the hand of Satan was in them.

And then that soldier whom God had cured by the hand of the boy, and showered with His mercy, stepped forward and contradicted the angry Chaldeans, and they beat him soundly, and it was with great difficulty that he extricated himself from the hands of his assailants, whose hearts were blinded by rage. And he wept and sobbed like a big baby, in his own words, for shame at the contempt that his comrades in arms were showing towards the God who works miracles and whose name is love, and their abuse of the illustrious prince of peace, the Jewish lad who had spoken with him in the tent, and cured him by the grace of his God.

Or-Nego suppressed the disorder, but not with a heavy hand as was his wont, since he understood the strength of feeling among his troops aroused by the Naaran episode. Naaran had been a valiant soldier and a popular officer, although not renowned for his intellect or his percipience.

Order was restored, in appearance at least. Chaldean soldiers continued to surround the young men and their wagon, and escorted them on the move. Their faces were blank and grim, their lips taut, and instead of bows and arrows, they held drawn swords.

Inside the wagon, the bitter altercation flared up again. Adoniah claimed with vehemence that it was a sacred duty to lend an attentive ear to the angry accusations of the mob, seeing that "the voice of the masses is the voice of Shaddai", giving them due and serious consideration, not forgetting the specific charge, heard over and over again, that these so-called miracles had been performed not by the hand of God but by the hand of the Destroyer, whose name is best not spoken aloud, and he is the one responsible for whatever has happened. And everything that Adoniah said was confirmed by Matthew, nodding his head vigorously and echoing his words.

Against Adoniah and Matthew, Mishael and Azariah and Gershon and Hananiah stood up in robust defence of their friend, adducing all kinds of signs and wonders in support of their argument that it is not in the nature of the Destroyer to perform miracles, since he has no interest in the welfare and the happiness of mankind – least of all in his sincere repentance and devotion to his Creator, his Name be blessed, and he who thinks otherwise is surely to be numbered among the disciples of the Destroyer, his soul in jeopardy and a bitter lot in store for him in the next world! And so the polemic raged on, with Gabriel and Uziel making their contributions too – sometimes on the side of Matthew and Adoniah, and sometimes supporting the firmly held opinions of the opposing camp – or saying nothing, as if the subject was of no interest to them at all.

Finally, Daniel spoke up for himself, saying that time would tell who was in the right, and there was no purpose to be served by arguing over issues of such depth and complexity. Furthermore, he went on to say, if decisive evidence of the mercy of God, the compassion and love of the Holy One Blessed be He, such as the spectacular recovery of the sick and the crippled, was not enough to convince – then what could mere words accomplish?

As the convoy passed by a wood, someone drew their attention to a stout oak-tree at the roadside. Still suspended from one of the lower branches was a length of rope, cut with a sword, the rope with which Naaran had hanged himself, and the mood turned ugly again.

In the long, shaded wagon, silence reigned. Outside, beside the wagon, Gershon was walking at a vigorous pace. It seemed the blazing of the sun did not bother him at all.

Gershon shielded his head and face with a cotton cloth, and did not heed the urgings of the youths, to climb into the wagon and let one of the younger men walk in his place. Daniel even tried to walk part of the way at his side, hoping that the older man would finally consent to go and sit in the shade, knowing there was a free place in the wagon. But Gershon wasn't listening, and this time it was the boys who gave in and stayed in their seats.

When evening came and the convoy halted for the night, there were some among the populace who furtively approached the surgeon and asked him where the young man's tent was to be set up, and between what times would he be available for consultation. The surgeon replied that by explicit order of Or-Nego, the convoy commander, the tent was not to be set up again, and this on account of the rioting that had taken place, leaving echoes that still reverberated in the air, the rioting in which these importunate ones had doubtless participated. The appellants expressed deep regret over everything that had happened, and went on to ask if it might be possible to approach the young man in the open, or in one of the wagons, whichever was most convenient for him, with the knowledge and consent of Or-Nego, and ask his advice. Again, the response of the surgeon was an emphatic negative.

It was out of the question. There was to be no contact with the young man, even from a distance. Those were the orders. Strict orders. There was potential danger to the youth, mortal danger, and it was Or-Nego's duty, by the king's command and his explicit instructions, to deliver him to the palace whole and healthy, without so much as a scratch on him. And if he failed in this mission then he, Or-Nego, the convoy commander, would be endangering his life. King Nebuchadnezzar was a man who did not know the meaning of compromise, who pretended to no one and demanded that his orders be obeyed to the letter as well as in the spirit. And as all this was known to Or-Nego, so it was known to his personal surgeon, and he thought it only right that it be known to all the travellers in the convoy, exiles and Chaldeans alike – and it should be made clear once and for all that no harm was to befall the young man, not only because Or-Nego was standing behind him and defending him at the risk of his own life, but most of all because the light of God was shining in his young face, and there could be no doubt he was under the personal protection of God, yes, God Himself, and who will dare defy God, contravene His commandments and fight against Him? Could such a man ever succeed in his defiance, cunning though he may be, and aided by all the unruly denizens of the depths of Hell?

Those who needed the young man's help were sent away empty-handed. And they returned to the camp, disappointed and ashamed, with no choice but to report to their friends the surgeon's emphatic rebuttal, and the mood was heavy and despondent.

"On your own heads you have brought this malignant evil!" had been the surgeon's final, conclusive statement, and all were forced to admit these were the words of the living God.

WHEN THE MIST CLEARS

In the month of Tishri, in the early dawn of the twenty-first day, the convoy climbed the heights of the towering Taurus range, and proceeding along the king's highway, came to the edge of a promontory, jutting out from the cliff-face.

The convoy halted, and the people turned to look to their left, at the broad valley beneath them, still buried under the milky-grey cover of a thick morning mist.

The mist caught the silvery rays of the rising sun and reflected them back into the vault of the sky in a glorious shower of sparks. As time passed, the mist rose gradually, dispersing and melting away, revealing, little by little, what lay hidden beneath it. In silence, the travellers watched as the mist cleared before their eyes, the wisps of it dispersing and melting in the air. And then the eyes of the observers opened wide and their hearts pounded, as the stunning vista was revealed to them.

Along the full length and breadth of the valley, stretching out at their feet like the bed of an ancient, dried-out sea, soared massive monumental walls, enclosing an area of ground of such vast proportions it was hard to encompass it with the eye. Framed by these towering walls, the roofs of a host of densely packed buildings rose into the void, gleaming in the sun of Tishri, and among them, reaching truly incredible altitudes, the domes of sumptuous palaces, sanctuaries and temples. A little to the right of the centre, the minaret of a tower cleft the fringes of the firmament itself, the tallest by far of all the buildings. The giddy height of the tower caused all who saw it to gape in amazement. It seemed as if the hand of man could never construct an edifice such as this, calling out a challenge to the Heavens.

All of the most majestic buildings, separated from the rest and taller than them, were surrounded by an inner wall which, judging by the way it refracted the light, could have been overlaid with marble, for the most part if not entirely, and it rose to the same height as the outer wall which so it seemed, must be utterly impregnable.

The eight youths and Gershon with them, still surrounded by armed guards, stood on the broad outcrop of rock overlooking the valley, and stared, entranced, at the sights revealed before their eyes.

Gershon sighed and said in a whisper, into which a strange fear had crept:

"Babylon!"

And Hananiah pointed to that loftiest of all the buildings, soaring high above all the others and said:

"The Tower of Babel!" – spoken with the sincere amazement of a child. And Matthew muttered grimly:

"Neither God nor man could breach those walls!"

Without looking at the speaker, Daniel declared:

"The earthquake that struck Bethlehem in the jubilee year buried the town under a layer of rubble a hundred cubits deep. If the Babylonians turn their backs on God, and conquer nations with the aim of oppressing their peoples – no relic will remain of this glorious spectacle, not one stone of those walls will be left standing, and this place will be nothing more than a haunt of vultures and buzzards, hyenas and jackals and carrion crows."

And suddenly all the enchantment of the scene faded, melting away and vanishing as if it never was. The clear, deep skies revealed to him their secret, the secret of the humility of the one who has attained eternity.

He remembered Bethlehem, devastated by an earthquake some seven years before. He accompanied his father, who visited the place as envoy of the king. The Chaldeans had not yet laid siege to Jerusalem; they were spoken of as a distant people, not yet encountered face to face. He asked if he might go with his father, and the minister Naimel gave his consent with a slight nod of the head.

At an early hour of the morning they walked along the road, most of it hewn out of the rock and a lesser part running between fertile fields of corn and barley. At the specific request of his father, the members of the escort did not carry weapons or ride on horseback, and the minister and his young son set the example. There were horses with them, but these were heavy draught-animals, pulling behind them some half dozen wagons laden with emergency supplies of food, blankets and clothing.

As they approached the settlement, three old men came forward to meet them, grim faced, with long white straggly beards. They greeted them with a silent bow.

The most distinguished looking of the old men began by apologising, in a grating, guttural voice:

"Our leaders and our chieftains perished in the earthquake and we are among the few who remain alive. We have come to greet you, and this on account of our advanced age, which enjoins upon us certain obligations in accordance with our holy Law. You are welcome to Bethlehem, in the name of the Lord our God!" – he concluded his speech without an excessive display of enthusiasm. In fact, every word that emerged from the old man's mouth was spoken in a dull, apparently lifeless monotone.

His father approached the old man, clasped his hand and hugged him to his breast, with an encouraging pat on the back, repeating the process with his two companions, and with a calm, sincere smile on his face, intended to inspire trust and confidence, he began:

"The king is deeply grieved by the disaster that has befallen your settlement, as are his ministers and generals and advisers, and all the people of Judah! And he has instructed me to convey to you his condolences and his confident belief that Bethlehem will be restored to its former state soon and quickly, and will again flourish and prosper as it has flourished and prospered in the past, and he has also sent a modest consignment of supplies to ease your suffering, by the grace and the mercy of God!"

The old men thanked him with the same mute bow of reverence and then turned and joined the deputation, walking down the narrow road leading to Bethlehem.

He never would forget the icy fear that gripped his heart when the spectacle was revealed before his eyes: black pits in the ground, like bottomless chasms, and at the sides of them remains of buildings, a wall standing like a rotten tooth and close by a flat roof preserved entire, besides a narrow, twisting black fissure crossing it from side to side, shattered and distorted utensils and severed limbs, human limbs – a skull, crushed and flattened, eyes still intact but the brain squeezed out, fingers covered in dust and blood, arms, feet...

His body shaking, he ran to his father and hugged him tight, searched for his hand and clutched it feverishly. For perhaps the first time in his life, and to his great relief, he felt the answering warmth of his father's hand, infusing his heart with solid confidence and easing the constricted blood vessels, and instead of vomiting or losing consciousness and collapsing there and then – he regained his composure and straightened his back, in control of himself.

They walked on slowly, towards the chaos and the destruction. The sound of sobbing and keening could be clearly heard in the distance. People with dishevelled hair and clothing, eyes flashing in feverish anger, and abysmal pain distorting their faces, dust in their hair and their beards, foreheads and cheeks pocked with brown markings, looking like corpses risen from their graves – watched the deputation approach without uttering so much as a whisper, like shadows, a swelling mass of morose humanity.

On reaching the central square of the settlement, his father halted the wagons and ordered the stern-faced officer of the guard to unload their contents at the end of the square and to station his men around the site.

And then someone emerged from among the shadowy figures and directed a stream of abuse at his father. The officer of the guard, hearing the abuse, immediately turned and with lightning speed grabbed the man by the neck and pulled him back roughly, evidently intent on beating him about the head. His father, the minister Naimel, forestalled him, ordering him to let the man alone.

"His grief has fuddled his mind," his father explained to the officer, obliged, against his will, to free his prisoner. The man turned this way and that, stooped to pick up a clod of earth and rising to his full height, flung it at his father, resuming his tirade:

"You there, ministers living in comfortable houses in Jerusalem, with your wives and your children by your side! You are not wanted here! You cannot heal our wounds with your hypocritical charity! Be off with you! And don't show your faces here again!"

The officer of the guard was about to punish this insolence, but before he could move he was set upon by other shadow-people, who knocked him to the ground, and his fate would have been sealed had his father not come running, tearing a pair of hands from the officer's throat and crying:

"In God's name, citizens and brothers, has it come to this?"

His voice was clear and calm, the voice of true authority, and the assailants withdrew, releasing the officer and retreating. The officer rose and shook the dust from his clothes and walked away in silence, in obedience to the minister's command.

And then the minister went among the shadow-people and spoke gentle words to them, and he did not hear the words because he was excluded from the circle and two men of the escort flanked him on either side, but the outcome was an unexpected change among the shadow-people surrounding his father, and suddenly a chorus of wailing broke out, with the sound of desperate and feverish weeping. And the shadow-people knelt before Naimel the minister and kissed his hands and robes and some even kissed his feet.

This he would never forget.

He was watching the scene with eyes wide open, quivering with the intensity of feeling, until he realised that he was weeping himself, and this weeping was purifying something deep in his soul, opening the door to a light as yet unknown to him, a living light saying clearly: "Trust in me!"

His friends stood rooted to the spot, mesmerised by the enchantment of the spectacle. He picked out the broad silver ribbon of the Euphrates, flowing at the feet of the high walls to the west. His eyes roved again over the tall, dense buildings of the city, sparkling in the sunlight with their facings of gold and silver and marble, the greatest city of the universe. Over there is the famous tower, the Tower of Babel, its foundations broad and solid and its pinnacle, a pinnacle of gold – like an arrow shot into the gleaming vault of the heavens, taking in the light of the sun and reflecting it in a riot of vivid colours. This tower also has no equal anywhere in the universe. Further on, the Hanging Gardens, one of the wonders of the world, and at the northern extremity of the city, secluded, surrounded by a wall and lustrous in marble and gold and colourful gem-stones – the palatial complex of His Majesty the King...

The youths, and Gershon with them, were simply insatiable, incapable of shifting their gaze from the domes, the towers and the walls – glories unlike anything they had ever seen before. The Chaldean officer appointed to escort and protect them declared once again, with pride that he made no effort to conceal:

"The palace of King Nebuchadnezzar, conqueror of the world!" – and with outstretched arm he pointed to that cluster of ornate buildings set apart from the rest.

"These buildings are superior in their grandeur and the genius of their construction to the Temple in Jerusalem and the palace of King Solomon!" – Adoniah exclaimed with a strange air of satisfaction.

"There is no building in the world, however splendid it may be, that may be compared with the Temple in Jerusalem and the palace of King Solomon, peace be with him!" Hananiah retorted, and proceeded to explain: "Over the Temple in Jerusalem and over the palace of King Solomon – the Spirit of God presides, as it presides over all the houses and the walls of the Holy City, thus infinitely superior to any other building or buildings anywhere in the world!"

"But the king of Babylon assaulted the walls of the Holy City and breached them, shook the foundations of the Temple and the palace of King Solomon and destroyed many houses!" – Uziel spoke in a tone of absent sorrow, without any argumentative intent, but Matthew did not hesitate to fill in the words which Uziel had left unsaid:

"Where was the Lord your God then, Hananiah?"

"He hid His face from us!" Azariah chipped in, adding: "On account of our many sins and the grievous misdeeds of our people!"

"Didn't Daniel tell us that God doesn't punish, because He is love?" Gabriel demanded to know.

"Hiding His face isn't the same as punishment," – Daniel intervened, in a steady, firm voice, without a trace of pomposity – "Hiding His face means – God turning away from those who don't want Him: *I was there to be sought by a people who did not ask, to be found by men who did not seek me. I said 'Here am I' to a nation that did not call upon my name.* With our arrogant tongue, wretched acts and contemptible thoughts we have banished God from our hearts, and drifted ever further from Him."

"*Banished* God, you say, what's that supposed to mean?" Gabriel persisted.

"We have demanded of Him that he leave us alone, let us manage our affairs as we see fit. The liar, the coveter, the adulterer – it's as if they are saying to God 'We don't want you!' and God who is love does not impose Himself in places where He is not welcome. And in a place where God is not welcome there is violence and destruction and ruin and disaster," he concluded in that tone of flawless sincerity, penetrating deep into the hearts of his hearers.

"I was right, then!" Adoniah cried with an expression of triumph and derision: "It is definitely possible to compare buildings – those in Jerusalem and those at our feet, since divinity no longer presides over those in Jerusalem or gives them any protection, and hence these buildings that we see before us are all the more superior to those that we have left behind – both in their grandeur and the ingenuity of their construction!"

And he saw fit to answer him with no change to the tone of his voice:

"Buildings over which the Holy Spirit does not preside are worthless, and all their beauty and their grandeur and their majesty are meaningless, the invention of mankind's concupiscent eye. Even the meanest hovel of the basest of beggars may be illumined with glorious light if he who dwells there is a man of faith. And he whose eyes are not blinded by concupiscence will see this light and rejoice in it, and for him, no building in the world, however majestic it may be, will be the equal of this hovel!"

A harassed Chaldean horseman appeared, and ordered them back into the wagon. The nine of them obeyed, reluctantly, but once in the wagon all of them, including Daniel, found suitable vantage points, and continued scanning the broad valley through the tattered flaps of the canopy. Some were still amazed by what they were seeing, while others curbed their amazement, and thereupon felt a quiet sense of satisfaction.

Gershon too was looking down at the valley and not shifting his gaze from it, but his thoughts were straying far away, to his homeland and his city, to members of his family, separated from him by vast distances, and he did not see what his eyes were perceiving but instead was filled with gloom and anxiety.

He too, like all the others, was still observing, but the beauty and the splendour revealed before him had lost all their vitality and looked like corpses, bereft of life and bereft of purpose, and he thought of what was beyond them, thought of the living light that is love, by whose grace the human race exists, and creation breathes, and there is hope.

"O my Father in Heaven, my God! You who stands behind all, and all is in You, You the creator of all whom no creature can touch, You, depending on nothing and all things depending on You, You standing above all and all things refreshed by You, exalted above the most exalted, raised higher than the highest. You are the infinite good and the absolute beauty that is the truth, and without You there is no truth, and all things tell of Your glory and sing to You anthems of praise.

"You, to whom all my longings are turned and in whom is all my hope. You, who are nothing but the fulfilment of my longings and my hopes, You, seeing Yourself in me. I shall not rest until I am absorbed in You utterly, with nothing left behind! O my Father in Heaven, my God – praise be to You, praise for all eternity!"

The winding road was broader now, paved with cobblestones of brown and grey, winding down steadily from the heights to the valley.

Travellers in the convoy seemed suddenly to come to life, revived and invigorated as they sensed the rigours of the journey were drawing to a close, fading away and vanishing as if they never were. Those on foot stepped out with redoubled vigour, horses were urged into a trot, and the creaking wagons lurched onward at a swifter pace.

Or-Nego tried to slow down the accelerated progress of the convoy, but realising this was impossible, abandoned the attempt and even allowed himself to be swept along with the general surge of enthusiasm, spurring on his horse. The horse too was well aware that the end of the tiresome journey was in sight, willingly responding to Or-Nego's commands and carrying him forward to the head of the long column.

The youths decided they had been sitting cramped together in the wagon long enough, and one after another they began climbing down and mingling with their mounted escorts, feasting their eyes on the vista of the long valley with its fringes kissing the distant lines of the horizon.

Only he and Gershon were left in the wagon, in the forward section behind the back of the Jewish driver, who had no need of his whip to urge on his pair of horses, towing the wagon with every appearance of enjoyment, and uttering whinnies of enthusiasm and alacrity.

Gershon turned to him and asked him:

"Is that the Tower of Babel that's mentioned in the Scriptures, where God confused the languages of the peoples who tried to reach Him?"

And he answered him:

"What is written there is only a parable. For those with open mind and pure heart, it is easy to see the moral."

"Could you try to explain it to me?" he asked, adding apologetically: "I've never been much of an expert in interpreting the Scriptures, and they are a closed book to me!"

"I too am no scholar, nor a paragon of saintliness, and I don't know to what degree my heart has been purged of the vanities of the world."

"But nonetheless!" Gershon pressed him and he answered him calmly:

"People, in their anger at one another, jealousy against one another, and concupiscence, have stopped understanding one another, man is estranged from his brother and they drive God out of their hearts. And in their folly and the wretchedness that they have brought upon themselves with their own hands, they have consulted together and decided to reach out to God and bring Him back to them, not by way of the love that is in the heart, but by way of worldly pride of which the Tower is the symbol, in other words – by way of arrogant scholasticism and intellectual snobbery."

"So that magnificent tower, rising to unbelievable height, and the handiwork of mankind, is nothing other than the fruit of human arrogance and pride?"

He nodded in assent.

"And the Temple in Jerusalem?"

"Was built for the sake of Heaven!" he declared, raising his eyes to the clearing, deepening vault of the sky.

THE GATE OPENS

As the sun rose to its full height, the convoy reached the fortified eastern wall, a menacing, haughty construction of dressed stone, and stopped there.

To their south, a broad gate opened, the Shamash Gate, and the convoy started streaming through it, a swollen river of people and animals, and the wagons rattling sturdily over the paving stones, the creaking of their wheels as rhythmic as a song, like the song of one who has been long absent from his home and roaming in foreign parts, and now he is back from his travels and is all relief and gratitude.

For a long time the convoy was making its way into the heart of the wondrous city, its fortresses not showing a friendly face and all of its buildings, to the very last of them, speaking of majesty and gloom. It was not until early in the afternoon that the wagon in which the young men were travelling reached the broad gate that stood wide open, the Shamash Gate, and came to Babylon. The wagon crossed a narrow alleyway and stopped before a squad of the royal guard, responsible for the inspections of customs. Or-Nego was standing there, and he explained something to the officer commanding the squad, who nodded his understanding and acquiescence.

Or-Nego stepped forward and asked Gershon to leave the wagon.

"This is where you must part company!" he declared with a rueful smile, and went on to explain: "The tanner must go to join the tanners, the boys – they're going to meet the King!" Even before he had finished speaking, Gershon had been grabbed by soldiers of the guard and hustled from the wagon.

"Don't forget me, boys!" he cried in a tone of pain and despair. "Daniel!" he called out as he was led away, "Don't you forget me!"

And Gershon just had time to hear the young man's voice ringing out clear and strong: "I won't forget you!"

Their wagon, still escorted by six armed Chaldeans, continued on its way, trundling noisily, yet placidly, over the paving slabs of the long, narrow street. To their left rose the gaudy temples of the gods, Adad and Shamash, and on reaching the crossroads they made out in the distance the white marble walls of the lofty temple of "Beth Nina", reflecting the rays of the setting sun.

"There's real Hebrew for you!" whispered Hananiah in a tone of misplaced awe, evidently referring to *Beth*, a Hebrew word of impeccable pedigree.

"The Chaldeans are the descendants of Shem, as we are, and their language is similar to ours, having the same roots," was Daniel's reply and he added: "But language apart, there is nothing we have in common with them. Our father Abraham left Ur of the Chaldees at God's command, never to return there: *"Go from your country and your homeland and your father's house to a land that I will show you!"* – he quoted from the Scripture, and Mishael completed the prophecy: *"And I will make you a great nation and I will bless you and magnify your name, and you will be a blessing!"*

Their wagon turned right, crossing a solid bridge of brown stonework and dressed masonry pillars, over the broad and normally turbid river, now flowing with strange serenity beneath their wheels, and then proceeded towards the inner wall, passing through another gate where the few soldiers on duty showed no inclination to stop them for inspection, contenting themselves with a glance of curiosity, and just a hint of bemusement.. When they entered the straight, broad streets of the inner city they noticed other wagons ahead of them, as well as the exiles who had made the entire journey on foot, and scores of Chaldean soldiers accompanying them. The Chaldean cavalry moved forward and took up their positions at the head of the column. And then they noticed that behind them too there were Chaldean horsemen, in closely packed and orderly ranks, and evidently enjoying themselves, smiling broadly and waving to the citizens starting to gather on both sides of the column of exiles.

They entered the centre of the city like a victory parade, hearing cries of approbation and applause from the spectators. All were dusty: the uniforms of the soldiers had turned grey and the clothes of the exiles were caked with dust, as were the manes of the horses and the canopies of the wagons. By contrast, the garb of the citizens of the capital was of startling cleanness, elegance even, and there was no shortage of scarlets and blues and purples, especially among the young women who left their houses to greet the newcomers, with candid smiles and cries of "Hurrah!"

"They have no shame!" Mishael exclaimed, and Azariah answered him:

"They say that the girls of Babylon aren't looking for Chaldean husbands, and that's by royal decree; the king wants to improve the Chaldean strain!"

"How can you improve such an inferior strain?" queried Matthew, winking at Adoniah who answered him:

"They're so stupid and so ignorant that any outsider marrying into them can't help but improve their racial stock!"

"And the Lord has commanded us not to consort with Gentiles," Uziel commented.

"Rather to wipe them off the face of the earth," Gabriel said by way of corroboration.

"And what's your opinion?" – Hananiah asked, turning to Daniel. He answered him:

"The verses you are quoting only tell us to erase from our minds all thoughts that are worthless and idolatrous, so that no trace or relic is left of them. He who purifies his mind from all things of a 'gentile' nature, from all worthless and idolatrous thoughts, such as thoughts of malice, avarice, adultery and deceit – such a man is fit to approach God and rejoice in Him and love Him with all his heart and all his might, and all his soul and all his intellect!"

"Your interpretations are bizarre!" Adoniah protested. "What I was taught by my master and teacher, Hananiel the priest – was that we are to put all Gentiles to the sword and destroy them, and burn down their homes and burn their crops too!"

"Only one who gives no thought to God could interpret the Scriptures in such a heinous fashion!" he retorted.

"Anyway, we can agree that modesty is not the outstanding quality of the young ladies of Babylon!" interjected Mishael, anxious to put a stop to the argument between Daniel and Adoniah while it could still be controlled.

They all sat in silence, watching the scene outside.

Dense ranks of girls stretched along both sides of the street, in flimsy clothing that concealed little and revealed a great deal, shouting "Hurrah!" and waving hands and coloured handkerchiefs, their bare arms gleaming. The wagon rolled on over the rough paving stones, as to their left appeared the solid foundations of the tallest tower in the world.

Not waiting to be asked, one of the Chaldean horsemen leaned towards them and explained:

"This is the Holy Ziggurat, the 'Tower of Babel' in your language, the only one of its kind anywhere in the world!" – the horseman's voice expressed a combination of pride, superiority and reverential awe. "That blue dome, overlooking vast spaces on the face of the earth," he added portentously – "is nothing other than the temple of Marduk, the bravest of all the gods, and the most valiant, conqueror of the world!"

Azariah could not let this go unchallenged:

"You Chaldeans, you're very good at building and at waging war – two kinds of fleeting illusion. We Jews, on the other hand, are distinguished by our faith in one God who has neither form nor body, who is in all and all is in Him, from whom everything comes and to whom everything belongs! The Jews will yet have the privilege of seeing the collapse of great buildings however impressive they may be, and the fall of powerful kings however wise and valiant they may be, and the ruin of mighty kingdoms, which have subjugated and enslaved other kingdoms by brute force of arms!"

The face of the Chaldean horseman turned dark with fury:

"Your tongue is a two-edged sword, contemptible Jewish slave!" – he hissed through his teeth. "If Or-Nego were not standing by you, guaranteeing your protection, your life would be worth nothing more than one of these cobblestones under my horse's hooves!"

"Or-Nego is not my defender, and I'm not the protégé of any Chaldean officer," Azariah retorted, his face pale: "The Lord my God is my deliverer and defender, and I am under His protection. My life is in His hands and He will do with it as He sees fit."

The Chaldean horseman could no longer control his rage. He took his whip, leather thongs studded with beads of lead, waved it high above his head and brought it down with great force, a vicious blow aimed at Azariah's exposed face.

The thongs of the whip whistled through the air, missed their mark, struck the canopy of the wagon and bounced back, with the sheer force of the impact – into the face of the infuriated Chaldean. The Jewish driver who had been a witness to the whole spectacle, brought the wagon to a halt – an unconscious, reflex action. The youths exchanged nervous glances. Daniel took his stand between the Chaldean horseman and Azariah:

"Ride on!" he commanded him. The clear, authoritative voice left the soldier no margin of doubt, and he spurred his horse and sped away along the column without pausing to consider what he was doing. The Jewish driver recovered his wits and not saying a word, set the wagon in motion again.

The column advanced. A few minutes later the horseman returned, and silently took his place alongside the wagon, looking to neither left nor right. On his fleshy cheek was a thin strip of dried blood.

Uziel asked Daniel:

"How could the horseman fail to hit Azariah?"

And he answered him:

"Neither whip nor sword can prevail over a son of God!"

The column passed through the inner wall by the gate dedicated to the god Marduk. A large proportion of the exiles had been brought here and they were separated and assigned to their work-places according to profession: workers in metals – to join the metal-workers, workers in wood – to join the woodworkers, with the same applying to tailors and building labourers.

Six wagons, half of them covered, continued to roll along the long, paved thoroughfare, and with them – some three dozen exiles on foot and almost the entire strength of the Chaldean army, riding before the wagons and behind them.

THE HOUSE OF OR-NEGO

The column approached a line of low buildings, built mostly of clay, enclosed by a low wall, crude and blackened. An order was given and the Chaldean horsemen, besides a handful of officers accompanying Or-Nego, turned to their right, passed through a wide open gate and were swallowed up among the low buildings.

"Those must be their barracks," Hananiah deduced correctly.

The walking exiles and the three open wagons also left the scene at this point. Or-Nego ordered the drivers of the three remaining wagons to continue on their way. Shortly after this they caught a glimpse, somewhere, at the edge of the fortified sector, like an extension to the lofty outer wall – of the ornate buildings of the royal compound.

"That's our destination!" – Matthew remarked, pointing to the buildings with the high walls, and façade of white marble still gleaming in the rays of the evening sun. But before they reached the palace, Or-Nego gave another order and the convoy halted before a spacious house three storeys high, painted red, with an iron gate and stone-built walls enclosing a substantial courtyard with garden and lawns.

As soon as the column had stopped, the iron gate was opened and some three dozen retainers and maidservants came out to meet them, neatly attired and faces expressing restrained delight bordering on reverence. And they approached the exiles remaining in the wagons and the Chaldean soldiers, greeting them with silent bows and helping them to dismount from the horses and the wagons. The wagons and the beasts were conducted to the stables, while the people stood in the large courtyard and waited. Or-Nego approached them and said with a faint smile:

"I shall be glad to entertain you for a while in my house!"

And his hospitality was warm and lavish indeed. Tables were set out, and on the softly textured cloths of pink and white were laid all kinds of delicacies, wines and liquor and mead and aromatic cordials mixed with water. The chairs were high and upholstered in deerskin and the guests, worn out by the endless rigours of the journey, were grateful for the opportunity to relax in comfort.

A girl some twelve years of age came and sat beside him, looking at him with wise and perceptive eyes, soft as velvet. The skin of the girl's face was the colour of alabaster, strangely offsetting the depth of her gaze.

"Who are you?" he asked her.

And she answered him:

"I am Adelain, the daughter of Or-Nego, commander of the army!" – she smiled gently and without looking away from his eyes she asked: "And who are you?"

"Daniel, son of Naimel, minister at the court of Judah."

"And where is your father?" the girl went on to ask.

"He fell in battle, fighting the Chaldeans."

"Oh!" the girl sighed softly. "I am so sorry! These wars and conquests bring nothing but grief and pain... to everyone!" She paused, and in a bid to change the subject she asked:

"You're not eating meat – is that a commandment of your God?"

"Yes," he answered her briefly.

"Not all of your companions are following your example!" she commented.

"It's not one of those commandments in the 'rather-die-than-transgress-it' class, and anyway, it's been relaxed over the years since my compatriots were incapable of upholding it. If they were to uphold it with joy and gladness and other people were to follow in their footsteps, there would be no more quarrels and disputes, battles and wars, no more grief and pain and destruction." His words were spoken softly, but with the full weight of earnestness.

She gave some thought to what he had said, poured into his cup a drink of honey mixed with water, poured some for herself and observed:

"So if mankind stops murdering animals, he won't murder members of his own species, is that it?"

He nodded in assent.

...One spring they found on the wooded summit of a hill behind the Mount of Olives, a wounded deer. A hunter had shot an arrow into his foreleg and injured him, but the deer had hidden from him so successfully that the hunter did not find him and returned home empty-handed.

The two of them ran to him, and the animal made no effort to escape or elude their grasp. He extracted the arrow carefully, and she removed the kerchief from her head, folded it over lengthways into a long strip and bandaged the bleeding wound. The eyes of the young deer expressed the full depth of searing pain and helplessness. He held the deer and caressed him, while Nejeen was treating him and binding his wound. Once the wound was bandaged, the deer seemed to recover his spirits, putting out his tongue and licking her hand and his.

"They have a soul, animals do, a beautiful soul that the Creator implants in them!" said Adelain.
He nodded again, and said:
"That is a fact that people ignore."

...And again there came to his mind the pale face of that other girl, and her eyes with their deep shade of blue, she sitting beside the wounded deer and asking:
"Do you believe that in the beginning all creatures ate only vegetables, as it's written in the Book of Genesis?"
"I believe it absolutely!" he answered her in a decisive voice, looking into her eyes which shone with a kind of luminous purity not of this world, eyes into which he never tired of gazing, sinking into their limpid and unfathomable depths, all tenderness and delight and freedom. It was then that he became aware of the futility of speech and conversation, all utterly superfluous. Language was merely a human device, invented in the Garden of Eden when mankind first sinned and needed words for the making of excuses. God is to be addressed with love and not in words.
He was afraid at first that she would break that holy silence in which he was sinking to the depths of her heart by way of her radiant eyes, bathing in her joy-inspiring light, a light disclosing the meaning of words such as "God", "eternity", "freedom", "love". But soon he understood that she, too, was sinking in the depths of his eyes and discovering, one after the other, treasures of freedom, eternity and love, and this holiness in the silence was no less dear to her than it was to him, and in fact, in the measureless depths that their eyes revealed in one another they had ceased to be "she" and "he" and become one in Him – the very essence of love.
Are these not longings? – he asked himself, taking heart and holding the wise gaze of Adelain, daughter of Or-Nego. And besides this gaze he sensed another, directed towards him from the other side of the table and watching him closely, not without a measure of satisfaction – the eyes of Or-Nego.
The look in Adelain's eyes was deep and, it could be said, wise beyond her years. But in comparison with *her*! Can anything be

imagined that even resembles *her*? Is a mountain stream to be compared with the sea, can the light of an oil lamp compete with the light of the sun in all its splendour?

He smiled. A discreet smile, meant for himself alone. He can look into the eyes of Adelain, daughter of Or-Nego, look into them as long as he pleases, in any way that he pleases and with as much intensity as he pleases, he can appreciate their depth, their beauty, their surprising, submissive tenderness – compared with *her* eyes these are the eyes of a precocious child, clever perhaps, but nothing more.

He was still looking into these eyes when for a brief instant a flame of strange light was ignited in them, flaring up and growing and the next moment – wavering and recoiling, as if the eyes had picked up something, some inkling, of what was going on in his heart. Had they picked up everything? He didn't know. He never would know.

Deep in the recesses of his soul he saw the light, the other light, the living light that gives life to the one whose heart is wide open to it, and he longed for it earnestly, with all his heart and might, at all times and always.

In vain Adelain tried to catch his eye. He was far away, travelling distances beyond measure, soaring to heights never before scaled, diving to depths never before plumbed. She abandoned the attempt. Sorrow was etched on the alabaster face and there was pain in her heart, and besides these – wonderment and reverence such as she had never experienced.

She did not dare disrupt the chain of his thoughts, and she waited patiently, hoping that soon he would once again give his attention to his surroundings. And so it was: his eyes seemed to have returned to him, glancing about the room as if just this moment he had entered and taken his seat among the convivial diners, eating and drinking with gusto, laughing aloud and regaling one another with stories of battles and wars, talking of a king who triumphed, and the future of the world under his sway.

When his glance rested on her he smiled, his eyes cleansed and their light gentle. And she, without thinking of what she was doing, suddenly leaned towards him and kissed the back of his hand. He pulled his hand away, astonished.

"There's no harm in this!" she assured him in a deep, adult voice: "It's our custom to kiss the hand of a saintly person as a mark of respect."

He had no answer to give to this. He took up his full goblet and thirstily drank the light liquid, flavoured with honey newly taken from the comb.

...The injured deer they carried to the courtyard of her house, and she continued tending him until the wound had healed, and then she asked what was the right thing to do: to keep him at home, although captivity was not to his taste and he had already tried to jump the high wall of the courtyard in a bid for freedom – or return him to the forest, where another hunter might be waiting for him with bow and arrow, ready to inflict a more lethal wound this time. And he answered her that the will of God should be done, and she asked what was the will of God, and he answered her – to trust in Him and not try to take His place. And so the deer was set free. And for a long time after this, whenever they were strolling among the pine trees on the hill behind the Mount of Olives, they would encounter the deer which in the meantime had grown to adulthood. And the deer would approach them and take from their hands the vegetation that they had picked for him, expressing his gratitude by licking their hands.

THE ROYAL PALACE

The three covered wagons, with their occupants, continued on their way towards the royal palace.

The gates giving access to the palace were broad, and their posts and lintels, like the gates themselves, were overlaid with blue marble and tablets of gold. The setting sun lit up the gold and the blue, which reflected the full intensity of its dazzling glare, and for a brief moment it seemed it was about to rise again before the gaping eyes of the exiles.

A heavy guard was posted on both sides of the main gate, and behind the guard stood two rows of musicians: pluckers of the cithara and horn-blowers, players of the lyre and of the viol known as *sabka* in the Chaldean tongue, the double flute or *somphonia* and the dulcimer or *psantarin*.

As the wagons advanced, they were surrounded by a retinue of soldiers who had marked the occasion by polishing their armour, burnishing their helmets and weaponry and even adding embellishments to the harness of their horses – and then the air was torn apart by a deafening, nerve-jangling fanfare of trumpets.

The young men looked up in surprise and alarm, and saw on the wall above the lofty gate a line of trumpeters, who had just now raised their instruments to their lips, emitting that terrifying sound. The trumpeters wore blue and gold livery, matching the gates of the palace admirably. From the brass trumpets hung standards of glossy tapestry, each showing three reclining lions embroidered in gold on a blue base. And before the youths had recovered their wits, the blare of the trumpets still resounding in their ears, this cacophony was supplemented by the no less strident sounds of the remainder of the orchestra: cithara, horn, lyre, viol, dulcimer and double flute.

"Those noises could raise the dead from their graves!" – was Gabriel's comment, and Matthew added:

"I think that's the intention!"

"It's their way of reminding visitors to the palace how privileged they are to be admitted, and how much deference is due to King Nebuchadnezzar, the wise and the valiant!" Uziel interposed.

"And I tell you this," – Hananiah joined in the conversation – "these sounds are nothing compared with the music of the Levites in the Temple! This racket resembles the barking of mad dogs, or the blood-curdling wail of a pack of hungry jackals!"

Meanwhile the trumpeters and the other musicians, having finished their recital, turned and disappeared among the buildings of the palace.

The wagons passed through the main gate, Or-Nego leading the way flanked by two senior officers, and the rest following behind.

In the extensive compound the soldiers and the wagons halted, and the young men alighted from their wagon along with the exiles from the other two wagons. On the instructions of a dark-skinned flunkey, the carters moved their empty vehicles to the eastern side of the square and disappeared behind an internal gate. The Chaldean cavalrymen dismounted and entrusted their horses to the care of nimble ostlers, who appeared from some hidden corner, and came in haste, taking the reins with an ostentatious display of deference.

A Chaldean officer summoned the group of older exiles and ordered them to accompany him. At a steady pace they turned in the direction of the western gate, its bronze doors seeming to open by themselves, without a sound, at their approach, and closing again once they had crossed the threshold, just as silently.

Left in the yard were the young men and the remaining Chaldean soldiers under Or-Nego's command. With a friendly smile Or-Nego invited the youths to accompany him and turned eastward, towards a big gate, both of its doors consisting of eight panels of beaten silver, the panels separated by cast gold, and in the centre of each panel, a flower with pearls for petals and an ingot of pure gold for a carpel. These doors also swung open silently before the guests.

The young men found themselves in a broad, high-ceilinged hall, furnished with chairs and tables and statues, all of them made of alabaster, and high, narrow windows, curtained with a white, transparent fabric, clean and lustrous. On entering the hall, they noticed two slaves wearing green loin-cloths, standing by the doors and opening and closing them as required, peering out into the courtyard through a spy-hole drilled into one of the panels.

"So much for Chaldean ingenuity!" commented Gabriel, relieved, on discovering the secret of the door-mechanism, which had bemused him at first.

"And what is to become of those who disappeared behind the bronze doors?" – Hananiah's question was addressed to no one in particular, but it was answered nonetheless.

Or-Nego turned to the inquirer and with the same friendly smile, replied:

"They have been assigned to serve the king as bakers and cooks and stewards, unlike you..."

"And how are we to serve the greatest king in all the world?" asked Adoniah, a tone of strange servility creeping into his voice, a tone emanating from confusion, distaste and fear.

And Or-Nego answered him:

"With your wisdom!"

From the eastern corner of the room a very tall man entered, in ceremonial attire: an elegant robe and a blue shawl, a white sash around his waist, and on his head – a purple turban. Gold embroidery fringed the robe and the shawl, the sash was studded with pearls and three diamonds sparkled on the turban. A long dagger, in a scabbard of stiff black leather encrusted with emeralds, a large red ruby set into the pommel, hung from the sash. The man wore shoes of thick soft linen, coloured bright green and with gold buckles. Hard on his heels came his seven minions, tall young men of fleshy build, wearing white sashes and turbans, red smocks and plain green britches, shoes of coarse material. Hanging from their sashes were curved swords in black leather scabbards.

The minions, who despite their youthful age were endowed with generous paunches, lined up behind their gaudily dressed master, silent and grim-faced. Their master bowed to Or-Nego, who returned his bow.

"In the name of the great God Marduk, defender of Babylon the fair and in the name of His Majesty King Nebuchadnezzar, the valiant and the wise, conqueror of the world, I welcome you, most highly esteemed Or-Nego!"

"On my behalf and on behalf of the soldiers under my command, all praise be to the great God Marduk, defender of Babylon the fair, and all glory and majesty to King Nebuchadnezzar, the valiant and the wise, conqueror of the world, and greetings and felicitations to Narazan the chief steward of the King's eunuchs, whose reputation goes before him!"

The two men bowed low to one another once more.

"These are the young men," Or-Nego resumed his speech, after a brief silence, serving to add weight to his greetings – "whom Ashpenaz chose from the remnant that was left in Judah! They are outstanding in wisdom and in knowledge of sciences, and in understanding. And they are greatly favoured by their God, who has endowed them with the faculty of seeing visions and interpreting dreams, and healing the sick, everyone according to the portion of divine grace allotted to him!"

"Blessings and salutations be upon you, most highly esteemed Or-

Nego, and upon the soldiers under your command! I see the children and I receive them from your hand and from this moment onward they will be my responsibility, and your task is done. In due course the King himself will no doubt express his gratitude to you, and his appreciation!"

"Blessings be upon you, Narazan the minister and steward of the eunuchs in the court of King Nebuchadnezzar, the wise and the valiant, conqueror of the world!" – and so saying Or-Nego turned and strode towards the heavy doors, with their panels of beaten silver and trimmings of gold and precious stones. Without a word spoken, one by one, the soldiers followed him and disappeared from view, whereupon the minister Narazan, chief steward of the eunuchs in the court of Nebuchadnezzar, turned to the youths with a smile of surprising tenderness on his round face, with its drooping jowls:

"Welcome to the court of the King of Babylon, the wise and the valiant, conqueror of the world!" – he greeted them, with a slight bow in their direction.

"And greetings to Narazan, most resourceful of ministers! All honour to the wise and the valiant King Nebuchadnezzar, conqueror of the world!" – Adoniah hastened to reply on behalf of them all, bowing in his turn. His companions followed his example.

"And now," the minister Narazan addressed them, his smile still broad and benevolent – "you shall tell me your names and I shall give you new names, as is the custom in the court of King Nebuchadnezzar!"

He approached Adoniah, bowed to him slightly and asked him:

"Your name?"

"Adoniah!" the youth replied with exaggerated readiness, and returned his bow.

"Adeshech you will be called! And your name?" – he asked Uziel, and when he gave his name, the minister changed it to "Uzen". Uziel bowed somewhat reluctantly, not much caring for his new name. Matthew was called "Marduk", and Gabriel's name was changed to "Bel". Gabriel liked his new name so much he almost prostrated himself at Narazan's feet.

The minister turned and fixed on him his dark and watchful eyes, peering from the depths of their fleshy sockets – with a hint of good-natured mockery which faltered and turned into amazement when he met that calm gaze.

"Belteshazzar!" – he cried, having barely heard the name of "Daniel", uttered by the young man, and he bowed low to the ground before him.

"Belteshazzar, the name of a God that is given to Kings alone! Will my Lord and my King forgive me?" Narazan asked himself. "He cannot now be called by any other name!" – he replied to the question that he assumed the King would ask. "The name came of itself, it echoed in my mind and lit up my heart, and left no room for any other name! This has been the name of this youth since the creation of the world!"

He was somewhat perplexed by that surprising look, the look of a born master, and yet despite this, deep in his soul Narazan felt a kind of strange pleasure – the eyes of the boy had touched the fringe of the edge of something over which the flesh has no dominion. And to complete his task of giving names, he called Mishael – "Meshach", Azariah – "Abed-Nego", and Hananiah – "Shadrach".

"And now," he addressed the young men again – "you are to scrub your bodies and remove the grime of the journey in the King's bathhouse, and then you will each receive three sets of formal clothing, as you are to resemble courtiers in every respect, and my men will conduct you to the quarters allocated to you in the precincts of the royal household!"

Uziel and Hananiah almost took a step forward, but thought better of it when they realised that Narazan, the minister responsible for King Nebuchadnezzar's eunuchs, was standing his ground, not making a move and showing no inclination to move, a clear sign that he had more to say before allowing them to leave the room.

"I am required to bring another matter to your attention," – Narazan spoke now in a louder voice and smiled broadly, although for some reason he had lost that air of good-natured mockery. In its place, a kind of stiffness showed in his flabby-jowled face, a look eloquent of authority and unmistakable superiority. "And this matter," Narazan continued, slowly and emphatically – "you are to register well in your young minds, and inscribe it on the clean tablet of your memories: you are nothing other than captives of war, sons of a foreign race that dared to rise up and resist the King of the Chaldeans, the great and awesome warrior, the conqueror of the world and he, the greatest King in the universe and the wisest of them all, has consented in his magnanimity to accept you in his court. You are the personal property of the King of Babylon, his indentured slaves, slaves in every respect. He will do with you just as the fancy takes him: raise you as high as the sky if he so pleases, or cast you down into the dust if he so pleases. Your young lives are in his hands – for better or for worse, for your benefit or to your disadvantage. You are destined, according to the will of His Majesty the King, to study the literature and language of the Chaldees, and all the wisdom and sciences of the Chaldees. And when your studies are completed, you will stand before him, before His Majesty the King and he will test you and decide your fate – honourable service as a retainer in the royal household, or the life of a serf in the royal copper mines."

The chief steward of the eunuchs took a deep breath, a substantial breath that was clearly audible, wiped the expression of domineering superiority from his face, and reverted to his jovial, benevolent style:

"I sincerely hope that you will all succeed in earning the grace and the favour of my sovereign, His Majesty King Nebuchadnezzar, the wise and the valiant!" – he concluded his peroration with felicitations that may well have come from the heart, but did little to cheer the hearts of his audience.

The young men stood motionless, stunned. For the first time since leaving their homeland, bitter reality had struck them in the face. This was a cruel blow, and it was real, not an illusion. No longer free men but prisoners of war, slaves in every respect, their fate surrendered, for better or worse, into the hands of a ruler not known for his compassion or his patience, rather for his severity and cruelty, for his petulant and vengeful personality.

For a moment it seemed to them they had been deceived and betrayed, led astray and cast into a cunning trap set before their feet, the next moment – they realised that what had been laid before them was nothing but the truth in all its painful ugliness. This was no goodwill visit and they were not welcome guests invited to honour the Chaldean King with their presence, but boys seized by force, without any consultation, without any consideration of their own or their families' feelings, and taken away by royal command to Babylon, to serve the King in ways and in roles that he would assign to them, according to his caprice or as Narazan had expressed it so neatly – "just as the fancy takes him".

Was it possible to guess in advance what would appeal, at the end of the day, to the fancy of this cruel King, who had indeed conquered the world, or substantial portions of it at least, including their homeland and their native city, Jerusalem the holy?

The tense silence that reigned in the ornate, expansive room was broken by Matthew:

"We can at least hope that the thoughts and the wishes of King Nebuchadnezzar will not be of the oppressive or the tyrannical kind, that his whims will not be too unreasonable, and that he will come to appreciate the benefits of our knowledge, the contribution that each and every one of us is capable of making to his people and his kingdom. It was for this reason after all that we were uprooted from faraway Judah and brought here!"

"And let us not forget our faith which is whole, pure and steadfast," Daniel exhorted them, his voice even and unruffled, inspiring confidence – "and let us trust in Him, with all our hearts and all our might, all our souls and all our minds, trust in our God, the one God, the truly valiant and wise, the compassionate and the merciful, the God who will never abandon us or consign us into the hands of the cruel and the sinful!"

His words restored some spirit to the young men. Constricted hearts began to beat again and among them all there was a sense of shared destiny and partnership, of mutual support, and standing as a team to confront whatever trouble might lie ahead.

Suddenly, Adoniah approached Daniel and silently held out his hand. And when the other clasped it warmly, he said, in a strained voice:

"Can you forgive me? I haven't always wished you all the best in the world, and I haven't always appreciated the qualities with which you're endowed, and I have been guilty of jealousy and malice directed towards you! Forgive me please, pardon me as a friend to a friend, as a man to his brother in destiny, gullible fool though he is!"

"Things like this happen between friends," he answered him gently, with a smile.

"And in my mind there isn't the slightest doubt that in your wisdom you will do your utmost to lighten this burden of ours!" – Adoniah went on to say.

"It's all in the hands of Heaven, and God is the one who will show us the way to salvation!"

"Do well, and be well!" – the minister responsible for the King's eunuchs waved a round, fleshy hand at them, studiously ignoring whatever comments and conversations he might have overheard and, his round face beaming benevolently once again, he left the hall.

Two of his minions approached the youths, bowing deferentially, and one of them said: "Be so kind as to accompany me!" and he set out towards the door from which Narazan had emerged and through which he had disappeared. He was joined by the other minion and they walked shoulder to shoulder, the boys following behind.

A long, lofty corridor, with light filtering through narrow slits in the walls, close to the ceiling – led them to a hall much more spacious than the previous one, its carved ceiling supported by round pillars faced with white marble. The high walls were constructed from greyish-white granite, and on the north and south walls and above the entrance there were fitted stone shelves laden with scrolls of parchment and clay tablets. Movable ladders gave access to the upper shelves. At the far end of the hall, on the west wall, there were carvings of all kinds of animals: antelopes, rabbits, foxes, snakes and especially – lions. All the creatures were crafted by a skilful hand, and shown in appropriate poses: the antelopes tense and alert, snakes lurking in crevices in the rock, foxes peering from their holes, rabbits fleeing in panic from some unseen predator, and lions – pouncing on their prey from every conceivable posture. At one end of the wall the figure of a man was carved, evidently a hunter, a sword and a dagger hanging from his belt, a spear slung on his back, a bow in his hand and the string drawn back, ready to loose an arrow at the lion that is leaping at him with the full force of his weight, claws out and eyes flashing murderous rage, mouth open and teeth exposed, chilling the heart of the viewer.

Five men sat in the hall at tiny tables, studying those tablets and scrolls. When the boys arrived, one of the readers looked up, gave them a brief, quizzical glance and returned to his studies with a somewhat resentful air. The others were either unaware of their presence, or chose to ignore them.

The youths were impressed by the carvings and especially – by the hunter taking such calm, careful aim with his bow, impervious to fear.

Hananiah turned to one of their guides and asked him if there were many hunters among the Chaldean people, and if they enjoyed hunting lions. The guide replied with dignity:

"The answer to both of those questions – is yes!"

"The Chaldeans must be brave!" – Gabriel commented, adding: "In our country there aren't many hunters, and most of them go after deer and antelope, not lions."

"According to the Torah, the flesh of predators is unclean," Mishael asserted.

"I'm sure even these people don't eat the flesh of lions!" Adoniah retorted, as if taking Mishael's remark more literally than was intended.

"In our country we have no use for a dead lion," Hananiah interjected, adding: "Its skin is of no commercial value and its flesh, as has been pointed out, isn't fit for consumption! Where we live, lions are killed when they prey on sheep or cattle, or attack human beings. Our King, David son of Jesse, peace be with him, wrestled with lions when he was a young shepherd, and Samson killed a raging young lion, *And he rent him as he would have rent a kid, and he had nothing in his hand –* killed the lion with his bare hands, as simple as that! Whereas the Chaldean needs bow and arrow and spear, and sword and dagger!"

Uziel turned to their guide and asked him:

"Why do the Chaldeans hunt lions?"

"For the hide that is taken from them," he replied.

"And of what use is the hide?" Mishael asked. The guide answered him:

"It testifies to the courage and manliness of the hunter, and people pay him respect accordingly. On solemn or festive occasions, hunters wear the skins of lions that they have killed, and earn acclaim."

"So the only use the Chaldeans make of the lion's skin is for show!" Hananiah concluded, addressing himself and anyone else who might still be interested in the topic.

And Uziel turned to the guide again and asked him:

"What is the purpose of this room, and where are you taking us?"

"This room is part of the royal library," the other answered him. "At this end, at the table, sits the librarian responsible for this department. The books themselves are set out on the shelves. There are books written on parchment scrolls, there are books inscribed on tablets of brass, wood or clay. The clay tablets are located on the wall to our right, and they are bound together with cords of hemp, straw or cotton. The tablets of brass and wood are on the wall behind us, the rolled up scrolls are on the shelves to our left. As for your destination," the guide went on to say – "you are to wait here a while until the baths are ready, and the slaves have filled the cisterns."

"Is it possible to take some of these texts and read them?" Azariah asked.

"With the permission of the official responsible for this department," the guide answered, and pointed to the librarian.

Azariah approached the librarian and asked his permission to look at the texts deposited on the shelves. Permission was given, and the librarian stipulated that after perusing the text Azariah should return it to him rather than replacing it on the shelf. He asked him which text he was interested in.

Azariah thought for a long moment and finally replied:

"One dealing with the customs and laws of the country."

The librarian asked a further question:

"Has the gentleman heard of our great law-giver from ancient times, according to whose precepts and commandments the realm of Babylon has been administered to this very day?"

Azariah confessed that, much to his shame, the name of this legislator was as yet unknown to him.

The librarian, who was wearing a livery of startling white, his shoes included, answered him:

"The renown of our law-giver has travelled far and wide, and there is no people or nation that has not heard tell of him. His name – Hammurabi, and I would consider it a great personal honour to set before you some of his enlightening precepts!"

The librarian left his table and turned to the shelves holding the clay tablets bound together with straw. He moved one of the ladders into the right place, climbed slowly and selected a bundle of tablets. Handing them over to Azariah, he reminded him:

"Bring them back to me!"

The youths gathered around Azariah and his tablets in one of the corners of their room, sitting down with their escorts at a long table. Azariah, who had imagined that the Chaldee letters would be similar to the letters of the Hebrew language, if not identical, was bitterly disappointed to discover that any similarity was entirely superficial, and of no help whatsoever to the reader of Hebrew. He was on the point of giving up the struggle and returning the tablets to the punctilious librarian, when one of their attendants volunteered his services, pointing out that he was familiar with the Chaldee language. The youths handed over the tablets to the attendant, who studied them and after considerable effort, began reading out disjointed words which gradually evolved into whole sentences:

If a man has an ox that gores and it is testified to his owner that he has gored and he has not cut off his horns nor kept the ox inside, and the ox then gores a man and kills him – half the sum of compensation shall be paid (Statute 251).

If a man puts out another man's eye, his own eye shall be put out (Statute 196).

If a man knocks out another man's tooth, his own tooth shall be knocked out (Statute 200).

"Surely this is nothing other than the holy Law of Moses!" exclaimed Gabriel, and Uziel added:

"Almost word for word!"

"Who came first – Hammurabi before Moses, or Moses before Hammurabi?" Matthew demanded to know.

"Judging by the year recorded on the tablet, Hammurabi was before Moses," Hananiah announced, sounding utterly dejected.

"In other words," Adoniah interjected in a tone of bitter triumph – "Moses copied from Hammurabi!"

"It is improper to make such remarks, even to think such thoughts!" – Daniel rebuked him, adding: "There is only one truth, and the truth is eternal and not subject to change. If there were more than one truth, if it were possible to make the slightest adjustment to it, it would not be the truth.

"Both those men touched it, the truth – and there was no question of one copying from the other! And they revealed it to us, the very same truth, Moses to the Children of Israel and Hammurabi – to the Chaldeans, and all this by the grace of God."

"And yet we are told that we, the Children of Israel, and we alone, are the Chosen People of God!" – Matthew voiced his protest, and Daniel answered him:

"The Chosen People of God is a people that sets an example to all the nations!"

LET ALL LIVING THINGS PRAISE THE LORD

Into the hall of the library came a slave wearing only a loincloth around his waist. He approached them and told them the bathhouse was ready and at their disposal. Two of their escorts rose and began walking towards the eastern entrance of the hall. Azariah returned the linked tablets to the librarian and thanked him on his own behalf and on behalf of his companions.

The "bathhouse" was a large, low building, constructed entirely of wood, in which there were three pools lined with marble, the first containing hot water, the second – lukewarm and the third – cold. Four swarthy-skinned slaves were waiting for them with porous pumice stones in their hands and gold powder in dishes at their feet.

One after another they ventured into the first pool, some crying out in protest at the heat of the water, others controlling themselves and entering the water without uttering a word. Within a few minutes their young bodies were acclimatised to the heat and they were beginning to enjoy it, their spirits rising, and Hananiah, having finally succeeded in dispelling from his mind the impression made on him by Narazan's last words – broke into song, with those well known verses from the one hundred and nineteenth Psalm of King David: *"Let your mercies come to me O Lord, your salvation according to your word, and I shall have an answer to the one who offends me for I trust in your word..."* The others soon joined in the singing, accompanying him until they reached the verse: *"I will lift up my hands to your commandments and meditate upon your statutes."*

The mood changed, and in place of dejection, came jubilation. Arguments were forgotten as if they never were. Distance from the homeland also faded somewhere among the gentle vapours of the hot water, and the very fact of being exiles in a foreign land not their own, prisoners of war, slaves – all this no longer seemed to matter.

The slaves joined the bathers, sprinkled some of the gold powder over their bodies and began scrubbing them with the pumice stones. In so doing they found the youthful spirits of the foreigners infectious, and joined in the singing with hoarse, hesitant voices, coping with the melody well enough but stumbling over the pronunciation of the words – understandably; unlike the youths, they did not have a lifetime of practice behind them. And as the mood became ever more cheerful, and enthusiasm soared and joy exceeded all bounds, Uziel suddenly changed direction and launched into the exultant, confident and triumphant strains of *"Praise God in his sanctuary, praise him in the firmament of his power, praise him for his mighty acts, praise him for he is great. Praise him with the sound of the trumpet, praise him with the lute and harp, praise him with the loud cymbals, praise him with the resounding cymbals, let all living things praise the Lord, Hallelujah!"*

The last line they repeated, in full voice, seven times, as was customary at Passover in the Temple, entirely forgetting where they were and the predicament in which they were placed. They sang and sang until they lost all sense of time, those sounds that bring solace to the soul, exalting the mind and moving the heart of man closer to his Creator, who is love, and arousing in this heart the firm desire to start again and never again return to what was, knowing that the longing for Him, the Blessed One, is the source of light and joy and freedom.

And as was also customary at Passover in the Temple, the youths turned to one another and exchanged handshakes. The slaves, infected once again by their enthusiasm, followed their example, extending hands to one another in a spirit of true fellowship and friendship.

After the hot, they bathed in the lukewarm water and then leapt with gleeful cries into the cold, emerging invigorated and refreshed, full of youthful strength and intoxicated with rapture. The slaves dried them with rough towels, anointed their long hair with oil and their bodies with unguents, and finally sprinkled them with rose water, its fragrance filling the bathhouse. In the closets set around the pools they found their new clothing – linen smocks of blue, purple and white, and cloaks of a thicker material with matching colours. There were also turbans and shoes, everything clean and pleasant to the touch. There was little in the way of ostentatious ornament, but each one of them received a gold brooch to fasten the wrappings of the turban, bearing the emblem of a rampant lion. The broad belts, made of linen, were fitted with silver buckles. On the upturned toe-caps of the shoes, rubies sparkled.

The slaves who had helped them dress pointed to the exit door of the bathhouse, where their escorts were waiting for them patiently, to conduct them to their quarters. Each of the young men occupied a cubicle, with a lace-curtained window overlooking extensive gardens. Under the window was a bed, and beside it a table with a clean white cloth covering, and an oak-wood chair. There was a closet and on the wall – a shelf. On the table stood an oil-lamp, with a stout wick – capable of emitting a powerful light.

And when evening fell and stars covered the sky, fatigue all at once overcame the young bodies and the boys took their leave of one another, went to their cubicles, climbed into their beds and immediately sank into deep sleep. And there were some among them who dreamed pleasant dreams, such that loosen the slumbering lips into an innocent smile, and there were some who saw nightmares. Among others, Uziel and Gabriel did not dream at all – sinking like stones into the dark waters of a deep well and waking only when the sun had risen, shedding the fullness of its light on the world of men, and the slave assigned the task of rousing them had arrived to shake them from their slumbers.

Breakfast was served in a long, low room, lit quite adequately by its many narrow windows, and it was pleasant to sit there at tables laden with all kinds of delicacies: succulent cuts of meat, choice wines, almonds and nuts, little bread rolls, and all kinds of vegetables and fruits, the pride of the fertile valley of Mesopotamia: dates moist and dry, light and dark, figs and mangoes and raisins and various concoctions blending the juices of the melon and the pumpkin.

The hall was buzzing with Chaldean youths of the same age as them, sons of ministers and dignitaries and close associates of the king, sent here to study Chaldee literature and language, etiquette, music and sciences, subjects which they too would be studying. A special table was set aside for them, the eight exiles from the Land of Judah. They took their seats and blessed the food, but before they had time to taste anything, Daniel turned to them and said:

"Friends and brothers, let's not contaminate ourselves with this meat and this wine which has not been prepared in accordance with our hallowed rituals! Eating such meat and drinking such wine is an offence against our Law. We should content ourselves with vegetables and fruits, nuts and almonds!"

"I don't think that would go down very well with those people," – Hananiah pointed to the waiters, who in addition to their other duties were keeping a close watch on the behaviour of the occupants of the hall.

"Let's try it and see what happens, and God will be with us!" he assured them.

"Without meat and wine, a meal isn't a proper meal!" – Matthew protested.

"A meal without meat and wine will weaken our bodies and impair our concentration too. How shall we endure the rigours of our studies, and how do you suppose we're going to fare in the tests?" – Uziel demanded to know, and he answered him:

"Any meal that is ritually clean, consumed with reverence and courtesy, gives strength to the body, pleasure to the soul, and clarity to the mind." And he added: "So let's avoid the pollution of meat and wine, and everything else we can eat with pleasure and with dignity, and our Father in Heaven and our God will shower His grace upon us, and we shall cope successfully with the studies and the tests."

A sneering smile twisted Adoniah's broad face:

"You're trying to win converts to your way of thinking, Daniel, and telling us what we can and what we can't eat and drink," – he drawled, continuing in a tone that somehow contrived to be both wheedling and exultant – "Even before all this you weren't a meat-eater or a wine-drinker. You're just following your father's example, and as for your interpretations of the Torah – they are weird!"

For a moment their eyes crossed – Adoniah's smouldering gaze and his own look, calm and sincere, concealing somewhere beneath it a kind of distant sorrow, at his inability to induce others to change. Both turned their eyes away, as it dawned on Adoniah too that there was no common ground between them, no path that could bring the two of them together – not even a narrow and twisting one.

"Speaking for myself, I'm not touching the meat or drinking the wine – only this wine!" he asserted, taking a piece of bread and some of the moist dates.

Without a word spoken, his example was followed by Hananiah, Mishael and Azariah. Uziel did likewise, slicing himself bread and swallowing a couple of dates, but then he changed his mind and chose a piece of meat from the display on offer, and poured himself wine, drinking his fill and gobbling the meat with gusto. Gabriel was drinking wine with a nonchalant air, and although at first he contented himself with fruit, in the end he too held out his hand to the dish of boiled meat, still steaming, selected a slice and stuffed it into his mouth, licking his fingers and chewing calmly.

Adoniah and Matthew were consuming meat and wine from the outset. Matthew gave the impression of one who for years has been hungry for meat and thirsty for wine, while Adoniah turned his meal into a performance: taking slices of meat between his fingers, moving them this way and that, flaunting them in the faces of all those present before cramming them into his mouth and chewing noisily.

The vigilant eye of one of the waiters noticed the strange behaviour of the group of four, abstaining from the meat and not drinking the wine. And the waiter came to them and said in a hesitant voice:

"You should eat the meat and drink the wine! This is meat of the highest quality – from the King's table, as is the wine! Such abstinence is an insult to the King and his solemn decree!"

The four of them looked at one another. His three companions seemed anxious.

"Will you submit to the Chaldean King, and defile yourselves with food that is unfit?" he asked them.

"Not I!" replied Hananiah firmly.

Mishael and Azariah also spoke up resolutely in his support. He turned to the waiter and asked him, politely but emphatically, to summon his superior. The waiter turned away and disappeared from the room.

A few moments later he returned with his superior – none other than Narazan, chief steward of the eunuchs. He greeted the four of them with a modest bow, his customary smile lighting up his heavy face. The four rose from their seats and returned his bow. He invited them to sit, and they complied.

"The waiter tells me that you are not treating the King's largesse with the respect that is appropriate, abstaining from his wine, which gladdens and strengthens the heart, and from the superb meat that he is providing for you! He also tells me he has warned you against any slight – whether real, potential or merely contemplated – upon the honour of the King – if, that is, you would rather stay in the palace than be sent to the copper mines in the mountains!" He chuckled, but behind the good-natured banter he was clearly anxious.

"We are not refusing the King's largesse, and we mean him no disrespect whatsoever!" he answered him in a clear but quiet voice, not intending his words to be overheard by the other diners, who were looking on with keen curiosity.

His reply reassured Narazan. It was a relief to him to know that he could negotiate with the young men without resorting to threats of punishment.

"All these fine foods that God has given to the sons of men, to enjoy them and to bless Him, set out in such abundance on these tables," the youth went on to say – "all come to us through the largesse of the King! Whether you nibble a date or gorge yourself on meat – you are enjoying the King's largesse, praising him, extolling his generosity and his refined taste! There is no difference between breaking one's fast with one or another element of the royal bounty, as both are of equal worth."

Narazan sighed and retorted:

"Meat is not of the same worth as fruits or vegetables. The former gives strength and the latter diminishes it! One who eats only fruits and vegetables and drinks no wine, will weaken, and even fall sick, and his thoughts will be impaired, likewise the meditations of his heart. He who eats meat and does not disdain the fine wine of His Majesty the King – is strong and of handsome appearance, proof against sickness, clear of thought and apt of speech, and the King delights in him, and for this reason he, the King, commands that he be given nourishing meat to eat, and invigorating wine to drink!"

"If that is the point at issue," he replied, a bright smile on his face, feeling lighter at heart as he saw a solution to the dilemma – "I suggest that we eat those portions of the King's largesse which we consider the most choice – nuts and almonds and pulses, fruits and vegetables, and bread, and if after ten days we appear worse than those who eat meat and drink wine, and we are feeble in comparison to them, and our thoughts more fuddled than theirs – then we shall bow to your will and join the ranks of the meat-eaters and wine-drinkers! If on the other hand we prove to be better looking and stronger than them – then you should withdraw your objection and allow us to continue eating good food in accordance with our Law, the holy Law of God!"

Narazan sighed again, and this time his sigh was deep and emphatic. The charm of this Jewish youth was working on him – in his appearance, in the crafting of his speech and the wisdom of his words. There can be no doubt – he told himself – that his God is with him and whatever he does will be blessed. Is it for him, Narazan the master of the King's eunuchs, to dare to defy any God? And supposing the whole business reaches the ears of the King, what then? In a hushed voice, as if imparting a secret or talking to himself, he said:

"I fear my Lord the King, who has decreed what your diet is to be! If you emerge from this more pale and haggard than the other children, my head will be forfeit!"

"The King only rules by the grace and with the consent of God!" he declared, fully aware of the momentous weight of his words: "And yet – I am asking for just ten days! If after ten days we are indeed pale and haggard, we undertake to eat meat and to drink wine, and if it is not so – we are freed from this obligation, and you will know that God is with us."

Narazan lowered his heavy head, in its turban of purple cloth, thinking over the young man's words, weighing them at length, and then he sighed for the third time, looked up and delivered his decision, almost in a whisper:

"Let it be as you say!" – and he turned and left the room.

From that moment on the astute waiter bothered them no more. On the contrary, he made things easier for them, putting neither meat nor wine on their table, and increasing the portions of fruits and vegetables and honey-water.

DENUR-SHAG

The Chaldee of literature was similar to Hebrew. And yet there were words which, while sounding like Hebrew expressions, meant something completely different, even the opposite. There was also a system of syntax, beguiling in its simplicity and acuity, but utterly alien to both Hebrew and Aramaic, and it required a great deal of effort and concentration to master it. The difference between the colloquial Chaldee that they had already picked up in the home land, and the original, written language was clearly evident.

Their studies were made easier by the teacher of Chaldee, Denur-Shag, a man forever smiling, witty and most important of all – a master of his subject, as conscientious as he was proficient. In addition to the new linguistic idioms he taught them the sciences too, including poetry and the art of rhetoric.

Denur-Shag always found a fitting way of enlivening his lessons, with pithy observations that often rendered the members of his class helpless with mirth. Thus for example, the preamble to the twenty-first statute of the Laws of Hammurabi, relating to the hire of an ox or an ass, should read: "If a man shall hire an ox..." By changing the order of the words to "If an ox man shall hire" he invented expressions such as "ox-man" or "ass-man" – creations both unexpected and contrary to logic. Banishing from his lessons all that was dry or solemn, he ensured that the "class of strangers" as this group was called, this mixture of the sons of other races, set apart from the Chaldeans – would both roar with laughter and absorb more readily the simpler rules of Chaldee syntax, learning them through the senses and growing accustomed to them without effort.

A lean man was the teacher Denur-Shag, short of build and with a large, round head, most of it bald, and kindly eyes that were often humorous, inwardly or overtly. He wore a grubby robe of coarse material, and a cloak, equally coarse and equally grubby, too big for him and trailing on the floor. On a number of occasions the teacher tripped and almost fell to the floor on account of this cloak, and yet he made no attempt to change it for one that would fit him better. His mishaps Denur-Shag took in good heart, even when one of his pupils had difficulty controlling his mirth. In such a case Denur-Shag would turn it all into a witticism, with a comment such as:

"That's what comes of trying to fly, and forgetting you're not a bird!"

The pupils, twenty-eight in number, members of various races and different nations: Sidonians and Parthians and Edomites and Moabites, three Egyptians and two whose nation and origin were cloaked in mystery, and two others, eyes aslant, from the distant land of Gog and Magog – sat on three long benches, pressed against three of the walls of the low but spacious room, at three long tables. The teacher's seat was by the entrance door – a chair, and a small table beside it. The boys etched with a stylus on the soft surface of clay tablets, and sometimes used a pen on parchment scrolls.

Above the teacher's chair, near the entrance door, was a long strip of parchment, the same hide from which the scrolls had been cut, and he used to write on it with a long splinter of wood dipped in red ink, pointing out the expressions, idioms, words or numbers that he meant to impress upon his pupils.

From the very first lesson there was a spark between him and Denur-Shag. Denur-Shag was endowed with a sharp eye for the discovery of qualities and strengths in his pupils, and he was also adept at recognising their deficiencies.

His attitude to him was exceptional – the teacher ignored him completely, although in this there was no intention to offend. From time to time he would call him to the front of the class, in order to demonstrate to the other pupils that a certain study-topic, contrary to their suppositions, was easily digestible, and he would put his questions to him. And he answered quietly and precisely, showing not only that the subject could be understood and taught, but that engagement with it could also be a pleasure.

In the first lesson, when his name was called and he rose to his feet as required, Denur-Shag stared at him, then his eyes lit up and he declared:

"See, the roles have been reversed – and he who should be the pupil of Belteshazzar is his teacher, and the one qualified to be the teacher of Denur-Shag is his pupil!"

He bowed respectfully to the teacher, and the other returned his bow. As far as most of the students were concerned, these opening words of Denur-Shag were not only enigmatic but quite meaningless. The Edomites on the neighbouring bench took it for a joke and laughed obligingly, eliciting no reaction from the teacher.

So from this time on, Denur-Shag ignored him, something accepted as natural and self-explanatory, and only rarely did he glance at the tablets on which he had inscribed his answers to the questions posed. This was a departure from his usual practice, which was to subject the tablets of his pupils to meticulous scrutiny, drawing their attention to the slightest error and insisting upon pinpoint accuracy.

In the third month of their studies, one day when lessons were over and before the second meal was served, Denur-Shag called his name: "Belteshazzar!"

He stood up from the bench, approached the diminutive man with the massive, balding head, bowed to him in conventional style and asked him:

"How can I be of service to the teacher?" – spoken in fluent Chaldee, much to the delight of his interlocutor.

"By doing me the honour of a visit to my home on a day of rest from study, meaning tomorrow!" the pedagogue replied.

He arrived at Denur-Shag's lodging and knocked on the door, once white but now liberally encrusted with a layer of congealed dust.

The door opened and a dark-skinned slave, clearly of advanced age, standing unsteadily on spindly legs, wearing only a loincloth and a linen head-covering, inquired in a croaking voice:

"Belteshazzar?"

"Correct!" he replied.

"Be so good as to come inside Sir!" – the slave stepped back hastily and made way for him, and in the short, dingy corridor he took his cloak from him and hung it on a hook, then pointed to a door which opened onto a spacious room.

In the middle of the room stood a heavy round table, made of polished cedar-wood, and around it three chairs of white wood, pine apparently, planed to a smooth finish.

Denur-Shag rose to meet him, shook his hand, invited him to sit in one of the white chairs and took his seat facing him. Then he clapped his hands and the elderly slave appeared and set a dish of dry dates on the table, also a jug of rose water and two large cups. The jug and the cups were made of glazed clay.

The teacher poured for his pupil and for himself, raised his cup in a gesture of benediction and drank from it.

"Denur-Shag, Sir, do you abstain from wine and meat?" he asked, having raised his cup to return his host's benediction and taken a few sips from it.

"No, not at all," he replied, "although I have heard it said that Belteshazzar abstains from wine and from meat. I have no questions to ask you on that subject. What I wanted to ask is – how do you find the fair city of Babylon, is it agreeable to you? Have you had much opportunity to make its acquaintance?"

"No," he confessed and added, "walking about the streets of a city holds no fascination for me. The precincts of the palace are spacious enough for exercise, and studying occupies most of my time."

"So you stroll in the lovely and well-tended gardens of the royal palace – alone or with a few of your companions?"

"Usually alone, because our free time does not coincide, but sometimes I will be accompanied by one or more of my friends."

"That is a wonderful thing, adding depth to the indelible riches of the soul!" – Denur-Shag spoke with pretended, ironical pathos – "But Babylon," he continued – "has rules of its own, rules of behaviour which should be observed. As the saying goes in ancient Chaldee: 'To keep your life, keep them!' – meaning, those rules of behaviour."

"We have been told nothing at all about them," he commented mildly.

"Nor will you be told! They are not written, these laws, not inscribed on stone or clay or parchment," he went on to explain – "but they emanate from the soul of man, Chaldean man that is. It is the law in Babylon's fair city, a law that is not to be transgressed, and it may be the law in other human societies too, societies of which I claim no expert knowledge – that a man who shuts himself away behind closed doors may be regarded as deranged, or arrogant, or a genius, but he will never be considered a normal and sane member of the community. Such conduct can have only one outcome," – he scanned him with a serene, expressionless look and added: "Jealousy!"

He took a date, lifted it to his dry mouth, removed the stone and put it in the clay dish, chewed thoroughly and added: "Jealousy, as you know, stirs up all kinds of trouble... of course, it is not for me to interfere in matters that are not my concern, and yet in spite of that – I feel I have a duty, a duty as an educator."

"Jealousy is not such a powerful force," he replied, explaining – "It is repelled by logic, among other things."

"Logic?" – Denur-Shag queried, as if asking himself a question. He added: "Even the definition of logic is not universally agreed! And if we try to call to mind those who are possessed of it, or who used to be, our task will be an easy one: they can be counted on the fingers of one hand

– and most of them have long since crumbled into dust!"

The teacher chuckled, his playful eyes bright with good will and affection.

"Dear, highly esteemed boy," he addressed him once more, holding up a hand to forestall any protest at the title thus awarded him – "some two dozen years ago a young man came here, full of hopes and with dreams and ambitions to spare, a scholar of literature and language, not only those of the Chaldeans, at all levels of antiquity; he was also familiar with the dialects of the Samaritans, and the Hebrews and the Egyptians, and he even knew a little of the raucous babble of that nation over the seas, which is reckoned, erroneously of course, to be the torch-bearer of human culture and wisdom and the harbinger of a glittering future.

"And this young man," – he returned to his theme – "was received with great honour and with the respect due to him by the king of that time, and he served him loyally. But he did not prosper for long, and he soon fell into disfavour. And the big head of that dreamy youth was nearly detached from his shoulders at the hands of the functionary responsible for this, the redoubtable Makphon-Mago, who is no longer with us, since his own black head was removed by his successor, Magaphan. Anyway, as I say, the sharp sword of the former was almost laid on the neck of that eager lad because…. because… I'm sure you can guess…" Denur-Shag smiled bitterly – "he preferred to stay indoors, confined to his quarters and never venturing out among people, knowing nothing of the frustrations and irritations of their humdrum lives. Not even taking a wife. Admittedly, in this last instance, the young man eventually changed his mind, changed it quite radically in fact, and married a young peasant woman, a total illiterate, who stayed with him just long enough to bear him two daughters. Whereupon the shrewd peasant woman decided to return to her parents' home in the village of her birth, and bring up her daughters there, rather than waste whatever years remained to her at the side of an idle, detached eccentric whose sole interest in life seemed to be staring at the heavens above and the earth beneath. And he was struck deaf and dumb when she made her justified complaints known, made them known repeatedly – in a voice so clear it could be heard from one end of the royal palace to the other. And she is still alive and well in her village, somewhere in the south of the country.

"And this young man was reckoned haughty, and all his successes in the service of the court were interpreted in this light, and were whispered in a thousand dialects and from a thousand mouths into the ears of the King, and he could no longer endure the relentless and unremitting pressure of the gossip, and like your hero of old, whose repute has come down to us, *He wished in himself to die*. But a king doesn't die, he has a slave to do it for him. And were it not for the teaching post which became vacant then, and which no other living person could be found capable of occupying with even symbolic success, were it not for that – I would not be here now, enjoying a pleasant encounter over a cup of clear honey-water and fruit from the Garden of Eden...

"Yes, it is my opinion that the palm-tree was planted first in the Garden of Eden," Denur-Shag went on to say, in an abrupt change of subject – "and there it grew and flourished. The palm-tree is wise and humble, and when it saw the fall of Adam and his bitter fate, its heart was broken beneath the solid bark and it wept and wailed, and turned to God, your God, the creator of all things, and entreated Him most earnestly to be allowed to join Adam in his exile and share his tribulations, and soothe as far as was possible the grief of his soul, and be his comforter. And the good and benevolent God gave his full consent, and the palm tree changed its abode – from the Garden of Eden with all its delights to the most remote and desolate corners of the world, where the sun beats down relentlessly and water is nowhere to be found – and there it flourishes, climbs to great heights and blooms, and digs its powerful roots deep down beneath the shifting layers of sand, finding pools of water invisible to the human eye and raising them to the surface and above, making life-giving springs and turning those corners of desolation and death into verdant oases, delightful to behold! And such is the story of the blessed palm-tree!"

And again the narrator took a dried date between two fingers, examined it closely, with tenderness and affection and even with love, blessing it and putting it slowly to his lips, with an air of intense appreciation.

He followed his example, taking a large date and consuming it with relish.

At the western window of the narrow, lofty room, overlooking the royal garden, the slender ray of an early sunset turned everything it touched to gold.

"You're supposed to be studying the principles of Chaldean mathematics now," Denur-Shag told him after a long silence, rising to his feet.

"Never mind the principles of mathematics, I'm more interested in the words of wisdom I've just had the privilege of hearing! Bless you, Denur-Shag, and may you prosper in this world and in the hereafter!"

"Bless you, Belteshazzar and whatever your destiny may have in store for you, for honour or for shame, for good or for evil, might and glory or great affliction – do not let yourself be a victim, trampled down by fate, but rise above it and take control of it!"

"How can you speak of might and glory and great affliction, of honour and shame?" he asked him, astonished.

"I see it branded with a seal of fire on your smooth forehead, see it living in the depth of your fearless eyes, hear it resounding in your clear and tranquil, finely modulated voice, feel it radiating from every movement that you make!

"No, I am not a prophet," Denur-Shag forestalled the question that he knew was coming, and added – "unlike your compatriots whose favourite hobby is prophecy. I am simply one of those unfortunates who have logic working in their brains and are still alive. Few of them are left, and becoming fewer all the time as the world is filled with conquerors and victors in war, and is split between slaves and masters, genealogies and races, peoples, tongues, nations, religions! Go in peace, Belteshazzar. Remember what you have heard here and be forever on the alert, and keep yourself in safety! And if you have no desire to do this for your own sake, do it for your admirers – for your compatriots who need you, and for certain teachers too who find themselves baffled, not knowing how to cope with a pupil who is unique in his generation, unique in his race and perhaps in all races, and these confused and weak-willed teachers cling to the hope that what their feeble hands have failed to accomplish, his young hands will yet bring to fruition. Go in peace!"

"And peace be with you, gentle master, my teacher and my mentor Denur-Shag!" – and he turned and left the room, took his cloak from the trembling hands of the elderly slave and returned to his lodging.

The ten days of the experiment were over, and Narazan appeared in the hall as his charges were eating their first meal of the day. Accompanied by the waiter he approached Daniel and his three companions. The four of them rose to their feet and Narazan gestured to them to sit, surveying them with a keen glance that gradually softened, and ultimately expressed nothing other than plain satisfaction.

"Your faces are so fresh and robust, so full of health and strength," Narazan declared, in a jocular tone – "anyone would think you've been gorging yourselves on the wild ox that's been served to the others!"

The waiter failed to appreciate the joke, and he hastily intervened:

"Heaven forbid, esteemed minister Narazan! All this time these youths have tasted neither meat nor wine and their diet has been only vegetables and fruit and sweetened water. I have kept a close watch on them!"

"There was no need to keep a close watch on them! None of these youths would ever tell a lie – they would sooner die!" – declared Narazan, steward of the eunuchs in the palace of King Nebuchadnezzar, and he concluded: "Serve them whatever food they ask for, from henceforward until their studies are completed!" – and he turned away and disappeared through the door of the dining hall, a genial smile on his face.

One day Denur-Shag appeared in the classroom in ebullient mood, bursting with eager enthusiasm. He put aside his tablets and parchment scrolls and began telling them, with characteristic verbosity, about peoples in distant lands, and especially those on the further shores of the great ocean, somewhere to the north-west, who invented the science of numbers, and who try to explain all the phenomena of the world, including the dispositions of the human mind and body and the greatness of God – in terms of numbers. And not content with adding one number to another, a simple enough process, and subtracting one number from another, which is equally simple – through copious study of numbers they have touched upon a new discovery or invention which they call "multiplication". And this word, which until now has served to signify the kind of vision typical to one who has imbibed a substantial quantity of the fermented juice of the vine, is now used to denote this remarkable and new-fangled invention.

They multiply number by number, and arrive at astonishing totals which could not have been foreseen at the outset. And in order that the process of multiplication may be understood by a broader spectrum of the populace, and diffused in the wider world, these inventive geniuses have recourse to two eminently simple concepts: "place" or "places" and "thing" or "things". "If there are four places" they say, "and in each one of them there are five things – the process of multiplication produces the number twenty." Indeed, logic tells us that this conclusion is correct. Anyone can prove it for himself. And they go on to claim, these inventors, that the art of multiplication applies to all cases and places and circumstances and times and occasions. And here, by chance or not by chance, they arrive at the miraculous number "zero", meaning – nothing at all. If in *no* place five things are located, according to their system, the system of multiplication, and of course such a thing does not accord with the healthy intellect, to say nothing of logic – the result is – zero... It emerges that in the process of multiplication, the "zero" is a lethal creature, like a great whale, consuming everything coming into its proximity, without distinction or consideration. The inventors have a remarkable formula at their disposal, as they express it: five times zero equals zero, and therefore, five equals a fifth part of zero, or – five equals zero; and here they plumb the utter depths of absurdity, but are incapable of admitting it!

Briefly, Denur-Shag taught them the numerical symbols and went on to say:

"What these clever people fail to realise is that here, before them, there is a warning signal; Heaven is telling them to revert to their humility before it is too late, since, and this my dear pupils you should inscribe firmly in your young minds – if they don't stop in time, they will finally bring this wonderful world crashing down in ruins and wreck utter destruction upon the human race. And even if this process continues for a thousand years, two thousand or three, this will be the final and inevitable consequence of "multiplication" for those who have recourse to it: it will set up a barrier between mankind and?..." – he turned with a question to his pupils, some of whom were listening attentively, some trying with varying degrees of success to make sense of what he was saying, and others staring blankly at the whitewashed walls of the classroom, thoroughly baffled.

"Belteshazzar!" he cried finally, and he stood up and completed the sentence:

"And God!"

"This will be the final outcome!" cried Denur-Shag with passionate emphasis, continuing: "Remember this well, inscribe it in your hearts, and pass it on to the generations that are to come! The intellectual arrogance of the west, that smug obsession with the science of numbers, will ultimately destroy everything that is pleasing in the aspirant soul of mankind! The soul of mankind longs and yearns for the truth, for what is beautiful and good, meaning – God. And it may that the sages of the west are unaware of what they are doing, and it may be there are some of them who will try to stop the wheel turning, and halt the race towards ruin and destruction before it is too late. We must wish them every success! But it seems to me that in the final analysis, that tiny minority, and it may in fact be one and one alone, the single wise man of his generation – will be the butt of laughter and mockery even on the part of his disciples, and his chosen disciple will be the one who betrays him! The evil instinct in man tends towards violence and destruction; it sets up a barrier between him and life, between man and God!"

Denur-Shag took a deep breath, and then another, and went on to say, his eyes flashing as he spoke:

"And in the east there lives a quiet people, strong and as multitudinous as the stars in the skies above and the sands on the sea-shore below. These people have slanting eyes that recall those of the fox or the snake, or both of them, and they are careful to avoid contact with strangers, and they keep to themselves the secret of the silk that is spun by worms feeding on mulberry leaves, and they make all their calculations using balls of string, and they conjure their dead and make them into gods. And they bow down to these gods and worship them, and their souls yearn for them, and they bring down on their own heads and on the heads of those whom they subjugate, nothing but ruination and death. And we, standing in the middle with a wise and valiant king ruling over us, need to know which way we are facing – towards the destruction and perdition of the west, or the ruination and death of the east, or are we to escape from the claws of one and the talons of the other and make a stand in our own right, and construct for ourselves a new way towards what is beyond destruction and perdition and above death and ruination, and we shall give our era a new name," – and Denur-Shag turned to his pupils and asked them: "What name would you give it, this new era?"

Since no one showed any inclination to answer his question, and there was silence in the hall, the teacher was forced to call on him again:

"Belteshazzar!"

He rose to his feet and declared without hesitation:

"The age of the sons of God!"

"And what are your reasons for naming it thus, the era of last hope?" – cried Denur-Shag, excitement kindled once again in his eyes.

"The Scriptures."

"Can you elucidate?"

The dialogue proceeded with animation and firm resolve, and it seemed that for the two participants all the others had ceased to exist.

"In our ancient Book of Psalms," he began in a tone of confident authority, his face radiant – "in the eighty-second psalm, the sixth verse reads: *I have said, you are God, and all of you sons of the Most High!*"

A look of deep happiness swept across Denur-Shag's excited features. He nodded to him in token of approbation, and added to this a deep bow of respect and appreciation, then straightened up, thinking something over. He turned to the rest of the class, his face suddenly changing expression, losing that look of keen enthusiasm and now showing nothing but exhaustion and mild dejection:

"Well," he said – "we have an answer here, and it may well be that other, different answers exist, but we shall content ourselves with this one and leave the others aside. Meanwhile, since our time is done and you must complete your riding lessons before the evening meal is served, be off with you, go in peace!" He withdrew, disappearing into the passageway.

The pupils rose, took up their writing tablets and exchanging lively conversation on the subject of the riding lessons they left the hall.

Adoniah approached him, hissing through his teeth:

"These words of yours are nothing but incitement to rebellion, and they will put your head in the noose that hangs from the execution pillar!"

He did not have time to reply – not that he had any intention of replying – before Matthew came from behind him, spitting bile:

"How long will you put on these airs of yours, son of Naimel the traitor?"

With lightning swiftness he took a firm grip on Matthew's shoulder.

"Take that back!" he cried, his eyes gleaming with a strange and intimidating lustre. Adoniah returned, to intervene at Matthew's side, but Azariah, Mishael and Hananiah immediately stepped forward to block his path, keeping him away from the belligerents. Gabriel and Uziel looked on from the side, curiously.

He squeezed Matthew's shoulder and went on squeezing, knowing he was inflicting pain, while the other howled like a beast led to the slaughter:

"I take it back, I take it back! Let me go!"

Slowly he removed his hand, allowing Matthew to flee, tears streaming down his face, to the long corridor, now almost empty. Mishael, Azariah and Hananiah came and stood beside him.

"Insolent boy!" hissed Hananiah.

"Denur-Shag admires you. Your answers really cheered him up, we saw his face!" Azariah saw fit to comment, intending to change the subject and encourage him.

"We are proud of you!" Mishael gave expression to his exultation, which had not yet abated.

"It's all by the grace and mercy of God!" he answered them and, a smile lighting up his face, walked with them down the corridor.

THE RACE

At the outset, lessons in riding were not included in the programme of studies. It was none other than the King himself who instituted them, saying it was not enough for his scribes and favoured servants to be skilled in the lore of tongues, in fine craftsmanship and the science of numbers – they must prove themselves valiant as well. He insisted that they be trained in equestrianism and stipulated that at the end of the course all the pupils were to compete in a horse race, according to the strict rules of ancient Chaldean tradition. And he, the King, would preside over this event.

A lean and nimble Numidian slave was their riding instructor. His name was Tabin and he treated them with the same respect and deference he would have shown to members of the aristocracy. Sometimes he compromised, deviating from the rigid requirements of the curriculum and not insisting that all the complicated manoeuvres be performed. He contented himself with demonstration, and with reminding the young gentlemen that in the final analysis, carelessness could cost them their lives.

Each of the pupils was given charge of a gelding or a mare, well fed and well groomed, and these were to be their mounts throughout the course, and afterwards.

He was allocated a young mare, alert and attractive, sharp-eyed and of quick intelligence, responsive to him and adept at sensing his mood, interpreting his wishes and fulfilling them. She was white and her name was Orelian, and the empathy between them grew stronger from one lesson to the next. No surprise, then, that no one was his peer in horsemanship. Even Tabin, their instructor, could not conceal his admiration. Matthew distinguished himself as well, although his technique consisted in goading his horse into a frantic gallop, the animal picking up speed in a desperate effort to rid himself of the troublesome rider and his vicious spurs. Despite this, in the practice races that the novices held from time to time, he never prevailed. He would whip and spur his horse into such a state of exhaustion that he stumbled on the turns and veered from the track, often rearing on his hind legs in a futile attempt to unseat his impetuous, brutal jockey.

Daniel's riding was characterised by a restraint which underlined his total control of his beast, winning the hearts of the spectators with his graceful movements and that rare understanding between horse and rider. The high-spirited Orelian needed no encouragement from whip or spur, from yelled commands or affectionate words whispered in the ear. She could read all her master's thoughts, and complied with absolute precision. She knew how to control herself and how to maintain speed on the turns, leaning slightly to one side. Her undulating, harmonious gait delighted the spectators and she invariably came in first, barely breaking into a sweat and as well tempered as ever, thus faithfully reflecting the personality of her rider.

As the course proceeded, the novices came to understand the meaning of the expression "according to the strict rules of ancient Chaldean tradition." In a special lesson, reticent as ever, out of respect and appreciation for his pupils, Tabin informed them that they would be required to jump over a ditch with deep, fast-flowing water at the bottom, which would sweep anyone who misjudged the jump into the foaming Euphrates. Many a rider, Tabin warned them, had either neglected his lessons or had panicked at the crucial moment, falling into the ditch instead of clearing it, bringing his young life to an end that was ignominious and highly regrettable by any standards. Not only this but King Nebuchadnezzar, the valiant and the wise, conqueror of the world, was demanding that the course of training be cut short, to finish the next month, with the full moon, twenty-seven or twenty-eight days hence, and on the day following the conclusion of training, a race was to be held; all riders to run the course which was to include jumping over the ditch three times, one after another, those who would live, to live, and those who would die – to die! This was the gist of Tabin's emotional address, and having spoken the Numidian slave led the group on a tour of inspection of the ditch, covered for the moment with heavy panels of brass.

This was a defensive moat of the old style, surrounding the royal palace and filling with the surging waters of the Euphrates whenever the sluice-gate was raised. In the course of time it was realised that the value of the ditch as a defensive measure was limited; having penetrated the Chaldean capital thus far, a potential enemy was unlikely to be deterred by it. Despite this, the ditch was not neglected and the sluice regulating the flow of water from the Euphrates was kept clear, in preparation for races such as this, the risk to the lives of the participants invariably attracting a large and variegated crowd of spectators, from the King himself and his courtiers to the lowliest of apprentices from the artisans' quarter.

So the days passed, and the quickened pace of the training began to bear fruit – the novices sat confidently in their saddles, and understood their mounts as far as their level of competence permitted, and preparations began for the fateful race.

The last week Tabin devoted to practising the technique of jumping the ditch. It was still dry at this stage and covered by those heavy brass panels, but by peering through the gaps between the panels one could gain an impression of the depth – an unnerving experience for the novices, who suddenly began paying more attention to their instructor, and carrying out the exercises required of them with all the thoroughness they were capable of. And so it was that by the middle of the week the horses were accustomed to jumping the ditch with its brass panels, no longer needing the encouragement of whip or spur as they approached the edge.

"When the panels are removed," Tabin used to warn them in his deep, hoarse voice – "the sight will be even less reassuring! Fear will definitely be a factor, and we must practise and practise until we could jump the ditch with our eyes closed!" Tabin bared two rows of gleaming white teeth in a rather awkward smile, and since nobody responded to the smile he continued in more earnest vein, warning that otherwise, one of them at least was bound to lose his young life, before getting to meet the King face to face and receiving the assignment he had set his heart on. "As for me," he went on to say – "I took part in this race some four years ago and I finished in third place. As a reward for this, the King took me out of the stables, and instead of shovelling horse dung from dawn till dusk, I became a riding instructor. Now, pay attention! The winners among you won't be given the most respectable assignments immediately, because you are still children, but the King will remember you, and when the time comes he will know how to reward the victor! King Nebuchadnezzar is valiant and wise, wise especially – and he won't forget to reward any man according to his deserts. The honest and the talented will find him a generous patron, the villain and the loser – he tramples into the dust!"

The young men listened to Tabin, the former stable-boy and took his peroration to heart, doing what was required of them with renewed vigour, omitting nothing, until they succeeded in putting the smile back on his face, a broad and radiant smile this time, a look of supreme satisfaction.

Two days before the day of the race, when the labourers were already busy erecting the stand for the King and his entourage, Tabin addressed the novices again and told them that he considered the jumps had been practised enough, and it was time to concentrate again on the issue of speed, or "acceleration" as he called it. He admitted he was not an expert in this field, and could only give the benefit of his own meagre experience; experience had taught him that the perfect matching of rider and mount was the key to acceleration, meaning – the horse should not feel insulted or degraded by rough treatment on the part of his rider, but on the contrary, should feel proud and appreciative of the one on his back, as eager as he to be first at the winning-post and exerting every effort to achieve this. "You need to be calm and considerate," he told them – "controlling yourself and not attacking the horse or riding in an abusive manner, which does no good at all but only harm. Excessive use of spurs is to be avoided too, as the only effect is to drive the animal out of its mind, meaning that both horse and rider are doomed to a sudden and unpleasant end." And here Tabin made it clear that his advice was intended for Matthew in particular, and he hoped Matthew would appreciate the importance of what he had said. Unlike him, Tabin, young Matthew was credited with some intelligence and could work things out rationally, and if he would only apply his talents to his riding, he would not only enjoy it, he could expect a successful outcome in the race, if not in first place, then in second or at least in third – like Tabin in his time.

"Most important of all," Tabin reminded them repeatedly, with hoarse emphasis – "listen for the sound of the trumpet! It's the signal for the start – and it's the only signal that you'll hear! Anyone who sets off too soon, will be disqualified and even if he comes in first, he'll be severely punished at the hands of the King, who is a stickler for order and self-discipline! Don't forget," he repeated in a more emotional tone than was his wont – "listen out for the trumpet!"

When his briefing was finished, and before they dispersed, the young riders pressed around him and asked him all kinds of questions, such as who, in his opinion, was most likely to win the race, and on whom would he lay a wager if this were permitted. He replied calmly that things such as these could not be foreseen or predicted in advance, and the whole of the business, including the identity of the winner, was in the hands of Heaven. If any of them was in direct contact with Heaven or its occupants, he should address his questions thither, and if regarded as worthy of it – he might even receive an answer. Speaking for himself, he wasn't in the habit of discussing things with Heaven or its occupants, and there was no point putting questions like these to him.

Once more they rehearsed the race from beginning to end, galloping along the broad and smooth track and jumping the ditch, still with its cover in place. It was estimated that the race would last no more than an hour.

The last day before the race was devoted to "relaxation of mind and muscles" as Tabin called it, and the young men were allowed to do whatever they pleased – short of touching strong liquor or eating anything to excess. Most of them split into groups of three and four and strolled along the outer wall, admiring the gigantic reliefs of lions, bulls and warriors. Some ventured beyond the fortified walls of Babylon and gazed at the mysterious, turbid waters of the Euphrates, flowing with a strange serenity towards the open sea.

At sunset the youths returned to their quarters, catching a glimpse on their way of the silhouette of the saluting stand that had been set up for the King and his entourage. It towered high above the race track and set in the middle of it was Nebuchadnezzar's throne, made of solid gold and ivory and adorned with precious stones and carvings telling of the history of Babylon and the exploits of its rulers.

His heart did not beat fast in anticipation of the race, unlike the hearts of the others. And if it had been possible to discern in him something resembling an emotion – this would have been a mild sense of grief, like a morning mist rising above an enchanted valley, watered by a bubbling, magical river.

It was obvious to him that there was jealousy and there was malice, and these had grown and intensified and turned into violent hatred – all of it directed at him.

If it had been possible to forgo the race, he would have done so willingly, but the slightest hint of reluctance on his part would have been misinterpreted, casting a heavy shadow of suspicion not only on him and his close friends but on the whole class and especially on the instructor. If it had been decreed that he was to compete in the race then he would do his utmost, invest all his strength and energy in the effort to win the victor's laurels.

He was awakened by the light touch of the slave assigned to this duty

"Sir!" he cried. "Sir!" he repeated, looking scared and flustered. "The time! The race! Sir!" The slave's command of the Chaldee tongue was less than impressive.

He leapt from his bed, washed face and hands in the water that the slave poured into the basin, put on a pair of blue riding britches, a white smock and a red sash, and set out for the compound in front of the palace.

His companions were already there, all of them without exception, as was Tabin, the instructor.

The firm lines of his face, his smooth forehead, serene eyes, every movement of his body spoke of freedom, enveloping him as in an aura of splendour and fearlessness, and spreading all around him a festive spirit. A shade of anxiety which had appeared on the Numidian's dark forehead vanished when he saw him.

"We're all ready!" he called to him with an air of joyful enthusiasm that he himself could not account for.

He approached them, affably shaking the hands extended to him, and in so doing, glimpsed the smiles of Adoniah and Matthew – the first expressing undisguised contempt, the second – something dark, intimidating, impossible to define.

The youths made their way to the spacious stables, where each of the horses had a stall to itself.

He examined the harness of Orelian, who whinnied affectionately at his approach, lowered her proud neck, put out her tongue and licked his hand as if to encourage him.

Did he need encouragement? – he asked himself, and brushed the question aside, preferring not to answer it.

He examined the knee-joints, ran his hand over the hooves. Everything seemed to be in order.

Driven by a sudden impulse he fell to his knees, put his hands together, looked up and said:

"Please, my Father in Heaven and my God, melt the hatred in the hearts of my enemies! Please, my Father in Heaven and my God, preserve us all from sudden death, and cleanse me of the last vestige of pride, the pride that I feel over my faith in You and my trust in You, my knowledge of You, and of Your truth, and of Your existence! Do not forsake me my Father in Heaven and my God, not even for a moment! Guide me always in the right way!"

He rose to his feet, and found himself face to face with Denur-Shag's frail and elderly slave.

"What brings you here?" he asked, astonished.

"My master Denur-Shag says, check the saddle and especially – what's under the saddle!" The slave recited his master's message, bowed low and, tremulous as ever, turned and disappeared the way he had come. For a brief moment he stood there, stunned and motionless, then recovering his senses he approached Orelian, carefully unfastened the girth and lifted the saddle. At the front end of it he saw a dark object, resembling a ball of lead. He tugged at it, and with some difficulty managed to pull it free. It was indeed a ball – but with a sharp and barbed spike embedded in it, and it had been concealed under the pommel, designed to pierce the horse's body at the crucial moment of leaping over the open ditch. Had the spike not been found in time, both his life and Orelian's life would have ended that day. He sighed a deep sigh of grief and revulsion.

He passed a hand over Orelian's erect and gleaming neck, and the mare turned her head back, put out her tongue and licked the caressing hand.

He tightened the straps of the girth, dumped the spike in a waste bucket, put his booted foot in the stirrup and with an agile movement, mounted the mare and rode out to the maidan.

It was a pleasant day to be outside, the air clear, the sky blue – and flawless.

On both sides of the long track, the crush of Babylonians was barely credible; they resembled a sea of heads, moving back and forth and heaving like waves. The crowd was held back by a triple cordon of tough-looking soldiers, with clubs and drawn swords in their hands. The atmosphere was festive. Colourful banners waved above the sea of heads, in front and behind.

He joined his companions and together they approached the starting line. Each one of the horses, which had been well trained, took its allotted place. The saluting stand reared up to their right. Surrounded by guardsmen with drawn swords, in gleaming armour and wearing gold helmets, holding shields of solid gold – sat the King on his high throne. They could not see the King's face, but they caught a glimpse of the crown on his head, consisting of several layers rising to a point of blazing gold, encrusted with precious stones and pearls the size of walnuts. The King's garments were all of gold brocade, adorned with so many gems and rubies it seemed that from the royal throne a new sun had risen, no less lustrous than the other. At the King's feet sat his courtiers, in tunics of variegated colours, festooned with jewellery.

The moment that the riders arrived on the track and took their places – the crowd broke into a loud chorus of applause, and now it was no longer a sea of heads but a forest of raised arms and waving flags, while the unrestrained cries of "Hurrah" made the very air vibrate and ear-drums were on the point of bursting.

Standing in the appointed place he noticed for the first time the line of trumpeters drawn up at the foot of the saluting stand, trumpets raised in their hands, poised and waiting for the King to give the signal. To the right of the trumpeters stood a line of drummers, huge drums hiding their faces and all of them built like wrestlers in the arena, with their massive shoulders and shaven heads, drumsticks raised in their hands.

He did not know what their function was, and regretted that Tabin had not mentioned their presence.

Suddenly, as if his thoughts had been overheard, the drummers struck a single, ear-splitting beat, and the riders had to exercise all their skill in controlling their steeds, keeping them firmly in position.

Following the drumbeat the tumult of the crowd was hushed and voices stilled, the waving of hands and banners stopped, and an eerie, unexpected silence reigned on both sides of the tracks. And then the silence was shattered by the strident blare of the trumpets.

He did not see when the King gave the signal. Deep in the recesses of consciousness something came alight and he and Orelian sprang forward like an arrow loosed from the bow of a skilled archer, one who never misses.

The start was perfect, and no less perfect was the running of Orelian. He could feel how his wishes were transmitted from his head to hers, becoming instructions that her body immediately obeyed. No longer were they two separate bodies but one, subject to the mastery of one mind and the sensibilities of one heart.

And as they approached the open ditch, the foaming of its waters clearly audible as they rose in spate, he had only to press lightly against her neck to feel how her body was poised, fearlessly, in anticipation of the well practised leap.

She leapt and hit the ground running, racing on with only the wind, tossing her mane back, to compete with her.

Moments after the first jump, he caught a glimpse of Matthew's furious glare. He paid it no heed, concentrating all his attention on guiding Orelian, at speed, into the sharp turn, and back to the ditch. And the mare went racing on as if possessed by a demon, leaving all the other riders far behind and receiving the loud applause and adulation of the spectators on both sides of the track, whose enthusiasm was such that they threatened to break through the cordon of grim-faced soldiers. As he passed in front of the saluting stand he saw how the elegantly dressed courtiers rose to their feet and shouted as one man, admiring the prodigious speed of Orelian.

Out of the corner of his eye he caught sight of a horse and rider, apparently exhausted but making desperate efforts to close the gap between them and overtake him at any price. He sensed that this frantic rider could be none other than Matthew, but he dismissed him from his mind, leaning forward on his horse's neck and leaping for the third and last time across the broiling waters. Only a parasang now separated him from victory. And then he sensed that something was happening behind him, something terrible, but he knew that any attempt to turn and look back would spell doom for Orelian and for himself.

He galloped and galloped, urging on his mount and never slackening his pace until he reached the winning post, leaving all his competitors far behind. And when he dismounted from Orelian and shook the hand of the agitated Tabin, he heard from his lips how Matthew, pressing on behind him, had come to the edge of the ditch and his horse, which had already jumped it twice, rebelled. He reared up on his hind legs and fell into the flooded ditch, taking his rider with him. Two horsemen who followed close behind Matthew saw what had happened but lost control of their mounts and one after the other they too tumbled into the raging torrent and perished. The water carried their bodies away to the Euphrates. This outcome was utterly unexpected and, as is the nature of facts – could not be reversed.

He was required to pass with Orelian before the saluting stand. He did this as if in slow motion, calm, relaxed, almost casual, hearing the loud applause of the courtiers and of King Nebuchadnezzar himself, who stood in his honour and ordered that the youth be given a purse of gold coins.

He bowed to the King and to his cheering courtiers, then turned and bowed to the crowds of spectators, who had recovered from the shock of the disaster that they had just witnessed and were bestowing on him all their affection and admiration, clapping their hands in his honour and pelting him with flowers, colourful little flags and sweetmeats, not to mention coins of bronze, silver and gold.

He returned to his quarters worn out by the day's events, washed and went to his cubicle intending to rest, only to find Denur-Shag waiting for him there.

Denur-Shag did not rise to greet him, and seemed in no hurry to congratulate him, but there was no mistaking his satisfaction at his protégé's success. His little eyes shone, and no amount of deep breathing could mask his delight.

"Do you want to know who planted the spike?"

"No!" he declared.

"You realise that whoever did this wasn't simply planning a harmless schoolboy prank?"

"I realise!"

But Denur-Shag was warming to his theme:

"He intended to send you to the world that's all good, with your horse thrown in for good measure, the majestic Orelian. Perhaps he feared you were going to obstruct him in his pursuit of some goal or other."

"Perhaps."

"I won't burden you with any more hints," Denur-Shag concluded.

They sat in silence for a long moment.

"How do you do this?" – he finally expressed his bemusement.

"Do what?"

"Expose this kind of villainy and nip it in the bud."

"I have ears and eyes in various corners of the court. Don't misunderstand me, I'm not in the habit of recruiting informers, but for some reason, people feel obliged to confide in me. As a matter of fact, it's not me they confide in so much as that doddering old slave of mine."

"Could it be that the 'informers' really don't want these things to reach you?" he asked.

"Anyone who knows my old slave knows perfectly well he would never hide anything from me, even if it cost him his life! There was a time," Denur-Shag continued with an amiable smile – "when this old slave of mine almost made it onto the menu for the royal lions. This is one of the traditional methods of execution in Babylon's fair city," he explained. "In the very heart of the King's ornate palace a lions' den has been constructed, and the inmates have been trained to prey on two-legged animals only, a diet of human beings in other words. Offer them wild ox – they're not interested. And this slave of mine, who was once a scribe, a calligrapher of scrolls, attracted some professional jealousy and was accused of worshipping gods other than the gods of Babylon, Marduk and Bel, who according to popular belief are the defenders of the Chaldean capital. They claimed they had proof of this and they almost succeeded in their conspiracy, and it seemed that the short walk to the lions' den was going to be the old fellow's last journey. But then he found an advocate, in the person of a balding teacher of outlandish philosophies and the Chaldee language. And this teacher took his life in his hands and stood before the King and caught the accusers in their own trap, and as there were three of them, the lions' loss turned into a profit.

"One way or another, what happened to my old slave left him paralysed, paralysis of the body and the tongue. For some time he lost both the power of movement and of speech. And even when he regained his faculties, he couldn't stop his hands from shaking and this was an affliction for which there was no remedy. Obviously, he was disqualified from his work as a calligrapher, and there was no choice but to send him to the slave market, with the proceeds going into the royal coffers as compensation for the loss of his services. Anyway, I managed to ransom him before he was officially put on sale, for a modest sum of money that I had at my disposal. And since then he's been with me, and the whole of the royal court knows that he's more devoted to me than a mother is to her children. Incidentally, that modest sum of money came to me courtesy of my wife, who lives in the country and sends her husband gifts from time to time, sweetmeats, rolls of fabric, sums of money. Of course, I only married her to please the King, and uphold the unwritten law of Babylon!"

"What law is that?" he asked, perplexed.

"A man who is mature and unmarried shows disrespect to the royal household. He is considered almost a rebel. By withholding his seed he fails to play his part in the increase of loyal subjects of the King, subjects who will uphold his rule, strengthen his arm and assist his conquests. No man who is fertile but unmarried may hold any official post in the court of the King. In certain cases, such a man will be deprived of all his rights and divested of his property."

"A strange business," he mused. "This means that all of us... that I?.."

"When the time comes it will be your duty to take wives!" – Denur-Shag nodded his mighty head.

He was silent.

Denur-Shag rose from his seat and said to him:

"Remember what happened today, and when the time is right and you are a close confidant of the King, who unlike other monarchs lives up to his nickname and is indeed wise and valiant, do everything you can to put an end to this horse race and the lethal ditch! Suggest instead a few simple fences, that a horseman can jump without paying with his life if he fails. Remember this!"

Denur-Shag left the cubicle.

Shortly after midnight someone knocked on the door.

He rose from his bed, turned up the flame in his oil-lamp and opened the door.

Before him stood Adoniah, holding a lamp.

"I don't mean to disturb you," he began apologetically and added at once – "I thought I should tell you not to reproach yourself over Matthew's untimely death. You weren't to blame. It was his obsession that drove him to it. That's all!"

Adoniah did not enter the cubicle, and showed no sign of wanting to. Nor did he invite him in.

"By the way," he continued as the flickering flame of his lamp revealed different parts of his face in turn, showing a uniformly unpleasant expression – "the other two fatalities were the slanty-eyes! That's a loss that shouldn't be too hard to get over! And one last thing, dear boy," he added – "After those three deaths on the race track, the King has decided that Tabin the Numidian failed in his duty as a riding instructor, and he's sent him back to the stable. Sweet dreams!" Adoniah turned and disappeared in the gloom of the corridor.

A clear and bright morning awaited him the following day. This was the day of rest after the race. The slave who was supposed to wake him failed to appear, but he awoke early anyway, rose, went for a dip in the communal bathhouse, and dressed in blue robe and cloak and a pair of comfortable and matching blue shoes. For a belt he wore a sash made of some glossy fabric, the handiwork of a renowned Chaldean seamstress.

He knelt in prayer and remained for some time on his knees, not uttering a word, his consciousness cleansed of thought. A kind of restrained gaiety arose in his heart. Is this the grace, the tangible grace of one who has the privilege of believing and knowing that his faith is the truth? – he wondered, or could this deep, simple satisfaction, untainted by fear, be called happiness? Is it possible to give a name to something that lies beyond the grasp of human language and of human comprehension?

He remained on his knees, his hands clasped, his head uplifted and his eyes fixed, unseeing, on the low ceiling.

His consciousness, unsullied by reflection of any kind, glowed in the infinite and became a part of it, became infinity itself. Time retreated and disappeared. The world of forms and of names grew pale, existed no longer. Nothing was left but He. The living light, love.

He went out into the royal gardens, ever luxuriant, ever a feast of thrilling colours, every tree a delight to see and every flower a thing of rare beauty, the air perfumed, the gardens shedding one shape and donning another and stretching away, so it seemed, to the faraway horizon, to the end of the world.

ADELAIN

In pleasant corners of the garden pure streams gurgled and birds trilled. In the centres of rounded patios, floored with fine mosaics, reflecting the light of the morning in soft shades, fountains of brass reared their heads and flung their jets of blue water high into the sky. The water descended in broad arcs and was collected in circular basins, lined in coloured marble. Ornamental fish, of all shapes and hues, swam serenely in the waters of these basins. Benches of polished wood, the work of skilled craftsmen, stood in the patio spaces, ranged around the fountains.

He sat on one of these benches, without a thought in his mind, gazing at the white foam of the surging water. Not far from the fountains one of the many doors of the royal palace was visible, guarded by sentries with broad-bladed, drawn swords in their hands. Time passed, and he did not know if it was the breakfast hour, but he did not feel hungry and preferred to go on sitting there on the bench, watching the fountains. And then he caught sight of one of the slaves, running among the trees and across the lawns, evidently looking for somebody – for him perhaps.

He stood up from his seat, to make himself visible, and sure enough the slave saw him there and hurried towards him. After the customary bows and salutations, the slave said:

"Sir has visitors!" – and he went on to explain – "The minister Or-Nego, general of the army and with him – a young lady. They are asking after you, Sir. No one knew where you had gone, so we have all been sent out to look for you. And here you are! They are asking after you, Sir!" the slave repeated, sounding flustered and confused, and he then fell silent and waited. He was a recent recruit to the palace staff, and nervous.

"You've given your message, go in peace!" he replied genially, with a smile. The slave was taken aback by the unexpected warmth of this response, and he bowed low, almost to the ground, before turning and retracing his steps to the palace. He knew he was supposed to follow, but instead he returned to his bench.

"Hail and greetings to the victorious rider!" – the voice came from behind him, and it resembled a song in its astonishing clarity and its harmony of sounds. He turned, and his eyes met the deep gaze of

Adelain, daughter of Or-Nego. This gaze reflected a sort of admiration, rising above itself and wanting to know nothing other than its object. And in this unfathomable admiration there was something perplexing and intimidating.

"Since the early hours of the morning we have been asking after him and seeking him, my father the minister, and I," – she spoke without shifting her gaze from his eyes for so much as an instant – "and I asked my father if we could come today and pay a visit... this morning, the morning after the remarkable victory that we witnessed yesterday! Winning in itself is of no great merit, but what a rider! My father, Or-Nego, is a fine horseman, and he taught me to ride too and we sometimes go riding together, and everything I dreamed of achieving and knew I would never achieve, nor would my father nor any of the horsemen of Babylon – I saw yesterday, set out before my eyes!"

"What are you referring to?" he asked, sensing a defensive note in his voice, wariness of something to which he was reluctant to submit.

"To that perfect blending of horse and rider. Every rider worthy of the name is aware of this blending between himself and his mount, but every honest rider will admit that such blending is far from perfect, and perfection belongs to the realm of self-deception, it is the stuff of dreams! And this firm, unshakable conviction was yesterday blown apart before my eyes, and I still cannot believe that I saw it and it was witnessed by others – it was real and not a fantasy!"

"That is something of an exaggeration!" he protested.

She did not acknowledge his protest and perhaps did not even hear the words he said. Her caressing gaze, expressing that breath-taking, intimidating admiration, went on sinking deep into his eyes, and he realised that his eyes too were not shifting from hers. Why? – he asked himself. Because he did not want to show any hesitation or worse than that – any fear? His question was left hanging in the air.

She went on to say, her speech rising like the singing of birds on a fine spring evening, flowing like a clear and fast-moving mountain stream:

"The horse knows the mind of his rider and behaves accordingly. An ugly mind will never succeed in taming a horse! The loyalty of a horse, its undying loyalty, is the reward of a beautiful spirit! But there exists another kind of spirit, which I had never known until yesterday, or dared to believe it could be real, a spirit that soars high above all others – and such a spirit the horse worships, erasing his own temperament entirely and performing, with a depth of satisfaction of which human beings cannot have the faintest conception, everything that this spirit requires of him, orders that are given and received – and yet unspoken!"

He admitted to himself that her perceptions of the innermost mind were profound, and she had done well in defining those mental processes which seemed to defy definition, and one so young! Somewhere, in the recesses of his soul, that other face came into view, those eyes that never failed to instil in him a refreshing serenity, a sense of steadfast joy. In its depth, this look resembled that of his interlocutor, but differed from it, as if an unbridgeable gulf separated them – in its sublime intensity.

He smiled, feeling himself immune from any violence that might befall him. And what kind of violence did he fear? – he asked himself. He has faith, and where there is faith, all violence fades away and vanishes as if it never was. Violence is nothing but the invention of people without faith. His broad, affable smile, embarrassed Adelain for some reason, and she fell suddenly silent and looked down.

"As I said, you're exaggerating!" – his voice remarkably clear, its confidence restored.

"I'm not exaggerating at all, not in the slightest, as he knows perfectly well!" she declared without raising her head, and he admitted inwardly that she was right.

"Should we try a less formal mode of address?" he suggested.

"By all means!" she replied warmly, looking up again, a bright and graceful light in her eyes, as she sought for his eyes, eager to sink into them once again.

"He..." she began.

"Call me Belteshazzar!" he corrected her.

"Yes," she conceded, "Belteshazzar. I'm sure he is committed to somebody, somewhere in his distant homeland... No, I'm not asking for information!" she declared – "Just trying to get things clear in my own mind. He must understand..."

"*You* must!" he corrected her again, with some vehemence.

"You must!" she echoed him. "There are relationships, human relationships I mean, relationships between a boy and a girl – of a different kind. And the strange thing is, until I met him, sorry – you – I wasn't prepared to admit this kind of thing existed! The kind of relationship that imposes no obligation at all, but on the contrary – is a call to freedom. And this special, surprising relationship is the source of unknown, unflagging joy! A person denies himself completely, in a way he never imagined himself capable of denying himself... completely!" –

she isolated the last word for the sake of emphasis and continued: "Absolutely and without any reservation, and he gains happiness for which the only fitting word is – infinite, or if you prefer – sublime!"

At the beginning of the last spring, when the atmosphere in Jerusalem was tense and hearts were heavy, and the prophet cried out in a loud voice "Thus says the Lord" – and no one paid him any heed, and instead of awakening hearts, he only aroused the wrath of the mob and inflamed pointless hatred – they sat in her garden, an extensive garden where every tree was in blossom and every flower in bloom, and the air was filled with their intoxicating scents. He spoke as if entrapped by a dream, repeating those lines that seemed to him to belong to another world, on a different, silvery star, where everything was perfect:

"You are as beautiful my dearest as Tirzah, lovely as Jerusalem, terrible as an army with banners. Turn your eyes away from me for they dazzle me. Your hair is like a flock of goats streaming down from Gilead, your teeth like a flock of sheep coming up from the washing, every ewe bearing twins and not one of them barren. Like a slice of pomegranate are your temples behind your locks... Who is this who looks out like the dawn, fair as the moon, bright as the sun, terrible as an army with banners..."

And here she concluded:

"Who is this coming up from the wilderness, leaning upon her beloved... Set me as a seal on your heart, a bracelet on your arm, for love is strong as death..."

"Love of what?" she asked as if talking to herself, without turning to him. And he heard his calm, steady voice replying:

"Of God."

This was not so long ago, the year that Jerusalem fell, and everything unfolded with such rapidity, and there was no knowing what the outcome would be, and events pursued one another, with new horrors every day. And that astonishing trust, in the grace and the love of God, was planted in him, to be his property from that time forward and for ever, and for this he would bless his Father in Heaven, his God, and praise him always.

He looked at her. The sun shimmered on her abundant hair, falling to her nape, wave upon wave, like the breakers of the sea, enslaved by the light of the moon, kissing the shore and nestling against it. And the song spoke of "a flock of goats, streaming down from Gilead."

He smiled – it was an innocent smile, friendly, pure.

"Is it possible," she began to ask, hesitant, wavering and repeating her question – "is it possible," she said, "to define this perfect union between horse and rider as something resembling – love?" She fixed on him the deep gaze of her eyes, tinged at the edges with melancholy, the melancholy of one who will not spare himself or the honour that is most precious to him, in the pursuit of an objective which in his eyes is exalted above all else and which he knows is incomparable.

"Love is a sacred word," he declared with some solemnity – "a word that we should refrain from expressing so long as we are engrossed in the profane, for 'Love' is the explicit name of God."

"So the one who loves, loves in divine fashion?" – it was partly a question, partly a statement.

"Loves God in divine fashion," he asserted.

She lowered her eyes and smiled. In her smile there was a sadness that was immeasurable and unquenchable and she subdued it forcibly, with violence almost, and without the flicker of an eyelid.

"On the matter of commitment," once again she brought up that strange word, which so surprised her with its very sound – "if it exists..."

"Man is committed to his God," he interrupted her, "out of desire to be close to Him, to know Him and to learn from Him what love is."

"Surely it's obvious what love is!" – she retorted, and it seemed that a cloud was removed from her white brow.

"What is it?" he asked with interest and for the first time noticed she was wearing festive clothing – a blue robe of fine but dense fabric, and around her delicate neck a string of tiny pearls which set off admirably the alabaster of her skin. A broad white belt of finely crafted leather enclosed her waist, with a gold buckle for a clasp, showing the emblem of a lily made up of white pearls. Over her robe she wore an open tunic, embroidered with gold threads, resembling chain-mail. Her feet were shod in white shoes of the same leather of the belt, with gold buckles that were precise, miniature replicas of the belt buckle with its pearl design. Her hair was swept back, tumbling to her shoulders.

She scanned him with an almost baffled look, as if astounded by his question and perhaps, irritated by it and indignant, and she answered him in her musical voice, redolent with youthful hope yet to be dashed.

"Sacrifice!" – and she saw fit to add: "Sacrifice offered willingly and gladly!"

He lowered his head. "Love is strong as death. No, not 'as death', but 'stronger than death'" he declared unequivocally. "Because love is life and the infinite and freedom, because love is God."

"Is that how you see it?" she asked finally.

"It's how I see it," he replied softly.

"And hence, to love means being happy," she declared with absolute seriousness – "and not being dependent on the object of your love."

"In other words, not being dependent on the reward of love which is love!" he declared.

"That is well expressed!" she cried with a kind of dignified enthusiasm, a maturity at odds with her age and her appearance.

And in spite of this, he thought, Babylon is different. Jerusalem is something else and the two of them are not to be compared, set against one another. The Holy Spirit rules everywhere, in Babylon as in Jerusalem, and Jerusalem bears its name.

In the days before the siege he used to go riding with Nejeen on little piebald ponies, like those of the Chaldeans. They used to leave early in the morning, sometimes before dawn, mounting their ponies and spurring them along unpaved roads, over steep wadis and swollen rivers, breathing deep into their lungs the stimulus of the fresh air, bearing within it the sharp fragrance of the radiant acanthus, and the open field, and above all else – the indelible odour of sanctity, the brooding sanctity of Jewish Jerusalem.

They rode without saddles and without needing bridles. The ponies too were whinnying with unrestrained glee, galloping freely as if this were its own reward, carrying them with the speed of the wind to wherever their fancy took them. They rode on and on, and lost all sense of time. At intervals they paused beside clear mountain streams where they sat side by side in alert and companionable silence, silence not marred by so much as the flicker of an eyebrow.

And at other times they halted beside raspberry bushes or, according to the season – at the feet of broad-leafed nut-trees, where they slaked their hunger, jesting and feeding one another with juicy raspberries and forest fruits and sometimes even strawberries, hiding in the undergrowth, or the milky, satisfying flesh of the walnut, cracked between two stones.

They rode on until noon, and sometimes till sunset and the fall of evening, returning with the rising of the first star in the pale sky, festive and replete with the fragrances of the day that had passed and the sanctity of the evening at hand.

His parents were not anxious for him. Her parents, on the other hand, used to come out from their home and ask passers-by if they had met them or seen them, when and where, even visiting his parents in search of a little reassurance.

"They will be back, God is with them!" his father declared, calm and confident.

And if indeed they were late returning, the clear mountain air turning blue and cold, and the stars rising one after another in the firmament of the sky, the minister Naimel used to climb to the top of the hill near their home, standing there like a statue and looking out towards the forest in the valley, shrouded by night, from which they were expected to appear.

And when they emerged from amid the last of the trees, Naimel would remain motionless, watching them as they approached. In those few, unique moments he could tell how deep was the minister's relief at seeing them – at seeing him in particular.

How he longed to please his father! How he delighted in his approval! He would urge on his piebald pony that did not know the meaning of fatigue, breaking into a proud and impetuous gallop and stopping right at his father's feet, then dismount with an agile, majestic leap, all youthful high spirits, stand before him and pronounce a blessing:

"Blessed be the day that has passed and the evening that has taken its place, by the grace of God!"

For a moment the minister Naimel would focus on him his clear, percipient eyes, and in that split-second he sensed the strange, intoxicating vibration, of something that is beyond human comprehension, beyond the love of a father for his son, beyond everything that people are assiduous in defining, devoting to it all their wondrous songs and emotional anthems.

"Praise be to God on High!" exclaimed the tall, statuesque patrician, always careful to hurt no one and fearing no man, and his whole being one single desire – to know the holy will of his God and perform it thoroughly. And then Naimel would approach her, pronounce the same benediction for her and say softly, as if it were an afterthought:

"Supper is served – in the hall," – meaning that her parents had been invited to dine with them that evening. And as all took their seats at the long, heavy table, there was something in the atmosphere that could be called a spirit of limitless harmony, a unity of fellowship that is the power whereby the world was created and the virtue whereby it continues to exist, the grace whereby anyone trying to undermine its foundations and destroy it will be subdued and utterly defeated.

The two families dined at their ease, as the servants set out the victuals on the table, in their minds that sense of unbounded admiration which fills the heart with the will to do everything that is possible – and more, for the sake of the object of it. And the only one capable of inspiring this kind of admiration was none other than his father, the dauntless minister Naimel.

He sensed this very same overwhelming flood of admiration, the same readiness to sacrifice everything for the sake of its object – in Adelain's eyes.

"You I strive to please my Father in Heaven and my God, and You alone! For it is You that serves as a bridge between me and my fellowmen, and without You and without Your love we are nothing but strangers to one another, dry fallen leaves, tossed by the wind!"

Those evenings when they returned from riding in the fields and the forest, the valleys and the rocky summits, on paths unknown to the map-maker, wading through surging rivers, those youthful evenings when they dined with their parents, it was clear to all present, parents and children alike, that in the fullness of time the two families would be united, and he and she would perpetuate the holy tradition of those who love God. It was plain and self-evident to both the families, to him and to her and to all their relatives, and no one needed to raise the subject or debate it from any angle whatsoever, and it was superfluous to ask or to answer questions about it. Everyone was sure this was the holy will of God, and His will would be done.

And this filled his heart with joy and inspired him with confidence – feelings that she shared, as did their parents and all their acquaintances.

"Is this not a commitment?" he asked himself and answered with another question: "Is the connection of the hand to the body a commitment of the hand to be connected to it?"

He laughed softly, a laugh that was all purity and freedom.

"If the idea ever appeals to you," Adelain began, her tone gentle and submissive – "come riding with me! There are fine horses in our stables, and bareback riding in the early morning on a sturdy young pony is a pleasure – to the steed, his rider and the whole world!"

"Riding is indeed a pleasure," he agreed – "but these days, I have obligations to the King."

"I think the King will gladly agree to whatever you ask!" – she expressed her firm conviction. "He loves horses and admires good horsemanship!"

"Nevertheless," he persisted, "I have to study and prepare myself for the King's examination."

"If it ever does take your fancy..." and before she finished her sentence he completed it for her:

"I'll remember!"

"I could sit here for fifty years at least!" she admitted, and her words were sincere – overwhelmingly, painfully so.

"If that is God's will!" he commented, not referring to her words.

"I am the handmaid of God!" she declared warmly and in a quaking voice she added: "Your God, that is, and your God will do with me as He pleases!" And suddenly she tensed and exclaimed: "The minister Or-Nego is waiting for us! He'll be worried sick, wondering where we are!"

"Let's go and calm his fears and soothe his anxiety!" he urged playfully, rising from his seat and stepping forward.

He did not notice her white hand, searching for his hand and left hanging in the air.

Or-Nego was sitting on a bench opposite the entry door to the young men's lodgings, perusing some tablets borrowed from the library.

They saw him from some distance away, as the footpath descended gently towards that low and extensive building in which the young foreigners were quartered.

"As regards my father's attitude towards you," – for some reason Adelain was whispering, leaning towards him slightly so that the fragrance of her breath assailed his nostrils – "it's rather complicated: enthusiastic on the one hand, servile on the other. He holds you in the highest possible esteem, and his admiration for you is measureless! I don't think that here, within the far-flung boundaries of Babylon you will find a single person... or just one perhaps," – she corrected herself – "who would worship you as my father worships you. He would be ready, as the local saying has it, to put both his hands in the fire for you!"

"Your father is a warm-hearted man and from the start he came into the world only to long for God and to yearn for Him, and I have no doubt that he's a man of faith and his faith is true and he loves God, and in the end he will worship his God with all his heart and all his might, and all his soul and all his mind!"

"It seems it is as you say," – she answered him, surprised and impressed for some reason, and skipping half a pace ahead of him, she turned to face him and studied his eyes with that strange gaze of hers, a blend of utter self-negation and submissiveness bordering on the abject.

"Aren't you cold?" he asked, pointing to her light clothing.

"If you're not cold," she retorted, pointing in her turn at his clothing, which was also on the light side – "why should I be?"

He smiled and asked instead of answering:

"Are all your seasons in this country as pleasant and as warm as this?"

"As a general rule – yes!" she answered him and added with dignity: "Were it not for the Euphrates and the Tigris, the whole of our land would be nothing but desert, a sea of sand, an arid waste, a haunt of buzzards and vultures but not of human beings!"

"It is a blessing from God, and we may suppose that many Babylonians believe in Him!"

"Many indeed," she retorted – "but those of true faith are very few!"

They approached Or-Nego, still engrossed in his tablets.

Or-Nego recognised their footsteps, light as they were, and he laid aside his tablets, turned his head and when he saw them, rose to his feet and took a step towards them, unable to conceal his excitement. His tanned, sincere features glowed with a rapture that could be neither repressed nor blunted, and he almost spread his arms to embrace them but thought better of it at the last moment. He stood his ground and tried, not without some effort, to assume an expression of dignity and restraint.

"You disappeared!" he exclaimed, and that unalloyed, radiant happiness sparkled once again in his eyes and swept across his face with its fringe of soft, chestnut-brown beard. "I wasn't worried!" he declared, adding: "As far as I'm concerned, you could have come back at sunset! I found something very interesting to read," he explained – "about horses and methods of training them. Our ancient patriarchs are of the opinion that it was the horse that first approached mankind, and not the other way round... God sent him to Adam to console him in his dejection following his departure from the Garden of Eden! An astonishing notion and a very interesting one," he declared. "Speaking for myself, I have no doubt it's the truth!"

"Bearing in mind that God is love," he commented after a vigorous handshake, "it naturally follows that He would seek to console mankind, the same mankind that rebelled against Him and defied Him, cast doubt on His truth and no longer wanted to stay in His company!"

"Is that the way you people interpret that ancient story of the departure from Eden?" Or-Nego asked with great interest, and Adelain turned to him again and fixed on him her subservient eyes, blind to all her surroundings save him.

"Not all of us," he retorted.

"A minority then?" – Or-Nego asked with a note of mild regret; the interpretation that he had just heard from the young man appealed to him much more than the official, institutional version, which spoke of expulsion and not of voluntary departure.

"A minority," he agreed.

"Very few earn His grace, to see the truth in the Holy Spirit!" declared Or-Nego.

He did not respond.

"With his permission," Or-Nego resumed, "let us go to his room. I have something to give him and Adelain, my daughter, also has a modest gift for him."

"I wish we could converse in a less formal style!" he insisted.

"If that is your explicit preference, then so be it!" – Or-Nego smiled broadly once again, picked up the bundle of tablets and strode towards the door of the accommodation building. He was wearing a robe of pale grey fabric with a deep fringe of gold braid. Over the robe he wore a long, light tunic of well tanned leather, the colour of honey, and from the belt of his robe hung a curved sword in a black scabbard. The hilt of the sword was solid silver, the pommel a big red stone. His shoes were of leather, the same colour as the tunic, and laced with a triple golden thread.

Hananiah was waiting for him in his room, but seeing Or-Nego arriving with his daughter, he acknowledged them with a bow and left.

"This scroll was given to me by a fellow officer who happened to be in the lower tannery works on the Euphrates!" – Or-Nego held out a small scroll, tied with a thread of straw.

He took the scroll, crossed the room to the window overlooking the royal gardens, untied the thread, opened the scroll and read:

In the name of God, make haste my most merciful master and rescue me from this accursed place, where I spend my days in backbreaking labour, toiling at a trade for which I have no aptitude! I acknowledge, it is for my arrogance and deceit that the Lord is punishing me and this is why I have fallen into this dark place of slavery, where the regime is harsh and the punishments grievous, where the spirit is deranged and the body wearied beyond endurance, both by the hard labour, and by the whips and scourges of overseers who delight in our pain. In the name of the Lord our God, help me, my young master!

In utter dejection, the eternally grateful, Gershon.

As he rolled the scroll again, a grim look on his face, Or-Nego commented:

"My friend is obliged to return to these places tomorrow, and he will perform any errand that you may ask of him!""Can he take a reply to the writer of this scroll, and a few coins?"

"By all means!"

He took a pen and wrote on a parchment scroll:

Patience! God never abandons one who turns to Him in humility of heart, as it is written: The Lord is near to all who call upon Him, who call upon Him in truth. Enclosed are a few shekels. God bless you!

He signed his name, added the date, rolled and tied the scroll, took the purse which the King had ordered he be given after the race, and gave the scroll and the purse to Or-Nego.

"I shall be grateful if your friend can give these to the man who entrusted the scroll to him."

"I foresee no difficulty there!" Or-Nego replied. "The writer of the scroll was sure he was going to have an answer, and he told my friend he would be waiting."

"And thank you again, Or-Nego. Thank you and thank your friend!"

"It was the very least I could do!" the officer retorted, sounding surprised and almost offended. "As for the race yesterday," – his voice shook with emotion that he was unable to restrain – "for as long as I can remember I never expected to see anything like it! In my mind there's not the slightest doubt that God has showered His favours on you!"

"If only I were worthy of it!" he replied rather wistfully.

"I shall return these tablets to the librarian and come back to collect Adelain – if that is agreeable to the pair of you!"

"Most agreeable!" declared Adelain with feeling, adding: "I'm not sure that our hearts can stand much more happiness than what has already been granted us today. So hurry back, my lord and father!"

"I shall see you shortly!" – the officer bowed low, and he returned his bow.

"And here is the modest gift that my Lord and father was kind enough to mention," – she turned to him after Or-Nego had left the room, took out a small package, untied the ribbon and opened it before him.

On the soft fabric, coloured deep blue, with running horses embroidered in gold thread, the work of a skilled craftsman, lay a pair of stirrups made of solid gold.

"These are the stirrups that I received the year that I came of age. They have brought me joy and happiness, as they symbolise my freedom and my independence, and if you consent to accept them, then this joy and happiness will go far beyond the joy and happiness that are the lot of humankind!" Her voice trembled with emotion, her eyes fixed despairingly on his, pleading with him to accept the gift, and not send her away disappointed.

He understood at once that his refusal to accept would hurt her deeply, and hurt her father too, the good and the loyal Or-Nego.

"They look so perfect in their design, and your joy and your happiness are reflected in every smallest particle of them. All that is left for me is to thank you for the gift and promise you it will be put to good use."

"Take care of them, Belteshazzar!" she cried, her lips contorted. She was on the point of breaking down completely, and her efforts to control the tremor of her treacherous voice and the impending tears were to no avail. She abandoned the attempt and tears filled her lovely eyes and streamed down her high-boned, alabaster cheeks, until he was compelled to offer her a clean linen cloth that was meant to be a head-covering.

She wiped away her tears, wiped again, then folded the cloth, put it to her breast and held it there a long time, silent, eyes staring at the floor, and finally said:

"And this I shall take with me!" – and without another word she kissed his hand and ran from the room, calling from outside: "I shall meet my father on the way. Peace be with you Belteshazzar, my master!"

He looked for Denur-Shag and found him, as he expected, in the hall of the library, where he was studying a tattered and crumbled scroll dealing with the rules of sowing and harvest in ancient Ur of the Chaldees.

"I have something to ask you," he announced after the customary exchange of felicitations.

"You mean to ask me," Denur-Shag deduced astutely – "if I am able and willing to turn aside from this important research that I am conducting into the ways of my forebears who by chance – not an altogether happy one – were your forebears too, and give my attention to whatever you have to say!

"It is worth knowing," – Denur-Shag leaned back in his chair with its upholstery of deer-skin stuffed with straw – "that the patriarch of your extraordinary nation was a Chaldean, like me and all my compatriots, from the fish-sellers in the Sunday market to King Nebuchadnezzar himself, the valiant and the wise, conqueror of the world. But in him, in that ancestor of your exceptional race, some change came about and his ears, unlike the ears of those I have mentioned, myself included, were opened. And he heard the Voice. Yes, the Voice of God. No other voice exists to be heard! All other voices are just incoherent babble, a variety of illusion, issuing from the lips of those who are engrossed in their dream, from which they are not easily awakened, a dream that is all too often a nightmare!

"He succeeded anyway, the patriarch of your peculiar race, in waking from the nightmare and hearing the Voice. And the Voice did not commend him for the ability that he demonstrated to awaken from that dreadful dream, since in the final analysis, such an awakening comes only through the explicit grace of the One whose Voice it is. Did you not know this?" – Denur-Shag asked for his corroboration and he nodded his assent, surprised and inexplicably happy to the very roots of his soul.

"A holy truth!" cried Denur-Shag, holding a finger up before his face to emphasise his words, and adding with all the earnest weight that he could muster, like a lecturer addressing an audience thirsty for knowledge:

"Without His emphatic mercies and His explicit grace, all the dreamers of this dream, innumerable as they are, would be swept into the maw of a certain volcano, known in your language, the so-called 'Holy Tongue' – as 'Gehenna' or 'deepest Sheol' or even 'Tofta' if Aramaic expressions are acceptable.

"This Voice, as I say, did not shower any compliments on the head of the ancestor of your people, nor did it sing him a lullaby or a paean of praise, nor did it promise him all the kingdoms of the world, all of which, in the final analysis, are His and all things own His sway. Nor is it His custom to coerce. On the contrary, He has respect for His creatures and does their bidding: if a dream is what they ask for, a dream they shall have!" Denur-Shag was enjoying his impassioned lecture and he added:

"The Voice of the Speaker addressed that exceptional creature who, fortunately or unfortunately for you, was the ancestor of your race and told him, no more and no less: *Go from your land and from your father's house,* or in other words – you have nothing to look for here because 'your land and father's house' are destined to suffer all the afflictions of the world and be wiped from it utterly, because violence and destruction are their heart's desire, and against this there isn't much that can be done! The man of little intelligence will learn only from bitter experience. As is well known, the wise learns from the experience of the less wise, and he it is who is destined to wake, to wake and hear the Voice!

"And since then your people have distinguished themselves with this ability: to wake up, wake up and hear the Voice. But over the course of time you have sunk into a strange kind of lethargy, an idle pursuit of your own shadows, which has made you arrogant and proud and unfeeling, deceiving and leading astray, and this quality of yours has been lost, meaning, not lost entirely – not a loss on the scale of the destruction of this universe – as there still are among you a few who have awakened from the dream and are hearing the Voice, but they are few and becoming fewer, disappearing from sight.

"Something else that remains to be pointed out, is that those who hear one who has awakened from the dream, who is awake and hearing the Voice – they prepare for him an especially warm and enthusiastic reception: putting him on the pyre, or on the cross, or simply pelting him with whatever stones come to hand." Denur-Shag smiled a soft and apologetic smile, was silent for a moment and then spoke again:

"Now that I have favoured you with my learned discourse, I am at your disposal and I am all ears, even if what you mean to tell me are the words of that Voice to which – as I have already warned you, my ears and the ears of my compatriots are deaf."

"It seems to me you're exaggerating a little!" – he smiled at him, enchanted by the flow of his speech and the nuggets of truth embedded there, despite the mild and inoffensive irony which added spice to his words.

"You're mistaken, young man!" he retorted playfully, and he thought he even winked at him – "A white horse wins a footling little race for you and you get ideas above your station... Anyway – what business brings you here?"

"If you prefer, we can go to my room or to your lodging, and I'll tell you there."

"I don't prefer that," – Denur-Shag declared with resolute emphasis – "You've just listened to me holding forth between these walls, so your humble words may as well be heard here as anywhere else!" – and he pointed to a high-backed chair on the other side of the table.

In the cavernous hall of the library, there was nobody other than themselves and the old librarian, immersed in the perusal of tablets at the other end.

"So be it," he agreed, pulled up the chair, sat facing him and began telling him about Gershon, about the close relative who was a tanner while he himself was a skilled and respected calligrapher of scrolls, about his decision to impersonate a tanner, to save his relative from exile and his family from poverty and hunger, a noble act indeed although less than entirely honest.

Denur-Shag acknowledged this last point with a nod of the head. "The believer doesn't need to distort the truth to save anyone's life," – he expressed his opinion – "All he needs to do is turn with his whole heart to the Creator of all souls – and his request will be granted!"

"Anyway," the other went on to say – "the state of this man, who is far from young – considerably older than me, and older even than you as it happens – is desperate! He sent me a letter, appealing for help."

"And what am I supposed to do to assist you in this humane enterprise, extricating your friend from the claws of despair?"

"Perhaps an assistant is required in the office of the royal calligrapher? An expert assistant! Are you not allowed to confer with members of the corps of clerks?"

"I used to be," replied Denur-Shag, "and officially at least, that permission was never revoked." He lowered his huge head, studying the big coloured tiles on the floor of the library and continued: "Since the episode of my old slave, I've done everything I can to steer clear of that department, and avoid contact with the staff who work there. When my route takes me anywhere near the place, I make a long detour through endless dreary corridors, extending my journey just so I won't be reminded of those days, when my faithful slave, who used to work there, was on trial for his life on fabricated charges. The experience wrecked him, physically and mentally."

"I'm sorry I turned to you," – his sorrow was genuine and he reproached himself for his lack of tact and consideration, for having raised the subject in such a clumsy way. "I'll go and ask myself!" he declared and rose from his seat to take his leave of Denur-Shag.

"Don't even dare think about it, my lad!" the pedagogue almost shouted, grabbing his pupil's arm and pulling him down again into his chair. "If ever any one of the foreign students should try to interfere, however innocently, in the workings of the royal secretariat, he would be expelled from the school immediately, however brilliant his academic record, and sent as an assistant to the copper smelters in the mines up in the hills – in that foul atmosphere you'd maybe survive for a year, but no more.

"Do you understand what I'm telling you?" Denur-Shag persisted – the expression on his face both serious and scared, as he had never seen it before or ever expected to see it.

He did not reply.

"And as for the request that you addressed to me," – Denur-Shag sighed, a sigh of relief – "don't push things, and let's see what the One with the Voice can do for all of us! Anyway" – he continued – "make your appeal. I daresay He's readier to hear your voice than mine. Yes, I too address Him now and then, but I can't always catch His attention. Obviously, my soul is still mired in the fog and isn't yet completely purged of doubt, unlike yours! And tomorrow, as you know, we shall meet in the classroom, and there will be a test on the ancient history of the Chaldeans. You have homework to do! When it suits me, I can be exceedingly severe to a pupil who wastes his time riding or in silly conversations with girls, aristocratic young ladies! Go in peace, Belteshazzar!" – he held out his round, little hand, and he shook it with warmth and gratitude.

Two weeks later, he was summoned to the reception hall.

"A visitor for you!" announced the slave responsible for rousing them, and did not elaborate.

Perplexed, he wondered who this might be – Adelain, or her father, or one of the other admirers he had gained on the day of the horse race? Or perhaps some unwelcome news awaited him there, in the ornate reception hall?

"Your will be done, my Father in Heaven, my God!" he murmured confidently. "All my desire, my Father in Heaven, my God, is to do Your holy and beneficent will with all my heart and might, all my soul and all my mind, at all times and always, amen and amen!"

A light shone in his heart, a solid resolve to accept everything with gratitude, with a blessing, with joy and with love. All that comes upon us comes only to awaken us to Him, our Father in Heaven who is love, to put us on the way to Him and to remove every obstacle from our path.

He went into the hall with that pure good cheer, that he had enjoyed as a child, glowing in his heart, that calm and contentment that nothing could spoil.

And then came the great surprise, that could not have been foreseen, overwhelming as a river in spate.

By the door sat a middle-aged man, thin, with ravaged face, but wearing clean and decent clothes.

"Gershon!" he cried and ran to him.

Gershon had difficulty recognising him, but when he saw him running, his hesitation faded, and he rose to meet him and fell into his arms.

"You saved me from the claws of darkness, brought me up from the pit of the grave, saved me from Gehenna, where the flames were already licking my body and now – the announcement has been made – I have been appointed assistant to the deputy assistant in the office of the chief calligrapher of His Majesty King Nebuchadnezzar, the valiant and the wise, the conqueror of the world!"

His tears fell, his lean body shook in the clean, cheap robe that he wore, and the outer garment, a crudely worked sheepskin coat that still reeked.

"I knew at once it was your doing, and the coins that you sent me, such a generous sum of coins!" he stressed with happy bemusement – "I shared them with my brothers in adversity, those miserable tanners who don't expect to live long on the bank of the Euphrates! And they thanked you. They thanked me too but most of all they asked me to pass on to you their gratitude and their blessing!"

"The gratitude and the blessing are due to God!" he declared solemnly and without a moment's hesitation.

For a long time they sat facing one another, enjoying their emotional reunion and asking and telling of their experiences. And then messengers came from the office of the royal calligrapher looking for Gershon, and asking him to accompany them. They parted with a promise to meet again soon.

He went in search of Denur-Shag.

He found him sitting in his home, drinking red wine and perusing the same crumpled parchment from two weeks before. When the slave announced him, he greeted him without rising from his seat, simply pointing to the vacant chair opposite him.

He sat down and waited. Denur-Shag laid the scroll aside, turned to him and said:

"First of all, there's no need to thank me! The little that I did was nothing but the fulfilment of a basic obligation. And in this instance, as you know, I served only as an instrument or, if you prefer, a pipe, a cracked and rusty pipe I regret to say – for the channelling of His grace, and I'm referring to the One with the Voice. And now, in accordance with an old and time-honoured tradition, which has plunged the members of our species into the morass in which they flounder even to this day – I am asking for something in return, a recompense for something which I did not do, but in which I played the part of an ineffectual midwife. Please listen to my request, which is far from modest!"

He leaned towards him, and continued earnestly:

"When the time comes and you have risen to a position of eminence – do something for the friends of your old friend, who have no advocate in the royal palace and no saviour. See their misery and lighten their yoke. I tell you, their yoke is heavy and their suffering unbearable! Will you remember this?"

He nodded his head in affirmation, and felt tears filling his eyes.

Denur-Shag noticed this, looked away and answered on his behalf:

"Of course you'll remember! Do you think the burden will be too much for you? One way or the other – do your best! And now my young friend, we should part company, as I am busy with this work of mine, studying the sensational history of your earliest ancestors. They were such weird and wonderful people, it's no surprise to find so many eccentrics among their descendents!"

He rose from his place, bowed low and hurriedly left the lodging of his Chaldean teacher and mentor. The old slave almost dropped his cloak as he handed it to him. As he went out into the darkness of the corridor, he could not stop the tears, they trickled as if of their own accord in a constant, unbroken stream, dripping from his chin to the stone floor and melting away without a sound.

A year elapsed and then another. Denur-Shag continued to teach, and toiled tirelessly to instruct the twenty-five young men remaining from the twenty-eight, in the ancient and the spoken Chaldee tongue, and in the learned precepts of Chaldeans and of others. He taught with energy and endowed every subject with breadth and depth, and the youths absorbed it according to their abilities. The riding lessons had been discontinued, but the youths were allowed to ride their horses twice a week, and on other occasions when there were urgent messages to deliver.

Adelain sent him short parchment scrolls on a regular basis, and beneath their playful style there was something buried deep, restrained and vibrant, something which gave him more grief than pleasure. Twice he went riding with her, and the outcome was tears on her part and awkwardness on his.

The minister Or-Nego used to bring him his daughter's scrolls, finely scripted by an innocent hand, on fine parchment with a thin stylus and in fragrant blue ink. He used to send her succinct replies, copying her light and carefree tone, but with the difference that in his case there were no hidden messages, no subtle hints.

He also received a scroll sent from the homeland with a party of exiles who came down to Babylon about a year and a half after them, and it perturbed him and added confusion to his confusion. Nejeen wrote to him and after describing the situation as tolerable and passing on blessings and greetings from his family, she concluded with the brief statement "Love is stronger than death" – the amended quotation as he used to recite it in those days.

For a while Nejeen occupied all his attention, and he sat at his desk in the schoolroom distracted and flustered, floundering in an empty void.

In one of the intervals between lessons Denur-Shag commented with typical irony:

"There are great hopes that seem constant, cherished in theory and wonderful in practice – and they expire at once and give up the ghost through the influence of a tender girl with pretty eyes!"

Denur-Shag was mistaken. No "tender girl with pretty eyes", no girl at all, could touch the sanctity of his hope. Rather, his mind was inundated with confusion that was not easily to be suppressed, as its roots were imbued with the power of the primitive. Light shone in this confusion, turning it into a founding principle of joy and rapture, something resembling a willingness to bear responsibility by virtue of his faith, and his unshakeable devotion to his Father in Heaven and his God. Matters became clearer to him in those days, and he laid aside his inner wrangling and invested all his energies in his studies, giving succinct, straightforward and lucid answers to Denur-Shag's questions, to the delight and profound satisfaction of the teacher.

In one of the lessons, when the boys were required to answer questions relating to wisdom, love, freedom and God, and failed utterly, one after the other, he gave an answer which amazed even Denur-Shag, who could not resist saying:

"There is one here among us, wearing the guise of a Jewish youth, who has no peer or equal in the chronicles of the human race, and whom no verbal description is adequate to encompass!" These words were spoken without thought, an expression of admiration that simply could not be contained – and after them the teacher lapsed into sudden silence, his lips sealed and only the giant head moving from side to side in a strange rhythm, as if he were talking to himself, continuing his speech without sound.

"I have to admit," he said finally, the spark still showing in his eyes, "I was carried away there just a little, the kind of thing that happens from time to time to an old goat like me! Experience of life, as you know, purges the human heart of all foolish expectations, and in this blessed instance all that is left for me is to refresh my parched soul, however infrequently it may happen, with the expectations of others.

"Be that as it may," Denur-Shag went on to say – "the days of the great test are drawing near, and then, without doubt, all will be revealed, meaning – your talents and your abilities, plain and unvarnished, unaided by the pedagogic enthusiasm of an old teacher who is so quick to lose all his sense of proportion! This quality – loss of sense of proportion," Denur-Shag pointed out – "is the one unmistakable sign by which you may recognise a gifted teacher! Remember this, and do not doubt the truth of what I say! Now," he concluded – "enough flights of fancy! We must come down to earth and consider the somewhat harsh legislation of Nebuchadnezzar the First, former king of the Chaldeans."

THE TEST

As Denur-Shag had said, the day of the great test was approaching. The King himself, in person, was expected to turn his attention to them and decide their fate.

At the feast of Bel, early in the spring, the youths were summoned to present themselves before the King in the assembly hall, the biggest hall in the royal palace and perhaps – the biggest in the whole world. So at least the Chaldeans believed, commoners and dignitaries alike, and so the King himself believed.

With the rising of the dawn people started streaming into the hall which was undeniably great – splendid, high-ceilinged and of vast and incomparable proportions, with a hundred narrow windows set high in the walls shedding gentle spring light. Round pillars of marble, likewise one hundred in number, supported the ceiling which was all reliefs and engravings in gold. The reliefs and engravings formed a continuous frieze, depicting the history of Babylon and its predecessor, Ur of the Chaldees, which was represented in the first circle in the centre of the ceiling; then there were throngs of herdsmen with their sheep and cattle followed by judges and lawgivers and leaders, and finally the image of Nebuchadnezzar the Second, the present King, charging into battle in his chariot, harnessed to four mighty horses, a heavy sword drawn in his hand.

Some fifty craftsmen had worked on the reliefs and they were artistic feats beyond belief, showing in meticulous and minute detail every item of clothing, and enlivening the faces of men and beasts with vivid expressions, paying them no compliments whatsoever and accentuating the cruelty of people and the fear and helplessness of beasts. At the eastern end of the hall, a giant stage had been carved out of granite, floored over with coloured marble, its superbly matching hues creating the impression of a lake lit by the rays of the sun on a bright spring morning. In the centre of the stage stood a throne, the throne of Nebuchadnezzar, made all of gold and ivory, the back – some ten cubits in height – and the arm-rests faced with innumerable tiny mosaic tiles. The seat of the throne was upholstered in glistening velvet all embroidered with threads of gold. On both sides of the King's throne there were chairs fashioned from silver with backs receding in height the further they were from the centre. These were intended for the

King's senior counsellors, five on each side. A further one hundred and fifty chairs, made of polished wood, a few with arm-rests and most without, were arranged in a semi-circle to the right of the royal throne, the seats of scribes and magicians, sorcerers and astrologers. Behind the King and his ten councillors a space had been cleared for the seventy-strong bodyguard, standing to attention, drawn swords gleaming in their hands, with helmets, breastplates and shields – all of pure gold.

At the front of the hall, opposite the stage, were one hundred seats for the dignitaries in the service of the King, and behind these were movable stools, the precise number unknown, for the use of the populace. Some spoke of five thousand, some of ten thousand and even more. Around the walls soldiers of the royal horse-guard took up their positions, swords sheathed but with clubs in their hands.

In honour of the occasion, twenty-five stools had been set up at the front of the stage, for the foreign youths whom the King was about to appraise.

The dignitaries knew their places. Other invitees, representing all strata of Chaldean society: craftsmen, merchants, agricultural labourers and clerics – needed the help of stewards to find the stools set aside for them. By the time the dignitaries began to arrive, the hall was already filled to overflowing.

The first to go up on the stage were the young men. After them came the scribes, the magicians, the sorcerers and the astrologers. A full hour passed before the trumpeters outside blew a short, ceremonial fanfare, heralding the arrival of the King.

The King himself entered from behind the stage, accompanied by his ten senior counsellors and seventy armed bodyguards.

Immediately the King had mounted the stage, all those present rose to their feet with deafening cries of "Hurrah!" and "Long live the King!" The cries echoed and re-echoed around the hall incessantly, and for a moment it seemed they would go on forever.

The King stood at the foot of his throne, facing the cheering crowd, bowed lightly, and when the hubbub did not stop but went on and even grew in volume, he bowed again, slowly and deliberately and raised his arm in a gesture of imperious authority, and the cries of adulation, which it had seemed would never end, were immediately silenced. The King turned and climbed the three steps to the throne, and took his seat, while a pair of dark-skinned slaves in white livery, armed with daggers, stepped forward with a footstool for the royal feet, and once the King had placed his bejewelled shoes there, they squatted on either side of the footstool, daggers at the ready.

For the first time since his arrival in Babylon he looked upon the face of King Nebuchadnezzar the Conqueror, attired in splendour and mighty in power. One snatched glimpse was enough – and already flickering in his mind, as if self-explanatory, were two words which expressed all that could be said, or needed to be said, about the King: "fearful majesty". If Nebuchadnezzar had been dubbed "fearful majesty", the title would have fitted absolutely his appearance of aggressive authority, his bronzed, uncovered features and his piercing, awesome gaze.

The King was wearing a red gown, and over it a blue mantle with gold embroidery, reaching to the floor, its fringe of white linen studded with precious stones. At his neck he wore a gold chain, with a pendant in the shape of a hand clutching a star, symbol of the god Bel. In his hand was a sceptre, a massive sapphire at its tip, and all of it pure gold inlaid with pearls and gems of various colours. A short two-edged sword in a gold scabbard, its hilt solid silver, glittered beneath the gown.

On his head the King wore one of his lighter gold crowns, encrusted with jewels. His long face, his shining, ample beard, neatly combed, wavy and black as night, with a ribbon of silvery threads, the high forehead, wide open eyes untouched by fear or trepidation, the straight, symmetrical nose – all spoke of might and impulsive dominion. The look in his eyes left no room for doubt: the King would not forgive anyone who tried, however innocently, to mislead him. The firmly crafted lips testified to an uncompromising devotion to the truth.

To a certain degree, the King reminded him of his father, the minister Naimel, but the differences were striking too: the aggressive honesty, the fearlessness, the might and the authority – were impetuous in the King, wild and intemperate, without Naimel's restraining qualities. King Nebuchadnezzar was incapable of forgiving; the minister was capable of looking deep into the soul of a man dependent on his mercy and always finding something there, something which, however minuscule it might be, was to the other's credit. King Nebuchadnezzar knew how to draw conclusions, to take decisions and implement them, with the force and the speed of lightning; the minister knew how to assess a situation in a fraction of a second, draw conclusions and act upon them – only when he was assured that such action would cause no harm to any innocent man. King Nebuchadnezzar was like a proud lion that has just emerged from his cage. He stands on a crag, raising his fearful and majestic head, shaking his mane and with his ferocious roar sending all the creatures in the land scurrying for cover. The minister Naimel was like an angel of God who comes down among mortals, his gleaming sword drawn in his hand, all eagerness to do the bidding of the one who sent him, and to do it thoroughly and flawlessly.

The face of King Nebuchadnezzar, with its strong lines, and the two deep furrows scoring his forehead, looked as if it had been sculpted from bronze, and it was the colour of gleaming bronze. He sat on the throne with such natural ease, it seemed that from the day of his birth he had been schooled and trained to accede to a royal throne – as if all the royal thrones in all the world had been designed for his exclusive use.

"Let the ministers ask their questions!" Nebuchadnezzar decreed in a voice that was not loud, but firm and resonant, as if uttered from a throat lined with metal. His words commanded respect, and instilled an obscure fear in the hearts of all present.

One after another the ministers began asking their questions, some of which had been prepared in advance and related to the various subjects that the pupils had studied. The King followed the questions and answers with interest, and it was evident that nothing escaped his ears and his eyes.

When the first round of questions was finished, when every one of the King's ministerial counsellors had asked what he had to ask, and each of the pupils had replied to the best of his ability, the King raised his arm, and the pupils huddled nervously on their seats, like defenceless chickens watching a predator approach.

The King pointed to several of the pupils, among then Uziel and Gabriel, whose answers to the questions had been generally sound, but expressed with timidity and effort, and not always with the clarity required and announced:

"Gardens and drains!"

At his signal, one of the beadles summoned these pupils and led them from the stage.

He located Denur-Shag among those seated on the movable stools, and saw him flinch as the King's stern verdict was heard. He looked away and, unconsciously, found his eye drawn towards the western end of the front row, where the Chaldean dignitaries sat in static seats. For a brief moment he caught the eye of Or-Nego, who acknowledged him with a wave of the hand and a glowing smile. Adelain sat beside him in white festive attire, detached from all those seated around her, a blue belt at her waist fastened with a shining gold buckle, a big amethyst inlaid in the gold. Her head was held high, her alabaster face remote and aloof and of stunning beauty, her high forehead expressive of wisdom, and her deep, calm and subdued look focused – unperturbed and without a trace of timidity – on him and on him alone. Like the look of a faithful dog, always attuned to his master's whims.

He returned his attention to the ministers who were questioning the nine remaining youths. These were questions relating to various kinds of calculation, profit and loss and commercial transactions. He gave answers that were precise and unemotional, as did Mishael, Hananiah and Azariah, his companions, although the last-named answered some of the questions after consideration that was a little over-long. In contrast to them came the animated answers of Adoniah. He almost lost control of himself, leaping up from his seat as the questions were heard and his answers given, and he could not resist offering additional answers of his own, over and above the conventional ones. The four remaining, a Sidonian, a Phoenician and the two who were of mixed race had difficulty answering in time and struggled with the solutions.

And again the King raised his arm, and the examiners stopped their questioning, and the royal decree reverberated through the hall, succinct and clear, leaving no room for comment, arousing admiration and instilling fear. The four who had found the questions too difficult, were assigned to the buildings and maintenance department, and Adoniah was sent to the trade and arbitration office. Then the King turned to those remaining and he himself asked each of them three identical questions, one after the other: What is the aim of proper government? How is this aim to be achieved? To what does each one of them aspire?

The first to be asked these questions was Azariah, who blushed and replied that the aim of proper government was the prevention of wars, and this could be achieved through peace treaties with neighbouring countries or the payment of indemnities, and he had no personal ambitions other than to perform faithfully whatever might be required of him. Next it was the turn of Hananiah, who declared that the aim of good government ("good" he said instead of "proper") was to promote religious faith in the hearts of the populace, and this could be achieved by the provision of more buildings dedicated to the worship of God, and his personal ambition was the strengthening and consolidation of his own faith. Mishael advocated the division of land among poor peasants, to be funded by levying higher taxes on those with more property than the average, and he hoped one day to be allowed to return to his home in Jerusalem.

King Nebuchadnezzar turned to face him directly, his dark eyes alert and penetrating as ever, and before he could answer, he recognised him and said:

"The victorious rider!" – this being the kind of compliment that the King was not accustomed to uttering lightly. "Now let us judge your prowess in the field of wisdom!" he added eagerly, and repeating his first question – "What is the aim of proper government?" – he received the brief reply:

"The well-being of the citizen."

"How is this to be attained?"

"By a ruler who sets an example to his citizens."

Suddenly a look of deep satisfaction washed over the noble and bronzed features of King Nebuchadnezzar, a satisfaction that was clear to all and marked with such intensity that one of the dignitaries could not restrain himself, but leapt to his feet and cried: "Long live King Nebuchadnezzar!"

And before anyone understood what was happening, the whole of the crowd was on its feet, chanting over and over again: "Long live King Nebuchadnezzar! Long live the King! Long life! Long life! Long life! Hurrah! Hurrah! Hurrah!"

The King rose from his seat, his face still flushed, bowed to the ecstatic crowd and then raised his arm in that gesture of authority that is not to be disobeyed, and the tumult stopped as if cut off with a knife.

The King returned to his ornate throne, every movement of his body expressing majesty, freedom and conscious glamour.

During the shouting which shook the very foundations of the hall, with its hundred marble pillars, and perhaps in spite of the cries, fit to deafen the heart as well as the ears, he absorbed that constant current which knew no obstacle, of boundless admiration, of worship without measure and without limit, of adoration that had neither kin nor comparison – and all of this emanating from a source somewhere in the vicinity of the seat of Or-Nego. He turned his head.

"What are your personal aspirations?" – the King repeated the third question.

"To give of my best to the people among whom I live and to my own people, from whom I am removed."

"Which of them do you prefer? Babylon over Judah or the contrary?"

Without hesitation and with astonishing clarity he replied:

"Judah over Babylon!"

There was silence in the hall. And the silence deepened and the whispers that arose in distant corners only served to emphasise it. The King's seventy bodyguards seemed to stiffen at their posts, hands firmly gripping the hilts of their swords, as if danger threatened the Chaldean King.

"Is this your answer to the King?" – the King's chief counsellor addressed him sternly.

"It is the answer of a nobleman!" – the King declared, sincerely impressed, thus putting an end to the whispering in the hall and allowing the members of his bodyguard to relax. The chief counsellor smiled faintly, both surprised and gratified.

"There is no clearer sign of noble birth than the telling of the truth!" the King added and turning to his chief counsellor he concluded:

"Be so good as to take into your service this young man, who in spite of his declared preference will be required first and foremost to contribute his remarkable talents to the service of the Chaldean people!"

Mishael, Azariah and Hananiah he divided among the other counsellors.

As Nebuchadnezzar rose from his high throne, concealed trumpeters blew a resounding fanfare in his honour, and all those seated in the hall rose as one and cheered their King, leaving the hall accompanied by his retinue and to the sound of loud and prolonged applause.

THE SHRINE OF BEL

Outside it was spring.

The moment he left the hall, one of the dusky slaves dressed only in a loin-cloth hurried to fetch Orelian from the stable, receiving a gold coin in return. The slave muttered innumerable words of gratitude, bowed low to the ground and retreated backwards, his black, bony hand clutching the generous windfall.

He had barely touched the bridle of the proud mare when he sensed Adelain approaching from behind, and finally standing beside him. She raised her deep eyes, which had suddenly changed expression and taken on a look of childish innocence, and for a moment they reminded him again of fresh wild flowers.

"All that I have to say," she began with dignity – "is pale and feeble and could not even come close to touching the emotion that fills my heart and perhaps – silence is the best expression of it!" She looked at him again and continued: "The truth is that for as long as I can remember, never have such words of refined wisdom been heard in Babylon as were heard today, and the way they were expressed, I mean – so concise, so conclusive! And as my father made the very same observation, and he is an authority on the history of Babylon, it's very unlikely that those two short sentences, summing up the whole science of enlightened government, have ever been heard in Babylon since its foundation, they or anything like them!"

"Let's not exaggerate!" He turned to her and suddenly realised that it was not a girl standing beside him but a woman, a young woman in her full bloom.

He did not so much as glance at her body, lithe and curvaceous as it had become, and despite an intense awareness that she wanted this, wanted him to take a look, longed for it, almost demanded it. Enough for him was the change in her eyes and her face: her eyes expressing charm and restraint combined, her face leaner and more finely sculpted.

"My father asked me to give you his regards. As I said before, he too was much moved by your audience with the King, and if before you enjoyed his admiration, from this time on he's close to worshipping you – and perhaps that's more than just a figure of speech. After all, worship is the natural successor to a certain brand of intense admiration. My father asked me if I appreciated the great good fortune that has befallen

Babylon, with the presence of 'this miraculous Jewish boy'. Those were his precise words. I answered him that 'this miraculous Jewish boy' was no longer a boy, not even a youth. We were discussing a young man who had gained the favour of his God, and who richly deserved that favour!"

"No creature of flesh and blood is worthy of the favour of God, it is given through His manifold mercies!" he declared earnestly, and then noticed that the young black filly at her side – thin-limbed, of graceful profile – was stamping restlessly.

"Shall we ride?" he suggested.

Without another word said she put her foot in the stirrup, and with a single, light movement, hoisted herself into the saddle. He noticed that her robe was folded into pleats, forming britches convenient for riding. Smoothly, effortlessly, he mounted Orelian.

"Anyway," she said before they set off – "my father wanted to express his heartfelt admiration to you himself, in person, and I persuaded him to let me do it for him, and now I'm not sure that I've done it right! Have I passed the message on properly?" she asked

"Properly and very thoroughly!" he declared with a warm, sincere and reassuring smile. "Where shall we ride to?" he asked.

"Have you ever gone walking at the foot of the great wall of Babylon?"

"No," he admitted.

"Perhaps this is the day to do it together. Strange though it may sound, I've never done a tour like that either. I know nothing of the most famous wall in the world, much to my shame!"

"What makes this wall different from all other walls in the world?" he asked with genuine interest.

"Sensational things are said about its height and the way it was constructed!"

They rode on serenely side by side, and he noticed that her mare was docile and obedient to her, a sure sign of an experienced rider with an understanding of horses.

They were close to one end of the wall, rising to a height of more than forty cubits, where steps had been constructed, giving access to the many archery-embrasures. Soldiers posted there acknowledged them with a raised hand, and they returned their greetings.

Soon the famous reliefs came into view – bulls, lions and horsemen, like those shown in the hall of the library, but on an infinitely larger scale. Lions pounced in fury, bulls tried to gore an unseen assailant, and horsemen charged with the light of battle gleaming in their eyes. And there were also beasts and men riddled with arrows or impaled on lances and swords, rolling on the ground, faces distorted by pain.

"A striking work of art!" he declared calmly and added: "And let's hope people learn from it and desist from killing!"

"That's not the purpose at all!" she retorted. "These images are designed to train people to kill, meaning that more wars and nightmares are in store for us. The marauding lion is still the symbol of manhood!"

He was silent. She was right. The lust for violence depicted here was the kind that lodges deep in the heart.

"If I had my way," she went on to say – "I'd scrape off all those horrible images of people and animals. I don't see how anyone could benefit from them!"

"What would you put in their place?"

Their docile mounts proceeded in time with the conversation, and when it was necessary, as at the moment that this question was asked, they stopped without being reined in, and waited patiently.

"I'd demolish the whole wall!"

Once again she was right. Where God is – walls are superfluous. She glanced at him sidelong, seeking his response.

"A dream for the distant future!" he retorted.

"And until then?"

"Let's leave the ugly wall of Babylon behind us and ride somewhere else."

They joined the broad royal highway, with its paved surface, and unprompted, the horses quickened their rhythmic pace

"We'll ride to the shrine of Bel!" she said. "There's a festival there today."

On the way they met a few riders, some of whom recognised them, especially the daughter of Or-Nego, and greeted them with a bow, while others passed them by, grim-faced and wrapped up in themselves, despite the fine and pleasant day that had descended on Babylon. Walkers were hurrying to one place or another, and there were carts too, harnessed to heavy-hoofed working horses, laden to overflowing, impeding and endangering the other traffic. When they reached the region of the shrines she drew his attention to a hill covered with flowers.

"Didn't you know about this?" she asked, and was surprised to hear his negative reply. "Look, it's a magic hill – and there's no ground underneath it!"

He followed the direction of her gaze and sure enough, he saw to his amazement that the entire hill with its abundance of flowers and young trees was suspended in the air.

"How?" – he wanted to know.

She answered him with a smile, for some reason tinged at the edges with sadness:

"There's a special way of planting a host of flowers like that on frames that are invisible to the eye. Those are the Hanging Gardens, one of the wonders of the world! They were planted as a wedding gift from King Nebuchadnezzar to his beloved bride, the Median princess Temior, who missed the flowers and the hills of her native land."

"King Nebuchadnezzar is a man of stature and of generous heart!" he declared.

"Any man who truly loves – has stature and a generous heart!" she retorted.

At midday they came to the shrine of Bel. This was a tall building with pointed roof, a garden of flowers and dwarf trees planted on it.

They went inside. In the depths of a spacious hall rose a statue some twenty cubits in height. At the feet of the statue glowed the gentle lights of grease-lamps. The huge mouth of the effigy, its nostrils and even its eye-sockets were exhaling flames of fire.

She anticipated his question before he had time to ask it and replied:

"It's a simple mechanism – the fire inside the hollow head is nourished by a constant stream of pure oil, and as the nostrils and the mouth and the eye-sockets are the only apertures, that's where the flames poke through. Of course," she went on to say – "someone has to maintain the fire, and also polish the statue so it shines all the time."

"The priests of Bel?" he asked.

"Priestesses," she corrected him.

"This idol is served by priestesses?"

"Priests too, but they're busy with the ritual. Care of the statue and maintenance of the fire in the head are entrusted to priestesses."

"And who are these priestesses?" he went on to ask, and she answered him:

"Winsome virgins, who dedicate themselves to the god. The lives of the priestesses of Bel are calm and tranquil, and they have no interest in worldly sensations. They believe that when their time comes, their souls will be united with the sublime soul of the god, and they will enjoy eternal bliss such as mortals are incapable of describing or experiencing. These virgins are also prophetesses, and when I visited this place last year one of them prophesied that I would either be the servant of a god coming down to earth in human form, or I would serve this idol."

"And do you believe such prophecies?" he asked, a note of indignation creeping into his voice.

"Absolutely!" she replied, her voice remarkably calm.

Unconsciously she touched his hand lightly, like the zephyr, a breeze at midday to caress the blossom of the apple-tree. He felt her touch and did not withdraw his hand, but did not encourage her either.

"In her time," she went on to say – "my mother wanted to be one of the virgin priestesses and worship Bel. She came here and put her request to the chief priestess. She looked at her with penetrating eyes, and a hint of maternal tenderness and told her this was no place for her (so anyway she described it to my father, the minister Or-Nego, and he repeated it to me). She told her that her service of the 'divine' – that's how the chief priestess put it, 'the divine', without mentioning any god specifically, not even Bel – would achieve its fullest expression at the side of a man of distinction, pure of heart and valiant in deed, who would bring her great happiness, and she would also bear him a daughter (so my father tells it and I'm repeating him word for word) and with the birth of her daughter her time on this earth would be at an end, and she would be gathered into the open fields of light where all the pure souls are privileged to walk.

"And as the priestess of the idol prophesied, so it was. My mother met my father and fell in love with him, and he returned her love, and their short life together was sublimely happy, and then I came into the world and, as had been foretold, my mother left us and her soul ascended to those wide open fields. And my father, the minister Or-Nego, the noblest of men, did not take a new wife to take her place, and he even told the King that he would rather die than consent to take another wife, as is the custom of the Chaldeans. And the King understood this, and my father's unbounded devotion to his first and his only wife touched him deeply, so at any rate people tend to believe, and I tend to believe or perhaps I should say, I would like to believe," – she corrected herself – "and he's an exceptional minister and counsellor and perhaps the only one in the King's service who has remained a widower and not taken a wife.

"As you will yet become aware," she went on to say without any change in the tone of her voice – "loyalty is the distinctive feature of this family, and nothing can prevail over it, not even the fires of Hell!" She looked away from him as she continued, her voice clear and every word audible:

"If I am not allowed to be by the side of the man I love, no other man will take his place, no one will defile my embrace and earn a place in my heart!" She turned to look at him again with those big eyes, lovely as velveteen flowers opening to the light.

In the late hours of the afternoon he returned to his lodging with heavy heart. Denur-Shag was waiting for him:

"I have come to take my leave of you," he sniffed. "Not for ever!" he hastened to add – "Not at all, not at all! We are sure to meet again in the long corridors of this forbidding building, that they call the palace of King Nebuchadnezzar, the wise and the valiant, conqueror of the world, His Majesty! And you would do well to remember all these titles. They are immeasurably important, and can sometimes mean the difference between life and death, especially when this King and conqueror of the world, the wise and the valiant, His Majesty – is in an eccentric mood, or should I say his normal mood. No other mortal can allow himself to indulge in such a mood, but it's nothing exceptional as far as the King is concerned.

"And today – ah! Today I enjoyed the performance! I emptied into my stomach all the pitchers of pleasure that I could take and believe me, this stomach of mine is bottomless, almost bottomless I should say! And in spite of that – today it was thoroughly satisfied, filled to the brim.

"According to the Chaldean perception, which differs from the perception of the inhabitants of those distant islands to the north-west – every play worthy of the name consists of three elements: plot, suspense, and a surprising and liberating conclusion. The plot of the play that I witnessed today came to its full fruition in the answer that was given to the all-conquering King, the wise and the valiant etc., no doubt affecting him to the very roots of his soul, which incidentally, in his case are not so difficult to reach. This was the plot, and the suspense which the plot engendered was the obligatory ritual cleansing, the ablutions – in this case, a bloodbath – the blood in question being yours.

"I almost saw you in the convivial company of that stalwart pair standing to attention behind the King, gripping the gilded hilt of the shining, naked, execution-sword, ready to brandish it over any neck that the King might point to.

"And then came the turn of the astonishing and liberating conclusion – no stalwart duo, no brandished blade, no blood – quite unlike the scenes normally staged for the King's benefit, taking account of his well-known tastes and proclivities. And instead of this – praise and jubilation! Incredible to relate!

"There is no doubt, no room for the shadow of a shadow of a doubt, that you are the chosen one, the most favoured of all by your God and the God of your fathers, who, according to your claim, is the one and the only, the exclusive God. And indeed, this has been proved, proved conclusively, incontrovertibly, before the forum of the people, in living marvels and miraculous spectacles – when your God freed you unharmed from the predatory claws of the roaring lion, always poised to spring. Till this day I had never witnessed such an impressive, conclusive scene, a scene that sets my heart quivering and makes all my limbs tingle, finally to release the heart from its quivering and my limbs from their tingling, bringing them joy instead, satisfaction and relief of the most exquisite kind!"

He breathed deep, like a man worn out after running a long distance, and gave him a sidelong glance suffused with tenderness and affection, concluding:

"I only came to wish you, in the name of your God and the God of your fathers and through His grace, stunning success in your new post in the office of the chief of the King's senior counsellors. Believe this or believe it not – I am proud of you!"

He shook his hand firmly and left the room which – so it seemed – he would now be obliged to vacate, transferring to grander and more spacious quarters, in keeping with the post allotted him in the government of Nebuchadnezzar the Second, King of Babylon.

THE PROPHET

BOOK II

NASHDERNACH

Working in the office of Nashdernach, the man appointed by the King to supervise his senior counsellors and reputedly an authority on the holy writings of the Jews, was fraught with tension. Runners came and went from early morning till late in the evening, even at times when Nashdernach was absent from the office, leaving their messages either orally, in which case the duty clerk made a written record with a stylus on finely crafted scrolls, or in the form of inscriptions on clay tablets, parchment or those thin, flimsy sheets of paper imported from Egypt, made from reeds and known as "papyrus".

For his part, the chief minister of the King's council made every effort to be present and to receive in person the dispatches arriving from all far-flung corners of the great kingdom, especially the oral reports, which were sometimes corrupted in transmission from one runner to another and from one clerk to another. If he suspected any such inaccuracy, the minister would personally interrogate the runner and force him to repeat the message over and over again, while a harassed clerk took dictation. If the several versions of the same material were inconsistent, as frequently happened, or even contradicted one another, a less common occurrence, Nashdernach would fume, abusing and berating the unfortunate runner and the fool who had entrusted him with the message, and sending him back the way he had come, accompanied by a runner of his own, who was instructed to report the minister's displeasure, demand an enquiry and return post haste with a clear and authenticated version of the original message.

At such times as this, the minister's extensive office was in a ferment: scribes and calligraphers running back and forth in search of more efficient styluses and better quality parchment, anxious to avoid any mistakes when taking dictation from Nashdernach, runners waiting tensely and changing places in the line, depending on how keen they were to be sent to that distant region from which the corrupted message had originated, secretaries consulting scrolls and tablets in search of all available information regarding the governors and agents of the Crown responsible for that particular locality. There were quieter days too, days of routine when no unrest had been reported in any of the regions and the provinces on account of some or other demand on the part of the King or those governing on his behalf; no one was complaining of an unreasonably oppressive regime or fomenting sedition.

A constantly irksome matter, naturally enough, was the tribute paid by conquered lands. Governors, chosen by the local populace, and agents acting on behalf of the Chaldean monarch, would sometimes make common cause with the residents of that territory or region or formerly sovereign state, and try every means at their disposal, from exploiting obscure points of Chaldean law to the offering of bribes, in the effort to reduce the tax to what they considered a more tolerable level. Thus for example, the merchandise sent in accordance with the treaty of submission, signed by the envoys of the King and representatives of the population of the vassal state, was not always of the quality explicitly required by the terms of the treaty. On the contrary, all too often these goods were of inferior quality, sometimes very inferior quality, so much so that Nashdernach took it upon himself to return them to the sender with a reprimand, a warning or even a threat, and this in spite of the expenses involved in returning the goods. And there were duplicitous agents who resorted to covering the inferior commodities with a thin top layer of goods of superior quality. If someone confirmed receipt of the merchandise without adequate inspection and reported it satisfactory, then the conspirators in the provinces had cause for celebration, while the people of Babylon had no option but to consume the flawed foodstuffs, gritting their teeth and swallowing the bitter pill. In many such cases Nashdernach demanded a thorough investigation of the issue, and the clerk who confirmed the receipt faced dismissal. In cases where responsibility was less easily assigned, the high quality material masking the inferior was simply sent to the palace for the use of the King and his court, and the remainder taken to the market and sold off cheaply – a highly unsatisfactory outcome. And if the business came to the King's knowledge, someone would pay for his carelessness, with a heavy fine or a lengthy term of penal servitude.

He was noted for his attention to detail and his diligence, qualities for which Chaldean clerks were not always renowned and especially – for his honesty. Whenever it was revealed, this uncompromising honesty aroused admiration – closely followed by jealousy, scorn and rejection. Nashdernach appreciated these qualities and came to depend on him when he needed to take decisions or prosecute somebody or other.

He did his work conscientiously and did not skimp on the hours of work, often staying on late in the office if some matter required urgent attention. And with this too he gained the esteem of Nashdernach and the jealousy of his colleagues. Furthermore, his handwriting was clean and legible and he wrote with remarkable speed to the minister's dictation which, in his angrier moments, tended to lack consistency and clarity, verging on the incoherent.

Late one evening a report of an imminent uprising in a remote southern province arrived on the minister's desk, this on account of a demand for the doubling of the rice quota sent to Babylon as tribute. The effect of the demand would be to add still further to the already wearisome burden of toil at every stage of the process – planting, harvesting, sorting, drying, packing and dispatch to the authorities in Babylon.

Nashdernach decided to send a punitive expedition to ravage the province and reduce its "feckless" inhabitants, as he called them, to "poverty and penury", and the only question in his mind was the scale of the expedition required, bearing in mind the expense involved and the need to obtain royal approval.

Nashdernach approached him as he was engaged in transcribing an illegible text onto clean parchment, gave him a sharp look with his oily, bloodshot eyes and asked him:

"Will one battalion suffice?"

"To start with," he replied.

"What's that supposed to mean – 'to start with'?" – Nashdernach retorted, angry and surprised.

"The first act of suppression will only be the beginning," he explained calmly, adding: "The revolt will spread, and people won't bother rebuilding the straw huts that have been torched; instead they'll set ambushes for Chaldean soldiers and attack them. This is their territory and they know all its dark corners, every tree and every stone, and if it comes down to guerrilla warfare the rebels will have the advantage and you'll have to send another expedition, and then another."

"In the end, the rebels will be crushed!" the minister declared, disbelieving the other's words, despite the confident tone in which they were spoken.

Ignoring the interjection, he continued:

"And on top of everything, you'll lose all the rice – all of it!"

"Expenses, expenses – and no revenue!" – Nashdernach grumbled.

Instead of answering, he went back to deciphering the ancient text.

The minister turned and began pacing up and down his spacious office, lit with numerous oil-lamps, his hands clasped behind his back. He was wearing a brown robe and a cloak of superior fabric, with no embellishment other than the silver medallion hanging on his chest, the symbol of his eminent status in the service of the King.

Having measured the length and breadth of his office once again, Nashdernach finally stopped by his desk and asked him:

"And what would you do in my place?"

"Without presuming to put myself in your place," – he looked up and calmly met his supervisor's gaze – "I would rescind the excessive demand for doubling of the rice quota."

"What makes you say it's 'excessive'?" – cried Nashdernach.

"The rebellion that it's provoked."

"They're just a bunch of idle no-hopers!" – Nashdernach complained.

"If they were idle no-hopers they wouldn't have completed even the original quota, and they wouldn't now be in such a mutinous mood, spoiling for a fight."

"If I reverse the decision," – the minister tried to explain – "I shall lose face in the sight of those barbarian populations, and they'll try to wriggle out of their existing obligations! Other lands and provinces will learn from them and follow their example, and the whole apparatus will unravel, with disastrous results!"

"The opposite is the case," he retorted evenly.

"How so?" his supervisor queried, a sceptical glint in his eyes.

"Only a strong ruler is capable of admitting his mistakes, and such an admission will arouse only esteem and respect in the hearts of the peoples under his sway. If you withdraw the excessive demand, you will gain the affection and appreciation of the local populations, and you will save the costs of a punitive expedition, and not run the risk of incurring royal displeasure. In addition, you will again receive the quota of rice as agreed in the treaty of submission, and it is very likely, that if you succeed in winning over the people of this province with incentives or expressions of your appreciation for their efforts – they themselves will decide to add to the existing quota, even if they don't go so far as to double it."

"You have a brain in your head!" exclaimed Nashdernach, clasping his fingers tightly behind his back. The minister turned sharply, sat down facing him and said to him:

"Listen to me, Belteshazzar! Put that work aside and listen!"

He did as he was asked, carefully folding the document and placing the work in progress under an ivory paperweight, then looked up at his supervisor serenely, his tranquil eyes cleansed from all the vanities of the world.

"Your advice is the best that there is, but that doesn't mean that I have to accept it and put it into effect! Not at all!" exclaimed Nashdernach. "However sincerely we may wish to do what is right – we are compelled to act in ways contrary to honest reason. And why is this?" he asked, and continued his impassioned speech without waiting for an answer: "It's because of the need to preserve this skin of ours," – and he pinched the back of his mottled hand – "We are concerned for our skin because there's no one who can be trusted! You have to understand – this idea, so logical and sensible, will be whispered in the ears of the King and presented in the most unfavourable light, as a sign of failure, the plan of an abject and spineless minister who can't manage his own affairs and worst of all – it will be taken as a slur on the honour of the King and a token of flawed loyalty. Pay close attention to what I'm telling you," Nashdernach stressed – "Disloyalty to the King, betrayal of the King's trust, well, you know the rest! Hard labour for the remainder of your life, confiscation of property, wife, sons, daughters, parents – on the streets!" He struck the table with his fist, so hard that the stylus left on it leapt into the air and fell to the floor.

He bent down, picked up the stylus, replaced it on the table, and responded:

"The esteemed minister is gravely mistaken!"

"What is that supposed to mean?" – once again Nashdernach fixed him with that oily stare of his, expressing wonderment and considerable curiosity.

"There is someone who can be trusted."

"Who?"

"God."

The minister froze in his seat and his fleshy mouth gaped open, like the mouth of a fish. A long moment passed.

"Who is this God that can be trusted. Are you referring to Bel or to Marduk? They both have a habit of abandoning their devotees in times of adversity."

"Neither one nor the other."

"Who then?"

"The God who created everything, who rules over everything, and who loves us as a father loves his children."

"And why then, if such a God indeed exists, who loves us as a father loves his children, and who created everything and rules over everything, why, I ask you, has this father-God cast us down to flounder in this Hell?"

In his deep, limpid eyes, a bright glow flashed for a moment, and he answered the minister Nashdernach, senior counsellor to King Nebuchadnezzar:

"Because people don't put their trust in him!"

Nashdernach pondered this, and after a long silence, he rose from his seat and resumed his pacing, back and forth, his step vigorous, hands clasped behind his back.

He returned to his copying work, and was on the point of finishing it, when Nashdernach called to him from one of the corners:

"And you trust in Him, who created everything and rules over everything, who loves us as a father loves his children?"

"With all my heart and all my might!" – was his clear and resonant response.

And sure enough, the minister Nashdernach changed his mind and decided against sending a punitive expedition. Instead he sent a deputation of conciliators who informed the inhabitants that the King, the valiant and the wise, the compassionate and the merciful had see their misery, and being well aware of their devotion to him and valuing their loyalty, he had decided to release them from the increased rice quota and even, in recognition of the respect and the warm feelings of esteem in which they held the King, to forgo the standard quota of rice for the current year, as a gesture of the goodwill, appreciation and gratitude that the King felt for them.

When the messenger-runner returned from the remote province he was so emotional he had great difficulty giving his report, describing how those unfortunate people had received the astonishing news, how they had hugged and kissed him and carried him shoulder-high, how they decided there and then, using their own meagre resources, to erect a temple to King Nebuchadnezzar, the wise and the valiant, the compassionate and the merciful, the one and only, and to worship him as a god, since only a god – those unfortunates claimed – could understand their feelings and the depth of their poverty, know of their oppression and bring it to such a conclusive and satisfactory end.

And the messenger-runner broke down in tears when he tried to describe the moving scenes to Nashdernach, sitting at his table, and all the clerks of the office listening to his disordered words; even those who were supposed to be recording them were utterly distracted from their task by the strength of the feelings that had gripped them.

Even the oily little eyes of the chief counsellor to the King of Babylon filled with tears that he was powerless to resist, and they glided over his round ruddy-red cheeks, and were absorbed into his bushy beard, flecked with silvery threads.

Finally, in a voice still defying his attempts to control it, the minister asked the messenger to leave the room, and not to return until he had composed himself; only then should he make another effort to dictate a succinct report for the benefit of the scribes.

When the minister's instructions had been followed, he rose to his feet and, snapping his fingers pleasurably behind his back, he approached him, leaned towards him and said:

"It seems, after all, He is worthy of our trust!"

IN MISHAEL'S LODGING

A year passed. And it came about one day that all of them, he and his companions, happened to be in one of the royal assembly rooms. The King's senior advisers were about to convene a meeting in this room, and their Jewish clerks had come to prepare the tables. Adoniah was there too, although he often left Babylon to travel to strange and distant lands where he traded in all the commerce of the world, from shoe-laces to slaves and concubines for the royal palace. Through all these dealings, he had made a handsome profit for himself.

One after another they entered the room, unable to restrain their joy at the unexpected reunion.

"Hananiah!" cried Mishael, almost embracing his friend.

"Mishael!" cried Azariah, and hurried towards him. The three of them exchanged handshakes and jovial slaps on the shoulder – and at that precise moment, although through separate doors – he and Adoniah made their entrance.

Adoniah hurried towards him and shook his hand vigorously, with surprising sincerity, then turned to the others and repeated the exercise, with warm handshakes, and even a slap on the shoulder for Azariah.

"How I've missed you, my friends and brothers!" he exclaimed – "And how good it is that God has brought us all together. My feet have trodden the wide open spaces of the world, places I never imagined I would go to, places I never knew existed! All those nations and tongues and peoples and principalities, living and subsisting on this continent of ours that is so full of surprises…. and most of all – I have missed you!" He turned to him again, this time with a convivial slap to the shoulder. "For some reason," he went on to say, his speech light and fluent – "It seems to me I haven't behaved towards you the way I should, and this has pinched my guts and weighed heavy on my heart! Anyway, blessed is the hour of our meeting, and this opportunity that I have to confess to you the sin I committed against you!"

"You're talking a great deal of nonsense!" he retorted. "I don't reckon you have ever sinned against me in anything!"

"Oh, I've sinned, you need have no doubt of that!" Adoniah insisted, the cheerful look on his face still bright, and growing brighter from moment to moment.

"And I tell you this too, my friend and brother!" Adoniah cried, shaking his hand again, a clownish grin flexing his fleshy lips: "I'm going to sin against you some more!"

The other three advanced, as Adoniah went on to say:

"You were good-looking even as a boy and now you've gone from strength to strength, what a brilliant career! Who would believe it? A courageous young fellow, a high-ranking courtier and a man of God as well! The frivolous young girls who chase me around would be scared off by you, living angel of God that you are, pure and unsullied, noble and brave, never to be tripped up by the sins of the flesh, and invincible – seeing that God Himself, in person, defends you and stands by your side, keeping you secure against evil or adversity! And why does God the all-powerful do this?" cried Adoniah, turning to Mishael, Azariah and Hananiah and answering his own question: "Because there is no one more worthy of it than him – no one! And who could possibly be jealous of such a man, doing everything in his power to dig a pit before his feet, to set a trap into which he will fall? This surely belongs to the dark side, the side that leads astray and causes delusions, the side of hypocrisy and seething anger, the serpent from the Garden of Eden, in other words, the side – to which I am totally committed!"

Hananiah intervened, his voice, in normal times so evenly modulated, turning harsh and almost menacing:

"All you're doing is fooling yourself! This power that you speak of can do nothing when it is revealed, in the open. It depends on cunning and deceit, and dark corners!"

"And perhaps," Adoniah interrupted him, "I really am cunning beyond belief and sufficiently degraded, a genius in that regard, to deceive you all and in particular, to arouse the superior compassion of Belteshazzar, and to blunt his eternal vigilance. Ha-Ha-Ha-Ha!" He shook his head with its mass of rust-coloured hair and beard and added: "I'm warning you – don't trust me!" Suddenly he turned more serious and wiped from his eyes the tears brought on by his wild laughter. "Don't trust anyone and take good care of yourselves, especially you!" – he pointed at him and laughed again.

He did not respond, but maintained his composure. Adoniah went on to say:

"You make me so angry, the anger of flesh and blood! Always the chief player, always in control of yourself, always standing in the right place, following the right road, always standing tall, to put it plainly – always a prig!" He turned to the remainder of his audience and asked gaily: "Don't you agree?"

"No!" the three companions replied with one voice, and as if they meant to protect him with their bodies, moved in closer and stood as a barrier between him and Adoniah.

"You seem to be drunk!" Azariah hissed between his teeth.

"Drunk, but not on wine!" Adoniah declared.

"What then, if not wine?" asked Hananiah and almost regretted his question, but the answer was not slow in coming.

When Adoniah spoke, his voice had changed and was calm and measured, although the arrogance of his mood was undiminished:

"On hatred!"

And suddenly, in an unexpected movement, Adoniah skirted the barrier of the three friends and stood facing him, fixed flashing eyes on him and asked:

"And you?"

"What?" he retorted in a clear, authoritative voice, not budging from his place.

"How much do you hate me?"

"I don't hate you."

"Pity me?"

"No."

"Afraid of me?"

"No."

"Despise me?"

"No."

"And you make no distinction between me," he hesitated for a moment, then completed his sentence – "and these, shall we say?" He pointed to the three friends, with a sweeping gesture of the hand.

"I do make a distinction."

"Them you love and me – you hate!" cried Adoniah in a tone of triumph, like one who has caught his quarry or exposed another as a liar.

"I think of them with pleasure, and of you – with great sorrow!" he declared.

Adoniah stood with head bowed and made no reply.

Mishael exploited the pause to issue an invitation:

"Come to my room this evening. I have some wine from the homeland, which we can drink with a clear conscience!"

In Mishael's lodging a surprise awaited them: besides the kosher wine, Gershon was sitting there – grey-haired now but looking fit in his clean clothing.

"You're all growing beards!" he cried, clearly finding the reunion an emotional experience – "Only a little while ago your faces were so smooth!"

They looked into one another's faces and perhaps for the first time realised they were no longer boys but men, young men with incipient beards.

"And have any of you taken wives yet?" Gershon asked curiously.

It emerged that Mishael, Azariah and Hananiah were soon to be betrothed to Jewish girls, precious finds indeed.

"There's no place for bachelors in the Chaldean administration!" Azariah explained.

"It's an immutable law," added Mishael.

The three of them had searched, and found in the environs of the city of Babylon a devout and decent Jewish community. The fathers of this community had no objection to marrying off their eligible daughters, knowing that the prospective grooms were not only Jews but were also functionaries in the service of Nebuchadnezzar.

"And what about you, Adoniah?" Gershon asked.

"I intend to marry a beautiful Egyptian princess, whose father, the prince, was taken captive by Nebuchadnezzar. The price that I shall pay for her – is her father's ransom!"

"And how can you afford the ransom? After all, a prisoner of such distinction will command a very high price!"

"The ransom will cost me nothing!" – Adoniah chuckled.

"How so?" Gershon persisted.

"The man who is holding him owes me a favour!" he declared, amused by the stony expressions of the others, and adding: "That's how things work in the wonderful world of commerce – you repay good with good, and evil with evil! As it says in our Holy Law – *an eye for an eye, a tooth for a tooth!*"

"And what if she induces you to change your religion?" Gershon went on to ask.

"Either she'll induce me, or I'll induce her. We are neither of us renowned for our faith or for our zealous observance of commandments!"

"Egyptian women turned the head of King Solomon, the wisest of all men!" – Mishael commented earnestly.

"Then I shall gladly follow in his footsteps!" – Adoniah chuckled again and sat down at the table.

Gershon was given the seat of honour at the head of the table, and he blessed the bread and the fruit of the vine and one after another they all read from the scroll of the Psalms that Adoniah had succeeded in salvaging from the homeland. Then they sang their favourite anthems and finally, resumed their personal conversations.

He asked Gershon about his work in the office of the royal calligrapher, and he answered willingly, as all listened attentively, telling them how he had already been promoted on account of his experience and his expertise; all agreed he had no equal in the skilled use of the sharpened Egyptian stylus, and in determining the quality of parchment and in mixing the ingredients of ink in the correct proportions, producing the colour required to make the text leap from the page, so that the reader would not only read and understand and be informed, but would also derive enjoyment from seeing the script, as a work of art in its own right. In the same way, a person who is fond of natural beauty or of weapons of war will enjoy the sight of a field or a forest or, *mutatis mutandis*, a sharp sword or a dagger, a bow and arrow or assorted spears. As for Chaldean writing, it was not complicated at all; on the contrary it was simple and easy to copy – and very satisfying. It was of course a cuneiform script, Gershon went on to explain, clearly glad of the opportunity to demonstrate his intimate knowledge of the subject, unlike the complex Hebrew script. Nevertheless – Gershon concluded with a smile and a conspiratorial wink – he preferred the Hebrew alphabet with all its complications to the pale and uninteresting Chaldean equivalent.

"And why is that?" Hananiah wanted to know.

"Because of the spirit that the Hebrew letter embodies."

"How so?" – Mishael expressed his sincere bemusement and added: "What makes you say that the letter embodies a spirit?"

And Azariah declared:

"The letter is dead and there is no spirit in it, never mind a living spirit!"

"You're wrong there!" Gershon answered him – "the letter is alive, and every language has a living spirit of its own!"

"What is the spirit of the Chaldean language, and what does the Hebrew language tell you?" asked Azariah, utterly baffled.

"The spirit of the Chaldean language is a spirit of arrogance. It is sure of itself, and it has a solidity to it and yet – it lacks depth and profundity.

The spirit of the Hebrew language on the other hand, aspires to the heights and is always trying, trying and trying again to reach the sky, the firmament which is the foundry of the language!"

"As the people, so is the language, and as the language so is the people!" – Hananiah tried to simplify the issue for himself, a faint spark of gratification in his voice.

Adoniah commented:

"If you carry on with this line of conversation, discussing the comparative merits of languages and peoples and nations and races, praising your own people and disparaging the Chaldeans, treating them with such open contempt – you'll be accused of insulting the nation and its monarch and fomenting sedition – and before you know it you'll be on your way to the copper mines in the bowels of the earth..."

"This is just a private conversation, between friends!" – Gershon retorted.

"Walls have ears!" – Adoniah put a finger to his lips as if warning of the dangers of idle talk and added: *"He who guards his mouth and tongue, is guarded against adversity* – so said the wisest of men!"

"In this room," he interjected, "there are ears of flesh and blood only." He meant to reassure Gershon, who responded:

"I spent long enough among the tanners on the Euphrates to learn what hardship means. No human being on earth could imagine what is going on there! No man sent down to the Euphrates to scrape animal skins for the Chaldean King will come out of there alive..."

"Except you, apparently!" Adoniah remarked with emphatic scorn.

"That was by the grace of God, the living God, the God full of mercy," declared Gershon reverently, with an involuntary inclination of the head.

"Why don't you tell us something about the Euphrates and the tanners?" Hananiah suggested.

Gershon looked at him again with a question in his eyes and, receiving his silent acquiescence, without hesitation and without a stumble, launched into his harrowing account:

"The river is broad at that point, so you can hardly see the other side, and it is shallow near the bank. The river bed is covered with stones and projecting rocks, creating all those swirling currents, and as if the currents weren't enough to cope with, the tanners have to stand barefoot on these stones and rocky surfaces from before dawn until the first star rises in the evening. There they stand, without pausing for a moment, scraping the crude skins fresh from the beasts, and causing serious injury to their feet. To begin with, you feel intense pain. As time passes, the pain is numbed, but walking becomes a very complicated process. You can tell a tanner by the way he walks – slowly, ponderously, picking up his feet like a goose. Here's the evidence!" – and with a quick movement, before anyone had the chance to protest, Gershon pulled off his shoes, unfastened the rags and revealed to the assembled company his bruised and battered feet, blackened toes deformed and folding under themselves, the very bones distorted. All looked on, and shuddered.

"What vicious beasts these Chaldeans are!" exclaimed Adoniah.

"How can you walk with your feet in that state?" asked Azariah.

"I manage, and every day I thank the living God for releasing me from that Hell, alive and with only this disability to cope with. God is full of grace and all powerful, doing great and marvellous things, going down into the depths to rescue those that He loves from the hands of the wicked, performing miracles and wonders. He is compassionate and kind and I shall bless Him and praise His name for as long as I live, and that's all there is to say!"

Carefully he wrapped his feet again and put on his shoes.

"Is there more to tell?" asked Mishael.

"And why don't the tanners leave that terrible place and seek employment elsewhere?" asked Hananiah.

"They have guards there, and overseers – guards with weapons at the ready, to prevent anyone leaving and overseers with whips – long, thick, black whips made from buffalo tails. A single blow from one of those could knock a healthy man to the ground. Somehow, my Lord rescued me from these floggings, but there are very few who can endure them. The overseers are fond of lashing the bare backs of the tanners, as we stand there naked as the day we were born in the dirty, frothing water, a wooden scraper in one hand and in the other – a vile-smelling animal skin."

"Didn't they supply you with clothing?" he asked.

"The new tanner is given a shirt, a loin cloth, a strip of coarse, untreated wool to wrap around the head, and a pair of shoes. But all this stuff disintegrates within a few days, leaving him without even a scrap of material to preserve his modesty. No other clothing is supplied. One issue is supposed to last you for life – not such a long time, admittedly.

"I never knew a tanner who endured this back-breaking toil for more than seven years. I was the oldest of them all, and no one expected me to last long. Within six months, a year at the most, they reckoned the overseer's whip would knock me down – and I wouldn't get up, not ever. They're a heartless, merciless lot those overseers; wild, ravening creatures are paragons of compassion compared with them!

"There were times when the work was proceeding to the full satisfaction of the overseers and the guards, and not one of the tanners was doing anything to disrupt the routine, all working in silence without looking up or attempting to move paralysed limbs, from before dawn until evening, and then one of the overseers cracks his black whip over a tanner who has caught his eye, and this merely as a means of relieving boredom or as he himself would put it, for the sake of exercise. The overseer's cronies come hurrying along to join in the fun, howling with raucous laughter, and the whips lash the body of the chosen victim until he collapses on the spot, falls in the water and usually doesn't come up alive..."

"It's as if you've described to us a scene from Hell," cried Hananiah – indignation, horror and revulsion blending in his voice.

"Hell is precisely what it is!" Gershon declared, adding: "In the evening they dole out a tiny portion of broth, broth made with rotten, foul-smelling rice or beans that don't smell any better. And sometimes that's the only ration. And then you sleep in straw booths on flimsy mats the colour of the ground, and just about indistinguishable from it, like garbage that's been left uncollected, to fester."

"It's a nightmare you've described!" Adoniah exclaimed.

"What can we do to ease those dreadful conditions?" – Azariah tossed the question into the air and unconsciously turned towards him.

One after another Mishael, Hananiah and Gershon followed his example, as did Adoniah, whose quizzical look was tinged by a strange air of tolerance, of one who recognises his own weakness and makes no attempt to conceal it.

He answered them solemnly, in a quiet but resolute voice:

"God will show us what to do, and soon!"

"And why has this God of yours left it so long, and why is He still waiting?" – the mocking note returned to Adoniah's voice.

"Because people don't turn to Him!" he answered him in the same tone, controlled but vehement.

"And if they turned to Him, would they be delivered?" Adoniah persisted.

"It is written: *The Lord is near to all who call upon him, all who call upon him in truth.* Every appeal to God that is truthful is answered at once, and in full!"

"And how can this God of yours satisfy the ravenous hunger of those wretched slaves?" Adoniah demanded to know, his tone provocative.

"He will send down manna, manna from Heaven!" he declared calmly.

"I've been roaming about this strange world of ours for more than a year. My horse's legs have covered vast distances, and it seems there is not a remote corner anywhere in which I haven't set foot. I have travelled to regions that have no language and no name, I have seen upright and honest children of the Torah, and scoundrels and buffoons who call themselves saints, I have known people of indelible faith whose lot in life is far from lavish, but never have I seen with my own eyes manna descending from Heaven!" Adoniah concluded, grating notes of anger creeping into his voice.

"Our fathers saw it," he answered him steadily, adding: "They ate of it and were satisfied."

"And instead of praising and thanking God," Gershon interjected hoarsely – "they began complaining and longed to return to the servitude of Egypt!"

"And these people that you happened to meet – honest and upright, people of faith and lovers of God," – Hananiah turned to face Adoniah: "Were they in a state of distress or of abject misery?"

Adoniah gave the matter some thought, his eyes straying to the smooth white ceiling.

"I'm not altogether sure..." he faltered, his head lowered – "but if I'm doing my best not to offend against the truth, then I have to say that in all my life I have never seen people so happy in their lot, so hospitable, always prepared to sacrifice something of their own for another. And you have to take care not to express any kind of wish in their presence!" Adoniah laughed a bitter laugh.

"Why is that?" asked Azariah.

"Because they'll move heaven and earth to make it come true! And if you're foolish enough to admire your host's shirt, you won't be allowed to leave the house without it – even if it's the only shirt he has and he's left with just a loincloth!"

A broad, radiant smile spread over the faces of his audience.

"You're not as unpleasant as you sometimes pretend to be!" – Hananiah approached Adoniah and slapped his shoulder.

"How do you make that out?"

"You're telling the truth, and you have described those godly people just the way they are!"

"And perhaps you're the gullible one, Hananiah, falling so easily into the traps that I set for you!"

"I don't think so, my friend and brother!" Hananiah smiled a gentle and reassuring smile – "And I am sure that when the time of testing comes, you will pass it with honour, as befits a son of our holy race, this race of prophets and kings and saints."

"Don't be quite so confident!" Adoniah retorted and turned to him: "And you, do you share Hananiah's child-like trust in me?"

"I do – and more!" he declared without hesitation.

Adoniah looked down again, and after a moment's silence turned to him and said:

"It slipped my mind completely!" – and he raised his hand as if drawing up a memory – "When I was in Jerusalem a girl approached me, not the kind of girl one normally meets on one's travels – and I'm talking about the purity in her face, the quiet courage in her dark-blue eyes, the seal of wisdom shining on her smooth forehead – and she asked me if I was going to Babylon and if I knew Daniel, son of Naimel, former minister of the royal household, and if so she wanted me to pass on her regards and best wishes, and if possible, this modest gift as well..." He thrust his hand into the pocket of his gown, pulled out a small packet and handed it to him.

With trembling fingers he unwrapped the bundle and found in it a parchment scroll and a tiny seven-branched candlestick made of silver – a real work of art.

His hand closed around the parchment scroll. He felt tears springing to his eyes, and made an effort to curb them, with some success. He took the candlestick and showed it to the assembled company. The skilfully beaten silver caught the flickering glimmer of the oil-lamps and grease-lamps in the room, shining with a pure radiance and reflecting the light back to those looking on, a gentle and conciliatory light.

"Did she ask about me?" – he turned to Adoniah, and the latter replied to him in a deliberately casual tone, in an effort to show complete indifference and the self-confidence which he so conspicuously lacked:

"She asked, oh yes – she asked!"

"And you told her?"

"I didn't want to disappoint her, and superb raconteur that I am, I could have told her a great deal about you. There is plenty to tell after all! On the other hand, I didn't want to confuse her either, and she was clearly preoccupied at the time, to say the least!"

He gave Adoniah a sharp, inquisitive, probing look until the latter flinched, recoiled involuntarily and fell silent.

"So what did you tell the girl?" asked Azariah, with a distinct edge of asperity to his voice.

"First of all," Adoniah grinned – "Nejeen isn't a girl any more, not the girl she once was. The years have passed and the girl has become a woman. A young woman of exceptional feminine beauty, whose equal is not to found anywhere on this earth, or possibly even in the Heavens above," and to the astonishment of his audience he attempted to reinforce his words with the most bizarre of arguments: "If a thief happened to be in her presence, a habitual thief, and he glanced once at her face if only for a moment – he would turn from his evil ways and return everything he had stolen to the rightful owners, or donate it to charity, and go to the Temple of God, and bow down before the Holy Ark, and fall face down on the floor in the fullest repentance. Such is the beauty of Nejeen of the house of Gamliel, and this is its special nature! However, I am no thief and am therefore absolved from repentance!"

"You're not answering the question, Adoniah!" – Azariah pressed him.

"Don't be so hasty, dear friend! Everything in its time! Didn't the wisest of men say, there is a time for everything? A time for peace and a time for war, a time to love and a time to hate? Well, I told the aristocratic young lady, Nejeen of the house of Gamliel, who it seems is also related to the royal family, about her sweetheart, who is doing great things in Babylon!" His sarcasm was venomous, and intended to hurt.

"Be careful what you say, Adoniah!" he warned, his voice icy.

"I haven't accused you of worshipping the spirits of the night," Adoniah retorted – "control your temper! It's true that you've visited the shrine of Bel," he continued with an air of secret, contemptuous pleasure, – "but you haven't changed your religion yet! I, on the other hand, stand accused of contemplating a change of religion for the sake of a foreign lady, the diametrical opposite of your Jewess... Well, so it goes, we differ in nature and in taste, and in the kind of people who are drawn to us, differ fundamentally..." Adoniah sighed a bitter sigh and added as if in conclusion: "Such is the way of the world and there's no remedy for it!

"'I know him!' I told her," he resumed his account, "and I had the privilege of seeing her wondrous exaltation of spirit, the brightness coming to life in her eyes, the brightness of fearless nobility, fine breeding, and for this reason I was quick to stress: 'I know him well! We both travelled to Babylon in the same convoy, and we studied in the same school. We even competed, at the behest of King Nebuchadnezzar, in horse-racing and steeplechasing, and as you can well imagine – he was the victor!'" Adoniah smiled a thin and calculated smile, was silent for a moment to deepen the impact of his words and add to the tension among his listeners, before continuing:

"Obviously, in this instance she needed to invest a lot of effort in the attempt to hide the surge of sublime emotion – and in my humble opinion, she's not accustomed to feelings of any other kind – that took hold of her.

"For her part, she was sure she had succeeded in curbing and concealing her emotions before it was too late, and I was happy to pretend to be unaware of her state of mind, because at that time it was my wish and my firm intention to reassure her and if possible – to cheer her up as well. The fact is, it is inconceivable that any creature should try to injure and offend one such as she, and if ever such a strange creature were to be found, he would deserve the soundest of thrashings. And yes, this is what I tried to do, I suppressed my noble inclination to make her happy, I tried to grieve and injure her – and I was soundly thrashed! Utter failure! And how did I try?" – he asked and answered for himself: "I tried by telling her of the Chaldean beauty who seduced Beltezhazzar (I revealed to her the proud Chaldean name that he bears) and led him to the temple of idolatry, the shrine of Bel, the Babylonian deity, and how they stayed there much longer than would be reasonably expected, and I stressed the point that all this information came from first hand, since I personally followed them there and waited, and waited a long time for them to emerge from the temple, and in the end, when there was still no sign of them, I gave up and left the place.

"I was sure I had succeeded in plunging a poisoned arrow into that sensitive heart, most wondrous of hearts... but not a bit of it!

"She turned to me and asked me why I had acted this way, and why I had followed them. Had I been appointed their bodyguard? And here I can tell you for sure that in her voice there was a clear intention to hurt me and to teach me a lesson, and expose my shameful behaviour to public view – and a threat like that always throws me off balance and sometimes numbs all my senses too. And that is what happened in this instance, and I turned to her and told her in all sincerity:

"It's because I'm jealous, my lady, I'm envious of him! Everywhere he outshines me and outclasses me, whether it's horse-racing or landing the best jobs, or making an impression on well-connected Chaldean women, and I'm sure you can't blame him for that! However, I shall fulfil my errand, if you still consider me suitable, if my conduct has not made you reconsider!' And what do you think she said? Can you have the slightest inkling of her response?" And without waiting for a reply he continued: "She said, 'Esteemed Sir, I trust you!' And that was it! With those words she trampled my soul into the dust! For a moment, I wanted to jump off the wall, but I didn't have the nerve!" Adoniah bowed his head, looked away and continued: "After we had parted company I thought of throwing the little package away, but then some instinct told me there might be something valuable in it and rather than discard it, I should take it to a silversmith and make some money from it. I opened the package and saw it was indeed a charming piece, but of little value. And I went further and read what was written on the parchment, I couldn't resist the impulse! And you," – he turned to him – "you can read it to us if you like, or shall I? Anyway, it says 'Love is stronger than death'."

He gave him a tolerant look, not particularly sympathetic but also devoid of hatred or abhorrence.

"You can pity me!" Adoniah resumed – "Pity me as much as you like. I'm more deserving of pity than any other creature in the world, and yet I don't ask for your compassion, I despise it. You can call me a scoundrel and challenge me to a duel with swords or spears or bare hands, or with bows and arrows – and I won't accept the challenge because I know perfectly well that you are superior to me in all these skills. But the day will come that I am longing for, when I shall tackle you in the way you least expect. Remember that. Remember it well!"

"You're out of your mind!" Gershon cried – "Crazy!"

"Not crazy exactly, a little deranged perhaps!" Adoniah corrected him, with a hoot of raucous laughter. He poured the remainder of the wine into his cup, gulped it down thirstily and noisily to the very last drop, put the cup down and said:

"Jerusalem is going to rebel! Remember what I'm telling you! Zedekiah is leading the Jewish people to catastrophe. Jeremiah is saying this too, but he's just repeating what his God is telling him, whereas I'm reporting to you what my eyes have seen and my ears have heard. If you want to save the lovely Nejeen," he turned to him suddenly – "fetch her here and do it soon!" And saying this he rose from his seat, and swaying a little on his short legs, left Mishael's lodging.

Adoniah's departure seemed to clear the air for those remaining, and all breathed more easily.

"The man's a fool, and he's talking nonsense!" Gershon exclaimed.

He did not respond, although the others expected him to. In the equable stillness that reigned in the little room, he asked Mishael if he was enjoying his work in the legal department.

Mishael answered willingly, telling them of a new law which had been proposed by the council of sorcerers, wizards and astrologers and would soon be presented to the King for his approval. According to the new law, the death penalty was to be imposed on anyone expressing contempt for the government of Nebuchadnezzar, however mild or good-humoured it might be. Now they were having to draft the law with all its clauses, and the senior legal adviser was doing his best to tone down the more stringent provisions. What was needed was an agreed and precise legal definition of "contempt".

Azariah described his work in the buildings inspectorate of the palatial complex, and the difficulty of finding enough assistants, or rather skilled artisans, for the work that needed doing. And since Babylon was not richly endowed with building labourers of the calibre required, he had suggested to his minister that skilled workers should be brought in from Judah. It seemed his suggestion had been accepted, and a convoy would soon be on its way, to recruit the Jewish artisans who were so sorely needed.

Hananiah was the assistant to the King's senior adviser on educational matters, and the work in that office was most agreeable to him. An edict was soon to be issued in the name of the King, according to which every child of the common people who proved adept and knowledgeable, would receive a full education at the King's expense. Preliminary surveys had shown that at least one out of every hundred plebeian children would benefit from this scheme, being educated free of charge by the best teachers in the land.

Later he returned to his own room, dismissed the slave who was preparing to serve his supper, turned to face Jerusalem, put his hands together and said softly:

"O my father in Heaven, my God, shining in the hearts of all men, bringer of peace, joy, truth and freedom, You are the one and the only true God, God the all-powerful, whose name is love!

"You are the God of the humble and the upright, the brave and the pure, the undaunted, and anyone who is born of You, who reaches out to You – overcomes the world!"

He rose to his feet, undressed slowly and climbed into his bed with a clear sense that the self within him had faded away into nothing, and all that was left was that perfect happiness, that the language of humans cannot even begin to describe.

THE TANNERIES ON THE EUPHRATES

On the anniversary of the repeal of the stern edict imposed on that remote region, in the matter of the rice levy, the office of the King's senior adviser, Nashdernach, was visited by a delegation representing the region. After the repeated bows and salutations, the delegation presented to the minister and his office clerks a gift of choice swine-meat, smoked in the traditional manner of that locality, and reels of coloured fabric of the finest quality.

Nashdernach was moved and he warmly thanked the members of the delegation, extolling for their benefit King Nebuchadnezzar the wise, the merciful and the valiant, conqueror of the world, and he expressed the emphatic hope that the people of this province not only would not disappoint His Majesty in any way, but would continue to demonstrate with signs and tokens their loyalty to him, and their appreciation of his beneficence and his generosity, this King who had dealt with them as a wise and loving father deals with his children.

The members of the delegation, twelve in number, were also moved, assuring Nashdernach there had been no need to raise the points that he had raised, and as proof of this they revealed to him that they themselves, of their own free will, and with a deep sense of gratitude that would never be erased from their hearts or the hearts of their children after them, had decided to do everything in their power to exceed the quota of rice imposed upon them, and also to treat the rice with special methods handed down among them since time immemorial, thus producing the finest-tasting rice to be found anywhere in the world, normally set aside for themselves and for their families.

Nashdernach entertained the twelve members of the delegation to superior wine from the royal cellars and wafers dipped in honey from the royal hives, and sent them on their way gratified and in good spirits.

The delegation left the office, and Nashdernach rubbed his hands together with emphatic satisfaction and a broad smile, approached him and said:

"I think we'll carry on believing in Him!"

He looked up at his superior, who was leaning towards him, awaiting his response. He said to him earnestly:

"There is another place where reliance on God and trust in Him would bear fruit worthy of the name!"

"What are you talking about?" Nashdernach pulled up a chair and sat facing him.

"The tanneries on the river Euphrates."

"Ah!" the minister retorted: "That business was brought to my attention not long ago, when we debated it in the general council. The feeling is that there's nothing to be gained by maintaining that plant and its idle work-force... oh yes, they are idle!" he insisted, noticing the spark of protest that flashed in his eyes: "The poor level of production doesn't justify the expense. Someone suggested those barefooted workers should be sent deep under ground, to the copper-mines, and given the opportunity to show how industrious they can be. We didn't discuss it at length, as there were more pressing and complicated issues to address, but the decision was taken to import hides from overseas. It seems that importation is preferable from every point of view, as the imported hides are much cheaper and of better quality. The decision hasn't yet been taken to the King for his assent, but we can assume it's going to be ratified soon. It's what the situation demands, the reality we have to face up to!" he declared, and was about to rise from his seat.

"If the esteemed minister will permit me!" he exclaimed, holding out a restraining hand and the other replied:

"Oh, why the formal manners, as alien to you as they are to me – call me Nashdernach! I'm perfectly capable of preserving my dignity even when I'm addressed by name!"

"You're right," he smiled and added: "I have a suggestion regarding this question of the tanners on the Euphrates."

"You're suggesting we trust in Him?" he asked, a faint smile extending his fleshy lips and flickering in his oily eyes.

"That's the first step," he declared in all seriousness and continued: "It seems to me it should be possible to increase levels of production and attain acceptable quotas in terms of time, price and quality, and then importation from abroad would be superfluous, no longer an option."

"How will you do that?" – Nashdernach expressed interest, settling back in his chair.

"Conditions need to be changed, meaning – conditions of accommodation and conditions of work!" he replied, adding: "After two months, I estimate, the tanners on the Euphrates will be producing hides in the quantity required and of the quality required – and more.

Nashdernach studied him with a probing look, and came to a

decision:

"You have two months!" He rose from his seat, approached one of his clerks and dictated a brief memorandum which he signed with the stylus that the clerk offered him, then returned to him, took from his finger a big ring bearing the King's seal, laid it on the table and said:

"This will be of use to you during these two months! The one who wears this ring is acting on behalf of the King, and every citizen of Babylon, soldier or civilian, must defer to him as if to the King himself and do everything to assist him in the performance of his task."

"I shall need a few armed men for an escort."

"Take a troop of twenty, commanded by..." Nashdernach pondered, and he suggested: "Or-Nego?"

"Or-Nego has more important things to do, but if he is free and agrees to go with you – you have my consent and approval. Don't forget – two months starting from today!"

Or-Nego agreed readily and personally chose the twenty soldiers who would accompany them. Two days later the deputation set out for the journey to the Euphrates, with Or-Nego in the lead.

A morning of searing heat descended on the land, while a boisterous breeze from the East dried the air and made breathing difficult. The horses whinnied, the soldiers were grim-faced and taciturn. At the Gate of Marduk they were stopped by sentries, but showing the ring bearing the King's seal was enough to have the gates opened, and men of the guard detachment stood to attention on either side of the door, their spears raised in salute. The same procedure was followed at the Shamash Gate, the fortified aperture in the outer wall. And here the Euphrates was revealed to them in all its glory: turbid, angry waves trying in vain to defy the ruthless onslaught of the east wind – waters heavier and more menacing than those of any other river in the world.

And perhaps – he mused inwardly, confronting the strange spectacle of the river – it isn't always like this, the ancient river, the Euphrates. Perhaps it's a mood that is turning it ugly, the east wind is provoking it and it's powerless to retaliate – as if it were human...

They advanced in a narrow file on a narrow path, paved with stones dredged from the river. At a steady canter they covered a distance of four or five Chaldean parasangs, until they reached the foot of an arid hill, topped by a long, low ridge. Stepping lightly the horses climbed the slope of the hill and stopped on the skyline. Stretched out before them was the tanners' camp of the Euphrates.

At the moment they arrived on the ridge, a half-naked, fleshy overseer, with a long thick whip made from a buffalo's tail, was lashing a strange creature which at best could be described as a walking skeleton, and a lean skeleton at that – hunched and naked, with bones protruding through the transparent embroidery of the skin that was filthy and covered with sores; skull, ribcage and pelvis all clearly visible. The blow from the whip set the skeleton reeling, and it fell to the ground and lay still. The overseer raised the whip, poised to strike again at the body recumbent in the sand.

"Stop!" he shouted in a voice that cut the air, sharper and perhaps more painful than the brandished whip.

The overseer froze where he stood and cautiously turned his shaved head, set on a short, thick neck, towards the ridge.

The arm raised in an unequivocal gesture, the line of silent, armed soldiers – spoke for themselves. The overseer's hand fell limply to his side, denied the pleasure of further assault on his skeletal victim, who seized the opportunity to crawl like an insect out of the range of the whip, making his escape on four legs and then on two, tottering like a drunkard.

Accompanied by Or-Nego, the soldiers following behind, he cautiously descended the hill. The overseer stood his ground, in sullen silence.

He ordered one of the soldiers to confiscate the overseer's whip. He handed it over sheepishly, all his confidence destroyed, and stooped, as if waiting for a blow that did not come.

"Call the commander of the camp!" he bellowed in the ear of the flustered flogger, who disappeared into a maze of flimsy hovels – little more than booths made of reed-thatch, supported by poles of rough, unplaned wood.

As far as the eye could see the shore was littered with these hovels, like tilting mushrooms in the forest, and beneath them, as Gershon had described, scraps of straw matting were visible. At the riverside itself, in long lines of at least fifty to a line, were the naked tanners, scraping the hides spread out on the water, working listlessly, as if liable to fall down and die at any moment.

He had counted some thirty such lines, when a tall, corpulent man appeared before him, wearing the faded cloak of a soldier and carrying a curved sword in a shining brass scabbard. He was accompanied by a half-naked, stout individual in a grubby loincloth, with a ring of coarse gold hanging from one ear. His face was so flabby that his eye-sockets were reduced to narrow slits. The man seemed unruffled and confident in himself, but it was possible to detect behind the narrow slits an alert and inquisitive look. He held another of those lethal whips made from buffalo tails.

"By what authority?" – the man with the sword chose to open the proceedings in a tone of indignation and menace.

"By authority of the King and on his behalf!" he declared, holding out his hand and displaying the ring.

"Oh!" – suddenly the man with the sword was all reverence: "All praise to His Majesty King Nebuchadnezzar, the valiant and the wise, conqueror of the world!" he cried in a fulsome, deliberate tone, and bowed ostentatiously, his overseer accomplice following suit.

"How can I be of assistance?" the camp commander inquired.

"You'll find out soon enough," he answered him. "Is there somewhere where we can talk?"

"Please be so good as to accompany me!" – the man with the sword repeated his obsequious bow and turned in the direction from which he had come, adding: "Distinguished guests from the Palace! An honourable visit such as this I haven't enjoyed since I was sent to this place, eighteen long, hard years! I'm used to getting petty officials, in a hurry. *Load up the hides!* or – *Is this all there is?* Or – *This isn't enough to pay for the beans that you eat!* And then it's – *If you don't meet acceptable targets this plant will be closed and the workers will all be sent underground to dig for copper. And you will have to face the King and invent good excuses for your failure!* That's it, year in, year out. The same words, the same haste, the same sacks of beans in exchange for treated hides, the same loads of fresh hides brought in for treatment. It's just the people who change. You know how it is – the ones who stay close to His Majesty the King, the valiant and the wise, conqueror of the world, climb the ladder of promotion, whereas with people like us," – he raised his arm in a gesture of sorrow and resentment – "it's a case of out-of-sight and out-of-mind!" Animal cunning, thinly veiled scorn, indignation and obsequiousness were blended in the voice of the chief officer of the tanners' camp.

Still on horseback they arrived at a large, tent-like pavilion, made of coarse cloth designed to repel the heat. Two of the camp attendants hastened to draw back the door-flaps, bowing low as they invited the guests to enter.

With an agile leap he dismounted from Orelian and handed the reins to one of the soldiers. Or-Nego did likewise and both of them went into the tent, leaving the soldiers to wait outside. Their hosts followed them, closing the door-flaps for the sake of privacy. The space enclosed within the tent was extensive indeed, crammed with tiny tables, a few chests, and stools and chairs of every conceivable description. In a corner, partly shielded by a thick curtain which had once been white, a bed was visible. Somehow, most of the stench of the camp had been excluded from this place, leaving behind only the mildest irritation to the nostrils.

A table was placed at their disposal and high-backed chairs, the most dignified ones that their obsequious hosts could find. They sat on one side of the table and the camp representatives on the other. Silence reigned in the shady interior of the tent.

The overseer's narrow eye-slits flashed with naïve curiosity. The mottled eyes of the tall and corpulent one with the faded military cloak twitched restlessly in their sockets, contemptuous perhaps, or arrogant, or simply trying to disguise the fear that had overwhelmed them.

"The King is far from satisfied with the standards of work and the goods produced in this place!" he began in a steady, even voice. "So, there are going to be changes in patterns of work and in methods of supervision, and in the duties of overseers and their superiors. It is all written down here, and signed personally by Nashdernach, senior counsellor to Nebuchadnezzar, the wise and the valiant King, conqueror of the world!"

He took a scroll from the inner pocket of his cloak and handed it to the camp commander. The latter squinted at it, in blank incomprehension. He realised that the man could not read, and neither could the overseer sitting beside him.

"I shall read the scroll to you!" he said, and he untied the ribbon, opened the scroll, and began to read:

"From this day forward the following arrangements are to be implemented in the tanners' camp by the river Euphrates:

"First clause – the labourers are to work from daybreak until midday. At midday, they will return to their quarters and eat a nutritious meal to include, besides lentils, rice or beans – also eggs, olives and such other vegetables as are available.

"Second – after this meal the labourers are to rest in their quarters for one hour, after which they are to work until sunset, and no later.

"Third – at the conclusion of their day's work, the tanners will receive a second meal, to consist of bread, onion and cheese, figs and dates.

"Fourth – in their free time the tanners will build themselves substantial huts, using proper construction materials, each of these units to accommodate two to four workers, and no more.

"Fifth – each tanner is entitle to receive two shirts, one cloak and two pairs of shoes per year, plus six loincloths.

"Sixth – the overseers are not to beat or lash the workers under any circumstances and for any reason. From this day forward, all whips belonging to the overseers are to be confiscated.

"Seventh – on the first day of every month, tanners, guards and overseers alike will receive payment from the royal treasury.

"And the final clause – any deviation from the provisions set out in this document, however slight, will be construed as an insult to His Majesty the King. A serious infringement will be regarded as treason."

He read through the document a second time and reminded his hosts that two further copies of it existed – one in the royal archive and one in the minister's office. He demanded to hear them repeat the full text of the scroll, sentence by sentence and clause by clause, then handed the scroll to the man with the sword, rose from his seat and commanded:

"Confiscate all the whips and bring them here!"

"We hear and obey," the two of them replied in unison, turning towards the door.

"You, wait a moment!" he called to the overseer with the slits for eyes.

"Sir?" he asked in a wheedling voice.

"Your whip!" – he pointed to the buffalo's tail wrapped around his arm. "On the table, now!"

"As you wish, Sir!" He left the whip on the table and turned to go.

"Do you think it's going to work?" Or-Nego asked, impressed and sceptical in equal measure.

"By His grace!" he answered him, with an upward glance.

Soon after this they left the tanners' camp behind their backs, every man of the escort troop carrying a dozen or so whips on the pommel of his saddle. Their hosts accompanied them to the slopes of the parched hill, where they bowed to them and prostrated themselves on the ground, and went on bowing and prostrating until they disappeared behind the ridge.

Or-Nego, his soldiers and he inhaled the fresh air with relief, as the stench faded away.

"My impression is that those scoundrels will hoodwink the workers and return to their evil ways," was Or-Nego's comment – "without whips admittedly, or perhaps that should be, without whips made from buffalo tails; and they won't give even a moment's thought to any kind of reform, to say nothing of the contents of the scroll, that they're supposed to have learned by heart!"

"Three days from now the first deliveries of food will arrive, consignments of nuts and almonds and eggs and fresh vegetables, and those consignments will remind them of our meeting and of the scroll that they have with them!"

"I think the consignments are more likely to inflame their primitive lust for profit," Or-Nego objected – "and they'll sell off the food and pocket the proceeds."

"We'll come back here in two weeks and see how the scheme has been implemented."

"That's the right idea," Or-Nego declared with the restrained enthusiasm that was his habitual tone – "we come back and check!"

They urged their horses on and quickly covered the ground. The hot wind had subsided. When they reached the gates the sentries did not delay them, but opened the gates as soon as they saw them approaching and stood to attention with spears raised in salute.

When they reached the forecourt of the royal palace, passing Or-Nego's spacious residence, the officer broke the silence, leaning towards him and saying:

"Adelain would be delighted if you would visit us!"

"Not this time, Or-Nego, begging her pardon and yours! I have much to do and Nashdernach is waiting for me."

Or-Nego was not offended by his refusal, and he appreciated this.

They parted company with an exchange of bows, agreeing to meet again two weeks hence for the return visit to the tanners' camp on the Euphrates.

If their first visit had astonished the supervisor of the camp and the overseer who was his acolyte, this time they were stunned into immobility, standing and gaping as the riders approached, like pillars of salt, or as if they had swallowed their tongues. The stench was as foul as ever, and the tanners were not noticeably more motivated than before, still standing in long silent lines in the turbid surf of the Euphrates, listlessly beating and scraping the hides. The overseers no longer brandished buffalo-tail whips, but used whatever implements came to hand – sticks, ropes or even stones with which they pelted their human targets, sometimes to encourage and sometimes as a release from boredom, a pleasurable pastime following the sumptuous meal that they had enjoyed at the expense of their workers.

There was no need for exchanges of words. The facts spoke for themselves. The man with the sword and his accomplice regained their wits and threw themselves down in the dust, even kissing the hooves of their horses, which whinnied and shied away from them. They wailed and wept, reeling off the names of wives and children and elderly parents who depended on them, and the supervisor ripped his faded cloak and beat his hairy chest and threw dust over his balding head, pulling out the whiskers of his greasy beard and howling incessantly. His assistant stripped stark naked and went on plastering himself with dust until he looked like a scarecrow.

They were both clapped into manacles and led to the tent where the previous encounter had taken place two weeks before.

Or-Nego and he took their places on the same high-backed chairs as before, the difference being that this time their interlocutors were grovelling tearfully at their feet. Two soldiers stood behind them, drawn swords in their hands.

He demanded that the guards of the camp and the overseers be summoned before him, and soon the tent was crowded with half-naked overseers and guards dressed in faded robes of indeterminate colour. He asked them if their superiors, the men now wallowing in the dust, had read them the King's edict, and the answers that he received were hesitant, mumbled and sometimes self-contradictory. Until one of the overseers came forward and said that their superiors had told them something about instructions from the King, and furthermore – there was among them a man who could read and write and he was asked to read them the contents of the scroll. His name was Harvud, and he was the scion of a distinguished family, fallen on hard times. He did as he was asked, reading the portentous words and even interpreting them for the benefit of the less educated among them. And then those two – and he pointed to the camp commander and his overseer acolyte – assaulted and abused Harvud and ripped the scroll to shreds, and threw the fragments on the ground and trampled them into the dust. And Harvud waited until the two of them had calmed down, and reminded them that according to the terms of the royal edict that they had just destroyed, they were guilty of treason and their lives were in danger. And they attacked him again and beat him with their fists, and not content with this they ordered that he be flogged. It was lucky for him that there was a shortage of whips in the camp, or he might not have survived the punishment.

"Where is this Harvud?" he wanted to know.

A lean young man, with flashing eyes and upright stance, wearing a faded but clean robe, stepped forward from among the group of guards and stood before him.

"You can read and write?" he asked him.

He nodded.

He handed him the copy of the scroll that he had brought with him and ordered him to read it aloud. In a ponderous but clearly audible voice he read out all the clauses one after the other and when he had finished, offered it back to him.

"Keep it!" he commanded, "And henceforward, you are to uphold it in the letter and in the spirit!" And in a solemn tone he added: "In the name of His Majesty the King I hereby appoint you the commanding officer of the camp of the tanners on the Euphrates!" From amid the massed ranks of the guards and the overseers a murmur of assent and deference was heard.

"And what's to become of us?" the former sword-bearer cried plaintively.

"You should lose your heads," he declared, the wailing of jackals accompanying his words – "for defying the King and disobeying his commandments! And yet – compassionate and merciful is His Majesty King Nebuchadnezzar, and since I have been appointed by the King's senior counsellor to do his will and judge in his name, I decree that you are to work as tanners for the remainder of your lives, and Harvud will supervise you and check the quality of your work, and if he has occasion to report the slightest infringement of the rules on your part, you will be led in chains before His Majesty and he will decide your fate!"

A nightmarish howl accompanied his last words, a kind of sound not easily identified as human, and evidently intended as an expression of gratitude for this show of leniency.

The supervisor's curved sword, in its brass scabbard, he handed over solemnly, before the eyes of the assembled company, to young Harvud, and there and then he had him swear faithful service to the King of Babylon and obedience to his laws and ordinances.

Once this oath had been sworn, they rose and left the camp.

About a month later, the first batch of hides worked by the tanners under the new dispensation was delivered, and it was more than satisfactory in both quantity and quality.

And when the day came, he accompanied Nashdernach and his three personal bodyguards on a further visit to the camp.

They arrived towards evening, when the tanners were sitting in rows on benches at tables, their faces bright and convivial. They were eating their second meal of the day, and all were wearing freshly laundered clothes. On seeing them they rose as one man to greet them, and even surprised them with an honorific anthem of their own composition, although it took three renditions for all the words to be deciphered:

There once was an angel who looked down on the earth, and he saw the suffering endured by the tanners on the river Euphrates. And the angel turned to the all-powerful God and told Him, weeping, my Lord and Father Almighty, God the all-powerful, I can no longer bear to look down on the earth at the dreadful plight of my brothers, human beings, the tanners by the Euphrates. Send me and I shall do all I can to ease their pain, expel those who beat and chastise them, bring their agony to an end and succour to their souls. The all-powerful God was pleased by the words of his angel, by his heart, a true heart of gold, and his generous spirit. And He sent him on his way with a blessing and dressed him in human form and called him Belteshazzar, and appointed him to serve King Nebuchadnezzar, His Majesty!

And the angel in human form did not delay, and he went to Nashdernach, chief counsellor to the King, to complain at the conditions of the tanners. And Nashdernach arose, and put on his finger the ring of authority, and sent him down to the river, to the tanners working there. And Belteshazzar, the angel in human form, went down to that dark and evil place, and summoned the guards and gathered the slavedrivers, and told them of the King's command – that they should no longer chastise his brothers, nor make their lives a misery, nor torment them with abuse and arduous labour – but should give them clothing, put food in their mouths and a roof over their heads, and payment in due time. And they tried to dupe him, swearing many an oath to obey his commandments but with other intentions. And the angel in human form knew neither rest nor sleep until he had completed his mission, returning to his human brothers, and casting in chains all those who had persecuted them, the tanners on the Euphrates, and he appointed a new chief, one with a human heart, and he turned their misery into joy and their pain into delight!

"They even mentioned me in their song!" Nashdernach declared, fighting back the tears – "Quite unjustly, of course…"

"With absolute justice!" he retorted, adding: "Without your consent, nothing could have been done!"

"Not my consent but His!" Nashdernach corrected him, with a reverent glance heavenwards, continuing in the same vein: "So, we shall go on trusting in Him!"

"At all times and forever!" he concluded.

"And what became of those two scoundrels, the former commander and his sidekick, the fat flogger?" Nashdernach asked Harvud, who accompanied them part of the way.

"They tried working in the kitchen at first, but they were dismissed from there on account of their laziness."

"Who dismissed them?" he asked with interest.

"The cooks themselves, who used to be their accomplices in thieving and embezzlement."

"And what are they doing now?"

"Beating the most rancid hides that we can find. Surprisingly, they're not making a bad job of it!" Harvud expressed his sincere bemusement.

"You'll make true tanners of them yet!" was Nashdernach's jovial comment.

ON FIGS AND NUTS

One of those glorious evenings, rare in Babylon but familiar in the homeland, when the sky is a regal cloak of velvet and the first stars are the jewels in the crowns of angels, chanting "All Hail" to the God above – one such evening the slave informed him that a gentleman named Denur-Shag was asking to see him.

When Denur-Shag entered the room he rose to meet him; the two of them shook hands warmly and exchanged affectionate slaps on the shoulder, looking into one another's eyes with undisguised pleasure.

The teacher's sparse beard, once blond, was flecked with threads of grey.

"Old age creeping on!" cried Denur-Shag with that lively, vigorous voice of his, seeing the look in the other's eyes.

"Among our people grey hair is not a sign of old age!" he commented mildly.

"What does it betoken then?" Denur-Shag asked with interest, sitting down on one side of the high, polished table, with its cloth embroidered in blue and silver stripes – an impressive combination.

"Wisdom!" he replied, taking his place on the other side of the table.

"One who is endowed with wisdom is endowed with it from birth!" declared Denur-Shag with dignity, leaning back as far as the chair would allow him. "It's a gift of God," he went on to say, "and it doesn't depend on beard or hair of any style or any colour!"

"All the same," he riposted, a smile rising to his face when he spotted a few oil-stains on the teacher's cloak, too big for him as usual – "as one grows older, so wisdom ripens and bears fruit!"

"Always assuming," Denur-Shag persisted – "that one was endowed with wisdom from birth in the first place!"

He made no further comment, and no attempt to challenge his guest's conviction.

It was then that the slave came in with a tray of inlaid silver bearing dried figs, almonds and nuts, a jug of honey-water and two clay cups.

"Is this your supper?" Denur-Shag asked curiously.

He nodded.

"An interesting meal, to be sure!" exclaimed Denur-Shag. "In content and in intention!" he added, and proceeded to explain: "The meal is modest but not frugal, nourishing but not fattening, mild but not bland!

It is very possible, esteemed master, assistant and right-hand man of the King's chief counsellor as you are – that I have things to learn from you, especially where suppers are concerned, and I shall be your most avid disciple!"

"If there's no other subject that will make you my disciple..." he began playfully, but Denur-Shag interrupted him:

"There is!" he cried eagerly, with all the enthusiasm of a pupil who has just chanced upon the right answer to a question and cannot wait to reveal it to the teacher.

"And that is?"

"Faith!" exclaimed Denur-Shag, bringing his tiny, round fist down with a resounding thump on the elegant table-cloth, as if stating an incontrovertible fact.

"Faith is the gift of God," he declared earnestly, concluding: "And faith is the mother of all wisdom!"

"And have you received this gift?" – Denur-Shag's eyes flashed.

"It's a gift that is offered to every human being, and it's up to him to decide whether to accept it or spurn it."

"I assume that *you* have accepted it!"

"By the grace and the mercy of God!" he asserted, in a voice blending reverence and joyous freedom.

Denur-Shag took a shelled nut, put it to his mouth, added half a fig and while chewing, slowly and deliberately, closed his eyes with an air of contentment and remarked:

"The nut and the almond and the fig – they also originated from the Garden of Eden!" As there was no response to this he cleared his throat, held his mighty head high, shifted restlessly in his seat and finally broached the issue that was the real purpose of his visit:

"As you know, there are laws that are written and laws that are unwritten, and both kinds are of equal force, imposing obligations, usually heavy ones, on mortal creatures, while threatening penalties for those who infringe or fail to uphold these laws, whether written or unwritten."

Again Denur-Shag took a large almond, fresh and appetising, wrapped it in half a fig before putting it in his mouth, as if this were some superstitious ritual, chewing with the same deliberation as before, closing his eyes again and adding a hedonistic smacking of the lips.

He waited for the teacher to continue, unsure where all this was leading.

Denur-Shag swallowed his mouthful, and resumed:

"Remember that the glorious kingdom of Babylon does not look kindly upon celibacy, and by remaining a bachelor you are refusing to contribute in any way to the increase and the prosperity of the population. This is a law that is not to be infringed, and there are penalties attached to it..." Denur-Shag chuckled pleasantly, adding: "This is a law that applies especially to those holding any kind of public office!"

"I haven't been approached about this yet."

"You will be!" Denur-Shag assured him, "And then you'll be in something of a predicament. You'll be made a generous offer that you simply can't refuse."

"Things don't seem to be as serious as all that!" he declared.

"I don't know what yardstick you use to judge the seriousness of things," Denur-Shag retorted, "but what I've just told you is what is going to happen, and is bound to happen – and happen soon!" And seeing the questioning look in his eyes he explained: "If you don't take the initiative yourself, it will be taken by your friends or those who consider themselves your friends. And you'll get a proposal that you can't reject and you can't ignore."

"I've already turned down one such proposal and I refused to discuss it, but in such a way as to leave no hard feelings behind."

"I can well believe it!" Denur-Shag concurred, adding: "But the next offer that you receive – and it's coming soon – is one that you can't afford to refuse or reject under any circumstances whatsoever."

"And who is the man whose offer, whatever it may be, I can't refuse or reject?" he demanded to know, sounding almost indignant.

"His Majesty the King!"

He weighed these words, astounded to the roots of his soul, and finally responded:

"Are my personal affairs discussed at such a high level?"

"In a tightly regulated state, like Babylon, citizens have no privacy and no personal affairs. The citizens of the kingdom of Babylon are loyal to their King and seek his approval, and they worship and revere him above any god or image of a god, and they hide nothing from him. In fact, they consider themselves honoured to keep no secrets from him. At any rate, that's the theory, and it explains why the citizens of Babylon are the most smug people on the earth! And if it is ever revealed that any subject, through negligence or forgetfulness, to say nothing of malice, has concealed any detail of his private life, this will arouse the justified anger of the King, and his fate will not be a good one, not by any means"

Changing the subject abruptly he asked:

"Aren't you going to join me in this agreeable meal?"

"I'm accustomed to praying before I eat."

"Go ahead then!" the balding, middle-aged man urged him genially.

"May the food that comes from Your hand sustain our hearts and purify us on our way to You! Amen and Amen!" – and immediately after the blessing he took a nut from the tray, wrapped it in half a fig and put it into his mouth, chewing steadily.

"You've been named as a candidate for several marriages," Denur-Shag went on to say. "The charming daughter of one of the King's senior officers has been mentioned, but if that idea doesn't appeal to you for reasons best known to yourself, then you will be offered one of thirty-seven beautiful princesses, daughters of the King himself, and whichever she is you cannot reject her without causing offence to her father, the King. You know perfectly well that such a refusal would be seen as a crude and premeditated insult to the honour of the Crown, and you know the penalty for that..." Denur-Shag drew his finger across his throat, a meaningful gesture.

"How can it be?" – he expressed his sincere bemusement – "How is it that so much priority is being given to such a peripheral, essentially pointless issue, as my future wedding?"

"In the royal palace, there is endless, unremitting activity," Denur-Shag sighed as he split the kernel of a walnut into two equal parts, with intense concentration. "A living, vibrant body is the palace of His Majesty King Nebuchadnezzar, and his courtiers never sleep, never take a moment's rest. They are pushing forward the affairs of state, and advancing their own interests and the interests of others, in the best possible way of course, according to their acute perceptions and clarity of thought. It may well be that somebody is anxious on your behalf, concerned at your bachelor status and afraid lest you fall into the embrace of the wrong woman, and is preparing for you, secretly and in a spirit of true friendship and fellowship worthy of the name – your future bride. Something which you would never regret, and which you might even find impossible to regret, and most important of all, as has already been made clear to you – something which you cannot under any circumstances reject or refuse. But if you have other ideas," Denur-Shag reverted to his equable tone of voice, assessing him with a quick glance and then turning away before continuing: "Move quickly and establish facts on the ground, anticipate, put the remedy in place before trouble strikes! And as far as my knowledge extends, and if my memory is not misleading me," the guest looked up and glanced at his host with an air of innocence – "this expression 'putting the remedy before the trouble' is a good old-fashioned Hebrew phrase, or I should say, it isn't a part of the new, 'progressive' language, or 'Jewish Hebrew' as it is currently called."

A warm glow filled his heart. He gazed at Denur-Shag, who had gone back to the choice nuts and the almonds and the figs, the lines of his face tensed as he studiously ignored his radiant look, expressing warmth, friendship and gratitude.

"It happens occasionally that someone has the opportunity to act as an envoy of Providence!" commented Denur-Shag, uncomfortable with the tide of gratitude flowing in his direction.

"Not everyone is endowed with that special grace, to be the redeeming envoy of Providence!" he retorted.

"You can be sure that these special people aren't balding teachers, who have to deal with artisans of all descriptions as well as ignorant dolts!" said Denur-Shag evasively, returning his attention to the almonds and nuts. He carefully poured himself a cup of honey-water, and drank it all down in one long gulp.

"These people are called true friends, and they are sometimes rated more highly than the ministering angels themselves!"

"Such concepts apply only to people of truly outstanding faith!" Denur-Shag protested, "And I can't claim the honour or the privilege of counting myself among them!"

"Not everyone who calls himself a believer is a believer, and not everyone who excludes himself from the category of believers is lacking in faith."

"Who then is the true believer?" Denur-Shag asked with genuine interest, the look in his eyes pure and childlike – and childishly innocent.

"He who loves God with all his heart and all his might, and his neighbour – as himself!"

"Just as I feared! Such people are prodigies!"

"They never see themselves as prodigies!"

"They truly don't see themselves as prodigies, or are they just pretending they don't see themselves that way?"

"They really and truly don't see themselves that way!" he insisted.

"In that case..." Denur-Shag hesitated "...in that case I suppose I could apply for membership of that unexceptional family of believers.

And by the way, if you're interested in Judah, where things appear to be going from bad to worse and nothing is as it should be – your fellow exile, whose Chaldean name is Abed-Nego and whose Hebrew name is Azariah, is putting together some kind of expedition, heading for Jerusalem to recruit skilled craftsmen. He has been given the necessary permits, and I advise you to talk to him at the first opportunity!"

He was distressed to hear of the state of affairs in his homeland – "going from bad to worse", evidently, and "nothing as it should be".

"The surprising thing," the guest remarked as if reading his thoughts, "is that a land such as your homeland, where one would suppose there are many people of faith, which appears from outside to be a place reserved exclusively for people of outstanding faith – is on the verge of catastrophe, and there is nothing anyone can do to prevent that catastrophe!"

"As I told you, not everyone who seems to be a believer or is called a believer or calls himself a believer – is a believer. People lie to themselves, and degeneracy sets in, and collapse is not far behind, with destruction closing the circle. Our great prophet, Isaiah, described it thus:

Then the Lord said: Because the women of Zion hold themselves high and walk with necks outstretched and wanton glances, moving with mincing gait and jingling feet, the Lord will give the women of Zion bald heads, the Lord will strip the hair from their foreheads. In that day the Lord will take away all finery: anklets, discs, crescents, pendants, bangles, coronets, head-bands, armlets, necklaces, lockets, charms, signets, nose-rings, fine dresses, mantles, cloaks, flounced skirts, scarves of gauze, kerchiefs of linen, turbans and flowing veils. So instead of perfume you shall have the stench of decay, and a rope in place of a girdle, baldness instead of hair elegantly coiled, a loin-cloth of sacking instead of a mantle, and burning instead of beauty, and your men shall fall by the sword and your warriors in battle."

Denur-Shag listened solemnly. When the recitation was over, he had his say:

"These words of the holy man of God – a vivid description of a state of affairs that leads always to failure and destruction! If your people had only the sense to grasp this, like that people that once dwelt in Nineveh, that put on sackcloth and ashes and the Lord revoked the doom that He had called down upon it– these disasters would not have befallen it. The same applies to all nations on the face of the earth, at all times and in all places, from time immemorial to the end of all the generations – those who cannot stop themselves in time, will be forever lost!" Denur-Shag declared, his brow wrinkled and sorrow in his eyes.

"The truth is always simple, and he who does not try to flee from it and does not reject it out of hand – no disaster in the world can befall him! And the contrary applies – he who ignores the explicit truth, his doom is sealed! As the doom of your people has been sealed in our times, and as the doom of the Chaldean people shall be sealed, likewise the doom of every other people and nation and race – if in the days to come they try to ignore the truth!"

"You are a prophet!" he exclaimed with warmth.

"Perish the thought, Beltezhazzar!" Denur-Shag protested, lifting up both hands before him as if to defend himself. "I am no prophet nor the son of a prophet, just a man endowed with a modicum of healthy intelligence!"

He rose from his seat, stretching his limbs.

"We have babbled on too long!" he sighed, gathering up the tails of his tattered gown, "And perhaps we have steered in directions that were not the most appropriate, or should I say – not the most practical. Still, we have not committed any sin, perpetrated any dastardly crime, broken any law, written or unwritten – nor have we neglected the issues of the day!" He raised his arm and held up a finger as a warning signal, then lowered his arm and spoke again as if simply making casual conversation:

"There is a certain energetic and exceedingly resourceful trader, who is doing great and wonderful things in the service of the King. One of the exiles of course – Chaldeans have never been renowned for their commercial acumen, only for what they call 'valour' – which translates as slavish devotion to instinctive violence. This exile, who is of the same age as you and arrived with you in Babylon and so it seems, is also a former pupil of mine, has access to every corner of the palace of King Nebuchadnezzar, His Majesty, the valiant and the wise. And he knows how to whisper, he's a master of the whispering art, as you might put it in your new-fangled style of Hebrew, but there's nothing entertaining, no novelty or fascination in the gossip that he peddles. It is highly probable that all this urgency to push you up the ladder of Chaldean propriety, to draw attention to your prolonged celibacy, and even to choose for you a well-connected bride, a Chaldean through and through – all this originates from the whispering of that trader. And you," he turned to him as if remembering the essence and dispensing with the inconsequential – "be well, my pupil hitherto, my master and my teacher henceforward!"

With a smooth, yet imperious movement, Denur-Shag raised a silencing finger to his pursed lips, and he restrained himself and did not respond. They repeated their exchange of firm handshakes and cordial shoulder-slapping, and the slave escorted the guest to the main door and saw him on his way.

BETWEEN THE WALLS

He asked after Azariah at his lodging. A servant told him he had gone to visit the parents of his betrothed, Havatzelet, of the family of Joseph Hannagid, who lived in one of the houses between the walls, beneath the carved lion, the last one on the north-eastern wall.

He left the residential apartments and before setting out in the direction of this house, sent word to Nashdernach that he expected to be absent from the palace for the rest of the day.

The climate was pleasant, with the sun tending westward and a light breeze blowing. He was in no hurry, and was glad to inhale the fresh air of the open spaces.

His time was divided, usually, between sitting in the office of the King's chief adviser and his quarters in the vicinity of that office. Sometimes he also dealt with official business in his home, and sometimes – until a late hour of the night. Because of his seclusion from the sun, involuntary seclusion as it was, and prolonged confinement within enclosed spaces, his cheeks were turning pale. Noting this, Nashdernach used to urge him to leave the office for recreation, despite the pressure of work, and if only for a short time, to mingle with people and breathe the outside air. "Conversation with simple folk," Nashdernach was fond of saying, "is a thousand times more refreshing and instructive than all the dry scrolls and tablets that are gathering dust in the royal library!" It was true, he often spent his few free moments in that library.

The open air cheered his spirits and he strode the broad royal highway at a brisk pace, skipping occasionally and feeling that his feet would gladly have sprouted wings and carried him far away, somewhere over the horizon, towards that bright iridescence, into the very enchanted heart of the light.

The road stretched the full length of the north-western wall and it was straight, gleaming, and teeming with people in a hurry, with horses and carts, with cattle and oxen uttering their restrained, resigned lowing, white foam dripping from their mouths. At the side of the road he caught sight of a man with grey hair and beard, staring blankly at a cart of which one of the two wheels had come off the axle and rolled away into the dust, while the she-ass was sprawled on the ground and the load, sacks of carobs for cattle-fodder, remained on the cart. The man stood beside the stricken vehicle, baffled and helpless.

He hurried towards him, bent down and tried to lift the cart and free the she-ass from the yoke. And then he realised just how heavy the cart was, realised too that the animal was showing no inclination towards moving, and all this time the owner of the cart was standing aside, staring at him in bemusement, as if he had lost all his senses. A crowd began to gather around, composed mainly of women, old folk and children, as most of the men were working at this time in the fields and the factories, and all of those present looked on with astonishment, clicking tongues and offering advice, and pointing out what had caused the cart to capsize – a paving-stone that had not been bedded in properly with the others; the carter should have paid more attention and steered his beast away from the obstacle, instead of bringing down all this trouble on his greying and balding head.

When he asked one of the youths to come forward and hold the shaft for him, and addressed the same request to an older man standing amid the spectators, both backed away hastily and disappeared into the crowd.

Again he gripped the shaft, exerting all his strength, and suddenly the she-ass came back to life and rose to stand on her feet, pulling the cart up with her, and before it could collapse again he supported its weight and shouted to the carter to fetch the wheel that was lying at his feet. The old man was jolted out of his stupor and he picked up the wheel and fitted it on the axle, and with a joint effort they heaved it into place. Once the cart was standing upright on both its wheels, he found the peg that held the errant wheel and secured it, hammering it home with a stone.

The old man hugged and embraced him, and showered him with thanks and benedictions and compliments, and invited him to come to his house between the walls, to be a guest beneath his roof and dine with him and his family.

He freed himself from the old man's grateful embrace, reminded him mildly that "all praises are due to God", and was about to turn and disappear into the crowd, when his ear caught something in the old man's exuberant and barely coherent litany of thanks – the reference to a house "between the walls".

"Is that where you live, between the walls?" he asked.

"Yes indeed, most generous of masters!" the old man replied, gratified by this sympathetic display of interest. "And I shall be delighted, as will all the members of my family be delighted, if my lord will honour us with a visit and sit down to dine with us..."

"At all events," he said smiling as he brushed dust from his cloak, "I shall accompany you to your house, and it may well be that we dine together yet, as I am on my way to visit one of the families living between the walls, under the last of the lion carvings."

"That is the place!" cried the old man, his eyes sparkling. "It must be the will of God, that I met you on the way and I can guide you to those houses between the walls," – and he turned and asked him in a more practical tone: "And the family that my lord is visiting, what is the name?"

"Joseph Hannagid," he answered him.

"He is my brother!" exclaimed the old man, raising his arms and waving them as an expression of astonishment. "Is he expecting you?"

"Not at all," he answered him.

"So why do you need to see him?" the old man asked, sounding disappointed.

"A friend of mine, named Abed-Nego, is betrothed to your brother's daughter, Havatzelet."

"Aha!" the old man expressed pleasurable surprise, drumming his fingers on his temples. "A-ha!" he repeated with emphasis and went on to say, "In my homeland of Judah they say that a lucky man such as yourself must be a saint because... because..." – the old man racked his brains, trying to dredge up the proverb he wanted.

"The one he is going to, comes to meet him!" – he completed it for him.

The old man, about to urge on his she-ass, turned to him and gave him a long look. His eyes were bright, tending towards green, glassy. Finally he asked:

"Is my lord a Jew?"

"He is."

"One of those boys who came with the betrothed of my niece, Havatzelet?"

"One of those boys," he confirmed.

"And your clothes tell me that you hold a senior post in the court of the King of the Chaldeans!"

"I wouldn't call it a senior post," he answered him with a smile, and suddenly felt a strange pang of resentment, for no good reason that he could think of. "I work in the office of one of the ministers, that's all. Like Azariah!" he concluded as if talking to himself.

"Like Azariah!" the other repeated like an echo.

The she-ass waited patiently for her master to pay her some attention, and he did so eventually, gripping the halter and tugging at it roughly with a cry of "Let's go!"

"My name is Raphael," the old man introduced himself and went on to say: "Today I have earned the privilege of performing a sacred service, helping a righteous man to find his way. What is my lord's name?"

"Belteshazzar."

"The Jewish name, I mean!" he insisted drily.

"Daniel."

"I think I have heard of you, and of your activities. Activities which are strange indeed!" – the old man snorted and added: "Or so rumour has it..."

The old man lowered his head, with an air of gravity, tugged at the halter with an effort and without turning to look at him, spoke again:

"I have saved my esteemed lord much toil and travail. It isn't easy to find the way to our house between the walls. The Chaldeans ignore us and would prefer to forget that we exist. To them, we are strange creatures, and they miss no opportunity to report us to the authorities, over the most trivial of matters. And they are quick to investigate, arresting innocent people and dragging them through the courts, and they are not content with warnings or with lenient fines, as is the way of the world, but they demand gold shekels, and the Chaldean shekel," the old man explained, "is worth twelve gold shekels from Jerusalem. And all this – for some footling misdemeanour!"

"And what are the crimes that the Chaldeans accuse you of?" – he listened intently to the old man's words.

"From disrespect or contempt, as they call it, towards some pompous official or other – to sedition and incitement to rebellion. And this of course we vehemently deny, with all the force that we can muster, and still we are dragged from court to court, paying lavish bribes until the charges are dropped. For sedition and incitement to rebellion there is only one punishment – death!" the old man concluded.

"Why pay bribes, when it's all down to slander?" he asked innocently.

"My lord has the demeanour of a dignified gentleman, and he has a wise look about him, and even his high forehead tells of intelligence – and yet his question is naïve, if he will excuse my uncouth tongue," – and without waiting for a response, the old man continued: "Venomous tongues and bloodshed have always existed and will exist until the coming of the Lord's Anointed. Until then – we must pay bribes, if we don't want to give the Chaldeans the pleasure of chopping off the heads of pious Jews!"

"I do not share your opinion!" he retorted with a touch of asperity, meant to ensure that his words would be heard, and indeed – the old man paid close attention, listening tensely.

"You have to trust in God and turn to Him, and lay your entreaty before Him and cleave to Him firmly and believe in Him – then everything will be settled properly, and peaceably, without bribes and lies and deception!"

"You speak with great eloquence, Sir!" the balding old man required, a bitter kind of smile passing like a shadow over his tanned, deeply wrinkled features. "This God of ours, Himself and in person, neglected us and abandoned us on account of our iniquities, and hid His face from us, till the uncircumcised and the Gentile, who knew him not, triumphed over His holy people and did with it as they pleased!"

"He did not neglect us nor abandon us – it is we who neglected and abandoned Him, and did what was evil in His eyes, and closed our ears lest we hear the word of His holy prophets!"

"I see, esteemed Sir, that you know a great deal, but in my humble opinion, all of your knowledge is flawed, flawed fundamentally! We have to fight the pagan and the Gentile, we have to defend Jerusalem the Holy City, destroy the Chaldean conquerors and put them to the sword, subdue them and annihilate them, leave no memory or vestige of them! And if God is truly with us and we are, as He says, His chosen people – then let this God of ours stand at the head of our armies and rout our foes, and bring a swift end upon our enemies."

The two men exchanged glances. The old man's eyes flared and burned with dry fire, zealous and vengeful; his eyes shone with a light that was all invincible strength.

For a brief moment, the old man looked away, yanking at the halter of the she-ass with quite unnecessary force. The unfortunate creature uttered a whinny of helplessness, or of weariness, or of both.

A portion of the route passed by in silence, and suddenly the old man turned to face him and said:

"Now I remember who you are, esteemed Sir, and the illustrious deeds that you have performed! At first I couldn't believe what I was hearing – the very notion that a man of intelligence, with Judah for a homeland and Jerusalem for a home town, could do the things that you have done! I refused to believe. But now, having heard your voice and listened to your words, I believe it absolutely! Was it not you who took pity on the race of the tanners, most of whom are pagan Chaldeans and only a minority are exiles, and you treated them with kindness, and brought them from death to life, and gave them food to eat and clothes to wear, so they might flourish and prosper, the better to conquer and enslave other peoples, as they have done with us, the chosen people of God... And we have heard of your compassionate heart and how you reduced the quota of rice demanded in tribute from an impoverished region, and were it not for this reduction they would have rebelled against King Nebuchadnezzar and shaken his power, and this would have helped us, the Jews, in our struggle against the Chaldean conqueror! Is it not incredible," the old man cried, his voice hoarse and strained – "an intelligent Jewish youth, strengthening the hand of the Chaldeans against his own people? Do you realise esteemed Sir what this means, does my lord even know *who he is*?"

He restrained and suppressed his swelling rage, keeping his temper, and answered the old man quietly:

"One who trusts in God, and trusts absolutely!"

The old man's wrath was seething, beyond any control. He turned on him and it seemed he was about to attack him with his fists, but then he tripped on an irregular paving-stone, stumbled and fell headlong in the roadway.

He leaned over him and tried to help him up. The old man pushed away his outstretched hands, but finally, seeing he could not possibly stand up unaided, he allowed himself to be helped, with an expression of revulsion and distaste, and once back on his feet he said:

"You are a sorcerer Sir, a sorcerer and a prig and..." – the word stuck in his throat and would not emerge from his dry mouth.

The old man's glassy eyes were livid with disgust. He gave him a baleful look, and without another word spoken, he gripped the halter of his she-ass once more, leading her with surprising tenderness, and continued on his way.

He was left standing, waiting for the old man to move on and disappear from view, but he stopped the cart, turned back and said in a low voice:

"I very much hope that his honour will not disgrace me, but will come with me as was agreed between us, before I spoke out so foolishly. When all is said and done, a man of my age is apt to be foolish! Please show me a little tolerance, and forgive and have mercy, and do not add further grief to my grief!"

Without another word spoken, he joined him.

Towards evening, when the sun had disappeared but not yet withdrawn its light, they turned northwards from the internal gate of Marduk and stood before the tall outer wall, at its eastern end, and here he realised the old man had been right when he spoke of doing him a favour, since he would never have imagined that below the last of the reliefs there was an aperture almost invisible to the eye, low down but just wide enough to squeeze through, and from this point a short dust path led down to a dense cluster of low buildings made of rough stone, standing on the narrow patch of ground with an air of brooding defiance and proud alienation.

The old man led him to one of the narrow entrances to an extensive building and said to him:

"This is where my brother lives, the family of Joseph Hannagid, that you are seeking! And forgive me if I have offended or insulted you, but Judah my homeland and Jerusalem its capital are very dear to my heart!"

"They are dear to the heart of every Jew," he responded calmly.

"No two hearts are alike!" declared old Raphael and he disappeared behind the cluster of silent houses.

He knocked on the door. An attractive girl opened it and asked what he wanted.

"I'm looking for my friend, Azariah!"

"Oh!" – and with a gentle, graceful movement the girl held the door wide open and said:

"He's here, and I'm sure he'll be glad to see you!" It was both question and statement. "Who are you Sir, and how shall I announce you?"

"Daniel," he said.

She ushered him into a dingy hallway, asked him to wait for a moment, went inside the house and called: "Az-ar-iah!"

He heard his friend's cheerful voice:

"Here I am!"

The girl called out again:

"A distinguished gentleman, looks like a scholar, his name is Daniel... I asked him to wait for you in the lobby."

Before she had finished the sentence Azariah was there before him, holding out a warm and firm hand to shake his, then drawing him into a long, low room, lit by a broad window.

In the room sat a middle-aged man, his face lean and an intense look in his eyes, with an air of confidence about him, the confidence of one who is well aware of his own worth.

"This is Saul, my future father-in-law," Azariah introduced him.

They bowed to one another in the Chaldean fashion.

"And this is Daniel, my friend from childhood. His Chaldean name is Belteshazzar," Azariah concluded.

"*That* Belteshazzar?" asked the man, who was sitting on the end of a broad bench which also served as a bed, made of unplaned wood and still smelling faintly of pine, strewn with mats as a substitute for a mattress.

"That Belteshazzar!" Azariah confirmed with a sigh, and invited his friend into one of the several side-chambers opening off the main room.

He entered the little side-chamber with its narrow, curtained window and prevalent gentle gloom, and sat down on the one chair. Azariah sat on the bed, made of the same wood as the other but rather more comfortably upholstered, with straw mattress, blankets and thick embroidered quilts, warm and woolly.

At the end of the room he noticed a narrow table covered with a cloth, bright blue in colour with fringes embroidered in white.

"What brings you here?" asked Azariah.

"That delegation setting out for Judah – when is it due to leave?"

"The day after tomorrow."

"I have a favour to ask of you!"

"I shall be happy to do it!" – Azariah gave him a clear answer, from the heart, and he was glad of this and felt more at ease.

"I want to ask Nejeen to come down to Babylon and marry me. I have written a few words..." He drew a tiny scroll from the pocket of his cloak, tightly coiled and carefully wrapped.

"I'm asking you to approach the leader of the delegation and talk to him – if, that is, you trust him. By the way, do I know him?" he asked.

"I rather think you do," Azariah replied, wrinkling his brow into a frown of ironical concentration. "After all," he continued smoothly, "at this very moment you are handing over a scroll to the leader of the delegation in person, as large as life! As to whether he can be trusted or not – that's a tough question to answer!"

They fell into one another's arms and broke into peals of limpid laughter that was all purity and irresistible youthful energy.

"So you are the one who is going?" he asked, detaching himself from his friend's embrace, and gazing at him with deep affection.

"I am the one!" Azariah replied.

"So," he sighed with relief, "you can tell her about the situation here, and pass on my greetings to my mother and my sisters and the baby, who hasn't been a baby for some time now..."

"You can rely on the leader of the delegation to say what he has to say and pass on what he has to pass on! Incidentally – how did you find me here? To this very day I have difficulty myself finding that strange doorway leading to the space between the walls... You've met my fiancée – so what do you think of her?" he asked.

"I think she's delightful!" he declared, adding: "As to your other question, about finding that strange doorway giving access to the Jewish quarter, and the quarter itself is just as strange – I doubt I'd have found it at all if I hadn't been assisted by a benefactor, called Raphael..."

"Saul's brother!" cried Azariah.

"That's him. He was my guide."

Azariah grew serious and seemed to withdraw into himself. Then he looked up and asked:

"And he didn't recognise you, didn't raise all kinds of rumours that have been going around here, in this strange community as you have described it?"

"He most certainly did, and at length!" he declared, laughing. "These Jews are zealots, but not zealous for their God, rather for their hatred!"

"They are strange, but not lacking in courage."

"That which drives and spurs on the zealot is not courage but pride," he declared and concluded – "and it is a dangerous thing, for him and for those who surround him."

"They have strange ideas," Azariah commented, with some hesitation.

"They mean to rebel against the King of Babylon?"

"To incite to rebellion."

"Incite whom?"

"The King of Judah, of course!" Azariah replied, adding: "Except that, so it seems, he doesn't need any encouragement. One way or another – they are in close touch with the homeland and they know everything that is going on there, to the minutest detail."

"What of the prophet Jeremiah?" he asked with some anxiety.

"King Zedekiah is scheming against him, but not in the same way that Jehoiakim used to do it. On the one hand, he draws him close and on the other – he incites his ministers to persecute him and put him in chains. Zedekiah is a man of troubled mind, and it seems he realises his revolt will not succeed and he will have to answer before his God and yet, he is forever making plans. He summons the prophet Jeremiah secretly, asks to hear the will of God, and the prophet tells him, and he disregards it. He lacks strength of character, and in the end he will bring down disaster upon his people, upon himself and upon his household!"

"And the family of Joseph Hannagid – whose side are they on?" he asked.

"They're inclined to support the zealots."

"And you?" he asked.

"Sometimes – I can't help but admire their courage, even though there is no faith there and as you have said – arrogance and conceit are at the root of it. In the early days I tried to talk them round, and when I realised no one was listening, I took a vow of silence on all these matters. The others have done the same. Mishael's future in-laws, on the other hand, are siding with Jeremiah, and for this reason they have been told to leave their house. They are outcasts here, and ostracised by the majority," Azariah explained.

"And have you been asked to take messages to certain people in Jerusalem, and carry messages back?"

"I've been asked," Azariah replied, giving him a measured look and adding: "I refused."

"How was your refusal accepted?"

"They had no choice but to accept it. Anyway, the important thing is that Havatzelet is standing by me, and it seems she's looking forward to leaving her parents' house."

"When will you be married?"

"On my return from Judah. Mishael and Hananiah too. Three weddings in one and perhaps" – he suddenly remembered and asked – "will there be four?"

"Perhaps," he replied, and Azariah concluded:

"We have here among us the righteous scion of a priestly family, and he is the one who shall marry us."

Havatzelet served milk in clay pitchers and dishes of honey. They said their blessings, drank the milk and tasted the honey. He rose to take his leave.

"We'll go together," said Azariah. "This isn't an easy place to get out of!"

"If you'd rather stay here, I can find my own way."

"No, it's time to go. I shall say goodbye to my in-laws, prospective in-laws I should say, and then I'll be with you." True to his word, Azariah disappeared briefly and returned to him.

Havatzelet accompanied them to the door of the house, wishing them well and replying to their blessings. She watched Azariah go with eyes full of longing, and he turned back to bid her one more farewell, from faraway, with a raised hand. And then the two of them walked following the narrow dust track with its slight upward incline, suddenly finding themselves at the end of the outer wall, facing the gate of Marduk.

THE DELEGATION SETS OUT

The next day he reported to Nashdernach and asked to confer with him privately. Nashdernach gave him a keen look with his tiny eyes, as if trying to work out what was bothering him, and without further ado he ushered him into a side-office, telling the clerks that they were not to be disturbed.

Nashdernach took his seat at a broad and heavy and highly polished table, on one side of it a selection of styli and on the other – scrolls of parchment, some blank and others covered with the cuneiform letters of the Chaldean script.

"Won't you sit down?" – Nashdernach pointed to a roughly hewn wooden chair, unpadded but comfortable enough.

He sat, and there was a moment of silence.

"I hope," the King's senior adviser began in his nasal, sometimes abrasive voice, "you haven't found another far-flung province where the inhabitants are clamouring for a tax rebate – or have you heard a rumour that the blacksmiths are unhappy with their working conditions?" Nashdernach spoke with mock-seriousness, and while speaking he picked up one of the scrolls and glanced at the contents, before hurriedly rolling it up and putting it back in its place.

"Neither of those is the case," he replied calmly, in all earnestness.

Nashdernach raised a short and bushy eyebrow, in token of surprise and bemusement, and he was indeed curious to know what Belteshazzar, his clerk, was about to say.

"It is my intention to marry."

"Aha!" The expression on his superior's fleshy face softened, as a smile broadened his lips and twinkled in his oily little eyes. "A most welcome statement! And what is more – a timely one!" he said emphatically, and proceeded to explain: "In an audience that I had with His Majesty the King, there was talk of you. When the King mentions your name, it is as if a smile lights up his stern face, and that is an exceedingly rare thing! 'The victorious rider' he calls you, and 'that clever lad from Judah.' And he has expressed his complete satisfaction over the episode of the rice levy, and the story of the tanners on the Euphrates gave him so much pleasure he actually clicked his tongue as a sign of approval, and all are agreed that such a thing has never happened before, at any rate not since he was crowned, and ascended the throne of the glorious kings of Babylon. And he, as I say, asked about you, and was particularly keen to know whether you are married or a bachelor, whether you have any commitment in the matter of marriage. And I had no choice but to admit to His Majesty that I had no precise knowledge of this and I would prefer not to speculate, however close to the truth such speculation might be, and I undertook to give him a full answer by the end of the week, or by the end of the day if the matter was considered urgent. And the King reassured me, saying the matter was not urgent, but all the same he wanted to know the position and would be pleased to receive my answer within three days. He went on to say that he considered this a most unsatisfactory state of affairs – a court official and his chief adviser not knowing the marital status of one of his senior clerks. I offered His Majesty fulsome apologies and begged for his indulgence, and he was kind enough to grant it."

He bowed to Nashdernach, a gesture directed not so much towards him as towards the King; the chief adviser appreciated this, and nodded with an air of complete satisfaction.

"As I informed you just a moment ago," the younger man responded, choosing his words carefully and speaking with absolute candour, "I am committed to marriage. There is a girl living in Judah who is destined to be my wife."

"And you have waited until this moment to tell anyone about this commitment of yours, myself included?"

"I suppose so," he admitted, adding: "I didn't realise it was a matter of such importance. In any case, I have asked the man leading the delegation to Jerusalem to find my future bride and bring her back with him – assuming, of course, that she hasn't had a change of heart. And not long ago she sent me a gift..."

With a dismissive gesture Nashdernach prevented him completing the sentence.

"If the girl has had a change of heart," he retorted with some warmth, "you stand to gain more than you lose! The King of Babylon, in person, is said to be arranging the most illustrious of marriages for you! As for bringing this girl to Babylon," he added in a changed tone of voice, "that is definitely the right thing to do! Incidentally, can you show me the gift that you mentioned, if indeed you have it with you?"

"It is with me wherever I go!" he replied, and drew out from under his robe the seven-branched candlestick, hanging on a slender silver chain.

Nashdernach rose, rounded the table, took the pendant in his little hand, probed it and turned it over, put it down finally, returned to his seat and exclaimed:

"That's a national symbol! Admittedly, Babylon isn't in the business of humiliating the Jews, and it hasn't forbidden them to cling to the national symbols that nourish their pride, although sometimes it seems that the Jews misinterpret the tolerance of His Majesty's government! Our great King has dealt with them generously and with justice, and has demanded no tax that is beyond their means, nor put one of his sons on the throne of Judah, letting Zedekiah rule instead, that young and not very promising man who has been appointed by the laws of Judah to sit on that throne! And Nebuchadnezzar, His Majesty, King of Babylon, the valiant and the wise, required one thing only, that the young Jewish king swear allegiance to him. And Zedekiah swore him a threefold oath, by his God, by the sacred scriptures that are said to be your life-blood, and by holy Jerusalem. He swore willingly and now..."

"What now?" he asked, a crease of concern showing on his smooth, open forehead.

"As I said before, you have done well in seeking to bring your betrothed out of Judah at this time, in these days," Nashdernach continued, ignoring the interjection. "Furthermore, I'm absolutely convinced that she has not had a change of heart!"

"How have you come to that conclusion?" he wanted to know.

"The gift that she sent you, and the very fact that you carry it with you wherever you go. There exists between you a deep bond that will not easily be broken. No, it will not be broken!" he declared confidently. "The girl will come here and will be your wife, and there's every reason to expect she will make an exemplary wife, and you will have joy in her and she will have joy in you. And so that she will be brought to Babylon in the style befitting her – befitting you, in fact, as senior clerk to the chief of the King's advisers, I shall order that a special wagon be added to the convoy, luxuriously appointed in the manner suitable for ladies of noble birth. I assume she is of distinguished lineage, is she not?"

"She is," he answered him, reluctantly for some reason.

"How do you know her?" Nashdernach went on to ask, and he realised that his interlocutor was trying to fill in the gaps in his knowledge about him, and this on account of the King's reprimand.

He answered him willingly:

"Our families were closely acquainted. Her father, like my own revered father, served King Jehoiakim. My father was killed in battle, one standing against many," – he thought it worth pointing out – "and her father disappeared. No one knows what became of him."

Nashdernach was satisfied. He could tell that his senior assistant was doing his best to help him, filling in the gaps that had led to the reprimand, and he gave him a warm look of gratitude and appreciation.

"Don't forget," he reminded him, "to check that the wagon I just mentioned has been added to the convoy. I shall give the order today. What's her name?" he asked.

"Nejeen of the house of Gamliel," he answered him.

"Nejeen of the house of Gamliel!" he echoed, slowly and pensively, as he perused the little parchment scroll that had been filled during the course of the conversation with dense cuneiform symbols – letters forming words and words forming three short sentences, peremptory in tone and relating to the special "luxury" wagon that was to be sent with the delegation.

"A most agreeable name!" He looked up and scanned him with inquisitive eyes. "The damsel Nejeen of the house of Gamliel!" he repeated in a tone of pleasure and respect. "She adds a degree of urgency to the entire mission!"

"And what is the reason for this urgency, if I may ask?" he inquired earnestly, his voice sincere and imbued with a strength of purpose that could not be easily resisted.

In reply, Nashdernach told him that matters were complicated, and deeply worrying:

"Something strange is happening in Judah, your homeland! Zedekiah, the young king, who sits on his throne with the backing of the Chaldeans, and with the consent of their King, seems to be devoid of any intelligence or any of the qualities appropriate to a monarch. He associates himself with a coterie of young men who are... how to describe them... let me think for a moment... frivolous one might say, or 'vain and reckless' in the language of your Scriptures. And even if he himself is not vain and reckless, if we turn once more to the wisdom literature of the Hebrews and one of your most beautiful hymns: *Blessed is the man who does not take his seat among the scornful* – the meaning is that a man, even one who is not scornful himself, may be tempted to associate himself with the scornful, and thus lose his last opportunity to avoid falling into this sinful state..." Nashdernach tried to smile, without success, and added: "I'm sure you are familiar with the rest of this glorious psalm!"

He nodded, feeling his heart shrinking within him.

"And this King Zedekiah has been induced, or persuaded, against his better judgment – if indeed he has anything of the kind – to appoint worthless characters such as these to be his ministers and advisers. And here you have a fine example of the magnanimity of our King, His Majesty, and his generosity and tolerance. He does not interfere with the internal affairs of Judah. He is content with a small and symbolic tribute, and the choice of ministers and advisers he leaves in the hands of the King, who rules with his consent and has sworn him an oath of allegiance. So Zedekiah proceeds to make his appointments, invariably the wrong ones, while our King, His Majesty, looks on from the sidelines, showing great patience and waiting to see how things develop.

"And something else you should know, my lad," Nashdernach continued, suddenly adopting an affectionate mode of address; his voice was warm, and rising in his eyes was a kind of distant sadness, musings of the heart drawn up from the depths of the soul. "This King of ours, His Majesty, whom I so admire – is the most God-fearing man alive! He will not take a single step without consulting God. He is the total opposite of the boy, Zedekiah, who sits on the throne of the kingdom of Judah, which had a glorious past and roots running deep, and used to be ruled by men whose way was lit by the fear of God! And the voice of God addresses Zedekiah directly and explicitly, morning and evening, warning of the disaster that he is inviting upon his people and upon himself, and calling on him to abandon his perversities. And he, this boy, closes his ears and refuses to listen, as did his predecessor, Jehoiakim!"

"Where does it come from, the voice of God that addresses him directly and explicitly?" he asked in a wavering tone, knowing that Nashdernach spoke the truth. And Nashdernach answered him willingly and at once:

"From the lips of Jeremiah the prophet."

His head slumped. It was as if whips had struck him down. Nashdernach realised that he had touched a sensitive point, and was silent.

After a lengthy pause, the Chaldean spoke again:

"Better perhaps not to inquire too deeply!"

"Not at all!" He looked up at once, his voice steadier now. "I'm eager to know all the details, if indeed you have details to give me."

"Indeed I have," Nashdernach sighed and added: "As with every sensible government, Babylon too has eyes and ears in the lands it has conquered, and in those it is yet to conquer. It's a disreputable business but – a practical necessity!"

"This 'business' as you call it doesn't say much for the faith of those involved."

"You're absolutely right!" Nashdernach agreed with him, adding: "This is a secret service, doing its work, disagreeable work, in the best possible way. From the point of view of faith, even wars are forbidden. *Not by force and not by power, says your God, but by my spirit.* Do you agree?"

"In all respects!" he stressed.

"Except that in the case of Judah there is no need for these 'eyes' and 'ears' operating secretly," the other continued. "Everything is done there in the light of day, in public. Perhaps Zedekiah knows that in the end all will be known, and hiding it is just a waste of effort."

"What is he doing now?" he asked.

"Fishing for support."

"Fishing where?"

"In Egypt."

He lowered his head again. This recurrent error on the part of kings of Judah and Israel. Egypt – the "broken reed".

"And preparations for revolt?" he asked, wanting to know for how long Nejeen would be safe.

"In the early stages. Let us wait – and hope!" Nashdernach sighed again.

"And pray!" the other added, thoughtfully.

At the order of the King's chief adviser, a special wagon was added to the convoy setting out for Judah, well upholstered and designed to withstand the rigours of the journey, however long it might be.

Taking the advice of Nashdernach he came and inspected the wagon: inside and out, shafts, suspension, upholstery, canopy, wheels, axles. All was to his satisfaction.

"By the decree of Nashdernach, chief adviser to the King, the delegation is not to depart until Belteshazzar, his senior aide, has authorised it!" Azariah proclaimed with joyful enthusiasm and handed him the papyrus sheet for his signature.

He took a pen and signed in red ink, under the few words stating that the extra wagon had been checked and found fit for travel – his Jewish name in full and alongside it the Chaldean name that he was growing accustomed to, Belteshazzar.

"I shall keep this certificate!" cried Azariah with youthful ebullience.

"In my mind there isn't the shadow of a doubt that seeing this signature of yours will set her heart a-flutter and fill it with joy!"

The delegation set out on its way.

THE MAN WITH THE DAGGER

One Sabbath he met with Hananiah and Mishael.

"We are on our way to visit the Jewish community, down there between the walls, and if you feel like joining us – you'll be very welcome!" Mishael invited him.

"What we are really doing is visiting our fiancées and their families!" Hananiah explained with a gentle smile. Mishael added:

"From what we hear, it seems you too will soon be in need of the priestly services of that community, just like us! Anyway, it will do you no harm to become acquainted with these Jews, most of whom trace their ancestry from genealogical scrolls that they have in their possession; a few are of priestly or levitical descent, and there is also a family descended from the Tribe of Benjamin. And the Jews have strange stories to tell about themselves and their community."

"Such as, for example?" he asked with amused interest.

"Such as, for example," Mishael proceeded to elaborate, in an entirely earnest tone of voice, "the story that their forefathers settled in the place before the outer wall was built, and this was many generations ago, in the time of King Solomon, and they came here in obedience to his explicit decree, or so they claim, these strange Jews! And those genealogical scrolls of theirs leave no room for doubt."

"And why did King Solomon command their forefathers to leave their native land and their patrimony and abandon their homes, and pitch their tents in foreign parts?" he asked, still in jesting mood.

"They have an explanation for this," Hananiah interjected with a grim look on his face, "and they whisper it among themselves like a secret that must not under any circumstances reach 'Gentile ears' or the 'house of the Gentiles' – as they are fond of repeating. According to their account, a mission was entrusted to them – to be the vanguard of the army of the greatest of all the kings of Judah, and in their opinion – greatest of all kings of the universe, the wisest of all men. They were to settle in foreign lands and when the time came, go out to meet his army, coming to take Babylon by storm, Babylon the wicked city, as they call it, as is the will and the commandment of God, and to destroy the homes of sinners and set them ablaze and above all, to tear down utterly the 'temples of Moloch' – their name for all the deities of Babylon – and smash his abominable idols and obliterate the lascivious wall-paintings and prove before all the nations of the world their right to be called the true heirs of Abraham their father, who did the same thing in his time and smashed the idols in the house of his pagan father."

"And how do they reconcile themselves to the fact that the armies of King Solomon did not come here, as they expected and as they hoped and, if their account is to be believed, as was promised to them by none other than King Solomon himself?"

Mishael was quick to answer:

"They don't reconcile themselves to it at all. Nor could it be said that they ignore it – they are aware of it, but they don't consider it rationally."

"So what do they do?" he asked, the humorous note fading from his voice.

"They wait. They go on waiting, from day to day, month to month, year to year, decade to decade, generation to generation, century to century. They wait in the belief, firm as iron, that the event will come about, and everything that has been spoken of and is awaited with yearning will be fulfilled, and when the army of Jewish liberation approaches, all the Jews will rise as one man and slaughter the pagans, and put them to the sword, and destroy, and smash, and ruin, and set ablaze, and they will go forth clean and purified to meet the holy army, and greet the King who stands at its head, and join forces with him, and they will deal ruthlessly with all the peoples who remain, leaving no vestige of them, no survivors and – in defiance of the edicts of Scripture and the precepts of the Torah – they will show no mercy to women, to the old or the young."

"There are some," Hananiah interposed, "who hold that there is a duty to show mercy to domestic beasts, that the beast is not infected by the pagan sin of its master, but the majority dismiss this argument with contempt, declaring that not even the beast is to be spared. And all of this passes from father to son and from teacher to pupil, as a great secret and a holy commandment, and this small community does everything in its power to stay confined within its walls, enclosed and shut off and separated, shunning involvement with the peoples around it, or as they put it, avoiding 'contamination' and preserving their 'purity' – and waiting with peerless, incomparable patience for the coming of salvation."

They left the royal palace and made their way on foot. The warmth was pleasant, with rays of sunshine sparkling in the clear air. It was easy to breathe air such as this.

"This climate is reminiscent of the homeland," Mishael commented.

"Except for the summer," he answered him and explained: "The summer here is arid and oppressive, and were it not for the Euphrates, Babylon would be nothing but a desert country."

Their gait was brisk and vigorous and yet – light and surprisingly steady, in a fashion not typical of men of their age.

"And how do you fit into this legend?" he asked as they walked.

"The beliefs and hopes of these Jews?" Hananiah answered with a question.

He nodded.

"Sometimes they are amusing!" Mishael laughed lightly. "Sometimes – they leave behind an unpleasant taste."

"How so?"

"It's because this zealotry is dark on the one hand and on the other..." Mishael deliberated, turning to him without slackening his pace and measuring him with a quizzical look, before concluding the sentence, with an air of absolute seriousness: "On the other hand, it arouses reverence and respect!"

"You're saying these people arouse reverence and respect? How?" he persisted.

"With their fanatical devotion to an idea," Hananiah interjected, "however grotesque and demented and mortally dangerous that idea may be."

"Do they appeal to God and seek His help?" he asked.

"There is a family of priests among them, so I suppose it is theoretically possible," Hananiah surmised

"To the best of my knowledge," Azariah commented, "they don't feel the need for any such appeal. They have unshakeable trust in themselves, and that is what turns their heads."

"Their belief in their mission is strong," Hananiah added.

"Their belief in God too?" he persisted.

Neither Hananiah nor Mishael could give him a clear answer.

"Sometimes," Mishael resumed, "they look demented, and sometimes – as mild as babies! The family of Deborah, my future bride, isn't among the zealots. Her father is a dedicated campaigner for peace and a man of innocent faith, and all the talk of insurrections and revolt and bloodshed and destruction, and royal missions to which they're supposedly committed – elicit from him nothing more than a tolerant smile. And my belief is that if only he could, Baruch, my future father-in-law, would leave this strange community behind and move to somewhere that isn't hemmed in by walls all around."

"Why doesn't he do that?"

"Because he has children who are all dependent on him, and his income is meagre," Mishael explained. He has a field and a few milch-cows, and hives some distance away – and that's all. And he's not renowned for his courage. He works his field and milks his cows and extracts his honey, and sells his produce in the market by the temple of Marduk. When he has cash in his hand, then he's in high spirits and he's a pleasant fellow to talk to, and when business is poor his heart is heavy and at such times he may turn to drink, quaffing the potent Chaldean liquor that is brewed from all kinds of toxic herbs, and he sits at home listless and morose, saying nothing. I have happened to be in his company in these disagreeable moments, and despite my best efforts to hold a conversation with him, if only for a moment, I've failed utterly."

"Simeon, the father of Hannah my future bride," Hananiah interjected, "is one of the fanatics. Unlike Baruch, whom Mishael mentioned just now, he isn't prone to changes of mood – he has a stern look on his face at all times, and you would think he'd been gloomy since the day of his birth. He says little, and there's no way of knowing what is going on behind that wrinkled brow, or buried deep in the recesses of his frozen heart. And yet, he showed some signs of pleasure when giving consent to the betrothal of his middle daughter, Hannah."

The morning sun was still high in the sky when the three of them turned aside from the broad, paved, royal highway, teeming with men and beasts, carts and wagons – and plunged into the dark passageway leading to the north-eastern wall. Soon afterwards they received an enthusiastic welcome at the house of Deborah, Mishael's betrothed, where Havatzelet and Hannah, future wives of Azariah and Hananiah, were also waiting for them. The three maidens were brightly dressed in freshly laundered festive costumes, coloured pink, blue and purple and trimmed with silver lace. Baruch, Deborah's father, pronounced the blessings, and his broad, round features shone with the light of exuberant high spirits.

"He must be trading at a profit!" Mishael whispered in his ear, smiling broadly, and sure enough, Baruch was quick to confirm his future son-in-law's hypothesis:

"Yesterday the Lord held out to me His generous hand, and bestowed upon me a share of those favours of His that gladden the heart. Everything that I took to the market of Marduk was sold in no time at all, and I made a handsome profit!"

"Damn him to Hell!" – a sour-tempered man entered the room, tall of build and heavy of movement, wearing a woollen shirt, coarsely sewn and coloured black, and breeches of the same colour. He identified him at once as Simeon, prospective father-in-law of Hananiah. "Curse the name and the memory of all pagan idols!" the newcomer stressed, accompanying his words with a grinding of teeth, and they realised it was Marduk he was referring to. Tucked into his broad black belt was a long-bladed dagger.

"For my part, I shall never mention his name again!" Baruch hastened to soothe these passions, adding: "All the honey and the fresh milk that I brought to that market," – he was careful this time not to give it a name – "was snapped up, pounced on, and in such a short space of time! God has indeed shown me His manifold mercies and not withheld His favours from me. Sit down my lords, let this table be your table, and my house your house. Let your hearts not be sad, and dispel gloom from your faces!"

"Is that a dig at me?" Simeon's rusty voice rasped over the heads of the assembled company.

"No, not at all! Such a thought never occurred to me!" Baruch tried to give his voice an emphatic edge. The angry frown on the brow of the questioner eased a little, as the host added: "I was referring to myself, and to anyone else who might be listening."

They moved to take their seats at a long table covered with white cloths, and by the time they arrived there the refreshments had already been served. He asked Mishael where the other members of the family were, and he in turn consulted Deborah.

"They have gone out," she replied, "to stroll in the fields outside the walls. We stayed because we knew you were coming, you and Hananiah. And your friend too, who is most welcome here!"

The table was laden with good things: milk in clay pitchers, red wine, pats of butter and cheese on broad fig leaves, dried figs, dates dried and moist, home-baked hallah bread and fresh honey, its sweet aroma still intact, and served in cups. Baruch recited the grace beginning "He who has given us life" and Simeon grunted something which was presumably meant to be an "Amen", and hosts and guests alike took plates from the pile at the end of the table and filled them with whatever they fancied.

The young ladies made an effort to restrain themselves and not share in the gluttonous frenzy that had gripped the menfolk, but to no avail, and it was not long before they were gobbling with equal gusto and seizing everything that their eyes coveted.

He was hardly aware of the first mouthful. Walking in the fresh air had sharpened his appetite, and the hallah bread still held the fragrance of the fields. He remembered the hallah offered to him in the low, shady houses outside the walls of Jerusalem. Friendly people, of simple ways and warm hospitality, somewhere in the distant homeland, had begged him to take the produce of their hands and bless the living God. He recovered his wits, and took no further share in the collective frenzy. His movements were measured, his eating sober. One after the other, Hananiah and Mishael followed his example.

The diners rose, and the girls began clearing the table while the men made their way to the main living room of the house and from there to a small lobby, the exit to the outside world. A light push and the heavy door swung open before them, revealing the spectacle he had least expected to see: a broad, cultivated field, extending to the ridge of a low hill, enfolding it all around and forming a close horizon. Above their heads stretched a blue sky, mottled with feathery clouds whiter than snow.

"We're outside the wall!" Hananiah enlightened him, seeing his bemusement.

"This field belongs to the community," Mishael added, "all of it!"

"To a few families," he corrected him mildly.

Somewhere, at the far end of the field, the silver ribbon of a flowing stream could be seen, and on one of its banks – a group of women and children. The women saw them and blessed them with raised hands, and they returned the greeting.

To their right, stood a stooping fig tree, with a thick trunk and dense foliage rustling in the light breeze, clearly inclining towards them as if offering shelter. They came and sat down beneath it.

"This is my portion!" he told them calmly, drawing lines in the air to indicate a modest area of land. "The territory that used to belong to my father," he explained, "was of considerable size – but it was divided! I have six brothers, and each received an equal share, as was the explicit will of my esteemed father. It was also a fundamental contravention of the rules laid down in the Holy Torah!" he added in a tone of mild indignation. "After all, I am the firstborn, and according to the Law…" he sighed and left the sentence unfinished.

Three men appeared from behind them, advancing quietly and

joining them. He recognised one of them – Saul, Azariah's future father-in-law. All three wore brown cloaks, bound at the waist with black leather belts.

"This is Nehemiah!" Simeon introduced a portly, broad-shouldered man – "And he is of priestly lineage!" he added with an air of superior satisfaction. "This is Gideon, one of Baruch's brothers, and beside him is Saul. His daughter, Havatzelet, is betrothed to your friend, Azariah!"

"When is this wedding due to take place?" Gideon asked.

"When the time is right," the priestly Nehemiah sighed, as the newcomers shook the hands of the guests and exchanged greetings.

"And that time is drawing near!" Simeon's rasping voice was heard again, as he tried to imbue his words with mystery and dark significance.

"What do you mean by that?" he asked.

"As the prophet has seen fit to tell us – the end of wicked Babylon is at hand. From that time on, all will be fire and destruction and mayhem – so the sooner this marriage takes place the better!"

No one responded to the impassioned words of the man with the dagger. He felt ill at ease, and turned to the priestly Nehemiah in search of corroboration.

"Is it all true, what he has said? You, as a priest and the son of a priest, are empowered to confirm or deny this."

"It is true, the statement is accurate!" retorted Nehemiah earnestly, a thick edge to his voice. He added, in a tone of stern authority: "The Lord will deal severely with all those who have not believed in Him, and who have perverted their ways and bowed down to idols and images, and have not repented in time – and that time is not far away!"

"We shall all be called upon then to do the Lord's work, and cleanse the land of pagans and Gentiles, who have derided the Holy Name of the Lord, and afflicted and scorned His people!" Saul concluded with eyes downcast.

"This will be the great day of the judgment of the Lord, the mighty and awesome warrior, the day of anger and of wrath, the day of fire and pillars of smoke, the day of death and vengeance, such as the world has never seen and the like of which it will never see again!" Simeon declared with grim intensity, lightly fingering the hilt of his dagger as he spoke.

Something in the depths of his soul was chilled with dread. Had it not been said of these people, that they have eyes to see and see not, ears to hear and hear not? And without the mercy of Heaven – where are they going?

"What is the sign portending this time?" he asked.

Simeon hastened to forestall the priestly Nehemiah, answering him:

"Zedekiah, the anointed of the Lord, who sits on the throne of David, who knows the times and knows what is to be – he will show us the sign for which we are waiting, and we shall put an end to Babylon the wicked, as is the commandment of our holy God, and set on fire all the temples of Moloch!

"And you boys," – Simeon rounded on them, his voice raised and with an unmistakable note of menace, "sitting at your ease in the palace of the pagan king and serving him, will have to decide – to go on pandering to the Chaldeans or to return to your God and cleave to Him and go forth to exact vengeance for His people, the holy nation. No one shall escape the wrath of God, as it is written: *If you soar like an eagle and make your nest among the stars, from there I shall bring you down!*"

He rose to his feet.

"I think it's time to leave!" he said, addressing his companions.

Without another word spoken, the two of them stood and joined him. Baruch accompanied them part of the way, and tried to reassure them, in a hesitant voice:

"Not everyone agrees with Simeon, not everyone will listen to him!"

He nodded thoughtfully.

As they left the passage, Nehemiah caught up with them, panting from the effort of running, stopped them with his hand, and turning to him he said:

"As you know, marriage is only one of the great commandments of the holy law of Moses! And as I am sure you have heard, the more generous the fee paid by the groom to the priest – the finer the wedding!" He winked conspiratorially, a strange smile twisting his thick lips, and stood his ground, watching them go. And when they had walked some distance and Hananiah looked back, Nehemiah the priest raised his arm and waved to them in valediction.

BELTESHAZZAR

He awoke with a strange sensation of weight and oppression. His heart was thumping and he was short of breath – *as if I have been plagued by a nightmare*, he thought – but he could not remember if he had dreamed at all. *It's a passing sensation!* he concluded, but still he could not overcome the feeling of suffocation. He tried to calm himself but knew that something was happening or was about to happen, and someone had been hurt or was about to be hurt.

He knelt at the head of his bed and joined his hands in prayer:

"If I have found favour in Your eyes and grace in Your presence, my Father in Heaven, my God, have mercy on those people who have departed from You and have rejected You, and whom disaster threatens!"

His consciousness was cleared and cleansed, and the sense of oppression eased before disappearing altogether. Tears welled in his eyes, tears of gratitude.

Without rousing the slave responsible for the household, he put on a gown and went to the bathhouse; after refreshing himself in cold water he felt almost inclined to burst into song. The cook was aware that his master was awake and he set about preparing his breakfast. When he entered the dining room, he found the table already laden with fresh and warm milk, honey, eggs, toasted bread, cheese and vegetables.

He arrived early in the office, and to his surprise, did not find it empty – Nashdernach, himself and in person, was pacing back and forth, the length and breadth of the office, in a state of obvious agitation, with twitchy fingers clasped behind his back. He did not sense his arrival.

He stood motionless. The first thought that occurred to him was that the trouble he had anticipated had come about and disaster had struck. Was Nashdernach the victim?

"Belteshazzar!" The Chaldean was startled to see him, and in the effort to cover the alarm apparent in his exclamation, hurriedly asked: "Do you always arrive so early?"

"No," he replied. "This morning I woke earlier than usual, with a sensation of weight and oppression, and I turned to my God and prayed, and the oppression disappeared as if it had never been."

"I wish I had somewhere to turn to!" Nashdernach sighed, and he saw that his face was pale and his eyes sunken.

"Except that, so it seems..." his supervisor hesitated, and added, as if going off at a tangent: "We Chaldeans were born under a very strange constellation, a gloomy and oppressive one! Saturn has, quite simply, stamped his seal upon us, or perhaps – it's just in our nature!" And while continuing to pace back and forth, from one end of the office to the other, he went on to say: "There's no denying it, trouble has come upon us, and disaster is set to strike some of the most eminent officials of the government, strike them mortally!"

"You too?" he asked, the composure of his voice shattered.

"No! Certainly not me. I'm not possessed of the qualities that the people I mentioned are endowed with, or are supposed to be endowed with, those upon whom this terrible blow has fallen. Lend an ear, Belteshazzar, and listen! Our King, His Majesty, the wise and the valiant, conqueror of the world – has dreamed a dream!" And seeing the mystified look in his face he hastily explained: "And this is the entire cause of the trouble and of the looming disaster. The King dreamed a dream," he repeated emphatically, "and his heart pounded, and he rose from his bed, and ordered the immediate summoning of all the soothsayers and magicians, the sorcerers, diviners and astrologers. And all those who were summoned came at once, consumed by panic and shaking with fear, and they stood dumbfounded in a semicircle at the foot of the high throne of the King. And the King, seated on his throne in all his pomp and majesty, addressed his flustered courtiers and made of them – to say the very least – a most unusual demand. It could be described as a demand the like of which has never been heard before. And included in this assemblage of soothsayers and magicians and sorcerers and astrologers was my brother-in-law, a genial fellow and a family man, who has no truck with the world of diviners and magicians and their dubious profession and their delving into mysteries, in any respect whatsoever – other than through the fact that his father was a talented soothsayer, a veritable wizard, as was his grandfather, and they, the father and grandfather, served the Kings of Babylon faithfully and were guests at their table and lived lives of comfort and ease. And my brother-in-law, in accordance with the enlightened laws of Babylon, inherited their appointment, along with all the trappings that belong to it.

"And since this dream that our wise and valiant King, His Majesty, so graciously dreamed, my brother-in-law, a peace-loving man of simple pleasures, has lived in the shadow of the deadliest danger!"

"The King demanded of all those soothsayers and magicians – that they interpret his dream?" he asked.

"Yes!" Nashdernach replied, and he stopped, turned and stood facing him, no longer fidgeting nervously with his fingers behind his back. "Precisely so! He demanded that they interpret his dream! But the problem is that not one of the King's eminent soothsayers, not one of his magicians, never mind all the rest," – Nashdernach raised both arms in a gesture of utter helplessness, as if pleading for the mercy of Heaven – "has the faintest idea what he is supposed to be interpreting!"

"The dream, surely!"

"The dream, yes, to be sure. Just as you say. To interpret the dream, explain it, solve it – that's the inimitable skill of these people! Tell them of a vision in which all the characters participating are split into two halves, and there are many of them, and the situations in which they are embroiled are strange and inexplicable, and they, these cunning readers of mysteries, will turn to you with broad smiles on their smug faces, bow to you and say: 'You are going to hear good news from relations and family, and bad news from one who is half a friend.' And if the news described as 'good' fails to satisfy you, your melancholia is directed at those who trouble you. And if the bad news changes its skin and becomes good – it is because you have sacrificed a bull-calf to the god and your sin is forgiven; and if you haven't yet sacrificed a calf, nor even so much as a dove to one or other of the deities – hurry up and do it, they will tell you – before it is too late!

"And the whole business is clear as the light of day, a matter of simple routine, except in this strange instance involving the King, our wise and valiant King!" – and Nashdernach thumped on one of the tables with his round little fist. "They are all intent on not sparing themselves hard work and travail in the effort to demonstrate their skill in the arts of interpretation, and even, within a short space of time, to attain a remarkable degree of unanimity, in their customary style, the only problem being – to the bewilderment and grief of all – there is nothing to interpret and nothing to explain!" Again Nashdernach raised both arms towards the ceiling."

"The dream!" he reminded him.

"Of course, the dream!" he repeated in a hollow voice. "This extraordinary royal dream... This time the King is not content with interpretation and explanation; the demand is a different one, involving a prelude to conventional interpretation and solution!" And

Nashdernach resumed his tour of the office, his fingers clasped behind his back.

"So what is His Majesty's pleasure?" he asked, intrigued.

The minister turned sharply and came hurrying towards him, staring at him with a look of despair and giving full voice to his woes:

"First and foremost he wants to be told what was the dream that he dreamed! Yes, absolutely!" – Nashdernach paused for emphasis. "Interpretation and explanation can wait. First and foremost he wants the dream revealed to him, the dream that he dreamed himself, in person, no one else. So, the King's spirit is troubled twice over: first on account of the dream itself and second – because this unique and special dream has fled from his memory! This, then, is the royal demand – that he be told what he dreamed! And as is his way, the King concludes his edict with the customary royal formula: 'If you do not reveal to me what I dreamed, and interpret the dream that I have forgotten – your blood be upon your heads!' Meaning, your blood will be spilled at the hands of the royal executioner. And the word of His Majesty the King is not spoken idly. This morning I was told of the execution of the chief of the sorcerers, and there will be more to come!"

And without a pause, Nashdernach continued, breathing heavily: "They are trying, the soothsayers and the magicians and the sorcerers and all the rest, to play for time, for they have no other way of resisting the cruel decree and forestalling the sword that is brandished above their necks. But the King can read their minds and he knows what they are thinking and he is incensed at them, and there is a rumour going about among the courtiers that he intends to wipe out his entire staff of seers and wizards, most of whom obtained their posts through family connections rather than through skill and expertise.

"And because there is no solution and no escape, some of those subtle sages are trying to point the finger at you, the Jewish exiles in the service of the King, you and your three companions, Shadrach, Meshach and Abed-Nego, as those who used spells and secret knowledge to make the King forget, and should now face the consequences of their actions! And there are others who oppose this malicious proposition, but who will gain the upper hand – it is too early to say!"

The keen look that he gave his interlocutor showed him that Nashdernach was among the opponents of the malicious proposition.

He looked down and made no response, and Nashdernach went on to say:

"And in the meantime my mild-mannered brother-in-law is so

terrified he has taken to his bed, and his body temperature is fluctuating wildly, his teeth chattering and his hands shaking, and he has neither saviour nor redeemer.

"Lord of the world, Belteshazzar!" cried Nashdernach in bitter despair, "Can you not appeal to your God, pray to Him, lay your entreaties before Him – plead for an end to the killing, and the repeal of that cruel decree?"

"With your permission, I shall sit for a moment!" he said and sat down at the table, hands clasping his temples.

Nashdernach stopped, quietly pulled up a chair and sat on it reversed, a cavalry officer's pose. His tense look followed every one of his movements, and in the gloom of his oily little eyes there rose the pale glimmer of a distant hope.

He laid his hands on the surface of the table, looked up and said:

"That mild-mannered brother-in-law of yours was in the wrong, pretending to be a magician or an astrologer and accepting payment that wasn't his by right, and the same judgment applies to all his colleagues, including those who are now making every effort to incriminate the innocent as a way of saving their own skin. I shall try to meet the challenge, and contend with the evil. For three days you shall not see me, and when those three days have passed, I hope I shall have an answer for you."

"And what is the purpose of those three days?" asked Nashdernach.

"Fasting and prayer" he replied and left the room.

He called upon Mishael and Hananiah and they, knowing what was afoot in the royal court, and having heard of the proposal to lay the blame upon them and sacrifice them as scapegoats, were troubled and fearful, not knowing how to behave and what to do. He addressed them and asked them too to fast and pray, so that the good God might see their oppression and also take pity on the soothsayers and astrologers of Babylon, and save them all from the hands of the executioner.

He shut himself away in his lodgings, and ordered his slaves not to disturb him and to admit no guests or visitors. All official business was to be referred to Nashdernach, his superior. And so he prayed and fasted, with pleas drawn from the depths of his grieving heart:

"The people have sinned, sinned in pretending to be what they are not and eating bread for free, bread that is not theirs!

"My God, my holy Father in Heaven, my lord and teacher and master!

You are love and you are all forgiveness and mercy, and they – they who do not know how to repent, let them be saved, by your grace, from the hands of the executioner, and their families spared from grief and penury and from the torments of fear. Give them the joy of Your pure love which whitens every sin, and ease their suffering, and bring them out of darkness into a great light!"

Indeed, his heart told him that more members of the royal household – wizards, astrologers and magicians – were bound to pay for their deception with their lives, their unfortunate families despoiled of their property and evicted from their homes. And this thought tormented and saddened him until he cried out in his prayers and in the depths of his grief, not rising from his knees day or night. He could no longer feel the limbs of his body, and it seemed to him it was not he but some other person, not known to him, who was kneeling there, clasping numb and frozen hands and praying without cease.

And suddenly he was visited by that familiar sensation, a feeling of cautious relief arising in the heart and spreading through every part of his body. And for the first time since embarking on his fast, he was aware of his limbs, emerging painfully from their torpor, and this in itself was a comfort.

He crawled to his bed, and with strenuous efforts that seemed to last hundreds of years, managed to climb into it. And then, as his body began to relax and to regain its vigour, he saw the dream that the King had dreamed, that troubled his heart but was forgotten when he awoke.

He called to his slave, and was surprised by the sound of his own voice, which was thin and barely audible. He had to muster his strength and cry out again to make himself heard, but to no avail. Nobody heard him and nobody came. An oil-lamp made of clay stood on the tiny table beside his bed and he pushed at it, knocking it to the floor. The lamp shattered, making a sound loud enough to reach the ears of his slave, who came running. He tapped on the door, and hearing the faint voice of his master, opened it.

The tanned face of the slave was alarmed, as were his bulging eyes, twitching in their sockets.

"Enter!" he cried, relieved to find that his voice was becoming clearer. The slave entered hurriedly and stood before him. Seeing the fragments of clay on the floor, he stooped and started picking them up.

"Leave those!" he commanded and added: "Go to Nashdernach at once, run to him! Tell him that the problem is solved! Run!"

No further urging was required. The slave was aware of the situation and of the exceptional circumstances involved: his master's prolonged fast, his lean appearance, the breaking of the lamp as an alarm signal, and the strange words about solutions and urgency – all of these gave him wings, and he ran out of the building, passing the sumptuous residences of the senior counsellors and reaching Nashdernach's house. He knocked on the great door, and panting heavily succeeded in transferring his panic to the footman, who ran up the stairs to alert his master, at that time in his night-shirt.

"Imp-p-p-portant message from Beltesh-esh-esh-azzar – s-s-something's s-s-solved, s-s-solved!" was the garbled message delivered by the stammering footman, but Nashdernach immediately understood what he was being told, and he changed his clothes and without another word spoken set out in pursuit of the messenger-slave. Despite his age – at least two decades older than the slave – he overtook him and arrived first at Daniel's bedside.

"So?" he asked him, breathlessly.

"The killing can stop!" he told him, his voice still thin and grating. "There is a solution! Go to Arioch, the chief executioner, and tell him I am ready and prepared to stand before the King tomorrow..."

"The Heavens be praised!" Nashdernach interrupted him with his high-pitched exclamation and added: "The solution has come just in time! Arioch, the chief executioner, wants your life and the lives of your companions, since the rumour going about the palace is that you are sorcerers, casting magical spells to destroy the sages of Babylon, and the King has decreed that your fate will be the same as that of the astrologers, and if you fail to tell him the dream that he has dreamed – you will be taken to the scaffold! And I asked Arioch to wait until first light, giving you time to fast and pray to your God, the all-powerful God, and he could expect a miracle that would stop the killing! This day alone," Nashdernach continued, "three more sages have been beheaded, and Babylon is plunged into grief over the bitter fate of its sorcerers and magicians, wizards and astrologers!"

Nashdernach shook his hand firmly and warmly, and retraced his steps at the same hectic pace, making his way to the house of Arioch, chief executioner to the King,

He dressed and sent his slave to summon his friends. When they arrived and stood before him, tense and nervous, he was quick to reassure them:

"The name of the Lord be praised from everlasting and to everlasting, to whom is all wisdom and might! He is the Lord of all and the One who changes the times, and all things own his sway and He it is who deposes kings and appoints kings, giving wisdom to the wise and understanding to the judicious, knowing things that are hidden from the eyes of mortals, and He is the one and the only light, the living light!"

And here he went down on his knees and his two companions did likewise, and he joined his hands and raised them, and went on to say:

"To You, my God and my Father, be thanks and praise, seeing that through your bountiful grace and your manifold mercies, and Your love that embraces the whole world, that conquers all – You have given us wisdom and strength and have revealed to us what we asked of You, the solution to the King's riddle and the dream that he dreamed, the dream on account of which many have died, and we too were in mortal danger, and You, in Your might and Your mercy, will save us from death in this foreign land, the land of our exile!"

He rose from his knees and his two companions followed his example, and they were light-hearted and in good spirits, praising God and jesting among themselves about the unwarranted terror that had gripped them. And meanwhile the kitchen slave informed them that, as the fasting was now over, a meal had been prepared and would shortly be served, and would the gentlemen be so kind as to take their seats at the table. He thanked his scullion warmly, and invited his friends to break bread with him.

Later that night he was visited by Arioch, the chief executioner.

He told Arioch: "You need slay no more of the sages of Babylon! Take me to the King tomorrow and I shall show him his dream!"

The following day Arioch was waiting for him in the avenue leading to the palace and the royal residence, and he was impatient, because the King's edict was still in force and if the solution failed to satisfy the King, then a grim fate was in store for him, his life in jeopardy.

Armed guardsmen opened the great door of the royal council chamber before them. At the end of the room stood the high throne of the King, three steps of cast gold leading to it, and the throne itself fashioned from gold and ivory, and Nebuchadnezzar seated there in all his regal splendour.

A broad strip of purple carpet stretched from the throne to the entrance, and on either side of the carpet troopers of the royal guard were drawn up, standing in motionless ranks face to face, wearing blue tabards embroidered in gold with the three recumbent lions that were the emblem of the royal household. Around their waists the guardsmen wore black belts with gold buckles, and each carried a gold shield in his left hand, and a broad-bladed drawn sword in his right. On their heads were gleaming helmets, likewise of gold.

So they entered, and Arioch hastened to lie full-length on the ground, and he did the same. Then they stood up and paced towards the King who sat on his throne awaiting them, until they reached the stool at his feet. They prostrated themselves once more before the King, and did not rise until so commanded.

For the second time he looked into the bronzed features of King Nebuchadnezzar, reminiscent in their composure and their ferocity of the face of a lion, crouching in his lair, confident of his power and ready at any moment to spring upon his prey.

The King wore blue breeches embroidered with gold, a white shirt also with gold trimmings, a broad white belt set with pearls and other precious stones, and a straight-bladed sword hanging from it in a gold scabbard, the hilt inlaid with silver and ivory.

"Speak!" the King commanded, his voice calm, clear and resonant, the voice of dominion and authority, not to be defied.

He bowed to him once more, and began:

The secret of which the King is asking – sages, wizards, astrologers and magicians could not explain to him. But there is a God in Heaven who reveals secrets, and He is telling King Nebuchadnezzar what is to be hereafter…

Your Majesty, thoughts came into your mind as you were in your bed, as you sought to know what is to be hereafter, and the Revealer of secrets showed what is to be. By the grace that has been bestowed on me, the secret has been revealed to me, so that I may stand before your Majesty and inform you of the solution, and you shall know the thoughts of your heart.

You looked, Your Majesty, and you saw before you a great and wondrous image. The head of the image – pure gold, the chest and arms – silver, the belly and thighs – brass. Legs of iron and the feet – partly of iron and partly of clay. As you looked on, a stone was hewn from a mountain, and not by any hand, and it struck the feet of the image, that were of iron and clay, and destroyed them and pounded them to dust. And then all was shattered together – the clay and the iron, the brass, the silver and the gold, and they became like chaff from the summer threshing-floor, and the wind bore them away, and no one know whither, and the stone that struck the image became a great and high mountain and filled all the earth. This is the dream, he concluded, his voice miraculously clear and limpid, like the voice of an angel, and the meaning of it I shall explain to my lord the King:

Your Majesty, you are the King, and the King of Kings, to whom God in Heaven has given the kingdom, the might and the valour and the glory, and wherever men dwell, and wherever there are beasts of the field and birds of the air, he has given you dominion over them. You are the golden head. After you, will come another kingdom inferior to yours, and another, a third kingdom of brass that shall rule the whole earth. And the fourth kingdom shall be strong as iron, for iron crushes everything, and as iron shatters and crushes, so it shall shatter and crush. And as for the feet that you saw and the toes, partly of clay and partly of iron, they will be a kingdom divided in itself, and it shall have something in it of the strength and fortitude of iron, while the other part will be brittle. As for the iron that you saw mixed with clay, when this is joined by the intermingling of the seed of mankind, there shall be no cleaving together, for iron does not cleave to clay. And in the days of those kings, the God of Heaven will set up a kingdom that shall never be destroyed, and no other people shall prevail over it, but it will shatter and crush all those kingdoms and it will last forever. And the stone that you saw, hewn from a mountain not by any hand, and shattering the iron, the brass, the clay, the silver and the gold – the great God has made known to the King what is to be hereafter. The dream is true, and its interpretation to be trusted.

Hearing his words, the King rose from his throne and descended the three gold steps, deeply moved, and he bowed to him and prostrated himself on the ground before him, and rising he clapped his hands and commanded the slave who appeared at once to bring offerings to Daniel and to anoint his feet with incense. Then he turned and addressed him, shaken to the very roots of his soul, his voice quaking:

"Truly, your God is the God of Gods and the Lord of kings, and of the kings of kings, and a revealer of secrets, even of this great secret!"

And the King sent word that the chief steward of the royal household be summoned, and he appeared in full ceremonial regalia, his clerk and slave following closely behind him, with a phial of ink in his belt, stylus and pen in his sleeve, and parchment scrolls in his pocket. And the King commanded that around the neck of Daniel the Jew, the revered Belteshazzar, there should be hung a gold necklace, with a pendant bearing the royal cipher, a sign and a symbol not to be ignored, and henceforward Belteshazzar was to be deputy to the King and all were to acknowledge his sway. He was to be the first and the chief of ministers, with authority over every official, clerk and counsellor within the palace and outside it. And the King ordered that he be allotted suitable remuneration, and given a house in the royal compound, and provided with as many slaves and maidservants as he wished for, and according to the King's own specific proclamation, all the soothsayers and wizards and magicians and diviners and astrologers in Babylon were to defer to him, to Belteshazzar, who would deal with them as he saw fit, with powers of life and death to be wielded entirely at his own discretion.

And Daniel bowed at the feet of the King, Nebuchadnezzar the valiant and the wise, conqueror of the world, and prostrated himself before him, and then rose to his feet and thanked him profusely for the honour done to him and for the recognition accorded to his God, the God of Gods. And he added that he had a favour to ask, and the King replied:

"Speak, and it shall be done!"

He reminded the King that he had companions who were scholarly and knowledgeable, God-fearing and God-loving, and loyal subjects of the King, and he asked that they be appointed his deputy ministers in all respects.

"So be it!" the King replied, beckoning to the chief steward of the royal household, and he hastily ordered the slave who accompanied him to record on parchment all of the King's edicts and stipulations, which would then be given to the copyists to transcribe in the proper manner; thus the King's will would be done in the great city of Babylon and throughout the Chaldean nation, and in every race and principality and state and country that the King ruled by right of conquest.

And so it was.

I AM YOUR SERVANT

He was given charge of a department adjacent to the royal council chamber, composed of five separate offices, and on the instructions of the King himself, he was assigned the largest of these offices, opening directly into the council chamber. His door was guarded by two sentries, men of the elite royal household corps. Three of the offices were allocated to Mishael, Hananiah and Azariah and one was left unoccupied. He was minded to offer this for the general use of the other ministers, but then an idea occurred to him and he decided to try to implement it.

One evening he knocked on the door of Denur-Shag's lodging, after dismissing the pair of bodyguards accompanying him.

The old slave opened the door cautiously, and the moment he saw him, he fell at his feet, prostrating himself before him.

"Get up, please! Please get up! There's no need for this!" There was a note of annoyance in his voice, which only added to the confusion of the slave, who now tried to scramble up from the floor and found the effort beyond him. He stepped forward and took the slave's arm , helping him to stand upright.

"My Lord," the slave mumbled, the pupils of his eyes dilated in abject fear, "my Lord and deputy King! Let this not be held to my discredit, may I rather gain grace and favour in Your Worship's eyes..." his voice trailed away.

"Calm yourself, my good man!" he addressed him mildly, adding in the same tone, "if Denur-Shag is at home, please be so kind as to inform him of my arrival, and ask if he is prepared to receive me!"

"Of course, my gracious Master, it shall be done at once!" In the slave's big eyes bewilderment was taking the place of fear, though without dispelling it completely. The words of the chief minister, the King's all-powerful deputy, were incomprehensible to him. Had he really heard it, with his own ears – this Belteshazzar, wearing the gold pendant with the royal cipher about his neck, wielding the power of life and death at will – asking permission of his humble master, the diminutive schoolteacher in the shabby cloak, to be received in his home? It made no sense to him at all.

Limping slightly the slave hurried into the house, and finding his master engrossed in one of his almanacs, he informed him in a quaking voice of the strange visit and the even stranger request.

And he answered him off-handedly:

"Tell him to come in!" – showing no sign of excitement or urgency, not rising from his seat or diverting his attention from the almanac.

The slave returned to the visitor, bowed down as low as he could without collapsing on the floor, and repeated his master's words:

"Tell him to come in!"

He entered the narrow, low and familiar house of Denur-Shag. The latter rose to meet him, with a firm handshake expressive of warmth and fellowship, and a look of satisfaction that he was unable to conceal.

"Be blessed, my friend, and may you continue to go from strength!" he cried, adding: "That gold necklace that hangs round your neck is many times heavier than its actual weight! Sometimes – you will have to defend it, defend it at the risk of your own life, and sometimes – hide behind it, and if you fail to conduct yourself properly this necklace will become for you that thick and knotted rope of notorious repute!" Denur-Shag returned to his seat and fell silent. The other began by saying:

"I came to ask you to participate in matters to which you are not indifferent!"

Without responding to this, Denur-Shag invited him to sit and called to his slave; when the latter opened the door a crack and peered through it, he asked him to fetch red, kosher wine, dates, goat's cheese and bread. The slave disappeared, to return moments later with everything that had been requested.

"How does he manage to get all these things?" he asked, intrigued.

"He's a very resourceful man," the host replied. "He knows what is where, and so he doesn't waste his time running around and looking for things, to the advantage of his master and his guests, and most of all – to his own!"

They both laughed, and then, with emphatic solemnity, Denur-Shag poured some of the clear liquid, the colour of the sunset or the ripe cherry, into two thick glass goblets, not of the finest quality, set one of them before him, raised the other in his hand and pronounced the blessing:

"May your all-powerful God be with you always!"

He replied with a brief blessing, giving thanks for food and wine, then picked up his goblet and drank from it, as did Denur-Shag, and put it down beside the long-necked earthenware bottle. And then he looked at his former teacher and asked him: "Well?"

Denur-Shag lowered his eyes, staring quizzically at the table for a while, before slicing the bread and transferring the soft cheese into clay dishes. Finally he looked up and said:

"There is no service that isn't the service of God. Even someone who has strayed far from Him and denies Him, in the final analysis is serving Him, even if this is not what he wants. Obviously, the correct and praiseworthy thing to do is serve God willingly, with love, and everyone with a brain should be asking himself if he is really doing this, and to what extent, and how. Your compatriots have the saying, *The voice of the people is the voice of God*, meaning, in my humble opinion, that anyone who serves the people, any people, faithfully and not with a view to profit, is serving God. And 'not with a view to profit' can be interpreted in certain cases to mean 'not in the bright light of publicity'. And service such as this is perhaps the one and only thing capable of bringing deep satisfaction, true satisfaction, and for this reason it is preferable that I don't accept an appointment in your office or more precisely – one of the offices allocated to you, as it has already been whispered in my ear that one of them is vacant." Denur-Shag grinned and added: "But I know for a fact that it wasn't for this that you approached me, even though as far as I'm concerned, it's all the same.

"If I thought that was where I belonged, I wouldn't have spurned your proposal without first delving into your motives – the overt and the covert ones! However," he continued, pushing his goblet towards him, "it's obvious to me that my place isn't there, and official posts and government offices are not for me, and moreover it's reasonable to assume that you know this, but to avoid the mistake of appearing heavy-handed, you came to me to hear me say it. Am I right?"

"You are right," he admitted to him, and to himself. The motive behind this visit – it was becoming clear to him – had been nothing other than the need to pay his former teacher the honour due to him, and somehow express his appreciation and his gratitude.

"Nevertheless," Denur-Shag went on to say with an air of clear satisfaction, "you won't be getting rid of me as easily as that! I shall stand by you, if the need arises – even if it isn't what you want. But I won't be on the sunny side of the street! I'll be lurking in the shadows, out of sight – and there I shall be at your service!"

They both resumed their sipping of the light wine, its delicate sweetness turning in the void of the mouth to distant flashes of song and fields of flowers.

Denur-Shag bit into his slice of bread, chewing steadily and with an air of undiluted pleasure, swallowed and continued:

"Your sudden rise to eminence has come as a shock to Babylon. Babylonians are by nature excitable, with a propensity towards the sensational, but the excuse for indulging their emotions that you've given them is in a class all of its own, virtually unique.

"It's reasonable to suppose that the coming days will have more surprises in store for us," Denur-Shag went on to say, speaking with unaccustomed gravity. "From the moment that Jews come to power in any country, that country will be blessed with chronic turbulence, enjoying ups and downs, miracles and wonders. Yes, it's a specific trait of your race, the Jewish race. They do very well serving as deputy to some king or other, or senior adviser to a governor, or treasury minister to a potentate. It's a different story when they take power into their own hands, and become the kings and the governors themselves. That's when everything falls apart, when the wheels come off the chariot! That's because the Jews were never meant to *do* things; their job has always been to have ideas, which others implement. Since the dawn of antiquity they were assigned the role of serving God, and He, God, is their only king, governor and leader and ruler. So anyone who sets out to imitate God, becoming king, conqueror or ruler, will ultimately encounter devastating defeat, and bring disaster upon his people and himself, is it not so?" he asked and he answered him:

"The role of imitating God was claimed by the power opposing him, the one who tempted mankind saying: *"You shall be as God"*

"If imitation isn't an option, what else is there?" asked Denur-Shag.

"Revelation," he declared, "meaning, the discovery of God in your own heart, and waking up to know yourself an inseparable part of Him."

"Outstanding!" enthused Denur-Shag, thumping the table top with his fist and setting all the utensils jangling.

Denur-Shag looked down again, pondering, and finally looked up and said:

"One way or the other, I have not a shadow of a doubt that the golden age of Babylon, as you predicted to the King, is close at hand and will soon be reaching its zenith, and why is this?" He was not expecting an answer and when none came, he went on to say – "Because Babylon, in these days of ours, is administered entirely by Jews! With the exception of the King himself. No one can compare with the Jews when it comes to conveying the blessing of God – to others, not to themselves. This is their fate as a race and a nation and a people until the coming of the last days, when God Himself shall rule His chosen people in His own kingdom, the Kingdom of Heaven!"

Again they sipped the kosher wine which Denur-Shag had thoughtfully provided, concluding their meal with the bread, freshly baked in the royal bakery and still smelling fragrant, accompanied by thin slivers of cheese.

"This Babylon, of today, is enjoying the festival that it owes to you, and is celebrating the saving of the lives of those wretched magicians, with the display of excessive exuberance and reverence – worshipping you in song and in dance and in procession – that is so typical. Tomorrow, according to the same norms and traditions – you will be envied and reviled, and those naïve and wretched magicians will look at you with jealousy and malice, and some will kindle virulent hatred of you, of which you will be only too well aware, and then perhaps, by God's grace, I can help you, standing in the shadows as I shall be!

"This is perhaps the role that God has enjoined upon me, and although I make no solemn vows or pledges, I shall fulfil this role of mine to the best of my ability, in other words – above and beyond what is to be expected and perhaps even – above and beyond what is tolerable and desirable." He raised his goblet, taking small and frequent sips until it was emptied, then putting the empty goblet before him, he spoke again:

"It has also come to my ears that you have succumbed to the Chaldean tradition that is linked to the superstitious belief that a bachelor is unfit to serve the State, and you are soon to marry. And of your future wife, it is said she is some fairy-tale Jewish princess."

"It is true, she is related to the royal household, but she is no princess," he replied.

"According to what is said in your writings, your God gave Adam the prospect of ascending and approaching Him, by creating him in His image and His likeness but not in His spirit, and He set the woman before him as a challenge. And if your first father, who you say is the father of every race and nation, had withstood the challenge of the woman as he should and not been tripped up by her – he would have earned the privilege of discovering the spirit of his creator in his heart and thereby knowing himself. Instead of this – he slipped and fell and showed the flesh to be as it is today – corruptible matter."

"It follows then that the penitent will regain his prospects, and he is the one who will find the spirit of his Creator in his heart," he completed his host's peroration.

"And how can man repent, and approach his Creator, and repair what he has spoiled, and know divine love?"

"By following the divine way that says: You shall love the Lord your God with all your heart and with all your might and with all your soul, and your neighbour as yourself!"

He stood up from his seat and bade Denur-Shag an amicable farewell. The host accompanied him to the door of the house and said to him as they parted company:

"Don't forget, my Lord and deputy to the King – I am your servant!"

WITHOUT MAKING A SOUND

His hands were spread on the top of the broad, oblong table, constructed of polished oak in its natural colour and heaped with rolled parchment scrolls and clay tablets, some separate and others strung together, alongside a selection of high quality styli and pens, and red and blue ink in phials of ivory.

Before he could begin the routine of the day, he heard a knock at the door, the light knock of his office slave.

"Enter!" he cried and the latter, a bright young lad from the northern isles, with a film of soft downy hair on his cheeks, dressed in blue livery, his Chaldean name Oshrich – opened the door and stood on the threshold.

Oshrich bowed to him, stepped inside, closed the door behind him, bowed again and on straightening up said: "A lady named Adelain is asking to see you, Sir!"

For some reason this announcement struck fear into his heart. He suppressed it and turning to Oshrich said: "I shall receive her in a little while!"

"You will call me, Sir?"

"I will call!"

As soon as Oshrich had left, he fell to his knees, raised his hands, palms together, and looking up at the sky, through the broad window behind his chair, began:

"Purify me I pray, my Father in Heaven, my God, guide me I pray, my Father in Heaven, my God. You are in me, my Father in Heaven, my God, and I in you, for ever and ever!"

The light of joy filled his heart, streaming in the void of his spacious, sumptuous office.

"For ever and ever I shall give thanks to You my Father in Heaven, my God! I thank You for the abundant grace that You have awarded me, and would that I were only worthy of it!"

He rose to his feet, took his seat at the table, clapped his hands once, twice, and the door opened. Oshrich stood on the threshold, bowing.

Rising to his full height he glanced at him, and for a long moment froze where he stood, motionless, his eyes reflecting utter astonishment, bordering on panic and veering towards reverence. Without realising what he was doing, the slave bowed down before him once again, prostrating himself at his master's feet as at the feet of a deity: his master's face was aglow with ethereal light.

"Be so good," he addressed him with an unfamiliar, musical lilt to his voice – "as to call the lady Adelain and ask her to come here!"

"As you wish Sir, so it shall be done!" Oshrich replied, his voice too seeming to deviate from its normal tone of restraint, and his face flickering with either a strange delight or with reverent fear.

Adelain entered. On her trim body a white dress, white as the virgin snow on the mountain tops. The dress was gathered at the waist in a broad leather belt of a deep velvet colour, its buckle silver studded with sapphires, and on her head was a turban the colour of her dress, fastened with a pearl brooch.

She turned upon him her big, deep, subdued eyes, and stood there tongue-tied and nervous, until a strange kind of merriment, excluding all else, took over her entire being.

"Good day to you, Adelain!" he greeted her, his voice vibrant, as if laden with confidence and hopeful tidings.

She did not return his greeting, preferring instead to express something of the intensity of the feelings that were making her heart flutter.

"Your face is radiant!"

"That's just the sun," he said with a modest smile, "the light of the sun on my face!"

"It isn't the light of the sun! You are a wonderful sight!" she insisted, the musical lilt of his voice now audible in hers, and her eyes absorbing and reflecting the purity in his eyes.

"How happy I am to be in your presence, to hear your voice, to be refreshed by the pure light that shines from your eyes!"

"Please be seated!" He pointed to the chair opposite his in an attempt to stem the flow of adulation, of compliments that were not to his taste, and he asked:

"What brings you here?"

"My desire to be, if only for a moment, close to you!" she declared sincerely, without hesitation, with none of the awkwardness that would be expected of a young woman in such circumstances.

Her candour took him aback. The thought crept into his mind that she was beautiful, and that her quivering voice could set hearts ablaze.

"I won't disturb you at all!" she declared, adding by way of explanation: "I shall sit by myself behind your back, without making a sound. You won't know I'm here!" she concluded, and without waiting for consent or rejection, she found a stool that had been left in a corner and saying not another word, sat herself down behind his back, not too close to him.

He had to admit that she was right; he was not aware of her presence. Even her breathing, which was not quiet, no longer reached his ears.

"You must do as you please!" he said without turning to face her. He unfolded a yellowing parchment scroll and settled down to read it.

Soon after Adelain's arrival, he called Oshrich and handed him a scroll to be passed on to one of his aides. And the slave was incapable of maintaining his composure or curbing his astonishment at the spectacle revealed to him: a young woman blessed with quite exceptional beauty, of distinguished family, judging by her attire – sitting on a low stool, tucked away in a corner of the office behind his master's back, and doing nothing and not making a sound, like a spare item of furniture, doing neither service nor disservice.

The bemusement reflected in the face of his slave made no impression on him, not because of the latter's clumsy attempts to hid it, but because he had completely forgotten Adelain's presence.

She sat without making a movement, as if she were not a body at all but a vapour, dispersing into the void and becoming a part of it. Furthermore, the matters he was supposed to be dealing with were urgent and demanded concentration and focus, and he spared himself no effort in working through each problem, understanding the implications and mastering the details and arriving at solutions, however abstruse and elusive the issues might be.

An hour passed, perhaps more than an hour. Again, Oshrich knocked on the door, entered and announced:

"The minister Nashdernach, chief of the King's advisers, requests an audience with you, Sir!"

"Show him in!" he cried.

Oshrich opened the door wide and stood back, bowing and making way for Nashdernach to pass by him.

The newcomer delivered his greetings and took a seat facing him, a friendly gesture.

"Did you know," he began, with a kind of tension in his voice that he was making an effort to conceal – and then Nashdernach noticed the young woman, sitting in silence on a low stool, in a corner, behind the other's back.

The chief of the King's advisers stared at her with his tiny, oily eyes, which were open wide, as wide as the eyes of a man who arrives at his workplace as usual and finds his father, long since dead and buried, sitting there grinning at him.

Nashdernach was struck dumb, unable to avert his gaze from the figure in white, sitting in silence as if detached from the world.

It was only then that the other remembered Adelain and the fact that she was sitting behind him. He turned, and the astonishment in his eyes changed rapidly into something that could be interpreted as a query, such as – *Well, what now?*

Without a word, without any acknowledgement whatsoever of the two men, Adelain rose and left his office.

Nashdernach lowered his gaze and sat for a while in silence. Finally he looked up and said, a twinkle in his oily little eyes:

"If I am not mistaken, she is the daughter of our valiant and illustrious commander, Or-Nego."

"She is indeed."

"This is a strange state of affairs. Women are strange, and that lady – she's in a class all of her own!" he asserted, going on to say: "I once heard of a woman, a relative of mine in fact, who loved a wise and handsome man, loved him with a love as strong as death, in the words of your scriptures. And his heart went out to her, and he asked her to marry him and be his wife – and she refused. Her love was so strong, she said, that it needed no physical contact. As simple as that! Have you ever heard of such a thing?" he asked.

"No," he answered him, adding, "but I understand your relative's attitude. Love is not dependent on the physical body, and distance and time do not exist where love is concerned."

"Anyway," Nashdernach resumed with a sigh, "that's how it was with my relative! The case caused something of a stir at the time, which is how I came to hear of it. She married no one and remained a virgin. A beautiful woman by all accounts. He on the contrary, married a wife and was divorced, and married again – and was divorced again. In the end he lived with a mistress. He didn't understand my relative's love and he used to complain that it wasn't love at all, but cruelty for its own sake. I don't know if the pair of them are still alive. To tell the truth, I just don't understand this kind of love," – Nashdernach expressed his bemusement with a shrug of the shoulders, "I mean, if she loves the man and she's going to be true to him, why not marry him and put him out of his misery? Is she afraid that this weird love of hers, or higher love if you prefer – let's not quibble over definitions – is she afraid that this higher love is going to be spoiled by physical intimacy?"

"The higher, the true love is eternal, and nothing can prevail over it, and it certainly won't be spoiled by any kind of contact," he replied.

"Why then, did this loving woman refuse to marry her lover?" Nashdernach persisted.

"I suppose that your relative reckoned marriage was liable to be harmful to him, and he wouldn't be prepared to do without physical intimacy, despite his repeated protestations to the contrary. And the proof of this – he separated from the wives in whom he sought this intimacy."

"Oh!" Nashdernach lowered his greying head, as if thinking through the implications, and then summing up for his own benefit:

"So she sacrifices herself on the altar of her higher love." And looking up again and fixing his little eyes on him he continued:

"As for *this* young woman, young and utterly delightful as she is – I reckon that the very fact of her visit to you and the time spent in your office, will do irreparable harm to her honour as a maiden and her good name as a woman, and she will no longer be eligible to marry according to the law, unless *you* marry her. And you're waiting for your princess from Judah! So things are becoming a little complicated, and this lady inspires admiration and compassion, and heart-ache as well. I suppose you could take her as a mistress? I'm sure she would agree to anything if it meant being close to you."

"I could never agree to that!" he protested.

"Your future wife would object?" asked Nashdernach, in a toneless voice.

"She wouldn't express any objection, but deep down she'd feel damaged. But even leaving that aside, the idea doesn't appeal to me."

"Why is that?" Nashdernach persisted.

"Because I don't believe in polygamy, and in my heart I know that polygamy is contrary to the will of God."

"Your forefathers married many wives, and to this very day the practice is tolerated among your compatriots!"

"The murder of animals and the consumption of their carcases are also practices condoned by the Torah, but this is a late version of it, a compromising version. It isn't the consummate worship of God, doing the true will of God."

"And is there to be no compassion for this young woman, no easing of her grief?"

"There is help for her," he declared, "but she has to consent to it."

"And how is she to do that?"

"By strengthening her faith in God, and loving Him with all her heart and mind."

"Aha!" exclaimed Nashdernach, his tone acknowledging that a valid and persuasive point had been made. And then he took a thick scroll from his pocket, laid it on the table, opened it and said:

"Now for the business in hand. We need to discuss the status of soldiers who are permanently disabled as a result of injuries sustained in war."

NEJEEN

With the onset of spring a wind from the east descends upon Babylon, gusting strongly day and night without respite, bearing on its wings grey dust from the roads and sand from the desert. People try to protect themselves from it by sealing the shutters of their homes and veiling their faces.

One such morning, when the east wind was beginning to subside, and the sky was peering through gaps in the swirling clouds of dust, he rose from his bed with a feeling of light-heartedness and merriment, bathed and dressed and went out to the broad veranda of his house, all awash with flowers, a rich tapestry of colours. He sat on a chair beside the oblong table, covered by a blue cloth with silver trim.

He knew the source of his exhilaration: *she* was coming.

How would she look? And what of the future relations between them? And the joy in his heart swelled and grew ever stronger, until it was no longer to be easily controlled or suppressed.

"My Father in Heaven, my God, what is the nature of this joy that fills my heart and thrills every fibre of my being? Is this joy pure? Are You the source of it? Does it have another source?"

"No my son! This joy arises and emanates from the fountains of my light, and it will not divert you from the way! Delight in it and bless it!"

The household slave was trying to attract his attention as he paced back and forth among the vases on the veranda, moving them this way and that, and when he finally succeeded and he looked back at him with a questioning glance, he bowed to him and informed him that Denur-Shag was asking permission to enter.

He broke off from his meditations and asked the slave to hurry and admit Denur-Shag to the house.

A few moments later, his former teacher was standing before him, trying to dissuade him from rising to meet him and to shake his hand.

"You shouldn't deprive us of the pleasure of prostrating ourselves before a person of exceptional authority!" he commented, adding in typical style: "Not that the exceptional is something that I care for particularly, but where persons of authority are concerned, it is the routine that repels – and I'm talking about smells here. Authority trapped in a frame of routine gives off a familiar smell, quite pungent and very similar, if not identical, to the smell that assails your nostrils in the vicinity of a slaughterhouse. In agriculture, for example, routine works wonders, and it's a boon to the farmer, to the land and to all of humanity, and its smell is clean. However, the routine that I like best of all is the routine of family life, paved as it is with petty disasters and delights."

He signalled to the slave, and he brought in figs, nuts and dates, an Egyptian jug made of the finest glass and containing honey-water, and matching goblets. The foodstuffs were served on small dishes that were smooth inside and out, gleaming white in colour and hand-painted in blue with images of trees, people and flowers – real works of art. Denur-Shag picked up one of the dishes, turned it over in his hand and studied it from every angle, finally declaring:

"Sent to you direct from the royal warehouse, I assume."

He confirmed this with a nod.

"I don't suppose that in the whole of Babylon there are exquisite objects such as these to be found, except in the possession of the King himself and now – in your possession too. I may be mistaken, and perhaps that clever trader who has the strange-sounding Hebrew name of Adoniah, and the equally strange Chaldean name of Adeshech, is among the few who own articles like these. As I'm sure you know, they are made by those faraway people with the slanting eyes, who weave silk fabrics made from caterpillars, or more accurately – from the cocoons of caterpillars, which, if allowed to live, would turn into winged butterflies of breath-taking beauty. Our faraway brothers are harsh in their treatment of these unfortunate caterpillars, stripping them of their cocoons and leaving them to die, naked and helpless, in excruciating pain. Such is the typical behaviour of mankind, and yet according to your sacred writings the first man was appointed to 'give names' to all living creatures, from the butterfly to the elephant, meaning – that man is supposed to defend them, and delight in them and love them, so that they will love him in return, and gladly provide him with wool and milk and with impressive displays of colour and movement.

"But here mankind has failed and has betrayed God's trust, and instead of 'giving names', mankind is deleting names from the list of living things, and is exploiting those that remain and tormenting them and preying on them. Was this your God's intention when He created mankind?"

"God is love," he responded evenly, while pouring honey-water into the goblets of fine Egyptian glass, "and love does not impose itself on the object of its love, love bestows freedom. Man is liable to make the wrong use of the freedom that he has been granted."

"I wouldn't say he was 'liable' to do that," Denur-Shag objected, taking the full goblet that was handed to him and raising it in a gesture of benediction, then taking a small sip from it. "Man has done it – and is still doing it, and is bringing down on his head all the disasters of the world."

Denur-Shag took a shelled nut, chewed it in his mouth for a while and before swallowing it said:

"Yesterday, at a late hour of the night, I had a visit from someone who is reckoned to be a relative of mine – by marriage," he saw fit to stress, and added for further clarification: "This is the family of my rustic wife, one of the most 'extended' in the kingdom. It has so many members that no one knows the precise number, but all of the people of that village, to the very last one of them, have close family ties between them and as you might say – they take responsibility for one another.

"And ever since I had the good fortune to marry a daughter of the village of these agreeable people – it's only logical and natural that, according to the rigid rules of that mutual responsibility, I should be acknowledged as a member of the tribe and of the family unit, and guaranteed their full support. To their credit I may say, they expect nothing from me in return.

"This relative, it turns out, joined some delegation or other and went away to Judah some months ago, and now he's glad to be back in Babylon. He had a specific job as a runner – carrying messages, letters, news and items of small value between members of the delegation, and between members of the delegation and outsiders. Exploiting his role as a harbinger, and using the expertise and the wealth of experience gained through this unconventional profession, he decided to precede the delegation, moving ahead like the vanguard of an army on the march, and he came to me yesterday, in the late hours of the night. And the boy didn't want to go to bed and rest from the rigours of the journey, perhaps because of the rigid rules of the mutual responsibility code – or perhaps he just wanted to share some of the impressions stamped on his peasant mind.

"Anyway, he sat down with me, this distant relative of mine, and while partaking of the modest repast which I served to him, he proceeded to tell me his story. And the story was a long one, extending into the dawn and even beyond, and it couldn't be described as interesting and pleasant to listen to either. This peasant boy is far removed from anything that could be called eloquence, and not much of a story teller, but that clan code demanded of him whatever it demanded, and I had to sit and listen closely because of my obligations under that ancient code – a fascinating object of study for anyone researching into ancient laws and customs, written and unwritten."

Denur-Shag returned to his drink, drained his goblet and without saying a word, took the bottle and refilled it.

He himself had not yet touched his drink, instead listening intently to the words of his guest.

"Are you bored?" Denur-Shag asked, taking a ripe date between two fingers and putting it to his mouth, without looking at him, as if ignoring his very presence and as if talking to himself.

And sure enough, the questioner did not wait for an answer, but went on to say:

"These words were by way of a preamble. And for some reason it seems to me – and 'seems' is just a sterile, evasive expression – it would be more accurate to say 'I'm sure', yes 'I'm sure' without any hesitation or prevarication, that the next part of the story will be of great interest to you. You can visualise it, and see the whole episode unfolding before your mind's eye!

"Well then," – Denur-Shag took another sip of his drink, "my relative told me that in the convoy travelling with the delegation there was a special wagon, with padding and upholstery, closed most of the time, and occupied by a wondrous Jewish princess. Wondrous, that is, in her beauty and also in her demeanour. My rustic relative referred specifically to an exceptional kind of behaviour, quite unfamiliar to him, something testifying to noble lineage or, as he tried to express it with his inferior eloquence, something showing that this lady was 'born to be a queen' – a common and hackneyed expression, but like so many such expressions, both succinct and accurate!

"And while on the subject of the exceptional behaviour of this Jewish princess, the one 'born to be a queen', my rustic relative told me that at one of their overnight halts, on the way back from Jerusalem, not far from Tyre, bandits got into the camp, tied up the two sentries who were supposed to be guarding the horses, and they were about to cut off their heads and steal the horses, leaving the convoy without any effective means of transport, stuck in the middle of nowhere, hopeless and helpless – when all of a sudden the Jewish princess appeared. She confronted the bandits, all five of them, and ordered them to untie the captives and set them free, to leave their booty behind and to go back to their haunts the same way that they had come. And this is the point: she didn't urge them, didn't plead with them, didn't cry or try to appeal to their compassion – no, she *ordered* them, in the clear voice of a born leader and commander. That is the testimony of the captives themselves, they saw her and heard her, and they were amazed by the glorious vision and by the regal sound of her voice. And no less impressed, so it seems, were the bandits themselves. Those five tough men obeyed her and even bowed to her, they released their captives, mounted their horses and rode away, leaving their booty behind, and disappeared into the darkness, as this was the third watch of the night. And the sentries who had been freed and had escaped with their lives did not know themselves for joy and even tried to offer some gift to the princess, but she flatly rejected any attempt to reward her, and when asked how she realised what was happening, unlike all the other members of the delegation who didn't wake or hear anything, and how she had mastered her fear – the Jewish princess explained that her wagon was parked close to the horses' enclosure, and with her sharp ear she heard the nervous whinnying of the horses and went to see what was afoot. As for fear, her comment was – anyone who trusts in God is exempted from fear. And as a direct result of this statement, referring as it did to the God of the princess, a number of Chaldeans converted there and then, following the lead of the two sentries who owed their lives to this God." Denur-Shag concluded his account and there was a long silence. Eventually he continued:

"This, in my humble opinion, is the least boring part of my story. According to my estimation, at this moment the delegation is crossing, or has just crossed, the bridge over the Euphrates, and it is due to arrive at the royal palace shortly after midday. If you want to meet the delegation in appropriate style, you have two hours in hand. As for me, I have no intention of staying around here and joining the reception committee, but before we part company, I shall tell you the third and final part of this story – yes, the story does have a third part!"

Denur-Shag leaned back in his chair and continued calmly:

"It turns out that my relative's visit to foreign parts, meaning Jerusalem, the sacred capital of Judah, had a profound effect on him. It wasn't just the emotional strain of distance from his native village, it was a traumatic spiritual experience that he had, by his own admission – the first such upheaval he has ever known.

"The youth told me of a man, the like of whom he had never seen before nor met before, not even in the great metropolis of Babylon. He had never dreamed that such a person even existed. A long, long beard, not neatly trimmed and plaited in the Chaldean style, but wild and unkempt, as is the hair of his head, and he wears a simple robe, a rope for a belt at his waist, and he walks about barefoot. Nothing remarkable so far – it could be that the man has eccentric tastes, or he could be short of cash. What astonished my relative was seeing the eyes of this man, eyes unlike any others he had known. One glance was enough to convince him this was the only pair of eyes in the world, the only eyes that could truly see. These eyes do not glitter or sparkle, but there is light in their depths, flaring up at intervals like a burning torch and at intervals subsiding, sometimes gleaming as bright as the sun. And yet these eyes are not troubled, on the contrary they are serene, with a serenity that is detached from all things, and that is why it is so potent, inspiring fear on the one hand and on the other, boundless admiration and exaltation of spirit.

"Anyway, this man walks the streets of Jerusalem, and speaks out in a clear and resolute voice, untainted by arrogance, and he turns to the people who follow him, and there are many who follow him, and he addresses them sometimes with stern words of reproof and sometimes with words of consolation and encouragement. And he always emphasises that it is not he who speaks but God, your God, speaking through him. And his words are an awesome warning – if the Jews do not learn to manage their affairs properly and proceed in the ways of reason – Jerusalem will be ruined and set ablaze. More than this – he demands there must be no revolt against the King of Babylon whom He, God that is, your God, calls 'my servant' – meaning, the one who does His will. And the reaction to this man, whose name by the way is Jeremiah, the priest from Anathoth, is entirely predictable. People respond to his conduct and the message that he brings in the traditional and time-honoured fashion: beating him with their fists and spitting in his face, waving sticks at him and pelting him with stones, yelling with the righteous anger of all patriots, 'Death to the traitor!' and leaving him to lie, barely conscious or not conscious at all, slumped at the roadside or in a corner of the marketplace. And there are indeed some who try to shield him from his assailants, but they are very few, and most of them old men, and their way of defending him is to stage public debates which, as you know, do more harm than good.

"Returning to that innocent youth, to whom I am tied by that reciprocal family code, attention should be drawn to something else that he said, an uncouth remark but vivid and significant for all that:

"He told me he had met a number of Egyptians, leaders among their own people, who disguise themselves as traders and simple folk and try to look like Jews in every respect, but their diction gives them away, as does their clothing. They are not used to the Jewish mantle, but to robes that flap in the wind, and when they try to move about in the tight confines of the mantle, it looks ridiculous and it betrays their origins. These Egyptians come and go in the court of King Zedekiah and this, like everything in the third and final part of my story, should engender surprise and raise questions and above all, strike fear into the heart. For it seems, and Jeremiah, the priest from Anathoth, confirms this wholeheartedly – darkness is descending on Jerusalem and a bloodbath is in store for Judah. And there is one question that is always asked before something happens that is supposed to happen – is this bloodbath inevitable?"

"No," he replied, "this bloodbath is not inevitable. There is no such thing as an inevitable bloodbath. As for the means of preventing it, it is the same as for any bloodshed anywhere in the world, past, present or future. Only one method is effective, no other."

"And that is?" Denur-Shag pressed him.

"Adherence to values."

"And what does that mean, 'adherence to values'?" Denur-Shag wanted to know.

"Devotion to the truth and the truthful."

"In other words, if people respect the truth in all things, in thought, in word and in deed – that is enough to avert a massacre?"

"It is enough!"

"Perhaps an exiled Jew, one who is in favour with King Nebuchadnezzar, could talk with those Jews who remain in their homeland, drinking their good wine and eating their sweet figs – and persuade them to mend their ways."

"If Jeremiah from Anathoth, through whom God speaks, failed in his mission – could an exiled Jew do any better?"

Denur-Shag pondered for a while, ignoring what remained of the refreshments, and thinking something through, weighing it inwardly at some length and finally asking in a faint voice:

"Why are the Jews such a stiff-necked people?"

He answered him calmly, although with a hint of bitterness in his voice:

"Because of the arrogance with which they are infected. They see themselves as standing above all other peoples and races and nations, and as long as they cannot cure themselves of this infection – disaster awaits them."

"But you are not like that," Denur-Shag protested, "nor are those three friends of yours!"

"Because our faith is the true faith," he explained.

"And the faith of your compatriots is not true faith?"

"Where there is arrogance, there is no room for true faith."

"And what is to be done to combat this fatal arrogance?"

"True faith is the only answer."

Denur-Shag rose heavily from his seat, shook his outstretched hand in silence and for a moment looked like a very old man, bowed under the weight of his years, defeated by life.

"Where are you rushing off to?" he addressed him kindly, still holding his hand and wishing he could give him some encouragement, however fleeting.

Denur-Shag looked up at him, and the expression of his face changed; the dejection dissolved, and a faint but steady light was ignited in the depths of his eyes.

"The Jewish princess is due to arrive at any moment! Anyone wanting to greet her had better hurry and make the necessary arrangement. And something else I shall tell you – there is hope for the Jewish people, and I wish there were just a small portion of it for the Chaldean people!"

"In what do you see this hope?" he asked.

"In that Jeremiah, the man of Anathoth, and in you and in those who are like you! Be well."

WITHOUT ANY CONNECTING THREAD

He could not believe what his eyes were seeing and his ears hearing. Nevertheless, it seemed to him there could be no sight more natural, more anchored in reality than this, no sound more familiar and responsive to his expectations than the voice he heard. On the one hand – it was as if the world had turned upside down and the new, without any connecting thread to what had gone before, was revealed to him in all the glory of its youth, while on the other – it seemed nothing had changed or was even capable of changing; the past being the present, and the present never deviating in the slightest degree from what used to be.

She stood before him, straight-backed, her long face pale, her forehead clear, a little arched, so pure it might never have been polluted by a deviant thought, or a less than exalted notion. And her eyes...yes, in her eyes there had been a change though it was barely perceptible. More precisely – the nature of the change was perceptible but not its extent. The luminous depths, familiar from days gone by, no longer knew any limit but flowed freely, from one eternity to another. The dark blue, that transported anyone seeing it beyond the furthest Heaven, was darker still, sometimes turning to the young violet of dusk.

The eyes resembled twin pools, deep, calm and smooth, drawing serenity and steadfast assurance from an unflagging source, and in the clarity of this source there was an astonishing wealth of tenderness, nobility and compassion.

It was Azariah who accompanied her to the threshold of his house, and after a firm handshake said awkwardly:

"I shall return later," and turned away.

The two of them shook hands and for a moment it seemed their hands would never be parted; then they parted them and gazed into one another's eyes with a look that was sincere, radiant, proud.

He began to speak, surprised at the sound of his calm, controlled voice:

"I very much hope that Babylon will be to your taste. It isn't Judah and it isn't Jerusalem!" he said, and heard her voice for the first time in eight years:

"God is everywhere!" – and her limpid voice was like a hymn of praise, of which he too was a part.

He repeated after her with a kind of joyful submission:

"God is everywhere!"

"I bring blessings and greetings from your mother, from your sisters and brother..."

"The baby!" he cried eagerly.

She smiled, and the high-ceilinged reception hall was swamped with light.

"He's eight years old!" she reminded him and added: "They asked me to tell you that they're proud of you."

"Why should they be proud of me?" he asked.

"Among other things," she answered him, "for interpreting the dream of the King of Babylon. Your mother says you are following in the path of our forefathers, who were commanded by God to make His will known to Jews and Gentiles alike."

"She's exaggerating!" he protested, in an attempt to dampen something of the admiration in her voice, which was indeed restrained but clearly perceptible. "What's your opinion?" he asked.

"What she says is the truth!" she replied simply, in her old style. "My mother's proud of you too," she added, "as are many of the citizens of Jerusalem..." Her voice quavered and her eyes fell.

"And there are also some who are not proud but angry," he suggested, and she confirmed it.

"There are indeed." Her voice was steady again.

He suggested they go to the veranda, and she followed him.

He sat down at the table as he had sat a little while before with Denur-Shag, noting inwardly that the strange, unfamiliar sensation of shining light, grace and quiet pleasure was taking over his entire being.

When the slave had served refreshments and a jug of warm honey-water, he resumed:

"I have heard about Jeremiah the prophet – how they are conspiring against him and humiliating him, how he has been beaten and persecuted!"

"It is true," she said, and suddenly the soft radiance of her eyes captivated him and he was all exaltation. He remembered the words of Adoniah, that one glimpse of her would be enough to persuade the worst of felons to mend his ways and repent.

My Father in Heaven, my God – he spoke to his heart, which was quivering with a rapture such as he had never known – *Am I worthy of this grace?*

And he heard her voice, offering strength and solace:

"Jeremiah the prophet has heard about you, too. When my uncle, my mother's brother, told him I was going down to Babylon to marry you, he took the trouble to come to us and he sat in our house three days and two nights, most of the time shut away in a room with the door locked, not saying a word and barely eating. Until finally he turned to me and said:

'Convey the blessing of God to your future husband and my blessing too, and tell him to be joyful and be glad, because his mission is ordained by God, a source of wonder and delight, and all the humble among my people will rejoice in him!' And seeing the look of astonishment on my face, the prophet added: 'Despite the contempt, and the ingratitude, the beatings and the abuse, the banishment and imprisonment to which the envoy of God is subjected, there shines in his heart the eternal joy of the awareness of God and the knowledge of Him! The reward of the envoy of God – is God Himself!'"

"That is indeed the truth!" he declared warmly, pouring out some of the honey-water for her and for himself, and taking only a tiny morsel of the bread. She asked him why he was abstaining from the lavish spread that was laid out on the table and he explained that earlier that morning he had been visited by a dear friend, the one who informed him of the imminent return of the delegation and her arrival – and they had broken their fast together.

"He wanted to cheer you up," she remarked casually, like him taking a small piece of bread and drinking thirstily from the liquid – light and refreshing and still retaining its warmth.

"He wouldn't miss an opportunity to gladden the heart of his friend!" he agreed, and smiled at her, a deep smile that she took in without raising her eyes, and her pale cheeks flushed slightly.

"Do you remember the bears?" he asked.

"I remember," she replied, looking up and calmly meeting his gaze. "Do you remember how many cubs there were?"

"Three!" he smiled again.

"And the colour of their fur?" she went on to ask, her voice light and vibrant with youth, as well as a sense of good-natured mischief.

He racked his brains, thought it over, seeing in his mind's eye the cubs and their mother... all standing there before him as if alive, and he even inhaled the peculiar balm of the air in the Jerusalem hills, but the colour of the fur of the cubs had vanished from his eyes.

"No," he looked up, admitting defeat. "I can't even remember if there was any difference between them. Do you?"

"One of them was very light, almost yellow, his brother was dark brown, and the youngest of all had tufts of brown fur on a lighter background." She laughed a full-throated, resonant laugh, pleasing to the ear, melodious as the laughter of a child.

They sat in silence, and the longer the silence lasted, so they felt the pleasure bridging the gap between them, redolent with faith and strong in its unflagging purity.

"How do you like the idea of bringing the marriage ceremony forward?" he asked, his tone calm and harmonious.

She answered him in the same tone:

"As you wish!"

"Would you like to see the house?" he asked.

"Gladly!"

He showed her round the two-storey house placed at his disposal, with its sixteen rooms and two halls, a large hall on the ground floor and a smaller one above. And then he showed her the seven-roomed apartment set aside for her, and introduced her two Chaldean chambermaids who greeted her with a bow. A spacious bed chamber linked her rooms to his.

"Do you approve of the arrangement of rooms?" he asked finally, as they sat facing one another in the parlour that was now hers.

"Very much so!" she answered him sincerely, and added: "Whatever pleases you, pleases me sevenfold. As it has been for as long as I remember!"

"I could say the same thing of myself," he smiled, and his smile again brought a flush to her cheeks: "Whatever pleases you, pleases me sevenfold!" He bowed lightly to underline his words.

"Your friend Azariah was very helpful to me, so please thank him in my name!"

"I'll thank him in my own name too! Azariah is a loyal friend and a devoted companion."

"We heard the rumour that you asked the King to appoint him a minister, and your other friends too, Mishael and Hananiah. In my humble opinion you did the best thing possible, and I have no doubt it will bear fruit."

"We work together, and by the grace and the mercy of God, we're trying to bring some relief to the peoples that Babylon has subjugated."

"That's what the prophet Jeremiah was saying – that your mission is a divine one and you could achieve a great deal – so he said, and you would also be tested by temptation, but God would always be with you to save you from death. Those were his explicit words and he went on to say you should be strong and take courage, as your words and your deeds will be the property of all generations of mankind yet to come, and there will be many who love you and more who hate you, and those who hate you are those who hate God and defy Him, and those who love you – are lovers of God who do His will."

"If only God will give the strength to cope with all of them!" he said, adding: "It is written in the Scriptures, *I am not jealous*, meaning that he who has earned the privilege of loving Him, the Blessed One, yearns for nothing else other than Him. All that he seeks, he seeks through Him, and all that he does, he does for the greater glory of His name, and all that he loves, he loves through Him and for His sake."

"May His name be forever blessed!" she pronounced the benediction in a remarkably even voice and raised to him her open, candid gaze, dismissing hypocrisy and banishing evil thought or malicious intent.

Again he was swept by that tide of pure delight and exuberance of spirit. He remembered Adoniah and asked her:

"Not long ago you sent me greetings through Adoniah, one of the exiles, who serves the King as a trader and a go-between."

"I remember him well," she replied. "A young man with all kinds of ideas running around in his head, not the kind of ideas likely to bring him closer to God. I entrusted to him a gift and a message for you."

He unbuttoned his shirt and showed her the seven-branched candlestick, hanging about his neck.

For a moment her eyes glowed with satisfaction, and then she went on to say:

"He told me certain things, some of which I was interested to hear."

"Such as?" he asked.

"Such as the horse race that both of you, it seems, took part in. At first he said he was crowned the winner, then he changed his story and said he almost won, and finally he admitted it was all lies and the winner was none other than you. Naturally I was pleased to hear this and I was proud as well. And then the man launched into a recital of gossip that I barely paid attention to, until he seemed to lose the thread and cut his speech short, stopping altogether and even apologising. Then he gave me some conflicting versions of his life story, saying how miserable he'd been, with no one to talk to or confide in, and then he declared with a kind of arrogance, to say nothing of pretentiousness, that the work he was doing was on behalf of the King of Babylon, and he was doing it well, and this role of his had opened up all kinds of opportunities for him, and he was seeing the world and gaining experience and most important of all – enjoying himself. Still, I see he did his task faithfully, and gave you what he was asked to give you!"

"He almost forgot!" he said lightly, with a chuckle.

"To tell you the truth," she replied – "I wouldn't have been surprised if he had forgotten. He looked so preoccupied."

"With what?" he asked.

"With himself!" was the clear and simple answer.

He took his leave of her, and told her chambermaids to prepare her a hot bath; they assured him it was already done. He watched the porters bringing in her belongings and for the third time that day, for no immediately obvious reason, he felt overwhelmed by glee and exuberance of spirit, and were it possible, at that moment he would have embraced the whole universe and given it all that was in him, and more.

Azariah he met the next morning, and he confirmed the rumours coming out of Judah, concerning Zedekiah and his rebellious intentions.

And Azariah went on to tell of the profound impression made by the interpretation of the King of Babylon's dream, and of people on the streets of Jerusalem saying: "See, a true prophet has arisen for us, and the Lord has visited His people and has sent His prophet to deliver us from the hands of strangers and from the yoke of the Chaldeans." And in the same breath, with the praise and the approbation, come the rage and the resentment – people of Jerusalem and Judah asking one another why is he, Daniel the Jew, fraternising with the Chaldean King, "the wicked King" as they call him, or "the heathen" and other such derogatory epithets. Why, they say, is this chosen son of our holy nation, our proud race that is set apart from all others, working in the service of an alien king, rather than serving us and our Jewish king? And to the question – how is this to be done, the startling answer is:

"He must threaten that King with ruin and destruction, if he does not lift his yoke from our necks!"

If they hear the answer to the other question – that it's his duty to preach the word of God before the King and before anyone else to whom God sends him, and this message that they want to convey to the King of Babylon is not from God! – they are incensed, those milling crowds of Jews, and they insist that every word spoken by a man such as this is the word of the living God, and if he has any interest in delivering his people from the Chaldean yoke, then he will not hesitate or prevaricate, but hasten to the enemy's lair and say what he has to say, and the tyrant will take fright, and he will restore the freedom of Jerusalem, and cancel his taxes, and never again dare to raise his hand against Judah. "Such are the words of the ignorant populace," Azariah concluded his account.

He did not reply to Azariah for better or for worse, but instead raised the subject of the weddings and asked him to discuss it with Mishael and Hananiah and let him know which day was acceptable to them for the raising of the canopy. With Azariah's approval, he would consult with Nehemiah, the priest of the community, to decide the order of service, and moreover he would choose a site and invite guests.

Azariah left his office and two days later returned to him with two dates that were acceptable to all three of them. He picked one of them and preparations for the wedding ceremonies, due to take place three weeks hence, began in earnest.

FOUR WEDDINGS

Long before the appointed time the Jews, members of the old community of Babylon, began streaming towards the maidan behind the wall, where the four wedding ceremonies were to take place. They left behind their daily labours, their curiosity urging them to come and feast their eyes on that prophet in whom the spirit of the Lord moved, who not only interpreted the dream of the dreadful King, as they called Nebuchadnezzar among themselves, but also saw in his mind's eye the same dream, an apparently impossible feat which had never been matched, which was beyond the ability of diviners and soothsayers the whole world over. It was certainly the grace of God that was revealed through this Jewish youth, known as Daniel in his homeland and here, in Babylon, as Belteshazzar, and the pagan King had the wisdom to acknowledge the miracle and to glorify Daniel, promoting him above all his other clerks and appointing him his viceroy, like the righteous Joseph in his time, to whom Pharaoh gave charge of the whole land of Egypt, wielding the power of life and death as he saw fit.

The wide open space, green and luxuriant, was crammed with bearded folk, wearing robes of all fabrics and colours known to man – ranging from the coarse and the dark, tending towards black or brown at best, the symbol of the meaner members of society – to the royal blue and the gleaming purple of fine linens and silks, embellished with all kinds of ornaments, from nuggets of silver and gold to precious stones of all kinds and colours. Almost all wore on their heads turbans of the same fabric as their robes, and broad sashes around their waists. Most wore shoes of leather or cloth, but a minority from among the less well-to-do proposed to attend the weddings barefoot, somewhat to the annoyance of their well-shod counterparts:

"They should be ashamed of themselves! If they had asked, we would have given them shoes as an act of charity. The truth is they're just lazy, it's in their blood, and it's a disgrace!"

And there were those who heard the indignant words of the complainers and declared explicitly that it was not up to the barefooted to come and ask for charity from the elders and the burghers of the community; the elders and the burghers of the community were supposed to know how poverty-stricken these people were, and supply them with whatever they needed. In any case, the bare feet of the barefooted was not necessarily evidence of laziness, but pointed, among other things, to the stinginess of the gentry, occasionally employing these barefooted workers and paying them virtually nothing.

One way or the other, they were all here, men, women and children, and everywhere there was jubilation, bridging the gaps between social classes and blurring divisions, the old and the new, the severe and the trivial.

Faces shone with cheerful radiance and even Simeon, father of Hanna, the destined bride of Hananiah, smiled into the rising sun and greeted his neighbour Baruch, Deborah's father, with a light bow and a firm shake, and a blessing of "So, to life!" that was almost free of any kind of resentment.

Also among the guests were Gabriel and Uziel, wearing the brown robes of minor officials. Adoniah had sent a message, regretting that he was unable to attend and exchange handshakes and good wishes with his old friends, as he had been sent on an urgent mission to the lands of the East, to repair trade links that had been disrupted by a series of obstacles and misunderstandings.

Nashdernach was present as the King's official representative. The four grooms for their part had invited Denur-Shag, and he arrived in a carriage drawn by six magnificent horses, hired at his own expense from the royal mews.

"At last, I shall see a Jewish wedding!" he exclaimed in typically jovial style, and tried to jump down from the carriage, and were it not for the grooms, who were standing there in line waiting to greet him, and who stepped forward and caught him just in time, he would have fallen flat on his face, treading on the tails of his elegant cloak, too big for him – as always.

Denur-Shag laughed heartily and after expressing warm words of gratitude he turned to them and said:

"I was testing your alertness! From now on it will be up to you to do everything you can, and more, to keep your wits sharp! This is one of the relatively few blessings that marriage confers on a healthy young man – it forces him to stay alert, and he has to learn how to put the remedy before the injury!"

Or-Nego was among the guests too, and with him Adelain. They met before the ceremony began. Or-Nego was wearing his parade uniform of blue shirt and white satin breeches, both embroidered in gold. On his broad blue sash, also with gold embroidery, hung a thin-bladed sword with gold hilt and a pommel of silver encrusted with pearls. The buckle of his sash showed a gold engraving of the three royal recumbent lions. His shoes were as white as his breeches.

Adelain wore a pink robe, hemmed in white. On the buckle of her sash was the engraving of a fig-tree on a background of cast gold. When he asked her what it represented she told him:

"It's the emblem of novice-priestesses in the shrine of Bel!" and gave him a long look. Behind the enforced gaiety, there was a deep sense of despair.

The two young women studied one another briefly, shook hands and exchanged greetings which sounded sincere. Then they were separated by the press of the crowd.

At his suggestion all four of them wore the same costume – white shirt and breeches, broad purple sash, white turban and shoes, all trimmed in gold. Belt and shoe-buckles were gold, the collars of the shirts embroidered in gold and on every turban was a blue jewel on a gold background. The brides on the other hand were dressed in various colours – blue, purple, white and violet, with matching belts studded with jewels of varying quality, size and colour.

The gigantic canopy was set up in the heart of the maidan, on a low stage, a slender wooden pole at each of its four corners supporting an awning of blue. In accordance with the custom of the place all the men, young and old, wrapped themselves in white and blue shawls, and the women covered their heads with kerchiefs. At the edge of the maidan stood the four couples, in line, while Nehemiah, resplendent in his priestly robes, took his place at the head of the procession and set off towards the canopy, as a young man walked at his right hand swinging the incense burner and the crowd made way for them. And the priest began in a guttural voice *"Blessed is the man"* – and the congregation gave the response, chanting with him *"who does not sit among the scornful".* And the couples advanced steadily towards the canopy and reached it to the swelling strains of the chorus, mounted the low stage and entered beneath the canopy.

The priest recited the nuptial contracts in that same guttural, well-lubricated voice, accustomed to recitation, and after the contracts came the blessings, and after each blessing the packed assembly replied "Amen!" as one man, and when the blessings were done the priest cried out in an awesome voice:

"If I forget you Jerusalem, may my right hand forget!" and he raised his arm aloft, and all the mighty crowd replied in the same tone and with the same gesture – *"If I forget you Jerusalem, may my right hand*

forget!" – until the air itself was shaken by the force of the vibration, and then all at once there was silence, and the priest repeated his energetic gesture and cried:

"Next year in Jerusalem!"

And the crowd repeated the same words with the same gesture as before and in the same awesome tone:

"Next year in Jerusalem!"

And when the moment came, and each groom sanctified his bride with the words "You are sanctified to me," the congregation ripped the void apart with cries of "Sanctified! Sanctified! Sanctified!"

And before the happy couples left the canopy, Nashdernach was invited to stand and to speak, to bless those who had just been united in the name of the King and of his Council.

The oration was brief, but was marked by a degree of vehemence which was clearly felt and which struck fear into the hearts of some members of his audience and embarrassed others, while there were some who were simply enraged by what they heard him say.

After congratulating the newly-weds in the traditional manner, and passing on to them the best wishes of the King and of the Court, and his own, and announcing the gifts that the King in his generosity was giving to them – lavish sums of money – he spoke briefly in praise of the community of Babylon, which according to him, had always demonstrated commitment and their loyalty to the Crown. And here he made the comment that as among the Babylonians themselves, among the Jews of Babylon too there existed a small and insignificant minority, promoting seditious ideas and trying to spread them among the members of the community at large. This effort was clearly doomed to failure, he assured them; after all, was there any group more fortunate than the Jews of Babylon, any benefiting more than they from the affluence and the freedom and the equality that the wise and valiant monarch, His Majesty King Nebuchadnezzar, had conferred upon all the nations and people under his sway, and he was confident that the decisive majority of the Jews of Babylon would take control of that insignificant minority and restore it to the ways of understanding and healthy reason, lest it invite disaster upon itself and upon the whole community.

Nashdernach concluded his clear and unequivocal speech with the exclamation:

"All praise to the King, the valiant and the wise, conqueror of the world, Nebuchadnezzar, His Majesty!" and he added to this "Long live the King!" The response to this was not the deafening chorus that might have been expected, but something more muted – and far from unanimous. Children and old men and some of the women took up the cry at full volume, as did a minority of the men. Among adult males some muttered the words reluctantly, others were silent, and tried to disguise their silence by turning to right and left and talking with their friends, others were ostentatiously silent, grim-faced and defiant.

Or-Nego pronounced a blessing too. He extolled the unique qualities of the Jewish people, a people distinct from all other races and nations, for better and decidedly not for worse, an asset of lasting value to the Chaldean kingdom in particular and to all races and nations in general. And here Or-Nego saw fit to stress that he had come to this conclusion through his close contact with the four bridegrooms and in particular with Belteshazzar, their leader, and to this very day – he went to say in his powerful, well-modulated voice, he was experiencing anew and reliving still the deep impressions made on him by that direct and dramatic first encounter. And he thanked God repeatedly for the privilege he had gained, and he was sure beyond any doubt, there was no people closer to God than the Jewish people, closer to the living God, and the salvation of the world and of all humanity depended on this people. And here his oration was interrupted by loud cries of "Hurrah!" and "Bravo!", accompanied by hand-clapping and foot-stamping, roars and whistles. And when the crowd had been hushed by the elders and dignitaries of the community, and the silence was broken only by a distant whistle or a faint cry of "Hurrah!", Or-Nego concluded his speech with the statement that all he really wanted to do was thank the grooms and their brides and the congregation for the honour of being allowed to attend the ceremony, and pass on special wishes for health and happiness from his daughter to Belteshazzar and his lovely wife.

Or-Nego stepped down from the stage, and the crowd resumed its chorus of cheering, hand-clapping and foot-stamping, which continued for a long time after he had disappeared from sight. Next to leave the stage were Nehemiah the priest and the newly-married couples.

Refreshments were served, and the foodstuffs were many and varied. Mostly meat dishes and all in abundance, with the wine flowing freely.

Denur-Shag approached him, a full goblet of wine in his hand and asked him:

"What's the meaning of those incantations, *If I forget you Jerusalem, may my right hand forget!* and *Next year in Jerusalem?*"

He admitted to Denur-Shag that he was no less puzzled himself. But then Baruch, Mishael's father-in-law, who was standing close by and overheard what was said, turned to them and explained:

"Those incantations have been part of the ritual of the Jews of Babylon since the community was founded, hundreds of years ago. They express the desire that will never fade for the return to Zion. And this will be fulfilled one day, and the Jews and all Israel shall return to their homes and dwell in Jerusalem the Holy, and worship God there until the end of all generations."

"Indeed, indeed!" Denur-Shag muttered, in genuine amazement, and commented: "Your people is indeed a stiff-necked people, but one with a vision! It seems that in the end this vision will be realised, even above and beyond what is hoped for!"

"So be it!" Baruch replied, and turned and disappeared into the crowd.

Oshrich, his office slave, who was now employed in his household as well, approached him and after offering warm congratulations, told him that some of the worthies of the community were asking his master to spare them a little of his time. They were sure he would not disappoint them, and they were waiting for him at the house of Simeon, Hananiah's father-in-law.

He did not deny their request, and leaving Nejeen in the company of her fellow-brides, he went with Oshrich to Simeon's house.

In a large and gloomy room sat about a dozen elderly men, wearing festive garb and prayer-shawls, who rose as soon as he entered and blessed him and wished him well. He was offered a seat, and when he had sat down, the hosts returned to their seats.

For a moment there was silence.

Simeon cleared his throat and began:

"We are very proud to welcome among us the King's viceroy, the wearer of the gold chain. We are grateful for the honour that he has conferred upon us and we congratulate him on his recent marriage, wishing every happiness to him and to his spouse!" And without any apparent connection to what had gone before he added: "The business of seeing the dream that the King saw and interpreting it, cannot but remind us of the saintly Joseph, who interpreted the dream of Pharaoh, King of Egypt, and rose to high office and when the time came – helped his brothers and his kinsmen and delivered them from the scourge of hunger."

And at this point somebody called out from the corner:

"The case of the saintly Joseph is not the same as the case of Daniel the man of God – a difference in favour of the latter!"

"What do you mean, Benjamin?" demanded Simeon, his thick brows knotting in menace.

Benjamin smiled awkwardly – a middle-aged man with light complexion and soft brown eyes, hair and beard in neat ringlets, clad in a robe of deep blue girded by a grey belt, and over his robe, like all the others present in the room, wearing a white shawl with gold embroidery:

"I mean," he replied, "that the saintly Joseph was required only to interpret the dream, whereas this man of ours, whom we are delighted to be entertaining in our midst, was required to reveal exactly what it was that the King dreamed, as the King himself had forgotten it, and only after revealing it – to interpret it. An important distinction!" the speaker added in an attempt to regain some of the self-confidence that Simeon's scowl had shaken.

"Both of them alike have served as glorious instruments in the hands of our God, Blessed be He, creator of Heaven and Earth!" Simeon declared, as if asking not to be interrupted again, or distracted from the main issue

Benjamin clearly had something to add, perhaps even points that he wanted to score over Simeon, but he kept his silence and seemed to shrink into his corner.

Simeon turned to him and asked him:

"Does your opinion differ from mine?"

"Not at all!"

"You are both glorious instruments in the hands of God?"

"And I am the lesser!"

Something resembling a smile twisted Simeon's heavy, dead lips.

"Do you hear that, Benjamin?" – he spoke without turning towards the one the words were directed at, and he pursed his lips again. The momentary spark that had shone in his dark eyes disappeared as it had never been.

"As I was saying," Simeon continued, "we are proud of you because you are a compatriot of ours, although few of us have had the good fortune to see the holy landscape of our homeland and to breathe its enchanted air. Still, it lives in our hearts and its fire will forever burn there, unquenched – until the time comes for our return thither, as it written *And the children shall return to their borders!* And we have no doubt that you will do everything in your power to ease our long time of waiting, marred as it is by suffering and abuse – and to shorten it as far as is possible, and hasten and bring forward that wondrous hour, the hour of our return to Zion!"

"It is not for me to hasten or bring forward the return of anyone to anywhere," he declared. "It is God who knows these things and God who decides them!"

"And what does God know, and what is he going to decide?" asked a man sitting close by, his voice low and barely audible, his garments suggesting that he was not among the elite of the community.

"It is God who knows when you will be worthy to return to your homeland and to your patrimony, and He it is who will decide the time," he replied.

The men stiffened. Someone shouted:

"Do you not think us worthy to return to Zion?"

"That is not for me to judge," was his answer. "God will decide."

"And we are sitting here at His command!" cried Benjamin, who had evidently mastered his confusion and regained his confidence, and he added: "So at least our fathers taught us!" The one sitting beside Benjamim leaned forward, with an emphatic movement, turned to him and said:

"We are here to safeguard the border of the holy kingdom of Judah, as was promised in our Scriptures. Surely that border is – the Euphrates!"

And at this point Simeon raised his voice, addressing him directly and saying:

"And it is your duty to assist us in this."

"In what?" he asked calmly, his eyes keen.

"In the destruction of the wicked kingdom!" shouted somebody amid the gathering, somebody he did not recognise.

He did not respond.

Silence fell in the room that was decorated with flowers, polished weapons and tapestries hanging on thick walls freshly daubed with lime – and yet in spite of this was sombre and chilly.

"I have heard much about your family," Simeon resumed his speech in a conciliatory tone, "from your friends and from many of the exiles who praise your father – a hero who fell honourably and died a martyr's death defending Jerusalem the Holy City! His memory be blessed!"

The gathering repeated after him in uncoordinated voices:

"His memory be blessed!" – and as they did so, rose fractionally from their seats.

"Yours, anyway, is the sacred obligation, as the loyal son of a valiant father and as a God-fearing man – to take revenge on his killers! As it is written in our Law, the Law of Moses – *an eye for an eye, a tooth for a tooth!* We shall all be with you and support you, and offer you all the help that you need and do as you command us to do, just so long as the death of your father, so much admired by all of us, does not go unavenged!"

All eyes were turned towards him, in tense anticipation, and in a kind of impossible innocence – with darkness at its core.

"It is written, *For I am merciful and I shall not bear grudges, forever!*" he replied, his voice reverberating in the stress-filled void.

After a long moment Simeon regained some composure and cried:

"You mean you're not interested in avenging your father's death?" – the tone of his voice resembled the snarl of a wild beast, ready to pounce and prey on whatever comes its way.

The one sitting beside Simeon echoed his protest:

"Will you refuse to take the field against the killers of your revered father, to fight them, strike a victorious blow and even die with honour – anything rather than do the bidding of one who ordered your father's murder?"

And Benjamin interjected:

"No Jew forgoes the honour that is due to him, and if it is decreed that he shall fall in battle, like his father, then fall he shall – there is no escape for him!"

And he replied:

"I do the bidding of no man and obey the will of no man, but of God alone! And because I obey His holy will, Blessed be He, I can stand against any man, be he a King of great renown, be they my brothers and compatriots, who are too blind to see!"

"And what is God commanding you now?" asked Simeon, clearly enraged.

"That which He commanded through the prophet Jeremiah!"

"Jeremiah is a traitor! A false prophet is Jeremiah!" Some of the men rose from their seats and waved clenched fists at him, their eyes shooting sparks.

"Jeremiah is the prophet of God, and all his words are the truth, the word of the living God!" – he cried in a clear, ringing voice, filled with unshakable, impregnable conviction.

"He who says that the Chaldeans shall defeat our holy people, this nation that the Lord chose from all the nations!" Benjamin intervened again from his corner.

"Jeremiah says," he insisted, "that if our people will not repent and mend its ways in time, nor cleave to the Lord, the loving Lord, nor uphold His holy Law that it swore to uphold – then it shall be trampled beneath the feet of its enemies."

"You too are an accomplice of this traitor!" cried the man who sat beside Benjamin, waving his fist menacingly.

"Jeremiah is the living voice of God, and anyone that does not obey him is defying and opposing God!" he declared.

Benjamin's neighbour stood up from his place, pushing his chair back noisily, apparently intending to attack him with his fists, and three others seemed ready to support him. Simeon hurried to his protection, shielding him and sending those who had risen back to their places. Then he turned to him and said:

"You have no intention, then, of taking up the sword to avenge the death of your revered father?"

And he replied:

"So long as I do the will of God, and hear His voice, I shall know for sure that my father is honoured and blessed in me!"

"It is the fault of people like you that our honour has been defiled, our people are oppressed and our enemies rejoice in our undoing!" raged Simeon.

"It is the fault of people who close their eyes from seeing and stop their ears from hearing the word of the living God, and call His prophet a 'traitor' – that calamity will come and disaster fall on our heads, and Judah will be ravaged and its people exiled from its land and dispersed among all the nations, to the ends of the earth!"

He turned and left the room, leaving its occupants stunned and stricken dumb.

JAHANUR

When it was that the King gave orders for the building of a gigantic statue in the valley of Dura, no one knew. It may be that it followed soon after those tempestuous days during which a dream was dreamed and forgotten, and the magicians and astrologers of Babylon were summoned to reveal and interpret it before the King, and when they failed Daniel came forward, the Jewish exile also known as Belteshazzar, and he revealed the dream and interpreted it, and earned high renown.

It may have been in the wake of these events that the King set to thinking and made his decision, and ordered the construction of this gigantic statue, sixty cubits in height, to stand in the heart of the valley of Dura and be a landmark visible from far away.

The building work proceeded, and Daniel paid no attention to it, nor did his friends, Mishael, Hananiah and Azariah. In their capacity as ministers they used to meet regularly to discuss matters of state, deciding which issues should have priority and precedence over others, which proposals should be dropped and which referred to the King for his approval. The business of the statue was never mentioned in their conversations, nor did it occur to them to imagine how fateful this statue would prove to be, how it would determine the course of their lives for the future.

One day Nashdernach came to his office, sat down facing him, cleared his throat and finally began:

"If I understand it correctly, the God that you worship is not one of those who are represented by images of clay or wood or iron or gold."

"That is correct," he answered him.

"And you are not permitted to bow down to any image, embodying any element of the divine, even of your own God?"

"Correct again!" he smiled.

"Even if the King himself commands you, and you know with absolute certainty that anyone disobeying the King's command shall surely die?"

"Even if the King himself commands me, and I know with absolute certainty that anyone disobeying the King's command shall surely die!" – he repeated Nashdernach's words with clear and earnest conviction, leaving no room to doubt his sincere intentions.

Nashdernach smiled awkwardly, rose from his seat, shook his hand warmly and left his office.

About a week later Nashdernach came once again to his office, and sitting down to face him in his customary fashion, told him:
"The King is asking to see you!"
He rose from his seat and followed Nashdernach, and the two of them entered the same hall in which he had revealed to the distraught King the dream that he had forgotten, and delivered a clear and succinct interpretation of it.

They passed between ranks of guardsmen standing to attention with swords drawn, bowed and prostrated themselves at the feet of the King, and when he had greeted them, rose and stood upright before him.

There was something of a gleam in the stern face of the King, in those bronzed features that did not know the meaning of fear, that struck terror into all those who saw them and set their heart-beat racing.

"My wish," said the King, addressing him, "is that you go to the mountainous northern region and to the town of Jahanur. You are to stay there a month, residing in the royal summer palace. Inspect the town and discover all that there is to know about it, and report to me on the number of inhabitants, their sources of livelihood, and how firm is their loyalty to the Crown!"

And Nebuchadnezzar turned to Nashdernach and said to him:
"For this month you are to take his place and do his work according to his instructions, everything to be put in writing and sealed by your hand!"

The two men bowed and prostrated themselves once again before the King, and saying in unison "His Majesty's will be done!" they withdrew, faces towards the throne and backs to the door.

On their return to his office, there was a certain awkwardness between them, for no apparent reason. He was entirely confident that Nashdernach was incapable of doing anything contrary to reason and integrity, and he was inclined to believe this was all down to caprice on the part of the King. Or perhaps this was the King's roundabout way of sending him to the hills for a period of rest and recuperation, although he had never complained of feeling overworked; on the contrary, he had fulfilled his duties conscientiously and gladly. Or was it the King's intention to treat him and his new bride to a honeymoon... But this explanation too failed to satisfy him.

"The whole of this business," Nashdernach said suddenly, "was arranged at my specific request!"

This admission by Nashdernach was utterly unexpected, and he gave him a startled look, though still without the slightest hint of suspicion or resentment, even in the depths of his heart. He waited for Nashdernach to clarify this remark and he did not have to wait long.

"About ten days from now the image that stands in the Dura valley will be dedicated, and the citizens of Babylon will be summoned by royal command to come and bow down to it, and anyone who does not come forward and bow to the image – will be thrown into the furnace! You will be among those summoned, and if you go to this place and refuse to bow to the image, in obedience to your God but in defiance of the King – you shall be thrown into the furnace. This is not what the King wants, nor is it what I want, your faithful servant! When the issue was explained to the King, just as I have explained it to you, he thought it over and came to his decision. As for that summer resort," Nashdernach continued with a cheerful smile – "there's no place that can match its beauty anywhere in the kingdom! It stands on a low hill surrounded by groves of pines with their sweet-smelling resin, and there are ancient vines in plenty, figs and olives and nuts and almonds, and bubbling streams. The inhabitants are hospitable, and the air is clear and invigorating!"

"And what is to become of my three friends, Shadrach, Meshach and Abed-Nego?" he asked, more interested in their fate than in lyrical descriptions of Jahanur.

"To the best of my knowledge," Nashdernach replied, "they are not required to be present at the dedication of the image, unlike you – the King's viceroy! And the solution that the King has devised for you is eloquent testimony – equivalent to that of a thousand witnesses – to the high regard and the warm favour in which he holds you. And this very day the leader of the council of Jahanur will be notified post-haste of your forthcoming visit and its purpose, and they are to prepare all the information that you require. I shall stay here, in your place, and do everything I can to expedite your projects in the best way possible, so you need have no concern on that account!"

He shook Nashdernach's hand firmly, and had to work hard to resist the impulse to embrace him – a mutual impulse as it was. They shook hands again, and slapped one another's shoulder, and when they parted, each noticed that the other's eyes were moist.

Before three days had elapsed, the convoy heading for Jahanur set out from the royal palace. One wagon sufficed for their possessions and they themselves rode in a light chariot, drawn by a pair of white horses.

As they approached the precinct of the shrines of the idols, they were halted by a procession of girls in white dresses, tallow candles burning in their hands, singing songs of praise and jubilation to Bel.

He recognised the virgin priestesses of Bel, and seeing Adelain among them he stepped down from the chariot and approached her, to wish her well on the completion of her noviciate and her acceptance into the order. She gave him a look that sprang from the very depths of her eyes, with a smile that seemed to combine youthful innocence with turbulence of spirit, and exclaimed:

"You are my God, to you I have dedicated myself and you I shall serve all the days of my life!"

Nejeen also stepped down from the chariot and held out her white hand, and the young priestess clasped the proffered hand tightly, as if it were a life-raft in a stormy sea, and giving her candle to one of her companions, fell into the arms of Nejeen and embraced her fondly, kissing her forehead. Then stepping back, she retrieved her candle and hurried to catch up with the rest of the procession, receding in the distance without a backward glance.

The staff of the King's summer palace sent representatives to meet the new arrivals, among them the chief councillor of Jahanur, Avarnam, a pleasant, silver-haired man who delivered a brief speech of greeting and welcomed them in the customary fashion. And so it was that they entered the township, accompanied by their twelve-strong bodyguards and the chief councillor on his elderly mare, with the steward of the household leading the procession.

At the gates of the palace, all of the King's retainers were gathered – clerks, footmen, cooks, grooms, gardeners, and there was even an aged court jester, who had not wanted to return to Babylon and had asked the King for permission to live out his days in Jahanur, permission which was granted. There was a total of fifty-four servants to maintain the palace with its seventy-eight rooms, halls and chambers.

The deputy steward came out to meet them, bowed low and offered them wine and bread, served on a gold tray covered by a white cloth, to celebrate their arrival. The maids and the servants followed his example, bowing low and holding the pose until the guests had passed them.

He replied to the greetings of the deputy steward and the leader of the town council, and expressed the hope that all would be conducted properly, and he assured them that he had no intention of changing their daily routine, and all the existing arrangements would remain in force. This was reassuring news for his audience, and there were smiles all around.

Out of the plethora of bed-chambers available, lavishly furnished and decorated in all colours known to man with the exception of black – they chose for themselves a spacious room on the upper storey, furnished in pink, with huge windows overlooking a fertile, verdant valley crossed by a foaming river, the rhythmic plash of its waters clearly audible.

She opened the window wide, and the air of the open spaces streamed into the room, bringing with it the light fragrance of wild flowers. At the end of the meadow, to their right, were thickets of pine trees.

"Nashdernach mentioned the scent of resin," he said, "and sure enough, I can smell it now!"

"The air and the atmosphere are both reminiscent of our homeland," she remarked.

"You're right," he agreed. "And the residents of Jahanur, will they be like our fellow-countrymen?"

"We shall have plenty of time to find out," she replied.

"I read some texts in the royal library about the inhabitants of this mountainous region in general and the inhabitants of Jahanur in particular. There is much that is known about them, and even more that is unknown."

Her calm gaze rested on him. Joy flooded his heart. How blessed he was in her!

He was not aware of the walls of the palace, the spaces in the room, all the heavy furniture, the light and pervasive scent of fields and pines, in a dream – of her perhaps, in any thought whatsoever.

The very fact of her presence prevented these things approaching him and disturbing that living depth that people fear to touch, even in imagination, lest they spoil the current of joy that is nourished by it.

The very fact of her presence brought him closer, in a closer communion than any he had known, to the one object of his love, none other than his Father in Heaven and his God, who is the infinite, freedom, love. How can he explain to himself this wonderful thing, that the very presence of someone could set him free from all that surrounds him, give him wings to soar away to the highest firmament, and to touch the Holy of Holies, to melt into it and to become a part of it?

Who is this someone who is setting you free, from herself and from yourself, so that you may awake to know yourself an inseparable part of the one, all-pervading love? Is she not the only object of your love, who is taking on, through the power of her love for you and by virtue of that love – human form?

Their eyes met. And it was only then that he realised that all his former conceptions of the sublime and of the pure were utterly meaningless. For the first time in his life he encountered the truly sublime and the entirely pure, these being nothing other than the inexhaustible, limpid and deep springs of love, the love that draws out from servitude to freedom, and from darkness into a great light.

He did not remember how long they had been standing in the spacious bed-chamber, but somehow he finally became aware that both the sky and the horizon had changed colour, turning through ever deepening shades of blue to the darker hues of regal velvet, studded with diamonds.

His eyes were in hers, and her gaze was his desire and his gaze was her delight, and the world of shapes and names ceased to exist, and with it time subsided, melted away as if it never was.

When he became aware of the knocking at the door, it had ceased to be as decorous and reverential as it was supposed to be. Then he remembered that throughout that day, while they stood by the open window, staring into one another's eyes, his glance melting into hers and her glance vanishing into the infinite freedom of his – in some place or another, under certain circumstances, and definitely without any reference to the time that had ceased to exist for them – there had indeed been persistent knocking, properly decorous and reverential at the start, but as the changes unfolded in the timeless void, so the knocking exceeded its normal limits, abandoning the last vestiges of respect and veering towards clamorous cacophony.

"Come in!" he cried.

The tall, wide door opened slowly, inch by inch, and one of the housemaids, the one responsible for the bed-chambers, peered inside and on seeing them froze where she stood, eyes gaping and tongue stuck to her palate. She remained there, petrified and dumbstruck, until he addressed her again, his voice gentle and reassuring:

"Are you the chambermaid?"

The tone of his voice did its blessed work.

"That is so, Sir!" she replied, her voice unsteady and still reflecting the shock that she had experienced on opening the door and looking into the room.

"That is so, Sir!" she repeated, this time with some of the balance restored to her voice. "Since this morning we..." she began awkwardly, paused and then resumed: "Your worships did not tell us what times would be convenient... for preparing the bed-chamber. And in the dining room too they are awaiting instructions. Clearly it is too late for the midday meal, but whatever your worships desire, so it shall be done. This is the time that we usually serve the evening meal, but we are ignorant folk, unfamiliar with the ways of the royal palace in the capital city, and we would be delighted if you would enlighten us! After all – it is dark outside, and the stars are in the sky and yet in this bed-chamber, there is light! Not a light such as candles give, nor the light of torches nor the light of a fire burning in the grate. A light such as we do not know and perhaps – it is only I, foolish and ignorant serving maid that I am, that does not know this light and has never seen the like!" Her voice shook and she was close to tears.

Nejeen hastened to say:

"You're neither stupid nor ignorant, and what happened here, really happened! And as my lord and husband has told you – the arrangements to which you are accustomed are not to be changed. We are running a little late, and in just a few moments we shall come down to eat our evening meal. This room is entirely to my satisfaction, and you need do nothing more here until tomorrow. What is your usual time for cleaning and tidying rooms?"

"Noon," replied the chambermaid, her confidence restored.

"Come back here tomorrow then, at noon!"

They did not part that night, or go to separate rooms. The night passed like a dream, or a fairy-tale that has never been told, or written.

The bright light of morning streamed in through the broad window that had been left open all night. A light, gusting breeze woke them with a caress, as a mother wakes her baby. He watched the white clouds drifting slowly, in ceremonious procession, across the deep blue of the sky, and they both admired once again the vista of meadows, river and groves of pine. The air shone, and the horizon sparkled in the distance like molten silver.

Having risen, they took turns bathing in the bath-house, with its three-fold arrangement of pools; the cold water of the final stage refreshed and invigorated them.

They broke their fast in an improvised dining room adjacent to the bath-house, and after thanking their attendants, went down to the stables to choose horses for themselves. Having so much time at their disposal, they could choose at their leisure. All the horses were of the finest quality, flawless thoroughbreds, well fed and properly trained.

They left the walls of the palace behind and spurred along the ridge of a gently sloping hill, on whose northern flank the inhabitants of Jahanur had built their white, somewhat decorative houses.

Generally these houses were built in the centre of a plantation or alongside an orchard or at the edge of a cultivated field. Beside each house, without exception, was a fig-tree in full bloom, and a number of the local residents were sitting at this early hour of the morning beneath their fig-trees, eating their morning snack in the shade of the branches.

It seemed that some of them noticed the two strange riders and hurried to inform the leader of the council, the silver-haired and agreeable Avarnam. He was not slow to arrive on the scene, his elderly and rather overweight mare panting and wheezing as if every step was an effort. He met them as they descended from the ridge, heading for one of the most picturesque streams they had ever seen.

"Be blessed in the name of God the most High!" Avarnam greeted them, raising his arm in an unconventional gesture, his face aglow.

"Blessings and all good things to you and to the good people of Jahanur!" he answered him cordially.

"If I may be of any service to your worships, it will be my delight and my most profound satisfaction!"

And before anyone could respond to these words, startling in their sincerity, Avarnam went on to say:

"As for the census of residents of Jahanur, it has already been done – a scroll has been prepared and will be delivered to you this very day, at the palace, by a representative of the community. According to this scroll, we have a population today of one thousand two hundred and sixty-one souls, men and women. And they are all the privileged descendants of those twelve ancient families, who lived in the past, the distant past I should say, in the ancient city of Ur, Ur of the Chaldees that is," he explained, and added: "In the aftermath of a certain episode, they abandoned the place and came to these hills and built the fertile and the prosperous township of Jahanur, the happy and the peace-loving settlement that you see today!"

At the mention of Ur of the Chaldees, the two of them exchanged bemused glances.

"This Ur of the Chaldees that you describe as 'ancient' – was it not prosperous in its time, and an agreeable place to live?"

"It seems that not everything was managed as it should be, and they did not all walk in the ways of virtue. And then that episode occurred of which I spoke – and a shattering and traumatic episode it was – and the twelve families, which exist today as they existed then, left their houses on the plain, houses built of clay, and climbed these hills and built for themselves the houses of stone and of wood that you have seen!" He stretched out his short arm in an expansive gesture, pointing to the houses with their friendly white facades, strewn across the slope of the hill at their feet.

"And our flock earned the blessing of Almighty God and flourished by His grace and has prospered ever since to this very day, and with the consent of the Holy One, will continue to flourish and prosper until the end of all generations!"

"Which 'Almighty God' is this?" he asked with great interest.

"The Creator of Heaven and Earth and all that is in them!" Avarnam answered him cheerfully, his resonant voice expressing a childlike innocence.

Hitherto she had refrained from taking any part in the conversation, assuming that in Jahanur, as in most eastern communities, women were excluded from men's conversations, and any contribution they made was likely to be ignored. But seeing the sincerity in Avarnam's face and the pure expression of his eyes, she felt confident enough to ask a question:

"Are the gods of Babylon your gods?"

Avarnam turned to her and without any change in his pleasant manner, in his air of fellowship and willingness to serve, he answered her:

"No, your ladyship! We differ from the Babylonians and their gods are not our gods, and their style of worship is not our style of worship!"

"Meaning?" he asked with mounting interest.

"We are forbidden to set up any image to any god, least of all to our God, Creator of Heaven and Earth and all that is in them. He must not be represented in any physical form."

"Since when has this ordinance existed?"

"Not since yesterday, or the day before!" Avarnam chuckled pleasantly, and while puckering his broad forehead as if trying to calculate times and dates he continued: "It has been our rule for many years, Excellency. And this is not to the liking of the Chaldeans living in the valley of the Tigris and the Euphrates who have claimed, with some justification, that we belong to them and are a part of their nation, as their language is our language. And we for our part claim, also with some justification, that although we have common roots there are also differences that divide us, and no faith is to be forced on us, least of all a faith that is not to our taste, that is fundamentally opposed to our conceptions and to the tradition in which we were nurtured – an ancient tradition indeed!" Avarnam declared with emphasis, still smiling his broad and captivating smile, expressing warmth, innocence and above all, a sincere willingness to serve and to oblige.

They both came to the conclusion, independently of one another, that Avarnam, leader of the council of Jahanur, was a most agreeable companion, and an affable interlocutor.

He went on to say:

"Not everything has proceeded smoothly. The Chaldeans, as is well known, are a people of resolute opinions, a nation of conquerors and valiant warriors, and they do not tolerate dissenters who refuse to accept their discipline, and bear their yoke – even if it is a small and peaceable community such as ours, doing no harm to anyone." Avarnam sighed and his plump mare shifted beneath him impatiently. He soothed her, patting her neck, and added:

"Nevertheless, they have not succeeded in imposing their will on us and we have not changed our religion – the same today as it has always been, although we have experienced setbacks and been treated like outcasts."

"And who has prevented the Chaldeans from imposing their will upon you and forcing you to change your religion?" he asked.

Avarnam turned his snow-white head to stare at him with a look of bewilderment, as if wondering how such a question could even be asked, the answer being so obvious and self-evident, and he replied with two simple words:

"Our God."

After the brief silence that followed, Avarnam went on to say.

"Our God, in whose hands are all things, and from whose hands all things come, He it was who defended our forefathers from the Chaldeans and from all the other troubles of the world, and He it is who guards us to this very day against anyone who would try to induce us to abandon our faith in Him for the sake of another religion."

"And what was the event that prompted your ancestors to dispense with idols and pictorial representations of the divine, to believe in God Most High, Creator of Heaven and Earth and all that is in them – and to abandon the ancient Ur of the Chaldees and move to the hills, founding the new Jahanur?" he asked.

"It is a fascinating story!" Avarnam declared emphatically, the broad, infectious smile returning to his face. "If you would like to know all the details as they are recorded in our ancient texts, you are welcome to visit the office of the community scribe and archivist, who records the chronicles of Jahanur and is an unrivalled expert in the interpretation of ancient writings. And he has it all preserved on parchment scrolls and on clay tablets. And as I said before, I shall be glad to be of service to you in any way I can!"

They made their way down to the building which housed all the municipal offices of the resort town, along narrow tracks winding between groves and orchards, crossing fast-flowing streams and lush meadows.

"What is the livelihood of the people of Jahanur?" he asked.

"Since time immemorial the people of Jahanur have been fruit-growers and tillers of the soil. They made all their own tools, everything needed for the home as well as for the field and the orchard, and sometimes they even traded with the surplus produce. As you see, every effort has been made to avoid contact with the outside world, disturbing no one and being disturbed by no one. Those who trade with other places are a very small minority, and most people born in Jahanur live here happily all their lives, finally being laid to rest in the ground that is celebrated in song. And if you need to know the extent of our loyalty to the Chaldean state and to His Majesty, it has never occurred to us to defy him in any way, and we shall continue to pay the tribute that is levied, punctually and in whatever medium is required – whether it be silver or gold, or textiles or wine or corn or fruit. Just so long as the Chaldeans leave us to ourselves, not stirring up religious dissension, opposing our true faith with their vain superstitions, and persecuting us for no fault of ours!" Avarnam looked back at him with an earnest, inquisitive expression.

And he replied in a tone of calm, genial assurance:

"I shall convey to the King what you have said, and my own impressions too I shall set before him. And how is it that a small town such as this, with a population of one thousand, two hundred and sixty-one, has a scribe and chronicler of its own?"

"Oh, that is a tradition among us, instituted after that extraordinary event that you will soon be hearing about, and it is a noble profession, requiring special skills, dedication and patience and above all, a strong and uncompromising devotion to the truth. It is the duty of the scribe and chronicler," – Avarnam warmed to his theme – "to inquire deeply and without prejudice into events and sayings until he arrives at the truth, and then he must record the truth, even if it is uncomfortable for him. And this is the proud inheritance of the Jaharan family, our family of scribes and copyists, whose scions have never omitted a letter, or added a single dot, or deviated to the tiniest degree from the texts that they transcribe. And all this work is done in a spirit of reverence, for the sake of Heaven, and every father in this family who teaches his son the sacred art, is also serving as a living example for him, of steadfast devotion to the truth."

"And who supports the scribe and his family?" she asked.

Without turning to face her, Avarnam replied:

"They support themselves. They have fields and orchards, and compiling chronicles does not occupy too much of their time. It is something that they do for the sheer pleasure of it – and as an act of reverence."

"And they have no slaves to assist them?" she persisted.

The leader of the council of Jahanur tugged at the reins and brought his mare to a standstill; she was glad of the respite, and took deep gulps of air into her elderly lungs.

"There you have touched on another of the principles that separate us from the Chaldeans and perhaps – from all other nations in the world!" And looking up towards the horizon, he explained:

"This faith of ours in one God, the God Most High, Creator of Heaven and Earth and all that is in them – is incompatible with slavery. It is a known fact that all human beings are brothers, sons of one Father, and how can you allow yourself to enslave your brother, taking from him the crop that he has planted with the sweat of his brow, and harvested with his own hands, allocating a meagre share to him and keeping for yourself the fruits of his labours? This is neither our inclination, nor our tradition!" he declared firmly, adding with an air of cheerful satisfaction: "You see? Without any recourse to slavery, our town has flourished and prospered, and all public matters are properly administered. And something else you should know: not one member of the council, not even the leader of the council, seeks any reward for his services to the public. All are happy to work in the Name of God, and for the sake of Heaven. And there are blessings everywhere!" he concluded, gently coaxing his mare into motion; reluctantly she resumed her clumsy gait.

"So you mean, you lack for nothing?" he asked.

"We lack for nothing, so it has always been and so it will always be, as long as we serve our God in faith and gladly obey His commandments."

Again they exchanged glances, with astonishment and wonderment in their eyes, and something resembling reverence.

Before the sun had risen to its zenith, they halted their horses at the foot of a low building, constructed of stone and freshly plastered, dismounted and hitched the reins to an iron ring beside the door. Avarnam knocked on the wide door, waited a moment and knocked again, this time with more vigour.

"Perhaps the scribe is working today in his field or his orchard, and has no leisure for his other activities," he suggested.

Avarnam smiled pleasantly and assured him:

"He's here! Writing a report on your visit, and your mission! But the moment he sits down at his desk and starts working, he becomes engrossed in the task in hand and detached from everything around him, and it's not easy to draw his attention to anything outside his texts!"

"Perhaps we shouldn't disturb him!" he said, trying to restrain Avarnam who was about to renew his onslaught on the door. "We can come back another time." But his intervention was too late, and the door shuddered under the hail of blows.

Avarnam looked up at him and once again wrinkled his brow, as if pondering his next words, but at that moment there was the sound of cautious movements from inside and the door swung open. On the threshold stood a man, with beard and hair sparse and flecked with grey, stooped posture and bright eyes, blinking in the sunlight.

For a long moment the man stood immobile, not sure what was happening, and then turned to them, smiled, bowed courteously, muttered something that sounded like "Welcome!" between thin and tight lips, then asked in a throaty, yet clear voice:

"How can I help you?"

Avarnam answered him:

"This is the King's envoy, who has come to inspect Jahanur. I'm sure you have already recorded the event in one of your scrolls."

The stooping man bowed again, in token of assent.

And Avarnam continued:

"We were talking of that episode that forced our ancestors to leave Ur of the Chaldees on the plain and settle in the hills, founding our beloved Jahanur. And they have expressed an interest in hearing more."

"Do they want me to read it to them from the old scrolls, which aren't easy to read, or would they rather hear it in my own words, in the oral tradition as is passed down from father to son and from teacher to pupil?"

"We'd like to hear it from you!" he said.

"I'll fetch some chairs and we can sit in the sun, which is pleasant at this time of year. It is dark inside, and the air dank and cold."

The scribe turned and bowed three times – once for each of the guests, and disappeared again behind the door with its mezuzah, returning a moment later with four stools. Then he fetched a tray with four apples on it, and a scroll wrapped in leather that had lost its original colour and turned black.

"These apples," he asked Avarnam, "were they grown here?"

"They were," he answered, not without pride. "The truth is," he added, "such fruit doesn't usually grow in places like this. But not everything depends on climate and quality of soil. In fact, very little depends on climate and quality of soil. A man and his work – they are the essence. If a man's work is done for the sake of Heaven – his labour is blessed and his fruit plentiful, and if a man's work is not done for the sake of Heaven, his work is cursed and his fruit blighted."

"There is no truth more holy than that!" he agreed.

"Part of the story," the scion of the Jaharan family began, his voice lucid and carefully modulated – "was recorded in this scroll by our ancestors. Anyone who knows how to decipher the language that preceded Chaldee is free to make use of this text – without taking it away of course, which is strictly forbidden. The script isn't easy to read, and the copying is in itself time-consuming. I myself have been making repeated efforts to transcribe the text onto fresh parchment, and even with the blessing and the help of God, the task will occupy a year of my time. Perusal is allowed only in my office, and with my help and supervision . One way or the other, the following is what is known to the people of Jahanur, regarding the ancient times."

Jaharan Ben Jaharan pronounced a brief blessing, bit into the juicy apple, and munching contentedly, resumed his account:

"Many generations ago the inhabitants of ancient Ur of the Chaldees, our ancestors, were worshippers of idols, like other nations and races in that locality. Their lives were apparently uneventful, as they did not stand out from their neighbours in any way. Like them they lived by rearing sheep and cattle, like them they worshipped innumerable idols and knew no serenity in their lives, neither joy nor satisfaction. And there were some who quarrelled with others over matters of religion or the distribution of land, and sometimes disputes erupted and often these turned into petty wars between tribe and tribe, between settlement and settlement, household and household, family and family. These wars claimed victims, and the relatives of the victims swore to avenge the deaths of their loved ones, and so it went on and on. And the idol-worshippers of Ur of the Chaldees, like the idol-worshippers of other places, carved their images out of wood and brass and stone, and bowed down to them and worshipped them, and offered them sacrifices and poured out before them their bitterness of heart – and all this to no avail. Until one day the son of one of the most illustrious sculptors arose and did something unheard of: he smashed the idols that his father had made and said to him: If these are really gods, let them avenge their injury!

"The father, who at first was seething with wrath at the impetuous act of his young son, was suddenly assailed by fits of laughter, wild and resounding laughter, for he saw with his own eyes that this young son of his was wiser than all the citizens of Ur of the Chaldees, with their reverence for images, images which he himself had created. But the sculptor soon stopped laughing, realising that his neighbours, friends and relatives were liable to see this act of his son as a very serious matter, and would vent their wrath on him, even stone him to death. So the sculptor called his clever son, gave him food and water and ordered him to go out to the desert and hide for a few days, allowing time for passions to cool and the affair to be forgotten. The son obeyed his father, took his knapsack and went away to hide in one of the caves in the desert, to the east of Ur of the Chaldees.

"No sooner had the son disappeared from his father's view, when the neighbours, his friends and relatives, having heard the sound of the idols breaking, came hurrying to discover the source of the terrible commotion – had some disaster occurred? And when they saw the shattered images, a great cry went up, and they flew into a panic and a rage, and began frantically wailing, tearing at their hair and their beards, ripping their clothes and scattering dust on their heads. And the rumour sprouted wings, and almost the entire population of Ur of the Chaldees came streaming to the door of the sculptor's house. And they demanded that the sculptor come out and admit the sin he had committed, and submit to the judgment of the crowd and receive his just deserts, meaning – death by stoning. And the sculptor was terrified, although relieved to know that his son was safe, and he came to the door of his house and promised to tell them the whole story, from beginning to end, omitting no detail, however small. And then his neighbours and relations and friends and fellow-citizens could decide what was to be done with him – whether it was to be life or death.

"Hearing the measured words of the sculptor the crowd was hushed, and in the tense silence that reigned in the open space before the house, the sculptor gave his version of events, revealing that last night, just after midnight, he heard a terrible din coming from his workshop and a deafening uproar, and he was jolted from his sleep and hurriedly went down to the workshop to see what was causing the racket, and he approached the door of the workshop, and though his heart was scared to death, he forced himself to touch the door, and opened it a crack, and stooped and peered through the crack. And what was revealed to him there was so dreadful, so terrifying, he immediately closed the door again and was minded to flee for his life while he still could. But knowing full well that in the morning he would definitely be summoned by the burghers and sages of Ur of the Chaldees to explain what had happened, and he would need a plausible account, he steeled himself again, opened the door and saw – Heavens above! – all the idols fighting one another, locked in vicious combat: the god of vineyards detached his stone arm and killed the god of rice with a single blow, and the god of rain held his heavy stone head in his hands and battered all his envoys and minions until they were wrecked beyond repair, and then the god of the forest attacked the god of vineyards and knocked him to the ground with a single blow, to be felled in his turn by the god of frost, who was killed by the god of the bears. The god of pregnant and nursing mothers slew at least a dozen minor deities, with the half of his body that he wielded as a weapon, but before the witness could identify the victims, the goddess of mammon took on all those who were still standing and laid them dead on the ground, and then she turned and saw the sculptor peering in at the doorway, shaking with fear, and she stormed upon him in a rage, but as she had been seriously injured in the course of the battle, she collapsed on the pile of slain gods and gave up the ghost too.

"For a long moment there was silence in the crowd listening

attentively to the words of the sculptor, until one of the renowned sages plucked up the courage to stand on a table and address all the citizens of Ur of the Chaldees, saying:

'How ridiculous we have been in our worship of wood and clay and iron and stone, and then here comes this wise sculptor, and he shows us how foolish we are, how incomparably ignorant!'

"And all at once the inhabitants of Ur of the Chaldees burst into gales of laughter, loud and long.

"And the sculptor asked for permission to conclude his story, for it had a conclusion, and the crowd respected his wish and was hushed. The sculptor admitted frankly that he was neither sage nor prophet nor thinker; such things were the prerogative of his young son, whom he had sent to hide in the desert until such time as the passions had subsided.

"The crowd laughed again, and the elders and the sages and the worthies of the community decided to send a deputation to bring the wise young man back to their city, as he was a precious asset to his community and his people, deserving to be their leader and their mentor, whose every command should be obeyed.

"The burghers of the town were as good as their word, and a dignified delegation set out and found the wise young man hiding in his cave, and they brought him back with great honour to his city and to his father. And the wise young man did indeed become their leader and their mentor and their governor, his every command obeyed. And in the fullness of time the young man revealed to them the existence of one God – Creator of Heaven and Earth and of all that is in them, who bears them only good will and shows them the way they should walk if they are to be saved, and to be the happiest of all men.

"And the boy, who grew in stature and in wisdom, gave then certain laws, which later the Chaldeans tried to copy and to adopt for themselves. These laws spoke of purification of the heart from the unclean, and its cleansing from every idolatrous or malicious or covetous thought. And the people of Ur of the Chaldees began studying these laws and adhering to them. And then it became known to them, to their grief and deep sorrow, that their neighbours were looking at them with a jealous eye and plotting against them and thinking ill of them, and hating them and informing against them. And it was at about this time, that God, the true God, commanded the son of the sculptor who had grown up and was a man and a leader of his people, to leave Ur of the Chaldees, his hometown, and never to return, and go to a place that

He, his God, would show him:

"*Go from your homeland and your father's house*, God commanded, and the man, whose name was Abram, obeyed, and bade farewell to his fellow citizens and his community, who respected him greatly, and he told them that Ur of the Chaldees was no longer a place for believers in the true God, and they should apply their minds to this and move to another place, and God would bless them, and afford them His protection, and defend them against their enemies and against all evil.

"And so indeed it was – Abram left his homeland and his father's house at God's command and twelve families of Ur of the Chaldees, believers in his God, followed his example, went up into the hills and founded Jahanur, and served the true God with all their hearts and minds, with all their souls and strength.

"This is the story as it is recorded in our writings," – Jaharan Ben Jaharan concluded, and held out to him the blackened scroll.

Slowly and carefully he untied the wrapper, which had stiffened over the course of the years, opened it and unrolled it until the first signs of writing appeared; this was one ancient language that even Denur-Shag had never taught. He rolled up the scroll again, wrapped it and handed it to Jaharan, who took it back into his office, and returned. Taking his seat again, he resumed:

"We have heard tell of what became of Abram, son of our little nation, and we know that he changed his name at God's command to Abraham, meaning 'Father of a great people', and this is not recorded in our writings as we didn't hear it from first hand, but it has been handed down from father to son and from teacher to pupil.

"There are sages among us," Jaharan explained "who teach the young the right path that they should follow. And these sages have much to say regarding the revelation of the Son of God, who will bring about the salvation of the human race, and who will be chastised and rejected and persecuted by many. And from hearsay we know that a great prophet arose to preach to the race of Abraham, and he heard the voice of God, and gave them laws, called the Torah. According to this Torah, men are commanded not to covet and not to commit adultery and not to bear false witness, commandments that we too accept, the difference being that we place more emphasis on purity of heart, so that adultery for example is forbidden not only in deed or in word, but above all – in the heart, in thought. And we believe with absolute faith that if the heart has not been purified – the Torah and the laws are nothing more than idle incantation."

He fell to his knees, bowing to the scribe of Jahanur and to the leader of the council and kissing the ground at their feet. Then he rose, shook their hands warmly and said:

"I wish there were many more like you!" – and taking his leave of Avarnam and Jaharan he mounted his horse and with Nejeen beside him, rode back to the King's summer palace. In their hands they held the apples they had been given, steadfast proof that all they had seen and been told was the truth.

In the room that he had set aside for an office, the scroll that Avarnam had mentioned was waiting for him.

He untied the ribbon and opened it: in clean, and cursive script – to the extent that Chaldean letters allowed for cursive forms – were the names of all the inhabitants of Jahanur, divided among the twelve families. There were also detailed notes relating to the history of the community and giving the names of its founders. The exceptional form of religion practised in Jahanur was also mentioned, and summed up in a single sentence: "They believe in the one, Almighty God, Creator of Heaven and Earth and of all that is in them."

He rolled up the scroll and placed it with the bundles they had brought with them.

An extensive veranda opened off the guest-room next to the bed-chamber, and they went out to inspect it. Like all the verandas of Babylon, this too was awash with flowers, their freshness testifying to the devoted care lavished upon them. They sat at a heavy table, of highly polished walnut wood, and with matching chairs. For a long time they were silent, trying to digest the riot of sensations stirring their minds. As the sun turned towards the west she began:

"How is it that this wonderful community of faithful upholders of tradition – and I say 'faithful' rather than 'fanatical' which is perhaps where they differ from our own people – has survived over the years untouched by destruction or neglect or the erosion of time, time which, it seems, has not changed it at all?"

Instead of answering her, he added a question of his own:

"If this community has indeed been preserved in this way, why has it not increased and multiplied, like any other community which has been spared from destruction, and grown inevitably into a great and populous nation? Think of our forefathers – seventy men who went down to Egypt, and their numbers grew and multiplied despite the yoke of servitude, and they returned to their land no longer a tiny band, but a race and a nation of some sixty thousand!"

She answered him equably:

"That is because of the strength of their faith, and the grace of God that rests upon them! They have remained as they are, neither suffering destruction nor growing and multiplying – and this because they have no interest in carnal pursuits for their own sake, and all the satisfaction that they need they find in their love of their God, loving him with all their hearts and minds, all their souls and all their strength."

"This marvellous community," he began, as if his thoughts and his mood were identical to hers, and his speech an extension of hers – "is a symbol of great hope and an example to all humanity of the faithful way of life. This community will never cease to exist, and no one will ever dare to attack and destroy it, as that would be tantamount to making war on God Himself!"

"And King Nebuchadnezzar," she said with no change in the tone of her voice, "did not send you here merely for rest and recuperation. This was a mission with a purpose!"

"That is indeed so!" he agreed. "Before I came here I read documents and scrolls, everything ever written about the community of Jahanur, and I found that it was all vague and elusive and unconvincing, because the compilers of reports simply did not have the mentality to comprehend the truth that the community of Jahanur embodies. And the King was exasperated by these unsatisfactory accounts, lines revealing less than they concealed, and when the opportunity arose to send someone on a tour of inspection, he took it."

They both looked out at the calm, pastoral landscape of Jahanur, bright with the radiance of the sunset.

"It is the grace of God that lights everything here!" she declared, and he added, as if to continue this train of thought:

"As our friends here in Jahanur have pointed out, blessing prevails where man is worthy of it. Regrettably, it can't be said of our compatriots that they have been blessed with that innocent and steadfast faith, faith for its own sake, that is rewarded by the grace of God!" There was bitterness in his voice and distant sadness. She turned to look at him, her calm gaze pouring into his eyes the unbounded freedom of her love, and he looked back at her, repaying her with the same love and the same freedom.

"Do you remember the wonderful story of the house of the Rechabites?" she asked.

He searched his memory for the name, but could not find it.

"At the beginning of his ministry Jeremiah the prophet was commanded to go down to the house of the Rechabites," she reminded him, and quoted:

"Go to the house of the Rechabites and speak to them, and bring them to one of the rooms in the house of the Lord and offer them wine to drink. So I fetched Jaazaniah son of Jeremiah son of Habaziniah, with his brothers and all his sons and all the family of the Rechabites. I brought them into the house of the Lord to the room of the sons of Hanan son of Igdaliah, the man of God, that adjoins the rooms of the officers above that of Maaseiah son of Shallum, the keeper of the threshold. I set bowls full of wine and goblets before the Rechabites and invited them to drink wine, but they said: We shall not drink wine, as our forefather Jonadab son of Rechab laid this commandment upon us, saying, You shall never drink wine, neither you nor your children. And you shall not build houses or sow seed or plant vineyards, and you shall have none of these things, but shall stay in tents all your lives, so that you may live long in the land in which you dwell. And we have obeyed all that our forefather Jonadab son of Rechab commanded us and have drunk no wine all our lives, neither we nor our wives, nor our sons, nor our daughters. We have not built houses to live in, or planted vineyards or fields. We have lived in tents, and obeyed all the commandments of our forefather Jonadab...

"And here with your permission I shall omit a few lines," she said without turning to him, "and move on to the end: *And to the house of the Rechabites Jeremiah said: These are the words of the Lord of Hosts the God of Israel, because you have obeyed the commandments of Jonadab your forefather, and followed his instructions and done all that he told you to do, therefore, says the Lord of Hosts the God of Israel – Jonadab the son of Rechab will not be deprived of a descendant, to stand before me for all time."*

After a short pause he responded:

"Hope is not yet lost for the people of Judah!"

The days passed one by one, and their tranquil radiance strengthened something in their hearts, but this was not faith, as their faith was already so steadfast it was beyond compare. Rather, it was what was shared between them that grew stronger and blossomed, striking deep roots and becoming an element of unity astonishing in its enduring vigour.

Most of the time they spent together and most of the time they kept their silence and did not converse between themselves, speech being superfluous. They did not need the voice to convey their feelings to one another, and the thoughts of one were revealed to the other without a word spoken. And the lasting pleasure prevailed over everything, even over mere satisfaction, and this was a pleasure that had nothing to do with the fleeting day or with the tender night. And their hearts beat with the same rhythm, until it seemed they were not two hearts divided one from the other but one heart alone – perceiving, feeling and thinking for two.

Often they went out on horseback, ascending to the low ridge or following the winding goat-track leading from one end of the settlement to the other. There was silence all around them, save for the steady murmur of the eddying streams which did nothing to impair it but rather accentuated it, as did the sound of their horses' hooves. There were days too when they went out walking, and their impressions then were sharper, as if closer to the primeval sources. Sometimes on their way they met a man or a woman of the locality who blessed them, and they never ceased to be amazed by the look of sincere humility, innocence and friendship. After meeting a woman advanced in years, her wrinkled face beaming, who urged them to take some of the nuts that she carried in her basket, and would brook no refusal, he said to Nejeen:

"From my father I heard a legend, or not so much a legend as a prophecy," – and as they climbed that winding goat path he continued: "The human race will destroy itself by driving God away, and all that will be left will be a tiny minority, people of simple ways who never considered themselves worthy of any distinction or prize, like the people of Jahanur for example, or the family of the Rechabites that you spoke of. And their precise number will be twelve thousand times twelve. And it isn't of the chosen ones that we speak, but those who have known God and delighted in Him secretly, and loved Him, and will not deny Him whatever the circumstances. In those one hundred and forty-four thousand souls God will reveal Himself in all His glory, and those souls shall be saved, turning from mortal to immortal, and God in them, and they in Him."

"So this is what lies ahead for the community of Jahanur, and for the future offspring of the family of the Rechabites!" she declared. "But what is to become of our people, which is astray in the ways of chaos and is far from God?"

"As the prophet said," he replied with a sadness that he could not hide: *"Would that my head were water and my eyes a fountain of tears, so I might weep day and night for the slain of my people!"*

THE BLAZING FURNACE

Midway through the month allotted to him, he felt a heavy weight growing in his heart, and he knew that disaster was imminent. She shared his premonition but revealed nothing to him – nor he to her – and both tried not to speak of what was in their minds, smiling at one another as if their smiles could instil confidence and equanimity. Until one morning he rose and said to her:

"We are returning to Babylon!"

And without saying a word in reply she set to packing their belongings, and felt some relief, knowing there was to be no more delay; trouble lay ahead and so long as they stayed here, they could do nothing to avert or forestall it.

He approached the steward of the household and ordered him to harness their chariot and to prepare the baggage wagon. In a few words he expressed gratitude for the hospitality that they had enjoyed, and declared himself fully satisfied, and the steward bowed to him, assured him that his commands would be obeyed, and gave instructions to his underlings.

About an hour before noon everything was packed and ready in the wagon, and they boarded their chariot, bidding hurried farewells to the staff of the household, slaves and serving-maids, and to Avarnam, who heard of their impending departure just in time and arrived in haste to give them his blessing. And as the royal chariot left the courtyard, Avarnam ran behind, calling out obscure words which at the time he did not understand:

"Accept the Son of the living God!"

On the way a vision was revealed to him, and he saw his three friends, Mishael, Hananiah and Azariah, standing in a ring of fire, laughing.

King Nebuchadnezzar made an image of gold, sixty cubits in height and six cubits in width. He had it set up in the valley of Dura in the province of Babylon. And the King sent out a summons to assemble the satraps, prefects, viceroys, counsellors, treasurers, judges, constables and all governors of provinces to attend the dedication of the image which he had set up. So they assembled – the satraps, prefects, viceroys, counsellors, treasurers, judges, constables and all governors of provinces – for the dedication of the image which King Nebuchadnezzar had set up, and they stood before the image, that Nebuchadnezzar had set up. Then the herald loudly proclaimed: O peoples and nations of every tongue, you are commanded, when you hear the sound of horn, pipe, zither, triangle, dulcimer, music and singing of every kind, to prostrate yourselves and worship the golden image which King Nebuchadnezzar has set up. Whosoever does not prostrate himself and worship shall forthwith be thrown into a blazing furnace. Accordingly, no sooner did all the peoples hear the sound of horn, pipe, zither, triangle, dulcimer, music and singing of every kind, then all the peoples and nations of every tongue prostrated themselves and worshipped the golden image which King Nebuchadnezzar had set up.

It was then that certain Chaldeans came forward and informed against the Jews. They said to King Nebuchadnezzar: O King, live for ever! Your Majesty has issued an edict that every man who hears the sound of horn, pipe, zither, triangle, dulcimer, music and singing of every kind shall fall down and worship the image of gold. Whosoever does not do so shall be thrown into a blazing furnace. There are certain Jews, whom you have appointed to serve in the administration of the state of Babylon – Shadrach, Meshach and Abed-Nego – and these men have paid no heed to Your Majesty's command. They do not serve your god, nor do they worship the golden image which you have set up.

Then in rage and fury Nebuchadnezzar ordered Shadrach, Meshach and Abed-Nego to be fetched and they were brought before the King. Nebuchadnezzar said to them: Is it by design, Shadrach, Meshach and Abed-Nego, that you do not serve my god or worship the golden image which I have set up? You have heard the commandment, that when you hear the sound of horn, pipe, zither, triangle, dulcimer, music and singing of every kind, you are to worship the image that I have made, and if you do not worship, you shall forthwith be thrown into the blazing furnace, and who is the god who can deliver you from my power?

Shadrach, Meshach and Abed-Nego said to King Nebuchadnezzar: We are not afraid to answer you in this matter. We have a God whom we serve, and he can save us from the blazing furnace, and deliver us from your power, O King. And even if we are not saved, be it known to Your Majesty that we will neither serve your God nor worship the golden image that you have set up.

Then the King was filled with rage against Shadrach, Meshach and Abed-Nego and he commanded that they be thrown into the blazing furnace. So these men were bound, in their cloaks and their breeches and their turbans and their other garments, and thrown into the blazing furnace. Because the King's command was urgent, and the furnace exceedingly hot, the men who threw Shadrach, Meshach and Abed-Nego into the furnace were themselves killed by the flames. And those three men, Shadrach, Meshach and Abed-Nego, fell bound into the blazing furnace.

Then King Nebuchadnezzar was amazed, and he rose in haste and said to his counsellors: Did we not throw three men bound into the fire? And they answered the King: Yes, Your Majesty. He answered: Yet I see four men walking about in the fire free and unharmed, and the fourth looks like the son of God. Nebuchadnezzar went to the door of the blazing furnace and said: Shadrach, Meshach and Abed-Nego, servants of God the Most High, come out, come here! And then Shadrach, Meshach and Abed-Nego came out from the fire. And the satraps, prefects, viceroys and royal counsellors gathered around and saw how the fire had not the power to harm the bodies of these men, and their hair was not singed and their garments were unchanged, and there was not even the smell of fire about them.

Then Nebuchadnezzar spoke out: Blessed is the God of Shadrach, Meshach and Abed-Nego, who has sent His angel to save His servants who trusted in Him, who disobeyed the royal edict, and would rather yield their bodies to the fire than worship any god other than their God. And it is my decree that any man, of whatever race or nation or tongue, who speaks ill of the God of Shadrach, Meshach and Abed-Nego, shall be cut in pieces and his house laid waste, for there is no other god who could save men in this way. And the King promoted Shadrach, Meshach and Abed-Nego in the service of the state of Babylon.

King Nebuchadnezzar to all nations and peoples and tongues in the world: may you ever prosper. It is my pleasure to tell of the signs and wonders that God the Most High has worked for me. How great are his signs, how mighty his wonders! His kingdom is an everlasting kingdom, and his dominion shall stand for all generations.

The vision that was revealed to him as he rode in the chariot, before arriving in Babylon, at once eased his heart and soothed his spirit. He smiled at her and said:

"Our God who is love has rescued his loyal servants from the King's furnace, namely Hananiah, Mishael and Azariah."

Her face reflected the relief that lit up his face, and the oppression that had tormented them lifted, melting away as if it had never been. As a field of wheat glows in the sunlight after a ferocious storm, so her face shone before him now, in all its youthful radiance.

He found Babylon in a ferment. Nashdernach was sitting in his office, his face ashen grey as the face of a corpse, his gloomy eyes sunk deep into their sockets, framed by the wrinkles of many sleepless nights.

Nashdernach rose to meet him and stood before him silent for a long moment, as if he did not recognise him or had lost his wits, but then he recovered himself, bowed low and vacated his place behind the broad table.

"It's all my fault!" he mumbled as if talking to himself, almost in a whimper, and then he clutched his outstretched hand, hugged him briefly and stood back, staring at him curiously, as the dilated pupils of his eyes gradually returned to their habitual state.

"I never imagined, it never occurred to me that the King's decree would apply to them as well, your three friends Meshach, Shadrach and Abed-Nego, and even when the decree was issued and they were forced to go to that valley and to follow the example of all the others, there was still hope that with all the confusion, and the noise and the crowds this would not be noticed – a few people defying the edict and not bowing down to that image. But there was jealousy in the hearts of the enemies of those three. The Chaldeans are by no means a people innocent of jealousy, but the Chaldeans were not the first to see them. Someone drew their attention, and he was neither a Chaldean nor a Sidonian nor a Mede. Someone pointed to those three, who were standing firm and not bowing to the image, in defiance of the King's command, and he whispered in the ears of the Chaldeans.

"So the matter was reported and they were brought before the King, who tried to mitigate their offence, asking them if it was 'by design' that they did what they did. If the three of them were to fall at his feet now, and confess that they had acted not by design but out of error and in all innocence, and now they were begging his forgiveness and appealing to his mercy, knowing he was generous of heart and great of spirit, showing mercy to all who deserve mercy – then they would be dismissed with a rebuke, and perhaps also relieved of some of their official duties, but their lives would be spared. They responded with vehemence that was utterly unexpected, defying that awesome King, Nebuchadnezzar, His Majesty, in the style of great warriors or saints, fearlessly and unequivocally, and thereby dealt a mortal blow to the King's pride, and his wrath was kindled.

"And I, who had thought of coming before him and falling at his feet and appealing for clemency on their behalf – I stopped myself just in time, realising that I would be doomed and they would not be helped! My death would be to nobody's advantage, least of all my own! And then, oh, then!" Nashdernach exclaimed, his eyes bulging wide open – "Then the miracle happened! Incredible to relate, a real miracle before our very eyes. The fire in the furnace didn't touch them at all, didn't even singe a hair of their heads or their beards. With my own eyes I saw," – the narrator pointed to his eyes – "and I couldn't believe what I was seeing. Even at this moment, I find myself shuddering, awe-struck, wondering if this was a dream that I dreamed or is my mind unhinged – did these things really happen? They did! And all praise and glory be to God the Most High, who saved His loyal servants from the fire. As King Nebuchadnezzar himself said, no other god could have done this. It happened, it happened before these eyes of mine. I saw and I witnessed. And once again I give thanks to the God of the Jews, to your God. Were it not for the miracle that He performed – I could not have endured the shame and the disgrace, of having deceived myself and deceived you, however innocently and unintentionally. Unforgivable – and my life would not have been worth living!

"I was sure your companions would not be forced to attend the ceremony of dedication of that image. And since it happened I have been wondering – why does your God, the true, the one God, the all-powerful – not deliver your people, rescue the whole of your race from the clutches of King Nebuchadnezzar, from the clutches of all the conquerors and kings of the world, as he has done for your three friends, Meshach, Shadrach and Abed-Nego?" He looked up at him with an air of innocent curiosity.

"Because my compatriots are not as devoted to Him as are Meshach, Shadrach and Abed-Nego, and they do not serve Him as Meshach, Shadrach and Abed-Nego serve Him, or trust in Him as they trust in Him!" he replied in a voice of remarkable serenity, a voice he hardly recognised as his own.

At his home, Denur-Shag was waiting for him. He rejected all offers of hospitality or refreshment and seemed in an agitated mood, quaking in every limb of his body, pacing this way and that, and mumbling to himself. For the first time since he had known him, he was not tripping on the flaps of his long, shabby cloak.

"The whole of this business," he said, sitting down opposite him and shaking his big, balding head to a rhythm all of his own, "has left me feeling utterly helpless, completely lost! It was a fateful moment, I should say – a moment of truth! You may find this hard to believe, but I actually tried to force my way through the crush and get to the King, with the idea of talking him into a compromise, exerting all my eloquence and persuading him to show mercy – and then this soldier comes along and clubs me over the head!" Denur-Shag touched his scalp gingerly, and he noticed a fresh, blue bruise.

"I lost consciousness," Denur-Shag continued, "but after that ignominious episode it suddenly became clear to me as daylight that deep down, I had no confidence at all in my ability to reach the King, stand before him, put my argument forward and drown him in a tidal wave of erudite words, thus attaining my goal. This being the case, it wasn't by chance that I passed so close to that coarse, rough-tempered soldier. In fact, I was hoping to be hit, and the man didn't disappoint me, he did a thorough job. This is the part of it that I just can't fathom out, and I reckon the best thing for me is a spell of voluntary exile, leaving Babylon and sorting some things out for myself. Perhaps I'll go to the countryside, stay with that estranged wife of mine – and suffer at her hands until I've atoned for my cowardice!

"And as for you," – he looked up at him, his eyes still troubled – "I'm sure you realised that that small community, the community of Jahanur, is distinct from all others, differing from its neighbours in an unbridgeable sense, not like, let us say, the difference between the Chaldean people and the Jewish people or any people you care to name. And the past of the community of Jahanur is shrouded in mystery, and other peoples have a strong interest in this past remaining hidden and shrouded in mystery. For if the past of the Jahanurians were ever to come into the light of day and be revealed before the eyes of all – then all wars and conquests and pomp and glory and lucre would cease to exist! And it is the opinion of these peoples, and of the leaders and chieftains they have chosen for themselves, that without these things their lives would be utterly pointless. Anyway, these peoples worship their gods, any gods, out of fear and hatred, and cannot bring themselves to believe that there is a God who is real and all-powerful, who will defend those whom He chooses to defend, and no one can do any harm to the one who is defended by the hand of God!

"The true God, oh yes!" cried Denur-Shag. "The true God!" he sighed and gave him a long look, a faint glow of distant hope beginning to take the place of the fear and unease. "We saw him in the fire of the furnace! I fall to my knees in fear and reverence and bow down to him!" and Denur-Shag knelt and raised joined hands towards the ceiling, crying "How good it is to know that You, the one God, the creator and the all-powerful – are real!"

Denur-Shag stood up from his kneeling posture, returned to his seat, gave him a sharp and uncharacteristically earnest look, and went on to say:

"And He, the true God, has taught me a lesson. He has proved to all of us, simpletons that we are, floundering around in all kinds of superstition and calling it 'faith' – that He is reality itself, the one and the only. And it is well that it happened the way it happened, and well that we were witnesses to the miracle, and well that our King, His Majesty, Nebuchadnezzar the valiant and the wise, at once acknowledged the true God, and repented of his anger, and declared the God of Meshach, Shadrach and Abed-Nego to be this God, and anyone daring to cast the slightest shadow of a doubt on this – his flesh shall be 'cut to pieces' and his home destroyed. A right royal decree indeed! And now, I'm ready to accept a cup of honey-water!"

That very evening he met Mishael, Hananiah and Azariah, sitting in Hananiah's spacious house. They had just finished their prayers. Their faces, which seemed to have matured almost beyond recognition, glowed. They held out their hands to him and took turns embracing him warmly, and weeping on one another's shoulder, shedding tears that were pure and purged of any hint of self-pity, like the spring rain that cleanses the fields and the plain.

And then the four of them sat and spent a long time looking into one another's eyes, inspecting one another, their looks expressing by turns wonder, reverence and joy, all the stronger for being held in check.

"The most marvellous thing of all," Hananiah began in a calm, controlled voice, welling up from the depths and not his own voice at all, "was that figure that descended into the furnace and was with us in the fire, untouched by the flames and driving them back!"

It was then he noticed that Hananiah's hair, including his beard and eyebrows, had turned completely white, like bleached wool.

He turned to look at Azariah and Mishael. Their hair too was streaked with grey, but was not like Hananiah's.

"You are wondering," Hananiah noted his expression and interpreted it correctly – "why my hair is all white, and the hair of Mishael and Azariah is merely turning grey. Listen then," Hananiah leaned towards him, pronouncing every word with emphasis. "My hair has turned white, because I am the one who spoke with him!"

"With whom?" he asked, taken aback.

"With the being in human form who came down into the furnace and rescued us from the fire. A figure of wondrous beauty, radiating love, speaking wisdom and bestowing freedom. We were so astonished at the sight we forgot where we were and all that we wanted – was to be with him until the end of all days. And he turned to me, and in that moment as we stood face to face, the light of his eyes sinking into mine, I was suddenly seized by an overwhelming sense of perplexity, wracked by shudders and spasms such as I never knew before, such as I never experienced nor ever will again! In fact, this wasn't so much perplexity as awe, and blended with it a feeling of joy from an unknown source, and a sensation of flying and soaring beyond the highest Heavens and becoming nothing, as insubstantial as the dust, and all of this – at one and the same time! And then I knew for sure that my hair had turned white and would never return to its former colour, though that was the least of my concerns! This divine figure, for it surely was divine, turned to me and asked me:

"Do you know me, Hananiah?" – and his voice was deep and clear, and keen, and painful.

"No, Master," I answered him sadly, for then I would have paid any price, given up my life even, if only I could have answered him gladly with words such as: "Yes, Master! I have always known you, and you I have served, serve and shall serve all the days of my life, in this world and the next!

"So," Hananiah continued – "my answer was 'No, Master'. And in spite of the grief that this answer caused me, or perhaps because of it, I asked: 'Who are you, Master?' And the answer was not slow in coming:

'I am the one who will be known in the fullness of time as the Son of God, and I shall be the touchstone for your people and for all other peoples! A tiny minority of your people will believe in me and be saved, and the majority that has neither purity nor truth, that will reject me, hate me and persecute me, slay me in the flesh and deny me – the majority shall not know salvation. And you, Hananiah, do you believe in the Son of the living God?'

"And I fell to my knees and said to him: 'I believe in the son of the living God with all my heart, as do my companions!' And he turned to Azariah and Mishael with his glorious light and they knelt at his feet and said to him: 'We believe!'"

He glanced at Azariah and Mishael and they nodded their heads as if in confirmation, their faces still aglow.

"And finally," Hananiah went on to say, "the Son of God revealed to us that the afflictions of the Children of Israel and of Judah will not come to an end until they believe in Him and accept Him. And at that moment the door of the furnace opened and King Nebuchadnezzar stood there staring at us, his whole body trembling as he declared: 'There is no God on the earth beneath or in the Heavens above other than the God of Meshach, Shadrach and Abed-Nego'."

Hananiah's story was told, and silence reigned in the room. Then Hananiah turned to him and asked:

"And you Daniel, do you believe in the Son of the living God?"

And without any hesitation he replied:

"With all my heart and soul!" – and only then did he remember the strange cry of Avarnam, the chief councillor of Jahanur: "Accept the Son of the living God!"

"Who do you think he is, this Son of God?" Azariah asked him.

"The future saviour of mankind."

"So how is he related to our God, who is one and one alone?" asked Mishael.

And he answered him, knowing it was the voice of another speaking through his lips:

"He is His embodiment!"

THE REBELLION

A year later, King Zedekiah rebelled. The Chaldean tax-collectors, coming to Jerusalem as they did every year, were sent away empty-handed.

The royal palace of Babylon was in uproar. Preparations were made for the dispatching of a punitive expedition, to be led, so it was rumoured, by none other than King Nebuchadnezzar himself.

Contacts between Babylon and the homeland were disrupted, and finally broken off altogether. In spite of this, there were still Jews arriving from Jerusalem. They saw themselves as refugees in the full sense of the word rather than exiles, and they told of what was happening there.

And so it was that he heard how the prophet Jeremiah had been assaulted by Zedekiah's minions, and had narrowly escaped stoning to death by the mob. Some of the elders and sages of the people had stood up and spoken out on his behalf, drawing attention to the similarities between his prophecies and those of his predecessors, and saying it should not be doubted it was God speaking through him; he was not to be persecuted or imprisoned lest the King and his ministers and the populace of Judah find themselves at war with God. But the words of the elders and the sages were to no avail, and there were instances when the inflamed mob turned its anger against them and attacked them, and some of them did as the prophet advised, packing a few possessions and leaving the rebellious city of Jerusalem, making their way, after many vicissitudes, to Babylon. After giving their reports to the King's representatives, who questioned them closely about the mood in Jerusalem, the activities of Zedekiah and his ministers and the common people, and the prophecies of Jeremiah, to which no one was listening – they recognised them as refugees and settled them in huts outside the walls. Those who had experience of agriculture were given plots of land to farm, skilled craftsmen were employed in the royal workshops, and scholars and intellectuals became clerks in the palace.

The newcomers were satisfied with their reception and grateful for everything, saying that all Jeremiah's predictions were coming true before their eyes, in spirit and in letter, including his assertion that anyone not rising in revolt against the Chaldeans would retain life and property intact; they had no reason to complain and nothing more to say – except to give praise and thanks to the King of Babylon – the envoy of God, according to Jeremiah.

And so it was that the four of them – Mishael, Hananiah, Azariah and he – happened to be together in Hananiah's office, listening to the report of one of the refugees, a clerk in the royal treasuries. He told them of the activities of an officer named Irijah, son of Shelemiah son of Hananiah, who detained Jeremiah at the Benjamin Gate as he was leaving the city, meaning to go to the land of Benjamin and hide there from the anger of the crowd and the machinations of the King's courtiers, and from the King himself, that unpredictable youth forever changing his mind and his policies.

And this man, Irijah son of Shelemiah son of Hananiah, raised a commotion in the marketplace and denounced Jeremiah as a traitor saying: "You mean to defect to the Chaldeans!" and Jeremiah replied: "That is a lie! I have no intention of defecting to the Chaldeans!" And the man did not believe him, nor did most of the crowd gathered there in the market-place, and they manhandled Jeremiah the prophet and put him in chains and brought him before the King. And the King disowned him, telling the ministers and the commoners: "Do with him as you see fit!"

And they threw Jeremiah into a pit in the prison yard. And there was no water in the pit, only mud, and Jeremiah began sinking into the mud.

King Zedekiah had a Negro servant, a eunuch, who well knew his master's mind, and how changeable it was. He was also, secretly, a supporter and a disciple of the prophet. And when the King's Negro servant heard that Jeremiah had been thrown into the pit in the prison yard, and was sinking into the mud, and did not have long to live, he approached the King and appealed to his compassion, saying: "My Lord the King, these men have done wrong in their dealings with Jeremiah the prophet, throwing him into a pit where he will sink and die!"

And the King commanded his Negro servant: "Take thirty men with you and haul Jeremiah the prophet out of the pit before he dies." And the servant assembled the men and went to the store-room of the palace under the treasury and took from there some cast-off clothing which he threw down to Jeremiah, with a rope. And the King's Negro servant said to Jeremiah: "Put these rags under your armpits, to ease the chafing of the ropes," and the prophet followed his advice. So they pulled Jeremiah out of the pit with ropes, and he stayed in the prison yard.

Then King Zedekiah had Jeremiah the prophet brought to him by the third entrance of the House of the Lord, and the King said to Jeremiah: "I have a question to ask you – speak and hide nothing from me!" And Jeremiah said to Zedekiah: "If I speak out you will kill me, and if I give you advice, you will ignore it!" And King Zedekiah swore a secret oath to Jeremiah: "As the Lord lives who gave us our lives, I shall not kill you, or hand you over to those men who seek your life!"

And Jeremiah said to Zedekiah: "This is the word of the Lord of Hosts, the God of Israel. If you go out and surrender to the officers of the King of Babylon, your life will be spared and this city will not be set on fire, you and your family shall live. And if you do not go out and surrender to the officers of the King of Babylon, this city will fall into the hands of the Chaldeans who will burn it to the ground – and there will be no escape for you!"

And here the story was suspended, as the refugee-narrator had urgent duties to attend to in his new post.

The four young men exchanged glances, all of them utterly perplexed and deeply worried by what they had heard.

"I suppose," said Mishael, "there is a chance that reason may prevail, when a ruler seeks to know what is the will of God, and God does not withhold His word from him, but informs him through His prophet what he must do if he is to live. And the ruler holds his fate in his own hands, his fate and the fate of his family and the fate of his people. All that is then required of the wise ruler is that he comply with the word of God and put an end to all his troubles and come out from darkness into a great light. Yet in this case, he does the opposite. The first step is sensible and gives grounds for hope – and yet without the second step it is worthless! It is an undeniable fact that the first step does not invariably lead to the second!"

"And why do those who take the first step not go on to take the second, which according to logic should follow from it?" Azariah queried.

He looked up at the ceiling and stared at it for a while, before lowering his eyes and saying, without addressing anyone in particular:

"Lack of faith."

And Mishael asked him:

"And is there no way to increase their faith and strengthen it?"

"There is," he declared, and added – "It's a question of repentance. This was an option that was offered to Zedekiah the King of Judah, and he rejected it out of hand."

"And what are we to do in these perilous times – and how can we help our compatriots and our families in Judah, and the unfortunate King, who is astray and leading others astray?"

"We must remain firm in our own faith, and strengthen it, and trust in Him, the Blessed One, and love Him with all our hearts and minds, our spirits and our might!"

"And this strengthening of faith and love of Him – will that help our compatriots and the hapless King Zedekiah, and our families in Judah?" asked Azariah.

"Increase of our faith and our love of Him will set out before every man, inasmuch as he is a man, the path to repentance, which leads on to salvation."

"So it is pointless, turning to God and asking for His guidance, if the one who turns and asks for guidance is lacking in faith!"

"As pointless as lighting a way in the darkness for one who has been blind from birth!"

They left Hananiah's office and went their separate ways – all of them in a mood of the most profound gloom.

Or-Nego sat facing him. It seemed that he had changed somewhat, having grown older and more circumspect. This was no longer the army commander who had boasted of punishing rebellious peasants and burning down their homes. Sitting there before him was a restrained man in the prime of life, who knew what lay before him and was determined to do the right thing, who was loyal to whatever seemed to him worthy of his loyalty. He remembered Adelain's story of the vows which Or-Nego made to his wife before she died – vows which he had kept. Truly, Nebuchadnezzar knew how to choose his men! If his army had a dozen more officers like Or-Nego, that army would be invincible.

The passage of the years had left their mark on his face and his body as well. This body had lost some of its litheness while gaining solidity. Two deep furrows scored his cheeks, as if to underline his firmness, while his gentle eyes had receded further into their sockets, their look of serenity, courage and congenial intelligence unimpaired.

Or-Nego had asked for this interview, in his capacity as a senior officer, but had insisted on waiting for his turn. As it turned out, the meeting was taking place a week after the original approach was made. They sat for a while in companionable silence, while he looked into those eyes that reminded him of Adelain's eyes – a little dry, and their lustre restrained – and made mental note of the more obvious changes that had come about since last he saw him. It was Or-Nego who eventually broke the silence:

"I'm supposed to be joining the King's army for the campaign against Judah, and I thought it right to come and see you beforehand and perhaps bid you farewell, even though the expedition won't be setting out for some time yet. And above all, the main purpose of my visit is to ask if you have any particular requests regarding your native city and your homeland."

"What do you mean, Or-Nego?" he asked him, sensing a faint awkwardness in the other, in that deep, benevolent look that reminded him so vividly of Adelain.

"If you like..." he hesitated momentarily, before continuing in a clear, steady voice: "I could use my discretion where your relatives are concerned. Tell me where they live – and I can deploy my troops in such a way that they're not harmed, they and their neighbours! I shall be glad to be of service – and Adelain will be glad too. This idea, of coming to you and offering my modest services appealed to her very strongly and perhaps," Or-Nego paused and pondered briefly, before revealing something that surprised him – though not the most shattering of surprises – "it was she who suggested it in the first place, knowing that nothing would give me greater pleasure... so, do you have any favours to ask of me, anything that's within my power to grant?" The soldier looked up and regarded him steadily.

He was in no hurry to reply. His eyes were fixed on Or-Nego's hands, laid on the polished table – good, broad hands, and most important of all – reliable.

"If you can't decide just now, I'll come back in two weeks or three, a month even. The expedition won't be setting out for at least another three months, possibly four, because the season has to be right and it takes time organising such a large and heavily-equipped force. Anyway, as you well know – it's all in the hands of Heaven!" He raised his hand and the look of serenity left him, to be replaced by that blend of reverence and hope that is the hallmark of the soldier and devout believer. "So think it over," he went on to say, "make up your mind and let me know. I shall return at a time of your choosing, and whatever you ask, I shall carry out with the utmost pleasure!" He bowed his head respectfully, as he concluded. And it was then that the voice was heard, emerging from his throat:

"You must do as King Nebuchadnezzar commands!"

Both men knew this was a commandment that could not be disobeyed, and it was not he who spoke but One whose will was incumbent upon both, to be done gladly.

Or-Nego stood up from his seat, took a step back and bowed to him, a full, deep bow of friendship, reverence and admiration, and so, still stooping, he retreated backwards towards the door, bowed again and went out without another word spoken.

Shortly after this he heard that Adoniah had returned from Jerusalem, and was brimming over with news and information about the rebellious city and its inhabitants, King Zedekiah and his court, and the prophet Jeremiah.

They met at Azariah's house. Beside a table that was laden with food and drink – ranging from honey-water to the choicest of wines – Adoniah reclined at his ease in a padded chair. He did not rise to greet him as the others did, but held out his fleshy hand as if dispensing a favour, smiling that characteristic smile of his – always hiding something behind the mask of ostentatious scorn.

"In your honour," he drawled, "your friends have chosen not to serve meat on their table!"

"Not just in his honour," Azariah objected hastily. "Since coming to Babylon, we too have willingly abstained from eating meat."

"Is that any reason to deny me, a meat-eater, my favourite food? What kind of hospitality is this?"

"It's precisely for reasons of hospitality, and the well-being of our guests, that we serve no meat on our tables!" Azariah retorted with a smile, this time succeeding in reproducing a hint of 'Adoniah-style' irony.

"A strange way of looking at things, in my opinion!" Adoniah replied, and for a moment it seemed that the sarcasm was wiped from his fleshy lips, as his round, ruddy head, with its dense fringe of beard and hair, moved slowly up and down in token of disapproval. "I have no choice then," he sighed, putting on an injured expression, "but to sample your menu and be like that lion, which at the end of time will eat straw for its prey and delight in wild herbs!" He took the goblet that the house-slave had filled with yellow wine, pure as a tear, cried "To life!" and took a long gulp. Laying down his goblet, he wiped his lips on a cloth that the slave handed him, and finally turned to the topic of the day:

"If you saw Jerusalem now, you wouldn't believe your eyes! It isn't the place we knew in our youth. Another Jerusalem has arisen to take its place, a proud and defiant city, the capital of a mighty kingdom, a city that will stand up to defend its honour, that is all splendour and valour.

And all its citizens, young and old alike, are rushing to arms and joining Zedekiah's army, to fight the Chaldean oppressor. And I tell you truly – they will fight like lions and they will prevail! Be sure to remember what I say. The great and the confident kingdom of Babylon will burst like a soap-bubble, and great days will return to Judah. A glorious future beckons, more glorious than anything man can imagine!" Adoniah reached for his goblet again and drank from it thirstily.

"And what of the prophet Jeremiah?" he asked, keeping his feelings in check.

"Our land is no stranger to cowards and traitors..."

"Watch your tongue! You have no right to judge the prophet of God!" His stern words reverberated around the room.

Adoniah was silent, flinching as if a whip had struck him, his tongue lolling from his mouth, and for a moment it seemed he had lost the power of speech. The next moment he regained some composure, and having tried to revert to his broad, sarcastic smile and failed, went on to say in a conciliatory tone:

"Forgive me, but I don't think that Jeremiah is serving his King, or showing any love for his people. Time will tell!" he added hurriedly, to forestall any interruption, and he resumed self-righteously: "If it really is God who is putting into his mouth the things that he says, preaching from morning to evening in the House of the Lord, in the market-places and the streets of Jerusalem – why do they arouse such anger?" He added, in an abrupt change of subject: "The King's servant saved him from certain death, and the King is holding him to witness what is yet to happen, when the day comes that Judah is liberated from the Chaldean yoke, and we storm Babylon and tear down its strongholds. And then it will finally be proved, for all to see, that the words of Jeremiah are not the words of the living God, but tales that he has made up for himself, for reasons known only to him..."

"Time will tell!" This time it was Hananiah who interrupted him, the tone of his voice much sharper than it had ever been known before, his face glowing in its frame of snow-white hair.

"You're right of course," Adoniah agreed, but went on to say: "Anyway, this Jeremiah that you call a 'prophet' has suffered so much violence and abuse that he's been uttering heart-breaking laments, even regretting the day he was born:

"Cursed be the day, he says, *when I was born, and be it ever unblessed, the day my mother bore me! A curse on the man who brought word to my father saying, a child is born to you, a son, rejoice! That man shall fare like*

the cities, which the Lord overthrew without mercy, and he shall hear cries of alarm in the morning and uproar at noon, because death did not claim me in the womb and my mother did not become my grave. Why did I come forth from the womb, to know toil and grief and end my days in shame?

"It wasn't because of the blows and the insults he received that the prophet said what he said," he pointed out in a steady voice that would brook no interruption, "but because of the violence and the ruin on the way, the destruction to come!"

"Permit me to disagree with you!" Adoniah answered him, after draining the entire contents of his goblet, wiping his lips again and signalling to the slave for a refill. "I don't believe that violence and ruin are the future of our people, this wise and wondrous, dauntless people! On the contrary, glory and praise are in store for it, and unbounded dominion over the earth and its fullness!" Adoniah cried, the enthusiasm flashing in his eyes. He sipped from the goblet, put it down again in front of him and declared with vehemence, unable to control his feelings:

"This is the golden age of Israel and Judah! Zedekiah is not standing idle, and envoys from Egypt are coming and going, and there are caravans of camels and countless wagons bringing weapons and provisions, and all the granaries are full, and if the city were to be besieged for ten years it could withstand it and not capitulate! But this time there will be no need to withstand a siege, for the Lord will deliver His people and lay His hand on the one whom Jeremiah calls His faithful servant, and fight him and destroy him long before there is any siege of Jerusalem, the Holy City, and his intentions shall be foiled and his conspiracy frustrated, and Babylon shall fall, never to rise again!"

"That kind of talk is liable to bring disaster upon our people, forcing Nebuchadnezzar to exact brutal reprisals and conquer our homeland and raze Jerusalem to the ground, as no foreign king has ever done before!" he insisted.

"That kind of talk, as you call it, is going to prove to be the truth, as you are all going to find out! Still, time will tell – and that's one thing on which we can agree! And now, if you have no objection, let's drink a toast to Zedekiah, King of Judah, and tomorrow's victor!"

He raised his cup, but they were slow to follow his example. They looked at him. Slowly he held out his hand, took his cup, raised it smoothly and said, in a voice that was not his:

"Long live Jeremiah, holy prophet of the Lord!"

This was a toast that they were glad to drink. Even Adoniah joined in – a triumph of thirst over principle, perhaps.

He barely tasted any of the fine and abundant foods on offer, tastefully prepared though it all was and attractively presented. Azariah was fortunate in having the services of a first-rate chef, from the northern provinces of the state of Babylon, regions renowned for fine craftsmanship and culinary skills.

"So here you are in Babylon, alongside this King, and you're singing his praises and extolling his wisdom," Adoniah began again, in a voice thickened by wine, "and you're impressed by his power and you speak of him with reverence and respect. And you give no thought to all the things that are happening out there in the world. Do you reckon that the whole universe is wrapped up within the lofty walls of this pagan Babylon? That is what you think, isn't it? Oh yes, and by the way," – and he raised his hand to forestall any interruption – "I've heard about that stunt with the furnace, and the miracle that you experienced, an impressive miracle by any standards, the finger of God, no less!" He nodded his round, hairy head, in token of wonderment. "And this naïve and gullible king, the pagan and gentile Nebuchadnezzar, falls in humble submission at your feet, and declares that your God is the only God. And I've heard talk too about the Son of God, the one who's going to split the Jewish people and set faction against faction. And I won't ask how you did it, and how the King was duped, and how you created the illusion of being inside the fire when in fact you were outside it, no doubt with the help of your accomplice, posing as the Son of God. No, I won't ask and I won't pry!"

The four of them exchanged glances, their eyes reflecting bemusement and perplexity, and something faintly resembling anger, resentment even. All at once they realised there was no purpose to be served by becoming embroiled in argument with him, and the best response to such slander was silence. And this thought nipped their anger in the bud and erased their resentment, giving way to sorrow and pity, and the four of them smiled barely perceptible smiles at one another and kept their silence, while their guest ranted on, piling words upon words and sentences upon sentences, paying no attention to his surroundings, and seeming at times to be talking to himself:

"And what have you gained from all this? What did you demand in exchange for this so-called miracle, performed before the goggling eyes of that ignorant pagan king, who was in such a hurry to proclaim yours the only God, and to threaten anyone denying this with summary execution. What did you ask him for?" – and without waiting for an answer – "He wouldn't have dared refuse you anything, he'd have done whatever you wanted, in the spirit and in the letter! Did it occur to you to ask him to liberate Judah from the yoke of his slavery, and ease the burden of his taxes? Did such a thought ever enter your heads, my dear friends?" he asked, and answered for himself exclaiming "No, no, of course not! You were content with your comfortable jobs and smart offices, and swanky houses, and all the precious gifts that the pagan King has been lavishing on you, holding you in such awe and reverence. And what do you expect to be called, other than pursuers of power and worldly glory? Is this how you serve your God – who rescued you, so you say, from the flames of the furnace – and whose deadly enemy you have been cosseting so courageously, King Nebuchadnezzar the pagan? Or perhaps you're relying on what your friend said, that nice Jeremiah:

These are the words of the Lord of Hosts, the God of Israel, to all the exiles whom I carried off from Jerusalem to Babylon: Build houses and live in them, plant gardens and eat their fruits. Marry wives and beget sons and daughters, and take wives for your sons and give your daughters to husbands, so they may increase and not dwindle away. Seek the welfare of the city to which you are exiled and pray for it to the Lord, since on its welfare your welfare depends. These are the words of the Lord: when a full seventy years have passed over Babylon, I will take up your cause and fulfil the promise of good things that I made to you, and bring you back to this place.

"Do you believe those words, are those the principles you live by? Oh, don't tell me, I'm really not that interested!" he exclaimed, waving a restraining arm in a gesture that was quite superfluous, as no one had any intention of responding.

"So you sit around idly, amassing wealth and acquiring ornate houses, your tables are creaking under the weight of fine foods, you wear the medals of pagan authority around your necks, you have grown fat, whereas I have been constantly on the move, forever devising strategies to elude my enemies, ignorant boors that they are – and me, you ignore, me you have left outside, left behind, like a severed limb that's no use to anyone. No one remembers me, no one calls on me – not even to bow to that ridiculous image set up by the idol-worshipping King! But I was there, I went on my own initiative, in person. And I saw the three of you," he pointed to Mishael, Hananiah and Azariah, "standing there and not bowing down, as stiff as statues and as proud as peacocks! You made me so angry! And I actually bowed down, made a point of bowing down, because of you! Or I should say, to be different from you, apart, untouched by your smug arrogance, close to the people rather than the ruling class!

"No one has ever offered me a prestigious job – to this very day. No one has ever put a necklace around my neck – let alone one of those pendants with the royal seal. I'm the one they forget, the one you've forgotten! And I'll tell you something – I'm grateful for this! In days to come you'll pay a high price for what you've been doing, and your joy will turn to grief, your pleasure to depression!

"Have I hurt your feelings?" – it was both a question and an exclamation, and the guest continued in a wheedling voice: "Can't you tell that I'm only joking! I have a sharp tongue, an errant tongue, and as the wisest of all men said, the tongue has the power of life and death! Anyway, at least here I can be myself, open the secrets of my heart to my friends and comrades... just a moment," he paused as if thinking something through – "when were you my friends and comrades? We met for the first time in that jolting wagon on the way to Babylon. Still, I shall call you my friends and ask you to forgive this provocative tongue of mine, that sometimes strays beyond the bounds of good taste. Anyway, accept my thanks and my warmest compliments, renowned miracle-workers and interpreters of dreams that you are, and be neither hurt nor offended. Pardon and forgive me. Even in the presence of the women I have dallied with, and there have been many of them, I could never confess and be my true self. Please, let me be a member of your group again, and don't think badly of me!" Again, the four of them exchanged baffled glances.

At a late hour of the night, Adoniah was finally defeated by the strong wine. His servants arrived, and carried him home.

He parted from Nejeen and went to his room for his night's rest. After a while, he heard Oshrich's soft knocking.

"Enter!" he cried and the door opened without a sound. Oshrich bowed low, and rising he said:

"Lord Denur-Shag is asking to see you, Sir!"

"Ask him to come in," he replied, wondering what urgent business had brought the dependable Denur-Shag knocking on his door at such a late hour of the night.

"Greetings and blessings!" Denur-Shag entered and immediately tripped on the flaps of his cloak and fell. He hurriedly took a step forward to catch him, but the guest managed to grab the back of a chair just in time.

"As usual!" exclaimed Denur-Shag, adding in the mock-serious tone that always brought a genial smile to the lips of his hearers – "The sense of balance of a one-day old baby who hasn't yet learned to walk on two legs! And it's a compliment, without a shadow of a doubt – a compliment!" he insisted, and in characteristic style, veered off at a tangent: "The baby, as you know, is distinguished by his innocent thoughts and purity of heart, and his trust in everything and in all people, and if it were possible for him to rule any people, he would bring it peace and happiness and most important of all – true equality and a final end to slavery. Yes, in my vision of the end of days, the rulers of all nations will be babies!"

Denur-Shag sat on the padded chair beside the broad table, covered with a white cloth and as a centre-piece, a crystal vase containing a rare flower of delicate fragrance, then took out from under his cloak a flask of wine, and laying it on the cloth, commented without looking up:

"From your homeland! Old Jerusalem wine, from the years before the crises and the conflicts. This was looted from the palace of King Jehoiakim, a renowned lover of fine wines who made a point of keeping a well-stocked cellar even when his granaries were empty. Anyway," Denur-Shag continued, looking up, "without the proper cups, glass ones I mean, this drink loses its special allure – its fragrance and the whole of that infusion of ancient flavours!"

He sat down opposite Denur-Shag, who seemed intent on drowning him in a deluge of words as a prelude, or a tentative overture, to the main point at issue, a weapon as yet unsheathed.

He clapped his hands and Oshrich appeared, bowed and awaited his instructions.

"Two glass goblets, please!"

There was silence in the room.

Denur-Shag treated him to a long, probing, inquisitive look, with, as always, an undercurrent of irony bordering on whimsy. He derived a strange pleasure from gauging the reactions of other people to the challenges that he set before them. Nevertheless, in this look of his, playful and challenging as it was, there was a sense of the warmth and the fellowship which are expressed in the willingness to share both in another's joy and in another's tribulation.

He responded to the challenge with a broad smile, and then noticed that those eyes, with the ironical and inquisitive look that was also warm and sympathetic – were weary, weary not in a casual or a temporary fashion, and for the first time in all the years that he had known his teacher, he feared for him.

Oshrich returned and placed before them a pair of thin-stemmed goblets of fine Egyptian glass, edged with a kind of tracery that was harmonious and of considerable aesthetic appeal.

Denur-Shag tugged at the wooden bung with its deerskin wrapper, and not without some effort, pulled it from the long neck of the flask. A thin vapour rose from the mouth of the flask. Carefully, almost reverently, Denur-Shag tilted the neck of the flask over the goblet set before the host and filled it half-full, then, with a similar flourish, repeated the process with his own. The clear, rosy liquid glided smoothly into the elegant glassware.

Having completed the task of pouring, Denur-Shag plugged the flask again, with deliberate movements, as if cautious of something, set it down beside him, raised his goblet and said:

"In your homeland, they drink a toast 'to life', meaning the true life in the realm of the legendary King-Messiah! Let's hope that in this story there is a spark of truth and optimism for the future, and let's drink in honour of the King-Messiah, urging him to come with all possible speed and put an end to strife and error. So, to life!"

"To life!" – he raised his goblet in turn and took a sip of the amber-coloured liquid. Denur-Shag was right – the wine was fine indeed, retaining its fragrance and with delicate flavours that refreshed the body and infused a sense of lightness and lustre. He was reminded of his homeland, the hills surrounding the Holy City, the road to Anathoth, the grove and the valleys, the enchanted air at nightfall, the paved streets, the temple of the Lord and the palace of the King, proud Jerusalem – long since trampled under the feet of foreign armies.

"All Jerusalem," the guest said softly, "the glory and the sanctity that hover above its temples and its houses and its alleyways, and give the air its special savour, and the hopes that have faded into nothing – all are embodied in this wine!"

"Denur-Shag, you have seen my thoughts and read my mind!"

The other did not respond.

They took up their goblets again and sipped from them with a strange sensation of loss and longing, blended with a distant hint of hope.

Denur-Shag wiped his lips, put down the goblet, and looked up at him, his little eyes dry and serious, and ominously acute.

"As you know," he began in a thoroughly practical tone, "our King, King Nebuchadnezzar, intends to march against rebellious Jerusalem and establish order there 'once and for all'. Obviously, 'once and for all' is a purely rhetorical expression. And although a dauntless warrior and a divinely appointed conqueror like this King of ours, is far removed from anything even remotely resembling literature or art or suchlike – he too cannot resist using borrowed expressions, by which I mean those that hover in the ether, with neither depth nor substance to them. 'Once and for all', at best, may be regarded as extending over one lifetime, no more, and there are various rogue elements that will, naturally, do everything possible to frustrate the purposes of this King of ours, His Majesty. And there can be no doubt that the King and his entourage are aware of this. And establishing order in Jerusalem on a 'once and for all' basis will not be achieved without pain and suffering and without the sacrifice of many lives, in other words – without war. And war usually begins before it is officially declared, *before the arrow is loosed and the shield wards it off*, as your prophet Isaiah puts it so well. And this war has already started, meaning here, in glorious Babylon. Zedekiah, the Jewish King, who reveres everything except God, refusing to hear His voice as conveyed to him by the prophet Jeremiah – is sly and cunning, as has been typical of losers since this world was created and will be so until its final destruction." Denur-Shag sighed, put the goblet to his lips and took a minute sip, replaced the goblet on the table and went on to say, broaching a subject apparently unrelated to all that had gone before:

"There are here, in Babylon, a number of Jewish families, citizens of long-standing to be sure, but Jewish in every respect. And they live in certain houses, built in the space between the walls, as a sign and a symbol that on the one hand they do not belong to Babylon, and on the other, they cannot afford to ignore it.

"And this strange community has put a proposition to King Zedekiah, or King Zedekiah has approached its elders with a proposition. One way or the other, and without the parties ever meeting face to face, something is being hatched between them that in any language would be called 'intrigue' or 'conspiracy', and this with the active collusion of those merchants, itinerant traders and wayfarers, who are the bridge between Babylon and Judah. And the plan is – to lie in wait for the King, who means to set out, two or three months from now, to bring Jerusalem to heel 'once and for all' – and strike him a mortal blow, thus making life easier for King Zedekiah, although all this is in defiance of the will of God, and the warnings uttered constantly, from morning to evening, by His prophet, Jeremiah.

"Everyone has his own plans," Denur-Shag stressed, going on to explain in the same tone, "and one of the couriers in the service of the Jewish community has a plan and an agenda of his own, or at least, that is the conclusion of my elderly brain." Denur-Shag raised his round hand, finger lightly touching his temple.

"It is possible that this courier, who is also attached to the royal trade mission, is eager to curry favour in the eyes of his King, and for this reason has chosen the route he has taken. In any case, the plan is known in all details and particulars to the soldiers of the royal guard and to the King himself. It has also been brought to my attention, but *that*, the King and his guard do not know. According to this ambitious plan, frightfully naïve in my opinion and for that reason, all the more dangerous and likely to succeed, a young man, an incorrigible fanatic, will arrive tomorrow, as darkness falls, at the south-eastern wall of the palace, a section of the wall that is overgrown with vegetation," the guest explained – "and not regularly patrolled. A narrow path, also neglected and overgrown, leads from the wall directly to the King's apartments and his private office. The young man is supposed to infiltrate this office, with a dagger concealed under his cloak, and if his luck holds and the King is present – attack him with the dagger and thus abort the whole of this expedition and the imposition of order 'once and for all' upon Jerusalem, which has been groaning under a heavy yoke since the day of its foundation to this very day. And confusion shall fall upon Babylon and someone will see in this the finger of God, and Zedekiah will be declared the winner of this war. We should also take into account the possibility – admittedly remote but just the kind of thing to inflame fanatical imaginations – that when Zedekiah marches in triumph through the land of the Chaldeans and takes Babylon by storm with his small but highly effective army, then that forgotten and outcast community will emerge from its anonymity, and they will exchange their hovels between the walls for the royal apartments, and rule over the pagan and dim-witted Chaldeans with a heavy hand and a firm purpose, and chastise them severely, as is written in one of the sacred books of that community. One way or the other," Denur-Shag sighed, fidgeting with his elegant goblet and twisting it between his fingers but not drinking any of the wine, the wine with its pleasant, twinkling reflections of the bright candle-light – "this young man, brave and resourceful as he may be, and armed with his dagger, will be awaited by heavies from the guard detachment, Chaldeans through and through, their swords drawn and clubs in their hands, the shackles for his wrists and ankles set out ready on the thorny ground. And all that remains for us is to finish the consecrated wine from the chosen land, and hope that the chosen people will come to its senses in time and listen, solemnly, to the voice of God and not to the voice of weak-minded novices or crafty tradesmen."

Denur-Shag raised his goblet and calmly sipped his wine. Rising from his seat, he shook the hand of his host and left the room without another word.

A few moments later he rode into the night, calmly and steadily urging on his horse, which needed little encouragement but bore him swiftly over streets now emptied of people, as the stars flicked in the violet, infinite void.

A little after midnight he came to the familiar houses between the two walls, all swathed in utter darkness.

Without dismounting from his horse, he knocked hard on the door of the family home of Joseph Hanaggid. It was not long before somebody called:

"Who is there?"

"Daniel! Open the door! This is urgent!"

The door opened. Saul, the father of Havatzelet, stood in the doorway, an oil-lamp in his hand.

"I must speak to you!" he said, jumping down from his horse and tying him to the hitching-post, and without waiting for an invitation, he rushed inside.

Saul closed the door behind him, and ushered him along the hallway and into the main living room of the house. Here he lit a dozen large oil-lamps, and every corner of the room was bathed in bright light.

"Speak!" Saul demanded. His face glowered, his voice was aggressive – but there was deep fear in his eyes.

"In the royal court there is talk of some kind of plot to murder the King, tomorrow at nightfall. The soldiers of the royal guard know when and where and how the assassin will strike. An ambush has been set for him and he has no chance of either doing the deed or evading capture. Take this to heart and act accordingly. And don't forget, it's the whole community that you're endangering, including women and children and the old."

"Wait here a moment!" Saul cried, clearly shaken. He took a lamp and left the room.

A few moments later he returned with Raphael, his elder brother, and a youth – lean, tall and wiry, with a pointed beard, black as pitch, lank hair and flashing eyes.

"This is Eleazar, of the family of Nehemiah the priest," Saul introduced him and added: "Please, respected Sir, tell him what you just told me!"

In a few words he repeated all that he knew.

For a long moment the four men stood in silence. No one sat. The bright flames of the lamps swayed calmly, this way and that.

Suddenly the young man turned away, and when he turned back a split-second later, he had a dagger in his hand.

"Death to the traitor!" he cried and lunged at him.

The two other men managed to restrain him, and with Daniel's help they wrested the dagger from his hand.

"I have done my part!" he said. He moved to the door and before leaving turned and blessed them: "May God have mercy upon you and upon your household!"

He went to his bed before daybreak and slept for a while, but fitfully. He got up finally and went to the window, feeling weary and heavy-hearted. The garden was in darkness and the sky turning pale, the last of the stars flickering and fading.

He was pleasantly surprised to find that the slave had already prepared a bath for him, and he spent some time lounging in the warm water. When he emerged and dressed in shirt and breeches of soft blue fabric, with a white sash, and entered the dining-room – the table was set. On the other side of the table sat Nejeen, in a pink robe. Her smile was radiant, and her face spoke of tenderness, her eyes – of love. She greeted him and rose as he approached the table. He returned her greeting mechanically, and did not seem to notice she was standing. She sat after he had taken his seat, and asked the maid who was serving drinks to fill his goblet with light wine. For herself she poured a cup of the mountain spring water that was brought down to Babylon in great wooden barrels.

He sipped the wine and felt its warmth restoring the vitality to his body and flushing his cheeks. How apt she was at guessing what he wanted and silently satisfying his desires, always finding a way of comforting him!

He looked up at her with eyes filled with gratitude.

She said as if answering a question:

"I saw you riding out in the night and I waited for you to return."

"What were you doing all that time?" he asked.

"I was praying," she smiled at him, a smile that opened up again before him a wondrous world of soft radiance, of song and harmony.

"Was it you who ordered the hot bath?"

She nodded. "Did you enjoy it?" she asked.

"It restored my strength."

"Praise be to God!" she exclaimed joyfully.

"Amen and amen!" he confirmed her blessing.

He was offered rye bread, a honeycomb, milk and butter. He felt his strength returning, with a healthy hunger that gratified him.

He offered her a buttered slice and took one for himself.

She thanked him and said:

"One morning, not long before the Chaldeans came, at the end of spring, you invited me to stroll with you to the grove of pines on the road to Anathoth. We walked along a path that could hardly be called a path because of the long, fresh grass that covered it. Once we had gone a certain distance, you held my hand, as if you wanted to protect and reassure me. I tried to convey to you that I wasn't afraid and your concern for me was unnecessary. We found the cave of a bear, or more precisely, a she-bear, and there were three little cubs there, full of energy and mischief. You had what was left of a honeycomb with you, and you gave it to me to share out among the cubs. I was the happiest girl in the world! And the main reason for this – I sensed how happy you were too, and what a delightful experience it was for you. At that moment – do you remember?" she asked curiously.

"I remember!" he exclaimed, going back to relive that exceptional, thrilling moment.

"At that very moment," she continued, putting the slice back on the plate in front of her, "we both sensed something strange, a heavy and clumsy presence, but not hostile. And then, I'm sure you remember, we slowly turned round and found ourselves standing, face to face, with the mother-bear, looking into her placid eyes."

"I remember!"

"She rubbed her muzzle, with more delicacy than you'd believe such a clumsy creature was capable of – on your shoulder and mine, and then she put out her tongue and licked your face and mine, and then she withdrew with a kind of contented purr and curled up in her corner, glancing at us with a look that seemed to say:

You play with my cubs! They're happy with you, and I'm happy to see them happy, and to see you happy!"

"And that's just what we did!" he reminded her. "We played and played for ages, we chased them and they chased us, and they climbed all over us and challenged us to catch them as they hid behind bushes and climbed trees. And all this time the mother was lying there contentedly, grooming her fur with her long, red tongue."

His marvellous wife had detected the tension that was troubling him and the fear that had penetrated deep into his heart, disturbing his rest and perhaps also souring his mood, and she had found just the right antidote, to assuage this fear and ease his depression – with the healing story of the she-bear and her cubs.

His face shone with warmth and gaiety, as did hers, and each of them had no desire other than to share this gaiety and this warmth with the other, rejoicing in the other's happiness, and finding relief and contentment in the relief and contentment of the other.

When he rose and passed by her, he kissed her silky hair, gathered at the back of her neck, as well as the hand that was held out to clutch his, and before he had time to say another word she kissed the back of his hand, a kiss that was tender and at the same time, deliberate and protective.

He worked in his office until evening, and after dining with his wife, invited her to join him for a stroll in the royal gardens. The walk refreshed them both, and they climbed the steps to their bed-chambers hand in hand.

When they woke the next morning, the palace was in a ferment, like an ant-hill turned upside down. It emerged that the prospective assassin had not abandoned his plan but only changed it – and had simply entered the palace by the main entrance. The man approached the gate and when asked to stand back in the customary manner and await clearance he pretended to obey, but the moment that one of the guards stepped forward to search him, he slipped past him and made a run for it, succeeding in getting as far as the royal gardens.

A pursuit followed, ending with the would-be assassin cornered in one of the felt-covered tool-sheds, some distance from the royal compound. The shed was surrounded by a tight ring of guardsmen, who called upon the fugitive to surrender of his own accord rather than wait to be taken by force. The summons was repeated, but there was no response. Just as the soldiers were about to launch an attack, a pillar of thick smoke was seen rising from the roof of the felt building, and immediately after it a massive flame leapt into the sky, and within moments the whole of the shed was ablaze. The soldiers did not lose their nerve, but found buckets, pans and other utensils and ran to fetch water from the nearby well. As they were busy dowsing the fire, a figure emerged from among the panels of felt, a human figure wreathed in flames and burning like a torch, shouting with the last remnants of his strength:

"Long live King Zedekiah! Long live Judah! Death to Nebuchadnezzar! Death to the ungodly Chaldeans!" – and a blazing hand still brandished a long dagger.

Still yelling, the burning figure fell, collapsed there and then and lay inert. As no one had any intention of intervening, the figure burned on to the end, until only ashes were left.

The day after the distasteful episode of the would-be assassin who was burned alive, there came to the royal palace a delegation of worthies from the ancient Jewish community of Babylon, and among them were Simeon and Raphael, Benjamin and Saul, who had been instigators of the assassination plot and its most ardent supporters. After they had been kept waiting for two days at the palace gate, the King agreed to receive them.

The members of the delegation all fell at the King's feet, and prostrated themselves reverently. After they had spent some considerable time kissing the cold floor of the reception hall the King commanded them to rise, and they rose to their feet one by one, assuring the King of their utter abhorrence of the criminal act committed by that deranged young man, whose sole intention had been to damage the exemplary relations, relations of peace, friendship, brotherhood and mutual trust that had always prevailed between the Chaldean people and the Jewish people, peoples which after all had shared roots and even similar laws, legal traditions mutually nourished – and they had come here to bow down before the King and affirm once more their unbounded loyalty to the Chaldean state and monarchy in general, and to King Nebuchadnezzar in particular. As was well known, since time immemorial they had spared no effort in demonstrating their fervent support of the Chaldean administration and glorious Babylon, which they saw as their homeland and their patrimony. And they offered the King an ancient sword which they said had once belonged to King Solomon himself, and one thousand gold shekels, of Babylonian coinage, as a contribution to the Chaldean war effort against the disloyal Zedekiah, and they welcomed this opportunity to denounce him publicly and disown any connection with him.

With a cynical sneer that he made no attempt to hide, the King rejected the sword and commanded that the thousand shekels be distributed among the poor and the needy of Babylon. He was minded to have the delegation forcibly ejected, but in the end he relented and let them go in peace, much to their relief. He had no quarrel with the Jewish community of Babylon as a whole, and besides, he reckoned that these men had humiliated themselves quite adequately without any help from him.

ADONIAH

Adoniah called upon Rafsi, the eunuch responsible for the east wing of the harem:

"I need to speak urgently with Anabil, the Egyptian woman that I brought here for His Majesty the King! Just for a few moments!" And before the giant could respond and send him on his way, he touched his swarthy arm and drew out a bulging purse from beneath his purple cloak. "One hundred gold shekels!" he whispered.

The eunuch seemed to be reconsidering his next move, his protuberant eyes fixed on that purse, and then, after inspecting his surroundings to be sure that the corridor was empty, with no living soul in sight, he snatched the purse as it was offered him and quickly hid it under his broad sash.

"Tomorrow, at sunset, in the perfumery, for a short time only! And I know nothing!" he whispered, adding emphatically: "The responsibility is all yours!" And with his head held high, and eyes scanning the ceiling with its carvings of cattle in bronze and lions in wood, he swept away in stately style, as indifferent to Adoniah as if he were a wall or a pillar.

Next day, at sunset, Adoniah slipped into the harem, turned towards the east wing, found the narrow corridor leading to the perfumery, and knocked on the low, white-painted door. A pale hand opened the door and he made a hasty entrance. The door was closed again without a sound.

"You're endangering my life!" Anabil fumed, irritation and impatience reflected in her big, dark eyes – handsome eyes, in which an inexperienced young man might have fancied he saw tenderness and devotion, and boundless submissiveness.

"I need you!" he whispered and added at once: "You are to tell the eunuch responsible for the wing that Belteshazzar, the chief minister and viceroy of the King, entered your bed-chamber at the seventh hour of the evening and tried to rape you!"

"What kind of nonsense is this!" she protested, staring at him coldly.

In his hand he held two bulging purses.

"In each of these," he pointed to the purses – "there are five hundred gold shekels. One of them is yours now, the other you will have when the deed is done."

"Why at the seventh hour?" she asked, still indignant.

"Because at the seventh hour he says his private prayers. No one will see him at that time or testify to that effect!"

"This is going to cost Belteshazzar his head!" she mused, as a broad smile of satisfaction, impossible to disguise, parted her sensual lips and exposed for an instant the flash of her teeth.

"Do you like him?" he asked.

"No!" she declared.

"Has he hurt you?"

"No," she replied grimly,

"He's hurt me!" he asserted.

"How?"

"Through his arrogance!"

"Yes," she agreed, her cold smile reflected now in her eyes as well. "Arrogance – that sounds like him!" and without any further hesitation she held out an eager hand and grabbed one of the two purses.

He turned around, opened the door a crack and stooped to peer out – the corridor was empty. Nimbly and without a sound, he slipped out and closed the door behind him. And so, unobserved by anyone, he left the harem of King Nebuchadnezzar, the valiant and the wise King, conqueror of the world.

Two days later the palace was shaken to its very foundations, and all those residing there were struck dumb with amazement on hearing reports of the shameful deed committed by Belteshazzar, the King's viceroy and senior counsellor. It seemed he was not immune from guilty passions after all, but had tried his luck with the young Egyptian concubine whom Adoniah had brought for the King a few months before, and who was indeed in the full bloom of her womanhood, sensuous and incomparably seductive, with charms that no man could easily resist. So even Belteshazzar had fallen from grace, and Anabil had rebuffed him and called for the help of the eunuch responsible for the wing, and he feared for his life and fled.

And when the story reached the ears of King Nebuchadnezzar, he ordered that both Belteshazzar and Anabil, his new concubine, be summoned before him. And the two of them came before the King, seated on his high throne of cast gold and ivory.

The viceroy bowed and blessed the King in the accepted manner, while Anabil sprawled on the floor at Nebuchadnezzar's feet and at once burst into bitter tears and loud lamentation.

The King commanded his concubine to stand and tell her story from beginning to end. And still whimpering, the Egyptian concubine described how Belteshazzar, in a frenzy of lust, had invaded her room the night before last at the seventh hour, and had assaulted her. She spurned his advances, but what strength did she have to resist a man? And she called out for help...

"Who answered your call?" the King interrupted her sternly. And she spoke out in praise of the prompt response of the one responsible for the east wing of the harem, none other than Rafsi, the eunuch.

And the King commanded that the eunuch responsible for the east wing of the harem be brought before him.

Rafsi arrived, flustered to the very roots of his soul, sweat glistening on his broad forehead. And he fell at the feet of the King and did not rise until permission was given, and then the King addressed him in a tone that did not bode well:

"Dirty, despicable wretch!" cried Nebuchadnezzar, incensed. "Why did you wait a day and a half before coming to me to report the scandalous activities taking place on your wing? You deserve to have that stupid head of yours removed from your shoulders!"

Rafsi prostrated himself again at the feet of the King and in a quaking and mumbling voice, confessed at once that it was all a fabrication.

Nebuchadnezzar commanded that they both be tortured with red-hot irons but before the irons touched their flesh, the truth came to light, and Adoniah was arrested at the King's command and brought before him in chains.

Adoniah adopted an air of baffled innocence and denied everything, declaring with fervour that he had never spoken to the eunuch or to the Egyptian concubine, and they had hatched a plot to make him a scapegoat. Clearly, they were enemies of the Jews, who felt they had scores to settle with the exiles of Judah. As for Belteshazzar, he was his best and most trusted friend, whom he had never known to do anything but good. It would never occur to him to describe him as "arrogant" – least of all in conversation with a bonded slave-woman!

Adoniah's protestations of innocence failed to convince the King, who silenced him and sentenced him forthwith to death by hanging.

It was then that Belteshazzar bowed to the King and asked for permission to speak. Permission was granted, and he proceeded to say:

"My King, live for ever! No word that His Majesty utters is ever to be ignored, and this wretched man is indeed worthy of the most severe of punishments – if it is proved beyond doubt that he has committed the heinous offence of which these witnesses have accused him, conspiring to incriminate his friend. Indeed, there is enough in the witnesses' accounts to cast a heavy shadow of suspicion on the King's commercial agent, but this is not conclusive, unequivocal proof, however likely it may seem. And because there is doubt, I venture to suggest that the sentence of death be commuted to hard labour in the mines in the mountains, so that no man's conscience needs to be troubled over the unproven guilt of this man, who persists in his claim that his hands are clean."

Belteshazzar's measured words eased some of the tension in the atmosphere, and opened the way to calm reflection and reconsideration.

For a brief moment King Nebuchadnezzar looked down as he pondered what had been said, before looking up again and declaring:

"It shall be as you say! This cunning knave shall have the benefit of the doubt and his head may remain on his shoulders. Instead he shall be sent for twenty-five years into the bowels of the earth, for hard labour in the bronze mines. He is to be bound in shackles which will not be removed until the very last day of his sentence has been served!

"The other two," the King thundered – "shall be put to death, and at once!"

Soldiers of the royal bodyguard swooped on the three malefactors and began dragging them towards the door.

The eunuch and the concubine uttered the most heart-rending shrieks, while Adoniah twisted round in his captor's hands to face the King and cried out to him:

"I have something important to say, my lord the King! Of the greatest importance, please hear me!"

And since the King showed no inclination to hear anything more from him, sentence having been passed, Adoniah shouted:

"I lied to my Lord the King! What these witnesses have said of me – is the absolute truth!"

"Stop!" cried the King, and his agent, in chains, was brought back to him and thrown down at his feet.

Adoniah was agitated, emotional and perhaps in pain as well, but he was not scared. Making no attempt to rise from the floor where he lay, he looked up at Belteshazzar and addressed his remarks to him, while panting heavily:

"All praise be to you! Your efforts to save me from the claws of death touched my heart, but the truth is, my fear of death is as nothing compared to my fear of hard labour and chains! You know how indolent and lazy I am, intent on fleeting pleasures... jealous too, and the most mean-spirited of men. Forget me, if you can, and I'm not asking you to mention me in your prayers! Peace be with you, Daniel, my brother! You are well rid of me – for I am your enemy! And you should know, you have many more enemies, so beware of them! And before I disappear from your life I must confess to another sin that I committed against you – the metal spike under the saddle of your horse, that was supposed to wreck your chances of winning the race, and bring your life to an abrupt end – it was my idea. I thought of it, and Matthew, the unlucky boy who died that day, was the one who carried it out.

"And all these years I have hated you for your success, and this hatred gave meaning to my life! And now, my life is ended, and the hatred is ended too. I am also the one who incited those who informed against Mishael, Hananiah and Azariah, bringing to their attention the way that those three stood erect while all of Babylon bowed to the golden image. Oh, how proud of them I was, and how I envied them! And how I hated them, and how eager I was to put them to the test, the severest of tests, to the end! And sure enough, I did it – and they withstood it! Pass on my warmest congratulations! Even at this moment, my heart is full of pride in you, and envy, at one and the same time. And as for you, peace be with you. I am swarthy, and not the prince of any haughty maiden's dreams!" And suddenly he turned where he lay and kissed the feet of the King's viceroy, and cried in a choking voice: "Forgive me and pardon me – if you can!"

"I forgive you and I pardon you, my brother Adoniah!" he said, and tried to raise him to his feet, but the soldiers of the guard forestalled him, dragged Adoniah up from the floor and made him stand, looking into the purple, enraged face of the King.

"Hang him!" commanded Nebuchadnezzar.

A MAN MUCH LOVED

BOOK III

AS DEEP AS THE SEA

King Nebuchadnezzar's preparations, to leave Babylon and march on Judah at the head of his army, were completed to the last detail. Supplies were requisitioned, both for men and for beasts. Weapons were distributed and polished meticulously, uniforms keenly inspected, and anything apparently old or deficient was replaced with new, the same process being applied to armour, helmets and shields; wheels of vehicles were checked and their axles greased, wagons were reinforced, and battering-rams and siege-engines mounted on the carriages specifically designed for the purpose. Commanders were appointed and duties assigned, decrees issued. Every officer, senior or junior, studied the orders according to which he was to operate and learned them by heart, and all rehearsed their battlefield tactics and fighting skills, drilling and training under the watchful eyes of their immediate superiors until every soldier knew his place in the formation, knew who stood next to him, knew the operation in which he was to take part, what he was to do – and why.

Warhorses were groomed, pack-animals and fodder animals prepared for their long journey. Prayers were issued too for the soldiers to learn, to be said privately or in times of crisis, in small or large groups, and so the mighty Chaldean army became a single organism, bound by the ties of unity and harmony, of freedom and initiative, and exuding confidence.

Gradually, as the training continued and muscles were flexed, even the expressions on the soldiers' faces changed, and the thinly disguised and habitual boredom, anxiety and suspicion – were replaced by looks of determination and self-assurance. Here and there, there were even smiles.

The Chaldean war-machine was built, assembled and lubricated with great precision, tried and tested and poised to strike – to punch a way through to its assigned objective, to trample down every obstacle in its path and inflict a crushing defeat on the enemy.

He watched all these preparations from a distance and felt a numb emptiness. He knew this was God's will, and this knowledge went some way towards cancelling out the emptiness; despite his best efforts, the feeling was not obliterated, only checked.

He also knew that the Chaldean war-machine was about to be launched against his own people, causing injury to his family, the blood of his blood and flesh of his flesh, his acquaintances and friends from long ago, and the blow to be inflicted would be intolerable – more cruel than any ever suffered by this race, stubborn and accustomed to affliction as it was.

"Oh my Father in Heaven, my God, whose mercies are as deep as the sea, is it a sin to ask you yet again to pardon and forgive this people of yours, frustrate its enemy and avert the impending catastrophe, so it may be saved?"

And in the depths of his heart he heard that calm and clear voice, addressing him:

And how am I to save this people when it does not want me, and rejects the salvation that I offer? I, whose name is love, and freedom, and truth!

He fell on his knees, tears choking him and his shoulders shaking in a silent whimper that contorted his lips:

"Blessed are you, my Father in Heaven, my God, giving understanding to the ignorant and pretending to no one, bestowing your love upon those worthy of it and making mortals into immortals! Blessed! Blessed! Blessed!"

He fell prostrate on the ground, wiped away his tears and stood again, and taking the place of the emptiness in his heart, the living light shone there.

On the eve of his departure, Nebuchadnezzar summoned him to his presence, a summons that surprised him. It occurred to him that the King might be in some kind of a quandary, needing to give vent to his thoughts, and this supposition proved correct.

The King was waiting for him in one of the private rooms of the palace, not intended for receiving guests or for plenary council sessions but reserved for the King and his innermost circle.

For the first time since knowing the King he saw him in his domestic attire, without any royal pomp or trappings of authority. A blue robe emphasised his erect stance; King Nebuchadnezzar was a statuesque man, but not tall. He wore no head-covering and his raven-black hair, here and there flecked with silver, was combed back, reaching his shoulders, while his beard, though neatly trimmed, was almost waist-length.

The garb surprised him, but not in the way that might be expected. It struck him that even in this decidedly domestic clothing, Nebuchadnezzar remained Nebuchadnezzar, a king to his very finger-tips, before whom bowing and kowtowing were axiomatic, instinctive expressions of respect for one elevated, by his very nature, above the common herd, destined to rule and radiating majesty by sheer force of personality.

The room was neither long nor broad, being circular or more precisely – oval, without ornamentation or decoration or regal trappings, but the very presence of the King invested it with a glamour that could not be erased or ignored.

It was absolutely forbidden to sit in the presence of the King without his express permission, and he could not remember a single occasion when this privilege had been granted. Most audiences were conducted standing, while he, the King, sat on his throne, quite indifferent to the weariness or discomfort of his interlocutor.

This time, in an unusual departure from convention, the King himself was standing to receive him, and he remained standing throughout the conversation. Although there was no shortage of padded chairs and divans in the room, he did not resort to any of them; sometimes while speaking he would slowly pace the length of the room, a habit which he took to be a token of the King's respect for him.

"God knows!" the King began – his voice resolute, metallic, the voice of one accustomed to issuing his decrees before the populace, a voice that would brook no interruption, a voice to stifle and silence the very thought of disagreement. There was no alternative but to heed this voice, and he knew that anyone whose heart was innocent of intrigue, whose spirit was pure, had nothing to fear from it; the very vehemence of the tone was such as to instil confidence and calm.

And the King went on to say:

"Oh, how I tried and tried again to avoid this situation, to avoid having to take this step! In my eyes, Judah has always been a lovely land, a land of unique qualities, the home of the Divine Presence, a land whose inhabitants have gained the favour of God, something denied other peoples.

"I respected the Jews, and the conquest of their land was never more than a strategic measure. I made no excessive demands of them, and they fared much better than most nations that have been defeated on the battlefield and occupied by foreign armies. I did no harm to the property of the Jews or the property of their king, or their places of worship, and wherever I breached the walls of Jerusalem, I ordered that they be rebuilt and restored. My only desire was to learn from the Jews! I wanted to know this God who is truth, enjoy the privilege of His revelation, the God who showed you the dream that I dreamed and then forgot – a task in which the Chaldean magicians and diviners, for all their world-wide renown, failed utterly. And the solution to the dream was also given to you by God, the God of truth! And this God Himself was revealed in all His glory to your three Jewish friends, the wondrous Meshach, Shadrach and Abed-Nego, saving them from the flames of the furnace!" The King walked slowly to one end of the room, and then retraced his steps and stood before him, going on to say:

"And in Judah of all places, the king whom I enthroned with my own hands, who persuaded me to appoint him king over his people and pledged allegiance to me in return, has risen against me and broken faith, and it is not me he is rebelling against but his God – it is Him he is defying and opposing!" Again Nebuchadnezzar walked slowly to that corner of the oval room where a table stood and on it, a black effigy of the god Bel, a cubit in height.

"And the angel of God, the prophet Jeremiah, warns the king repeatedly, and it is not of me that he warns him, but the perverted ways in which he has chosen to walk, refusing to obey his God, the God of the Jews. And this is beyond my understanding: I, Nebuchadnezzar, the pagan, the idol-worshipper – am more devoted to your God and believe in Him more fervently than your own king! The prophet Jeremiah, holy angel of God, prophesies of me and calls me God's servant, while your king stops his ears and will not hear! I shall never understand it! And I tell you this!" – he moved closer to him, his eyes flashing sparks of fire: "This time it is all over! Zedekiah shall pay the full price of his treachery. He and his gang of cronies!

"Zedekiah consulted the Lord, the Lord who does not pretend, and He answered him, telling him that the Temple in Jerusalem is no longer a sacred site, for wicked men have defiled it, and Zedekiah at their head, and it is fit only to go up in flames, and I give you my word – I shall burn down the tainted sanctuary of the traitor Zedekiah!" There was no need for the King to raise his voice to express his rage, and he spoke without any change of tone.

The King, in his blue robe with the delicate gold embroidery at the collar, resumed his steady pacing, then stopped before him, studying his face keenly and evidently expecting a response.

And the response came, in a clear and tranquil voice that seemed to come from faraway:

"Why does King Nebuchadnezzar, who believes in God, the God of truth who created Heaven and Earth and all that is in them – still worship idols?" He nodded towards that black effigy of Bel.

Nebuchadnezzar was taken aback by the question, but not unduly offended. Indeed, he chuckled as he replied, with a sidelong glance at the image:

"If I were to discard Bel altogether, I would be deceiving myself, for I'm still committed to him. But the day will come when by the grace of the God that you serve I shall do whatever is the right thing! And my question to you is this: what will be the ultimate fate of your compatriots if you have kings like Jehoiakim, who tore up Jeremiah's scroll in which the living words of God were inscribed and threw it in the fire, and persecuted Jeremiah cruelly, and Zedekiah, against whom I am taking the field tomorrow, who refuses to hear the word of the Lord as spoken by His prophet, and does not heed his warnings?"

And as an answer to the King's question was explicitly required, he declared:

"Evil and bitter will be the fate of my compatriots! Affliction will pursue affliction, disaster will replace disaster, and destruction invite further destruction. Because my compatriots have scorned their creator and defender and discarded Him, and have spurned Him and all the angels He has sent to them to warn them against the evil that they are bringing down upon their heads. But in the end, my unhappy people will repent of their misdeeds, and this through the grace and the mercy of the God who loves them. And the final outcome for this stubborn and quarrelsome race will be its return to God, and this return will bring about the salvation of all the peoples of the world, all nations and tongues and principalities!"

The King's eyes were fixed upon him, their expression keen and bold like the look of a panther, and conveying admiration and joy – the joy of a king that is always held in check, and is thus all the more pure and sublime.

Nebuchadnezzar bowed low before him and said:

"Truly, your people is nothing other than the people of God!"

The King's words did nothing to reassure or console him. Their effect was the opposite. In his heart a cloud of depression descended. As he was well aware, and as the King had confirmed, a people of God existed. Was it really his people? Would a people of God behave as his people had behaved, treat its God as his people had treated its God? What was the definition of a people of God, and who were its constituent members? And the answer sprang into his consciousness of its own accord and was inscribed there:

Those who know that His name is love.

And for His people… yes, for His people He is grieved. And His grief is deep. If only they would awaken from their blindness and their vain delusions and see what lies ahead. Prophets were sent to them, to warn them constantly against the ruin and destruction that are in store. And they do not listen, and they pay no heed, stubborn and arrogant as they are, trusting in their own strength. And bitter, oh how bitter will be their destiny!

He did not know what time he reached his home. He was eager to see Nejeen, and talk with her, feel her closeness. She's sure to be asleep by now, he reflected gloomily. He bathed to refresh himself, went to his room, stripped off his clothes and climbed into the broad bed. And here a surprise awaited him: Nejeen was there. Under the blanket, on the other side of the bed.

"How did you guess?" he asked, in a bemused, shaky voice.

"Guessing had nothing to do with it," she answered him in that calm tone of hers that never failed to instil tenderness and joy. "I was drawn here."

"How so?" he persisted.

"I realised how much you need me just now!"

Their bodies drew closer, and arms entwined. Her breath had a fragrance unrivalled by any of the perfumes of the world; it was the balm of the countryside and the freshness of the field, and the purity of the constant heart.

"You should know…" he began to say, meaning to tell her how hard it was to imagine his world without her, but before he could utter another word, he heard her saying, almost in his ear:

"God is real! And as the prophet says, *Cursed is the man who trusts in man, and he goes on to say, Blessed is the man who trusts in the Lord!*"

"But there are times when man is divine," he pointed out. "It's written in the Scriptures: I said, you are God, and all of you sons of the Most High!"

"That is true," she said, and turned on him the tranquil lustre of her eyes. He felt the depression melt and the tension dissolve.

"And what of the King?" she asked.

"He's troubled!" he replied with a smile.

"Jeremiah calls him 'my servant Nebuchadnezzar'," she commented.

"There is none worthier than him to bear that title," he said, recalling all that had been said that evening. "God is with that man!" he concluded.

"You like him then!" she declared.

"Admire him!" he retorted.

"And you say he's worthy of the title Jeremiah has given him?"

"No one is more so!" he confirmed.

"And yet – he's a worshipper of idols!"

"It's ingrained in him. But it seems the time isn't far away when he'll put all that behind him!"

Oh my Father in Heaven, my God, how can I thank you for bringing me so close to this beloved body, not so much a body as a beam of pure light, emanating from you, with the fragrance of wild flowers and the warm youth of the springtime, never flagging and never failing, praising you and telling of your glory, and knowing your name, as I know it. For all that comes from your hand is good and beautiful, wise and brave. For you are love and you are my love!

They exchanged no more words, and even their breathing did nothing to impair the harmonious silence, binding the two bodies in a loving and inseparable union, of heavenly provenance and heavenly aspiration.

He was not aware of the passage of the night, or the retreat of the distant line of the grey horizon, fading away into nothing. He was not aware of time or its indications. He melted into her utterly, and she ceased to exist as a body apart, and became him.

The rising dawn found them in each other's arms, silent, non-existent, knowing the love of God, and known to Him.

They broke their fast on the veranda that was all flowers and verdant green. The air was clear, the skies high aloft, and there was silence everywhere. They both knew something was about to happen, something far from pleasant, and they were going to witness it. And they did not fear it, since their togetherness was absolute, and their sole desire was to dispel grief and gloom – each from the heart of the other.

They smiled as they drank the honey-water and tasted the fresh bread with butter and honey.

And this blessed silence overhanging the void was suddenly, rudely shattered by the thunder of drums and cries of "Long live the King!"

The air vibrated to the sound, and the cutlery on the table jangled.

Without a word spoken they both rose from their seats, lithe young bodies standing firm and eyes seeing the space extending from the gates of Nebuchadnezzar's palace to the gates of Zebava and Urash. He moved forward to the rail and leaned on it. She remained behind.

In the ninth year of the reign of Zedekiah over Judah, in the month of Sivan, the first day of the month, the army of Nebuchadnezzar, King of Babylon, was poised and ready to leave Babylon and march to war against Judah and Jerusalem. And the army was great and powerful, with foot-soldiers and cavalry and war-chariots, siege-engines and battering-rams.

And the army was drawn up in regiments, battalions and platoons, with flags and standards, along the northern wall, stretching from the palace to the city gates, more than five Chaldean parasangs. And the city of Babylon, greatest and fairest of all the cities of the world, was too small to contain this vast army. And as the King and his retinue, in the purple robes of war and mounted on stately horses, took their places before the massed ranks, drums rolled and the army raised a great cheer, shouting in chorus "Long live the King!" – and all of Babylon resounded to the awesome sound and the ground shook underfoot and the foundations of houses and of gaudy temples quaked, and there were some among the populace who thought this was the end of the world, and the dead were rising for judgment.

And the King and his retinue mounted a stage constructed for the purpose, still on horseback, and the soldiers and the people of Babylon saw the King and his closest aides in all their finery, the gold trappings and accoutrements of the King and his horse, and the silver ornaments of the retinue, men and horses alike – all gleaming in the bright light of the rising sun.

And Nebuchadnezzar spoke, and all listened attentively to the words of the Chaldean King:

"God has called me to rule over this land, and in His manifold grace, He has given everything into my hands! So I rule with the consent of God and I act with the courage that has been given to me, and with the valour and wisdom bequeathed to me. And the King of Judah, whom I made King over his people, the Jewish people, swore an oath of allegiance to me, by his holy books and in the presence of the priests who serve his God, and his ministers were witnesses. And I have never pressed him to do anything, or tempted him into anything, and I did not force him to rule, or burden him with taxation, as I have done with other peoples that I conquered by force of arms, other peoples that God placed beneath my feet. And he was like a son to me, whom I appointed to rule in my stead in the land of Judah, the nation that has offended sorely before God. And this child, who without me would not have lasted a day on his throne, has rebelled against me and rebuffed my envoys, men of distinction, the elite of Babylon, and sent them away empty-handed, with contempt, refusing to pay even the paltry tribute required under the terms of his oath. And in my wrath I turned to my gods and asked them what is be done to an insolent rebel, and they answered me, the gods that I serve: Set forth with this army and invade Judah, and lay siege to Jerusalem, and teach this upstart, who owes his throne to you, a bitter lesson!

"I swear by all that is sacred to me, I shall show this foolish boy neither mercy nor compassion, and from me he can expect no kindness, only cruelty. I am marching on rebellious Judah to smash and to shatter and to ruin, not to plant or rebuild or restore! I, Nebuchadnezzar, King of Babylon, conqueror of the world, go forth into this war as envoy of the gods of Babylon, and as envoy and servant of the God of the Jews, and I shall return from it the victor!" the King concluded his oration.

And the army, and with it all the citizens of mighty Babylon, who had come out into the streets or stood on the roofs and the balconies, to see the King and his army and his retinue and hear his address, replied to the King with a rousing chorus of "Long live the King!" and "God speed the King!" and "Death to the traitor Zedekiah!" and "Down with the rebels!" – until all ears rang to the sound.

And the horns were blown and the trumpets sounded, and the great bass-drums and then the kettle-drums took up the rhythm of the march, and the heavy gates of the city swung open, and the army was on the move, like a tidal wave advancing with irresistible force, sweeping aside anything that stands in its way.

Standing at the railing of his veranda, with its profusion of flowers, he looked down at the crowds and heard their cries and their acclaim, and his heart was heavy, and when Nejeen approached quietly and stood beside him, he repeated in an unsteady voice the words of the prophet Isaiah:

"And he will hoist a signal to nations far away, he will whistle to call them from the ends of the earth, and see, they come quickly. None is weary, not one of them stumbles, not one slumbers or sleeps. None has his

belt loose about his waist, or a broken thong to his sandals. Their arrows are sharpened and their bows all strung, their horses' hooves flash like shooting stars, their chariot-wheels are like the whirlwind. Their growling is the growling of a lioness, they snarl like young lions, which roar as they seize the prey and carry it away, beyond deliverance. They shall roar over it on that day like the roaring of the sea. If a man looks out over the earth, he will see darkness closing in, and the light turning dark on the hill-tops."

SERAIAH BEN-NERIAH BEN-MAHSEIAH

About a year after King Nebuchadnezzar set out for Jerusalem at the head of his army, a Jew of diminutive stature arrived in Babylon, clad in a faded cloak and a threadbare shawl, his beard sparse and his back stooped, and a feverish look in his eyes, which flashed and darted about in their sockets. At first it was assumed he had lost his wits and was not entirely sane, but finally, when he insisted most vehemently on seeing the King's viceroy, none other than Belteshazzar, on the grounds that he had been entrusted the task of bringing him news from the homeland, initial impressions were revised. Belteshazzar was informed, and he sent for the man.

It was a fine and glorious morning in late spring. The air was clear and buoyant, the sun shone and its warmth was pleasant; flowers opened their gaudy calices and thirstily imbibed the sacred light of their Creator, and birds trilled tunefully.

The window of his office was wide open, overlooking the city of Babylon that was bathed in the tranquil radiance of a youthful morning.

The man, reputedly from Jerusalem and asking to see him, was admitted.

He did not bow or show any sign of deference. Crook-backed and of indeterminate age, he looked worn out. His clothing was worn and tattered, his reddish-brown hair and beard unkempt, his greenish eyes livid and suspicious.

"My name is Seraiah Ben-Neriah Ben-Mahseiah," he introduced himself, and when the other rose to greet him and extended his hand, he did not clasp it but merely touched it absently with his own, as if his mind were elsewhere, detached from his surroundings.

"Would you like to sit?" he smiled, in an effort to reassure the man and restore some semblance of lucidity to him; it seemed he was either seeing visions or engrossed in a dream.

"Sit?" he echoed blankly, staring in utter incomprehension. It took him a few moments to realise what had been said, whereupon he exclaimed, "Oh yes, sit!" – and did so, cautiously, facing him across the table and looking tense.

"From Jerusalem I come, the steadfast city that is encompassed by foreign armies, besieged by Nebuchadnezzar King of Babylon and his troops. Jerusalem," he declared emphatically, "is hungry for bread, and thirsty for water, and is sorely afflicted! And if the truth be told, the full and naked truth – Jerusalem is dying, yes, dying! And I would not have left the place, deserting it in its hour of greatest need, had I not been expressly instructed to do so, had a mission not been entrusted to me. A mission on behalf of the Lord Blessed be He, and His loyal servant and holy prophet, none other than Jeremiah of Anathoth, of the priestly line! He it was who asked me to take on this mission and leave the beleaguered city, pleading and cajoling until I finally consented. For myself, I would rather stay with my compatriots and die an honourable death than survive in a foreign land!"

His voice was monotonous, as if he were reciting texts that he had learned by heart or praying in the Temple, and there was not the slightest movement of body or limbs to accompany the flow of his speech. It seemed he was not aware of everything he was saying, or even whether the other was paying attention to him or not. His weary, bulging eyes were transfixed in sudden alarm on the top of the broad table, as if there was something strange about it, strange and menacing.

"Will you take breakfast with me?" he asked him pleasantly, adding at once – "I would consider it an honour!"

The fugitive raised his unkempt head for the first time since entering the room, and looked him in the eye. It seemed he was still surprised to find himself in these surroundings and in this company.

"Breakfast?" he repeated like an echo. "With the greatest pleasure, gracious Sir, Lord Belteshazzar!"

"If you like, you can call me Daniel!" he said, in an effort towards further cordiality.

"Yes, Daniel!" he agreed, and resumed his monologue: "Two missions were entrusted to me by the prophet Jeremiah, and it is my sacred obligation to fulfil them in the letter and in the spirit. One is directed to you, the other to the exiles of Babylon. And on account of these missions I had to make a hasty departure from my home city, Jerusalem the ever holy, leaving behind me friends and family and knowing for sure I would never see them again with these eyes of mine, nor they see me. I didn't even say goodbye to them, with the one exception of my eldest son, Nathaniel, who is serving in King Zedekiah's army. I also told him about the double mission imposed upon me. Unlike most of his comrades in arms, he doesn't believe that the prophet Jeremiah is siding with the Chaldeans. He encouraged me, telling me this mission of mine is the Lord's work, and everything that Jeremiah prophesied has come about, and disaster awaits us because we defied the Lord our God and did not heed His voice, and the wheel has turned too far to be stopped, and the King of the Chaldeans can no longer be appeased, and Zedekiah knows all of this, and knows too that nothing is left for him and the beleaguered citizens of Jerusalem, other than embrace the Holy Name and die with honour. Yes, this is what my firstborn son told me, Nathaniel, may God prolong his years and fill them with joy and prosperity! And he wished me well in my mission, saying I had done the right thing approaching him and giving the news only to him, sparing the other members of my household pointless grief and upset. He would tell them himself when the time seemed appropriate and besides, my departure was not in itself an occasion for distress and lamentation. Despite the rigours of the long journey on which I was embarking, from Jerusalem to Babylon, I need have no fear of danger, as the Lord would be with me, protecting me from my enemies and allowing no harm to befall me. I had been appointed a divine messenger, and as our sages have assured us, a divine messenger is not in peril, but will always arrive in safety. And as he said – so it has proved. Here I am, treading the soil of Babylon, and here I am before you!"

The heavy door of the office opened, and Oshrich bowed and waited in silence for his instructions.

"Breakfast please – and an extra jug of warm milk for my guest!"

Oshrich bowed again and disappeared behind the closed door.

"And how is the prophet Jeremiah faring?" he asked with interest.

"He has been abused and imprisoned, then released and now he has disappeared from sight! God took pity on him and hid him from his persecutors, those who have eyes to see and see not, ears to hear and hear not. Only the King, in his terror and confusion, consults him secretly and hears his words – hears but does not obey. He's afraid of the Chaldeans and he dreads the Jews, and he is pinning all his hopes on the Egyptians, expecting them to arrive at the last moment and extricate him from the pit that he's dug for himself! The fact is," the guest declared, "where faith is lacking and there is no knowledge of God – hunger and plague and the sword take their place, and ruin and destruction are not far behind. We have been clearly told – *Not by strength and not by might but by my spirit* – and who listens to this now?

"King Zedekiah did try to reverse his policy and negotiate with the Chaldeans, but his ministers and advisers objected, reminding him that he was the one who incited them to rebel in the first place, and it was far too late to change anything."

A heavily laden tray was set on the table. Fresh bread, milk steaming in clay jugs, butter, cheese, honey, olives, pears and apples – produce of the mountainous regions, fresh from the verdant plantations of fair Jahanur.

The guest swooped on the food and said no more. It was clear that he had been hungry for a very long time. Not wanting to embarrass him, he took only a small morsel of bread for himself and drank half a cup of warm milk, but the other was not at all abashed, and such was his hunger, it seemed nothing else existed for him. When he had consumed everything on the tray, leaving only a few crumbs of bread and a scrap of butter, the guest wiped his mouth with the back of his hand, shook crumbs from his tattered cloak, lifted his head and looked at him, this time with an air of satisfaction.

He clapped his hands and Oshrich came and removed the tray, giving the guest a damp cloth and wiping a few stray crumbs from the table.

"About you," Seraiah Ben-Neriah Ben-Mahseiah resumed, "I have heard many strange things! There are some who say you have defected to the Chaldeans, and others who say that even if they saw it with their own eyes, they would not believe it. They remember your father, the minister Naimel, who fell in battle, one standing against many – the memory of the saints be blessed!" He added as if it were an afterthought: "Your family has survived, your mother, your two sisters, one of whom has married, and your younger brother.

"It is said of you that you asked one of Nebuchadnezzar's senior officers to look after your family when the city is stormed and keep them from any harm. That's what the trouble-makers are whispering, and the gullible swallow the bait and complain – 'What about us? Don't we count as family?' It's all just rumours. Anyway, your name is widely known in Judah and it arouses both admiration and acute dissension. People are very disappointed that you didn't succeed in influencing the pagan king and turning his heart towards mercy and compassion, persuading him against marching on Jerusalem in a mood of fury, determined to exact his revenge!"

"Is there any way other than the way of the Lord?" he saw fit to comment.

"Perhaps!" the guest averted his gaze, blinking and finally said: "Who knows which is the way of the Lord that we should follow?"

He answered him:

"The prophet Jeremiah knows!"

"Oh, yes," the messenger admitted awkwardly, "the prophet Jeremiah. "He preaches and proclaims the way of the Lord all day long – and no one listens, no one obeys the Lord's commandments. And yet, people are yearning for something, they long for salvation"

"What kind of salvation?" he asked.

"Salvation of the soul, of course!" Seraiah Ben-Neriah Ben-Mahseiah retorted.

"And that is in the Lord!"

"You are right," the guest said thoughtfully, "and your words are akin to those of the prophet Jeremiah, the holy one of God! And he is always standing at your side, defending every word that you say and letting no one malign you. And it is well known among the citizens and the defenders of Jerusalem, and in the populace at large, that anyone who stands beside Jeremiah and believes his words, also stands beside you and believes your words!"

"And my family?" he asked, and almost regretted the question.

"They are all on your side, as you might expect. Blood is thicker than water, as they say, and members of your family enjoy all the honour and respect that they are entitled to, and no one dares make any comment about you in their presence. And your relations are convinced that whatever you think, say and do – it is God who puts it in your mind, your mouth, your hand, and this will be for the good of Judah and even, so they say, the good of all peoples wherever they may be, all nations and races and tongues, and in the end – your name will be praised!"

"And how are the stocks of water and food in the city?"

"The situation could not be worse! Food is scarce and water even more so. The kosher animals, young and old alike, were slaughtered long ago and their meat distributed among the people. And the same was done with the fowls and after them it was the turn of the horses – with the exception of a few that the King is keeping for his escape when the wall is breached. But even fodder and straw are in short supply, and what state these horses will be in when the hour of crisis comes, and whether they will have the strength to carry the King and his bodyguards – nobody even wants to know. The King is trying to reassure his people, and at one point, as a gesture of goodwill and a demonstration of obedience to the ordinances of the Torah, he liberated all the slaves and the maidservants held by his ministers and viziers. But immediately after the public ceremony of liberation, the ministers and viziers took them back into servitude, as before! And Zedekiah did not protest but pretended he hadn't noticed – he hadn't heard or seen or understood. But God sees the thoughts of all hearts. And He sent Jeremiah to the King, and he told him the words that the Lord put into his mouth:

These are the words of the Lord the God of Israel, I made a covenant with your forefathers on the day that I brought them out of Egypt, out of the land of slavery. These were its terms: within seven years each of you shall set free any Hebrew who has sold himself to you as a slave and has served you for six years; you shall set him free. But your forefathers did not listen to me or obey me. And you did what was right in my eyes when you proclaimed an act of freedom for the slaves and made a covenant in my presence, in the house that bears my name. But you too have profaned my name, in that you have taken back the slaves you had set free and you have forced them, both male and female, to be your slaves again. Therefore these are the words of the Lord: You did not obey me when you declared an act of deliverance for your kinsmen and your neighbours, so I shall declare a deliverance for you, says the Lord, a deliverance to the sword, to plague and famine, and I shall make you repugnant to all the kingdoms of the earth!"

The guest sighed, his brow wrinkled, his face fallen:

"It's all up for the people of Jerusalem and the land of Judah! And I'm sure you know how to conduct your affairs according to the word of the Lord and walk in His ways! And I can only hope that you continue thus until the end of your days on this earth, and then all will profit by your example – Jews and Gentiles alike! As a man sows, so shall he reap!"

The guest's head slumped forward, and his chin almost touched his chest. Silence descended in the spacious office and he felt no inclination to break it. There was a long and awkward pause.

Seraiah Ben-Neriah looked up again, and his eyes were moist, his face pale and his brows contorted, and when he spoke again, his voice was hoarse and grating:

"The two missions entrusted to me by the prophet Jeremiah, the holy one of God! One of them is for the exiles of Babylon, and the word has already gone out and they will all come when evening falls and gather on the bank of the Euphrates to hear the word of the Lord, and the second mission concerns you, the great minister Daniel, whose Chaldean name is Belteshazzar!"

And the envoy rose to his feet, and with all the vigour that he could muster, delivered his message:

"Thus says the God whose name is the Lord of Hosts, the God of

Israel: Be strong and be brave, my servant Daniel! Wherever I have sent you, you have prospered, and I shall send you to more places yet! Do not be afraid of them and do not be anxious, for I am with you to save you. And I have given you to be as a sign and a token to all nations and races and tongues on the face of this earth, and to your people Israel! And I have revealed to you great secrets and awesome mysteries such as no living man has seen before! Be strong and be brave, my servant Daniel, for no harm shall befall you and I am with you, to keep you in all your ways!"

And saying this, the envoy bowed low, retreated backwards to the door and disappeared from the office, leaving him stunned and shaken to the very roots of his soul.

Before sunset, both he and Nejeen went down to the Lugelgira Gate, in the northern sector of the lower wall, and on arriving there they found a great crowd of exiles, also some former acquaintances from the ancient Jewish community of Babylon, standing on the bank of the Euphrates and waiting for whatever was due to happen. Mishael, Hananiah and Azariah were there too, with their wives.

People were grim-faced and taciturn, greeting one another with nothing more than a slight inclination of the head, and no spoken benedictions. When Mishael, Hananiah and Azariah approached them, they said nothing and asked no questions, waiting with the others.

And when the sun began to slip behind the low ridge of the mountains, mustering the last vestiges of its light, and the air, clear and blue-tinted, seemed to underline the tense silence, and evening descended – from somewhere or other that man appeared, none other than Seraiah Ben-Neriah Ben-Mahseiah, holding a parchment scroll, and his whole demeanour expressing dignified indifference to his surroundings. He walked through the crowd and seemed to see no one. And he took up his position on the bank of the broad, smoothly-flowing Euphrates, the bank that sloped down to the edge of the river where water lapped the pebbles.

And then the man's voice was heard, and it was clear, firm and decisive, not like the voice that he had heard in the morning in his office. The man said:

"Hear, you exiles, the instructions given by the prophet Jeremiah to Seraiah Ben-Neriah Ben-Mahseiah: *When you come to Babylon look at this, read it all and say: Lord, you have declared your purpose to destroy this place, and leave it a habitation for neither man nor beast. It shall be a wasteland for ever. And when you have finished reading the scroll, tie a stone to it and throw it into the Euphrates and say, So shall Babylon sink, never to rise again after the disaster that I shall bring upon her!" And Seraiah Ben-Neriah Ben-Mahseiah took a stone, and tied it to the scroll, and threw it into the river Euphrates.*

And the scroll sank and the deep waters covered and swallowed it, and it was never seen again.

THE SIEGE

For three years Nebuchadnezzar laid siege to Jerusalem, proud capital of Judah. He pitched his tent on the top of a hill overlooking the beleaguered city. At the apex of the tent, the royal standard fluttered, in all its grandeur: three gold recumbent lions, skilfully embroidered on a blue background. The sheets of the tent were azure and purple, inlaid with gold and furnished on the inside with heavy tapestries. At dawn, the gold fittings reflected back the rays of the rising sun, and at sunset they were ablaze – a symbol of awesome power.

The hill on which the tent was pitched was named after the prophet Samuel, who anointed the first two kings of Israel and Judah, Saul of the tribe of Benjamin, who fell on his own sword never to rise again, and David, the highly praised son of Jesse, to whom the people gave the affectionate title, "Sweet singer of Israel". He it was who laid the solid foundations of the dynasty of kings, enduring from that time until this. Nebuchadnezzar used to sit on a throne of ivory in the doorway of the tent, looking down at the city, where the defenders huddled day and night over the archery embrasures in the wall, poised to repel any attack.

The King was not aware of the passing of the days, nor the changing of the seasons. His anger was not abated; on the contrary, it grew ever more intense, but it was restrained, just as a seething heart may be restrained beneath a thin veneer, only to erupt with terrible force, casting ruin and destruction in all directions.

In the early days of the siege King Zedekiah attempted a number of sudden sorties outside the wall, and some of them succeeded, as his light cavalry took the enemy by surprise and penetrated deep into the Chaldean battle lines, inflicting heavy losses, setting fire to vital equipment and stocks of food, and sowing mayhem and destruction before returning in triumph to their citadel, leaving behind them only a few casualties of their own and a handful of prisoners. The aggressive spirit and warlike qualities of the Jews made a deep impression on the Chaldean troops, and did nothing to boost their morale. The King found it necessary to address his soldiers and inspire them with the same absolute confidence in final victory that beat in his own heart. And having delivered his speech, Nebuchadnezzar proceeded at once to sit in judgment, ordering the execution of three of his senior officers for lack of alertness and failure to foresee events; twelve soldiers were also beheaded for dereliction of duty, and delay in the lighting of the warning beacons. The heads of the defaulters were impaled on spears and prominently displayed in the centre of the camp.

As for the twenty-three Jews captured by the Chaldeans, eleven of them seriously wounded, the King ordered that they be hanged in full view of the walls of the besieged city, and the bound bodies be left there, dangling in the breeze for six nights and seven days, as a grim warning to their fellow citizens that mercy was no longer to be expected and any Jew falling into the hands of the Chaldeans faced certain death.

The bodies of the hanged men wilted in the heat, with a virulent and all-pervading stench, and the ravens, which had pecked out their eyes on the first day, began ripping apart their livid flesh, especially the flesh of their faces, and exposing their skull-bones. It was a fearful sight. After a week the King ordered that the corpses be cut down and thrown to the jackals.

These measures taken by the King all proved their worth, and following the execution of the Chaldean defaulters and the hanging of the prisoners, the sorties mounted by Zedekiah failed, one after the other, and instead of leaving scores of his enemies slain on the battlefield, the King of the Jews paid a heavy price in lives sacrificed on his own side, as well as losing many horses that could not be replaced. While pondering his next move he suspended the sorties, and seldom sent his horsemen outside the walls.

Nebuchadnezzar was also looking for ways to break the deadlock, and he devised, and put into effect, a classic diversionary tactic. Four regiments of Chaldean fighters with wall-scaling equipment attacked the besieged city from four directions. Ladders were raised and put against the walls, and ropes with grappling hooks were thrown, taking hold. The Chaldeans climbed these ladders and ropes like acrobats, were repulsed and climbed up again, in a continuous cycle, and the defenders were in no doubt that this was a genuine attempt to storm the walls and break into the city. Zedekiah summoned all his forces to the places where the walls were under attack, and concentrated them there, with the aim of repelling at any price the persistent attacks of the enemy and preventing the storming of the city. This was what Nebuchadnezzar expected.

At the western end of the wall of besieged Jerusalem, a small gate was inset, neglected perhaps, but apparently secure, consisting of a pair of double doors, locked and bolted, which could be opened only from the inside. And even if the gate were to be opened, this would contribute little to the success of an attack, since two stalwart defenders on the other side would have been sufficient to deny access to the narrow passage. For this reason, little thought had been given to the proper defence of the gate, and in the heat of the battle that Nebuchadnezzar had ignited, even the few men stationed there were called away to take part in a battle that was considered crucial.

Furtively, some half a dozen grappling hooks were thrown over the neglected gate, and trained Chaldean soldiers, agile as monkeys, climbed the ropes and, as the King expected, found on the other side not one single defender. The Chaldeans lost no time pushing back the rusty bolts and opened both doors to their comrades who were waiting outside, clearing the way, narrow as it was, into the besieged city.

The Chaldeans streamed in a thin but constant trickle, one after the other, into the rear fortress of Jewish Jerusalem. More than five hundred warriors had crawled through the aperture and were poised to attack, before one of the Jewish defenders of the wall noticed them. He raised the alarm and ordered the blowing of the horn, pointing with his blood-stained sword at the Chaldean forces, stealing in behind their backs.

Zedekiah, who was trying to rally his troops on the wall and happened to be close by, realised at once the scale of the danger, and the disaster that would engulf the city if this steady infiltration were not stemmed immediately, and calling up the two elite divisions of the palace guard, he threw them into the attack.

The battle was bloody, claiming many lives on both sides. The Chaldeans succeeded in setting fire to a number of huts serving as stores for food and fodder, and Zedekiah's bewildered soldiers found themselves having to fight the flames as well as the enemy, and their ranks were thrown into confusion. The Jews resisted tenaciously, but it was the Chaldeans who gained the upper hand and Nebuchadnezzar, standing at the door of his tent and watching the progress of the battle, ordered the trumpeter to sound the retreat.

Step by step, not turning their backs on the enemy, the Chaldeans withdrew as victors, inflicting severe losses on the defenders of the city even as they retreated.

The army of Judah had clearly suffered a crippling defeat, one from which it might never recover. In the immediate vicinity of the gate alone, the bodies of more than twelve hundred Jewish fighters were counted, precious food and fodder for horses had gone up in flames, and all of this added to the dejection of the townsfolk, whose numbers were growing ever fewer, and fuelled the sense of despair. The burden of grief was heavy, and bereavement depressed even the most hardened warriors, men renowned for their courage.

Following the success of Nebuchadnezzar's ingenious stratagem, the King promoted and showed special favour to two of his senior officers, one of whom, Or-Nego, had shown remarkable initiative and valour in that battle; although surrounded by some twenty Jews with drawn swords, and the last man in the retreat, he did not despair but attacked ferociously and carved a path through the tight circle, picking up a wounded commander on the way and carrying him to safety.

At the beginning of the month of Elul, there remained in Jerusalem neither water to drink nor food to eat, besides two dozen horses belonging to Zedekiah, and they too were emaciated for lack of nourishment. People lay down in the alleyways and expired beneath the scorching sun of Elul, and there was even the temptation, resisted only with great difficulty, to eat human flesh – not that this would have been of any avail, since thirst was an even greater scourge than hunger and it claimed many victims. And those who remained alive crawled like shadows among the silent buildings, their only desire being to find a drop of water or a scrap of food, and since there was neither, they were reduced to licking cold stones in damp cellars, or chewing cloth or leather looted from the bodies of the dead.

Only one man was still on his feet, despite his exhaustion, and he walked among those sprawled helplessly in the alleyways and in the shadow of houses, and he seemed not to be aware of them, his gaze fixed on the clear sky, soon to be masked by the bluish haze of evening, and a gleam in his eye; not the gleam of the insane, but the deep, inner light of one who has detached himself from the vanities of the world and is all obedience to what is beyond them, a living and life-giving light.

Those sprawled in the streets of the city knew the man, but did not try to address him or ask for his help. And yet there was one middle-aged woman, dying on the steps of her house, her clothes covering only a fragile skeleton, and when she saw the man, a strange, living flame was kindled in her eyes, her lips moved, and turning to him she whispered:

"Jeremiah, prophet Jeremiah – where are you going?"

The prophet heard her voice and understood her, and answered her:

"To Zedekiah, to the King!"

Hearing this, a strange kind of peace spread over the woman's face, and at that moment she gave back her soul to her Creator. And the walking man bent down and closed her eyes, and at the very touch of his fingers her face softened into a faint smile, a smile of the ease that she knew only after her death.

When Jeremiah arrived at the royal court, the first stars were already gleaming in the blue sky, and it was blessedly cool after the blazing heat of the summer day.

He found the King among his courtiers, and all were running hither and thither and engaged in frantic activity: leading the few horses that remained out of the stables, saddling them and loading them with gold ornaments and bags crammed with precious stones, changing their gaudy clothes for simple leather jerkins to disguise themselves as farmers or artisans, intent on slipping away from the palace and leaving the city before it was captured.

Jeremiah surprised them and they stopped their work for a long moment, standing silent and awkward.

First to recover was the King, and he turned to him and said:

"If you want to come with us and save yourself from the Chaldeans, I have to tell you we have no spare horse for you, and you can't share a horse with anyone either, as the horses are tired and there are loads to be carried too, and the Chaldeans will be chasing us..."

"Listen to the word of the Lord, Zedekiah!" the prophet interrupted him, and he raised his voice and it was clear and bold, a delivery that surprised his hearers, since the man from whose throat it emerged was utterly exhausted, like all the beleaguered inhabitants of the Holy City.

"Thus says the Lord of Hosts, the God of Israel," the prophet thundered, *"You shall not escape from the hands of the Chaldeans! Your efforts and your hopes are in vain. Before sunrise you will fall into the hands of your enemies, and they will take you before the King of the Chaldeans, my servant, and you shall see him face to face and you will not escape from their hand, and this city shall be burned to the ground!"*

One of the ministers who had just saddled his broken-down horse turned to the King and said:

"This man deserves to die!" – and drawing his sword he lunged at Jeremiah, but he lost his footing and fell heavily to the ground, injuring his arm on the blade of the sword. Blood flowed from the deep gash. Letting go of the sword the man struggled to his feet, took a faltering pace towards his horse and bound the wound with a piece of cloth taken from his saddlebag, and with a look of terror in his eyes he called out to his companions and to the King:

"Come on, let's get out of here before this man brings disaster down on our heads!"

"And I have this to tell the King," added Jeremiah, speaking in a totally different tone, faint but clear: *"This was the word of the Lord of Hosts, the God of Israel, If you go out now and surrender yourself to the ministers of the King of Babylon, you shall live and this city will not be burned. You and your household will be safe. But if you do not go out and surrender yourself to the ministers of the King of Babylon, this city shall be given into the hands of the Chaldeans and they will burn it down, and you will not escape them.* And you – King Zedekiah, who asked to hear the word of the Lord and when it was told to you, did not listen to it and did not follow it, but remained obstinate, and rebelled against the King of Babylon, the servant of the Lord, and fought against him, and fought against the Lord and the living God – see whither your actions have brought you! Perhaps now you will kneel and fall upon your face, and plead for the mercy of the Lord, for He is kind and merciful and long-suffering, not vengeful or a bearer of grudges, and He will hear your prayer and succour you!"

King Zedekiah mounted his horse, turned to face Jeremiah and said to him:

"Too late, my prophet! It's all over! If your God chooses, in his manifold mercies, to save me from the hands of the Chaldeans, He will save me without me asking it of Him and if not – I shall know He is not the God who promised to David his servant that his descendants would sit for ever on his throne! Peace be with you!"

The riders urged their horses on with whips and reins, and the horses left the rear courtyard of the palace with faltering and reluctant steps, famished as they were and thirsting for water.

In the eleventh year of the reign of Zedekiah, on the ninth day of the fourth month, the city was breached. And all the ministers and generals of the King of Babylon came and took their seats by the central gate.

Seeing this, Zedekiah, King of Judah, and all his warriors took flight, escaping by night from the city through the royal gardens and the gate between the two walls, into the wilderness. The army of the Chaldeans set out in pursuit, and overtook Zedekiah in the desert wastes of Jericho.

King Nebuchadnezzar summoned Or-Nego to him, and when he

stood before him asked him:

"I know that before you left Babylon you visited Belteshazzar, the one who stands in such favour with his God, and his God is always at his side, protecting him from all harm, and when you visited him what was the subject of your conversation, and what did you ask him and what was his answer?"

Or-Nego bowed before the King, sitting in the middle gate of the conquered city on his ivory throne, and rising he told him:

"I asked him if he, Belteshazzar, the King's viceroy and chief magus in all the lands that the King has conquered, had a request that I could fulfil."

"What kind of request did you have in mind, Or-Nego?"

"I meant, Your Majesty, that if it were his wish, I could find out the whereabouts of his family and offer them the King's protection, keeping them from all harm, and if he so desired – bring them to him in Babylon."

"You should know, Or-Nego, that you cannot do such things without asking my permission and obtaining my explicit consent, and if you do not ask my permission and do not obtain my explicit consent, you are defying the King and betraying his trust, and for that the penalty is death!"

"I know, Your Majesty, that is the case, and I did not mean to take any step, large or small, without bringing it first to the attention of the King, asking his permission and obtaining his consent..."

"So why have you not done so?" the King interrupted him impatiently, without waiting for the rest of the sentence.

"My King, live for ever," Or-Nego bowed low before King Nebuchadnezzar whose anger, it seemed, was growing more intense – "I did not come before my lord the King, or ask his permission and consent, then as now..."

"You admit then, you had no intention of approaching me and asking for my permission and consent!" the King interrupted him again, and in his stern, penetrating eyes a flame was kindled, a flame that also reflected, strangely, keen interest and a certain curiosity – like the light, perhaps, in the eyes of a predatory beast that has caught his prey and holds him securely, and yet the prey offers spirited resistance, which both surprises and amuses the predator.

"I did not ask for the King's consent and did not intend to, because there was no need for it!" Or-Nego concluded.

"How so?" cried Nebuchadnezzar, unable to conceal his

bemusement.

"Belteshazzar did not ask me to locate his family and relatives, to protect them and bring them to Babylon, and to my question, could I help him in any way, he answered with one short sentence..."

"Which was?" the King pressed him impatiently.

"Obey the King's command!"

For a brief moment the King remained open-mouthed. The flame in his eyes and the flash of anger faded all at once. If the King were capable of feeling embarrassment or anything akin to shame, at that moment he would have tottered under their weight. And yet the King's lips softened into a perceptive, and quite unexpected smile. The rough-hewn, bronzed face flushed suddenly like the face of a child who has received a precious gift and does not know how to express his gratitude to the giver.

"There's a true man for you!" he declared conclusively, rising from his throne and, perhaps for the first time ever, slapping Or-Nego's shoulder in a gesture of comradeship and amity. Then he paced this way and that, returned to his throne, and seemed to be thinking deeply. Finally he looked up, and addressed his senior commander:

"Nevertheless, we must do something for that exalted man of God! Go down to the city, at once, and ask after his family and relatives and if you find them – give them food to eat and water to drink, and tell them that by my order they are to be taken to Babylon, to be reunited with their beloved son and brother!"

"As my lord the King commands, so it shall be done!" exclaimed Or-Nego, much relieved. He bowed low once more and hurriedly withdrew from the King's presence.

Or-Nego went down to the residential quarters of the city, to the winding alleyways and little squares, the neglected gardens, overgrown with nettles and thistles and brambles, and the dried-up wells, and everywhere he turned he saw only corpses, victims of the great hunger, skeletons wrapped in rags with staring eyes, crying out to the skies. As he walked on he ordered one of his platoons to dig graves and start burying the dead.

He was desperate to find at least one living person, and his heart sank, surrounded as he was by bodies, sprawled on the ground or leaning against the walls of houses and abandoned orchards. Finally, he found an old man huddled over a bone that a Chaldean soldier had thrown him, gnawing it like a famished dog. He leaned towards him, held out a hunk of bread and a lump of cheese, and when the other snatched them from his hand and gave him a suspicious look, offered him a flask of water. When he saw the flask, life was revived in those sunken eyes, and he took it with shaking, skeletal hands, and drank his fill, then broke off a piece of the bread, stuffed it into his mouth and chewed slowly, with intense concentration, and without saying a word. He seemed quite unaware of Or-Nego's presence, as even his eyes were totally absorbed in the methodical process of eating.

This continued for some time, the man eating and Or-Nego watching him and waiting patiently. As he watched he realised this was not an old man after all, but someone much younger than he seemed at first, with hair not yet streaked with grey, and his eyes, as he ate, regaining their youthful gleam. When the meal was finished, and the last crumbs were swept into his mouth, the man looked up at him and said abruptly:

"If you want to kill me you can do it now – though it's a mystery to me why you bothered to feed me first!"

"I have no intention of killing you!" he replied, in what he hoped was a mild and reassuring tone.

"Why not?" – the man looked puzzled. "Isn't that what all Chaldeans do – cutting off our heads, we who are powerless to resist, shooting us full of arrows, impaling us with spears and burning our homes!" He pointed to the plume of smoke spiralling up behind his back.

"Listen to me!" Or-Nego retorted, pronouncing every syllable clearly, "I have no intention of doing you any harm. But I have a question to ask you."

"And if I refuse to answer your question – you'll kill me then?" the Jew challenged him.

"No!" Or-Nego insisted.

The other lowered his head and sank deep into his thoughts. And looking up again he said:

"I don't know why – but it seems to me you're not like all the others. Go on then, ask your question!"

"Among us in Babylon," Or-Nego began, "there lives a certain distinguished Jew named Daniel, whom the Chaldeans call Belteshazzar."

"Aha!" the living skeleton responded instantly, "Who has not heard of this Daniel? Of his outstanding success in the court of the Chaldean King and his appointment as viceroy, like the righteous Joseph who was viceroy to the Pharaoh, the King of Egypt, correct me if I'm mistaken!" The man's animation seemed completely restored.

"You're not mistaken," Or-Nego assured him, listening intently to his words.

"Except that he, Daniel, unlike the righteous Joseph, our ancestor," the Jew continued, a note of bitterness creeping into his voice, "has shown no interest in his brothers and has not served them as Joseph served them! And opinions of him are divided, as there are some who say he has done well and we should be proud of him, others who say he has done ill and we should be ashamed of him. And as for me, I shall not say if I was engaged in this debate, and which side I took! And this because of the sudden weakness that I feel. Your food has indeed revived me, but my stomach is not accustomed to it, and I shall have to go somewhere and lie down to rest. So please, hurry up and ask your question while I'm still capable of answering you!"

"Do you know anything of the family and relatives of Daniel?" he asked, stooping to hear everything the man said. Once more, the deep-sunk eyes of the living skeleton stared at him with a look of revulsion and suspicion.

"What are Daniel's family and relatives to you?" he demanded tetchily, and added as if talking to himself, "I remember now. I didn't side with him. We all hoped he would persuade his patron, the King of Babylon, not to bring all this affliction and destruction down on our heads, the ruins that you see before you. And our hopes were dashed. There was the prophet Jeremiah too. Oh yes, the prophet Jeremiah! I tell you, he's the one you should turn to. He can answer your question! My mind is clouding over and I can't help you, but Jeremiah is still wandering around somewhere. I don't want any involvement in this and I need to go and rest – if your Chaldean soldiers will let me." His tongue heavy and his speech slurred, he concluded, "Go in peace – and if you have any more bread, I'll take it gladly."

He handed him all the contents of his knapsack, gave him the flask of water and hurried away to seek out the prophet. Encountering one of his lieutenants he ordered him to inquire and report to him immediately if a Jewish man had been seen walking among the ruins, as he needed to speak to him urgently. He also demanded a fresh supply of bread and water.

His lieutenant, a sprightly young man, unusually cordial by Chaldean standards, bowed low and answered him:

"I've seen him myself, the prophet Jeremiah, behind that block of buildings, and you can be sure he's still there, as he's tending the starving and the King's orders are that he be given everything he asks for. He's not the kind of man you could ignore, or fail to be impressed by. As for the bread and water, take mine Sir, if you please!"

He thanked his lieutenant, took the bread and water from him, and rounding the block of buildings, came out into a square bathed in sunlight and ringed with black smoke. Sprawled there in confusion were the emaciated bodies of men and women, some still alive – others not.

He saw the prophet tending those who still showed signs of life, giving them milk to drink, and he understood immediately what his lieutenant had said – this was indeed a man who could not be ignored, who could not fail to impress. He looked like a creature not of this world. His eyes stared as if in an empty void and yet – they were deep and something shone in them, something beyond the comprehension of flesh and blood. Or-Nego tried to define to himself what it was that he saw in the prophet's eyes, and he could not avoid using words like "God" and "God-like" – although he instinctively recoiled from anything smacking of sacrilege. Finally, as he focused all his attention, involuntarily, on those eyes, he felt an easing of the tension in the heart, and the words "God" and "God-like" no longer seemed sacrilegious.

He approached the man and, making no conscious decision to do so – bowed down and prostrated himself on the ground. When he stood up again, those eyes were fixed on him, penetrating deep into his heart and filling it with a quiet joy that could have been defined as hope. His instinct was to bow to him again, but something stopped him. Perhaps, the will-power of the man who gazed at him steadily, not saying a word.

"Prophet Jeremiah," he began in a tremulous voice that surprised him too. "May I ask you a question?"

"Ask!" the man exclaimed, his voice like the crashing of waves on a rocky shore, reflecting back the light of the sun.

"Among us, in Babylon," Or-Nego explained, still nervous and his voice hesitant, "lives a man known as Daniel, a man of God, who drew up from the pit of oblivion the dream that our King dreamed and interpreted it by the grace of God. And Daniel has family and relations in this city. And I have no intention other than to offer them help, so far as I am able, and thus reward the man of God!"

"There is nothing that you can do and as for rewarding him," – that clear voice rang out, the voice that reached into the very souls of those who heard, setting all the fibres a-quiver – "it is for God to reward him, the God who is always by his side! And you should know Sir, that Daniel's family, his blood-relations, his mother, his sisters and brother – have all perished. By the sword and by hunger and by fire. One of his sisters married a man and he was killed in the battle on the walls. She herself was trapped in the ruins of her burning house and expired, a one-day old baby in her arms. His mother's funeral, I conducted personally. She and her son died of hunger. His younger sister took her own life. And you, man of Babylon, you know Daniel and you know of his holiness?"

"I know him and I know of him, Sir!" Or-Nego answered him, his voice quavering again, as he bowed and prostrated himself at the feet of this miraculous man.

"Do you believe in the God of Daniel, who is my God?"

"I believe!" Or-Nego heard his own voice, as if it were the voice of a stranger.

"With absolute faith?"

"With absolute faith, Sir! And to prove my faith," Or-Nego added, "I mean to accept the rite of circumcision!"

"Circumcision in the flesh can wait – you must first purify your heart!" warned Jeremiah, adding: "All the sons of Israel and of Judah are circumcised, but what does this circumcision of the flesh avail them, if they are gentiles at heart?"

"What does it mean, Sir, to be a gentile at heart?" the Chaldean officer asked, still on his knees. "Tell me, so I may avoid it."

"It means estrangement from the living God and the worship of idols, namely the idol of greed and the idol of deceit and the idol of adultery! Anyone who abandons the worship of these idols, even if he be uncircumcised – is a son of God! And the one who worships them, even if he be circumcised – is a gentile at heart and an enemy of God! The iniquities of the sons of Judah and the sons of Israel, circumcised though they are, are more grave than the iniquities of all the uncircumcised nations. For the sons of Judah and the sons of Israel knew what had to be done and they did not do it, while the other nations do not know what has to be done and yet sometimes – they do it! So purify your heart first, and only then will the fleshly rite avail you!"

Or-Nego rose to his feet and asked the prophet:

"And what fate does God have in store for my homeland, the place that made me what I am?"

And Jeremiah turned to him, and declared:

"Grievous is the offence of your homeland and the place of your nurture has sinned, turning away from the living God and cleaving to idols and abominations. Listen and I shall reveal to you what the fate of Babylon shall be:

"And Babylon shall become a heap of ruins, a haunt of jackals, a place of horror and derision with no inhabitant. Together they roar like young lions, they snarl like the whelps of a lioness. I shall cause their drinking bouts to end in fever, and make them so drunk they will writhe and toss, then sink into unending sleep never to awake, says the Lord. I will bring them like lambs to the slaughter, rams and he-goats together. Sheshak is captured, the pride of all the world taken. Babylon has become a horror among the nations. The sea has surged over Babylon, she is covered by its roaring waves. Her cities have become waste places, a land dry and desolate, a land in which no man lives and through which no mortal passes. I will punish Bel in Babylon and make him spew up what he has swallowed, and nations shall no longer flock to him. The wall of Babylon has fallen. Come out of her, O my people and let every man save himself from the anger of the Lord. Then beware of losing heart, fear no rumours spread abroad in the land, as rumour follows rumour, year by year, violence on the earth and ruler against ruler. Therefore a time is coming when I will punish Babylon's idols and all her land shall be put to shame, and all her slain shall lie fallen in her midst. Heaven and earth and all that is in them shall sing in triumph over Babylon, for marauders from the north shall overrun her, says the Lord. Babylon must fall for the sake of Israel's slain, as the slain of all the world fell for the sake of Babylon. You have escaped from the sword, go, do not stand still, remember the Lord from afar and call Jerusalem to mind. We are ashamed at what we have heard, and our faces are covered with confusion, for strangers have entered the sanctuaries of the Lord. Therefore the days are coming, says the Lord, when I will punish their idols and all through the land the wounded shall groan. Though Babylon should reach to the skies and make her high towers inaccessible, marauders will come to overrun her, says the Lord. Cries of grief shall be heard from Babylon, sounds of destruction from the land of the Chaldeans. For the Lord is despoiling Babylon and will silence the hum of the city, as the waves roar like a mighty torrent. For the marauders have come to her, to Babylon, her warriors are captured and their bows broken, for the Lord will repay in full, I shall make her ministers and her wise men drunk, her viceroys and governors and warriors, and they shall sink into endless sleep, never to awake. This is the word of the King, whose name is the Lord of Hosts."

AT RIBLAH

Zedekiah was caught as he attempted to escape, put in chains and brought to Riblah, by order of Nebuchadnezzar. And all the sons and daughters of Zedekiah were transported to Riblah, in the province of Hamat, for judgment. And King Nebuchadnezzar sat in judgment upon Zedekiah, his ministers and advisers, and all his household and his servitors.

The King sat on his high throne, with the three red-carpeted steps before it, with the purple cushions and arms of ivory, and the back that was ivory and gold, and above the King's head a great stone was suspended, a sapphire known as the "stone of justice", spreading all around its cold and menacing lustre. The very sight of this stone was enough to make a grown man shudder, make him recall all his wrongdoings and move him to remorse, even to confession and repentance – and to strike terror into the hearts of all those called to account before the King.

So Zedekiah was called before the King, and at his side all his sons and daughters and ministers and advisers and priests and generals. And Zedekiah fell at the feet of King Nebuchadnezzar, and the bronze shackles binding his hands and feet clattered on the marble floor of the judgment chamber. And Zedekiah cried out to the king in a loud voice:

"I have sinned and transgressed both against my lord the King and against God, and my iniquity is too heavy to bear, and yet I venture to appeal to my lord the King, to his merciful heart and his tolerant hand, if not for myself then for all those who now stand at my side – those who are blameless and have done no harm to anyone and whose only fault is in their association with me, and those whom I incited to do those things that should not be done! And on their behalf I address my plea to His Majesty the King, whose is noble of spirit and incomparably magnanimous of heart, a fair and a righteous judge who does no injustice to any man!" And Zedekiah beat his head on the steps of the throne and wept bitterly.

When Nebuchadnezzar delivered his reply, his booming voice resounded around the high walls of the palace of Riblah and set the very air a-quiver:

"According to your own words I shall judge you, wretch who called himself a 'king' and is now blubbering like a contemptible slave caught pilfering from his master! It was I who made you a king and placed you on the throne of dominion, putting a sceptre into your hand and hanging a gold sword at your waist, and you swore by your God and your holy writings, of which you say your whole life is in them, and vowed to keep faith and see to it that your people would know only good things, not bad, and worship its God and praise its judicious king! And instead of this you betrayed – not me but your own God, that God who sees the hearts of men! And when you said 'I believe!' you showed your contempt for the very notions of faith and reverence! Why did you not give thought while there was still time to those for whom you now ask my mercy and forgiveness, begging me to spare them? And yet it was your fervent claim, when you were first questioned, before you were brought here to face me, that they incited you to rebellion, and had you not listened to them you would not have risen against me, disgracing yourself and breaking your solemn vows.

"You surely know that the King is the final arbiter, and he has the competence to accept or spurn the advice of any man, listening to the words of the wise and silencing the mouth of the fool!

"Who would even think of saying such things but a simpleton and a craven wretch, who does not know the meaning of honour... And your weeping and your whimpering will avail you nothing – I do not hear them! You have kindled my wrath, and it blazes unabated! Scores of thousands have paid with their lives for your stupidity and greed, your betrayal of your people and your God! The voice of Jeremiah, through whom God speaks – you did not hear, paying more heed to the voice of your counsellors, those of whom you now say, 'they incited me!'

"Mercy shown to one such as you is no mercy, but an insult to all mankind. Justice you asked for – a holy word that is alien to you as you are alien to it – and yet justice you shall have!"

And the King of Babylon slew Zedekiah's sons before his eyes; he also put to death all the ministers of Judah in Riblah. Then he put out Zedekiah's eyes, bound him with fetters of bronze, brought him to Babylon and cast him into the prison.

In the fifth month, on the tenth day of the month in the nineteenth year of the reign of Nebuchadnezzar, King of Babylon, Nebuzadaran, captain of the King's bodyguard, came to Jerusalem and set fire to the house of the Lord and the royal palace. All the houses and mansions of Jerusalem were burnt down. The Chaldean forces with the captain of the guard pulled down the walls are round Jerusalem. Nebuzadaran captain of the guard deported the rest of the people left in the city, those who had defected to the King of Babylon and any remaining artisans. The captain of the guard left only the meanest class of people to be vine-dressers and labourers.

The Chaldeans broke up the pillars of bronze in the house of the Lord and the trolleys and the sea of bronze and took the metal to Babylon. They also took the pots, shovels, snuffers, tossing-bowls, saucers, and all the vessels of bronze used in the service of the temple. The captain of the guard took away the precious metal, whether gold or silver, of which the cups, fire-pans, tossing-bowls, pots, lamp-stands, saucers, and flagons were made. The bronze of the two pillars, of the one sea and of the twelve oxen supporting it, which King Solomon had made for the house of the Lord, was beyond weighing. The one pillar was eighteen cubits high and twelve cubits in circumference; it was hollow and the metal was four fingers thick. It had a capital of bronze, five cubits high, and a decoration of network and pomegranates ran all round it, wholly of bronze. The other pillar, with its pomegranates, was exactly like it. Ninety-six pomegranates were exposed to view and there were a hundred in all on the network all round.

THE RETURN OF THE KING

Babylon was in festive attire. The day before, the advance party of fast riders had arrived, having whipped and belaboured their horses relentlessly, till their mouths dripped blood and foam and two of them even collapsed on the spot and died of exhaustion – and informed the dignitaries and elders of the greatest city on earth that the victorious army, with the King at its head, was approaching his capital and was due to arrive at the Shamash gate, at the latest, two days hence in the early hours of the afternoon. The dignitaries made haste to recruit slaves and maidservants and set up pavilions and stands alongside the road leading from the Shamash Gate to the royal palace. One particularly ornate stand was erected near the royal palace, and it was assumed that here the victorious King, accompanied by his senior commanders, would take the salute of his troops and address the massed ranks of the parade.

This stand was bedecked with heavy and glossy fabrics and fine linens of blue and purple, and a regal throne was placed in the centre of it. The other stands, intended for the use of the aristocracy of Babylon, the priests and the magicians and the soothsayers, were set up on the northern side of the route, near the wall. The balconies and windows of houses, the sanctuaries of the gods and the wall itself were adorned with a plethora of luxuriant flowers of every shape and colour, flags and pennants and tapestries. Dense chains of flags and banners were also suspended above the route of the march, between house and house, between temple and temple, between the wall and poles erected specifically for this purpose and garlanded with flowers. Little silver bells were concealed among the flowers, tinkling softly in the gentle breeze, and everywhere there were standards emblazoned with the insignia of distinguished families, the insignia of the city of Babylon, the ancient symbols of the Chaldean kingdom, and in pride of place, above the central saluting stand, was the ensign of the royal household, with its three golden lions on a blue ground.

An orchestra of harpists, pipers, horn-blowers, players of the psaltery and the sackbut, was stationed by the grand Shamash Gate, waiting in bright sunshine to welcome the victors home.

Since the early morning a great crowd had been assembling on both sides of the triumphal route, on the wall, on the balconies and roofs of houses and temples. The colours of the flowers and the banners and the tapestries were enriched by the sunlight and for a moment Babylon, the greatest city on earth, resembled a great garland of glorious blooms, of the kind that enthusiastic people offer to their gods in token of gratitude for their grace and their generosity and their forbearance of the weaknesses of mankind. And just as the flustered messengers had predicted, the first ranks of the vanguard of the army were seen in the valley of Nukar in the early hours of the afternoon. A detachment of horsemen headed by three trumpeters approached the Shamash Gate, and on their arrival the trumpeters raised their gleaming instruments and blew a short fanfare, a signal to the others to take up their parade formation, sitting upright in the saddle and holding their lances at the vertical.

These soldiers were greeted by a shout of applause as they cantered through the gate without pausing there and stopped about a half a parasang further on. And then King Nebuchadnezzar was seen riding his horse at the head of the main body of his troops, flanked by his two senior commanders, clad in armour of pure gold, and wearing a gold, conical helmet with a gleaming diamond inset at the apex, reflecting back the light of the sun and dazzling anyone who caught its rays. The helmets of his two escorts were solid silver.

Behind the King, mounted on his mighty charger, white as snow as were the horses of his outriders, came the seventy-strong royal bodyguard mounted on horses black as night and with gold shields, and next in line were the horn-blowers and trumpeters with instruments at the ready and the drummers pounding out the rhythm of the march.

As soon as the King was seen approaching the Shamash Gate, the orchestra struck up with the popular marching song known as the "Anthem of Victory" or "Praised be the Gods" according to the ancient Chaldee version. The rousing strains of the song, sweeping across the parade ground, had the expectant crowd breaking into cries of "Long live the King!" and "Gods of Babylon, preserve the King!" and "The King is our God!" and similar spontaneous exclamations. Then the King's trumpeters and horn-blowers raised their instruments and emitted three abrupt and intimidating blasts, and the crowd was hushed into silence.

The King approached the wide open gate, decked as it was with flowers, banners, tapestries and bells. And here he was met, as tradition demanded, by three of the elders of the city of Babylon, in colourful costume and with silver medals hanging about their necks. Bowing low before the King, seated aloft on his gilded saddle, they offered him bread and wine on a gold tray and greeted him: "In the name of the Gods of Babylon, we welcome the victor home from the battlefield!" And the King answered them: "Greetings to the fine folk of Babylon, its good citizens and all the peoples that the Gods of Babylon have placed beneath my sway." And without dismounting from his horse, he took a small piece of the brittle bread and sipped from the goblet offered him.

At that moment the orchestra, silenced by the fanfare of the trumpeters and the horn-blowers, resumed the playing of their anthem, and to the strains of the orchestra and the cheers of the onlookers, the King finally entered the city and made his way in stately procession towards the triumphal route, passing the precinct of the shrines, while the advance formations that had awaited him fell in behind. And the massive, jostling crowds on the main thoroughfare caught the first glimpse of their monarch, and all cried with one voice "Long live the King" and the whole city reverberated to the sound, and this time the trumpeters and the horn-blowers and the drummers were unable to compete with it. And the shouting continued unabated until the King had passed through the crowds and reached the stand prepared for him, where he dismounted from his horse and took his seat on the throne.

Behind the first contingent of warriors the Babylonians had an opportunity to inspect the vast hoard of booty brought from Jerusalem: gold implements and ornaments and whole pillars looted from the Temple that had been sacked and burnt, and from the palace of the Kings of Judah built by Solomon, most glorious of all oriental monarchs. Seventy open wagons, laden to overflowing, carried the spoils of war, and the multitudes feasted their eyes on them, staring with a kind of appalled fascination. And trailing behind the wagons came the prisoners, barefoot and clothed in tatters, and chained together.

Bound in bronze shackles, led by a gigantic Negro slave, with only rags to cover his livid blue flesh and black holes instead of eyes, Zedekiah, King of Judah stumbled along, falling frequently before being brusquely hoisted back onto his feet and forced to march on.

When the troops came to a halt, two horsemen took Zedekiah from the black hands of the slave, one lifting him onto his saddle and the other supporting him from the side, and he was brought to the stand where Nebuchadnezzar, King of Babylon, victor and conqueror, was enthroned. Once on the stand, Zedekiah tottered and fell before the throne, and from his parched lips emerged the word "Water!" – spoken in Hebrew, Aramaic, colloquial Chaldee and ancient Chaldee, all the languages that he knew.

The man standing beside the prisoner, an officer in purple uniform, raised questioning eyes to the King, and the King nodded. The officer held the mouth of a long clay bottle to the lips of the prisoner, who drank thirstily of the reviving liquid, his gullet, behind the dusty, unkempt beard, bobbing up and down at a rapid rate. When he had finished, he turned his head away, and the officer corked the bottle and put it back in his sabretache. Drops of water on Zedekiah's beard glistened in the sunlight like morning dew.

The King stood up from his throne, to address the crowds and his troops, speaking in a clear, metallic and resonant voice, clearly audible from far away.

"I, King Nebuchadnezzar, by the grace and consent of God, King of mighty Babylon and of the nations of the world that I have conquered at God's behest and by my own valiant hand – I fought the rebellious King of Judah and defeated him, and slew before him all his minions and all his household and then put out his eyes. His city I set ablaze, and I demolished its walls to the foundations. Such is the fate in store for all those who break their vows to their God and betray my trust!

"I, the Chaldean King Nebuchadnezzar, ruler of the peoples, nations, tongues and races which God has given into my hands, I the conqueror of the world, have accomplished what I set out to do, and so may I continue, for as long as God allows me!"

As the King concluded his brief oration, again that awesome cry arose from innumerable excited mouths and took hold in the city like fire, growing ever stronger and louder, and defying all the efforts of the King's stewards to restrain and control it. And the King, clearly gratified, gave the signal, and the massed ranks of the army moved forward for the final phase of their triumphal march, weapons gleaming and flags flying proudly, dragging behind them the seventy wagons laden with looted treasure. And the cheering of the crowd continued unabated, as the army saluted its victorious King, once more enthroned in splendour.

He and his three friends, Mishael, Azariah and Hananiah, stood on the roof of his house and watched the parade and heard the speech of the victorious King, and saw his sumptuous attire and the pathetic rags of the defeated King, the empty holes of his eyes and the bronze fetters binding his hands and feet. They witnessed the triumphal march of the army, and could not fail to see the seventy wagons, carrying all the gold and silver which had enriched the palaces and temples of Jerusalem since the days of Solomon.

Mishael exclaimed:

"The prophet Isaiah predicted everything that we are seeing today. Long ago, in the time of Hezekiah, the righteous King, he declared that all the wealth of Jerusalem would be taken to Babylon."

"Which verses are you referring to?" Hananiah asked, and it was Daniel who answered the question:

"It was when the deputation arrived at the court of King Hezekiah, and to impress his Chaldean visitors he showed them all the wealth of the palace, as it's written:

At this time, Merodach-Baladan son of Baladan, King of Babylon, sent envoys with a gift for Hezekiah, for he heard that he had been ill and was well again. Hezekiah welcomed them and showed them all his treasury, silver and gold, spices and fragrant oil, his entire armoury and everything to be found among his treasures. There was nothing in his house and in all his realm that Hezekiah did not show them. Then the prophet Isaiah came to King Hezekiah and asked him: What did these men say and where have they come from? They have come from a faraway country, Hezekiah answered, from Babylon. Then Isaiah asked: What did they see in your

house? They saw everything, Hezekiah replied, there was nothing among
my treasures that I did not show them. Then Isaiah said to Hezekiah: Hear
the word of the Lord of Hosts. The time is coming when everything in your
house and all that your forefathers have amassed until this day, will be
carried away to Babylon. Not a thing shall be left, says the Lord.

"Well, it is the will of God, the Holy One, so we should not be too despondent!" was Azariah's comment.

And he reminded them:

"Judah will yet rise from its ruins, and Jerusalem shall be built – according to the prophet Jeremiah, who specified a period of seventy years. For seventy years the exiles of Judah shall remain in Babylon, and at the end of that time they shall be awakened and return to their land. And we must do all that we can for these exiles, so they remain united and are not destroyed or dispersed, perish the thought, or assimilated. We have to strengthen their faith and bolster their yearning for the home that they left behind. This is the task entrusted to us, by the grace of God and for the glory of His name!"

He turned away from the flat roof and went down into his house, taking leave of his three friends.

He went to his bed chamber and walked out on the broad veranda, all awash with flowers. He sat on a low bench and felt the gentle warmth of the sun, and saw nothing but the bright blue of the sky and the white clouds silently drifting.

And suddenly he felt a miraculous joy rising from his heart, a living bliss that took over his entire being.

THE SEVEN SEASONS

About a month after the King's triumphal procession through the streets of Babylon, Or-Nego came to the gate of his house, pulled on the ring hanging from the mouth of a tiny lion's head made of bronze, setting a silver bell jangling, and when the footman appeared, asked him to announce his arrival to his master.

He was glad of the visit and shook the army chief's broad, bony hand warmly, ushering him to the veranda where Nejeen was sitting.

She rose from her place, bowed lightly to Or-Nego, picked up the embroidery that she was working on and left the veranda.

Or-Nego stood as if rooted to the spot, stunned and nonplussed, and it was only when Nejeen passed by him, and he dimly remembered having seen her on her wedding day, that he recovered himself and returned her salutation with a deep bow that convention and the circumstances did not in fact require. And although the woman had disappeared from his field of vision, and they both took their seats at the table, he was still agitated and he stared into the void, beyond the flowering bushes that swamped the veranda and gave it the appearance of a living garland. Finally, shrugging off the shock, he looked up and spoke:

"Your wife – a living angel of God! And she has the demeanour of a queen. She reminded me of my own wife – may her soul rest in the gardens of the righteous! Rare women such as these," he added, "arouse in the heart a powerful aspiration to do what is most exalted, to sacrifice oneself for the glory of their name, fulfil their desire even before it is expressed, inscribe their names in letters of fire on the peaks of the loftiest mountains. And all this – out of a joy that is not to be believed, bliss that has no peer on the face of the earth! Surely, she is the woman meant for you!" Or-Nego declared, with more animation than was typical of him. "There is one such to a race, two in the entire universe! Like my princess, whom God bestowed upon me in His grace!"

"It is indeed as you say," – something of the strange and pure exuberance was conveyed to him and stuck to him: "Love is divine and is stronger than all things, it will never be impaired nor fade away, and sacrifice – is its joy!"

"So praise be to God!" exclaimed Or-Nego, a look of mellow acceptance on his face, "God who has shown us the power of His love through human creatures of such perfection!"

"Blessed be He for ever and ever!"

They were served fruit and honey-water, poured into the delicate goblets of Egyptian glass, and after another benediction, they raised their goblets and sipped from them. And then there was silence, and the longer it continued, the gloomier was Or-Nego's face.

He sighed, shifted in his chair and finally said:

"When we were in Jerusalem... with the knowledge of the King and at his explicit request, I inquired of your relations and members of your family."

"You mean," – he had tensed without realising it – "you were to locate them and bring them to Babylon?"

Or-Nego nodded his greying head.

"They refused and did not want to come?" he asked.

The guest lowered his head and did not say a word. A long moment passed.

His face turned pale, his heart seemed to stop beating.

"There was no one to bring?" he asked at last, his voice hollow.

Or-Nego looked up. His eyes were moist.

He mourned for his mother and his sisters, and his brother who was only a young boy when he was taken. He went down to the oratory that the exiles had set up outside the walls, with the King's permission, where they used to gather every eve of Sabbath and end of Sabbath, and on festivals and holy days, and there for a whole month he recited chapters from the Psalms. For his benefit, the oratory was opened on secular days too. Mishael, Hananiah and Azariah joined him. And so, every morning, the four of them would set out to walk the five parasangs, crossing the wall and coming to the oratory, where a congregation awaited them. And the priest pronounced the blessing, and levites played the harp as he chanted one after the other the ringing anthems of King David, and the congregation answered "Amen and amen". And at the end of the month he made a generous donation for the upkeep of the building, for the priest and the levites and the beadle, and for the poor of the community.

He did not neglect his pressing duties, and his days of mourning did not interfere with them. He also prayed at home for the souls of all his family.

About a week after the conclusion of the mourning period, he was summoned urgently by the King, who had once again dreamed a dream that troubled his spirit. Not one of his multifarious diviners and magicians had succeeded in interpreting the dream.

It was a hazy day, the air listless and the sun hiding behind low clouds, grey and looming, shedding warmth but only the dimmest of light on a world that was silent, devoid of life.

The King was waiting for him in the oval chamber. This time the King wore his full ceremonial regalia, which only served to underline the unease in his face.

He bowed to him, and while bowing the thought occurred to him that he was bowing to the murderer of his family and his relatives. But this thought did not take root, as it was essentially alien to his nature. Instead of this, the name of Zedekiah came into his mind and was fixed there. That Zedekiah, who heard the word of God and was warned by His holy prophet, Jeremiah, and was stubborn and refused to do what he was required to do, thereby denying succour and deliverance to himself and to all of his people, including Daniel's family. Was Zedekiah, who broke his sacred oath, not the real murderer?

He cleared his consciousness of all these thoughts and looked again at the face of the King. No, he felt no resentment, certainly no hatred against this man, who by the grace and with the consent of God ruled over a great people. Even for the wretched Zedekiah, who brought about the destruction of his land and the slaughter of his people, he bore no grudges.

"Ah, Judah!" the King sighed as if reading his thoughts. "How I wish those people could have been left in peace, as it says in your writings – every man under his vine and under his fig-tree. But they did no heed the warnings and they left me no choice! It is not enough merely being a king, it is my duty to act as a king, before whom the whole world kneels, whose every word is obeyed. And sometimes," he added, his voice changing and seeming to quiver, "the man before whom the whole world kneels, has to kneel himself before his heart's delight, and still she is not content! And he is ready and willing to lay at her feet whatever she desires, and the one thing which it is not in his power to give her – to bring her homeland to his land – that is what she asks for? Does it sound you like a reasonable request?" the King asked.

"No," he answered him, sensing something of the intensity of the King's pain.

"And I really did try!" he exclaimed. "I brought the landscape of her homeland here, to the very heart of Babylon, my capital. Those hanging gardens that I'm sure you have seen, reckoned one of the wonders of the world – I planted for her. 'There are hills' she said 'in my homeland, and abundant flowers.' I built her a hill of flowers, such as no eye has seen, no ear has heard described, that has no equal on the face of the earth. And she was happy – for a week! Then her face was sad once more. 'Yes' she said, 'you have built a hill for me, with many flowers of glorious colours and delightful fragrance, and they closely resemble the flowers of my homeland, but the air is different, and the light is harsh and dazzling. I long for the balmy air of my homeland, and yearn for its gentle light.' So she tells me. And obviously the air I cannot give her, nor soften the light of the sun of Babylon. Not even God Himself can bring the air of one land to another, or change the sunlight!"

"Nothing is beyond the power of God," was his comment.

"Anyway, He hasn't answered my prayers! Neither my God, nor the God of the princess, Temior, the most glorious woman on the face of the earth! And because I could not bear to see her in her grief, and despite my love for her, which will never falter or fail, I sent her back to her home. And she returns my love – in letters... and that is all!"

"What you have just described could be a unique expression of truly divine love!" he remarked after hearing the King's heart-rending story.

"Meaning what?" the King demanded to know, his brow wrinkling.

"Working for her happiness and taking no account of your own pain!"

Nebuchadnezzar chuckled that surprising, melodious chuckle of his and his teeth flashed against the pitch blackness of his beard, and he knew how strong were his feelings of friendship and admiration for this man.

"I still miss her! And all my wives and concubines, and they are many, cannot expunge her image from my heart. But I don't visit her, despite constant and repeated invitations on her part to go to the palace that I built for her in her homeland, that to this day I have not set eyes on!"

"Why does His Majesty not visit his heart's beloved?" he asked.

"Too busy!" the King declared, turning suddenly serious as the matter that had troubled him and led to this urgent summons returned to the forefront of his mind. His face was grim.

And the King began:

"I, Nebuchadnezzar, was at my ease in my home in the luxury of the palace. As I lay on my bed, I saw a dream which terrified me, and fantasies

and visions which came into my head dismayed me. So I summoned into my presence all the wise men of Babylon to make known to me the interpretation of my dream. Then the magicians, the soothsayers, the astrologers and diviners gathered together and before them I related my dream, but they were at a loss and could not interpret my dream. And lastly I have called upon you, Belteshazzar, named after my god, knowing that a spirit of divine holiness is in you, and there is no secret that is not known to you. Listen then, and hear my dream, and interpret it for me!

As I was looking I saw a tree of great height at the centre of the earth. The tree grew and became strong, reaching with its top to the sky and visible to earth's farthest bounds. Its foliage was lovely, and its fruit abundant, and it yielded food for all. Beneath it the wild beasts found shelter, and birds lodged in its branches, and from it all living creatures were fed. And as I lay on my bed I saw a holy angel coming down from Heaven. And the angel cried out in a loud voice: 'Cut down the tree, lop off its branches, strip away the foliage, scatter the fruit, let the wild beasts flee from its shelter and the birds from its branches, but leave the stump with its roots in the ground. Bind him in fetters of iron and bronze! He shall eat the grass of the field and be washed in the dew of Heaven and share the lot of the beasts in their pasture. And in place of the mind of a man, he shall be given the mind of a beast. And seven seasons shall pass over him. This is the judgment of the angels and the command of the holy ones. Therefore the living will know that the Most High is sovereign in the kingdom of men: he gives the kingdom to whom he will and he may set over it the humblest of mankind!'

"This is the dream that I, King Nebuchadnezzar, have dreamed and you, Belteshazzar, shall interpret this dream of mine and expound it to me! Though all the wise men of my kingdom are unable to tell me what it means, feeble and lazy as they are, and deserving to be cast out of my sight – you can tell me, since the spirit of the holy God is in you!"

He stood rooted to the spot, and what he saw in his mind's eye shocked and dismayed him. He was silent a long time, until the King addressed him again, exclaiming:

"Belteshazzar! The dream and its interpretation should not alarm you. Speak, and I shall hear you!"

He looked up, and gazing intently into the eyes of the King, gave his response:

"My lord the King, this dream should be for your enemies and its interpretation for those who hate you! The tree which you saw growing and becoming strong and its top reaching to the sky, its foliage lovely and its fruit abundant, yielding food for all, wild beasts sheltering beneath it, and its branches a lodging for the birds of the air – it is you, my King. You have grown and become strong, and your power has grown and reaches the sky, and your kingdom stretches to the ends of the earth. And you saw a holy angel coming down from Heaven and he said: 'Cut down the tree and destroy it, but leave the stump with its roots in the ground. Bind him with fetters of iron and bronze, and he shall eat the grass of the field and be washed in the dew of Heaven, and share the lot of the beasts in their pasture, until seven seasons shall pass over him.' This is the judgment of the Most High, imposed upon my lord the King. You shall be banished from the company of men, and shall live with the beasts of the field, you shall eat grass like oxen and the dew of the ground shall wash you, and this you shall endure for seven seasons, until you know that the Most High is sovereign over the kingdoms of men, and he gives power to whomsoever He chooses. And as for the commandment to leave the stump with its roots – this means that your kingdom will be restored to you when you have learned that God is sovereign over the heavens and the earth alike."

The King's face fell, and his mind was in agony, which he tried in vain to suppress. And without waiting for Nebuchadnezzar's response, Daniel addressed him again, the pain clearly audible in his voice:

"Therefore, King Nebuchadnezzar, my King, be advised by me! Atone for your sins with charity, and for your wrongdoings with magnanimity towards your captives, and if someone is unable to pay your taxes – pardon him! You may yet enjoy the favour of Heaven, and see your own debts cancelled!"

The King drew himself up to his full height, a strange flame flickering in his eyes as he cried:

"What kind of a king is he who is alarmed by prophecies such as these, softening his heart and abasing himself and becoming a laughing-stock among men! I shall pardon no man, nor give charity. If anyone should presume to punish me, then let him try. I am ready for him!"

He bowed sadly and left the oval chamber without saying another word.

Days passed, weeks and months. And at the festival of Bel, something happened to King Nebuchadnezzar. The King's slaves and his loyal bodyguards told anyone who was prepared to listen, that suddenly Nebuchadnezzar had run up to the roof of his palace and cried out in a loud voice: "I am King Nebuchadnezzar, King of Kings, all peoples serve me and bow down at my feet, and there is no creature in the Heavens above or the earth beneath that does not bend the knee to me! I am Nebuchadnezzar who built the great city of Babylon for a royal residence, by my own might and for the glory of my majesty, the King who rules over all, the valiant and the wise, I am he!"

As the King was still speaking, a voice was heard from the Heavens: *Your kingdom has passed from you!* And the voice went on to tell the King, to the dismay of the slaves and the bodyguards who heard it all:

You shall live with the beasts of the field, and eat grass like the ox, and seven seasons shall pass over you, until you learn that the Most High is sovereign over the kingdoms of men, and he gives power to whomsoever he chooses!

Scared out of their wits, the men ran to tell the ministers and viziers what they had heard. And the ministers and viziers rejected the reports of the slaves and bodyguards and declared they must be out of their minds; they would believe only what they were told by the King himself. The men must be drunk, and they had better stop their mouths and hold their tongues, because the King would yet ascend his throne and sit in judgment, and words such as these were tantamount to sedition against the Crown, and everyone knew the inevitable penalty for this!

So the bodyguards and the slaves held their tongues and said no more of what they had seen and heard, much to their alarm, and did not even discuss it among themselves, partly for fear of the gallows and partly out of respect for the King, their King, whom they admired and dearly loved.

The King disappeared.

And as time passed and he was not seen in the palace, nor was he attending meetings of his council – his whereabouts were a mystery to all, though no one dared speak of it or pass comment. Finally, the sages of Babylon and the King's ministers met to discuss the issue, and they came up with a typically Babylonian formulation: "The thoughts of a king are not like the thoughts of the common people, nor are his ways their ways!" But the state of affairs persisted, and when a whole month had passed, it was obvious that the King was not in his palace, and he had told no one where he was going or when he would return. And it was decided that an effort must be made to find him.

At first these searches were conducted discreetly, under the guise of casual tours of Babylon and its environs, but as this process failed to bear fruit, the hunt for the King became a public issue, with inquiries extending to the remotest provinces and most far-flung corners of the empire. And the more thorough and meticulous were the searches, the clearer it became to the investigators that there was no trace of their King and no prospect of finding him.

There was no alternative but to convene a plenary session of the supreme royal council.

The issue was discussed by the ministers and councillors, the viziers, governors, satraps, courtiers and dignitaries, and nothing was resolved. Some suggested that a temporary replacement for the King should be appointed; others held that such an appointment could not be considered until it was known what had become of him. Others proposed that the King's eldest son could succeed to the throne, which would be his anyway in the fullness of time. Finally they turned to Belteshazzar and asked for his opinion.

He rose from his seat and addressed the assembled councillors:

"Let us wait – for seven seasons! And in the meantime we should do our best to rule and administer all the peoples and races and nations and tongues of the great kingdom of Babylon in a proper manner. If after seven seasons the King has not been found and he does not return to rule as before – we shall meet again and adopt one of the resolutions that has been proposed here. But this you should know," he went on to tell the King's attentive minions – "According to the King's dream and its interpretation, he is required to be absent from his palace for seven seasons, so he may learn a lesson and be wiser on his return, ruling his kingdom and guiding his people in the most enlightened way!"

"But where is the King?" asked one of the ministers impatiently. And he answered him:

"He is where God has sent him and He, God, is watching over him."

"And perhaps he has been killed, and we know nothing of it, and we are making no effort to hunt down and punish his killers! We shall be a laughing-stock throughout the kingdom!" another minister protested, prompting a measured reply from Nashdernach:

"If he had been killed in an accident, or murdered, we would have found his body. We have conducted the most thorough search that Babylon has ever known and no nook or cranny, no dark corner has been left unexplored – and nothing has been found! And there is something else," Nashdernach continued, looking keenly at the other members of the council, a strange spark igniting in his eyes. "Not long ago we heard the strange story of a certain farmer who went to the forest to cut wood, and suddenly a frightening figure leapt out of a thicket, his hair and beard unkempt and covering the whole of his body, which was horribly dirty and had the most vile stench, his fingernails long and crooked like the talons of a bird of prey. And this strange creature attacked the unfortunate farmer and snatched from him the meal that he had prepared for himself, bread and cheese and onion, and while bolting it down in the most revolting fashion imaginable, he was shouting over and over again, with the glazed eyes of a drunkard or a maniac: 'I am King Nebuchadnezzar, the valiant, the wise and the terrible! I am the mighty King, Nebuchadnezzar! I am King Nebuchadnezzar!' And swallowing the last mouthful the creature shouted yet again in the ears of the farmer, who was scared out of his wits – 'I am the King!' and he beat his hairy, filthy chest and exclaimed: 'Heaven and earth shall serve me! All shall obey my command!" And at that moment the lightning flashed, the sky was lit by a blinding light, thunder rolled and the rain came down in torrents, and the creature fled for his life into the thickets, wailing and whimpering with fear.

"That is the story," Nashdernach sighed, and his oily eyes scanning once more the faces of the assembled company, he concluded:

"I support Belteshazzar's proposal, and I call upon all of you to join me in supporting it!"

The resolution was accepted unanimously.

QUEEN TEMIOR

The "seven seasons" passed, and Babylon was still standing. At first, rumours of the King's disappearance led to unrest among the populace, and crowds converged on the royal compound with shouts of "We want the King!" and "The King of Babylon lives!" and "Give us our King!" Some of the ministers demanded that the protesters be treated with a firm hand and forcibly dispersed; the royal horse guards should deal with them, men not renowned for their tolerance. Nashdernach was vehemently opposed to this, and he asked to be allowed to address the rally. The council of regency, deputising for the King, agreed, and a stage was erected for him. Nashdernach mounted the stage and stood on the red-carpeted podium, without escort and without bodyguard, alone in the seething heart of the turbulent crowd. Once the chief of the King's senior advisers had spoken, the crowd began to drift away and finally dispersed, without any need to send in the cavalry. And this was Nashdernach's address to the agitated throng:

"Dear citizens of Babylon! I am happy to see you, and my heart is filled with pride, knowing your concern for our wise and valiant King, Nebuchadnezzar, His Majesty, concern that is shared by me and by my fellow ministers. But I have heartening news for you, our wise and valiant King is alive and well!" And here there was a long pause, until the shouts of "Long live the King!" and "The King lives!" had subsided. Nashdernach went on to say:

"God entrusted a special mission to the King and he, our glorious monarch, took it upon himself to fulfil this mission in the spirit and in the letter. There cannot be the slightest shadow of a doubt that our wonderful King, His Majesty, will succeed in his task and bring peace and ever more prosperity to his people, enough to satisfy all their expectations. And my duty and yours, his most beloved people – is to wait patiently until the King returns in triumph!" And Nashdernach stressed in conclusion:

"Remember, dear and beloved citizens of Babylon, the freedom that His Majesty has given you, and the happiness and the security that you enjoy under his enlightened rule, and now – go back to your fields, your trades and professions, lest you incur the ire of the gods, in whose eyes idleness is the most detestable attribute of man, and who rate the lazy with less favour than grave-robbers – and may all your enterprises be blessed!" And saying this, Nashdernach raised his arm in a gesture of salute and left the improvised stage accompanied by cries of support and approval and declarations of loyalty to the King, and all dispersed and went their separate ways, without further disturbance.

With the passing of the "seven seasons", on the anniversary of the disappearance of Nebuchadnezzar, Nashdernach came to his office, and after a firm handshake, sat facing him in silence for a while, looking troubled, and finally said, in a hushed and furtive tone:

"The seven seasons are up!" This was not so much a statement of fact as a probing question, demanding an answer – and the answer came:

"The day is not over yet!" he said with a breezy smile.

A bemused look crept into Nashdernach's tense features. He swallowed his saliva and went on to say:

"If by tomorrow His Majesty has not yet returned – we shall convene a plenary session of the Council."

"So we shall," he responded.

"I have already summoned the ministers for the third hour of the morning."

"Excellent!"

"And you, I assume, will honour us with your presence?"

"I shall be there," he assured him, his voice limpid and untouched by hesitation or deliberation.

Nashdernach rose, shook the other's hand warmly, and his lips fluttered, easing into a faint smile that drove the cloud of gloom from his face.

"You're a strange creature!" he exclaimed, but in the voice of one who has not abandoned hope.

Changes and transformations came about in his life in those seven years. Two sons were born to him; the older was named Naimel after his father, and the younger – Gamliel, after his father-in-law. Sons and daughters were born to his three friends too.

They approached Denur-Shag and asked if he was prepared to educate their children. He declined, treating them to a typically prolix and erudite sermon, consisting in the main of self-denigration and a claim of total ignorance of anything relating to the education of infants, as opposed to boys. They asked him if he could recommend an alternative candidate and he nominated Aniran, a middle-aged man from the islands in the north, who had taught young children in his homeland and, according to his own account, had been tutor to the crown prince of those islands until his detention at the hands of the Chaldeans.

Aniran proved a good choice, as was evident from the immaculate manners of five year old Naimel and four year old Gamliel, and from the moulding of their personalities. He did not see his children every day; Nejeen did her best to adjust their daily routine to his, but the latter was subject to abrupt changes, and the former was not so easily altered. In any case, before going to bed he would pass their room and see them asleep, and the sight of them filled his heart with a quiet joy and brought a prayer of thanksgiving to his lips, and he knew his sons were very dear to him but God, who gave them to him – Him he loved most of all.

At a late hour of the afternoon, one of the soldiers of the royal guard detachment burst into his office, his slaves chasing after him and threatening him with all kinds of lurid punishments for this outrageous breach of protocol, and he fell at his feet in a state of extreme agitation, every muscle of his body shaking, and when the slaves arrived, brandishing their clubs and drawn swords, he ordered them not to harm him. He told the soldier to stand and say what he had to say.

And the man rose from his knees, his forehead covered in sweat, his big black eyes bulging wide open in fright, and his voice shaking as he said:

"The King! The King is coming! Or perhaps... it isn't the King!" The flustered soldier added: "A kind of a man, wearing a loincloth of leaves of the forest, who claims that he is Nebuchadnezzar and demands that I summon Belteshazzar. He has the voice of a leader and commander and he is standing outside the gate. My fellow sentry refuses to admit him, but he too is dumbfounded and scared to the marrow of his bones – since the voice of this stranger is so like the voice of the King, and his eyes too, are like the King's eyes, and by what right do we refuse a King admittance to his own palace? He calls on you by name: 'Belteshazzar,' he says, 'the man who revealed my first dream and interpreted the second, call him at once and do not delay, lest you arouse my anger and I have your carcases hung from this gate that you're pretending to guard!'

"So here I am, Excellency, Lord Belteshazzar, viceroy of the King, and in the name of Bel and the name of great Marduk, save us from this dreadful predicament of ours!"

And sure enough, this was Nebuchadnezzar, his hair grown and his beard awry, his fingernails long and crooked and most of them broken, his eyes still bright, but their wild impetuosity gone for good. He no longer resembled a lion or a volcano, but rather a stately horse, powerful and attractive to the eye, yet knowing full well that he has a master, and it is the master who holds the reins.

He fell at his feet, bowing down to the ground before him, and he ordered that the gates be opened and the King be admitted with all due ceremony. He was to be bathed, and dressed in his full regal attire.

The rumour of the King's return brought the ministers scurrying from their offices and all came running to see him, although not all of them believed their eyes. Some whispered that caution and vigilance were required here, lest this were some charlatan seeking to exploit the situation and deceive them, while others kept their doubts in their hearts and dared not express them aloud. Daniel and Nashdernach knew for a fact that it was the King, back from the exile imposed on him by Heaven. And it was then that the most extraordinary thing happened, something entirely unexpected which stunned them all.

The King strode down the long corridors, so familiar to him, passing the offices, as ministers and slaves followed and his bodyguard cleared the way for him, but instead of repairing to his private apartments, he climbed the steps to the roof of his palace.

He stood on the roof, and in full view of all, knelt and prostrated himself on the ground and kissed the marble tiles, and then raised his tousled head towards Heaven and cried out in a loud voice:

"Your name be magnified O God, creator of Heaven and Earth and all that is in them, may It be praised and glorified for ever and ever. You are the one Almighty God and there is none like you! You are the one who crowns kings on this earth, who gives them their kingdoms and takes their kingdoms away.

"And I, Nebuchadnezzar, returning to my palace by your grace and with your consent, praise and extol the King of kings of kings whose every act is truth and all his ways are just. The one who exalts himself he casts down, and the one who humbles himself, he lifts up!"

Seven days and seven nights Babylon celebrated the return of the King to his palace, and on the eighth day, when the festivities were ended and the streets of the greatest city in the universe were empty, as its inhabitants returned to their trades and vocations, seven ornate carriages, each one harnessed to six horses, passed through the gate of the walled city, the highest and grandest of them all, the Gate of Orash and turned in the direction of the royal palace.

When the carriages halted at the palace gates, from the largest and most ornate of all, with horses white as snow – a woman emerged who seemed hardly mortal; dressed in blue and white trimmed with gold and bedecked with pearls, a gleaming and slender coronet on her head, surmounted by a flawless sapphire, her brown eyes deep as a forest from some fable of long ago, her face as fair as the dawn and her rosy lips smiling. Nothing about her resembled flesh and blood; she was like moon light in tangible form.

All the doors of the palace were opened before her, until she arrived in the innermost chamber where the King sat enthroned, perusing a scroll, his ministers and courtiers and bodyguards around him. When he saw her he rose and took a step towards her. And Temior, the Median princess, fell at her husband's feet and cried:

"I wish to live no longer in the palace in my homeland, and never again shall I be parted from you. I was grieved to hear what had befallen you, and these seven seasons my eyes have not ceased shedding tears, and my heart never tired of reproving me for my conduct. And I know it is only you I long for, only you I desire, and King Nebuchadnezzar is my King and my lord, always and for ever!"

And the King stooped, and raised his queen to her feet, and as all his servants and slaves and ministers looked on, the eyes of the wise and valiant King – in which storms used to rage, which used to flash with volcanic fire – filled with tears. He broke down and sobbed, his shoulders shaking.

And all the King's servants and slaves and ministers opted at this moment for discreet departure from the inner chamber, and the King was left alone with Temior, his beloved, for whom he had built the Hanging Gardens of Babylon, and for whose sake he had filled the grounds of the palace with lawns and trees and fountains and flowers in bloom at all times of the year, for whom he longed all the days of his life and whom he saw in his dreams at night, tormented by her absence but keeping it all a closely guarded secret.

The joyful news of Temior's return to the bosom of her husband was the pretext for yet more celebrations, a pretext which Babylon, like any other city in the world, was quick to exploit. The King himself joined in the festivities, and ordered the slaughter of seven hundred fatted cows and innumerable sheep and fowls – their meat to be distributed among the poor of Babylon. And tables were set up in the streets, each with space for a thousand diners, and as if this were not enough, the King went on to give orders for the distribution of clothes to the needy, the building of accommodation for the homeless, and the provision of work for the unemployed; half of the gold and silver stored in the royal coffers was to be shared out among the poorest citizens.

And the indigent and down-trodden of society, enjoying these unexpected bounties and eating and drinking as the guests of the King, were unstinting in their praise of Nebuchadnezzar, as they were transformed overnight into respectable citizens freed from the indignity of poverty, and no longer forced to go barefoot and sleep in the streets or the fields, or to search in vain for employment.

And the King, accompanied by his exquisitely beautiful wife and a handful of bodyguards, strolled among the revellers, greeted with exclamations of loyalty and obeisance and giving benedictions in reply, hearing jokes and telling jokes and laughing with the rest of them, and taking the opportunity to be become acquainted with the personal concerns of his subjects: how could they be helped, were they being mistreated and if so – by whom?

Some time after this festival, the like of which Babylon had not known since the day of its foundation, and would in all probability never know again – the King summoned his ministers and dictated to them a series of new laws, a supplement to the code of laws which had existed for centuries. His instructions were the following:

"No slave shall be required to work for more than ten hours in the day, from the hour of sunrise to the hour of sunset. Anyone who infringes this rule – his slave shall be set free.

"No child under ten years of age shall be employed to work in the fields or in construction. Anyone who infringes this rule – his fields shall be confiscated or his building demolished.

"Women are not to be set to work in the buildings of roads or of houses, even if they are convicted felons. Anyone who infringes this rule will be fined twenty gold shekels and if he is a state employee, he will be dismissed.

"Every man is entitled to approach the authorities and demand employment, and the authorities are required by this statute to find him suitable employment. Any man who refuses to accept the work thus offered him, and has no reasonable excuse, shall be exiled from his land.

"Public buildings are to be set up, and anyone who cannot afford a home of his own can lodge there in exchange for a monthly rent, at a level to be determined by the ministers, in accordance with his income.

"Any pauper who falls ill is to be treated at the expense of the state.

"Freedom of religion and worship is guaranteed, so long as one man's observance does not interfere with that of another."

These supplements which King Nebuchadnezzar added to the existing legal code of his realm brought about many improvements in the lives of the citizens of Babylon and its environs, and boosted his prestige among the populations of all the lands that he had conquered, and lands beyond the boundaries of his empire.

The King personally designed the building in which the homeless were to be accommodated; the apartments were spacious and airy and greatly appreciated by the grateful tenants.

Among the ministers and courtiers and advisers and all who were close to the King, it was said that since his return from the forest, after the seven seasons, he had changed in two significant ways:

Firstly – he was serving his God and praying to Him three times every day, and appealing to Him in humility, resignation and calm acquiescence, not – as in the past – with bombastic tirades and outbursts of anger.

As to the second issue, the close associates of the King and members of his household had nothing meaningful to say about it, but it was clear to all of them that it did indeed exist. Until one day Belteshazzar, alias Daniel, heard from the lips of Denur-Shag a word that fitted the elusive concept admirably.

Sitting with him on his veranda, and in merry mood having imbibed liberal quantities of young red Chaldean wine, Denur-Shag uttered in passing the word "mellowing". The King had "mellowed" indeed. He was no longer in the habit of ordering summary executions, and he was not as quick as he used to be to send convicted felons to penal servitude in the subterranean copper mines. Not only this, but more and more frequently, and to the surprise of all, the King was seen strolling in his garden – and smiling. And this smile of the King infected all his aides and ministers and advisers, his slaves and servitors and took over the whole palace, emerging thence into the streets of Babylon and descending to the Chaldean populace, dispelling gloom and spreading good cheer. People did not ask one another what was the reason for this startling, and in the eyes of many, blessed change in the personality of the King, as expressed in his new patterns of behaviour and demeanour. What was making the King smile? – it was a secret, but an open secret, known to all: it was the proud and elegant Median princess, Temior.

Shortly after the return of Temior to her husband the King, he began disbanding his army of concubines, and of the ten wives in his harem the only one he retained was Domilin, a middle-aged woman whose son, Belshazzar, was destined to inherit the throne in due course. She was happy to be the companion of Queen Temior and to oversee the management of the household.

Offered generous financial settlements, the nine remaining wives of Nebuchadnezzar were returned to the families whence they had been taken. Six of them were content with this arrangement and even welcomed it; three felt hurt and insulted.

Nebuchadnezzar suggested they should go to the islands of the north, where there was no stigma attached to a woman who lost her virginity before marriage – especially if she was rich. Only one family took his advice, going down to the great sea and setting sail for those islands. The others remained in a state of deep dudgeon, but their complaints went unheard.

The "mellowing" of Nebuchadnezzar was most clearly demonstrated in his response to the request put to him by Or-Nego.

Since his return from Judah, Or-Nego had kept his distance from people, living in seclusion and going out only when it could not be avoided. Some considered his behaviour eccentric, but so long as he did his duty impeccably, no one thought to probe too deeply into his personal affairs. Such was the respect that they felt for him, and the reputation that he had gained, and the confidence placed in him – it was reckoned he must know what he was doing.

He visited him on a number of occasions – during the period of the "seven seasons" and afterwards. He could tell Or-Nego was worried about something.

"God!" Or-Nego remarked in the course of one of their conversations, his voice thick and soft – "There is no greater pleasure on earth than to serve Him with all your heart and might, to worship him at all times and always, and love Him truly. And seeing your sincere efforts, He may entrust a holy mission to you. Not like the mission that was entrusted to the prophet Jeremiah, I know I am not worthy of that! All that I seek is a way to serve Him, your God I mean, the one my heart longs for, who in my eyes is the God of truth. And what a shame it is that Adelain, my daughter, has chosen to serve a god that is nothing but an idol! But I have no intention of trying to persuade her otherwise. Lectures will do no good. Only by the grace of God, reflected in the bounty given to all who long for Him, only thus can miracles be worked. It is not anything that I can do, of that I am absolutely sure!"

"Do you often meet Adelain?" he asked.

"Visiting her is as difficult for me as it possibly could be. Not that I don't want to visit her, see her, hear her voice, do her any favour she might ask for. But as I say, it isn't easy for me."

"Why is that?" he persisted, undeterred by Or-Nego's long and keen glance.

"Because she only wants to talk about you and your wife, nothing else! And such conversations work her up into a highly emotional state, and I reckon that if I stay away the subject won't be raised, and life will be easier for her. In time, perhaps, though it's something I don't dare even dream about – she will attain some peace of mind and the memory of all this will fade away into nothing!"

Or-Nego sighed, and as the other did not respond, he added by way of explanation:

"She doesn't ask about you directly. She knows I don't like it, and knows too that it doesn't redound to her honour, which is my honour as well. She doesn't ask directly, but those eyes that she fixes on me – the inestimable dolour behind them, pain that will not be assuaged until I have brought up in conversation some topic relating to you, or mentioned your name in one context or another. Then her face lights up, there is an easing of tension and for a moment she seems soothed, almost happy, a bright look in her eyes.

"And I don't think this is healthy, which is why I tend to stay away from the shrine of Bel, especially as he is no longer my god!" Or-Nego smiled wryly.

He had nothing to say to Or-Nego, not even a word of consolation. He did not regret inducing him to speak of Adelain, but decided that henceforward he would ask him no more questions about her.

"Do you believe?" he asked his guest.

"Interesting!" the latter replied. "That other man of God, the one whose like I have never seen, excepting you, asked me the very same question."

"And what was your answer?"

"I believe."

"If you believe, there is always a way open to you!"

"And that is?" – something was awakened in the eyes of the

Chaldean.

"Pray! Address yourself to God, and He will give you an answer. He will never abandon you, and He will always bring solace to your soul. Turn to Him!"

"And if I haven't yet taken the rite of circumcision?"

"If your heart is pure and you truly believe – God will answer your prayer."

"As that other wonderful man told me," Or-Nego responded eagerly, "I should purify my heart first."

"He gave you sound advice!"

"All the same," Or-Nego resumed after a long moment of deliberation, "I still intend to submit to the rite. All that I did in Judah, the fearful slaughter that I took part in, these things give me no peace. For me the rite will be an act of sacrifice, a token, however meagre, of my deep remorse. And your God, who is my God and to whom I cleave with absolute faith, may yet forgive me and pardon me."

"He is kind and merciful, and long-suffering," he answered him, and added: "And His name is love!"

"Of that I am absolutely sure!" Or-Nego declared, his voice shedding the last traces of the dejection that had clouded it thus far, "I only have to say it, and my heart is filled at once with joy and delight!"

"So, turn to Him!" he urged him.

Or-Nego was admitted to the Covenant of Abraham in a ceremony in the old community of Babylon conducted by Nehemiah the priest, and three days of pain and bleeding followed, and he said not a word to anyone. By the fourth day the worst was over, and he was glad in the knowledge that he had suffered for a sacred cause.

The old Jewish community of Babylon, which had tried in vain to come to terms with the extended community of the exiles, was no longer the community that had once dreamed the great dream of the Kingdom of the House of David, extending from the Red Sea to the Tigris and the Euphrates. A pall of gloom had descended upon it, since the first rumours were heard of the victory of the Chaldeans and the destruction of the Temple and the fate of King Zedekiah, blinded and living among slaves in Nebuchadnezzar's prison. And yet, the majority of its members still would not admit that Jeremiah was the holy prophet of God, and everything he predicted had come true and was coming true even now, and as God's mouthpiece on the earth he must be obeyed, and they should fortify themselves with patience and wait for the seventy years to elapse – whereupon He, Almighty God, His name be blessed, would restore the exiles of Babylon to their homeland and the place of their nurture, and they would build their houses again and repair the ruins of the Temple and the royal palace and the city walls. No, the people of the ancient community of Babylon were in no mood to compromise. To them, Jeremiah was a traitor who had brought disaster upon Judah by weakening the resolve of its defenders, in league with those exiles who had accepted senior appointments in the Babylonian administration and for some reason were thought to be a cut above the rest.

So the two communities remained, the veteran and the newly-arrived, separated from each other, mutually alien and sometimes mutually hostile. But the worship and the liturgy as practised by the veterans were highly regarded, and their Bet Midrash was the preferred setting for the circumcision of sons born to the exiles too. Despite their antipathy to the exiles, the mohels could not refuse to admit their sons to the Covenant of Abraham, which is a commandment; he who shirks it might just as well declare himself an outcast from Israel and from Judah.

On his recovery from the painful operation, Or-Nego asked for an audience with King Nebuchadnezzar, and put to him a strange request, that in the distant days of the past the King would have rejected out of hand; in former times the suppliant himself would have thought long and hard before daring even to broach the subject.

But, as has already been noted, this was a different age and different days, unsullied by the past. And the King smiled and listened patiently as Or-Nego, his senior commander, told him that he wanted to serve the God he believed in, the God, that is, who saved his three ministers, Abed-Nego, Meshach and Shadrach from the flames of the furnace, and revealed to his senior aide, Belteshazzar, the nature of the King's first dream and the interpretation of the second, and he, Or-Nego, was asking for the King's permission to go to Jerusalem, or rather to the smoking ruins of Jerusalem, to build a hostel there for the service of wayfarers, offering them a warm welcome and warm hospitality, food and drink and a place to lodge for the night and if necessary, they would be provided with clothing too. They would be sent on their way with a blessing, and all of this was to be free of charge – in honour of the God in whom he believed and to sanctify His name.

For a long moment Nebuchadnezzar stared at him as if seeing nothing. Then he asked him:

"All of this – why?"

"It is to atone for the wicked things I did in those places, and the dreadful slaughter that I was a part of, and to receive the forgiveness and pardon of God, if indeed I am judged worthy of them."

And the King asked Or-Nego if he would accept an allowance of one thousand gold shekels per year, to cover his expenses. Or-Nego bowed and prostrated himself before the King and answered him:

"My King, live for ever! It is a generous offer, Your Majesty, but if I am to serve my God, I must trust in Him absolutely. He will provide for me and keep me from all harm, He will strengthen me and ease my woes, if indeed I am judged worthy! If the King so desires, he may distribute those thousand shekels among the Jewish exiles, some of whom are still living in penury."

"It shall be as you say, my faithful servant Or-Nego!" cried the King. "May God make your ways prosper and extend His protection over you and keep you safe from all evil, and bless the labours of your hands, whereby you sanctify His name!"

Or-Nego bowed low before his King and withdrew, walking backwards as he left the regal chamber, and not looking at the face of Nebuchadnezzar whom, every day that he lived, he had revered.

Before setting out on his way, Or-Nego met him again, along with Mishael, Hananiah and Azariah, and they told him the story of the Son of God who was with them in the furnace and kept the flames from harming them, and released the bonds in which they were tied.

"He is the one who is to come," said Mishael, "and He shall redeem his people Israel, the people that knows Him, for whom the worship of God is not yet a mere recitation of words!"

And Daniel said, echoing Mishael's assertion:

"All our prophets have foretold Him, the God who will take on flesh to endure the suffering of mankind in the flesh, to atone for the sins of men and to stand as an example and an inspiration to them!"

And Hananiah added:

"Many more good people will follow in your footsteps and do as you are doing. Some will choose seclusion out of devotion to their God, and others will sanctify His name through the service of their fellow-men!"

And Or-Nego set out for the long ride to Jerusalem, in his saddle-bag one loaf of bread and a flask of water, and by the grace and the love of God he reached Jerusalem and built his hostel from the scorched bricks of the ruined buildings; before long he had opened his door to welcome inside the weary travellers and itinerants, washing their feet, feeding them with whatever God provided, praying with them and singing psalms, offering them sleeping-mats that he had woven himself – and to anyone who lacked clothing he gave whatever he had, until his last shirt and his last shabby cloak had gone. But he was not left naked because God saw him, and affluent people passing by the house considered it a divine duty to donate clothing, and even food when his larder was bare. His Hebrew name was Isaac Hameir, and over the course of time he came to be known as Saint Isaac.

At about this time Denur-Shag resolved to ask the King to cancel the horse-races, in which the competitors were required to jump the open ditch, thus endangering their lives for the entertainment of the spectators.

So he approached the King who received him cordially, and not only heard him out but was delighted by what he heard. He smiled that bright smile of his, infusing warmth and confidence in the hearts of all who observed it, and gave his answer:

"How marvellous are the ways of the God that you call 'love', and I believe that is indeed His name. I was insane and it seemed to me my life was over – and he cured me of my insanity and purged me of pride, and gave back to me my heart's desire, my Queen Temior, most wondrous of women. And he has given me happiness such as I never dreamed could even exist. And as for this idea of yours, to stop the killing in the horse-races – this is surely inspired by God! This very day I shall issue the decree and the race in its present form will end forthwith. The ditch will be filled in, and replaced by a simple hurdle, that may be jumped with no risk to the horse or the rider.

"And I tell you something else!" the King cried in his enthusiasm. "We are laying the foundations of a new style of horse-racing that will take over the world and persist over the years and the generations and ages. And those who witness it will enjoy it and those taking part will be glad, since their lives will not be in danger, and no one will know its origin, from whence it came, and who devised it!"

THE ROYAL COUPLE

Queen Temior celebrated her forty-fifth birthday, and to mark the occasion King Nebuchadnezzar organised a garden-party in her honour. And at the Queen's specific request, invitations were limited to a very small number: the King's ten senior counsellors, headed by Nashdernach, and the four ministers of Judean origin, namely – Belteshazzar, Meshach, Abed-Nego and Shadrach, with their wives.

The Queen chose a spacious corner of the garden, with its verdant lawns and lush flowers, blooming in all seasons of the year, and mosaic paths strewn with fragments of gold, gleaming in the moonlight and reflecting back the gentle lustre of the stars.

The paths led the guests to a circular patio, with a fountain at the centre of it, and water gushing from the beaks of four swans of solid gold, their necks intertwined, and cascading in graceful arcs into the marble basin, sparkling with ever-changing colours. The tops of the tables set up beside the fountain were panels of ivory covered by white cloths with silver trimmings; the legs were cast gold.

Drinks were served in silver goblets, and all the tableware was pure gold, burnished well.

At the central table sat the royal couple: the King resplendent in his blue robes with their gold tracery, his white sash and the short sword suspended from it, with gold scabbard and silver hilt - and the Queen in white robes likewise trimmed with gold. The crown on the King's head was gold, studded with sapphires, while the Queen's slender coronet, in the shape of interwoven clover-leaves, was encrusted with diamonds. The Lady Domilin, in deep purple, sat beside the royal couple with her son, Belshazzar the heir to the throne, a feckless youth in his early twenties, resembling his father only in his curly beard. With his broad face and narrow forehead he tended to take after his mother, and his watery eyes betrayed the profligacy of the libertine.

An orchestra hidden from view played soft music as the refreshments were served. One by one the courtiers toasted King Nebuchadnezzar and Queen Temior and wished them long life and happiness.

The King rose from his seat, thanked the well-wishers and said:

"The life of man is paved with surprises and novelties, and mine has been no exception! Whatever a man aspires to and hopes for, he shall attain it, so long as he is the faithful servant of his God. For God is the unflagging source of all hopes, and He is their fulfilment. Blessed is the man who trusts in Him!

"And to my wife, my best beloved, dearest of all to me – I wish all the happiness that God gives to those of courageous spirit and pure heart, happiness of which none is more deserving than she! And to all those present here – may your enterprises be blessed, and may you find joy in your spouses and contentment in your issue!"

"So be it!" – the chorus rang out, as goblets were raised and drained at a single gulp. The slaves were quick to refill the crystal glassware.

And then a troupe of Indian dancers appeared, combining sinuous and startling gestures of hand and eye with the conventional steps of the dance, movements that were both graceful and suggestive – and all to the sounds of flutes.

Mishael, who was sitting beside him, commented:

"They say that in the course of time, troupes of dancers will not be enough, but the entire population will be out there, dancing and playing!" To which he responded in all seriousness:

"That will be the first sign of the ultimate degradation of the human species!"

On the improvised stage, a variety of performers appeared in succession: fire-eaters and sword-swallowers, conjurors putting doves in helmets and pulling out rabbits, while others ignited quantities of powder, creating strange explosive sounds and projecting balls of fire into the sky, to the amazement of the revellers, who applauded loudly. To conclude the entertainment, three clowns with painted faces leapt onto the stage and after performing some impressive bodily contortions, recited humorous verses, poking irreverent but innocuous fun at the King and the Queen, the party-goers, the Chaldean race and the entire population of Babylon.

The wine flowed freely, relaxing inhibitions, and when all the appetizing refreshments had been consumed, the King rose to take a stroll in the garden, the guests following.

Nashdernach accompanied the King. Queen Temior, who throughout the festivities had been gazing fixedly at Nejeen, approached her and greeted her. Nejeen returned her greeting with a deep bow, and without another word the Queen took her arm and led her on a leisurely circuit of the garden, following the sparkling mosaic paths. The gentle light of many lanterns and the reflections of the moon and stars flickered at the feet of the strollers.

He walked with Mishael, with Hananiah and Azariah following, and behind them came the three wives, Havatzelet, Deborah and Hannah, chatting together in hushed tones. Other guests walked with their wives, while the crown-prince Belshazzar accompanied his mother,

As they strolled on, he caught a glimpse of the King, leading Nashdernach into the palace. It seemed that Mishael noticed this too. Some important business that cannot be delayed! – he thought.

"Have you heard the latest news about Or-Nego, or Isaac Hameir as he is now?" Mishael asked him, and when he responded with a quizzical look, went on to say:

"He really has built a house and turned it into a hostel. And there are people of other races too, who stayed on in Judah and have been inspired by his example – building themselves huts in that vicinity and worshipping with him, praising the Almighty God day and night, without a pause, even when they are eating their frugal meals, even when working in the fields. Do you believe such a thing is possible?" – he was asked and he replied:

"I believe it absolutely."

"One of the exiles who happened to be there, on his way to do business in Egypt and stayed among them for a while, was impressed by the strength of their commitment and the purity of their qualities, and he said that if ten such men had lived there in the time of Zedekiah, Judah would have been spared and Jerusalem not burned to the ground. And it is fine work that they are doing there," Mishael warmed to his theme, sensing the keen interest of the others, "ploughing small plots of land – one man harnessed to the plough and the other guiding him, as they have no animals, and they sow with eagerness and reap with joy – it is all team-work, and everything is shared in common. In the first year their produce was meagre, but now with God's blessing they have enough to supply their needs. And while working in the fields or at any other business, they never tire of reciting verses from the Psalms and the praises of God are for ever on their lips, and they ask His pardon and thank Him for all the good things, all the bounteous grace that He has bestowed upon them. They have planted trees as well – fig and olive and pomegranate – and they rear and tend them with care, and eat their fruit and share it with any chance visitor. They don't waste their time in idle talk, and their guests have a simple choice to make: either to pray with them or to keep their silence. The people gathered around Isaac Hameir converse only in passages drawn from the Scriptures. Nevertheless, as this exile told me, there is always good cheer in their abodes, and their eyes reflect the pure wonderment of children. The exile's heart went out to them and he says he would willingly have stayed there, if his family and household in Babylon did not depend on him."

"These righteous people," the other retorted solemnly, "are the last hope of the race of Israel and of Judah and indeed, the last hope of all humanity. And the more that they grow in number, and the stronger is their faith – the closer will be salvation, and the love of God will be acknowledged by the majority, and thus the threat of violence and destruction will be averted. But if the faith of some becomes a matter of lip-service only, then in the course of time deceivers will spring up among them, and hypocrites and charlatans, and violence and destruction will be inevitable. But these people, following the lead of Isaac Hameir, have begun sowing the good seed in the world, and this seed will never go to waste."

"They bear the light in their hearts!" Mishael asserted, in a hushed and emotional voice.

"They don't bear the light," he corrected him, "they are the light!"

It seemed they had completed a full circuit of the garden, as they were again approaching that doorway where, not long before, the King had disappeared, in the company of Nashdernach, his chief minister. At that moment, the two of them appeared again. The King's face was grim, Nashdernach's eyes were moist.

"Do you see what I see?" asked Mishael, sounding perplexed.

"Yes," he answered him and did not elaborate, feeling a dim sense of foreboding.

The party was over. The revellers bowed low to the royal couple, to the Lady Domilin and to her son, the egregious Belshazzar, heir apparent to the throne.

When they went to their bed-chamber, sleep eluded them. Perhaps on account of the mixed impressions they had absorbed that day, or perhaps for some other reason, something not easily identified that was troubling them.

He asked her about Queen Temior, who throughout the walk had not left her side, and Nejeen answered him with enthusiasm:

"Queen Temior is a wonderful woman! She has something of the purity of the maiden about her, as if nothing unclean could ever sully her.

"She spoke about you, saying you are nothing other than a god come down from Heaven in human form, and a divine mission has been entrusted to you. All this she can tell from the look on your face and its beauty, which she says is spirit and not of this world. As for me, she said I am an angel whose task it is to stand at your right hand in your struggles against the forces of evil, to rejoice in your joy and share in your victory. And then she went on to say, as if moving to another topic: 'I know that yours is the happiness in which the Shekhinah prevails, as indeed is mine, and we should, both of us, thank God day and night for that conjugal bliss which is the lot of no more than a score of couples in all the universe. God has smiled on us, and we are both numbered with that chosen few!'" And Nejeen continued:

"Temior told of herself, and described two parents devoted to their only daughter and committed to her utterly, seeing no purpose to their lives except in bringing her happiness and indulging her every whim. As for her husband, he is deeply sorry that she has born him no son, only two daughters who cannot succeed him, while his heir, Belshazzar, is a disappointment to him, although he does not say so. And she, for her part, behaved towards him like a spoilt child, and it seems she will never forgive herself for this after all that he has done for her, those hanging gardens that he built for her, reckoned one of the wonders of the world. And she persisted in her misery until he sent her back to her parents, though this was very painful for him. And she knows that everything he did he did for love, for love of her, wanting only her happiness. Yes, he sent her back to her home and her homeland and her illustrious parents, of the royal house of Media, with a tolerant smile on his face but with eyes sunk deep in their sockets, showing the strain of sleepless nights. How could she treat him so – to this day it is beyond her understanding. And this because above all and after all – there is no man in the world to compare with him and she loves him; she loved him then, loves him now and will always love him.

"And the Queen was thoughtful, and for a while we walked on in silence, filling our lungs with the glorious fragrance of the royal gardens. And suddenly the remarkable Queen Temior stopped dead and looked at me and said: 'When I was brought to him on the morning of my wedding day and saw him for the first time in my life, I thought my heart had stopped beating. Body and mind – I was all ablaze, with a fire so intense I was scared of myself! I wanted to run for my life, escape while I still could, flee from him, hide from him. I never imagined such a powerful attraction could even exist, sweeping everything before it like a mighty river in spate. I wanted to be by myself, to think things through, weigh up the arguments and come to the right decision. And that is why I behaved as I did!' And so saying she linked her arm in mine and before we had walked more than a couple of paces she whispered in my ear as if imparting a secret: 'If your husband is a god who has taken on human flesh, King Nebuchadnezzar, my husband, is the most perfect human being alive! He is kind-hearted and generous, a man of dauntless courage and regal stature – a model to be followed by all peoples and kingdoms of the earth, wherever they may be, an example to all enlightened rulers! And he has one great love in his life, one love, for one wife. And he trusts in God with all his heart and mind, and to Him he dedicates all his acts, and through Him he loves as only he knows how to love – with unflagging devotion, with sacrifice! And I tell you something else,' Temior said in conclusion, 'and remember this well.' And she declared with a force that set my heart quaking: 'When the King dies – his Queen shall die with him!'"

He did not tell her of his conversation with Mishael. He stared up at the ceiling with its dense crop of carvings, showing incidents from the Holy Scriptures of the Jews. Here is Abraham, dressed as a shepherd, a shepherd's crook in his hand, leading his flock, and his eyes not watching the sheep but gazing upwards, to the sky. Could he follow in the footsteps of Abraham, be like him?

He did not remember if he closed his eyes in sleep, or stared all night at the images on the ceiling, thinking of the patriarchs of his race and their actions, and their legacy. If there is any hope for my people it is in the hands of a righteous few, like Or-Nego, or Isaac Hameir as he is now called; their task is to awaken the spirit of the people and renew its youth, and light its path and guide its steps towards the hope that is distant and seems not to exist... And then he thought he heard footsteps in the next room, hesitant, furtive footsteps, and suddenly he was fully awake. He sat up on his bed and waited, and he did not have to wait long before hearing a soft, timid tap at the door.

"Enter!" he heard his calm voice reverberating in the room, and saw Nejeen's wide open eyes, following his movements uneasily.

The door opened a crack, and the footman spoke without looking inside:

"Excellency, please forgive your servant! Lord Nashdernach has asked that you be wakened, and he is waiting for you in the parlour!"

"I shall come at once!"

Nejeen watched him as he dressed, and he caught a glimpse of the warmth and the brightness of her eyes. She sat up as he approached her, kissed his outstretched hand and held it to her heart, saying softly, in a tone of voice evoking unfathomable depths of affection:

"God be with you!"

He kissed her forehead and went.

In the parlour Nashdernach was sitting, in the same clothes that he had worn for the garden-party. It was clear that he had not slept that night.

"King Nebuchadnezzar, glorious King of Babylon, has given back his soul to his Maker," he reported in a dry voice, trying to hold back the tears but failing, breaking down and sobbing, his round shoulders shaking. It was some time before he regained control of himself, wiped his eyes and nose with a handkerchief and said:

"I came to inform you, because you have been chosen to accompany me in the funeral procession and give support to Queen Temior. Yes, he died in her arms. The physicians say it was his heart that failed him. He was sixty-eight years old – crowned King at the age of twenty-five, he reigned forty-three years and God was with him, and he was good to his people, and good to all the races and nations and tongues that he conquered and annexed. He was a man of dauntless courage, integrity, sincerity and incomparable loyalty; he believed firmly in his God and he loved Temior, his Queen, in a way that only a king is capable of loving... As to the physicians and their diagnosis, I have nothing to say. They are the ones who must decide, in the final analysis and we cannot quarrel with their conclusions – nor is there any point, as nothing will bring the dead back to life!

"I'm sure you noticed yesterday, how he took me aside during the garden-party. He did everything he could to avoid drawing attention, but I saw you when we went into the palace and when we came out, and you saw us, and you no doubt had conjectures and speculations of your own – and if ever there was a time for conjecture and speculation, this was it!

"What he told me went far beyond anything I ever heard him say before. He foresaw his death, and reckoned he had only hours to live. And visions such as this are not vouchsafed to anyone, save by the will of God!" Once more, Nashdernach wiped his red eyes and nose.

"Blessed be the Judge of truth!" he exclaimed, adding: "And how is Queen Temior faring? Does she have anyone to comfort her in this fateful hour?"

"You wouldn't believe it, but she has composed herself in a way beyond the understanding of ordinary mortals! As befits a queen and as befits her! She sent for me, and I found her sitting on her throne in the reception hall. As you may know, recently King Nebuchadnezzar, may he rest in peace, commanded that another throne be set up beside his, a precise copy of his own, but she opposed the idea and in the end, her wishes prevailed. So the throne set up there for her was lower, and more modest both in dimensions and decorations. And this was where she was sitting, cool and restrained and you might almost say – frozen, speaking in a clear and articulate voice. She commanded me to make all the necessary arrangements for the royal funeral, but not to have the coffin constructed at this stage; she has yet to decide on the shape and the dimensions and the materials to be used. And all are anxiously awaiting her instructions, as it is no small undertaking to build a coffin of gold or even of silver – overnight! And meanwhile the body is laid out on a big table in the council chamber, and she has dressed the King in his robes of blue and purple, like a man of war going off to battle, and she it was who combed his hair and trimmed his beard, and sprinkled perfume on his face, and put the crown on his head, and King Nebuchadnezzar seems to be alive and smiling into the void above him, although his eyes are closed. Again – it was she who closed his eyes!"

"And after hinting at his imminent demise – what other instructions did the King give you in the course of that conversation?" he asked bluntly, and was answered:

"He told me to keep a close eye on the heir to the throne, Belshazzar. He considered him unfit to succeed him, and was sorely disappointed in that Temior bore him only daughters, two daughters, as you know, and according to the law of Chaldean succession – and as I understand it, the same law applies with your people – a daughter cannot accede to her father's throne and rule in his stead. There are those who reckon this law should be changed – but meanwhile it remains in force and it must be obeyed! So, Belshazzar was the cause of much concern to his father, and most of our conversation revolved around the part I was to play as his guide and mentor, offering sound advice and averting, to the best of my ability, the disintegration of the Kingdom, and the destruction of Babylon that has been predicted. Yes, these were the King's explicit instructions. His last will and testament.

"And his words alarmed me and weighed heavily on my mind, and the King saw this and he noticed my tears as well, and like you he pretended he saw nothing. And that is really why I am here, taking the liberty of rousing you at this early hour, as you are a loyal friend, before whom I can open my heart, and ease the heavy burden of grief that I bear over the death of our King. I feel comforted already! And it is our duty, as I said before, to present ourselves to Queen Temior and stand beside her in her time of grief, and if necessary, support her when she accompanies her husband on his last journey. The grave, according to his command, will be dug in that corner of the garden where yesterday he celebrated his last festival, in honour of Temior's birthday – the woman he loved above all others! There will be a procession, and the coffin will be transported on the funereal carriage of the Kings of Babylon, harnessed to ten black horses, passing through the streets of Babylon, and giving the citizens an opportunity to pay their tearful farewells to the King, and in the temples of Bel and Marduk, the priests will pray for the repose of the King's soul. And he will be brought back to the palace tomorrow and buried in the afore-mentioned plot, near the fountain, the place where the King knew his last happiness on this earth."

"Have all the necessary arrangements been made, and all the instructions issued?" he asked, in an effort to subdue the shock and the distress he felt as a result of all that he had heard.

His question seemed to bolster Nashdernach's flagging spirits.

"Instructions have been issued! The twenty-one days of mourning have already begun, and everything is in readiness for the funeral procession! Once the Queen has told us precisely what she has in mind, regarding the design and construction of the coffin, all will proceed smoothly. We know what the dimensions of the coffin will be, so at least we can start putting the frame together, and thus avoid any delay."

He gave him a long, keen look and said solemnly:

"Don't make any hasty assumptions over the dimensions of the coffin!"

"What do you mean?" demanded Nashdernach, genuinely baffled. "Are you telling me those dimensions are going to be changed?"

"It's a distinct possibility!" he declared, and did not elaborate.

As evening fell, Nashdernach came looking for him again, and found him sorting out some unfinished business in his office, assisted by one of his clerks.

He had never known Nashdernach so agitated

"You knew!" he exclaimed, in a high-pitched yell that was not typical of him.

Eliciting no response, he proceeded to explain:

"She has done this! Queen Temior has done this! No one can determine the cause of her death. Yes, she was found lifeless on her couch, in all her royal finery, a diadem on her head and a scroll in her clenched fist, bearing the text: Bury me beside my husband, his arm around my shoulder. That is all. Learned doctors and eminent physicians, of Babylon or of other lands – not one of them is capable of establishing the cause of her death. They say, 'she has done this', as I said myself, but they understand nothing.

"She did not take her life – did not thrust a dagger into her heart or harm herself with any implement, did not swallow poison or a potion – all this is clear. And her face, so serene, so happy indeed, tells us she did not expire from excess of grief. No, far from it! The only reasonable explanation is – she simply wanted to go with her husband, the one great love of her life – and her wish was granted. Do you think such a thing is possible?" he asked, and he answered him:

"If desire is strong and true, nothing can resist it, and God the merciful and the loving will not impede it, or put obstacles in its way!" he declared, his voice vibrant with the intensity of his awe and admiration of the Queen.

"And you guessed!" Nashdernach exclaimed.

"Not at all. The Queen herself, Her Majesty, confided in my wife yesterday, that if her husband were taken from her, she would go with him and not stay for one more day without him."

"That is well said!" Nashdernach declared, impressed. "And what precious treasures they are, women like these! In all the world you won't find more than half a dozen who are their equals!"

"These are not women, but queens!" he declared, adding: "They were born queens, they live as queens and they die as queens. Even after their death – queens they will always remain!"

The funeral procession caused mayhem and tumult in the streets of Babylon. The report that the Queen had gone to join her husband and champion, her heart's true love, rather than live without him a single day, and the King, who loved her all his life, would still walk beside her even in the world of shadows, and the delight that they had known in each other was not to be curtailed but would continue into the next world, stronger than ever and lasting for ever – all of this impressed the common folk and moved them beyond measure. The procession was an exhibition of solidarity, rapture, triumph, joy and pain. People shouted and jostled, some were knocked down and trampled to death by the frenzied crowd, while others were so overwhelmed by the surges of raw emotion that their hearts could not cope with the pressure – and failed them.

All the ministers and officers of the state took part in the funeral procession, from the most senior to the most junior, and there was no need for any special decrees or proclamations, as all came willingly – whether out of firm attachment to the King and the royal household, or as an expression of human warmth and affection.

On a black horse, with black saddle and harness, Belshazzar, heir apparent to an illustrious father, Nebuchadnezzar the Second, rode at the head of the procession.

The frivolous youth tried to force upon his face a look of grief and pain, but he soon tired of this, and as he abandoned the effort to pretend to emotions that he did not feel, his face took on an expression of intense boredom. Detached from his surroundings and recoiling from the heaving mob and the contorted, anguished faces, he finally turned all his attention to his horse's neck and the bobbing, twitching ears. Something about them struck him as comical, and he had difficulty suppressing a fit of giggles.

The heir's mother, Domilin, rode in a small, covered carriage harnessed to a brown horse. Dressed all in black she followed her son, her face pale and set.

He sat with Nashdernach on the broad seat of the funereal carriage, as both of them gazed at the calm faces of the King and his Queen, lying in a simple coffin of oak, not yet sealed. And in accordance with the explicit request of the Queen, the King's arm was draped around her shoulder, and it was as if she knew it, and was enraptured. Nebuchadnezzar seemed to be smiling too. The sight of the royal pair, not separated even in death, infused in him a lively sense of uplifted spirit, wonderment and quiet joy.

The representatives of the citizenry and the elders of the people delivered eulogies of their King and Queen, and not one of them could resist the onset of tears. One wept in the middle of his eulogy, another at the beginning of it, another at the end, and yet another from beginning to end, without a pause. The people filing past the coffin also sobbed and wailed, and paced slowly with heads bowed.

The coffin was placed in the centre of the shrine of Bel, and although all the six broad gates of the shrine were open wide, they were too narrow to accommodate the constant, dense stream of mourners.

The ministers had their say too, but they did not weep. The voice of Nashdernach, like his words, expressed nothing but a strange happiness, a blend of spiritual exaltation, awe and respect.

He did not eulogise the King, or go into the shrine. The image of the royal couple in the open coffin remained clearly before his eyes. The bitterness of death had not parted the lovers. In his heart he was kneeling at their feet, bowing with reverence and admiration.

The next day the coffin was moved, and again he sat with Nashdernach in the funeral carriage. Wrapped up in his thoughts he was not aware of the tormented gaze of a pair of dark eyes, fixed on him unflinchingly, and when he was roused from his reverie and turned his head, he caught sight of the shadow of a priestess of Bel lurking in the crowd, and he knew this was Adelain.

The cortege returned the way it had come, with the priests of Bel and Marduk in their black robes leading the way, and acolytes in white habits following in the rear, swinging incense-burners and chanting hymns from the liturgy of Bel, the excited crowd joining in the responses. And all of Babylon hummed to the sound. It was as if the dead had risen and were shouting their hollow reproaches in the ears of the living, who responded to them with raucous howls.

The gravediggers had done their work well, and the pit was dug in the precise spot where, two days before, the King and his wife had sat, happy and loving, with their household around them.

The coffin was lowered on ropes, closed, and buried beneath the light, sandy soil of Babylon. A big marble slab was set down on the heap of earth, and with this, the tomb was sealed. And the ministers filed past the freshly-dug grave one by one, bowing to the silent tumulus and each of them reciting in turn a verse from the "victory song" of Marduk.

He too walked past the grave, bowed and recited a verse from the Psalms: *"Blessed is the man whose strength is in you!"*

The following day, Belshazzar was declared King of Babylon, and crowned in a coronation ceremony utterly devoid of pomp or pageantry – and this at the specific request of the young man, who disliked crowds and wanted to keep his public appearances to a minimum. Nashdernach warned him that he risked offending the plebeians and the patricians of the city alike, and he should at least invite the civic elders to attend his coronation, but his advice was flatly rejected. Belshazzar was stubborn, and refused to concede anything, and the ceremony proceeded in the presence of only his senior ministers.

Nashdernach had no choice but to spread the rumour that the young man was distraught, still in mourning for his father and not yet ready to face his subjects.

BELSHAZZAR

A week after his coronation King Belshazzar convened a meeting of the supreme royal council, now called the Great Council of the Crown. Belteshazzar and his three companions were not among those invited.

The four friends met in his office.

"This does not bode well!" Azariah remarked, in a voice full of dread.

They exchanged glances, going on to scrutinise one another's features.

The faces of Mishael and Azariah were both scored with wrinkles. Hananiah's forehead seemed to be higher and broader than before.

On his own, rather elongated face, there was no sign of wrinkles. The fair skin of his forehead had become fairer still and its purity was perfected, lit by the bright glow of wisdom. The depth of his eyes was unfathomable, with vision capable of seeing the invisible. His matching eyebrows, straight nose, cheek-bones high as the sturdy, silent peaks of mountains, pale lips sheltering in their lee – completed the picture. His hair and beard were neatly combed, now flecked with grey. His stance was upright, and anyone seeing him could not fail to take courage, his heart filled with reverent joy.

He smiled and said:

"God is our Lord, and in Him we shall trust, accepting everything that befalls us with blessing and with thanks, with gladness and love!"

"Let us bless Him indeed!" exclaimed Azariah, his confidence restored, and Hananiah added his voice to the chorus:

"May your name be magnified and praised, lauded and glorified, for ever and ever, amen!"

"Amen and amen!" they all responded, before going their separate ways and about their separate business.

Towards evening, Denur-Shag came to visit him. He was in a highly charged emotional state, making every effort to conceal his perturbation behind the mask of a faint and ironical smile. Still smiling, he responded with a bow to Nejeen's greeting as she passed him, and took his customary seat in the parlour, then produced a leather flask from the folds of his tattered cloak, placed it on the table, and proceeded to explain:

"Ordinary wine! From the late harvest of the vineyards in my wife's village, fresh from the vats! I received a batch last week. Nothing 'vintage' about it, and all the healthier and more efficacious for that! None of that confusion of tastes that vintage wines arouse between tongue and palate, and yet the result is the same – dulling the senses and blurring consciousness – what more could anyone ask for? Clay cups, if you please, this has to be done properly!"

The clay cups were provided, and Denur-Shag pulled out the crude wooden stopper from the neck of the flask and poured the wine into the receptacles with an air of unaccustomed solemnity; the forced, ironical smile was gone. He was in no hurry to taste the drink, but remained for a long moment engrossed in himself, as if working something out – repeatedly.

"You remember your offer," he began slowly, his head still bowed, displaying his bald patch in all its glory – "to install me in one of your offices?" He looked up, giving him a long and thoughtful glance. "I rejected the offer, and I have to confess to you that I don't regret it, not in the slightest! I have learned over a long lifetime, and it's the fruit of my accumulated experience – never to regret a decision, even when it's the right one!" He grinned at his own witticism, and the other responded with a faint smile.

"And then – if your memory still serves you, I told you this didn't mean I wasn't going to serve you. On the contrary, if the circumstances required it, I would definitely serve you, with or without your consent! And in reality, such a need has not arisen, then or now." The grin had faded from his eyes, and once again his face took on that untypical expression of solemnity and gravity. He continued, with slow and deliberate articulation:

"And what I didn't ask myself then was, at what time would I stop serving you? It seemed to me then this time was very far away, and might not ever arrive. And now, it has come to me as a terrible surprise, mixed with a certain sense of relief – although 'terrible' and 'relief' are not words that sit naturally together – to find that this time has arrived! As of this evening, my service of you is terminated. Not that I won't be glad to go on being of service to you in any way, but from a professional point of view, in the corridors of the palace – I shall not longer have the opportunity to achieve this."

"Have you been dismissed?" he asked.

"Not exactly!" Denur-Shag answered him, pushing one of the cups towards him and taking the other, recited a benediction – "Blessed is He who gives us the wine!" – and drank thirstily, with big, noisy gulps.

He replied "Amen" and sipped the wine. It certainly did not have a 'vintage' taste, and it might not even be ritually pure, but it had a sharp, youthful tang that was most agreeable.

Denur-Shag wiped his mouth with his hand and fingered his sparse beard, pushed the cup away from him, as if it were an unwelcome distraction, and went on to say:

"I have a brother-in-law. In fact, I have more than a dozen brothers-in-law. Decent fellows all of them, well-rooted in the soil, countrymen in every respect. One of them left the plough and the sickle behind and made his way to the big city in search of his destiny, which according to his way of thinking, the sheer determination of a countryman who has lost interest in the people and the landscapes of his village – meant a well-paid and distinguished occupation. And sure enough, through assiduous burrowing in all the nooks and crannies of the royal household, and commendable commitment to the ploys of self-advertisement, flattery and bribery, he was taken on as deputy assistant to the deputy assistant to the minister responsible for the building of roads in greater Babylon. And here he proved remarkably successful; his sterling qualities stood him in good stead and he was never dismissed or disciplined on account of excess of dedication to the task in hand. He had a true countryman's instinct for sharp practice, and he coped admirably with all the scheming that went on in that department.

"As luck would have it, this brother-in-law of mine was invited to join the personal staff of his minister, and in this capacity he was present at a meeting of what used to be called the Supreme Royal Council and has now been renamed, in presumptuous style – the Great Council of the Crown. His role was to serve the minister as a gofer, bearing great bundles of scrolled maps – specifically designed to confuse anyone rash enough to enquire about programmes of repair and construction of roads.

"In the event the new sovereign, our friend King Belshazzar, showed no inclination to inspect these maps, and throughout the session of the Council my unfortunate brother-in-law was obliged to stand, bearing that heavy load of spurious scrolls in his arms and under his armpits, a posture causing him extreme discomfort and even pain. As a way of distracting himself he chose a most novel method, such as only a shrewd countryman would think of – listening to what was said, and in this specific case – to the speech of the young King!" Denur-Shag held out his hand and picked up the cup, raised it to his lips with a shaking hand and drank, his thirst undiminished.

"This new King, who has the seed of genius firmly planted in his brain, a seed that is bound to burgeon and flower, bearing remarkable fruit which we and people of like mind will have to find ways of coping with – the King came up with an expression that is novel not only from a political point of view and from the perspective of the natural sciences, but linguistically as well! He coined a linguistic idiom such as has never been heard before, and he spoke it in the hearing of his attendant ministers and in the hearing of my pagan-rustic brother-in-law. King Belshazzar spoke, may Heaven preserve us – of blood-purity! Do you realise to what an extent the speaker has outclassed all those who ever misused the word 'purity' in the past, who twisted it to mean all kinds of things – and he has succeeded, in the most remarkable way, in linking it to the word that is the furthest removed from it – 'blood'! And indeed we cannot deny that here there is a truly exceptional manifestation of effrontery and imagination, an assault on hallowed precepts – linguistic and not only linguistic.

"My brother-in-law was stunned, as indeed were all those present, and in particular he noticed the devastating effect on the spirits of the King's most senior adviser – Nashdernach, growing old now, as we all are!

"According to my brother-in-law, with his own eyes he saw the blood drain from that man's cheeks when the King coined that original phrase, and the change was so sharp and abrupt and conspicuous, my brother-in-law swears by all he holds sacred that he couldn't help but be aware of it, and I tend to believe him!"

Denur-Shag drank from his cup again until it was empty, and pushing it away with the back of his hand, went on to say:

"And without any recourse to arcane language, the King referred to those Jews who have 'crawled in like maggots' – a colourful metaphor but hardly original – and infiltrated the royal palace, and had known how to flatter his father who, in Belshazzar's opinion, was gullible in spite of his valour and wisdom, and had risen to great heights and obtained all kinds of senior appointments and – no more and no less – had opened the way to the contamination of the pure blood of the proud sons of Babylon. And it is a fact, the King went on to say, that this blood is the blood of those who were defeated in battle, who fled for their lives and were subdued, whereas the pure blood of the Chaldeans, is the blood of victors in war, of aristocrats, the conquerors and the undefeated. And hearing these words my brother-in-law felt, according to his own account, that some new spirit had entered him, and he had suddenly grown taller and stronger, and he finally realised where he came from and where he belonged, and why he had taken on this employment. I didn't interrupt him at this stage and I let him prattle on with the irrepressible enthusiasm of a country boy who knows that town-dwellers exist only for the purpose of explaining to him what he has known all along, things that have been plain to him since the day he was born.

"And this inventive King of ours continued to expand on the theme of that particular kind of 'blood', the blood of the exiles from Judah who, by surreptitious means, had infiltrated the court of the Chaldean King, and taken over wide swathes of his mighty capital city. And here the eloquent orator needed an illustration, and one was conveniently to hand – the community between the walls, and the new community, established alongside the holiest site in the capital, the temples of the proud, victorious gods of the Babylonians; obviously, everything possible must be done to halt this insidious penetration, burn out the infection before it is too late. And he, the King, failed to understand how the community between the walls – from among whom that assassin had emerged, intent on killing the King, his father, before being burned alive by the gracious intervention of Bel and Marduk – how this community was not only still in existence but was even prospering, and for some reason his father had not given the order to burn the homes of the murderers and raze that settlement to the ground, slaughtering the males and taking the females into servitude and distributing the cattle among the poor, 'pure-blooded' peasantry of the kingdom. That last sentence in particular inflamed that arid patch in my kinsman's brain that is called imagination, and he told me that if his hands had not been full of scrolls he would have clapped them, and if protocol did not allow this, he would certainly have rubbed them together in token of satisfaction and pleasurable anticipation. But this particular delight was denied him, and he had no option but to maintain his immobile and heavily laden stance.

"The King's last words were in fact a question, addressed to that Nashdernach, his most senior adviser who, you will remember, had turned as pale as a statue, and whose cheeks had yet to regain their colour, and he clicked his tongue and bowed low and said in a tone that in my brother-in-law's opinion was supposed to sound forceful but came over as cracked and hollow: 'Your father, may his soul rest in Bel's kingdom of light and truth, did not smite this community, because he wanted to draw closer to Babylon all races and nations and peoples and not to make outcasts and enemies of them. Your father the King taught us that the mighty kingdom of Babylon is composed of many races, and speakers of many languages, and the essence of good government lies in identifying what is shared and consolidating it, and shunning whatever is divisive, instilling in the hearts of all citizens the sense of unity and the knowledge that they are all equal before the gods and before the law and before the King. Furthermore – your father was never in favour of collective punishment. He used to maintain that collective punishment is merely a sign of weakness on the part of the one who punishes, and the victims are aware of this and are therefore more likely to be defiant than compliant.'

"These arguments, so my brother-in-law says, made no impression whatsoever on the King. He rejected them utterly, and although he didn't say this openly, his face answered for him. Disregarding the advice of his senior minister, the King proceeded to issue a series of edicts:

'The burden of taxation imposed on the Jews is to be increased and as a first step, the tax on property will be trebled, and the poll tax will be doubled with the birth of every additional child. Strict limits will be imposed on the property that Jews are allowed to own, and everything above this limit will be confiscated by the Crown. And finally – the Jewish ministers are to be dismissed from their posts forthwith, expelled from their offices, removed from the palace and exiled to the furthermost corners of the empire. And at this point Nashdernach asked if he might speak again, and permission was granted.

"The senior councillor bowed once more to the King, but according to my brother-in-law, in a noticeably perfunctory fashion, for form's sake rather than a display of genuine respect, and he said:

'Your father, the most glorious King in all the world, may his memory be forever blessed, whose name is inscribed in the chronicles of all peoples and races and will never be erased from them – he it was who gave these prestigious posts to those Jewish ministers who had proved their loyalty to him and to the Chaldean people, who were endowed with rare qualities and imbued with the spirit of their God. If their appointments were to be annulled this would be an insult to the institution of the monarchy and a slight on the great and glorious name of King Nebuchadnezzar, your father. The word of a king is not to be taken lightly, in his lifetime and after his death – if his heir truly respects him as is fitting – with the respect that is due between one king and another, or if Your Majesty prefers, between an illustrious son and a magnanimous father...'

"And at this point, my brother-in-law says, with the benefit of his acute percipience and shrewd understanding, it was clear that not all of the ministers were in agreement with their chief. He, the brother-in-law, had noticed the satisfied expressions that had greeted the King's decree demanding the expulsion of the Jewish ministers, and the indignation shown on the same faces in response to the senior councillor's speech in defence of his Jewish friends, and it was then that my kinsman came to the firm conclusion that right was on the side of those demanding eviction of the Jews. Anyway, why should your country be ruled by any foreigners, let alone by Jews, a people trounced and subdued by your heroic national army! The narrator paused here, no doubt expecting fulsome approval of his intuition and intelligence, but in this he was disappointed, and he had no option but to go on and tell of the dispute that flared up between the councillors and the courtiers, to which the King put an end, saying it was his command that the Jewish ministers vacate their offices and also their official houses, with the exception of Belteshazzar, whom the Chaldean people respected for some reason; Belteshazzar was to be expelled too, but at a later date. And he declared that issues of 'blood-purity' would be discussed no longer, in this session of the council at least. They were to address the next items on the agenda, and he expected them all to be as efficient and conscientious as they had been in his father's time, if not more so.

"He then demanded that on the open land to the north of the palace, another should be built, of the same dimensions and the same grandeur, certainly no less, and this palace should comprise a number of extensive halls dedicated to the purposes of recreation and entertainment. It was the duty of his loyal ministers to fill his palace with concubines and all kinds of entertainers – musicians and singers and clowns, to celebrate the dawn of a new era in the annals of Babylon, the era of liberty.

"He insisted that all the halls of entertainment, without exception, should have walls panelled in gold and ceilings of ivory – and to pay for this he ordered the increase of all existing taxes by a quarter, and imposed new taxes on basic commodities like bread and water. Every living man must contribute to the wealth of the royal coffers in return for the privilege of living and breathing, since there is no experience more pleasurable and rewarding to man than living and breathing – and eating and drinking, courtesy of the King and his ministers! And here, my brother-in-law tells me, the faces of all the ministers fell, and he is sure that his fell too, and the hands clutching the bundles of scrolls shook – both from the pain and the numbness of his fingers, maintaining their stubborn grip, and from the unwelcome news that his relatives and his family and he himself were soon to be levied exorbitant taxes on food and drink, as well as for the privilege of living and breathing. Then the King dissolved the first meeting of the Great Council of the Crown, and his senior adviser asked for a private audience with him and stayed behind. He himself, my kinsman I mean, had to trail along behind his master and return all the scrolls to the shelves in the road surveyor's office, unopened and unread. It seemed that the building and upkeep of public highways were not issues of great interest to the King, certainly not worth discussing.

"On a personal level, this rustic relative of mine, with his new found city ways, was not displeased over the 'pure blood' issue; in his humble opinion, as he explained to me with true and unfeigned rustic humility, it could reasonably be expected that new opportunities would be available, new prospects of climbing the ladder of promotion as appointments became vacant, and all good and upright Chaldeans, with pure Chaldean blood flowing in their veins would enjoy true prosperity at last, justifiably proud of their undefiled racial purity.

"At this point I thought it my duty to draw his attention to certain facts, simple and eminently rural facts, having to do with my less than total conviction of the purity of my own blood. As for him, I was prepared to swear any number of sacred oaths, before all the gods and goddesses of the world, that there is nothing even remotely pure-bred about him, and I have no doubt at all that were the matter to be investigated, it would be easily proved that there is an appreciable quantity of hybrid blood flowing in his veins, as there is in his sister's veins, she being none other than my sainted wife, every detail of whose family-tree is familiar to me. And it would take only one friend, no less ambitious for promotion than he, to catch the eye of some minister or other and whisper in his ear, for the contaminated state of his blood to be established beyond doubt, shattering his hopes and stalling his career, perhaps for ever.

"And here I can tell you that the face of this brother-in-law of mine, self-styled man about town and dedicated hedonist, fell in the most pitiable fashion, and if I am to be utterly truthful I must admit that the spectacle of a peasant with ideas above his station brought crashing down to earth, aroused in me the purest form of pleasure, malicious enjoyment of another's misfortune."

Denur-Shag filled his cup again and took a few deep gulps before replacing the cup on the table and pushing it away from him. He seemed suddenly calm, with some of his freshness restored.

"And I have something to tell you," he resumed, "or rather – a secret to share with you, not that it's a secret any more. I'm resigning, in fact I have resigned. Yes, I've done with all this!" he declared with a kind of satisfaction that was both portentous and despairing: "This very morning, I resigned – and my resignation was accepted there and then! It's not just that I doubt the purity of my Chaldean blood. Forty-one years of service have come to a glorious end, an inevitable, pre-ordained end if you like. One way or the other, I feel at ease! I'm going back to the countryside, to live with my dear wife. I'm almost longing for the nerve-grating voice she's been blessed with, like the shriek of an angry crane. You know what people say: 'There's nothing that's all bad.' The trumpet-voice of my wife is the song of the nightingale compared with the incoherent mumbling that's all you hear from the new breed of sycophants hanging around the young King. And when I say 'new breed' I'm referring to those veteran government officials who will soon be getting a new lease of life, scrabbling to ingratiate themselves with the young king and hang on to their sinecures. Such is the marvellous nature of humankind – the "crown of creation"! Always prone to innovation and change and whatever is most likely to promise advancement, or progress if you prefer – either way, it's the greasy pole. And this brilliant notion of 'blood-purity' puts every man and woman in the right place. It's blood that decides and not, perish the thought, abstract things like intellect, talent, generosity or integrity. Even among your own people, the old idea of blood-purity holds sway, and that is what pushes you from crisis to crisis and from disaster to disaster. You should have learned from experience. To put it another way – experience isn't going to teach you or tackle that stubborn streak of yours, and your future is shrouded in mist.

"As for living in the country... people are always saying, scholars and simpletons alike, that to live to the full – you need to be in the bosom of nature! Everyone aspires to it, and the subject is written about, and more will yet be written, and there is great enthusiasm, among writers and readers alike, and only someone who tires of literature goes to the country and lives there. I suppose I'm an exception to that rule. And days in the countryside are clear and the nights are starry, so very rustic in every sense, and to me they are as alike as two drops of water. If however you see anything appealing in the way of life that I have chosen for myself, being of sound mind and after careful consideration – I should be delighted to be your host – all of you, the whole family, in the verdant village of my charming wife, with the sweet voice… which from this day forward, will be my village too! You know that in the countryside, unlike the city or the large metropolis, there is always space to be found, space to live or space by any other definition, since supply exceeds demand by such a wide margin. And the air is healthy, scented with the aroma of garlic and onions, and there's no shortage of fields and plains and arable land. And agriculture – work to purify the soul and the meditations of the heart and even – the blood. Come! I shall be waiting for you!"

He parted from Denur-Shag with a tight hug and a firm handshake.

THE DEATH OF NASHDERNACH

The next day, arriving at his office, he found Nashdernach sitting at his desk and waiting for him.

He sat down facing him and as he did so, noticed how much the man had aged: his oily little eyes had almost disappeared in the depths of sorrow and indignation and their strange glow – was the glow of mortal sickness. His face looked wasted and grey, wrinkled and shrivelled, and it seemed his whole body was racked by numbing fatigue. His puffy hands, laid flat on the table-top, quivered spasmodically. His cloak and his robe were crumpled and ill-kempt and worn in careless fashion – not at all the way things used to be.

He felt sorry for the man, and decided he needed prompting. He said: "I'm having to leave my office and my house..."

"No, not the house!" – Nashdernach seemed to come to life and raised his hand in a blocking gesture. In an anxious voice, its equilibrium lost, he continued: "It's only the office, and that will only be for a limited period of time. Until the King's mood changes... Yes, yes, this is a mood!" he stressed, evidently trying to convince himself – "And like any mood it will melt away and disappear as if it never was. King Belshazzar is prone to sudden changes of mood!"

He noticed that Nashdernach was referring to the King without using the customary honorific titles.

"We shall have to learn to cope with them!" Nashdernach continued in the same cracked and uneven tone. "Not you, I mean, but us...his remaining ministers. I tell you, if it weren't for the vows I made to his illustrious father, the wisest of kings, I wouldn't stay in Belshazzar's palace one moment longer! And no one would stand in my way or try to stop me. I'd give back to the King everything I've received from him and return to the mountain province where I grew up, where my family still owns a smallholding. But..." He broke off, stammering unexpectedly, and seemed on the point of keeling over.

"Nashdernach!" he cried, thoroughly alarmed. "It's as you say," he added in a vigorous tone – "we're going to cope!"

"That's right! Quite right!" Nashdernach answered him, clutching at the table for support. "And yet, in spite of the promise I made to my King, Nebuchadnezzar – may God watch over his ways in the world that is all good – I have tendered my resignation. Yes, I have tendered it! After long deliberation that could fairly be described as agonising, I told this boy – if you'll pardon the expression, King Belshazzar I should say – that although I had promised his illustrious father I would stand at his side through good or ill and support him in word and deed, and for that reason I had not left my post when he came up with that pernicious idea of 'blood-purity' – in the final analysis, faced with his incorrigible stubbornness, I intended to withdraw from all official responsibilities while I still had some of my dignity intact. And I said that if his father was looking down from high, I was sure he would forgive me, and not be too disappointed by the inadequate performance of his former minister, to say nothing of his current heir! And then he relented and granted my request."

"What request was that?" he asked, trying to steer the conversation in a less abstract direction, and also to allow Nashdernach time to recover himself.

"Didn't I tell you? Oh – I forgot. Well then," he picked up the thread again, in a rather more composed tone of voice, "I was sure you wouldn't agree to stay in your house, if your three friends were evicted from theirs. Was I right?"

"You were right. In fact, there are two things I have been meaning to tell you: one is that you are not to blame for any of this, the other is that I won't agree to anything which would separate me from my three good friends, Meshach, Abed-Nego and Shadrach. So I'm telling you now, I shall vacate my house when they vacate theirs, and I intend to inform King Belshazzar to that effect. I don't need his favours. God is my King and my patron and Him I serve!"

"No! No!" cried Nashdernach, repeating his blocking gesture, this time with an air of panic. "Don't do that!" and he added at once: "There's no need for it!"

"How so?" he asked, surprised.

"As I told you," Nashdernach tried to raise a smile to his weary face but failed, and his face retained the greyish gloom of the terminally ill – "in spite of the promise I made to my noble King, Nebuchadnezzar, may he be exalted even in the world of truth – I tendered my resignation, and I made it clear I would play no further part in the administration of the government unless he revoked his decision to evict Meshach, Abed-Nego and Shadrach from their homes in the precincts of the palace. And he, the young King, was silent for a while, studying me with a look that could have reflected anything other than intelligence, and thinking something over and finally he said: 'It shall be as you say, old man!' – that's what he called me, 'old man'. And I swear to you he knew very well just how grievous this insult was, twisting a phrase that in other circumstances could have been an expression of affection, and doing it deliberately. 'I cannot, unfortunately, dispense with your services just now!' the boy grinned at me and said in conclusion: 'Their offices they will still have to leave!' I made no response to this, I just bowed and left the room, that room with its air so balmy and fresh, its furnishings so familiar to me, where so often I listened to the stirring speeches of the King, Nebuchadnezzar the valiant and the wise, King of Kings!" His voice shook, but with a perceptible effort, he succeeded in stifling the tears that were imminent.

"My thanks to you, dear Nashdernach!" he cried. "In my humble opinion, you really didn't need to go to all this trouble! I would have been quite willing to leave behind the house that King Nebuchadnezzar, whom the prophet Jeremiah called 'God's servant' was so gracious as to give me. We are people of faith, and the upheavals of this world and the vicissitudes of fate can do nothing to dismay us so long as our hearts are true to God, trusting in Him and eager to do His will!"

"No!" Nashdernach objected, so faintly he was barely audible, but then he mustered up his last reserves of strength and added in a voice that was almost steady: "You don't have to thank me – I am the one who should be thanking you, for always treating me with more respect than I deserve, and there is no reason why you should leave the house that my great King gave to you as a token of his gratitude and esteem. And I feel I should apologise to you for the way that the successor to our beloved King is behaving! On the basis of what I have just been saying, I shall no doubt be accused of sedition and betrayal of trust, and I shall freely confess to any such charge. They may do with my grey head as they please!"

Nashdernach rose.

He rounded the table and clasped the old man's trembling, outstretched hand and then, although neither of them could have said how it happened, they fell into one another's arms and embraced warmly, and when they parted and Nashdernach went his way, he sensed that he was walking with restored confidence.

The new taxes were imposed, and exacted without mercy, causing resentment not only among the Jewish exiles but among all the variegated racial and ethnic communities of Babylon.

Jewish reactions to the dismissal of the four ministers and their eviction from offices in the palace were mixed – sometimes contradictory and sometimes surprising. There were those who were angry and affronted, seeing these dismissals not only as a national slur but as a personal insult as well, and demanding some response. On this side, much to his surprise, stood the decisive majority of the long-standing community of Babylon, and among the latter there were some who revived old memories and claimed that if they had not been prevented from acting as they had intended, the state of affairs now would be very different – ignoring the fact that their plan had been exposed and could not be put into effect.

There were others who approved of the dismissals, saying that the days of the righteous Joseph were gone for good, and Jews should not accept positions of temporal authority; by so doing, they only served the interests of the gentiles and made themselves into scapegoats, to be sacrificed in times of trouble. Their constant refrain was that the acceptance of such roles never did the Jewish people any good, bringing down upon them disaster after disaster, and feeding them gall and wormwood. They backed up their arguments with persuasive proofs drawn from the recent and the distant past, citing the case of the Pharaoh who succeeded the good Pharaoh and "knew not Joseph" – and afflicted the Jewish people sevenfold. And naturally there were some who found a malicious satisfaction in the turn of events, and others who were envious of any benefits obtained from the gentiles by members of their own race, especially wealth and power and prestige.

But the Jews made no further attempts to subvert the Chaldean state, and it never occurred to anyone to plot the murder of "the wicked king" as they called Belshazzar. The elders and dignitaries of the community warned their flock against indulging in any foolish ideas and trying to rid themselves of the heavy yoke laid on their shoulders – the taxes and the confiscations, the restrictions and the discrimination. Any blow struck against authority would lead to reprisals, punishing not only the culprits and their families but the entire Jewish people. Rather than this, the elders and dignitaries advised them – they should all repent, exiles and veterans alike, give glory to God and fast and pray, wear sackcloth and scatter ashes over their heads, and the cruel decrees would yet be rescinded. And the elders and dignitaries evoked the miracle of Nineveh, where the citizens were not even Jews, not the chosen people of God, and yet when Jonah called upon them in His name to repent, they obeyed him, fasted and prayed and wore sackcloth and scattered ashes on their heads, and all the evil that was supposed to fall upon them was averted, and came to nothing.

So the Jews suppressed their resentment and opted for docility rather than defiance, but the same could not be said of the Chaldeans. In the course of one of the grand processions through the streets of Babylon, for which the young King had acquired a taste, there was an attempt on his life. The would-be assassin, wielding a sword, was foiled just in time, and beaten to death by the King's bodyguards. His bruised and battered body was later hung at the crossroads, as an example to others.

Nashdernach was of the opinion that the man had not acted alone, and the matter required thorough investigation before another attempt was made, this time perhaps with more success. But Belshazzar did not want to listen, and even Nashdernach's advice that he wear body-armour whenever he left the palace – a suggestion which all the ministers and advisers supported unanimously – he rejected with contempt.

On the anniversary of the death of Nebuchadnezzar the entire royal entourage set out on a lavish procession of mourning. King Belshazzar rode on a black horse, with Nashdernach to his right, and to his left, the commander of the royal bodyguard.

When the procession was forced to close ranks in order to pass by the corner of the alleyway leading to the square before the palace, a poisoned arrow was shot. It was aimed at the King, but missed its mark and instead struck Nashdernach, his chief minister. He fell from his horse, barely conscious, and was immediately picked up and placed in one of the luxurious carriages transporting the King's innumerable concubines. A physician was summoned, and he examined the wounded man and declared he did not have long to live.

King Belshazzar turned his horse and rode back to the carriage. Bending over Nashdernach he asked if he had any last request; he promised it would be honoured. He answered him: "Don't harm the Jewish exiles!" – and gave back his tormented soul to his Maker.

The one who shot the arrow was never caught, and Babylon was rife with rumours. Some alleged that the assault had been planned by the King's ministers and advisers, who regarded Nashdernach as a thorn in their flesh, and carried out at their instigation and at their expense. Others claimed that King Belshazzar himself had hired the assassin, to be rid of the old man who had never been one of the court sycophants and who always protested vigorously against anything that seemed to him too imperious or contrary to law and to justice.

Babylon mourned its chief minister and all the Jews of Babylon, veterans and exiles alike, dignitaries and aristocrats, pedlars and peasants, followed the coffin and lamented the loss of a true friend who would not easily be replaced.

In the funeral procession the four of them met and walked for a while side by side, in silence. Then he addressed them, saying:

"We trust in God, and rejoice in Him at all times and always, and live His existence, loving Him with all our heart and might, all our soul and all our mind, and we know for sure that pure souls will come to Him, Nashdernach among them!"

"That is our fervent wish!" Azariah sighed, staring at the ground. And Hananiah said:

"It seems that the circle has closed, an era has come to an end. The era of King Nebuchadnezzar, servant of God."

And Mishael added, in corroboration of this:

"As our friend Daniel prophesied to the late King – the golden age under his wise rule has come to an end, and the death of Nashdernach, his right-hand man and loyal retainer, is a further sign that that time is over."

"Next will be the age of silver," he responded calmly, adding, "And if Belshazzar proves unworthy of it, he will not be the one who presides over it!

"Let us praise the Lord above, maker of Heaven and Earth and all that is in them, who has blessed us with His grace and opened our hearts to love Him at all times and always, with all our heart and mind, might and soul, amen and amen!"

And all joined in the response: "Amen and amen!"

THE FEAST

King Belshazzar convened a meeting of the Great Council of the Crown and demanded of his senior ministers and advisers that he be brought detailed plans for the expulsion of all the Jews from the kingdom of the Chaldeans and first and foremost from its capital city, from mighty Babylon. No trace of them should be left behind.

The rumour spread within the communities of Babylon and outside them, as the King made no secret of his intentions; on the contrary, he deliberately let the news leak out, and derived a malicious pleasure from the plight of the Jews, who could not sleep at night for fear and horrendous expectations.

The elders and the dignitaries of the flock called for fasting and prayer, and privations of body and mind. He joined Mishael, Hananiah and Azariah in a prolonged and rigorous fast; they put on sackcloth and tore their hair and sprinkled ashes on their heads, and prayed to God to deliver the people from disaster and overrule the King's ruthless decree.

The date for the expulsion of the Jews from Babylon, so people said, had been fixed although nobody knew it except the King himself and one of his more sinister henchmen, a gloomy misanthrope named Nasathan, who had emerged from obscurity after the demise of Nebuchadnezzar.

Members of the other ethnic groups living in Babylon were already eyeing up the houses and hovels that would soon be vacated by the Jews, becoming the property of whoever was first to grab them, while the Jews themselves were sitting and praying in the new oratory that they had built for themselves, with Nebuchadnezzar's blessing, on the outskirts of the town, and no one slept or tasted food and all were tense with expectation and foreboding, not knowing what the future held for them. One of the ministers took the risk of reminding the King of his promise to Nashdernach. He had personally witnessed the death of Nashdernach, his memory be blessed, and had heard his last request and Belshazzar's undertaking to fulfil it. By way of response to his minister, the King ordered his bodyguards to eject the man from his palace; they complied and did such a thorough job of it that the minister returned to his home with bandaged head and a black eye.

King Belshazzar was satisfied with all that he had done and excited at the prospect of what he was yet to do. He invited his friends, and there were many of them, to a great feast that was to continue whole days and nights – until the day of the enactment of the decree, when a crack squad of Chaldean soldiers would begin the process of evicting the Jews from their homes, and expelling them from all the territories under Babylonian rule.

Warmed by the wine, Belshazzar gave the order to fetch the vessels of gold and silver which his father Nebuchadnezzar had taken from the sanctuary at Jerusalem, so that the King and his ministers, his mother, his wife and his concubines, might drink from them. So the vessels of gold and silver that had been taken from Jerusalem were brought in, and the King and his ministers, his mother, his wife and his concubines drank from them. They drank wine and praised the gods of bronze and iron, of wood and stone. Suddenly the fingers of a hand, a human hand, appeared and wrote on the wall of the palace opposite the lamp, and the King saw the hand as it wrote.

At this the King was filled with dismay, and his mind was in turmoil, his limbs limp and his knees knocking together. He called loudly for the magicians, diviners and astrologers to be brought to him, and addressing the wise men of Babylon he said: 'Whoever can read this writing and tell me its interpretation shall be robed in purple and honoured with a chain of gold round his neck, and he shall rule over Babylon, with only the King and his viceroy outranking him.' The King's wise men came and they could not read the writing nor interpret it for the King.

The King was scared out of his wits, and his ministers were at a loss. Hearing what had happened, the King's mother came and addressed him: 'Long live the King!' she said, 'Calm yourself and do not be dismayed. There is a man in your kingdom who has in him the spirit of the holy gods, a man who was known in your father's time for his intelligence and his wisdom. King Nebuchadnezzar, your father, appointed him chief of the magicians, the diviners and astrologers. This Daniel, whom the King named Belteshazzar, has the gift of interpreting dreams, explaining riddles and solving problems. Call upon Daniel, and he will give you the interpretation.'

Then Daniel was brought before the King, and the King said to him: 'Are you Daniel, whom the King my father brought from Judah? I have heard that you possess the spirit of the holy gods and that you are a man of clear understanding and exceptional wisdom. The wise men and the sorcerers have just been brought into my presence to read this writing and tell me its interpretation, and they have been unable to interpret it. But I have heard it said of you that you are able to give interpretations and to solve problems. So now, if you are able to read the words and tell me what they mean, you shall be robed in purple and honoured with a chain of gold round your neck and you shall rank as third in the kingdom!'

Then Daniel replied to the King: 'Your gifts you may keep for yourself, and give your rewards to another. Nevertheless I will read this writing to your majesty and tell you its interpretation.

'The Most High God gave your father Nebuchadnezzar a kingdom and power and glory and majesty, and because of this power which he gave him, all peoples and nations of every tongue trembled before him and were afraid. He put to death whom he would and spared whom he would, he promoted them at will and at will degraded them. But when he became haughty, stubborn and presumptuous, he was deposed from his royal throne and his glory was taken from him. He was banished from the society of men, his mind became like that of a beast, he lived with the wild asses and ate grass like oxen, and his body was bathed in the dew of heaven, until he came to know that the Most High is sovereign over the kingdom of men and sets up over it whom he will. But you, his son Belshazzar, did not humble your heart, although you knew all this. You have set yourself up against the Lord of heaven. The vessels of his temple have been brought to your table, and you and your ministers, your wives and your concubines have drunk wine from them, and you have praised the gods of bronze and iron, of wood and stone, which neither see nor hear nor know, and you have not given glory to God, in whose charge is your living soul. And this hand has been sent and it has written this inscription, and this is what is written: 'Mene mene tekel u-pharsin'. And the interpretation: 'mene' – God has numbered the days of your kingdom and brought it to an end; 'tekel' – you have been weighed in the balance and found wanting; 'u-pharsin' – and your kingdom has been divided and given to the Medes and Persians.'

The following day Belshazzar the Chaldean King was murdered. This time it was a member of his household who assailed him, a young officer of the guard whose parents, in the countryside, had been evicted from their home and left destitute for failing to pay the new taxes when they were due, and his brother and his two sisters had been sold into slavery.

The young officer approached the King, bowed as if wishing to inform him of something, and on rising he severed the neck of Belshazzar with a single stroke of his sword, as swift as lightning. Impelled by the force of the blow, Belshazzar's head bounced on the floor and rolled to the feet of the dumbfounded guards, who had no idea what they should do or how they should deal with their superior officer.

The latter took advantage of the confusion and jumped from a window into the royal garden. Here he was detained by a fellow officer of the guard, who realised something was amiss when he saw his colleague escaping through the window. The assassin was chained and imprisoned in the palace dungeons.

News of the King's death spread rapidly through Babylon and outside it. It seemed no one was too distressed about it. Darius the Mede, uncle of Temior, the late queen, came to the Chaldean capital at the head of a small army, and the Chaldeans did not resist him but threw the gates of the city wide open to him and to his troops.

Darius was crowned King of Babylon and sat on the throne of Nebuchadnezzar, and ordered the immediate abolition of the taxes that Belshazzar, his predecessor, had imposed on the inhabitants of Babylon, as well as the special taxes levied on the Jewish communities. Darius reinstated the sacked ministers to their posts, and first and foremost the four ministers of the Jewish exile, namely Belteshazzar, Meshach, Shadrach and Abed-Nego. The brave minister who had dared to remind Belshazzar of Nashdernach's dying wish, Darius promoted, appointing him chief adviser in place of Nashdernach, and on the latter's tomb he ordered the placing of a marble plinth, twenty cubits in height and bearing the inscription in letters of gold inlay "The municipality of Babylon mourns its faithful son". The King's murderer, Darius hanged on the grounds that "No man should raise his hand against one crowned King with the consent of God, no matter how he has behaved," but his family was pardoned and had their property restored, and his brother and sisters were released from servitude. They also received a generous sum in compensation for their suffering and humiliation.

Gershon, who had voluntarily left the office of the royal calligrapher, did not change his mind despite an official invitation and the promise of promotion. He found a refuge with Simeon of the house of Avinoam, Hannah's father and the father-in-law of Hananiah, and the two of them spent days and nights recalling the great days of the Hebrew nation and its past glories, and bemoaning the troubles besetting it at present.

Gershon expressed the opinion that the root of all the people's woes was to be found in its lack of faith and in its pursuit of temporal pleasures, including power and fame, and its enslavement to them. Simeon on the other hand maintained with undiminished stubbornness that those sons of the people who had accepted positions of authority in the service of pagan rulers were responsible for all the problems, and this because they disregarded the interests of their own race and would rather ingratiate themselves with the infidels. At the end of the day, none of the experiences of the Jews had come about through any agency on the part of God. God ruled His own kingdom, meaning the kingdom of Heaven, and the world below He entrusted into the hands of men, and as men sowed so would they reap, as the sages used to say.

Gershon disagreed with his sparring partner but without undue heat or vehemence, as some of the other's arguments he could accept. The statement that man reaps what he has sown – with that he concurred wholeheartedly.

One way or the other, Gershon found a roof and a lodging with Simeon of the house of Avinoam, Hananiah's father-in-law, and whenever the occasion arose he exchanged cordial greetings and good wishes with the four friends, his former travelling companions.

With the ending of the siege of Jerusalem and its conquest by Nebuchadnezzar, Gershon tried to ascertain what had become of his family and his brother-in-law, Jacob Ben Eliezer, without much success. Someone said that all the members of his family had survived, including his brother-in-law and his sister and their children, who had left Jerusalem before the siege began and found refuge in Egypt. Someone else said his brother-in-law had been seen fighting on the walls of the city, and his fate was unknown. Gershon had to be content with these snippets of information, from sources of dubious reliability, but he was convinced, or rather he succeeded in convincing himself – that if his relatives had perished, he would have heard. He preferred to believe the version according to which they had left Jerusalem before Nebuchadnezzar arrived to lay siege to the city, and found a place of safety in Egypt, and in this he found some reassurance.

Gershon was contented with his lot, helping Simeon to write letters to the authorities, and performing the same service for the burghers of the community and the simple folk, and for this work of his he received a nominal stipend. As time passed he stopped taking an interest in the world around him and sank into a kind of easeful slumber, like an old man coming to the end of his road and wanting only to be gathered to his ancestors without suffering or pain.

THE FOUR BEASTS

At about this time, visions began to rise before his eyes, and, and at night he was visited by dreams that perturbed and unsettled his mind, making a deep impression upon him. And in the morning, on rising from his bed, he would remember every single detail of these dreams which – more than they were nightly happenings in the sleeping hours – were living events and not the fruit of delusion.

To avoid disturbing Nejeen in her sleep, he went back to sleeping in his own room. He reckoned he should apologise to her for this, but she forestalled him:

"It does no harm, you sleeping in your own room, if that is really what you want. For my part, I shall stay in the room that we share."

He bowed to her, as a mark of appreciation for her considerate approach, and sat down with her to eat breakfast. And when the meal was over and the maid had cleared the table, while they were still sitting there, face to face, he finally broke the silence, telling her of one of the dreams that he had dreamed, or more accurately – had seen.

She listened with rapt attention and when he had finished his account, she remarked that in her humble opinion it was important, and perhaps even his duty, to record the dream in writing, word for word as he had told it to her.

He weighed her words carefully, and after some thought came to the conclusion that she was absolutely right. He went to his private study with its window overlooking the palace gardens, and its cool and refreshing ventilation, sat at his desk and recorded, as Nejeen had suggested, word for word:

In my visions of the night I saw a great sea stirred by the four winds of heaven, and four huge beasts coming up out of the sea, each one different from the others. The first was like a lion with eagle's wings. I watched as its wings were plucked off and it was raised from the ground and made to stand on its feet like a man, and it was given the mind of a man. Then I saw another, a second beast like a bear. It was standing to one side and had three ribs in its mouth, between its teeth, and it was commanded: Arise and gorge yourself with flesh! After this I saw another, a beast like a leopard, with four bird's wings on its back; this creature had four heads and was invested with sovereign power. Next in my visions of the night I saw a fourth beast, dreadful and threatening, and very strong, with iron teeth. It munched and devoured, and trampled underfoot all that was left, and it differed from all the others in that it had ten horns. As I was looking at the horns, I saw another horn, a little one, springing up among them and three of the first horns were uprooted to make space for it. And in that horn were eyes like the eyes of a man and a mouth speaking proud words.

And I watched and I saw thrones set in place and one ancient of days taking his seat, in a robe as white as snow and the hair of his head like pure wool. Flames of fire were his throne and its wheels blazing fire. A flowing river of fire streamed out before him, and thousands upon thousands served him and myriads upon myriads attended his presence. And the court sat and the scrolls were opened.

Then because of the proud words that the horn was speaking, I went on watching until the beast was killed and its carcass destroyed and given to the flames. The rest of the beasts, though deprived of their sovereignty, were allowed to remain alive for a time and a season. And in my visions of the night I also saw one like a man coming with the clouds of heaven, and he approached the Ancient of Days and was presented to him. To him were given sovereignty and glory and kingship, so that all people and nations of every language should serve him, and his sovereignty was to be an everlasting sovereignty which should not pass away, and his kingship such as should never be impaired.

My spirit was troubled, and disturbed by the visions that came into my head. I, Daniel, approached one of those who stood there, and I saw he was known to me, but I could not say from what place and from what time I knew him, and yet there was friendship and fellowship in his eyes, and I asked him to explain to me the meaning of all these things. And he told me the interpretation: These great beasts, four in number, are four kingdoms that shall rise from the ground, and after them the saints of the Most High shall receive the kingly power and shall retain it for ever and ever. Then I asked to know the meaning of the fourth beast, the beast that was different from all the others, more dreadful, with its iron teeth and bronze claws, munching and devouring and trampling underfoot all that was left. And I wanted to know the meaning of the ten horns on its head and the other horn which sprang up and at whose coming three of them fell – the horn that had eyes and a mouth speaking proud words and appeared larger than the others. And as I watched, that horn was waging war with the saints and overcoming them, until the Ancient of Days came, and judgment was given in favour of the saints of the Most High, and the time came, when the saints gained possession of the kingly powers. And my *informant told me: The fourth beast signifies a fourth kingdom that shall arise on the earth, that shall differ from all other kingdoms and shall devour the whole earth, tread it down and crush it. The ten horns signify the appearance of ten kings in this kingdom, after whom another king shall arise, differing from his predecessors, and he shall humble three kings, and he shall speak defiance of the Most High and shall oppress the saints of the Most High, and he will seek to change the customary times and the laws, and the saints shall be delivered into his hands for a time and times and half a time. Then the court shall sit and he shall be deprived of his sovereignty, so that in the end it may be destroyed utterly. The kingly power, sovereignty and greatness of all the kingdoms under heaven shall be given to the people of the saints of the Most High. Their kingly power is an everlasting power and all sovereignties shall serve them and obey them. This is the end of the account. And as for me, Daniel, my thoughts perturbed me greatly and I turned pale, and I kept these things in my mind.*

One evening in late summer, with a light breeze bearing in its wings the invigorating moisture of the Euphrates, he sat with Nejeen, Naimel and Gamliel on the veranda, shaded by flowers and foliage, and read to them the dream-vision as he had recorded it in writing.

His reading was remarkable for its lucidity, for the careful enunciation of the words and the balanced expression of emotion, such that all the pictures, one after the other, were clearly drawn before the eyes of the listeners, vivid and stirring, impossible to erase.

For a long time after he had finished reading they remained silent, shaken by the strong impression that the vision had left in their hearts. And the rhythmic gusting of the wind and the soft rustling of the leaves of the climbing-plants only underscored the silence. Out of the corner of his eye he looked at his sons: young Gamliel, wrapped up in himself, too much so perhaps, his absorption doubtless recalling that of the man whose name he bore. Naimel, on the other hand, radiated a kind of quiet freedom, natural and self-explanatory, his smooth forehead speaking of intelligence and his eyes fearless. With his air of pleasant serenity, he resembled his father. A warm sense of well-being suffused his heart.

Both Gamliel and Naimel were youths who impressed all those who saw them with their bodily strength and fine appearance, their manners and their prudence.

About a week earlier, the four of them – Nejeen, Gamliel, Naimel and he – had gone out riding beyond the walls, on the paved roads leading to the southern hills. They were all skilled riders, and the excursion inevitably turned into a race. At the start of the race, the boys set out at a hectic pace, but Nejeen and he soon had the measure of them, and their fine steeds needed little encouragement; they overtook their sons and arrived unchallenged at the finishing point that had been agreed, a ruined building at the corner where the road took a sharp turn, for the ascent to the peaks.

When all had assembled at the rendezvous near the ruined building, the four horses were snorting and breathing heavily, and the clothes of the riders were stained with broad patches of sweat.

Naimel gave him a look of frank admiration, and at that moment it occurred to him: this was exactly the way he used to look at his father, absorbing the warmth in his father's eyes until he did not know himself for joy.

Gamliel asked:

"How do you do this, Father?"

"How do I do what?" – he smiled equably.

"You're not wearing spurs, you're not sticking spikes in your horse's flanks and you never use a whip – and your mare carries you along like a storm-wind, to wherever you choose to go!"

"I talk to her, you see – in her own language!"

"Whatever you're doing, it definitely works!" Naimel exclaimed.

Nejeen, who had been gazing at him proudly throughout this exchange, started telling the story of the race that King Nebuchadnezzar, may he rest in peace, used to organise during the early years of his reign, a race for life and death – and this father of theirs, a youth at the time, a mere boy, had emerged the victor, through the grace and the love of God.

Gamliel broke the silence that reigned on the veranda, asking:

"Does the Ancient of Days have no shape or body?"

"That's right, my boy!" he answered him solemnly. "God has neither shape nor bodily form, but in dreams and visions everything is expressed in symbols, since there is no other way. Even the beasts in the vision are symbols, and their horns are symbols – as was clearly explained to me."

"And the whole of that vision – has to do with the end of days!" Naimel put in; it was part question, part assertion.

"The cycle of humanity has turned – or at least, that is true of the part of it which cleaves to God. There will no longer be rulers and kings and despots of various kinds – only God alone, God who is love, and every man who knows what love is will be awakened in Him and become Him."

The sky turned blue and the stars were rising – clear and close at hand, sparkling in their silent, teeming lustre, like the light stored in the hearts of those who long for God and delight in doing His will.

"And what is to be done to be worthy of this grace and this love, turning to God, and awakening in Him and becoming Him?" Naimel persisted.

"You have to love," he answered him.

ABIRIUCH

The Jewish communities, the old one as well as that of the exiles, greeted the miracle that had befallen them, on hearing that the "irksome Belshazzar" had perished in such an ignominious manner, that his policies had been revoked, and that rights, property and dignity were to be restored to the Jewish minority. In some respects, the Jews were better off than they had been even in the time of Nebuchadnezzar: free assembly was now permitted, as were religious processions, and authorisation had been given for the building of the temple on the site of the old oratory. Official funding had been guaranteed, and construction was already under way. Not content with one temple, the communities demanded two, so that each congregation could have its own place of worship, and this was also sanctioned. Joy was unbounded and jubilation soared sky-high and all praised the Lord and blessed the living God, with prayers of thanksgiving for the miracles granted to them, and for the grace and compassion that He had bestowed upon His people – this stubborn, sinful, mutinous and unruly people. And there were those who wept and beat their breasts and made solemn vows to observe the Torah and uphold it in letter and in spirit, as is written: *And you shall love the Lord your God with all your heart and all your might and all your spirit* – and many, many repented.

And the priests of both communities composed prayers for the long life and well-being of Darius the Mede and for the prosperity of his realm, and a deputation of elders and dignitaries came to bow at the feet of the King and to offer him a gift – an ancient Torah scroll, a wilted parchment on which, according to tradition, the sacred text had been inscribed by none other than Joshua Ben Nun himself. The King, an enthusiast for antiquities, was much moved to hear this story and almost wept for joy, since he greatly admired that warrior of ancient times, whom even the sun obeyed, and whose conquests were all at the behest of God and for the glory of God. Following this episode the Jews, who had been well aware of his interest in antiquities and his admiration of Joshua and had acted accordingly – rose still higher in the King's estimation.

Darius was sixty-two years old on his accession to the throne in Babylon. And he chose to appoint one hundred and twenty satraps to administer his kingdom, responsible for the governance of all the peoples, nations and tongues of his realm; to take charge of the one hundred and twenty satraps he appointed three senior ministers, of whom Daniel was one. In fact, he was minded to appoint Daniel chief of all his ministers and governors, to rule in his stead and to report to him regularly on all that was happening in the land. And all this because he recognised in Daniel the spirit of the almighty God, whom all men must obey and whom no man can defy; whatever Daniel blessed would be blessed, whatever he cursed – cursed.

Such things were not to the liking of the two remaining ministers and the newly appointed satraps. They invoked the memory of Belshazzar, who had not tolerated foreigners in his palace, and they regretted his untimely death, and looked with jealously at Daniel, alias Belteshazzar, whose origin was Jewish and who was nothing more than an exile brought to Babylon by King Nebuchadnezzar, who in the opinion of many wise men had thereby made a grievous mistake, and instead of enhancing the power and the repute of his realm had achieved the opposite result. Such were the topics of conversation among the satraps and the two ministers, repeated day after day, until it became evident that all were unanimous, with only one dissenter – a young man who was a newcomer to the court. The uncle of the young man had been a confidant of King Belshazzar and had enjoyed favour and promotion in his service, attaining quasi-ministerial status, and he did not look kindly on what he considered the "misguided" views of his nephew who, in defiance of the collective wisdom, was taking the side of Belteshazzar, the King's viceroy, and speaking out on his behalf. After consultation with his colleagues, the uncle took it upon himself to tackle this nephew of his and urge him to consider the issues, appreciate the facts as they stood and understand some essential truths, abandoning his stubborn position and returning to the fold while there was still time. And when persuasion proved fruitless, stern reprimands achieved nothing, and sweet words fell on deaf ears, the uncle suggested that his nephew remember to whom he owed his career in the palace and his appointment as one of the one hundred and twenty satraps; how dare he ignore and defy his patron and benefactor in such a brazen manner?

And since even these stern words of reproof, uttered by a man reckoned among the outstanding intellectuals of Babylon, failed to hit the target, threats were raised: the young satrap was warned, unequivocally, that if he held to his dissenting opinion and continued to support the Jewish Daniel, neither he nor his family could expect to enjoy the hedonistic pleasures of this life, or indeed enjoy anything in life.

As it turned out, young Abiriuch proved to be a man of exceptional stubbornness, stubbornness of almost Jewish proportions. He could not be shifted from his position by a fraction, and so there was no alternative but to accept this and treat him accordingly: one hundred and nineteen satraps and two ministers ostracised Abiriuch and no longer greeted him or called upon his services. And they were meeting daily and debating ways of finding some pretext to blacken the name of Belteshazzar before the King, so that former glories would be restored, and never again would a foreign voice, let alone a Jewish voice, be heard in their council chamber.

So all the satraps, rated the wisest and most astute of men, and the ministers set above them were hunting for that pretext that would destroy Belteshazzar's reputation, this man whom the King proposed to appoint his deputy, whose sway all of Babylon must acknowledge. And despite all the energy and the guile invested in the project, those enthusiastic researchers could find nothing, no indictment that could be laid against the minister Belteshazzar, alias Daniel, to incriminate him before the King. The man seemed utterly flawless, and there was no blemish on his record, great or small, and wherever he went he kept his hands clean, and never so much as said a vulgar or abusive word, or lost his temper; perhaps there really was a divine spirit in him, as the King believed, and he could not be tackled in this way.

So among the satraps there was a degree of uncertainty and a mood of dejection, and some of them began looking more kindly at Abiriuch, the outcast and exchanging greetings with him, while others turned to superstition and sought remedies in charms and spells and incantations, but despite the doubts and misgivings, all were united in their refusal to accept defeat. They believed in the assertion, the decidedly reasonable assertion, that there was no such thing as a totally flawless man, and it was only their frailty and incompetence that had prevented them finding any stain on the cloak of that Jewish exile. With courage, persistence and patience, they could yet achieve their hearts' desire.

And they renewed their efforts, assiduously searching and enquiring, and still they found nothing. It seemed that for the time being the project was doomed and would simply sink into oblivion. There was nothing for it but to submit to the yoke of the Jewish minister of the Median king, whose eyes, so they averred, were blind. And Abiriuch was no longer treated as a pariah and was beginning to feel happier and more at ease, when one fine day a satrap from the southern territories – a man with bald head, projecting paunch, and a broad smile on his freckled, shapeless face – mounted the podium and called for silence. Silence fell, whereupon he demanded that all pay close attention to what he was about to say; there was a solution to the problem, and that stain on the cloak of the Jewish exile had finally been found.

There was silence in the spacious council chamber, and all those seated there held their breath. If someone had accidentally dropped a stylus, it would have sounded like a thunderclap.

And the portly man proceeded to address them, saying with a cunning smile, and in a smug voice:

"According to a royal decree that was issued not long ago at my instigation, any man who within the next thirty days, shall worship any god, bow down to this god and bring before him his prayer and his petition, without first addressing his prayer and his petition to His Majesty King Darius, shall be thrown into the lions' pit. And my faithful Libyan slave, knowing his master's anguish and his fervent wish, called me and drew my attention to the fact that this Daniel is failing to comply with the explicit command of the King that I instigated, and he kneels in his house and three times in a day he prays with hands joined to his God, his face turned towards Jerusalem, the ruined capital of the Jews, and the windows of his house are open wide, and anyone can look inside and see him at prayer, this most senior of ministers!

"So I accompanied my Libyan slave and at the appointed time I watched the house and observed the conduct of Belteshazzar, and indeed it was exactly as my slave told me. I had to check it for myself, since only the testimony of a free man is valid according to the laws of our enlightened kingdom. And now my esteemed colleagues, distinguished ministers and governors of the empire of Babylon, we have no option but to put the God of the Jews to the test, and see if he can indeed rescue his loyal disciple and dauntless servant from the maw of the lions!"

Loud applause echoed around the high walls of the great council chamber in response to these inspirational words on the part of the satrap from the south, and there was a feeling of relief in the air. All those present turned to one another and exchanged handshakes and hugs and mutual congratulations on the success and good fortune that one of their own parochial and chauvinistic gods had granted them, as a reward for their perseverance and commitment to the sacred objective.

And it was then that the brazen Abiriuch, a man apparently incapable of dissembling and possessed of stubbornness worthy of a Jew, leapt onto the speaker's podium and cried:

"And He, God, will protect him, as he protected his three friends from the flames of the furnace in the time of His Majesty King Nebuchadnezzar! "

The words spoken by the young man, although no one was likely to take them seriously or be influenced by them, sowed some confusion among those who were busily exchanging congratulations and handshakes and hugs, and for a moment their resolve seemed to be faltering, but this was a fleeting moment, quickly forgotten in the surge of collective euphoria.

A delegation was formed, consisting of twenty-one men – nineteen of the most pompous of the satraps and the two ministers, nominally Belteshazzar's deputies. And the delegation rose, left the hall and made its way to the garden in the heart of the royal palace, where Darius was usually to be found at this time of the day, feeding his favourite goldfish. And sure enough, the august delegation found the King there beside the goldfish pool, surrounded by members of his household and the royal bodyguards. And the delegation asked to be received in urgent audience, and their request was granted. The senior of the two ministers bowed at the King's feet and began:

"Long live King Darius! All the ministers, deputies and satraps, councillors and governors, with one exception, a young man not yet versed in the ways of authority and the dignity of power – have consulted together and resolved to uphold the ordinance of the King and enforce the prohibition issued by the King, according to which, whosoever shall, within thirty days, address a prayer or an entreaty to any god or man other than you, Your Majesty, or without your express permission, shall be cast into the lions' pit. And we have no doubt that you, Your Majesty, will uphold this prohibition in the letter and in the spirit, since it emanates from you and we look to you, our King, to provide an example to the many populations beneath your sway and to your loyal courtiers, by implementing the laws that you have decreed in your wisdom and the prohibitions that you have promulgated so fearlessly!" Again the speaker bowed down to the ground, almost kissing the lush grass at the King's feet, as all the members of the royal entourage listened in silence to the words of the bizarre plaintiff.

Rising to his feet again, the latter resumed:

"Daniel, otherwise known as Belteshazzar, whom you propose to appoint as governor over all of the kingdom that God has given you, acting as your deputy, despite his knowledge of the commandment emanating from the King, and the strict prohibition that he imposed, forbidding any man to address a plea or offer prayer to any god or man other than the King himself – he goes to his house where the windows of his chamber are open wide, and bows down on his knees before his God, and prays to Him and praises Him as he always has and always will, without regard for the King's ordinance. You are the one who promulgated this law, and its terms are very clear, and you it was who decreed that anyone infringing it is to be thrown into the lions' pit. Such is the plain and literal meaning of the law and the prohibition, Your Majesty!"

The King was grieved at heart and his spirits fell, as his thoughts turned to Daniel, or Belteshazzar, who was very dear to him, and he looked for ways to save him from the malicious conspiracy of his governors and ministers, and until the setting of the sun he was bandying words with the members of the delegation, arguing over every clause of this law and its precise interpretation, and the traditions of the Medes and the Persians. But all his efforts to save Daniel were to no avail, and the ministers and the governors were gaining the upper hand. And when they saw how great was the King's affection for Daniel the Jew, their malice and their jealousy mounted to a higher pitch than ever, and they said to the elderly King Darius:

"You should know our Lord the King that there is one immutable rule in the kingdom of the Medes and the Persians: no law that is inscribed by the hand of the King, nor any prohibition sealed by his hand – is ever to be revoked. And not one utterance of the King is to be idly discarded!"

Then the King ordered that Daniel be brought before him.

And Abiriuch ran to warn Daniel even before his colleagues had arrived in the royal garden to seek an audience with the King, and rushed into his home, and when the guardsmen on duty detained him, he insisted that he had urgent business with the minister.

He heard the commotion, and he came out and demanded the young man be released. The guardsmen withdrew, freeing the uninvited guest, who fell on his knees and bowed to the ground at Daniel's feet; on rising again, he proceeded to tell him:

"Abiriuch is my name. and this name will not tell you much, perhaps nothing at all! If I may remind you of forgotten things – I am the son of that Chaldean soldier whom you cured when you were still a boy being brought to Babylon with the convoy of exiles, do you remember Sir?" – the young man asked very politely, his troubled eyes fixed on Daniel's.

"I remember it well!" he replied with a smile, and a beam of light dispelled the anxiety from the young man's eyes, replacing it with a spark of hope.

"That is not the issue that brought me here, although I should be glad to discuss it with you at another time!"

And the young man continued, in a more even tone:

"My father passed away with your name on his lips, and for that reason he did not suffer; indeed, you could say he was happy to leave this world for the next. When my uncle, my mother's brother, secured my promotion to the rank of satrap-designate, my father summoned me, on his death-bed, and told me:

'Abiriuch my son, remember the words that I say to you now! In the royal palace there resides a man whose Chaldean name is Belteshazzar, and his Hebrew name Daniel, and as I have told you before, he is the one who cured my infirmity, a feat beyond the ability of human medicine, and rescued me from fearful pain, and he is a man of great spiritual strength, to whom the gods lend their grace. Any King who honours him as he should and heeds his advice, will be strengthened and advanced, his realm will prosper and his government flourish, and any ruler who spurns him and rejects his advice out of hand, will be doomed. And you, in the prestigious post that you have attained, should serve our King with loyalty and devotion, and always stand at the right hand of Belteshazzar, or Daniel, and honour him in everything and observe his commandments, even if he does not address them to you directly. Be even more faithful to him than you are to the King himself. For everything that you do out of respect for the truth and loyalty to this holy man – God will repay you sevenfold, and for everything that is not done out of respect and loyalty to him, he will punish you in the same measure!'" The young man paused and studied the expression on his face before continuing:

"And now all the governors and the satraps and the two ministers who are supposed to be your deputies, have consulted together and they are looking for an excuse to topple you! For a long time they have been searching in vain for such an excuse, and now they have discovered that you are kneeling down and praying to your God, with the windows of your house open, for all to see, and this in contravention of the explicit command of King Darius, whereby no man may address prayer or entreaty to any god or man other than the King himself, and anyone breaking this law shall be thrown into the lions' pit." Again the young man peered awkwardly into the other's face and realised, to his amazement, that his expression was quite unchanged. And he went on to say, with fervour, pretending more confidence than he really felt:

"I have not the slightest doubt, Sir, that your God, the High and the Almighty, will save you from the jaws of the lions, as he saved your friends from the flames of the furnace. And my only reason in coming here is to make your close acquaintance, and hear your voice and to express my deep admiration, and my belief that in everything you do you will succeed, always and for ever."

Again the young man bowed before him and before he could be stopped, kissed his feet. Standing up, he blessed him and turned to go. And he responded to him without knowing it was he who spoke, and in his own voice:

"My God will surely save me, and you – trust in Him!"

For a brief moment, astonishment flashed in the young man's dark eyes, the next moment – he was gone.

Nejeen heard the commotion as the guardsmen chased Abiriuch, and was on her way to the porch when she heard the youth's agitated voice, and stopped to listen. As the satrap disappeared from view, she was standing by her husband's side, saying quietly, in her way, looking into his eyes with love undiluted:

"I heard it all. How pitiable they are!" She wound her arms around his neck and added: "I shall always be wherever you are! And as you are an inseparable part of your God, so I am an inseparable part of you! Should I call the children?" she asked.

"No!" he said.

And she knew his confidence had been restored to him, and his faith was firm, and he clearly knew what she knew with the same clarity, that God was with him.

As evening fell, the King's envoy arrived, a tall man of imposing appearance, in gold helmet and gold breastplate and accompanied by three guardsmen, armed from head to foot. And he called on him to accompany him at the King's command, as he stood accused of a serious offence – for which the punishment was death in the lions' pit.

He received the announcement with a natural ease and composure that baffled the envoy and his escorts in equal measure.

"Let's be on our way!" he said, bidding farewell to no one, and still wearing his domestic attire and footwear.

THE PIT OF LIONS

...A few days after Succoth he rode with his father along the twisting shepherds' paths on the approach to Ein-Gedi. The sun had just emerged from its sheath, and the limpid air sparkled with a lustre reflecting both tenderness and solemnity, and the light balm born aloft by the breeze filled the heart with the joy that is unique to Jerusalem and Judah, the joy of holiness.

The horses ambled along at an easy pace, making steady progress.

They passed by a grove of tall holm-oak trees, and far away they could hear the silky murmur of the bubbling streams of Ein-Gedi. And it was not long before they caught sight of the first houses of the village of Hephtzi-Bah, at the foot of the Jerusalem hills – white buildings winking at them through the trees.

Early-rising farmers greeted them with blessings as they drove their bleating sheep and goats from their pens.

They went down to the house of Eleazar Ben Berechiah, whose son served in his father's office, and found him sitting with his three young sons, two daughters, wife and mother-in-law, at the breakfast table.

They all rose to meet them, and the minister Naimel was quick to reassure them, saying they were on their way to the summit of Ein-Gedi, and Ephraim son of Eleazar was in good health, and if Eleazar had no objection – they would leave their horses in his stable.

The Berechiah family welcomed the visit, and above all were relieved to hear that their son Ephraim was well, and they gladly took it on themselves to guard the horses until their return.

They urged them to drink a cup of milk, fresh and bubbling still. His father knew that refusal would offend the family, and he accepted the offer. They sat at the table, pronounced the benediction and quaffed the milk which tasted sweet and light and was refreshing and invigorating. They took their leave of them and set out on foot, following the old and narrow goats' path, its imprint barely perceptible, climbing up through the tall holm-oaks, casting their shade on the solid ground. Soon the village disappeared behind them, and the silence of the young morning enveloped them again.

He had come to understand, even at ten years old, that his father would never take him anywhere or go out walking with him, unless the journey held some lesson for him, some intellectual exercise, which was invariably accompanied by a pleasant surprise. So he was expecting a surprise, and it was not slow in coming: as they walked along the downward path of the tall cliff, overlooking the Dead Sea, he made out on a broad plateau a kind of fawn-yellow mass, blending in well with its surroundings but somehow distinguished from it by some quality that at first he did not recognise. All at once, as they approached the yellowish mass, they realised it was something alive, and moving.

With measured pace they came closer, and then the surprise – that yellowish mass was nothing other than a lioness. And not far from the lioness crouched the lion.

He could not remember afterwards exactly what it was that made him feel no particular emotion other than that pleasant sense of surprise; was it the smooth, balmy morning with its easeful air and serene light – or was it the confidence that his father inspired in him, walking steadily by his side, without any change in facial expression or tone of voice?

He realised at once that his father's attitude to these large predators was exactly the same attitude that he showed to features of the landscape – a rock, a tree, a bush. And he followed his example. They drew closer to the lions until they, the two of them as one, were revealed in all their regal splendour: their firm, powerful bodies crouching without a hint of unease on the solid ground, the calm gaze of their eyes moving over their faces with a kind of casual indifference.

They came closer still, as his father drew his attention to the nimble flight of a pair of birds unknown to him, darting around them and chirruping melodiously.

"That's the wagtail!" Naimel told him, pointing.

And then the lioness rose and with slow, leisurely tread, her head held high, she approached them and rubbed against his father's thigh and then, with great caution, turned to nuzzle him, her head on a level with his head and her muscular back on a level with his shoulder. It was a pleasant sensation – and strangely gratifying. He remembered a hazy thought occurring to him – something about all living creatures blending into a higher symmetry, a symmetry that is all praise of the living God. And after the lioness came the lion, approaching them and following the example of his mate. And the two beasts did not leave them; on the contrary, they accompanied them on their way – the lioness to his right, and the lion to his father's left – their muscular, yellowish bodies undulating slightly as they walked, the mane of the lion swaying to the rhythm.

The lion tried to scratch his mane with his paw, but failing in the effort he approached his father and nudged him again, as if asking him for something. His father stood his ground, stooped and ruffled the majestic mane, probing until he found what he was looking for – two ticks deeply embedded in the skin of the animal. He removed them one after the other. A nudge of gratitude, and they were on their way again.

When they reached the summit of the rock the beasts stood their ground, and then took their leave of them with deep guttural growls, but muted – as if saying: "We have enjoyed your company, please visit us again!" All the same, he was glad to clutch his father's hand and feel its reassuring warmth.

"Lions," his father told him without releasing his hand, "are very special creatures. They can sense the spiritual being of a man and act accordingly. As a rule – the lion does not prey on mankind, but it will hunt down a coward and expend its wrath on the sinner and the fool, and it will kill a murderer. Sometimes, the kings of olden days used to throw to the lions men accused of crimes. If the charge was valid, the miscreant was eaten; if the man was innocent, the lions did him no harm. When the kingdom of God is established on the earth, lions will eat straw, as was prophesied by Isaiah Ben Amotz."

"And why do they hunt prey now?" he asked.

"Because mankind, in rejecting God, has exerted a malign influence on all living and growing things, inanimate things too. And the beast longs for the time when he shall eat straw, and prey no more."

"When will this time come?" he asked.

"When mankind is born anew!" – his father smiled, and his smile, inspiring confidence and igniting the spark of hope, made his heart beat faster. He let go of his father's hand and ran up the narrow path, leaping from rock to rock and skipping across a brook, like a young gazelle in the first flush of freedom.

His father caught up with him and so, at a run, they reached the springs of Ein-Gedi, washed in the foaming water and drank their fill, before returning to Hephtzi-Bah. They mounted their horses and rode the narrow paths, crossing familiar territory on the homeward journey.

O my father in Heaven, my God! Guide me in the ways of humility, and I shall sanctify your name as is fitting, and I shall delight in you at all times and always, and I shall not fear what flesh can do to me!

When he glanced at the face of the King, for a moment he was shocked by his appearance: the King had aged suddenly and looked like an old man dealt a mortal blow and knocked to the ground, falling – never to rise again. His cheeks were wrinkled and their normal rosy hue had changed to an earthen grey. His eyes were dim with weariness and his breathing was heavy. He wanted to reassure him, if only with a look, but had no opportunity to do so.

"You have disobeyed my commandments – you, my viceroy-designate!" The voice croaked, a sound so empty and so dry it seemed the very fabric of his lungs had decayed beyond repair. "And since you have left me no choice," Darius sighed – "I hereby command that you be thrown into the pit of the lions, and the God that you serve, may He protect you from their jaws!"

"Indeed," he had time to say, "my God shall surely save me!" And the quiet confidence that his words expressed shook all those present to the very fibres of their souls; they turned to stare at him in wonder, and in the eyes of his accusers, a sudden flash of fear was clearly visible.

So he was thrown into the lions' pit, and a great boulder was brought and laid against the entrance to the pit, and the King sealed it with his seal and the seal of his ministers, so it could not be moved without this being detected. And King Darius returned to his palace and fasted, and cancelled the courtly entertainments arranged for that evening, and he could not sleep and did not close his eyes all that night.

And before daybreak, the King rose from his bed weary and in a dejected mood, and he hastened to the pit, where the seal on the boulder was unbroken, and cried out in a quavering voice, almost without hope

"Daniel, servant of God, are you alive, Daniel? Could the God that you serve and in whom you trust save you from the jaws of the lions?"

The King's voice fell silent. He saw his loyal guardsmen standing by, ready to support him or carry out any orders he might give.

And then the voice was heard. And for a moment no one knew where it was coming from; they reckoned it was the wind that was deceiving them, mimicking a voice; a voice rising from afar, from the depths of the earth, but speaking with perfect clarity:

"Long live the King! The God whom I serve sent His angel to stop the mouths of the lions, for I have earned the favour of my God, and before you too, my lord the King, I have committed no offence, nor sinned in any way whatsoever!"

And suddenly the King's spirits were restored to him and he stood erect once more. And he called the men of his guard and ordered them to move the boulder from the mouth of the pit and lower a rope to Daniel, and they drew him up from the lions' pit, and not one of the beasts made any attempt to spring at him and all remained frozen where they stood, because an angel had stopped their mouths.

And there and then King Darius issued a hasty edict, and he sent the guards to fetch at once the twenty-one slanderers from the community of satraps and governors, and to throw them into the pit, with their children and their wives and all the members of their households. And before they had even touched the floor of the pit, the lions were upon them and ripping them to shreds.

And then the King summoned his scribes and his secretaries and dictated the following decree:

"To all peoples and nations of every language throughout the whole world, Greetings! It is my command that in all my royal domains, men shall fear and revere the God of Belteshazzar, who is the living and the everlasting God, whose kingdom shall never fail, nor his power come to an end. He is the saviour and deliverer and a worker of signs and wonders on the Earth below and in the Heavens above, who sent his angel to stop the mouths of the lions and saved Belteshazzar, known also as Daniel, his loyal servant, from their clutches."

And this Daniel prospered during the reigns of Darius and of Cyrus the Persian.

ZEDEKIAH

After the upheavals that affected the government of Darius the Mede in Babylon, his capital, the young Abiriuch was appointed to lead the one hundred and twenty satraps and governors, most if not all of whom had been replaced by new personnel – men loyal to the King who had not served in any capacity in the court of Belshazzar and had not been among his cronies.

No one was more pleased by this arrangement than young Abiriuch himself, working under the immediate supervision of Belteshazzar, the man he admired most of all, and reporting to him on affairs of state and on conditions in the outlying provinces and territories of the empire. Belteshazzar would then take his proposals to the King and confer with him; these audiences invariably concluded with the King agreeing to Belteshazzar's proposals and acting accordingly.

One day, when Abiriuch had finished reading to him from the scrolls in his hand, had heard his comments and noted them in red ink on the margins of the scrolls, and it was time for them to part company with the mutual benediction "May God light your way!" – Abiriuch remained seated and did not extend his hand in the usual fashion. The King's viceroy noticed this odd behaviour and looked up at him with a quizzical air. Abiriuch shifted uneasily in his chair, looked away, drummed lightly with his fingers on the table-top and finally ventured to say:

"In the King's prison, in the cellar, among the tanners and the cutters of parchment, there is a man whom Nebuchadnezzar brought back from the ruins of Jerusalem; he is blind and his hands and feet are chained, and I have been told that he is sick and his condition is serious – and his days are numbered. I thought this information might be of interest to the King's viceroy," Abiriuch explained and added: "The man's name is Zedekiah and so they say, he was the last King of Judah and lived in Jerusalem before it was sacked."

He thanked Abiriuch warmly, and confirmed that the information was indeed of great interest to him. As soon as the young man had gone on his way, he left his office and set out in search of the King.

He found Darius in the palace garden, tending his goldfish in the basin beneath the fountain. The King's face radiated goodwill and equanimity, his bright eyes sparkled with the innocence of a child, the grey hair that framed his big, round head set off the rosy glow of his forehead and cheeks, while his broad and red nose testified to a penchant for strong liquor.

"They multiply in this season!" the King exclaimed with enthusiasm, responding with a nod to the deep bow of his viceroy.

"The goldfish, I mean!" the King added, by way of clarification. "Theoretically, this isn't their breeding season, but I suppose if they are feeling contented and relaxed they get the urge to propagate, just as people do in those conditions!" It seemed that the unseasonable fecundity of his fish both intrigued and amused the monarch.

He responded to the King's smile with a smile of his own – typically warm and sincere. He felt a deep affection for King Darius, and knew that essentially he was a tolerant and amenable man, easily pleased. The image he projected, of a caring and attentive grandfather, distributing gifts with a generous hand, was more in keeping with his personality than the traditional regal epithets of "warrior" and "conqueror". Darius returned his affection in like measure, secretly admiring him and openly trusting him.

Now he waited to be asked why he had sought this unscheduled audience, and after a few more comments regarding the eccentric habits and exquisite pedigree of his goldfish – to say nothing of their astounding beauty – Darius turned to him again with that attentive, avuncular smile:

"What urgent business brings you here?"

"Long live the King!" he began, knowing this was a salutation guaranteed to reassure Darius, who was becoming increasingly conscious of his age. "In the prison, in the cellar, among the tanners and the leather cutters, a man is confined in chains. He was blinded by order of King Nebuchadnezzar, and he was the last of the royal line of the Jews, King Zedekiah!"

"Ah!" exclaimed Darius, making no effort to remove the jovial smile from his face – "Zedekiah the rebel! He who brought down ruin upon his land and disaster upon his people! How is he faring?" he was curious to know.

"He is sick, and his sickness is mortal. I ask the King's permission to take him into my house, so he may know a little ease before he returns his soul to his Maker!"

"You really want to do this, ease the suffering of a rebel who did not listen to the voice of God, warning him of disaster? You Jews have more than your fair share of holy men, prophets and seers and saints – it's kings that you're short of! With most nations, the opposite is the case. The question is, which is preferable? And to this question – there is no answer!" the King declared with undiminished good humour. "As for that wretch who has fallen ill, if his condition is indeed terminal, then by all means take him into your house and make his last days comfortable. He might yet find it in himself to repent and express some regret over his blunders, some remorse for the calamity which he brought down upon his compatriots. May your God go with you!"

He bowed again, and withdrew. Accompanied by two armed guards, he made his way to the dungeon.

The former king he found sprawled on a threadbare mat, on the coarse stone floor of the prison. At first sight it seemed he was dying. The hair of his head and his beard had turned completely white, but looked dirty and ragged – there was nothing venerable about it, nor any dignity in his general air of decrepitude. His cheeks and his narrow, domed forehead were lined with deep furrows.

"By your leave, my lord King Zedekiah!" – he addressed him in Hebrew, and saw the tremor of surprise that set the lean and wasted body quivering beneath the ragged, stained robe. "From this day forward, I shall be honoured to serve as your host, in my home which is not far from here. And I extend this offer with the explicit permission of King Darius."

"Who... who are you... Sir?" His voice resembled the sound of water, bubbling in a cracked gutter-pipe.

"I am Daniel, whose Chaldean name is Belteshazzar. I was exiled to Babylon in the days of King Jehoiakim."

"Aha!" the prematurely aged man remembered, sitting up on the mat with a perceptible effort, and gasping with the strain of speech: "Daniel...Belteshazzar... I know you! The former right-hand man of King Nebuchadnezzar who did nothing to save his land or deliver Jerusalem, the holy city! But you, Daniel... or Belteshazzar... don't misunderstand me! I'm not blaming you!" And in the same breath he went on to say: "You have every right to castigate me for the error of my ways, and my failure to heed the warnings of Jeremiah, the words of the living God." Zedekiah seemed on the point of collapse, but he recovered sufficiently to say:

"Now... it is your pleasure to invite me into your home. I shall not resist! Even if I were minded to resist – I don't have the strength... Blindness, and confinement in this damp dungeon have taken their toll..."

"I must beg your pardon, King Zedekiah, for having forgotten your very existence. I am ashamed of this, and I ask you to forgive me!"

"But Daniel, my lord and master, viceroy to King Darius, even if you had remembered me, you could not have helped me! Nebuchadnezzar would not have changed his mind. Nebuchadnezzar was a king, a king to his fingertips, a king and only a king. I knew him well! He it was who gave me my throne, he who crowned me a king, and he who had me swear in the name of my own God to keep faith with him, and he who slaughtered before my eyes all the members of my family, everyone who was dear to me, and it was he who gouged out these eyes of mine and threw me into this prison, so I could relive in my mind all my foolish deeds and torment myself to distraction over the fate of my people and my family and my own fate. Nebuchadnezzar was not the flexible type; once he had made up his mind, there was no shifting him. And Belshazzar? Ah – Belshazzar!" – a kind of smile twisted the blind man's bluish lips – "He was no friend to you, Daniel, wise counsellor that you are, knowing secrets, seeing visions, interpreting dreams by the grace of God – I heard of Belshazzar and of his scheming against you, and I was glad! I said to myself, even this man of God is not immune from punishment. Well, he deserves it! And I expected Belshazzar to go further, and throw you out of his palace, perhaps even banish you to the fever-ridden swamps of the southern provinces. Or he might chain you, as I was chained, and throw you into the dungeons.

"I enjoyed these thoughts, and I wasn't ashamed of them and unlike you, I ask no forgiveness for them... they were the only consolation that I had, in my agony of body and mind, my utterly hopeless state. Anyway, pleading with Belshazzar on my behalf wouldn't have got you anywhere, it certainly wouldn't have released me from this furnace!

"So, that leaves Darius. Old Darius was much impressed by the miracle of the lions' pit. It was the talk of the day among the slaves and artisans of the prison, a miracle guaranteed to impress the pagans, and I have to admit, it impressed me too – to the depths of my soul. And I was filled with pride: to think that a son of my race, an alien and an outsider, considered no better than sub-human no matter how many distinctions are awarded him - had proved his courage and his strength of spirit! And most important of all – he had proved that God loves him, and loves his people too, this race renowned for its stubbornness but also for its faith and its prophets and its visionaries. I was proud of you! And here, in the prison, I again enjoyed some prestige on your account. I say again, because the same thing happened in the time of Nebuchadnezzar, with the episode of your three friends in the blazing furnace. Before that they had despised and reviled and humiliated me, and sometimes I was punched or kicked, or robbed of the scraps of food that some charitable soul had put into my hand. The slaves here are insolent and disrespectful, and there's no limit to their cruelty to anyone who has fallen from grace, descending from the heights to the depths. And that was the way I was treated, until the miracle of the furnace. Then I was shown nothing but deference and respect – for a whole month. The truth is, they were afraid of me, as one belonging to that race whose God can save his servants from the flames of the furnace. But as is usually the way with reverence that is based on fear, this was soon forgotten and they reverted to their former ways – assault and abuse and contempt – until along came your miracle of the lions, sparing you but ripping your adversaries to shreds. This time I had lower expectations, not trusting the slaves and bondswomen here, having seen their volatile nature. But the miracle in itself impressed me, and as I have said – I was proud of you! And I must confess to some remorse for the pleasure that I felt when Belshazzar, the foolish King, attacked you and undermined your status..."

"But I still feel it is I who owes you an apology," he interrupted him, "I am at fault, having forgotten you!"

"Well, you have my forgiveness, although I don't see your forgetting as any kind of a sin! On the contrary, my blindness and all the things inflicted on me, the cruelty and the torture – have helped me greatly. I tell you, Daniel my friend, if a different fate had been allotted to me, and after all that my eyes had witnessed, I had been given a comfortable home and attended by servants, looking upon the world with the same eyes that saw the murder of my sons and daughters – I would have put out these eyes myself! Nebuchadnezzar was a wise king, wise and valiant as they called him, and rightly so. He granted my last request, although I never put it to him, and he showed me mercy – as the valiant and the wise are always capable of showing mercy! In his mercy and his wisdom, and his courage – King Nebuchadnezzar enabled me to live out a life that I was capable of enduring, without losing my mind and without taking my own life – either because of what I had done, or because of what my eyes had seen. Ah, how considerate to me was Nebuchadnezzar! I was grateful to him. Yes, deep in my heart, I was grateful. From that day to this, and all days that are yet to come! My own days are numbered, and I know this and I'm glad of it. For these few remaining days of mine I shall take up your offer and accept the hospitality of your house, lie in a bed and eat food other than the scraps left over by slaves. And these shackles – would you be so kind as to have them removed?"

He ordered the guardsmen to remove the shackles and they picked up the prisoner and carried him to the anvil in the prison yard, where the smith detached the chains with a few deft blows of the hammer and discarded them.

Zedekiah's lean body was washed, the bruises inflicted on him by the shackles were soothed with wine and anointed with oil, his hair and his beard were combed and he was dressed in a blue robe – the colour that promotes health and conveys the blessing of the angels – and a cloak, also of blue, though this was something he was unlikely to need.

The blind king was too weak to stand on his feet, and food was brought to him in his bed. But in spite of the many delicious meals offered to him, Zedekiah ate very little, and even the light young wine, from the verdant vineyards of Jahanur, was not to his taste. His body seethed with fever and yet, on the skin of his cheeks, drawn taut over the bones of the skull, there was a strange smirk of satisfaction and bitter disdain. The smirk did not extend to the blind holes of his eyes, which resembled open graves.

Whether on account of his fever, or on account of a longing repressed for so many years, Zedekiah talked, and talked like a raging torrent, not caring whether his words were heeded or not. In fact, the whole family, Nejeen, his sons and he, sat in a half-circle around Zedekiah and listened to his impassioned words:

"I know you are a miracle worker, and God pays heed to you and answers your prayers, and you have cured people who were beyond the help of other mortals. I have been told it all! And my plea to you is this, and remember it well and comply with it. Do not pray to your God on my behalf! Don't ask Him to grant me pardon and compassion and love and health and long life. Not only because, as you know so well, I am the last man on earth to be worthy of the grace of God, or His mercy or His love, but also and most of all – because I have no wish to add further days to the span of my life! To put it as plainly as I can – I don't want to go on living! On the contrary, I long with all my heart and soul, my spirit and my mind, to be gathered, and soon, to my people and to my ancestors. If indeed," – and again the strange smirk flickered on the lips of the speaking skull that was Zedekiah – "they are willing to accept me in their company. There is hope in my heart that they will indeed accept me; Jeremiah said quite plainly that I would be buried amid the tombs of my fathers, and nothing said by Jeremiah is to be taken lightly! It was God who spoke through him, again and again. And I listened and I believed, but I did not have the strength to resist my ministers!"

Zedekiah was silent for a while, then bowed his head and declared in a changed voice:

"Now I am adding sin to my sin and folly to my folly! I was quite capable of imposing my will on my ministers, but I chose not to do so. I acted with cunning. I incited others to stand before me and urge me to spurn Jeremiah and ignore his words. To the last moment of their lives they thought I had been incited by them, and it never occurred to them that the opposite was the case.

"Jeremiah was warning me of the folly of my ambitions, even before I became King. And at the very moment that I swore allegiance to Nebuchadnezzar, I knew that I was going to break this vow; I had no intention of keeping faith!

"I always yearned with a yearning stronger than Hell itself to acquire praise and respect, to be a King, and not just of a small country that is all obsessed with a worn-out, antiquated faith, that the world derides and ridicules, but to rule over many lands, over half the world, the whole world! This was my ambition, and I longed for it so much that it hurt, I was going out of my mind! And God, who reads minds and looks into hearts, was quick to send me His holy prophet, to warn me against the effects of my lunacy while there was still time. And then it occurred to me I could get the better of Jeremiah, and of the one who sent him! What stupidity!" – the narrator chuckled, a hollow, bitter sound – "Any man of the meanest intelligence would realise that this is the shortest route to the edge of the abyss, to the torments of Hell – and only I, the young and the ambitious, could see no further than the end of my nose, or see where my insanity would lead me, or more precisely – I closed my eyes and refused to open them. God, like a father loving his rebellious and unruly son, never tired of making His voice heard to me, with promises – and with warnings of the dangers awaiting me. Such was my folly, I rejected them all! I longed to wallow in silver and gold, and all the riches of the world. In my mind's eye I saw my palace soaring into the Heavens, its walls of pure gold, its roof of ivory and silver, and its pinnacles sparkling with precious stones. I saw myself dressed in crimson and purple, accompanied by liveried escorts, mounting my high throne, and the rulers of all peoples and nations prostrating themselves at my feet and kissing the floor, and the crowd bowing before me and extolling my name and crying out with one voice: 'Long live the great King, the King of Kings of Kings, the divine Zedekiah!' All this I was seeing at night in my bed, and sometimes when I was awake, walking in my garden. And I had no rest, I was forever conspiring, and inciting with guile disguised as innocence everyone who could be incited, meaning – everyone! And to the very last moment I believed that my luck would change, and all would turn out in the way that I wanted, and my dream take on skin and sinew and become reality. I was like a sleepwalker!

"And God thought otherwise, and I was unable to make Him my ally!" He breathed heavily, gargling sounds emerging from his throat and spittle glistening on his thin lips – pink spittle that did not augur well.

"Perhaps your honour would like to rest a while?" Nejeen suggested with urgent tenderness, trying, with some success, not to reveal the pain and compassion which this man aroused in her heart.

"A few hours from now, rest will be all that's left to me!" Zedekiah snorted again, chuckled faintly and suddenly turned his skull to face them, fixed on them the blank stare of his empty eye-sockets and cried anxiously:

"Will you fulfil the prophecy of the holy Jeremiah and send my body to Jerusalem, for interment in the burial ground of my ancestors?" His voice betrayed tension and agitation of mind, which he made no attempt to conceal from his hearers.

"It will be done!" he assured him calmly, in a steady voice, a tone to inspire confidence.

Zedekiah made a sound that could have been interpreted as a sigh of relief, and went on to say, but at a slower pace and without the same ardour, almost as if he was beginning to relax:

"All that has befallen me I brought upon myself, with my own hands! You may not believe this, but it's a fact: even being blind and after all my tribulations and the disaster that I brought upon my people – I still cherished ambitions. I thought to myself that even a blind ruler could still be a ruler, capable of earning respect and esteem, and enjoying all the worldly pleasures that he desires. A blind ruler, indeed!" Again he chuckled, but with mounting bitterness. "When Nebuchadnezzar died it seemed to me someone might yet call upon my services, someone would attack Babylon and conquer it, and then come to me, in this stinking dungeon, unfasten my fetters and restore to me my former glory! What a fool I was, an incorrigible fool! Even the death of Belshazzar gave me reason to hope! And only lately have I begun to perceive the unbearable darkness of my soul. And I have woken up to the simple truth, that the one who abandons his God and leaves Him far behind is nothing other than a creature deranged! And so I was – until the death of Belshazzar. It was then that I began to retreat and to recoil in disgust – from myself! Could this be a sign, a portent of God's willingness to forgive me for my mistakes, my folly and my grievous sins?"

The speaking skull turned slowly towards him, with a strange urgency, the holes of his dead eyes fixed on him. And he answered him:

"God does not hide his face from those who return to him with full repentance!"

"Perhaps I have repented," Zedekiah mumbled hesitantly, as if probing the recesses of his soul – "but I'm not sure that it's full repentance! This is a wearisome question which will be answered for me in the full glare of truth a few hours from now, when I leave this world to go to the next!"

Zedekiah stretched out on the soft mattress, stuffed with sweetly smelling dried flowers, and said no more. The silence lengthened and one of the sons made a move as if meaning to leave, thinking the invalid was asleep, but he was mistaken.

"Please be so good," Zedekiah spoke in a hollow voice, but not lacking in force, "as to be patient a little longer, and sit beside me until I give my soul to my Maker. I want to say what I have to say to the end, and confess it in full. And this in the hope that saying it will help me in some way when I step beyond this," – he tilted his head upward – "and I'm still not sure that it has all been said. And even if it has all been said, I would not want to be left alone in this my last hour, and if you are doing all this in a dutiful spirit, I can assure you that I won't be trying your patience for much longer!"

"You have no reason to worry on that account, King Zedekiah!" he told him. "We shall sit here, all of us, all the family, my wife and my sons, for as long as this is what you want."

And after a long silence, broken by Zedekiah's heavy breathing and loud, irregular gurgles, he addressed his host again:

"People are incapable of truly appreciating what has been put into their hands. If they could do this, most conflicts could be avoided. And this is because their faith is not true faith, and deep down they are hypocrites and sceptics!

"I used to consult God before every action that I was contemplating, and I complied with His word – so long as it suited my convenience, and accorded with my aspirations. And it was necessary for me to experience all the horrors of a lost war, the failed attempt to flee from Nebuchadnezzar's soldiers, the humiliation of capture, being forced to watch the execution of all my household and then endure the gouging of my eyes, the binding in chains and the casting into the dungeon, to crawl between the legs of slaves in search of a crust of bread or a sip of water – it took all this to make me understand the simple truth and know myself for a fantasist and a hypocrite, a coward and a traitor! And I give thanks for this. This truth is worth all my afflictions, and no price is too high to pay for it!"

A dry, persistent cough interrupted his speech. Again he sat up on the bed, in a desperate effort to control the coughing, but without success. There was a blue tinge to his face, and an ooze of blood glinted at the corner of his mouth and trickled down his chin. For a brief moment Zedekiah was silent, as the coughing seemed to abate. And he cried out in a hoarse voice, low but quite clear:

"May He be blessed and magnified, praised and glorified, the God who is love!"

And his head sank forward on his chest, and he was no longer in the land of the living.

As he had promised, he sent the body of Zedekiah to Jerusalem in a special cortege and there, so it was reported, he was buried in the graveyard of the Kings of Judah, in a modest ceremony attended by few.

"May his memory be blessed!" he replied when asked about him, and with this the episode was ended and the circle closed.

KING DARIUS

King Darius fell ill and took to his bed. And all the physicians of Babylon, men whose renown was spread throughout the kingdom and even beyond its borders, were summoned to attend him. And the physicians pontificated and inquired, and examined the King. Some said it was the King's liver that was ailing, some said it was his heart, while others were convinced that the problem was with his bowels. There were even those who declared that the King's heart, bowels and liver were all in a parlous state; this on account of the monarch's style of living and the fact, which could not be denied, that he was no longer a young man.

So the famed luminaries of Babylonian medicine gave the King herbal treatments and also prescribed incantations and charms, and recommended special diets. The King did all that required of him, taking the medications and bathing in cold water, and eating raw pigeon-meat and the flesh of young crocodiles, put on amulets and listened to incantations, and stood in the sun, and practised physical exercises. Instead of easing his physical symptoms and improving his state of mind, these remedies only made his sickness worse. And the King dispersed the quacks forthwith and expelled them from his palace and paid no more heed to their advice and threw away their medications, and called upon the wizards and the necromancers. And they worked their spells and brought in dancers costumed as monsters who danced before the King for hours on end in an effort to exorcise his demons, and they taught him special prayers which he should say, and all of to no avail. And the King sank into black depression, for long days and nights.

Meanwhile, Cyrus, King of Persia, went to war against Babylon, and crossed its frontiers and invaded the outlying provinces, storming remote outposts. And the mighty army of Cyrus the Persian marched on the Chaldean capital, Babylon, greatest of all the world's fortified cities. And the King's counsellors did not know how to break the news to him, and he heard them whispering among themselves beside his sick-bed, thinking him asleep. And he opened his eyes, and demanded to know what was being talking about and why they were so anxious. And when the counsellors hesitated to reply, he insisted that he was not to be deceived; they were to tell him everything that they knew and conceal nothing from him.

And the chief minister approached the King, bowed low and informed him that Cyrus, King of Persia, was intent on conquering Babylon and was advancing with a great army to lay siege to it.

For a moment an ugly cloud passed over the face of Darius and he looked utterly dismayed, but the next moment he brightened and ordered his ministers and senior counsellors to go and fetch Belteshazzar, otherwise known as Daniel, the King's viceroy, as he wanted to talk with him privately. The ministers complied with the King's demand, bowed to the invalid one after the other and left his bed-chamber, and sent word to Daniel, summoning him to a confidential audience with the King.

So Daniel left all his other work and went in haste to the King's bedchamber. Sick though Darius was, he showed no symptoms of pain or fever; on the contrary, he was smiling and evidently on the way to recovery.

"Belteshazzar my friend!" the King began – "Until this day I have refrained from bothering you with this infirmity of mine, but in this critical state of affairs, with Cyrus the Persian, a truly astute and courageous King, advancing towards my capital city and intent upon attacking it, I am left with no choice other than to consult you regarding this affliction which is draining my energies and plunging me into gloom. What must I do to be rid of this disease, so I can rise from my bed and stand at the head of my troops and offer Cyrus some stiff resistance?"

And Daniel bowed at the King's feet and answered him:

"Long live His Majesty! I can tell the King a way whereby he may put an end to this malady and be cured of his sickness, so he may stand firm on his feet and resist the army of King Cyrus – and it is the way of modesty, fear of God and utter humility."

"What are you talking about?" Darius asked gruffly, some tension showing in his face which had lost its rosy hue and turned grey, his eyes sunk deep in their sockets. His viceroy proceeded to explain:

"The style of life to which Your Majesty is accustomed is to be abandoned once and for all. You must abstain from indulging in wine, meat and women! Eat vegetables and a little bread, and drink only fresh water or honey-water, and there should be no more dalliance with women for as long as you live. And your strength will be restored to you and you shall again be a stalwart King, your natural vigour unabated, and on the face of all this earth there will no enemy who is a match for King Darius!"

For a moment the King froze, his mouth agape and his eyes open wide in bemusement, but then he recovered himself and laughed, lying back on the bed.

"Why should I live a life without wine, meat and women?"

"For God's sake, and to do His will."

The King gave him a long and quizzical look, then sighed and said solemnly:

"I understand, these are the words of the living God that you are speaking, though personally I would prefer a short life and a few days on the earth to abstinence from meat, wine and women! Be blessed, Belteshazzar, and be assured – I have always seen you as my friend!"

A few days later he heard that the King had recovered and risen from his bed and was tirelessly training for the forthcoming battle, practising his swordsmanship and spear-throwing, and even shooting arrows with bows of horn and cherry-wood.

Meanwhile, Cyrus the Persian arrived at the head of his army before the lofty walls of Babylon and set his siege. Persian troops surrounded the perimeter in a dense cordon, blocking the supply of provisions to the greatest city in the world, allowing no one to enter or leave.

King Darius laughed on hearing news of the siege and he said in the War Council that Cyrus would need a great deal of patience and self-control, since in Babylon, the fortified capital, there were stocks of food sufficient to feed the population for five years at least. If King Cyrus were indeed as astute as he was reputed to be, and dauntless too, then he would know which was the correct and the logical course of action, and mount a massive frontal assault designed to storm the walls, in which case he, King Darius, could promise Cyrus the Great – a solemn promise of one King to another – a surprise which would not be at all to his taste.

But matters evolved according to patterns hidden from the eyes of mere mortals, and did not accord with the King's expectations. Cyrus the Persian proved he was indeed astute, and a peerless master of stratagems too. The unpleasant surprise, of which King Darius spoke, took on skin and sinew and became a reality, and yet the one surprised was not Cyrus the Persian but Darius the Mede.

One morning, on a day of searing heat, the citizens of Babylon rose and were astonished to find that there was no water in their wells. All their sources of water had dried up overnight.

Anxious and tense, Babylonians began gathering in groups, angrily demanding to be told what was happening. In a move that was quite unpremeditated, the thirst-stricken populace converged on the royal palace and milled about the gates, with only a handful of trusty guardsmen to keep them at bay.

When the news reached the King, he convened a meeting of the War Council and ordered an investigation. It soon became clear that Cyrus had done something which no one could have foreseen – he had diverted the course of the Euphrates, thus drying up all the water-sources of Babylon. And while this information had a devastating effect on the army commanders present at the meeting, it did nothing to detract from the equanimity and the vigour of the King; for some obscure reason, he seemed positively delighted.

"Our friend Cyrus is challenging us to leave the safety of our defensive walls and confront him on the battlefield, face to face. As he is leaving us no other option, let us gladly accept his invitation and go out to meet him in the open, where we shall harry him with our sharpened arrows and fend off his arrows with our shields, hurl our long lances, draw our burnished swords and hack his soldiers down. To the colours!" cried Darius, and for the first time since he was taken ill the healthy, ruddy colour was fully restored to his grey, wrinkled cheeks.

They dressed the King in his armour, hung a knight's sword at his waist, put a long Chaldean lance in his right hand and a gold shield in his left. He was mounted on a powerful horse, sleek and adorned with gaudy trappings. And so King Darius the Mede rode out from his palace, followed by the royal horse guards and the sovereign's escort, gold shields sparkling in the sunlight and the blades of their drawn swords dazzling.

The crowd, seeing the King in his resplendent armour, forgot its anger and was fired with enthusiasm, uttering ear-splitting cries of "Long live the King!" and "Praise and glory to our King!" and "Victory to the mighty Darius!"

His personal contingent reinforced by two extra brigades of cavalry, and his infantry held in reserve, the King ordered that the great Shamash Gate be opened before him and he rode out of Babylon to confront his enemy.

The King lost no time in charging at one of the advance units of Cyrus' army, inflicting a decisive defeat and setting out in pursuit. And then, as he raised his heavy sword with a mighty flourish, he suddenly reeled in the saddle, as if he was losing consciousness, and he collapsed and fell at his horse's feet, his gold shield lost, lance broken and helmet dented. The officers following closely behind him reined in their mounts and hurried to help their King as he sprawled on the ground, closing around him in a tight circle and stripping off his armour.

"I always hoped I would die on the battlefield!" King Darius wheezed, gasping for breath. "God has answered my prayer! Cyrus – he was slow, too slow. He missed his chance to stick an arrow in me, not even one single arrow..." The exhausted King gulped air into his lungs and cried: "He is your King now!" And saying this he breathed his last, as a broad smile spread across his face, the cheerful expression, so characteristic of him in days gone by, restored in full.

Babylon capitulated to King Cyrus without further bloodshed. And the new King held a lavish funeral for his predecessor, a royal funeral in every sense, conducted with reverence and solemnity. The citizens of Babylon, attending the ceremony en masse, appreciated this generous gesture on the part of Cyrus and felt reassured.

And so a new era began, the reign of Cyrus, that shrewd and courageous King, far-sighted and resourceful, doing everything in his power to ease the lives of his subjects, by the grace and with the blessing of God.

THE WISE, AND THE TEACHERS OF RIGHTEOUSNESS

He knew that during the reign of Cyrus the Persian there would come to an end the seventy years of exile decreed upon his people, as it had been prophesied by Jeremiah in the name of the Lord.

The Jews of the exile, and likewise those Jews of the old community who had studied the passage of time and noted the signs, knew that the period of exile was drawing to a close, and they would soon be returning to Judah and to Jerusalem, where the glories of the past were to be restored. And deep down in their hearts they also knew that so long as they failed to respect and observe the commandments of the Torah, this was not going to happen. And he was witness to a remarkable phenomenon – the rebirth of a people and the renewal of a nation. Fathers taught their children to serve and to love God, and furnished them with a living example. And children gladly followed in their fathers' footsteps, suppressing their baser instincts, eschewing pride, and maintaining high standards of honesty and integrity in commerce and in employment.

At the Sabbath Eve prayer, in the new and spacious synagogue of the exiled community, built not far from the Shamash Gate, he recognised among the worshippers a white haired man, the friend of Uziel and Gabriel. When the prayer was finished and the congregation dispersed, he approached him and asked of them. And he answered him willingly and thoroughly:

"The two of them went down to the islands of the north. They never really settled down in these parts; they didn't marry either, and bachelors are not well regarded in Babylon. They did make efforts to marry but there was always something unsatisfactory – an unattractive bride, awkward prospective in-laws, insufficient dowry – or they themselves failed to impress. So they never married, or were even seriously betrothed. Nor was it easy for them to uphold the commandments which the whole of the community, with the exception of a small minority, is happy to observe. Finally, that small minority decided, with one accord, to go down to the islands of the northern seas and no longer be numbered among their people, the Jewish people. They asserted that accident of birth is not the arbiter of destiny, but it is the inclination of the heart that tells a man where to go and with whom to associate. They were told it is not enough to want to belong to any particular race; you have to consider how willing that race will be to admit and accept you into its midst. Although proximity of blood is no guarantee of harmony and unanimity, the course of action that they were proposing would turn them into aliens among all the nations, a strange plant in whichever race they chose to belong to, and they would be spurned.

"But they refused to listen to any advice, gathered together a few possessions and set out in a northerly direction. And before they went, Uziel turned to me and with these ears of mine I heard him say these words:

'Whether the nations of the world accept us or revile us, it makes no difference, for better or for worse, to me and to my fellow-travellers, since our own people do not want us and have spewed us out!' Then he turned and went to join that group of renegades from Israel and Judah, and set out for the north."

At about this time he recorded, at Nejeen's suggestion, a dream that had been revealed to him, and this was the text that he wrote:

And I saw in a dream that I was by the river Ulai. I looked up and there I saw a ram with two horns standing between me and the stream. The two horns were long, the one longer than the other, growing up behind. I watched the ram butting west and north and south. No beasts could stand before it, no one could rescue from its power. It did as it pleased, making display of its strength. While I pondered this, suddenly a he-goat came from the west skimming over the whole earth without touching the ground; it had a prominent horn between its eyes. It approached the two-horned ram that I had seen standing between me and the stream and rushed at it with impetuous force. I saw it advance on the ram, working itself into a fury, then strike the ram and break both its horns; the ram had no strength to resist. The he-goat flung it to the ground and trampled on it, and there was no one to save the ram.

Then the he-goat made a great display of its strength. Powerful as it was, its great horn snapped and in its place there sprang forth towards the four quarters of heaven four prominent horns. Out of one of them there issued one small horn, which made a prodigious show of strength west and east and towards the fairest of all lands. It aspired to be as high as the host of heaven, and it cast down to the earth some of the host and some of the stars and trod them underfoot. It aspired to be as great as the prince of the host, suppressed his regular offerings and even threw down his sanctuary. The heavenly hosts were delivered up, and it raised itself impiously against the regular offerings and threw truth to the ground. In all that it did it succeeded. I heard a holy one speaking and another holy one answering him, whoever he was. The one said, How long will the period of this vision last, and how long will iniquity bring desolation and the holy place be trodden down? And the answer came: For two thousand three hundred evenings and mornings, and then the holy place shall emerge triumphant.

As I, Daniel, was seeing this vision I was trying to understand it. Suddenly I saw standing before me one with the semblance of a man; at the same time I heard a human voice calling to him across the bend of the Ulai: Gabriel, explain this vision to this man. And I sensed his look of friendship and fellowship, so familiar to me, but I could not remember from where and from when. He came to me where I was standing, and I was alarmed and fell prostrate, but he said to me: Understand, O man, the vision points to the time of the end. When he spoke to me I fell to the ground in a trance, but he grasped me and made me stand up where I was. And he said: I shall make known to you what is to happen when the wrath is ended, for this is an end to the appointed time. The two-horned ram that you saw signifies the kings of Media and Persia, the he-goat is the kingdom of the Greeks, and the great horn between his eyes is the first king. As for the horn which was snapped off and replaced by four others – four nations shall rise out of that nation, but not with power comparable to his.

In the last days of those kingdoms, when their sin is at its height, a king shall appear, bold and a master of stratagem. His power shall be great and he shall wreak havoc and shall succeed in everything he does and bring destruction upon great nations and a holy people. With his keen intelligence he shall succeed in his crafty designs. He shall devise great plans and when they are at their ease bring destruction upon many and challenge even the Prince of princes, and he shall be broken but not by human hand. And the revelation which has been given of the evenings and the mornings is true, but you must keep the vision secret, for it points to days far ahead. And as for me, Daniel, my strength failed and I lay sick for a while, then I arose and attended to the king's business, but I was perplexed by the vision and could not understand it.

He collapsed and needed some days to recuperate. And as he lay on his bed of sickness, given to contemplation, he asked himself again and again, what future had been decreed for his people. And the question disturbed his rest and nagged at him without respite. None of the visions that appeared to him was capable of answering it or resolving it. And then as he began to overcome his weakness and recover from his infirmity, and friends and relatives were coming to wish him well, he imposed a strict fast upon himself.

He fasted for twenty-one days, and when the fast was done, turned to his Father in Heaven, to his God, and prayed to Him from a broken heart, begging most fervently for the forgiveness of his people, despite all their mistakes. He asked that they be purified in faith and strengthened in piety, human as they were and of volatile temperament, and not to be trusted; as the prophet said, *Cursed is the man who trusts in man, and Blessed is the man who trusts in God.*

When his prayers were concluded, he was visited by another dream, which he recounted in these words:

On the twenty-first day of the first month, I found myself on the bank of the great river, that is the Tigris. I looked up and saw a man clothed in linen with a belt of pure gold around his waist. His body gleamed like topaz, his face shone like lightning, his eyes flamed like torches, his arms and feet sparkled like a disc of bronze, and when he spoke his voice was like the voice of a multitude.

I, Daniel, alone saw the vision, while those who were near me did not see it, but great fear fell upon them and they stole away, and I was left alone gazing at this great vision, but my strength left me and all my energy was gone. I heard the sound of his words and when I did so, I fell prone on the ground in a trance. Suddenly a hand touched me and pulled me up on to my hands and knees. He said to me: Daniel, man much loved, attend to the words that I am speaking to you, and stand up where you are, for I am now sent to you! When he addressed me I stood up trembling, and again I sensed that gentle look of friendship and fellowship, so familiar to me, though I could not say from where and from when, and he said to me: Do not fear, Daniel, for from the first day that you applied your mind to understanding and humbled yourself before your God, your prayers have been answered and I have come in answer to them. And the prince of the kingdom of Persia resisted me for twenty-one days, and then Michael, one of the chief princes, came to help me and I remained there with the kings of Persia. And I have come to explain to you what will happen to your people in days to come for this too is a vision for those days. And when he spoke these words to me I hung my head and was struck dumb. Suddenly one like a man touched my lips, and I opened my mouth and addressed him as he stood before me: Master, this vision has left me at a loss and I have no strength left. How can my master's servant presume to speak with my master, since my strength has failed me and no breath is left in me? Then the figure touched me again and restored my strength. He said: Do not be afraid, man much loved, peace be with you, be strong, be strong! When he spoke to me I recovered my strength and I said: Speak master, for you have made me strong! And he said: Do you know why I have come to you? I must now go back to fight with the princes of Persia, and as soon as I have left, then the prince of Greece will appear. But I shall tell you what is written in the book of truth, and I have no ally at my side other than Michael, your prince!

And the man told me all that lay in store for my people, and for all other peoples in the world, a bitter fate indeed, with no chance of escape and only the faintest of hopes – depending on repentance, true penitence and absolute piety.

Oh, my Father in Heaven and my God, you know that whenever this people of yours has repented, and put on sackcloth and fasted and bemoaned its sin – it has withdrawn its repentance the very next day, and neither it nor its sincerity are to be trusted – unless you bring this people back, so that it never again falls by the wayside or turns away from you, bringing upon itself affliction after affliction, disaster after disaster and wreck and ruin! Bring us back and we shall return, O Lord our God, our beloved Father and King, as you spoke by the mouth of your faithful servant Jeremiah, the man of Anathoth:

The time is coming, says the Lord, when I will make a new covenant with Israel and Judah. It will not be like the covenant I made with their forefathers when I took them by the hand and led them out of Egypt. Although they broke my covenant, I was patient with them, says the Lord. But this is the covenant which I will make with Israel after those days, says the Lord, I will set my law within them and write it on their hearts, and I will become their God and they shall become my people. No longer need they teach one another to know the Lord, for all of them shall know me, high and low alike, says the Lord, for I will forgive their wrongdoing and remember their sin no more.

And the speaker went on to say:

At that moment Michael shall appear, Michael the great captain who stands guard over your fellow-countrymen, and there will be a time of distress such as there has never been since they became a nation till that moment. But at that moment your people shall be delivered, every one who is written in the book. And many of those who sleep in the dust of the earth will wake, some to everlasting life and some to everlasting reproach.

And the wise shall shine like the bright vault of heaven, and those who have taught righteousness to many shall be like the stars for ever and ever. And you Daniel, keep the words secret and seal the book until it is time for the end. Many shall run hither and thither and knowledge shall be increased!

And I, Daniel, looked and saw two others standing, one on the bank of the river and the other on the opposite bank. And one said to the man clothed in linen who was above the waters of the river, How long until these portents cease? And he lifted to heaven his right hand and his left and swore by him who lives for ever: It shall be for a time, times and a half, and when the holy people ceases to be dispersed all these things will come to an end. I heard but I did not understand and I said, Master, what will be the end of these things? And he said, Go your way, Daniel, for the words are secret and sealed until the time of the end. Many shall be purified and refined, but the wicked shall continue in wickedness and will not understand, but the wise shall understand. From the time that the daily offering is cancelled, and the abomination that is all desolation, there shall be an interval of one thousand two hundred and ninety days. Happy is the man who waits and lives to see the completion of one thousand, three hundred and thirty-five days. But go your way to the end and rest, and you shall arise to your destiny at the end of the age!"

And he wrote everything down as he was commanded, but weakness overtook him again and he collapsed on his bed. This was not a mortal sickness, but both heart and flesh were wracked with pain.

Nejeen sat at his bedside, or stood at the window with her back to him, so quiet he was barely aware of her presence. And his sons came to visit him every day, standing silent in the sickroom, trying to suppress their grief and to hide it from him and from their mother, then mumbling a blessing and leaving as unobtrusively as they had arrived.

And then one day he was surprised by a most welcome visitor, none other than Avarnam, the chief councillor of Jahanur in the distant mountains.

The man was leaner than before, and his whitened hair gleamed like molten silver; in his eyes was the same childlike warmth, and on his face, the same good-natured and captivating smile.

"I came here on official business and I heard you were sick," he began in a sweetly lilting voice, like the soft tinkling of a spring in the depths of the forest. "As a matter of fact," he added, "this is not an illness like any other, but God wants you to rest on your bed and ponder all the things that He has seen fit to reveal to you, the secrets that you have proved worthy of knowing. Of course, the truth is there is no such thing in this world as a secret, but if a man has no desire to understand meaningful things and rejects them out of hand – that is what is called a 'secret'! And you, man much loved, have never closed your heart to meaningful things, those that illumine this existence of ours from end to end, and you love the Lord your God with all your heart and might and mind and spirit, and your neighbour as yourself, and thus you have been proved worthy of what has been revealed to you, and capable of understanding it, and God, who is love, has set out everything before you!"

"How is it that you call me 'man much loved'?" He was astonished, and a spasm shook his body. "How did you know that I was called thus by the angel of God in the form of a man?"

"As I told you just now," Avarnam chuckled – a pure, limpid sound like the song of a bird soaring into the bright blue firmament – "meaningful things are revealed to those worthy of them and capable of understanding them. And if I have been found worthy, like you, then both of us, together, are sharing the same experience and seeing and hearing the same meaningful things. And each of us has his own mission, and you did not know your mission until the day that the visions visited you, whereas my mission, I have always known." And Avarnam gave him a look that was keen, but also radiant with warmth and understanding.

And all of a sudden the thought came to him like a flash of lightning, and at once, he realised: that look, that ray of light, he had known and recognised in every single one of his visions, and the one who gave this look had been present in the visions, close to him, conveying friendship and fellowship, and it was he who came to him when he fell to the ground and set him on his feet...

As he gazed into Avarnam's face with a look of growing wonder, the other nodded gravely as if confirming what had not yet been put into words.

"They say of us," Avarnam explained, "that we are thirty-six in number, and it is by our merit that the world exists, and we see and are not seen – meaning that very few have seen us, the fewest of the few, and they are the chosen, and you are one of them. And remember!" – Avarnam raised an emphatic finger – "Only the wise and the teachers of righteousness, they and only they shall be redeemed!"

And before he could ask him who were these wise ones, and how were teachers of righteousness to be recognised, Avarnam answered him in the same tender and affectionate tone of voice, an ever irresistible force:

"Those who are wise are the believers, and the teachers of righteousness are the humble. And the people that is wise and capable of teaching righteousness – that is the Chosen People of God!"

- The End -

Some other Fiction works by Shlomo Kalo:

LILI
ATHAR
KIDNAP
ERRAL
THE DOLLAR AND THE GUN
THRILLER
FOREVERMORE
THE TROUSERS - Parable for the 21 Century
THE FANTASTICAL ADVENTURES OF LESUTENLIEB

These titles and others are available at **www.y-dat.com**.
They are being gradually Introduced into **Amazon.com**.